CHAOS WALKING

CHAOS WALKING

PATRICK NESS

SCIENCE FICTION

THE KNIFE OF NEVER LETTING GO Copyright © 2008 by Patrick Ness
    Publication History: Candlewick Press hardcover, May 2008
                            Candlewick Press trade paperback, July 2009
THE ASK AND THE ANSWER Copyright © 2009 by Patrick Ness
    Publication History: Candlewick Press hardcover, September 2009

First SFBC Science Fiction Printing: July 2010

Published by arrangement with
Candlewick Press
99 Dover Street
Somerville, Massachusetts 02144

Visit The SFBC online at http://www.sfbc.com

ISBN 978-1-61664-537-3

Printed in the United States of America.

CHAOS WALKING

Contents

THE
KNIFE OF
NEUER
LETTING
GO

For Michelle Kass

IF WE HAD A KEEN VISION and feeling of all ordinary human life, it would be like hearing the grass grow and the squirrel's heart beat, and we should die of that roar which lies on the other side of silence.

George Eliot, *Middlemarch*

PART 1

1

THE HOLE IN THE NOISE

THE FIRST THING you find out when yer dog learns to talk is that dogs don't got nothing much to say. About anything.

"Need a poo, Todd."

"Shut up, Manchee."

"Poo. Poo, Todd."

"I said *shut it*."

We're walking across the wild fields southeast of town, those ones that slope down to the river and head on toward the swamp. Ben's sent me to pick him some swamp apples and he's made me take Manchee with me, even tho we all know Cillian only bought him to stay on Mayor Prentiss's good side and so suddenly here's this brand-new dog as a present for my birthday last year when I never said I *wanted* any dog, that what I *said* I wanted was for Cillian to finally fix the fissionbike so I wouldn't have to walk every forsaken place in this stupid town, but oh, no, happy birthday, Todd, here's a brand-new puppy, Todd, and even tho you don't want him, even tho you never asked for him, guess who has to feed him and train him and wash him and take him for walks and listen to him jabber now he's got old enough for the talking germ to set his mouth moving? Guess who?

"Poo," Manchee barks quietly to himself. "Poo, poo, poo."

"Just *have* yer stupid poo and quit yapping about it."

I take a switch of grass from beside the trail and I swat after him with it. I don't reach him, I don't *mean* to reach him, but he just laughs his little barking laugh and carries on down the trail. I follow after him, switching the switch against the grass on either side, squinting from the sun, trying not to think about nothing at all.

We don't need apples from the swamp, truth be told. Ben can buy them at Mr. Phelps's store if he really wants them. Also true: going to the swamp to pick a few apples is not a job for a man cuz men are never allowed to be so idle. Now, I won't *officially* become a man for thirty more days. I've lived twelve years of thirteen long months each and another twelve months besides, all of which living means I'm still one month away from the big birthday. The plans are being planned, the preparayshuns prepared, it will be a party, I guess, tho I'm starting to get some strange pictures about it, all dark and too bright at the same time, but nevertheless I will become a man and picking apples in the swamp is not a job for a man or even an almost-man.

But Ben knows he can ask me to go and he knows I'll say yes to going because the swamp is the only place anywhere near Prentisstown where you can have half a break from all the Noise that men spill outta theirselves, all their clamor and clatter that never lets up, even when they sleep, men and the thoughts they don't know they think even when everyone can hear. Men and their Noise. I don't know how they do it, how they stand each other.

Men are Noisy creachers.

"Squirrel!" Manchee shouts and off he goes, jumping off the trail, no matter how loud I yell after him, and off I have to go, too, across the (I look round to make sure I'm alone) *goddam* fields cuz Cillian'll have a fit if Manchee falls down some *goddam* snake hole and of course it'll be my own *goddam* fault even tho I never wanted the *goddam* dog in the *goddam* first place.

"Manchee! Get back here!"

"*Squirrel!*"

I have to kick my way thru the grass, getting grublets stuck to my shoes. One smashes as I kick it off, leaving a green smear across my sneakers, which I know from experience ain't coming out. "*Manchee!*" I rage.

"Squirrel! Squirrel! Squirrel!"

He's barking round the tree and the squirrel's skittering back and forth on the tree trunk, taunting him. **Come on, Whirler dog,** says its Noise. **Come on, come get, come on, come get. Whirler, Whirler, Whirler.**

"Squirrel, Todd! Squirrel!"

Goddam, animals are stupid.

I grab Manchee by the collar and hit him hard across his back leg. "Ow, Todd? Ow?" I hit him again. And again. "Ow? Todd?"

"Come *on*," I say, my own Noise raging so loud I can barely hear myself think, which is something I'm about to regret, you watch.

Whirler boy, Whirler boy, thinks the squirrel at me. **Come get, Whirler boy.**

"You can eff off, too," I say, except I don't say "eff," I say what "eff" stands for.

And I really, really shoulda looked round again.

Cuz here's Aaron, right here, rising outta the grass from nowhere, rising up and smacking me cross the face, scratching my lip with his big ring, then bringing his hand back the other way, closed as a fist, catching my cheekbone but at least missing my nose because I'm falling into the grass, trying to fall away from his punch, and I let go of Manchee's collar and off he runs back to the squirrel, barking his head off, the traitor, and I hit the grass with my knees and my hands, getting grublet stains all over everything.

And I stay there, on the ground, breathing.

Aaron stands over me, his Noise coming at me in fragments of scripture and of his next sermon and **Language, young Todd** and **the finding of a sacrifice** and **the saint chooses his path** and God **hears** and the wash of pictures that's in everyone's Noise, of things familiar and glancing flashes of—

What? What the forsaken—?

But up flies a loud bit of his sermon to block it out and I look up into his eyes and suddenly I don't wanna know. I can already taste the blood where his ring cut my lip and I don't wanna know. He *never* comes out here, men *never* do, they have their reasons, men do, and it's just me and my dog only ever but here he is and I don't don't don't wanna know.

He smiles down at me, thru that beard of his, smiles down at me in the grass.

A smiling fist.

"Language, young Todd," he says, "binds us like prisoners on a chain. Haven't you learned anything from yer church, boy?" And then he says his most familiar preaching. "If one of us falls, we all fall."

Yes, Aaron, I think.

"With yer mouth, Todd."

"Yes, Aaron," I say.

"And the effs?" he says. "And the geedees? Because don't think I didn't hear them as well. Your Noise reveals you. Reveals us all."

Not all, I think, but at the same time I say, "Sorry, Aaron."

He leans down to me, his lips close to my face, and I can smell the breath that comes outta his mouth, smell the weight of it, like fingers grabbing for me. "God hears," he whispers. "God *hears.*"

And he raises a hand again and I flinch and he laughs and then he's gone, like that, heading back toward the town, taking his Noise with him.

I'm shaking from the charge to my blood at being hit, shaking from being so fired up and so surprised and so angry and so much hating this town and the men in it that it takes me a while till I can get up and go get my dog again. *What was he effing doing out here anyway?* I think and I'm so hacked off, still so raging with anger and hate (and fear, yes, fear, shut up) that I don't even look round to see if Aaron heard my Noise. I don't look round. I don't look round.

And then I do look round and I go and get my dog.

"Aaron, Todd? Aaron?"

"Don't say that name again, Manchee."

"Bleeding, Todd. Todd? Todd? Todd? Bleeding?"

"I know. Shut up."

"Whirler," he says, as if it don't mean nothing, his head as empty as the sky.

I smack his rump. "Don't say that neither."

"Ow? Todd?"

We keep on walking, staying clear of the river on our left. It runs down thru a series of gulches at the east of town, starting way up to the north past our farm and coming down the side of the town till it flattens out into a marshy part that eventually becomes the swamp. You have to avoid the river and especially that marshy part before the swamp trees start cuz that's where the crocs live, easily big enough to kill an almost-man and his dog. The fins on their backs look just like a row of rushes and if you get too close, *WHOOM!* – outta the water they come, flying at you with their claws grasping and their mouths snapping and you pretty much ain't got no chance at all then.

We get ourselves down past the marshy part and I try to take in the swamp quiet as it approaches. There's nothing to see down here no more, really, which is why men don't come. And the smell, too, I don't pretend it don't smell, but it don't smell nearly so bad as men make out. They're smelling their memories, they are, they're not smelling what's really here, they're smelling it like it was then. All the dead things. Spacks and men had different ideas for burial. Spacks just used the swamp, threw their dead right into the water, let 'em sink, which was fine cuz they were suited for swamp burial, I guess. That's what Ben says. Water and muck and Spackle skin worked fine together, didn't poison nothing, just made the swamp richer, like men do to soil.

Then suddenly, of course, there were a whole lot more spacks to bury than normal, too many for even a swamp this big to swallow, and it's a ruddy big swamp, too. And then there were no live spacks at all, were there? Just spack bodies in heaps, piling up in the swamp and rotting and stinking and it took a long time for the swamp to become swamp again and not just a mess of flies and smells and who knows what extra germs they'd kept saved up for us.

I was born into all that, all that mess, the over-crowded swamp and the over-crowded sematary and the not-crowded-enough town, so I don't remember nothing, don't remember a world without Noise. My pa died of sickness before I was born and then my ma died, of course, no surprises there. Ben and Cillian took me in, raised me. Ben says my ma was the last of the women but everyone says that about everyone's ma. Ben may not be lying, *he* believes it's true, but who knows?

I am the youngest of the whole town, tho. I used to come out and throw rocks at field crows with Reg Oliver (seven months and eight days older) and Liam Smith (four months and twenty nine days older) and Seb Mundy who was next youngest to me, three months and a day older, but even he don't talk to me no more now that he's a man.

No boys do once they turn thirteen.

Which is how it goes in Prentisstown. Boys become men and they go to their men-only meetings to talk about who knows what and boys most definitely ain't allowed and if yer the last boy in town, you just have to wait, all by yerself.

Well, you and a dog you don't want.

But never mind, here's the swamp and in we go, sticking to the paths that take us round and over the worst of the water, weaving our way round the big, bulby trees that grow up and outta the bog to the needly roof, yards and yards up. The air's thick and it's dark and it's heavy, but it's not a frightening kind of thick and dark and heavy. There's lots of life here, tons of it, just ignoring the town as you please, birds and green snakes and frogs and kivits and both kinds of squirrel and (I promise you) a cassor or two and sure there's red snakes to watch out for but even tho it's dark, there's slashes of light that come down from holes in the roof and if you ask me, which, granted, you may not be, to me the swamp's like one big, comfy, not very Noisy room. Dark but living, living but friendly, friendly but not grasping.

Manchee lifts his leg on practically everything till he must be running outta pee and then he heads off under a bush, burbling to himself, finding a place to do his other business, I guess.

But the swamp don't mind. How could it? It's all just life, going over itself, returning and cycling and eating itself to grow. I mean, it's not that it's not Noisy here. Sure it is, there's no escaping Noise, not nowhere at all, but it's quieter than the town. The loud is a different kind of loud, because swamp loud is just curiosity, creachers figuring out who you are and if yer a threat. Whereas the town knows all about you already and wants to know more and wants to beat you with what it knows till how can you have any of yerself left at all?

Swamp Noise, tho, swamp Noise is just the birds all thinking their worrisome little birdie thoughts. **Where's food? Where's home? Where's my safety?** And the waxy squirrels, who are all little punks, teasing you if they see you, teasing themselves if they don't, and the rusty squirrels, who are like dumb little kids, and sometimes there's swamp foxes out in the leaves who you can hear faking their Noise to sound like the squirrels they eat and even less often there are mavens singing their weird maven songs and once I swear I saw a cassor running away on two long legs but Ben says I didn't, says the cassors are long gone from the swamp.

I don't know. I believe me.

Manchee comes outta the bushes and sits down next to me cuz I've stopped right there in the middle of a trail. He looks around to see what I might be seeing and then he says, "Good poo, Todd."

"I'm sure it was, Manchee."

I'd better not get another ruddy dog when my birthday comes. What I want this year is a hunting knife like the one Ben carries on the back of his belt. Now *that's* a present for a man.

"Poo," Manchee says quietly.

On we walk. The main bunch of apple trees is a little ways into the swamp, down a few paths and over a fallen log that Manchee always needs help over. When we get there, I pick him up around his stomach and lift him to the top. Even tho he knows what I'm doing, he still kicks his legs all over the place like a falling spider, making a fuss for no reason at all.

"Hold still, you gonk!"

"Down, down, down!" he yelps, scrabbling away at the air.

"Idiot dog."

I plop him on top of the log and climb up myself. We both jump down to the other side, Manchee barking "Jump!" as he lands and keeping on barking "Jump!" as he runs off.

The leap over the log is where the dark of the swamp really starts and the first thing you see are the old Spackle buildings, leaning out toward you from shadow, looking like melting blobs of tan-colored ice cream except hut-sized. No one knows or can remember what they were ever sposed to be but best guess by Ben, who's a best guess kinda guy, is that they had something to do with burying their dead. Maybe even some kind of church, even tho the spacks didn't have no kind of religion anyone from Prentisstown could reckernize.

I keep a wide distance from them and go into the little grove of wild apple trees. The apples are ripe, nearly black, almost edible, as Cillian would say. I pick one off the trunk and take a bite, the juice dribbling down my chin.

"Todd?"

"What, Manchee?" I take out the plastic bag I've got folded in my back pocket and start filling it with apples.

"Todd?" he barks again and this time I notice how he's barking it and I turn and he's pointed at the Spackle buildings and his fur's all ridged up on his back and his ears are flicking all over the place.

I stand up straight. "What is it, boy?"

He's growling now, his lips pulled back over his teeth. I feel the charge in my blood again. "Is it a croc?" I say.

"Quiet, Todd," Manchee growls.

"But what is it?"

"*Is* quiet, Todd." He lets out a little bark and it's a real bark, a real dog bark that means nothing but "Bark!" and my body electricity goes up a bit, like charges are going to start leaping outta my skin. "Listen," he growls.

And so I listen.

And I listen.

And I turn my head a little and I listen some more.

There's a hole in the Noise.

Which can't be.

It's *weird*, it is, out there, hiding somewhere, in the trees or somewhere outta sight, a spot where yer ears and yer mind are telling you there's no Noise. It's like a shape you can't see except by how everything else around it is touching it. Like water in the shape of a cup, but with no cup. It's a hole and everything that falls into it stops being Noise, stops being *anything*, just stops altogether. It's not like the quiet of the swamp, which is never *quiet* obviously, just less Noisy. But this, this is a shape, a shape of *nothing*, a hole where all Noise stops.

Which is impossible.

There ain't nothing but Noise in this world, nothing but the constant thoughts of men and things coming at you and at you and at you, ever since the spacks released the Noise germ during the war, the germ that killed half the men and every single woman, my ma not excepted, the germ that drove the rest of the men mad, the germ that spelled the end for all Spackle once men's madness picked up a gun.

"Todd?" Manchee's spooked, I can hear it. "What, Todd? What's it, Todd?"

"Can you smell anything?"

"Just smell quiet, Todd," he barks, then he starts barking louder, "Quiet! Quiet!"

And then, somewhere around the spack buildings, the quiet *moves*.

My blood-charge leaps so hard it about knocks me over. Manchee yelps in a circle around me, barking and barking, making me double-spooked, and so I smack him on the rump again ("Ow, Todd?") to make myself calm down.

"There's no such thing as holes," I say. "No such thing as nothing. So it's gotta be a something, don't it?"

"Something, Todd," Manchee barks.

"Can you hear where it went?"

"It's quiet, Todd."

"You know what I mean."

Manchee sniffs the air and takes one step, two, then more toward the Spackle buildings. I guess we're looking for it, then. I start walking all slowlike up to the biggest of the melty ice-cream scoops. I stay outta the way of anything that might be looking out the little bendy triangle doorway. Manchee's sniffing at the door frame but he's not growling so I take a deep breath and I look inside.

It's totally empty. The ceiling rises up to a point about another length of me above my head. Floor's dirt, swamp plants growing in it now, vines and suchlike, but nothing else. Which is to say no *real* nothing, no hole, and no telling what mighta been here before.

It's stupid but I gotta say it.

I'm wondering if the Spackle are back.

But that's impossible.

But a hole in the Noise is impossible.

So something impossible has to be true.

I can hear Manchee snuffling around again outside so I creep out and I go to the second scoop. There's writing on the outside of this one, the only written words anyone's ever seen in the spack language. The only words they ever saw fit to write down, I guess. The letters are spack letters, but Ben says they make the sound *es'Paqili* or suchlike, *es'Paqili*, the Spackle, "spacks" if you wanna spit it, which since what happened happened is what everyone does. Means "The People."

There's nothing in the second scoop neither. I step back out into the swamp and I listen again. I put my head down and I listen and I reach with the hearing parts of my brain and I listen there, too, and I listen and listen.

I listen.

"Quiet! Quiet!" Manchee barks twice real fast and peels off running again, toward the last scoop. I take off after him, running myself, my blood charging, cuz that's where it is, that's where the hole in the Noise is.

I can hear it.

Well, I can't *hear* it, that's the whole point, but when I run toward it the emptiness of it is touching my chest and the stillness of it pulls at me and there's so much quiet in it, no, not quiet, *silence,* so much unbelievable silence that I start to feel really torn up, like I'm about to lose the most valuable thing ever, like there it is, a death, and I'm running and my eyes are watering and my chest is just crushing and there's no one to see but I still mind and my eyes start crying, they start crying, they start *effing crying,* and I stop for a minute and I bend over and Jesus H. Dammit, you can just shut up right now, but I waste a whole stupid minute, just a whole stinking, stupid minute bent over there, by which time, of course, the hole is moving away, it's moved away, it's gone.

Manchee's torn twixt racing after it and coming back to me but he finally comes back to me.

"Crying, Todd?"

"Shut up," I say and aim a kick at him. It misses on purpose.

2

PRENTISSTOWN

WE GET OURSELVES outta the swamp and head back toward town and the world feels all black and gray no matter what the sun is saying. Even Manchee barely says nothing as we make our way back up thru the fields. My Noise churns and bubbles like a stew on the boil till finally I have to stop for a minute to calm myself down a little.

There's just no such thing as silence. Not here, not nowhere. Not when yer asleep, not when yer by yerself, never.

I am Todd Hewitt, I think to myself with my eyes closed. *I am twelve years and twelve months old. I live in Prentisstown on New World. I will be a man in one month's time exactly.*

It's a trick Ben taught me to help settle my Noise. You close yer eyes and as clearly and calmly as you can you tell yerself who you are, cuz that's what gets lost in all that Noise.

I am Todd Hewitt.

"Todd Hewitt," Manchee murmurs to himself beside me.

I take a deep breath and open my eyes.

That's who I am. I'm Todd Hewitt.

We walk on up away from the swamp and the river, up the slope of the wild fields to the small ridge at the south of town where the school used to be for the brief and useless time it existed. Before I was born, boys were taught by their ma at home and then when there were only boys and men left, we just got sat down in front of vids and learning modules till Mayor Prentiss outlawed such things as "detrimental to the discipline of our minds."

Mayor Prentiss, see, has a Point of View.

And so for almost half a stupid year, all the boys were gathered up by sad-faced Mr. Royal and plonked out here in an outbuilding away from the main Noise of the town. Not that it helped. It's nearly impossible to teach anything in a classroom full of boys' Noise and *completely* impossible to give out any sort of test. You cheat even if you don't mean to and *everybody* means to.

And then one day Mayor Prentiss decided to burn all the books, every single one of them, even the ones in men's homes, cuz apparently books were detrimental as well and Mr. Royal, a soft man who made himself a hard man by drinking whisky in the classroom, gave up and took a gun and put an end to himself and that was it for my classroom teaching.

Ben taught me the rest at home. Mechanics and food prep and clothes repair and farming basics and things like that. Also a lot of survival stuff like hunting and which fruits you can eat and how to follow the moons for direkshuns and how to use a knife and a gun and snakebite remedies and how to calm yer Noise as best you can.

He tried to teach me reading and writing, too, but Mayor Prentiss caught wind of it in my Noise one morning and locked Ben up for a week and that was the end of my booklearning and what with all that other stuff to learn and all the working on the farm that still has to be done every day and all the just plain surviving, I never ended up reading too good.

Don't matter. Ain't nobody in Prentisstown ever gonna write a book.

Manchee and me get past the school building and up on the little ridge and look north and there it is, the town itself. Not that there's all that much left of it no more. One shop, used to be two. One bar, used to be two. One clinic, one jail, one nonworking gas stayshun, one big house for the Mayor, one police stayshun. The Church. One short bit of road running thru the center, paved back in the day, never upkept since, goes to gravel real quick. All the houses and such are out and about, outskirts like, farms, meant to be farms, some still are, some stand empty, some stand worse than empty.

And that's all there is of Prentisstown. Populayshun 147 and falling, falling, falling. 146 men and one almost-man.

Ben says there used to be other settlements scattered around New World, that all the ships landed about the same time, ten years or so before I was born, but that when the war started with the spacks, when the spacks released the germs and all the other settlements were wiped out, that Prentisstown was nearly wiped out, too, that it only survived cuz of Mayor Prentiss's army skills and that even tho Mayor Prentiss is a nightmare coming and going, we at least owe him that, that cuz of him we survive alone on a whole big empty woman-less world that ain't got nothing good to say for itself, in a town of 146 men that dies a little more with every day that passes.

Cuz some men can't take it, can they? They off themselves like Mr. Royal or some of them just plain disappear, like Mr. Gault, our old neighbour who used to run the other sheep farm, or Mr. Michael, our second-best carpenter, or Mr. van Wijk, who vanished the same day his son became a man. It's not so uncommon. If yer whole world is one Noisy town with no future, sometimes you just gotta leave even if there ain't nowhere else to go.

Cuz as me the almost-man looks up into that town, I can hear the 146 men who remain. I can hear every ruddy last one of them. Their Noise washes down the hill like a flood let loose right at me, like a fire, like a monster the size of the sky come to get you cuz there's nowhere to run.

Here's what it's like. Here's what every minute of every day of my stupid, stinking life in this stupid, stinking town is like. Never mind plugging yer ears, it don't help at all:

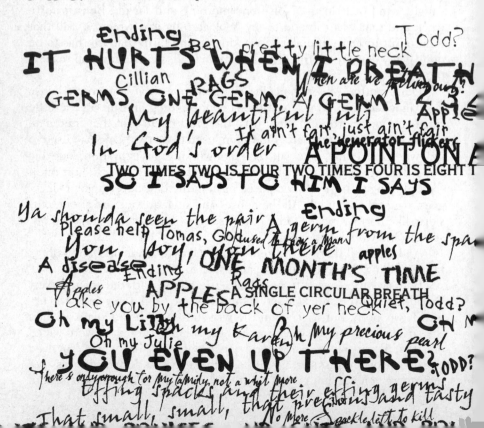

TS "AND BRUISES AND CUTS AND BRUISE

Oil the barrel but keep the oil free from the stock   they'll be men

What I wouldn't give for a real beefburger

What if he asks about the sheeps!   I AM AND ALL IS IN GOD'S ORDER.

TIE YER HANDS TOGETHER

Please don't let the fever take my Justin   WITH SOME ROPE

Oh my Esther, my Esther oh my beautiful girl   Apples

ONE MONTH   Prentiss'll have the first go

How are we ever getting outta here!

How are we ever getting outta here! oh here!

WHAT HAVE WE DONE, OH, MY LORD?

Todd?

I'll kill him   A disease, a germ, from the spacks

WE'LL RUN OUTTA MILLET   Ending   BEFORE W:

I AM A POINT AND THE POINT IS ME   I'll just have the one more and go   Cillian

Tense sous   One hundred nineteen days without rain

LOOK AT THE TINY HANDS   course not, Do Apples

Yer a liar, sir   A 3 2 1   the holiness of the silence

When are   sit   you to yer face

I'VE FORGOTTEN HER FACE

HOLD YER THOUGHTS IN A LINE, A LINE, A LINE   a germ, remember that

ONE MONTH'S TIME   guts are red   NOTHING BUT BEASTS

Keep the boy from their hands somehow, God

THE WOOD IN MY HANDS   rags

OH MY   OH MY NORMA   Oh my Kelly

DISCIPLINE, MEN!   JADE   Oh my Karla

How are we ever getting outta here?

IRCLE ON A POINT ON A CIRCLE

S EIGHT IS SIXTEEN   CUTS AND BRUISES AND CUT

THAT HEWITT BOY   Todd?

THE ANTS GO MARCHING TWO B

The way she used to

1 2 3 4 4 3 2 1

ent, found and unfound and found again

OU THERE ARE NO PAINKILLERS LEFT

Hold strawberries for winter, neither

hold you, hold you down, hold you

times sixteen is thirty-two two times thirty-two is sixty-four

EN STRIKES THE HOUR   Rags

LIP THE BOLT OVER, INSERT THE FIRING MECHANISM

Nail one two three, nail one two   CHARLIE

NOTHER OVER HERE,   cockroaches

months time, one months time

I AM AND ALL IS IN G   blasted blasted blasted

One ~~THIS IS IN GOD'S ORDER WHO~~nding

SHUT UP, PLEASE GO
SHUT IT UP

And them's just the words, the voices talking and moaning and singing and crying. There's pictures, too, pictures that come to yer mind in a rush, no matter how much you don't want 'em, pictures of memories and fantasies and secrets and plans and lies, lies, lies. Cuz you can lie in the Noise, even when everyone knows what yer thinking, you can bury stuff under other stuff, you can hide it in plain sight, you just don't think it clearly or you convince yerself that the opposite of what yer hiding is true and then who's going to be able to pick out from the flood what's real water and what's not going to get you wet?

Men lie, and they lie to theirselves worst of all.

In a for instance, I've never seen a woman nor a Spackle in the flesh, obviously. I've seen 'em both in vids, of course, before they were outlawed, and I see them *all the time* in the Noise of men cuz what else do men think about except sex and enemies? But the spacks are bigger and meaner looking in the Noise than in the vids, ain't they? And Noise women have lighter hair and bigger chests and wear less clothes and are a lot freer with their affecshuns than in the vids, too. So the thing to remember, the thing that's most important of all that I might say in this here telling of things is that Noise ain't truth, Noise is what men *want* to be true, and there's a difference twixt those two things so big that it could ruddy well kill you if you don't watch out.

"Home, Todd?" Manchee barks a bit louder down by my leg cuz that's how you gotta talk in the Noise.

"Yeah, we're going," I say. We live on the other side, to the northeast, and we're going to have to go thru the town to get there so here it comes, as fast as I can get thru it.

First up is Mr. Phelps's store. It's dying, the store is, like the rest of the town and Mr. Phelps spends all his time despairing. Even when yer buying stuff from him and he's polite as can be, the despair of him seeps at you like pus from a cut. Ending, says his Noise, Ending, it's all ending and Rags and rags and rags and My Julie, my dear, dear Julie who was his wife and who don't wear no clothes at all in Mr. Phelps's Noise.

"Hiya, Todd," he calls as Manchee and I hurry by.

"Hiya, Mr. Phelps."

"Beautiful day, ain't she?"

"She sure is, Mr. Phelps."

"Beaut!" barks Manchee and Mr. Phelps laughs but his Noise just keeps saying Ending and Julie and rags and pictures of what he misses about his wife and what she used to do as if it's sposed to be unique or something.

I don't think anything particular in my Noise for Mr. Phelps, just my usual stuff you can't help. Tho I must admit I find myself thinking it all a little bit louder to cover up thoughts about the hole I found in the swamp, to block it out behind louder Noise.

Don't know why I should do this, don't know why I should hide it.

But I'm hiding it.

Manchee and me carry on walking pretty fast cuz next is the gas stayshun and Mr. Hammar. The gas stayshun don't work no more cuz the fission generator that made the gas went kerflooey last year and just sits there beside the gas stayshun like a hulking ugly hurt toe and no one'd live next to it except Mr. Hammar and Mr. Hammar's *much* worse than Mr. Phelps cuz he'll aim his Noise right at you.

And it's *ugly* Noise, *angry* Noise, pictures of yerself in ways that you don't want pictures of yerself, violent pictures and bloody pictures and all you can do is make yer own Noise as loud as you can and try to sweep up Mr. Phelps's Noise in it, too, and send it right back to Mr. Hammar. Apples and Ending and fist over hand and Ben and Julie and Peaut, Todd? and the generator is flickering and rags and shut up, just shut up and Look at me, boy,

And I turn my head anyway even tho I don't want to but sometimes you get caught off-guard and so I turn my head and there's Mr. Hammar in his window, looking right at me and One month, he thinks, and there's a picture from his Noise and it involves me standing on my own but somehow even more alone than that and I don't know what it means or if it's real or if it's a purposeful lie and so I think about a hammer going into Mr. Hammar's head over and over and he just smiles from his window.

The road curves round the stayshun past the clinic, which is Dr. Baldwin and all the crying and moaning men do to doctors when nothing's really wrong with 'em. Today it's Mr. Fox complaining about how he can't breathe which would be a pitiable thing if he didn't smoke so much. And then, as you pass the clinic, God Almighty, you get the stupid, stupid bar which even at this hour of the day is just a howl of Noise cuz what they do there is turn the music up so loud it's meant to drown out Noise but that only works partway and so you get loud music and loud Noise and worse, *drunk* Noise, which comes at you like a mallet. Shouts and howls and weeping from men whose faces never change and just horrorpilashuns of the past and all the women that used to be.

A whole *lot* about the women that used to be but nothing that makes any sense, cuz drunk Noise is like a drunk man: blurry and boring and dangerous.

· It gets hard to walk around the center of town, hard to think about the next step cuz so much Noise is weighing on yer shoulders. I honestly don't know how men do it, I don't know how *I'm* going to do it when I become a man 'less something changes on the day that I don't know about.

The road bears up past the bar and to the right, going by the police stayshun and the jail, all one place and in use more than you might think for a town so small. The sheriff is Mr. Prentiss Jr. who's barely two years older than me and only been a man for a short while but who took to his job well and quick and in his cell is whoever Mayor Prentiss has told Mr. Prentiss Jr. to make an example of this week. Right now it's Mr. Turner who didn't hand over enough of his corn yield to "the good use of the whole town," which just means he didn't give no free corn to Mr. Prentiss and his men.

So you've gone thru the town with yer dog and you got all this Noise behind you, Mr. Phelps and Mr. Hammar and Dr. Baldwin and Mr. Fox and the extra extra Noise from the bar and Mr. Prentiss Jr.'s Noise and Mr. Turner's moaning Noise and yer still not done with the Noise of the town cuz here comes the Church.

The Church is why we're all here on New World in the first place, of course, and pretty much every Sunday you can hear Aaron preaching about why we left behind the corrupshun and sin of Old World and about how we'd aimed to start a new life of purity and brotherhood in a whole new Eden.

That worked out well, huh?

People still go to church tho, mainly cuz they have to, even tho the Mayor hisself hardly ever bothers, leaving the rest of us to listen to Aaron preach about how we're the only thing each of us have out here, us men together, and how all of us have gotta bind ourselves in a single community.

How if one of us falls, we all fall.

He says that one a lot.

Manchee and me are quiet as possible going past the front door of the Church. Praying Noise comes from inside, it's got a special feel to it, a special purply sick feel like men are bleeding it out, even tho it's always the same stuff but the purply blood just keeps on coming. *Help us, save us, forgive us, help us, save us, forgive us, get us outta here, please, God, please, God, please, God,* tho as far as I know no one's never heard no Noise back from this God fella.

Aaron's in there, too, back from his walk and preaching over the prayers. I can hear his voice, not just his Noise, and it's all sacrifice this and scripture that and blessings here and sainthood there and he's going on at such a rattle his Noise is like gray fire behind him and you can't pick out anything in it and he might be up to something, mightn't he? The sermon might be covering for something and I'm beginning to wonder if I know what that something is.

And then I hear Young Todd? in his Noise and I say, "Hurry up, Manchee," and we scoot our way along real quick.

The last thing you pass as you crest the hill of Prentisstown is the Mayor's House which is the weirdest and hardest Noise of all cuz Mayor Prentiss—

Well, Mayor Prentiss is different.

His Noise is awful clear and I mean awful in the awful way. He believes, see, that order can be brought to Noise. He believes that Noise can be sorted out, that if you could harness it somehow, you could put it to use. And when you walk by the Mayor's House, you can hear him, hear him and the men closest to him, his deputies and things, and they're always doing these thought exercises, these counting things and imagining perfect shapes and saying orderly chants like I AM THE CIRCLE AND THE CIRCLE IS ME, whatever that's sposed to mean, and it's like he's molding a little army into shape, like he's preparing himself for something, like he's forging some kind of Noise weapon.

It feels like a threat. It feels like the world changing and leaving you behind.

1 2 3 4 4 3 2 1 I AM THE CIRCLE AND THE CIRCLE IS ME 1 2 3 4 4 3 2 1 IF ONE OF US FALLS WE ALL FALL

I will be a man soon and men do not run in fear but I give Manchee a little push and we walk even a little faster than before, giving the Mayor's House as wide a curve as possible till we're past it and on the gravel path that heads on toward our house.

After a while, the town disappears behind us and the Noise starts to get a little bit quieter (tho it never never stops) and we can both breathe a bit easier.

Manchee barks, "Noise, Todd."

"Yesiree," I say.

"Quiet in the swamp, Todd," Manchee says. "Quiet, quiet, quiet."

"Yes," I say and then I think and I hurry and say, "Shut up, Manchee," and I smack him on his rump and he says, "Ow, Todd?" but I'm looking back toward the town but there's no stopping Noise once it's out, is there? And if it was something you could see, moving thru the air, I wonder if you could see the hole in the Noise floating right outta me, right outta my thoughts from where I was protecting it and it's such a small bit of Noise and it'd be easy to miss in the great roar of everything else but there it goes, there it goes, there it goes, heading right back toward the world of men.

}

BEN AND CILLIAN

AND JUST WHERE do you think you've been?" Cillian says as soon as Manchee and I come into view off the path. He's lying down on the ground, deep into our little fission generator, the one outside the front of the house, fixing whatever's gone wrong with it this month. His arms are covered in grease and his face is covered in annoyance and his Noise is buzzy like mad bees and I can already feel myself getting angry and I haven't even properly got home yet.

"I was in the swamp getting apples for Ben," I say.

"There's work to be done and boys are off playing." He looks back into the generator. Something makes a clunk inside and he says, "Dammit!"

"I said I wasn't playing, if you'd ever listen!" I say but it's more like a shout. "Ben wanted apples so I was getting him some ruddy apples!"

"Uh-huh," Cillian says, looking back at me. "And where might these apples be then?"

And of course I'm not holding any apples, am I? I don't even remember dropping the bag I'd started to fill but of course I must have when—

"When what?" Cillian says.

"Quit listening so close," I say.

He sighs his Cillian sigh and here we go: "It's not like we ask you to do so much around here, Todd"– which is a lie –"but we can't keep this farm running by ourselves"– which is true –"and even if you ever finish all yer chores, which you don't"– another lie, they work me like a slave –"we'd still be playing a catch-up to nothing, now wouldn't we?"– and this is true, too. The town can't grow no more, it can only shrink, and help ain't coming.

"Pay attenshun when I talk to you," Cillian says.

"Tenshun!" Manchee barks.

"Shut up," I say.

"Don't talk to yer dog that way," Cillian says.

I wasn't talking to my dog, I think, loud and clear enough to hear.

Cillian glares at me and I glare back and this is how it always is, our Noise throbbing red with hassle and irritashun. It's never been so good with Cillian, not never, Ben's always been the kind one, Cillian's always been the other one, but it's got worse as the day approaches when I'll finally be a man and won't have to listen to any more of his crap.

Cillian closes his eyes and breathes loudly once thru his nose. "Todd–" he starts, his voice a bit lower.

"Where's Ben?" I say.

His face hardens a little more. "Lambing starts in a week, Todd."

All I do to this is say again, "Where's Ben?"

"You get the sheep fed and into their paddocks and then I want you to fix the gate to the east field once and for all, Todd Hewitt. I have asked you at least twice before now."

I lean back on my heels. "'Well, how was your trip to the swamp, Todd?'" I say, making my voice go all sarcastic. "'Well, it was fine and dandy there, Cillian, thank you for asking.' 'Didja see anything interesting out there in the swamp, Todd?' 'Well, funny you should ask, Cillian, cuz I sure did see something interesting which might explain this here cut on my lip that you ain't asked about but I guess it'll have to just wait till the sheep are fed and I fix the *goddam fence!*'"

"Watch yer mouth," Cillian says. "I don't have time for yer games. Go do the sheep."

I clench up my fists and make a sound that sounds like *awwghgh* which tells Cillian that I just can't put up with his nonreason not for one second longer.

"Come on, Manchee," I say.

"The sheep, Todd," Cillian calls as I start walking away. "The sheep first."

"Yeah, I'll do the ruddy sheep," I mutter to myself. I'm walking away faster now, my blood jumping and Manchee's getting excited from the roar of my Noise. "Sheep!" he barks. "Sheep, sheep, Todd! Sheep, sheep, quiet, Todd! Quiet, quiet in swamp, Todd!"

"Shut up, Manchee," I say.

"What was that?" Cillian says and there's something in his voice that makes us both turn around. He's sitting up by the generator now, his full attenshun on us, his Noise coming right at us like a laser.

"Quiet, Cillian," Manchee barks.

"What does he mean 'quiet'?" Cillian's eyes and Noise are searching me all over.

"What do you care?" I turn again. "I got ruddy sheep to feed."

"Todd, wait," he calls after us but then something starts beeping on the generator and he says "Dammit!" again and has to go back to it tho I can feel all kinds of asking marks in his Noise following me, getting fainter as I head out to our fields.

Blast him, blast him and all, I think, in more or less those words and worse as I stomp across our farm. We live about a mile northeast of town and we do sheep on one half of the farm and wheat on the other. Wheat's harder, so Ben and Cillian do most of that. Since I was old enough to be taller than the sheep, that's who I've taken care of. Me, that is, not me and Manchee, tho another one of the false lying excuses why he was given to me was that I could teach him to be a sheep dog which for obvious reasons – by which I mean his complete stupidity – hasn't worked out as planned.

Feeding and watering and shearing and lambing and even castrating and butchering, I do all these things. We're one of three meat and wool providers for the town, used to be one of five, soon be one of two because Mr. Marjoribanks oughta be dying from his drink problem any day now. We'll fold his flock into ours. I should say *I'll* fold his flock into ours, like I did when Mr. Gault disappeared two winters ago, and they'll be new ones to butcher, new ones to castrate, new ones to shear, new ones to put in pens with ewes at the right times, and will I get a thank you? No, I will not.

I am Todd Hewitt, I think, the day just keeping on not making my Noise any quieter. *I am almost a man.*

"Sheep!" say the sheep when I pass their field without stopping. "Sheep!" they say, watching me go. "Sheep! Sheep!"

"Sheep!" barks Manchee.

"Sheep!" say the sheep back.

Sheep got even less to say than dogs do.

I've been listening out for Ben's Noise over the farm and I've tracked him down to one corner of one of the wheat fields. Planting's done, harvest is months away, so there's not so much to do with the wheat at the minute, just make sure all the generators and the fission tractor and the electric threshers are ready to start working. You'd think this would mean I'd get a little help with the sheep but you would be wrong.

Ben's Noise is humming a little tune out near one of the irrigashun spouts so I take a turn and head across the field toward him. His Noise ain't nothing like Cillian's. It's calmer and clearer and tho you can't see Noise, if Cillian's always seems reddish, then Ben's seems blue or sometimes green. They're different men from each other, different as fire and water, Ben and Cillian, my more or less parents.

Story is, my ma was friends with Ben before they left for New World, that they were both members of the Church when the offer of leaving and starting up a settlement was made. Ma convinced Pa and Ben convinced Cillian and when the ships landed and the settlement started, it was my ma and pa who raised sheep on the next farm over from Ben and Cillian growing wheat and it was all friendly and nice and the sun never set and men and women sang songs together and lived and loved and never got sick and never never died.

That's the story from the Noise anyway so who knows what it was actually like before? Cuz then of course I was born and everything changed. The spacks released their woman-killing germ and that was it for my ma and then the war started and was won and that was it for pretty much the rest of New World. And there's me, just a baby, not knowing nothing bout nothing, and of course I'm not the only baby, there're loads of us, and suddenly only half a town of men to take care of all us babies and boys. So a lot of us died and I was counted among the lucky cuz it was only natural for Ben and Cillian to take me in and feed me and raise me and teach me and generally make it possible for me to go on being alive.

And so I'm kinda like their son. Well, more than "kinda like" but less than actually being so. Ben says Cillian only fights with me all the time cuz he cares about me so much but if that's true I say it's a funny way to show it, a way that don't seem much like caring at all, if you ask me.

But Ben's a different kind of man than Cillian, a *kind* kind of man that makes him not normal in Prentisstown. 145 of the men in this town, even the newly made ones just past their birthdays, even Cillian tho to a lesser degree, they see me at best as something to ignore and at worst as something to hit and so I spend most of my days figuring out ways to be ignored so as I won't get hit.

'Cept for Ben, who I can't describe much further without seeming soft and stupid and like a boy, so I won't, just to say that I never knew my pa, but if you woke up one day and had a choice of picking one from a selecshun, if someone said, here, then, boy, pick who you want, then Ben wouldn't be the worst choice you could make that morning.

He's whistling as we approach and tho I can't see him yet and he can't see me, he changes the tune as he senses me coming to a song I reckernize, Early one mo-o-rning, just as the sun was ri-i-sing, which he says was a favorite of my ma's but which I think is really just a favorite of his since he's whistled and sang it for me since I can remember. My blood is still storming away from Cillian but I immediately start to feel a little calmer.

Even tho it *is* a song for babies, I know, shut up.

"Ben!" Manchee barks and goes running around the irrigashun sctup.

"Hello, Manchee," I hear as I round the corner and see Ben scratching Manchee twixt the ears. Manchee's eyes are closed and his leg is thumping on the ground with pleasure and tho Ben can certainly tell from my Noise that I've been fighting with Cillian again, he don't say nothing but, "Hello, Todd."

"Hi, Ben." I look at the ground, kicking a stone.

And Ben's Noise is saying Apples and Cillian and Yer getting so big and Cillian again and itch in the crack of my arm and apples and dinner and Gosh, it's warm out and it's all so smooth and non-grasping it's like laying down in a brook on a hot day.

"You calming down there, Todd?" he finally says. "Reminding yerself who you are?"

"Yeah," I say, "just, why does he have to come at me like that? Why can't he just say hello? Not even a greeting, it's all 'I know you done something wrong and I'm gonna keep at you till I find out what it is.'"

"That's just his way, Todd. You know that."

"So you keep saying." I pick a blade of young wheat and stick the end in my mouth, not quite looking at him.

"Left the apples at the house, didja?"

I look at him. I chew on the wheat. He knows I didn't. He can tell.

"And there's a reason," he says, still scratching Manchee. "There's a reason which ain't coming clear." He's trying to read my Noise, see what truth he can sift from it, which most men think is a good enough excuse for starting a fight, but I don't mind with Ben. He cocks his head and stops scratching Manchee. "Aaron?"

"Yeah, I saw Aaron."

"He did that to yer lip?"

"Yeah."

"That sunuvahoor." He frowns and steps forward. "I just might have to have words with that man."

"Don't," I say. "Don't. It'll just be more trouble and it don't hurt that much."

He takes my chin into his fingers and lifts my head so he can see the cut. "That sunuvahoor," he says again, quietly. He touches the cut with his fingers and I flinch away.

"It's nothing," I say.

"You stay away from that man, Todd Hewitt."

"Oh, like I went running to the swamp *hoping* to run into him?"

"He ain't right."

"Well, holy crap, thanks for that bit of info, Ben," I say and then I catch a bit of his Noise that says One month and it's a new thing, a whole new bit of something that he quickly covers up with other Noise. "What's going on, Ben?" I say. "What's going on with my birthday?"

He smiles and for a second it's not an entirely true smile, for a second it's a worried smile, but after that it's a smile true enough. "It's a surprise," he says, "so don't go looking."

Even tho I'm nearly a man and even tho I'm nearly getting on up to his height now, he still bends down a little so his face is level with mine, not too close to be uncomfortable, just close enough so that it's safe and I look away a little bit. And even tho it's Ben, even tho I trust Ben more than anyone else in this crappy little town, even tho it's Ben who saved my life and who I know would do it again, I still find myself reluctant to open up my Noise about what happened in the swamp, mainly cuz I can start to feel it pressing on my chest again whenever the thought gets near.

"Todd?" Ben says, looking at me closely.

"Quiet," Manchee barks softly. "Quiet in swamp."

Ben looks at Manchee, then back at me, his eyes going all soft and asking and full of concern. "What's he talking about, Todd?"

I sigh. "We saw something," I say. "Out there in the swamp. Well, we *didn't* see it, it hid, but it was like a rip in the Noise, like a tear—"

I stop talking cuz he's stopped listening to my voice. I've opened up my Noise for him and am remembering it as truthfully as I can and he's looking at me something fierce and from way behind me I can hear Cillian coming and he's calling "Ben?" and "Todd?" and there's concern in his voice and in his Noise and Ben's is starting to buzz a little, too, and I just keep thinking as truthfully as I can about the hole we found in the Noise but quietly, too, quietly, quietly, so as to keep the town from hearing if I can and here comes Cillian still and Ben's just looking at me and looking at me till finally I have to ask.

"Is it spacks?" I say. "Is it the Spackle? Are they back?"

"Ben?" Cillian's yelling it now as he's coming across the fields.

"Are we in danger?" I ask Ben. "Will there be another war?"

But all Ben says is, "Oh, my God," real quietlike, and then he says it again, "Oh, my God," and then, without even moving or looking away, he says, "We have to get you outta here. We have to get you outta here *right now.*"

4

DON'T THINK IT

CILLIAN COMES RUNNING UP but before he says anything to us, Ben cuts him off and says, "Don't think it!"

Ben turns to me. "Don't you think it neither. You cover it up with yer Noise. You hide it. You hide it as best you can." And he's grabbing my shoulders as he's saying it and squeezing tight enough to make my blood jump even more than it already is.

"What's going on?" I say.

"Did you walk home thru town?" Cillian asks.

"*Course* I walked home thru town," I snap. "What other effing way is there to get home?"

Cillian's face tightens up but it's not with being pissed off at me snapping, it's tightening up with fear, fear I can hear loud as a shout in his Noise. They don't yell at me for "effing" neither, which makes it all somehow worse. Manchee's barking his head off by this point, "Cillian! Quiet! Effing! Todd!" but nobody's bothering to tell him to shut up.

Cillian looks at Ben. "We're gonna have to do it now."

"I know," Ben says.

"What's going on?" I say again, all loudlike. "Do *what* now?" I twist away from Ben and stand looking at them both.

Ben and Cillian take another look at each other and then back at me. "You have to leave Prentisstown," Ben says.

My eyeballs go back and forth twixt theirs but they're not letting nothing go in their Noise 'cept general worry. "What do you mean I have to leave Prentisstown?" I say. "There ain't nowhere else on New World *but* Prentisstown."

They take yet *another* look at each other.

"Stop doing that!" I say.

"Come on," Cillian says. "We've already got yer bag packed."

"How can you already have my bag packed?"

Cillian says to Ben, "We probably don't have much time."

And Ben says to Cillian, "He can go down by the river."

And Cillian says to Ben, "You know what this means."

And Ben says to Cillian, "It doesn't change the plan."

"WHAT THE EFF IS GOING ON?" I roar, but I don't say "eff," now do I? Cuz it seems the situashun calls for something a little stronger. "WHAT EFFING PLAN?"

But they're still not getting mad.

Ben lowers his voice and I can see him trying to get his Noise into some kinda order and he says to me, "It's very, very important you keep what happened in the swamp outta yer Noise as best you can."

"Why? Are the spacks coming back to kill us?"

"Don't think about it!" Cillian snaps. "Cover it up, keep it deep and quiet, till yer so far outta town no one can hear you. Now, come on!"

And he takes off back toward the house, running, actually *running*.

"Come on, Todd," Ben says.

"Not till someone explains something."

"You'll get an explanashun," Ben says, taking me by the arm and pulling me along. "You'll get more than you ever wanted." And there's so much sadness to him when he says it that I don't say nothing more, just follow along running back to the house, Manchee barking his head off behind us.

By the time we make it back to the house, I'm expecting—

I don't know what I'm expecting. An army of Spackle coming outta the woods. A lineup of Mayor Prentiss's men with guns at the ready. The whole house burning down. I don't know. Ben and Cillian's Noise ain't making much sense, my own thoughts are boiling over like a volcano, and Manchee won't stop barking, so who can tell anything in all this racket?

But there's no one there. The house, *our* house, is just as it was, quiet and farm-like. Cillian busts in the back door, goes into the prayer room which we never use, and starts pulling boards up from the floor. Ben goes to the pantry and starts throwing dried foods and fruit into a cloth sack, then he goes to the toilet and takes out a small medipak and throws that in, too.

I just stand there like a doofus wondering just what in the effing blazes is going on.

I know what yer thinking: how can I *not* know if all day, every day I'm hearing every thought of the two men who run my house? That's the thing, tho. Noise is *noise*. It's crash and clatter and it usually adds up to one big mash of sound and thought and picture and half the time it's impossible to make any sense of it at all. Men's minds are messy places and Noise is like the active, breathing face of that mess. It's what's true and what's believed and what's imagined and what's fantasized and it says one thing and a completely opposite thing at the same time and even tho the truth is definitely in there, how can you tell what's true and what's not when yer getting *everything*?

The Noise is a man unfiltered, and without a filter, a man is just chaos walking.

"I ain't leaving," I say, as they keep doing their stuff. They don't pay me no mind. "I ain't leaving," I say again, as Ben steps past me into the prayer room to help Cillian lift up boards. They find what they're looking for and Cillian lifts out a rucksack, an old one I thought I'd lost. Ben opens the top and takes a quick peek thru and I can see some clothes of mine and something that looks like—

"Is that a book?" I say. "You were sposed to burn those ages ago."

But they're ignoring me and the air has just stopped right there as Ben takes it outta the rucksack and he and Cillian look at it and I see that it's not quite a book, more a journal type thing with a nice leather cover and when Ben thumbs thru it, the pages are cream-colored and filled with handwriting.

Ben closes it like it's an important thing and he wraps it inside a plastic bag to protect it and puts it in the rucksack.

They both turn to me.

"I ain't going nowhere," I say.

And there's a knock on the front door.

For a second, nobody says nothing, everyone just freezes. Manchee's got so many things he wants to bark that nothing comes out for a minute till he finally barks "Door!" but Cillian grabs him by the collar with one hand and by the maul with the other, shutting him up. We all look up at each other, wondering what to do next.

There's another knock and then a voice comes thru the walls, "I know yer in there."

"Damn and blast," Ben says.

"Davy ruddy Prentiss," Cillian says.

That's Mr. Prentiss Jr. The man of the law.

"Do you not think I can hear yer Noise?" Mr. Prentiss Jr. says thru the door. "Benison Moore. Cillian Boyd." The voice makes a little pause. "Todd Hewitt."

"Well, so much for hiding," I say, crossing my arms, still a little annoyed at it all.

Cillian and Ben look at each other again, then Cillian lets go of Manchee, says "Stay here" to both of us and heads for the door. Ben shoves the sack of food into the rucksack and ties it shut. He hands it to me. "Put this on," he whispers.

I don't take it at first but he gestures with a serious look so I take it and put it on. It weighs a ton.

We hear Cillian open the front door. "What do you want, Davy?"

"That's Sheriff Prentiss to you, Cillian."

"We're in the middle of lunch, Davy," Cillian says. "Come back later."

"I don't think I will. I think I need to have a word with young Todd."

Ben looks at me, worry in his Noise.

"Todd's got farmwork," Cillian says. "He's just leaving out the back. I can hear him go."

And these are instructions for me and Ben, ain't they? But I ruddy well want to hear what's going on and I ignore Ben's hand on my shoulder trying to pull me toward the back door.

"You take me for a fool, Cillian?" Mr. Prentiss Jr. says.

"Do you really want an answer to that, Davy?"

"I can hear his Noise not twenty feet behind you. Ben's, too." We hear a shift in the mood. "I just want to talk to him. He ain't in no trouble."

"Why you got a rifle then, Davy?" Cillian asks and Ben squeezes my shoulder, probably without even thinking.

Mr. Prentiss Jr.'s voice and Noise both change again. "Bring him out, Cillian. You know why I'm here. Seems like a funny little word floated outta yer boy into town all innocentlike and we just want to see what it's all about, that's all."

"'We?'" Cillian says.

"His Honor the Mayor would like a word with young Todd." Mr. Prentiss Jr. raises his voice. "Y'all come out now, you hear? Ain't no trouble going on. Just a friendly chat."

Ben nods his head at the back door all firmlike and there ain't no arguing with him this time. We start stepping toward it slowly, but Manchee's kept his trap shut for just about as long as he can bear and barks, "Todd?"

"Y'all ain't thinking about sneaking out the back way, are ya?" Mr. Prentiss Jr. calls. "Outta my way, Cillian."

"Get off my property, Davy," Cillian says.

"I ain't telling you twice."

"I believe you've already told me about three times, Davy, so if yer threatening, it ain't working."

There's a pause but the Noise from them both gets louder and Ben and I know what's coming next and suddenly everything's moving fast and we hear a loud thump, followed quick by another two, and me and Ben and Manchee are running to the kitchen but when we get there, it's over. Mr. Prentiss Jr. is on the floor, holding his mouth, blood already coming from it. Cillian's got Mr. Prentiss Jr.'s rifle in his hands and is pointing it at Mr. Prentiss Jr.

"I said get off my property, Davy," he says.

Mr. Prentiss Jr. looks at him, then looks at us, still holding his bloody mouth. Like I say, he ain't barely two years older than me, barely able to even get a sentence out without his voice breaking, but he's had his birthday to be a man so there he is, our sheriff.

The blood from his mouth is getting on the little brown hairs he calls a mustache and everyone else calls nothing.

"You know this answers the asking, doncha?" He spits some blood and a tooth onto our floor. "You know this ain't the end." He looks right at my eye. "You found something, dincha, boy?"

Cillian aims the rifle at his head. "Out," he says.

"We got plans for you, boy." Mr. Prentiss Jr. smiles bloodily at me and gets to his feet. "The boy who's last. One more month, ain't it?"

I look to Cillian but all he does is cock the rifle loudly, getting his point across.

Mr. Prentiss Jr. looks back at us, spits again, and says, "Be seeing you," trying to sound tough but his voice squeaks and he takes off as fast he can back to the town.

Cillian slams the door behind him. "Todd's gotta go *now*. Back thru the swamp."

"I know," Ben says. "I was hoping—"

"Me, too," Cillian says.

"Whoa, whoa," I say, "I ain't going back to the swamp. There's Spackle there!"

"Keep yer thoughts quiet," Cillian says. "That's more important than you know."

"Well, since I don't know nothing, that ain't hard," I say. "I ain't going nowhere till someone tells me what's going on!"

"Todd—" Ben starts.

"They'll be coming back, Todd," Cillian says. "Davy Prentiss will come back and he won't be alone and we won't be able to protect you from all of them at once."

"But—"

"No arguing!" Cillian says.

"Come on, Todd," Ben says. "Manchee's gonna have to go with you."

"Oh, man, this just gets better," I say.

"Todd," Cillian says and I look at him and he's changed a little. There's something new in his Noise, a sadness, a sadness like grief. "Todd," he says again, then suddenly he grabs me and hugs me to him as hard as he can. It's too rough and I bash my cut lip on his collar and say "Ow!" and push him away.

"You may hate us for this, Todd," he says, "but try to believe it's only cuz we love you, all right?"

"No," I say, "it's not all right. It's not all right at all."

But Cillian's not listening, as usual. He stands up and says to Ben, "Go, run, I'll hold 'em off as long as possible."

"I'll come back a different way," Ben says, "see if I can throw 'em off the trail."

They clasp hands for a long minute, then Ben looks at me, says "Come on" and as he's dragging me outta the room to get to the back door, I see Cillian pick up the rifle again and he glances up at me and catches my eye and there's a look to him, a look written all over him and his Noise that this is a bigger good-bye than it even seems, that this is it, the last time he ever expects to see me and I open my mouth to say something but then the door closes on him and he's gone.

5

THE THINGS YOU KNOW

I'LL GET YOU TO THE RIVER," Ben says as we hurry across our fields for the second time this morning. "You can follow it down to where it meets the swamp."

"There ain't no path that way, Ben," I say, "and there's crocs everywhere. You trying to get me killed?"

He looks back at me, his eyes all level, but he keeps on hurrying. "There's no other way, Todd."

"Crocs! Swamp! Quiet! Poo!" Manchee barks.

I've stopped even asking what's going on since nobody seems to want to tell me nothing so we just keep on moving past the sheep, still not in their paddocks and now maybe never getting there. "Sheep!" they say, watching us pass. On we go, past the main barn, down one of the big irrigashun tracks, turning right at a smaller one, heading toward where the wilderness starts, which pretty much means the beginning of the rest of this whole empty planet.

Ben don't start talking again till we get to the tree line. "There's food in yer rucksack to last you for a bit but you should make it stretch as far as you can, eating what fruit you find and anything you can hunt."

"How long do I gotta make it last?" I ask. "How long till I can come back?"

Ben stops. We're just inside the trees. The river's a hundred feet away but you can hear it cuz this is where it starts rushing downhill to get to the swamp.

Suddenly it feels like just about the loneliest place in the whole wide world.

"You ain't coming back, Todd," Ben says, quietly. "You can't."

"Why not?" I say and my voice comes out all mewing like a kitten but I can't help it. "What'd I do, Ben?"

Ben comes up to me. "You didn't do anything, Todd. You didn't do anything at all." He hugs me real hard and I can feel my chest start to press again and I'm so confused and frightened and angry. Nothing was different in the world this morning when I got outta bed and now here I am being sent away and Ben and Cillian acting like I'm dying and it ain't fair and I don't know why it ain't fair but it just ain't fair.

"I know it ain't fair," Ben says, pulling himself away and looking me hard in the face. "But there *is* an explanashun." He turns me around and opens my rucksack and I can feel him taking something out.

The book.

I look at him and look away. "You know I don't read too good, Ben," I say, embarrassed and stupid.

He crouches down a bit so we're truly face-to-face. His Noise ain't making me comfortable at all.

"I know," he says, gentlelike. "I always meant to try and spend more time—" He stops. He holds out the book again. "It's yer ma's," he says. "It's her journal, starting from the day you were born, Todd." He looks down at it. "Till the day she died."

My Noise opens wide.

My ma. My ma's own book.

Ben runs his hand over the cover. "We promised her we'd keep you safe," he says. "We promised her and then we had to put it outta our minds so there was nothing in our Noise, nothing that would let anyone know what we were gonna do."

"Including me," I say.

"It had to be including you. If just a little bit got into yer Noise and then into the town . . ."

He don't finish.

"Like the silence I found in the swamp today," I say. "Like that getting into town and causing all this havoc."

"No, that was a surprise." He looks up at the sky, like he's telling it just how completely a surprise it all was. "No one woulda guessed that happening."

"It's *dangerous*, Ben. I could feel it."

But all he does is hold out the book again.

I start shaking my head. "Ben—"

"I know, Todd," he says, "but try yer best."

"No, Ben—"

He catches my eyes again. He holds 'em with his own. "Do you trust me, Todd Hewitt?"

I scratch my side. I don't know how to answer. "Course I do," I say, "or at least I *did* before you started packing bags I didn't know about for me."

He looks at me harder, his Noise focused like a sun ray. "Do you trust me?" he asks again.

I look at him and yeah, I do, even now. "I trust you, Ben."

"Then trust me when I say that the things you know right now, Todd, those things ain't true."

"Which things?" I ask, my voice rising a little. "Why can't you just tell me?"

"Cuz knowledge is dangerous," he says, as serious as I've ever seen him and when I look into his Noise to see what he's hiding, it roars up and slaps me back. "If I told you now, it would buzz in you louder than a hive at honey-gathering time and Mayor Prentiss would find you fast as he could spit. And you *have* to get away from here. You have to, as far away as you can."

"But where?" I say. *There ain't nowhere else!*

Ben takes a deep breath. "There is," he says. "There's somewhere else."

I don't say nothing to that.

"Folded in the front of the book," Ben says, "there's a map. I made it myself but *don't look at it,* not till yer well outta town, okay? Just go to the swamp. You'll know what to do from there."

But I can tell from his Noise that he's not at all sure I'll know what to do from there. "Or what I'm gonna find there, do you?"

He don't say nothing to that.

And I'm thinking.

"How did you know to have a bag already packed?" I say, stepping back a little. "If this thing in the swamp is so unexpected, why are you so ready to chuck me out into the wilderness today?"

"It was the plan all along, ever since you were little." I see him swallow, I hear his sadness everywhere. "As soon as you were old enough to make it on yer own—"

"You were just gonna throw me out so the crocs could eat me." I'm stepping back farther.

"No, Todd—" He moves forward, the book still in his hand. I step back again. He makes a gesture like, okay.

And he closes his eyes and opens up his Noise for me.

One month's time is the first thing it says—

And here comes my birthday—
The day I'll become a man—
And—
And—
And there it all is—
What happens—
What the other boys did who became men—
All alone—
All by themselves—
How every last bit of boyhood is killed off—
And—
And—
And what actually happened to the people who—
Holy crap—
And I don't want to say no more about it.
And I can't say at all how it makes me feel.

I look at Ben and he's a different man than he always was, he's a different man than the one I've always known.

Knowledge is dangerous.

"It's why no one tells you," he says. "To keep you from running."

"You wouldn't've protected me?" I say, mewing again (shut up).

"*This* is how we're protecting you, Todd," he says. "By getting you *out*. We had to be sure you could survive on yer own, that's why we taught you all that stuff. Now, Todd, you have to go—"

"If that's what's happening in a month, why wait this long? Why not take me away sooner?"

"We can't come with you. That's the whole problem. And we couldn't bear to send you off on yer own. To see you go. Not so young." He rubs the cover of the book with his fingers again. "And we were hoping there might be a miracle. One where we wouldn't have to—"

Lose you, says his Noise.

"But there ain't been no miracle," I say, after a second.

He shakes his head. He holds out the book. "I'm sorry," he says. "I'm so sorry it has to be this way."

And there's so much true sorrow in his Noise, so much worry and edginess, I know he's speaking true, I know he can't help what's happening and I hate it but I take the book from him and put it back in the plastic and into the rucksack. We don't say nothing more. What else is there to say? Everything and nothing. You can't say everything, so you don't say nothing.

He pulls me to him again, hitting my lip on his collar just like Cillian but this time I don't pull away. "Always remember," he says, "when yer ma died, you became our son, and I love you and Cillian loves you, always have, always will."

I start to say, "I don't wanna go," but it never comes out.

Cuz *BANG!!* goes the loudest thing I ever heard in Prentisstown, like something's blowing right up, right on up to the sky.

And it can only be coming from our farm.

Ben lets me go real quick. He ain't saying nothing but his Noise is screaming Cillian all over the place.

"I'll come back with you," I say. "I'll help you fight."

"No!" Ben shouts. "You have to get away. Promise me. Go thru the swamp and *get away.*"

I don't say nothing for a second.

"Promise me," Ben says again, demanding it this time.

"Promise!" Manchee barks and there's fear even in that.

"I promise," I say.

Ben reaches behind his back and unclasps something. He wriggles it for a second or two before it comes unlatched completely. He hands it to me. It's his hunting knife, the big ratchety one with the bone handle and the serrated edge that cuts practically everything in the world, the knife I was hoping to get for the birthday when I became a man. It's still in its belt, so I can wear it myself.

"Take it," he says. "Take it with you to the swamp. You may need it."

"I never fought a Spackle before, Ben."

He still holds out the knife and so I take it.

There's another *BANG* from the farm. Ben looks back toward it, then back to me. "Go. Follow the river down to the swamp and out. Run as fast as you can and you'd better damn well not turn back, Todd Hewitt." He takes my arm and grips it hard. "If I can find you, I'll find you, I swear it," he says. "But you keep going, Todd. You keep yer promise."

This is it. This is good-bye. A good-bye I wasn't even looking for.

"Ben—"

"Go!" he shouts and takes off, looking back once as he runs and then racing off back to the farm, back to whatever's happening at the end of the world.

6

THE KNIFE IN FRONT OF ME

C'MON, MANCHEE," I say, turning to run, tho every bit of me wants to follow Ben as he's running cross the fields a different way, just like he said, to confuse anyone out looking for Noise.

I stop for a second when I hear a bunch of smaller bangs from the direkshun of the house which gotta be rifle shots and I think of the rifle that Cillian took from Mr. Prentiss Jr. and all the rifles that Mayor Prentiss and his men have locked away in the town and how all those guns against Cillian's stolen rifle and the few others we got in the house ain't gonna be much of a fight for very long and it gets me to wondering what the bigger bangs were and I realize they were probably Cillian blowing up the generators to confuse the men and make everyone's Noise so loud they can't hear even the whisper of mine way out here.

All this for me to get away.

"C'mon, Manchee," I say again and we run the last few feet to the river. Then we take a right and start following the river downhill, keeping away from the rushes at the water's edge.

The rushes where the crocs live.

I take the knife from its sheath and I keep it in my hand as we move along fast.

"What's on, Todd?" Manchee keeps barking, which is his version of "What's going on?"

"I don't know, Manchee. Shut up so I can think."

The rucksack's banging into my back as we run but we keep going as best we can, kicking thru river shrubs and jumping over fallen logs.

I'll come back. That's what I'll do. I'll come back. They said I'd know what to do and now I do know. I'll go to the swamp and kill the Spackle if I can and then I'll come back and help Cillian and Ben and then we can all get away to this somewhere else Ben was talking about.

Yeah, that's what I'll do.

"Promised, Todd," Manchee says, sounding worried as the ridge we're going along is getting closer and closer to the rushes.

"Shut up," I say. "I promised to keep on going but maybe keep on going means coming back first."

"Todd?" Manchee says and I don't believe it either.

We've gotten outta hearing distance from the farm and the river veers away east a little before it enters the top of the swamp so it's taking us away from the town, too, and after a minute there ain't nothing following us as we run 'cept my Noise and Manchee's Noise and the sound of the running river which is just loud enough to cover the Noise of a hunting croc. Ben says that's "evolushun" but he says not to think about it too much around Aaron.

I'm breathing heavy and Manchee's panting like he's about to keel over but we don't stop. The sun is starting to set, but it's still light as anything, light that don't feel like it's going to hide you. The ground is flattening out and we're getting down closer to river level as it all starts turning to marsh. Everything's getting muddier and it's making us slow down. There's more rushes, too, can't be helped.

"Listen for crocs," I say to Manchee. "Keep yer ears open."

Cuz the water from the river is slowing and if you can keep yer own Noise quiet enough you can start to hear them out there. The ground's got even wetter. We're barely making walking pace now, sloshing thru mud. I grip the knife harder and hold it out in front of me.

"Todd?" Manchee says.

"Do you hear them?" I whisper, trying to watch my step and watch the rushes and watch out for Manchee all at the same time.

"Crocs, Todd," Manchee says, pretty much as quiet as he can bark.

I stop and I listen hard.

And out there in the rushes, out there in more than one place, I can hear 'em. **Flesh**, they're saying.

Flesh and **feast** and **tooth**.

"Crap," I say.

"Crocs," Manchee says again.

"C'mon," I say and we start splashing along, cuz we're in muck now. My shoes start sinking with each step and water's coming up over the top of 'em and there's no way to go 'cept thru the rushes. I start swinging the knife as we go, trying to cut any rush that's in front of me.

I look ahead and I can see where we're going, up and to the right. We've made it past the town and it's the part where the wild fields come down by the school and meet up with the swamp and if we get thru this marshy part here we'll be on safe ground and can get onto the paths that head into the dark of the swamp.

Was it really only this morning I was here last?

"Hurry up, Manchee," I say. "Almost there."

Flesh and **feast** and **tooth** and I swear it's getting closer.

"C'mon!"

Flesh.

"Todd?"

I'm cutting my way thru rushes and pulling my feet outta mud and **flesh** and **feast** and **TOOTH**.

And then I hear **Whirler dog**–

And I know we're done for.

"Run!" I yell.

And we run and Manchee lets out a frightened yelp and leaps past me but I see a croc rear up outta the rushes in front of him and it jumps for him but Manchee's so scared he jumps even higher, higher than he really knows how, and the croc's teeth snap on empty air and it lands with a splash next to me looking mighty pissed off and I hear its Noise hiss **Whirler boy** and I'm running and it jumps for me and I'm not even thinking and I'm turning and I'm pushing my hand up and the croc comes crashing down on top of me and its mouth is open and its claws are out and I think I'm about to be dead and I'm thrashing my way back outta the muck up onto the dry part and it's on its hind legs coming after me outta the rushes and it takes a minute of me yelling and of Manchee barking his head off before I realize that it's not actually coming after me no more, that the croc's dead, that my new knife is right thru its head, still stuck in the croc and the only reason the croc's still thrashing is cuz I'm still thrashing and I shake the croc off the knife and the croc falls to the ground and I sort of just fall over too in celebrayshun of not being dead.

And it's when I'm gasping for air from the rush of my blood and Manchee's barking and barking and we're both laughing from relief that I realize that we've been too loud ourselves to hear something important.

"Going somewhere, young Todd?"

Aaron. Standing right over me.

Before I can do nothing he punches me in the face.

I fall backward onto the ground, the rucksack digging into my back and making me look like an upturned turtle. My cheek and my eye are

just singing with pain and I haven't even moved properly before Aaron's
grabbing me by my shirtfront and the skin beneath and lifting me to my
feet. I yell out from how much it hurts.

Manchee barks an angry "Aaron!" and goes for Aaron's legs, but
Aaron doesn't even look before kicking him outta the way hard.

Aaron's holding me up to look him in the face. I can only keep the
one non-painful eye open to meet his.

"Just what in the name of God's bounteous, glorified Eden are you
doing down here in the swamp, Todd Hewitt?" he says, his breath
smelling like meat and his Noise the scariest kinda crazy you never
wanna hear. "Yer sposed to be at yer farm right now, boy."

With his free hand, he punches me in the stomach. I try to bend
over with the pain of it but he's still holding on to my shirtfront and the
skin below.

"You gotta go back," he says. "There's things you need to see."

I'm gasping for breath but the way he says it catches my ear and
some of the flickers I'm catching in his Noise make it so I can see a little
bit of the truth.

"You sent them," I say. "It wasn't me they heard. It was you."

"Smart boys make useless men," he says, twisting his gripping hand.
I cry out but I ruddy well keep talking, too. "They didn't hear the quiet
in my Noise. They heard it in *yer* Noise and you sent them to me to keep
them from coming after you."

"Oh, no, Todd," he says, "they heard it in yer Noise. I just *made sure*
they did. I made sure they knew who was responsible for bringing danger to our town." He grits his teeth into a wild smile beneath his beard.
"And who should be rewarded for his efforts."

"Yer crazy," I say and boy is it ever true and boy do I wish it wasn't.

His smile falls and his teeth clench harder. "It's mine, Todd," he
says. "Mine."

I don't know what this means but I don't stop to think about it cuz I
realize instead that both Aaron and I have forgotten one important
thing.

I never let go of the knife.

A whole buncha things happen at once.

Aaron hears *knife* in my Noise and realizes his mistake. He pulls
back his free fist to make another punch.

I pull back my knife hand and I wonder if I can actually stab him.

There's a breaking sound from the rushes and Manchee barks,
"Croc!"

And all at the same time, we hear **Whirler man**.

Before Aaron can even turn, the croc is on him, clamping its teeth onto his shoulder and grabbing him with its claws and pulling him back toward the rushes. Aaron lets go of me and I fall to the ground again, clutching at all the bruises he's left on my chest. I look up and I see Aaron thrashing in the muck now, fighting with the croc and the fins on the backs of other crocs heading his way, too.

"Outta here!" Manchee's barking, almost shrieking.

"Too effing right," I say and I stumble to my feet, the rucksack knocking me a little off balance and my hurt eye trying to peel open but we don't stop and we run and we run and we run.

We get out of the marshes and run along the bottom of the fields to the start of the swamp path and we run into the swamp along it and when we get to the log that Manchee always needs help over he just sails right over it without even stopping and I'm right behind him and we're running our way to the Spackle buildings just like we were this morning.

And the knife is still in my hand and my Noise is thudding so loud and I'm so frightened and hurt and mad that I know beyond any shadow of a thought that I am going to find the Spackle hiding in his Noise hole and I am going to kill him dead dead dead for everything that's happened today.

"Where is it?" I ask Manchee. "Where's the quiet?"

Manchee's sniffing away like mad, running from building to building, and I'm doing my best to calm my Noise but there don't seem any chance of that.

"Hurry!" I say. "Before it runs—"

And it's barely outta my mouth before I hear it. The rip in the Noise, as big and horrible as life itself, I can hear it a little bit away, behind the Spackle buildings, behind some bushes.

It ain't getting away this time.

"Quiet!" Manchee barks, all keyed up, and he runs past the buildings and into the bushes.

And the quiet moves, too, and tho I can feel the pressure in my chest again and the terrible mournful things coming into my eyes, this time I don't stop, this time I run after my dog and I don't stop and I take in my breath and I swallow away the pressure and I wipe the water from my eyes and I grip the knife and I can hear Manchee barking and I can hear the silence and it's just around this tree just around this tree just around this tree and I'm yelling and I'm going round the tree and I'm running at the silence and my teeth are bared and I'm screaming and Manchee's barking and—

And I stop.

I stop right there in my tracks.

I don't, I do absolutely *not* put down the knife.

There it is, looking back at us, breathing heavy, crouched at the base of a tree, cowering from Manchee, its eyes practically dying from fright but still trying to offer up a pitiful threat with its arms.

And I just stop.

I hold my knife.

"Spackle!" Manchee barks, tho he's too chicken to attack now that I've held back. "Spackle! Spackle! Spackle!"

"Shut up, Manchee," I say.

"Spackle!"

"I said *shut up!*" I shout, which stops him.

"Spackle?" Manchee says, unsure of things now.

I swallow, trying to get rid of the pressure in my throat, the unbelievable sadness that comes and comes as I look at it looking back at me. Knowledge is dangerous and men lie and the world keeps changing, whether I want it to or not.

Cuz it ain't a Spackle.

"It's a girl," I say.

It's a girl.

PART II

7

IF THERE WAS

IT'S A GIRL," I say again. I'm still catching my breath, still feeling the pressure on my chest, *definitely* still holding the knife way out in front of me.

A girl.

It's looking back at us like we're gonna kill it. It's hunched down in a little ball, trying to make itself as small as possible, only taking its eyes off Manchee to snatch quick glances of me.

Of me and my knife.

Manchee's huffing and puffing, his back fur all ridged, hopping around like the ground is hot, looking as charged up and confused as I am, tho completely hopeless about keeping in any way cool.

"What's girl?" he barks. "What's girl?"

By which he means, "What's a girl?"

"What's girl?" Manchee barks again and when the girl looks like it might be about to make a leap back over the large root where it's huddling, Manchee's bark turns into a fierce growl, "*Stay, stay, stay, stay, stay . . .*"

"Good dog," I say, tho I don't know *why* it's good what he's doing but what else can you say? This makes no sense, no sense at all, and everything feels like it's starting to slip, like the world is a table tilted on its side and everything on it is tipping over.

I am Todd Hewitt, I think to myself but who knows if *that's* even true anymore?

"Who are you?" I finally say, if it can even hear me over all my raging

Noise and Manchee's nervous breakdown. "Who are you?" I say, louder and clearer. "What are you doing here? Where did you come from?"

It looks at me, finally, for more than just a second, taking its eyes off Manchee. It looks at my knife, then it looks at my face above my knife.

She looks at me.

She does.

She.

I know what a girl is. Course I do. I seen 'em in the Noise of their fathers in town, mourned like their wives but not nearly so often. I seen 'em in vids, too. Girls are small and polite and smiley. They wear dresses and their hair is long and it's pulled into shapes behind their heads or on either side. They do all the inside-the-house chores, while boys do all the outside. They reach womanhood when they turn thirteen, just like boys reach manhood, and then they're women and they become wives.

That's how New World works, or at least that's how Prentisstown works. Worked. Was meant to, anyhow, but there ain't no girls. They're all dead. They died with their mothers and their grandmothers and their sisters and their aunties. They died in the months after I was born. All of them, every single one.

But here one is.

And its hair ain't long. *Her* hair. Her hair ain't long. And she ain't wearing no dress, she's wearing clothes that look like way newer versions of mine, so new they're almost like a uniform, even tho they're torn and muddy, and she ain't that small, she's my size, just, by the looks of her, and she's sure as all that's unholy not smiley.

No, not smiley at all.

"Spackle?" Manchee barks quietly.

"Would you effing well *shut up*?" I say.

So how do I know? How do I know it's a girl?

Well, for one, she ain't no Spackle. Spackle looked like men with everything a bit swelled up, everything a bit longer and weirder than on a man, their mouths a bit higher than they should be and their ears and eyes way, *way* different. And spacks grew their clothes right on their bodies, like lichens you could trim away to whatever shape you needed. Product of swamp dwelling, according to another Ben-best-guess and she don't look like that and her clothes are normal and so there ain't no way she's a Spackle.

And for two, I just know. I just do. I can't tell you but I look and I see and I just know. She don't look like the girls I seen in vids or in Noise and I never seen no girl in the flesh but there she is, she's a girl and that's that. Don't ask me. Something about her shape, something about her smell, something I don't know but it's there and she's a girl.

If there was a girl, that's what she'd be.

And she ain't another boy. She just ain't. She ain't me. She ain't nothing like me at all. She's something completely other else altogether and I don't know how I know it but I know who I am, I am Todd Hewitt, and I know what I am not and I am not her.

She's looking at me. She's looking at my face, in my eyes. Looking and looking.

And I'm not hearing *nothing*.

Oh, man. My chest. It's like falling.

"Who are you?" I say again but my voice actually *catches*, like it breaks up cuz I'm so sad (shut up). I grit my teeth and I get a little madder and I say it yet again. "Who are you?" and I hold out the knife a little farther. With my other arm, I have to wipe my eyes real fast.

Something's gotta happen. Someone's gotta move. Someone's gotta do *something*.

And there ain't no someone but me, still, whatever the world's doing.

"Can you talk?" I say.

She just looks back at me.

"Quiet," Manchee barks.

"Shut it, Manchee," I say. "I need to think."

And she's still just looking back at me. With no Noise at all.

What do I do? It ain't fair. Ben told me I'd get to the swamp and I'd know what to do but I *don't* know what to do. They didn't say nothing about a girl, they didn't say nothing about why the quiet makes me ache so much I can barely stop from ruddy *weeping*, like I'm missing something so bad I can't even think straight, like the emptiness ain't in her, it's in *me* and there ain't nothing that's ever gonna fix it.

What do I do?

What do I do?

She seems like maybe she's calming down. She's not shaking as much as she was, her arms aren't up so high, and she's not looking like she's about to run off at the first opportunity, tho how can you know for sure when a person's got no Noise? How can they *be* a person if they ain't got no Noise?

And can she hear me? *Can* she? Can a person with no Noise hear it at all?

I look at her and I think, as loud and clear as I can, *Can you hear me? Can you?*

But she don't change her face, she don't change her look.

"Okay," I say, and I take a step back. "Okay. You just stay there, okay? You just stay right there."

I take a few more steps back but I keep my eyes on her and she keeps her eyes on me. I bring my knife arm down and I slide it outta one strap of the rucksack, then I lean over and drop the rucksack to the ground. I keep the knife in one hand and with the other I open up the rucksack and fish out the book.

It's heavier than you'd think a thing made of words could be. And it smells of leather. And there's pages and pages of my ma's—

That'll have to wait.

"You watch her, Manchee," I say.

"Watch!" he barks.

I look inside the front cover and there's the paper folded in just like Ben said. I unfold it. There's a hand-drawn map on one side and then a whole buncha writing on the back but it's all a big block of letters which I ain't got the calmness of Noise to even try right now so I just look at the map.

Our house is right at the top and the town just below with the river Manchee and I came down off to one side leading into the swamp and that's where we are now. But there's more to it, ain't there? The swamp keeps going till it starts being a river again and there's arrows drawn along the riverbank so that's where Ben is wanting me and Manchee to go and I follow the arrows with my fingers and they lead right outta the swamp, they lead right to—

WHUMP!! The world goes bright for a second as something clubs me upside the head, right on the sore spot where Aaron punched me; and I fall over but as I'm falling I swing the knife up and I hear a little yelp of pain and I catch myself before I fall all the way down and I turn, sitting down on the ground hard, holding the back of my knife hand to the pain in my head but looking at where the attack came from and it's here that I learn my very first lesson: Things with no Noise can sneak right up on you. Sneak right up on you like they ain't even there.

The girl is on her butt, too, sitting on the ground away from me, holding on to one of her upper arms with her hand, blood coming from twixt her fingers. She's dropped the stick she hit me with and her face is all collapsed in on itself with what she must be feeling from that cut.

"WHAT THE HELL D' YOU DO THAT FOR?" I shout, trying not to touch my face too hard. Man, am I sick of being hit today.

The girl just looks at me, her forehead still creased, holding her cut. Which is kinda bleeding a lot.

"Stick, Todd!" Manchee barks.

"And where the hell were you?" I say to him.

"Poo, Todd."

I make a *Gah!* sound and kick some dirt at him. He scrabbles back, then starts sniffing at some bushes like there ain't nothing unusual going on in the world. Dogs got attenshun spans about as long as a match-stick. Idiot things.

It's starting to get dark now, the sun really setting, the already dark swamp getting even darker, and I still don't have no answer. Time keeps passing and I ain't sposed to wait here and I ain't sposed to go back and *there ain't sposed to be a girl.*

Boy, that cut really is bleeding on her.

"Hey," I say, my voice shaky from the charge running through me. *I am Todd Hewitt,* I think. *I am almost a man.* "Hey," I say again, trying to be a little calmer.

The girl looks at me.

"I ain't gonna hurt you," I say, breathing hard, just like her. "You hear me? I ain't gonna hurt you. As long as you don't try to hit me with no more sticks, all right?"

She looks at my eyes. Then she looks at the knife.

Is she understanding?

I lower the knife away from my face and bring it down near the ground. I don't let go of it, tho. With my free hand, I start looking thru the rucksack again till I find the medipak Ben threw in. I hold it up.

"Medipak," I say. She doesn't change. "Me-di-pak," I say slowly. I point to my own upper arm, to where the cut is on her. "Yer bleeding."

Nothing.

I sigh and I start to stand. She flinches and scoots back on her butt. I sigh again in an angry way. *"I ain't gonna hurt you."* I hold up the medi-pak. "It's medicine. It'll stop the bleeding."

Still nothing. Maybe there ain't nothing in her at all.

"Look," I say and I snap open the medipak. I fumble with one hand and take out an antiseptic pad, tearing away the paper cover with my teeth. I'm probably bleeding from where first Aaron hit me and then the girl, so I take the pad and rub it over my eye and eyebrow. I pull it away and yep, there's blood. I hold the pad out to the girl so she can see it. "See?" I point to my eye. "See? It stops things bleeding."

I take a step forward, just the one. She flinches but not as much. I take another step, then another and then I'm next to her. She keeps looking at the knife.

"I ain't putting it down, so just forget it," I say. I push the pad toward her arm. "Even if it's deep, this stitches it up, okay? I'm trying to help you."

"Todd?" Manchee barks, full of asking marks.

"In a minute," I say. "Look, yer bleeding everywhere, okay? And I can fix it, all right? Just don't get any ideas about any more ruddy sticks."

She's watching. And she's watching. And she's watching. I'm trying to be as calm as I really don't feel. I don't know why I'm helping her, not after she whacked me on the head, but I don't know what to do about anything. Ben said there'd be answers in the swamp and there ain't no answers, there's just this girl who's bleeding cuz I cut her even tho she deserved it and if I can stop the bleeding then maybe that's doing something.

I don't know. I don't know what to do, so I just do this.

The girl's still watching me, still breathing heavy. But she ain't running and she ain't flinching and then so you can hardly tell at all she's turning her upper arm toward me a little bit so I can reach the cut.

"Todd?" Manchee barks again.

"Shush," I say, not wanting to scare the girl anymore. Being this close to her silence is like my heart breaking all over the place. I can feel it, like it's pulling me down into a bottomless pit, like it's calling for me to just fall and fall and fall.

But I keep my nerve, I do. I keep it and I press the antiseptic pad on her arm, rubbing the cut, which is pretty deep, till it closes a bit and stops bleeding.

"Ya gotta be careful," I say. "That ain't a permanent heal. You gotta be careful with it till yer body heals the rest, okay?"

And all she does is look at me.

"Okay," I say, to myself as much as anyone cuz now that that's done, what's next?

"Todd?" Manchee barks. "Todd?"

"And no more sticks, all right?" I say to the girl. "No more hitting me."

"Todd?" Manchee again.

"And obviously my name's Todd."

And there, just there, just there in the fading light, is there a little beginning of a start of a smile? Is there?

"Can you . . . ?" I say, looking as deep into her eyes as the pressure in my chest allows. "Can you understand me?"

"Todd," Manchee's barking picks up a notch.

I turn to him. *"What?"*

"Todd! TODD!!!"

And then we can all hear it. Pounding thru the bushes and breaking branches and running footsteps and Noise and Noise and oh, crap, Noise.

"Get up," I say to the girl. "Get up! Now!"

I grab my rucksack and put it on and the girl's looking terrified but in a not-helpful paralyzed way and I shout "Come on!" to her again and I grab her arm, not thinking about the cut now, and I try to lift her to her feet but all of a sudden it's too late and there's a yell and a roar and a sound like whole trees falling down and me and the girl can only turn to look and it's Aaron and he's mad and he's messed up and he's coming right for us.

8

THE CHOICES OF A KNIFE

HE'S ON US IN THREE STEPS. Before I can even try to run, he's coming at me with his hands out, grabbing my neck, smashing me back against a tree.

"You little FILTH!" he screams and presses his thumbs into my throat. I scrabble at his arms, trying to slash at him with the knife, but my rucksack has fallen and the strap has pinned my arm back against the tree so he can pretty much go on strangling me for as long as it takes.

His face is a nightmare, a horrible thing I'm not gonna stop seeing even if I ever get outta this. The crocs took his left ear and a long strip of flesh with it going right down his left cheek. You can see his teeth through the gash and it's causing his left eye to bulge forward like his head's been caught in mid-explosion. There are other gashes on his chin and neck and his clothes are torn and there's blood practically everywhere and I can even see a croc tooth sticking out of a fleshy tear on his shoulder.

I'm choking for breath but not getting any at all and you can't believe how much it hurts and the world's gone spinning and my brain's going funny and I have this stupid little thought that Aaron didn't survive the croc attack after all, that he died but he's so pissed off at me that dying didn't stop him from coming here to kill me anyway.

"WHAT ARE YOU SMILING AT?" he screams, little bits of blood and spit and flesh spraying onto my face. He squeezes my neck harder and I can feel myself throwing up but there's nowhere for it to go and

I can't breathe and all the lights and colors are flowing together and I'm dying and I'm going to die.

"*AAH!*" Aaron suddenly jerks back, letting me go. I drop to the ground and throw up all over everywhere and take in a huge gasping breath that makes me cough in a way like I'm never gonna stop. I look up and see Manchee's snout wrapped around Aaron's calf, biting it for all he's worth.

Good dog.

Aaron slams Manchee sideways with an arm, sending him flying into the bushes. I hear a thump and a yelp and a "Todd?"

Aaron whirls around to me again and I just can't stop looking at his face, at the gashes everywhere that no one could have survived, no one, it's not possible.

Maybe he really is dead.

"Where's the sign?" he says, his torn expression changing real quick and looking around in a sudden panic.

The sign?

The—

The girl.

I look, too. She's gone.

Aaron whirls again, this way, that, and then I see him hearing it the same time I do, hearing the rustle and snap as she runs, hearing the silence as it flows away from us, and without another look at me, he takes off after her and he's gone.

And just like that, I'm alone.

Just like that, like I have nothing to do with anything here.

What a stupid day this has been.

"Todd?" Manchee comes limping outta the bushes.

"I'm okay, buddy," I try to say and get some of it out despite the coughing, even tho it ain't true. "I'm okay."

I try to keep breathing thru the coughs, forehead on the ground, dribbling spit and barf everywhere.

I keep breathing and these thoughts start coming. They come all uninvited, don't they?

Cuz maybe that could be it, couldn't it? Maybe it could be over, simple as that. The girl's obviously what Aaron wants, whatever he means by "the sign," right? The girl's obviously what *the town* wants, what with all the ruckus over the quiet in my Noise. And so if Aaron can have her and the town can have her, then that could be the end of it, right? They could have what they want and leave me alone and I could go back and everything could be like it was before and, yeah, it would probably be no good for the girl but it might save Ben and Cillian.

It might save me.

I'm just *thinking* it, all right? The thoughts rush in, that's all.

Thoughts that this could be over as soon as it started.

"Over," Manchee murmurs.

And then I hear the terrible, terrible scream that of course is the girl getting caught and that's the choice made, ain't it?

The next scream comes a second later but I'm already on my feet without even really thinking it, slipping off my rucksack, leaning a bit, coughing still, reaching for more breath, but the knife in my hand and running.

They're easy to follow. Aaron's torn thru the bushes like a bull and his Noise is throwing up a roar and always, always, always there's the silence of the girl, even behind her screams, which somehow makes it even harder to hear. I run as best I can after them, Manchee on my heels, and it ain't more than half a minute before we're there with genius me having no idea what to do now I've got here. Aaron's chased her into a bit of water about ankle-deep and got her back up against a tree. He's got her wrists in his hands but she's fighting him, fighting and kicking for all she's worth, but her face is a thing so scared I can barely get my words out.

"Leave her alone," my voice rasps but no one hears me. Aaron's Noise is blazing so loud I'm not sure he'd hear me even if I yelled. THE HOLY SACRAMENT and THE SIGN FROM GOD and THE PATH OF THE SAINT and pictures of the girl in a church, pictures of the girl drinking the wine and eating the host, pictures of the girl as an angel.

The girl as a sacrifice.

Aaron gets both of her wrists in one of his fists, fumbles off the cord belt of his robe, and starts tying her hands together with it. The girl kicks him hard where Manchee bit him and he hits her across the face with the back of his hand.

"Leave her alone," I say again, trying to make my voice louder.

"Alone!" Manchee barks, still limping but still ferocious. What a ruddy good dog.

I step forward. Aaron's back's to me, like he don't even care I'm here, like he don't even think of me as a threat.

"Let her go," I try to shout but it just makes me cough some more. Still nothing, tho. Still nothing from Aaron or anyone.

I'm gonna have to do it. I'm gonna have to do it. Oh man oh man oh man I'm gonna have to do it.

I'm gonna have to kill him.

I raise the knife.

I've raised the knife.

Aaron turns, not even fastlike, just turns like someone's called his name. He sees me standing there, knife in the air, not moving like the goddam coward idiot I am, and he smiles and boy I just can't say how awful a smile looks on that torn-up face.

"Yer Noise reveals you, young Todd," he says, letting go of the girl, who's so tied up and beaten now she don't even try to run. Aaron takes a step toward me.

I take a step back (shut up, please just shut up).

"The Mayor will be disappointed to hear about yer untimely departure from the earthly plain, boy," Aaron says, taking another step. I take another step, too, the knife in the air like it's of no use at all.

"But God has no use for a coward," Aaron says, "does he, boy?"

Quick as a snake, his left arm knocks into my right, sending the knife flying out of my hand. He hits me in the face with the flat of his right hand, knocking me back down into the water and I feel his knees land on my chest and his hands pressing down on my throat to finish the job but this time my face is underwater so it's going to be a lot faster.

I struggle but I've lost. I've lost. I had my chance and I've lost and I deserve this and I'm fighting but I'm not nearly as strong as I was before and I can feel the end coming. I can feel me giving up.

I'm lost.

Lost.

And then, in the water, my hand finds a rock.

BOOM! I bring it up and hit him on the side of the head before I can think about it.

BOOM! I do it again.

BOOM! And again.

I feel him slide off me and I lift my head, choking on water and air, but I sit up and raise the rock again to hit him but he's laying down in the water, face half-in, half-out, his teeth smiling up at me thru the gash in his cheek. I scrabble back from him, coughing and spluttering, but he stays there, sinking a little, not moving.

I feel like my throat is broken but I throw up some water and can breathe a little better.

"Todd? Todd? Todd?" Manchee says, coming up to me, all licky and barky like a little puppy. I scratch him twixt the ears cuz I can't say nothing yet.

And then we both feel the silence and look up and there's the girl standing over us, her hands still tied.

Holding the knife in her fingers.

I sit frozen for a second and Manchee starts to growl but then I realize. I take a few more breaths and then I reach up and take the knife from her fingers and cut the cord Aaron bound her wrists with. It drops away and she rubs where it was tied, still staring at me, still not saying nothing.

She knows. She knows I couldn't do it.

Goddam you, I think to myself. *Goddam you.*

She looks at the knife. She looks over at Aaron, lying down in the water.

He's still breathing. He gurgles water with every breath, but he's still breathing.

I grip the knife. The girl looks at me, at the knife, at Aaron, at me again.

Is she telling me? Is she telling me to do it?

He's lying there, undefended, probably eventually drowning.

And I have a knife.

I get to my feet, fall down from dizziness, and get to my feet again. I step toward him. I raise my knife. Again.

The girl takes in a breath and I can feel her holding it.

Manchee says, "Todd?"

And I have my knife raised over Aaron. One more time, I've got my chance. One more time, I've got my knife raised.

I could do it. No one on New World would blame me. It'd be my right.

I could just do it.

But a knife ain't just a thing, is it? It's a choice, it's something you *do*. A knife says yes or no, cut or not, die or don't. A knife takes a decision out of your hand and puts it in the world and it never goes back again.

Aaron's gonna die. His face is ripped, his head is bashed, he's sinking into shallow water without ever waking up. He tried to kill me, he wanted to kill the girl, he's responsible for the ruckus in town, he's gotta be the one who sent the Mayor to the farm and cuz of that he's responsible for Ben and Cillian. He deserves to die. He deserves it.

And I can't bring the knife down to finish the job.

Who am I?

I am Todd Hewitt.

I am the biggest, effing waste of nothing known to man.

I can't do it.

Goddam you, I think to myself again.

"Come on," I say to the girl. "We gotta get outta here."

9

WHEN LUCK AIN'T WITH YOU

AT FIRST I don't think she's gonna come. There's no reason for her to, no reason for me to ask her, but when I say to her, "Come on," a second time more urgently and gesture with my hand, she follows me, follows Manchee, and that's how it is, that's what we do, who knows if it's right, but that's what we do.

Night's well and truly fallen. The swamp seems even thicker here, as black as anything. We rush on back a ways to get my rucksack and then around and a little bit farther away in the dark to get some distance between us and Aaron's body (please let it be a body). We clamber round trees and over roots, getting deeper into the swamp. When we get to a small clearing where there's a bit of flat land and a break in the trees, I stop us.

I'm still holding the knife. It rests there in my hand, shining at me like blame itself, like the word *coward* flashing again and again. It catches the light of both moons and my God it's a powerful thing. A *powerful* thing, like I'd have to agree to be a part of *it* rather than it being a part of me.

I reach behind me and put it in the sheath between my back and the rucksack where at least I won't have to see it.

I take the rucksack off and fish thru it for a flashlight.

"Do you know how to use one of these?" I ask the girl, switching it on and off a coupla times.

She just looks at me, as ever.

"Never mind," I say.

My throat still hurts, my face still hurts, my chest still hurts, my Noise keeps pounding me with visions of bad news, of how good a fight Ben and Cillian managed to put up at the farm, of how long it'll take Mr. Prentiss Jr. to find out where I've gone, of how long it'll take him to be on his way after me, after *us* (not long at all, if he ain't already), so who ruddy cares if she knows how to use a flashlight. Of *course* she don't.

I get the book out of the rucksack, using the torch for a light. I open up to the map again and I follow Ben's arrows from our farm down the river and thru the swamp and then outta the swamp as it turns back into river.

It's not hard to find yer way outta the swamp. Out on the horizon beyond it, you can always see three mountains, one close and two farther away but next to each other. The river on Ben's map goes twixt the closer one and the two farther away ones and so all we gotta do is to keep heading toward that space in the middle and we should find the river again and follow it. Follow it to where the arrows keep going.

Keep going to another settlement.

There it is. Right there at the bottom of the page where the map ends.

A whole other place.

As if I don't have enough new stuff to think about.

I look up at the girl, still staring at me, maybe not even blinking. I shine the flashlight in her face. She winces and turns away.

"Where'd you come from?" I ask. "Is it here?"

I point the flashlight down at the map and put my finger on the other town. The girl don't move so I wave her over. She still don't move so I sigh and pick up the book and take it over to her and shine the flashlight on the page.

"I," I point to myself, "am from here." I point to our farm north of Prentisstown on the map. "This," I say, waving my arms around to show the swamp, "is here." I point at the swamp. "We need to go here." I point at the other town. Ben's written the other town's name underneath, but – well, whatever. "Is this where yer from?" I point to her, point to the other town, point to her again. "Are you from here?"

She looks at the map but other than that, nothing.

I sigh in frustrayshun and step away from her. It's uncomfortable being so close. "Well, I sure hope so," I say, studying the map. "Cuz that's where we're going."

"Todd," Manchee barks. I look up. The girl's started to wander around in circles in the clearing, looking at stuff like it means something to her.

"What're you doing?" I ask.

She looks at me, at the flashlight in my hand and she points thru some trees.

"What?" I say. "We don't have time—"

She points thru the trees again and starts walking there.

"Hey!" I say. "*Hey!*"

I guess I have to follow.

"We gotta stick to the map!" I duck under branches to follow her, the rucksack getting caught left and right. "Hey! Wait up!"

I stumble on, Manchee behind me, the flashlight not much good against every ruddy little branch and root and puddle in a great big swamp. I keep having to drop my head and tear the rucksack free of stuff so I can barely look ahead enough to follow her. I see her standing by a fallen, burned-looking tree, waiting for me, watching me come.

"What're you doing?" I say, finally catching up with her. "Where're you—"

And then I see.

The tree *is* burned, *freshly* burned and freshly knocked over, too, the unburned splinters clean and white like new wood. And there are a buncha trees just like it, a whole line of 'em, in fact, on either side of a great ditch gouged outta the swamp, now filled with water but piled-up dirt and burned plants all around it show that's it gotta be a new thing, like someone came thru here and dug it up in one fiery swoop.

"What happened?" I swing the flashlight along it. "What did this?"

She just looks off to the left, where the ditch disappears into darkness. I shine the flashlight down that way but it's not strong enough to see what's down there. Tho it feels like *something's* there.

The girl takes off into the darkness toward whatever it might be.

"Where're you going?" I ask, not expecting an answer and not getting any. Manchee gets twixt me and the girl, like he's following her now instead of me, and off they go in the dark. I keep my distance but I follow, too. The silence still flows from her, *still* bothers me, like it's ready to swallow up the whole world and me with it.

I keep the flashlight shining over every possible square inch of water. Crocs don't usually come this far into the swamp but that's only usually, plus there's red snakes that're poisonous and water weasels that bite and it just don't feel like luck is bothering with any of us today so if something can go wrong it's probably gonna.

We're getting closer and I shine the flashlight down to where we're heading and something starts glinting back, something that ain't tree or bush or animal or water.

Something metal. Something *big* and metal.

"What's that?" I say.

We get closer and at first I think it's just a big fissionbike and I wonder what kind of idiot would try to ride a fissionbike in a swamp cuz you
can barely get 'em to work over flattened dirt roads much less water and
roots.

But it ain't a fissionbike.

"Hold up."

The girl stops.

Whaddya know? The girl stops.

"So you can understand me, then?"

But nothing, as ever nothing.

"Well, hold up for a sec," I say cuz a thought's coming. We're still a
bit away from it but I keep flicking the flashlight over the metal. And
back over the straight line that the ditch makes. And over the metal
again. And over all the burned stuff on either side of the ditch. And a
thought keeps coming.

The girl stops waiting and heads off toward the metal and I follow.
We have to go around a big burned log, still lazily smoking in one or two
spots, to get to the thing and when we do it's much bigger than the
biggest fissionbike and even then it looks like it's only part of an even
bigger something than that. It's crumpled and burned in most places
and even tho I don't know what it looked like before it crumpled and
burned, it's obviously mostly wreckage.

And it's obviously wreckage of a ship.

An airship. Maybe even a *space*ship.

"Is this yers?" I ask, shining the flashlight at the girl. She don't say
nothing, as usual, but she don't say it in a way that could be agreement.
"Did you crash here?"

I shine the flashlight up and down her body, up and down her
clothes, which are a bit different than what I'm used to, sure, but not so
different that they couldn't have belonged to me once upon a time.

"Where'd you come from?" I say.

But of course she don't say nothing and just looks off to a place farther into the darkness, crosses her arms, and starts heading off there. I
don't follow this time. I keep looking at the ship. That's what it's gotta
be. I mean, *look* at it. A lot of it's smashed beyond recognishun but you
can still see something that might be a hull, might be an engine, even
something that might have been a window.

The first homes in Prentisstown, see, were made from the ships the
original settlers landed in. Sure, wood and log homes got built after, but
Ben says the first thing you do when you land is build immediate shelter
and immediate shelter comes from the first supplies to hand. The
Church and the gas stayshun back in town are still partly made outta

metal hulls and holds and rooms and such. And tho this heap of wreckage is pretty pounded, if you look at it right, it might be an old Prentisstown house that fell right outta the sky. Right outta the sky on fire.

"Todd!" Manchee barks from somewhere outta sight. "Todd!"

I go running round to where the girl disappeared, round the wreckage to a part that seems less smashed up. As I run past, I can even see a
door that's been opened out the side of one wall of metal a little way up
and there's even a light on inside.

"Todd!" Manchee barks and I shine the flashlight over to where he's
barking, standing next to the girl. She's just standing there looking down
at something and so I shine the flashlight and see that she's standing by
two long piles of clothes.

Which are actually two bodies, ain't they?

I walk over, shining the flashlight down. There's a man, his clothes
and body pretty much completely burned away from the chest down.
His face has burns, too, but not enough to disguise that he was a man.
He has a wound on his forehead that woulda killed him even if the
burns hadn't but it don't matter, does it, cuz he's dead either way. Dead
and lying here in a swamp.

I swing the flashlight over and he's lying next to a woman, ain't he?

I hold my breath.

It's the first woman I ever seen in the flesh. And it's the same as the
girl. I never seen a woman in real life before but if there was a real-life
woman, that's what she'd be.

And dead, too, of course, but nothing as obvious as burns and a
gash, not even blood on her clothes so maybe she's busted up on the inside.

But a woman. An actual woman.

I shine the flashlight at the girl. She don't flinch.

"That's yer ma and pa, ain't it?" I ask, my voice low.

The girl don't say nothing but it's gotta be true.

I shine the flashlight over the wreckage and think of the burned
ditch behind it and it can only mean one thing. She crashed here with
her ma and pa. They died. She lived. And if she came from somewhere
else on New World or if she came from somewhere else altogether, don't
matter. They died, she lived, and she was here all alone.

And got found by Aaron.

When luck ain't with you, it's against you.

On the ground I see drag marks where the girl musta pulled the
bodies out of the crash and brought them here. But the swamp ain't for
burying anything but Spackle cuz after two inches of dirt you pretty
much just get water and so here they sit. I hate to say it but they do

smell, tho in the overall smell of the swamp it ain't as bad as you'd think, so who knows how long she's been here.

The girl looks at me again, not crying, not smiling, just blank as ever. Then she walks past me, walks back along the drag marks, walks to the door I saw open in the side of the wreckage, climbs up, and disappears inside.

10

FOOD AND FIRE

HEY!" I say, following her over to the wreckage. "We can't be hanging around—"

I get up to the door at the same time she pops out, making me jump back. She waits for me to step outta the way, then climbs down from the door and walks past me, carrying a bag in one hand and a coupla small packets in the other. I look back at the door and stand on tiptoes, trying to peek in. It all looks like a wreck inside, as you'd expect, things tumbled everywhere, lots of busted everything.

"How'd you live thru that?" I ask, turning around.

But she's got herself busy. She's put down the bag and the packs and has taken out what looks like a small, flat green box. She sets it down on a dryish area of ground and piles some sticks on top of it.

I look at her in disbelief. "There ain't time to make a—"

She presses a button on the side of the box and – *whoosh* – we've got ourselves a whole, full-sized, instant campfire.

I just stand there like a fool, my mouth wide open.

I want a campfire box.

She looks at me and rubs her arms a little bit and it's only then that I really realize I'm soaking wet and cold and achy all over and that a fire is just about the closest thing to a blessing I can think of.

I look back into the blackness of the swamp, as if I'd be able to see anyone coming. Nothing, of course, but no sounds neither. No one close. Not yet.

I look back at the fire. "Only for a second," I say.

I walk over to the fire and start warming up my hands, keeping my rucksack on. She rips open one of the packs and throws it to me and I stare at it again till she dips her fingers into her own pack, taking out what must be a piece of dried fruit or something and eating it.

She's giving me food. And fire.

Her face still has no kinda expression at all, just blank as a stone as she stands by the fire and eats. I start eating, too. The fruit or whatever are like little shriveled dots but sweet and chewy and I've finished the whole pack in half a minute before I notice Manchee begging.

"Todd?" he says, licking his lips.

"Oh," I say, "sorry."

The girl looks at me, looks at Manchee, then takes out a small handful from her own pack and holds it out to Manchee. When he approaches, she jerks back a little like she can't help it and drops the fruit on the ground instead. Manchee don't mind. He gobbles it right up.

I nod at her. She don't nod back.

It's full-fledged night now, dark as anything outside our little circle of light. You can only even see stars thru the hole in the treetops made by the crashing ship. I try to think back over the last week if I heard any distant booms from the swamp but anything this far out could've been drowned in the Noise of Prentisstown, I spose, and been missed by everyone.

I think of a certain preacher.

Nearly everyone.

"We can't stay," I say. "I'm sorry about yer folks and all but there's others that'll be after us. Even if Aaron's dead."

At Aaron's name, she flinches, just a little. He must've said his name to her. Or something. Maybe.

"I'm sorry," I say, tho I don't know what for. I shift my rucksack on my back. It feels heavier than ever. "Thanks for the grub but we gotta go." I look at her. "If yer coming?"

The girl looks at me for a second and then uses the tip of her boot to knock the burning sticks off the little green box. She reaches down, presses the button again, and picks up the box without even burning herself.

Man, I *really* want one of those things.

She puts it in the bag she brought outta the wreckage with her and then brings the strap of the bag over her head, like her own rucksack. Like she was planning on coming with me even before now.

"Well," I say, when all she does is stare at me. "I guess we're ready then."

Neither of us moves.

I look back to her ma and pa. She does, too, but only for a second.

I wanna say something to her, something more, but whaddya say? I open my mouth anyway but she starts rummaging in her bag. I think it's gonna be something to, I don't know, remember her folks with or make some kind of gesture or something but she finds what she's looking for and it's only a flashlight. She flicks it on – so she *does* know how they work – and starts walking, first toward me, then past me, as if we're already on our way.

And that's it, like her ma and pa ain't just lying there dead.

I watch her go for a second before saying, "Hey!"

She turns back to me.

"Not that way." I point to our left. "That way."

I head off the right way, Manchee following, and I look back and the girl's coming after us. I take one last quick look behind her and as bad as I want to stay and look thru that wreckage for more neat stuff, and boy do I, we gotta go, even tho it's night, even tho nobody's slept, we gotta go.

And so we do, catching sight of the horizon thru the trees when we can and heading toward the space twixt the close mountain and the two farther away mountains. Both moons are more than halfway full and the sky is clear so there's at least a little bit of light to walk by, even under the swamp canopy, even in the dark.

"Keep yer ears open," I say to Manchee.

"For what?" Manchee barks.

"For things that could get us, idiot."

You can't really run in a dark swamp at night so we walk as fast as we can, me shining my flashlight in front of us, tripping our way round tree roots and trying not to tromp thru too much mud. Manchee goes ahead and comes back, sniffing round and sometimes barking, but nothing serious. The girl keeps up, never falling behind but never getting too close neither. Which is good, cuz even tho my Noise is about the quietest it's been all day, the silence of her still presses on it whenever she comes too near.

It's weird that she didn't do nothing more about her ma and pa when we left, ain't it? Didn't cry or have one last visit or nothing? Am I wrong? I'd give anything to see Ben and even Cillian again, even if they were . . . Well, even if they are.

"Ben," Manchee says, down by my knees.

"I know." I scratch him twixt the ears.

We keep on.

I'd want to bury them, if that's what it came to. I'd want to do *something*, I don't know what. I stop and look back at the girl but her face is just the same, just the same as ever, and is it cuz she crashed and her parents died? Is it cuz Aaron found her? Is it cuz she's from somewhere else?

Don't she feel nothing? Is she just nothing at all on the inside?

She's looking at me, waiting for me to go on.

And so, after a second, I do.

Hours. There's hours of this silent nighttime fast creeping. Hours of it. Who knows how far we're going or if we're heading the right way or what, but *hours*. Once in a while, I hear the Noise of a nighttime creacher, swamp owls cooing their way to dinner, swooping down on probably short-tailed mice, whose Noise is so quiet it's barely like language at all, but mostly all I hear is the now-and-then fast-fading Noise of a nighttime creacher running away from all the ruckus we must be making by tromping thru a swamp at night.

But the weird thing is there's still no sound of nothing behind us, nothing chasing us, no Noise, no branches breaking, nothing. Maybe Ben and Cillian threw them off the trail. Maybe the reason I'm running ain't so important after all. Maybe—

The girl stops to pull her shoe outta some mud.

The girl.

No. They're coming. The only maybe is that maybe they're waiting till daybreak so they can come faster.

So on and on we go, getting more and more tired, stopping only once so that everyone can have a private pee off in the bushes. I get some of Ben's food outta my own rucksack and feed small bits to everyone, since it's my turn.

And then more walking and more walking.

And then there comes an hour just before dawn where there can't be no more.

"We gotta stop," I say, dropping the rucksack at the base of a tree. "We gotta rest."

The girl sets her own bag down by another tree without needing any more convincing and we both just sort of collapse down, leaning on our bags like pillows.

"Five minutes," I say. Manchee curls up by my legs and closes his eyes almost immediately. "Only five minutes," I call over to the girl, who's pulled a little blanket outta her bag to cover herself with. "Don't get too comfortable."

We gotta keep going, no question of that. I'll only close my eyes for a minute or two, just to get a little rest, and then we'll keep on going faster than before.

Just a little rest, that's all.

I open my eyes and the sun is up. Only a little but ruddy well up.

Crap. We've lost at least an hour, maybe two.

And then I realize it's a sound that's woken me.

It's Noise.

I panic, thinking of men finding us and I scramble to my feet—

Only to see that it ain't a man.

It's a cassor, towering over me and Manchee and the girl.

Food? says its Noise.

I *knew* they hadn't left the swamp.

I hear a little gasp from over where the girl's sleeping. Not sleeping no more. The cassor turns to look at her. And then Manchee's up and barking, "Get! Get! Get!" and the cassor's neck swings back our way.

Imagine the biggest bird you ever saw, imagine it got so big that it couldn't even fly no more, we're talking ten or twelve feet tall, a super long bendy neck stretching up way over yer head. It's still got feathers but they look more like fur and the wings ain't good for much except stunning things they're about to eat. But it's the feet you gotta watch out for. Long legs, up to yer chest, with claws at the end that can kill you with one kick if yer not careful.

"Don't worry," I call over to the girl. "They're friendly."

Cuz they are. Or they're sposed to be. They're sposed to eat rodents and only kick if you attack 'em, but if you *don't* attack 'em, Ben says they're friendly and dopey and'll let you feed 'em. And they're also good to eat, a combo which made the new settlers of Prentisstown so eager to hunt 'em for food that by the time I was born there wasn't a cassor to be seen within miles. Yet another thing I only ever saw in a vid or Noise.

The world keeps getting bigger.

"Get! Get!" Manchee barks, running in a circle round the cassor.

"Don't bite it!" I shout at him.

The cassor's neck is swinging around like a vine, following Manchee around like a cat after a bug. **Food?** its Noise keeps asking.

"Not food," I say, and the big neck swings my way.

Food?

"Not food," I say again. "Just a dog."

Dog? it thinks and starts following Manchee around again, trying to nip him with its beak. The beak ain't a scary thing at all, like being nipped by a goose, but Manchee's having none of it, leaping outta the way and barking, barking, barking.

I laugh at him. It's funny.

And then I hear a little laugh that ain't my own.

I look over. The girl is standing by her tree, watching the giant bird chase around my stupid dog, and she's laughing.

She's *smiling*.

She sees me looking and she stops.

Food? I hear and I turn to see the cassor starting to poke its beak into my rucksack.

"Hey!" I shout and start shooing it away.

Food?

"Here." I fish out a small block of cheese wrapped in a cloth that Ben packed.

The cassor sniffs it, bites it, and gobbles it down, its neck rippling in long waves at it swallows. It snaps its beak a few times like a man might smack his lips after he ate something. But then its neck starts rippling the other way and with a loud hack, up comes the block of cheese flying right back at me, covered in spit but not hardly even crushed, smacking me on the cheek and leaving a trail of slime across my face.

Food? says the cassor and starts slowly walking off into the swamp, as if we're no longer even as interesting as a leaf.

"Get! Get!" Manchee barks after it, but not following. I wipe the slime from my face with my sleeve and I can see the girl smiling at me while I do it.

"Think that's funny, do ya?" I say and she keeps pretending like she's not smiling but she *is*. She turns away and picks up her bag.

"Yeah," I say, taking charge of things again. "We slept way too long. We gotta go."

We get going on yet more walking without any more words or smiling. Pretty quick, the ground starts to get less even and a bit drier. The trees start to thin out some, letting the sun directly on us now and then. After a little bit, we get to a small clearing, almost like a little field that rises up to a short bluff, standing just over the treetops. We climb it and stop at the top. The girl holds out another pack of that fruity stuff. Breakfast. We eat, still standing.

Looking out over the trees, the way in front of us is clear. The larger mountain is on the horizon and you can see the two smaller mountains in the distance behind a little bit of haze.

"That's where we're going," I say, pointing. "Or where I think we're sposed to go, anyway."

She sets down her fruit pack and goes into her bag again. She pulls out the sweetest little pair of binocs you've ever seen. My old ones back home that broke years ago were like a breadbox in comparison. She holds them up to her eyes and looks for a bit, then hands 'em to me.

I take 'em and I look out to where we're going. Everything's so *clear*. The ground stretching out before us in a green forest, curving downhill into proper valleys and dales as it starts to become real land again and not just the mucky bowl of a swamp and you can even see where the marsh starts turning back into a real river, cutting deeper and deeper canyons as it gets closer to the mountains. If you listen, you can even hear it rushing. I look and I look and I don't see no settlement but who knows what's around the bends and curves? Who knows what's up ahead?

I look behind us, back the way we came, but it's still early enough for a mist to be covering most of the swamp, hiding everything, giving nothing away.

"Those're sweet," I say, handing her the binocs. She puts them back in her bag and we stand there for a minute eating.

We stand arm's length apart cuz her silence still bothers me. I chew down on a piece of dried fruit and I wonder what it must be like to have no Noise, to *come* from a place with no Noise. What does it mean? What kind of place is it? Is it wonderful? Is it terrible?

Say you were standing on a hilltop with someone who had no Noise. Would it be like you were alone there? How would you share it? Would you want to? I mean, here we are, the girl and I, heading outta danger and into the unknown and there's no Noise overlapping us, nothing to tell us what the other's thinking. Is that how it's sposed to be?

I finish the fruit and crumple up the packet. She holds out her hand and shoves the rubbish back into her bag. No words, no exchange, just my Noise and a great big nothing from her.

Was this what it was like for my ma and pa when they first landed? Was New World a silent place all over before—

I look up at the girl suddenly.

Before.

Oh, no.

I'm such a fool.

I'm such a stupid goddam fool.

She has no Noise. And she came from a ship. Which means she came from a place with no Noise, obviously, *idiot*.

Which means she's landed here and hasn't caught the Noise germ yet.

Which means that when she does, it's gonna do what it did to all the other women.

It's gonna kill her.

It's gonna kill her.

And I'm looking at her and the sun is shining down on us and her eyes are getting wider and wider as I'm thinking it and it's then I realize something else stupid, something else obvious.

Just cuz I can't hear any Noise from her don't mean she can't hear every word of mine.

11

THE BOOK OF NO ANSWERS

No!" I say quickly. "Don't listen! I'm wrong! I'm wrong! It's a mistake!
I'm wrong!"

But she's backing away from me, dropping her own empty packet of
fruit things, her eyes getting wider.

"No, don't—"

I step toward her but she takes an even quicker step away, her bag
dropping to the ground.

"It's—" I say but what *do* you say? "I'm wrong. I'm *wrong*. I was thinking of somebody else."

Which is the stupidest thing to say of all cuz she can hear my Noise,
can't she? She can see me struggling to think of something to say and
even if it's coming out a big mess, she can see herself all over it and besides, I surely know by now there's no taking back something that's been
sent out into the world.

Dammit. Goddammit all to hell.

"Dammit!" Manchee barks.

"Why didn't you SAY you could hear me?" I shout, ignoring that she
ain't said a word since I met her.

She steps back farther, putting a hand up to her face to cover her
mouth, her eyes sending asking marks at me.

I try to think of something, *anything* to make it all right, but I ain't
got nothing. Just Noise with death and despair all over it.

She turns and runs, back down the hill and away from me as fast as
she can.

Crap.

"Wait!" I yell, already running after her.

She's going back the way we came, down across the little field and disappearing into the trees, but I'm right behind her, Manchee after me. "Stop!" I shout after her. "Wait!"

But why should she? What kind of reason could she possibly have to wait around?

You know, she's really amazingly fast when she wants to be.

"Manchee!" I call and he understands me and shoots off after her. Not that I could really lose her, any more than she could lose me. As loud as my Noise is chasing her, her silence is just as loud up ahead, even now, even knowing she's going to die, still as silent as a grave.

"Hold on!" I shout, tripping over a root and landing hard on my elbows, which jolts every ache I've got in my body and face, but I have to get up. I have to get up and go after her. "Dammit!"

"Todd!" I hear Manchee bark up ahead, outta sight. I stumble on a bit and get my way round a big mass of shrubs and there she is, sitting on a big flat rock jutting outta the ground, her knees up to her chest, rocking back and forth, eyes wide but blank as ever.

"Todd!" Manchee barks again when he sees me, then he hops up on the rock next to her and starts sniffing her.

"Leave her alone, Manchee," I say, but he doesn't. He sniffs close at her face, licks her once or twice, then sits down next to her, leaning into her side as she rocks.

"Look," I say to her, catching my breath and knowing I don't know what to say next. "Look," I say again, but nothing else is coming.

I just stand there panting, not saying nothing, and she sits there rocking till there don't seem nothing else to do but sit down on the rock myself, keeping a distance away outta respect and safety, I guess, and so that's what I do. She rocks and I sit and I wonder what to do.

We pass a good few minutes this way, a good few minutes when we should be moving, the swamp getting on with its day around us.

Till I finally have another thought.

"I might not be right." I say it as soon as I think it. "I could be wrong, you see?" I turn to her and I start talking fast. "I got lied to about everything and you can search my Noise if you want to be sure *that's* true." I stand, talking faster. "There wasn't sposed to be another settlement. Prentisstown was sposed to be it for the whole stupid planet. But there's the other place on the map! So maybe—"

And I'm thinking and I'm thinking and I'm thinking.

"Maybe the germ was only Prentisstown. And if you ain't been in the town, then maybe yer safe. Maybe yer fine. Cuz I sure can't hear nothing from you anything like Noise and you don't seem sick. So maybe yer okay."

She's looking at me and still rocking and I don't know what she's thinking. *Maybe* probably ain't all that comforting a word when it's *maybe yer not dying.*

I keep on thinking, letting her see my Noise as free and clear as I can. "Maybe we all caught the germ and, and, and, yeah!" I get another thought, a good one. "Maybe we cut ourselves off so the other settlement wouldn't catch it! That must be it! And so if you stayed in the swamp, then yer safe!"

She stops rocking quite so much, still looking at me, maybe believing me?

But then like some doofus who don't know when to stop, I let that thought go on, don't I? Cuz if it's true that Prentisstown was cut off, then maybe that other settlement ain't gonna be too happy to see me strolling in, are they? Maybe it was the other settlement that did the cutting off in the first place, cuz maybe Prentisstown really *was* contagious.

And if you can catch the Noise from other people, then the girl can catch it from me, can't she?

"Oh, man," I say, leaning down and putting my hands on my knees, my whole body feeling like it's falling, even tho I'm still standing up. "Oh, man."

The girl hugs herself again on the rock and we're back to even worse than where we started.

This ain't fair. I am telling you this ain't fair at all. *You'll know what to do when you get to the swamp, Todd. You'll know what to do.* Yeah, thanks very much for that, Ben, thanks for all yer help and concern cuz here I am and I ain't got the first clue what to do. It ain't fair. I get kicked outta my home, I get beaten up, the people who say they care for me have been lying all these years, I gotta follow a stupid map to a settlement I never knew about, I gotta somehow read a stupid book—

The book.

I slip off the rucksack and take out the book. He said all the answers were in here, so maybe they really are. Except—

I sigh and open it up. It's all written, all words, all in my ma's handwriting, pages and pages and pages of it and I—

Well, anyway. I go back to the map, to Ben's writing on the other side, the first chance I've had to look at it under something besides a flashlight, which ain't really for reading. Ben's words are lined up at the top. *Go to* are the first ones, those are definitely the first words, and then there are a coupla longer words that I don't have time to sound out yet and then a coupla big paragraphs that I *really* don't have time for right now but at the bottom of the page Ben's underlined a group of words together.

I look at the girl, still rocking, and I turn my back to her. I put my finger under the first underlined word.

Let's see. *Yow? You,* it's gotta be *you. You.* Okay, me what? *M. Moo? Moose? Moosed? You moosed. You moosed?* What the hell does that mean? *Wuh. Wuh. Warr. Warren? Tuh. Tuhee? Tuheem. You moosed warren tuheem?* No, wait, *them.* It's *them.* Course it's *them,* idiot.

But *You moosed warren them?*

Huh?

'Member when I said Ben tried to teach me to read? 'Member when I said I wasn't too good at it? Well–

Well, whatever.

You moosed warren them.

Idiot.

I look at the book again, flip thru the pages. Dozens of them, dozens upon dozens, all with more words in every corner, all saying nothing to me at all, no answers of any kind.

Stupid effing book.

I shove the map back inside, slam the cover shut, and throw the book on the ground.

You *idiot.*

"Stupid effing book!" I say, out loud this time, kicking it into some ferns. I turn back to the girl. She's still just rocking back and forth, back and forth, and I know, I know, okay, I *know,* but it starts to piss me off. Cuz if this is a dead end, I got nothing more to offer and she ain't offering nothing neither.

My Noise starts to crackle.

"I didn't ask for this, you know," I say. She don't even look. "Hey! I'm talking to you!"

But nothing. Nothing, nothing, nothing.

"I DON'T KNOW WHAT TO DO!" I yell and stand and start stomping around, shouting till my voice scratches. "I DON'T KNOW WHAT TO DO! I DON'T KNOW WHAT TO DO!" I turn back to the girl. "I'm SORRY! I'm sorry this happened to you but I don't know what to do about it AND STOP EFFING ROCKING!"

"Yelling, Todd," Manchee barks.

"Awwghh!" I shout, putting my hands over my face. I take them away and nothing's changed. That's the thing I'm learning about being thrown out on yer own. Nobody does *nothing* for you. If you don't change it, it don't get changed.

"We gotta keep going," I say, picking up my rucksack all angrylike.

"You ain't caught it yet, so maybe just keep yer distance from me and you'll be okay. I don't know but that's all there is so that's what we gotta do."

Rock, rock, rock.

"We can't go back so we gotta go forward and that's that."

Still rocking.

"I KNOW you can HEAR me!"

She don't even flinch.

And I'm suddenly tired all over again. "Fine," I sigh. "Fine, whatever, you stay here and rock. Who cares? Who ruddy cares about anything?"

I look at the book on the ground. Stupid thing. But it's what I got so I reach down, pick it up, put it in the plastic bag, back in my rucksack, and put my rucksack back on.

"C'mon, Manchee."

"Todd?!" he barks, looking twixt me and the girl. "Can't leave, Todd!"

"She can come if she wants," I say, "but—"

I don't even really know what the *but* might be. *But* if she wants to stay here and die all alone? *But* if she wants to go back and get caught by Mr. Prentiss Jr.? *But* if she wants to risk catching the Noise from me and dying that way?

What a stupid world.

"Hey," I say, trying to make my voice a little gentler but my Noise is so raging there's really no point. "You know where we were heading, right? To the river twixt the mountains. Just follow it till you come to a settlement, okay?"

Maybe she's hearing me, maybe she ain't.

"I'll keep an eye out for you," I say. "I understand if you don't wanna get too close but I'll keep an eye out for you."

I stand there for another minute to see if it sinks in.

"Well," I finally say. "Nice knowing ya."

I start walking away. When I get to the big stack of shrubs, I turn back, giving her one more chance. But she ain't changed, just rocking and rocking.

So that's that then. Off I go, Manchee reluctantly on my heels, looking back as much as he can, barking my name all the time. "Todd! Todd! Leaving, Todd? Todd! Can't leave, Todd!" I finally smack him on the rump. "Ow, Todd?"

"I don't know, Manchee, so quit asking."

We make our way back thru the trees to where the ground dries out, to the clearing and up the little bluff where we ate our breakfast and looked at the beautiful day and I had my brilliant deducshun about her death.

The little bluff where her bag still lies on the ground.

"Oh, god*dammm*it!"

I look at it for a second and it's one thing after another, ain't it? I mean, do I take it back to her? Do I just hope she finds it? Will I put her in danger if I do? Will I put her in danger if I *don't*?

The sun's fully up now and the sky as blue as fresh meat. I put my hands on my hips and take a long look round like men do when they're thinking. I look at the horizon, look back the way we came, the mist mostly burned off by now and the whole swamp forest covered in sunlight. From the top of the bluff, you can see out over it, over where we drove our feet into oblivion by walking it all. If it were clear enough and you had powerful enough binocs you could probably see all the way back to town.

Powerful binocs.

I look down at her bag on the ground there.

I'm reaching for it when I think I hear something. Like a whisper. My Noise leaps and I look up to see if the girl's following me out after all. Which would make me more relieved than I want to say.

But it ain't the girl. I hear it again. A whisper. More than one whisper. Like the wind is carrying whispering on it.

"Todd?" Manchee says, sniffing the air.

I squint into the sunlight to look back over the swamp.

Is there something out there?

I grab the girl's bag and look thru it for the binocs. There's all kinds of neat crap in there but I take the binocs out and look thru 'em.

Just swamp is all I see, the tops of swamp trees, little clearings of swampy bits of water, the river eventually starting to form itself again. I take the binocs away from my face and look them over. There are little buttons everywhere and I push a few and realize I can make everything look even closer. I do that a coupla times and I'm sure I can hear whispering now. I'm sure of it.

I find the gash in the swamp, the ditch, find the wreckage of her ship, but there's nothing there except what we left. I look over the top of the binocs, wondering if I see movement. I look thru them again, a little nearer to us where some trees are rustling.

But that's only the wind, ain't it?

I scan back and forth, pressing buttons to get closer and farther away, but I keep coming back to those rustling trees. I keep the binocs trained on a kinda open, gully-type thing twixt me and them.

I keep the binocs there.

I keep the binocs watching, my guts twisting as maybe I'm hearing whispering, maybe I ain't.

I keep watching.

Till the rustling reaches the clearing and I see the Mayor himself come outta the trees on horseback, leading other men, also on horses.

And they're heading right this way.

12

THE BRIDGE

THE MAYOR. Not just his son but actually the *Mayor*. With his clean hat and his clean face and his clean clothes and his shiny boots and his upright pose. We don't never actually get to see him much in Prentisstown, not no more, not if yer not in his close little circle, but when you do, he always looks like this, even thru a pair of binocs. Like he knows how to take care of hisself and you don't.

I push some more buttons till I'm as close as I can get. There's five of 'em, no, six, the men whose Noise you hear doing those freaky exercises in the Mayor's house. **I AM THE CIRCLE AND THE CIRCLE IS ME,** that kinda thing. There's Mr. Collins, Mr. MacInerny, Mr. O'Hare, and Mr. Morgan, all on horses, too, itself a rare sight cuz horses are hard to keep alive on New World and the Mayor guards his personal herd with a whole raft of men with guns.

And there's Mr. ruddy Prentiss Jr., riding up next to his father, wearing a shiner from where Cillian hit him. Good.

But then I realize that means whatever happened at the farm is definitely over with. Whatever happened to Ben and Cillian is done. I put the binocs down for a sec and swallow it away.

I put the binocs back up. The group's stopped for a minute and are talking to each other, looking over a large piece of paper that's gotta be a way better map than mine and—

Oh, man.

Oh, man, you gotta be *kidding*.

Aaron.

Aaron comes walking outta the trees behind 'em.

Stinking, stupid, ruddy effing ruddy Aaron.

Most of his head is wrapped in bandages but he's pacing the ground a little way's back from the Mayor, waving his hands in the air, looking like he's probably preaching even if no one looks like they're listening.

HOW? How could he have lived? Doesn't he ever effing *DIE*?

It's my fault. My stupid effing fault. Cuz I'm a coward. I'm a weak and stupid coward and cuz of that Aaron's alive and cuz of that he's leading the Mayor thru the ruddy swamp after us. Cuz I didn't kill him, he's coming to kill me.

I feel sick. I bend over double and hold my stomach, moaning a bit. My blood is charging so hard I hear Manchee creep a little ways away from me.

"It's my fault, Manchee," I say. "I did this."

"Your fault," he says, confused and just repeating what I said but right on the money, ain't he?

I make myself look thru the binocs again and I see the Mayor call Aaron over. Since men started being able to hear animals' thoughts, Aaron thinks they're unclean and won't go near 'em so it takes the Mayor a coupla tries but eventually Aaron comes tromping over to look at the map. He listens while the Mayor asks him something.

And then he looks up.

Looks up thru the swamp trees and sky.

Looks up to this hilltop.

Looks right at me.

He can't see me. No way. Can he? Not without binocs like the girl's and I don't see any on the men, never saw *anything* like 'em in Prentisstown. Gotta be. He can't see me.

But like a great pitiless thing he raises his arm and points, points it directly at me, like I'm sitting across a table from him.

I'm running before I can even think, running back down the bluff and back to the girl as fast as I can, reaching behind me and pulling out my knife, Manchee barking up a storm on my heels. I get into the trees and down and round the big mess of shrubs and she's still sitting on the rock but at least she looks up as I run to her.

"Come on!" I say, grabbing her arm. "We gotta go!"

She pulls back from me but I don't let go.

"No!" I shout. "We have to go! NOW!"

She starts hitting out with her fists, clonking me a coupla times on the face.

But I ain't letting go.

"LISTEN!" I say and I open up my Noise for her. She hits me once more but then she's looking, looking at my Noise as it comes, seeing the pictures of what's waiting for us in the swamp. Check that, what's *not* waiting for us, what's making every effort to come get us. Aaron, who won't die, bending all his thoughts to finding us and coming this time with men on horseback. Who are a lot faster than we are.

The girl's face squishes up, like she's in the worst pain ever and she opens her mouth like she's going to yell but nothing comes out. Still nothing. Still no Noise, no sound, no nothing at all coming from her.

I just don't get it.

"I don't know what's ahead," I say. "I don't know nothing about nothing but whatever it is, it's gotta be better than what's behind. It's *gotta* be."

And as she hears me, her face changes. It clears up to almost blankness again and she presses her lips together.

"Go! Go! Go!" Manchee barks.

She holds out her hand for her bag. I hand it to her. She stands, shoves the binocs in, loops it over her shoulder and looks me in the eye.

"Okay, then," I say.

And so that's how I set off running full out toward a river for the second time in two days, Manchee with me again and this time a girl on my heels.

Well, *past* my heels most of the time, she's ruddy fast, she is.

We go back up the hill and down the other side, the last of the swamp really starting to disappear around us and turning into regular woods. The ground gets way firmer and easier to run on and it's sloping more downhill than it is up, which may be the first piece of luck we've had. We start catching the actual river in brief glances off to our left side as we go. My rucksack's bashing me in the back as I run and I'm gasping for breath.

But I'm holding my knife.

I swear. I swear right now before God or whatever. If Aaron ever comes in my reach again, I will kill him. I ain't hesitating again. No way. No how. I ain't. I swear to you.

I will kill him.

I'll ruddy well kill him.

You just watch me.

The ground we're running on is getting a bit steeper side to side, taking us thru leafier, lighter trees and first closer to the river and then away from it again as we run. Manchee's tongue is hanging out of his mouth in a big pant, bouncing along as we go. My heart's thumping a million beats and my legs are about to fall off my body but still we run.

We veer close to the water again and I call out, "Wait." The girl, who's got pretty far in front of me, stops. I run to the river's edge, take a swift look round for crocs, then lean down and scoop up a few handfuls of water into my mouth. Tastes sweeter than it really should. Who knows what's in it, coming outta the swamp, but you gotta drink. I feel the girl's silence lean down next to me as she drinks, too. I scoot a little ways away. Manchee laps up his share and you can hear us all taking in great raking breaths between slurps.

I look up to where we're going, wiping my mouth. Next to the river is starting to become too rocky and steep to run on and I can see a path cutting its way up from the riverbank, going along the top of the canyon.

I blink, as I realize.

I can see a path. Someone's cut a *path*.

The girl turns and looks. The path goes up and along as the river drops below it, getting deeper and faster and turning into rapids. Someone *made* that path.

"It's gotta be the way to the other settlement," I say. "Gotta be."

And then, in the distance, we hear hoofbeats. Faint, but on their way.

I don't say another word cuz we're already on our feet and running up the path. The river falls farther and farther away beneath us and the larger mountain rears up on the other side of the river. On our side there's a thick forest starting to stretch back from the clifftops. The path's clearly been cut so men would have a place to travel down the river.

It's more than wide enough for horses. More than wide enough for five or six, in fact.

It ain't a path at all, I realize. It's a *road*.

We fly along it as it bends and turns, the girl ahead, then me, then Manchee, running along.

Till I nearly bump into her and knock her off the trail.

"What're you doing?!" I shout, grabbing onto her arms to keep us both from falling off the cliff, trying to keep the knife from accidentally killing her.

And then I see what she's seeing.

A bridge, way on up ahead of us. It goes from one cliff edge to the other, crossing the river what's gotta be a hundred feet or more above it. The road or path or whatever stops on our side at the bridge and becomes rock and dense forest beyond. There's nowhere to go but the bridge.

The first shades of an idea start to form.

The hoofbeats are louder now. I look back and see clouds of dust rising from where the Mayor is following.

"Come on!" I say, running past her, making for the bridge as fast as I can. We pound down the cliff top path, kicking up our own dust,

Manchee's ears flattened back, running fast. We get there and it's way more than just a footbridge, six feet wide at least. It looks like mostly rope tied into wooden stakes driven into the rock at either end, with tight wooden planks running all the way to the other side.

I test it with my foot but it's so sturdy it don't even bounce. More than enough to take me and the girl and a dog.

More than enough to take men on horseback who wanted to cross it, in fact.

Whoever built it, meant it to last.

I look back again down the river at where we've run. More dust, louder hoofbeats, and the whispers of men's Noise on its way. I think I hear young Todd but I'm only imagining it cuz Aaron'll be way behind on foot.

But I do see what I wanna see: this bridge is the only place where you can cross the river, from back where we've run to miles farther ahead as you look.

Maybe another piece of luck is coming our way.

"Let's go," I say. We run across and it's so well made you can't even see twixt the gaps in the planks of wood. We might as well still be on the path. We get to the other side and the girl stops and turns to me, no doubt seeing my idea in my Noise, already waiting for me to act.

The knife is still in my hand. Power at the end of my arm.

Maybe at last I can do some good with it.

I look over where this end of the bridge is tied to the stakes in the rock. The knife has a fearsome serrated edge on part of the blade, so I choose the likeliest looking knot and start sawing on it.

I saw and saw.

The hoofbeats get louder, echoing down the canyon.

But if there suddenly *ain't* no bridge—

I saw some more.

And some more.

And some more.

And I'm just not making no progress at all.

"What the hell?" I say, looking at where I been cutting. There's hardly a scratch there. I touch the serration on the knife with my finger and it pricks and bleeds almost immediately. I look closer at the rope. It looks like it's coated in some kind of thin resin.

Some kind of ruddy tough, steel-like resin that ain't for cutting.

"I don't believe this," I say, looking up at the girl.

She's got her binocs to her eyes, looking back the way we came down the river.

"Can you see 'em?"

I look down the river but you don't need binocs at all. You can see
'em coming with yer own two eyes. Small but growing larger and not
slowing down, thundering their hooves like there's no tomorrow.

We got three minutes. Maybe four.

Crap.

I start sawing again, fast and strong as I can, forcing my arm back
and forth hard as I can make it, sweat popping out all over the place and
new aches forming to keep all the old ones company. I saw and saw and
saw, dripping sweat down my nose onto the knife.

"C'mon, c'mon," I say thru my teeth.

I lift the knife. I've managed to get thru one tiny little bit of resin on
one tiny little knot on one huge effing bridge.

"Goddammit!" I spit.

I saw some more and more and more. And more and more than that,
sweat running into my eyes and starting to sting.

"Todd!" Manchee barks, his alarm spilling out all over the place.

I saw more. And more.

But the only thing that happens is that the knife catches and
I smash my knuckles into the stake, bloodying them.

"GODDAMMIT!" I scream, throwing the knife down. It bounces
along, stopping just at the girl's feet. "GODDAMMIT ALL!"

Cuz that's it, ain't it?

That's the end of everything.

Our one stupid chance that wasn't a chance at all.

We can't outrun the horses and we can't cut down a stupid megaroad
bridge and we're gonna be caught and Ben and Cillian are dead and
we're gonna be killed ourselves and the world is gonna end and that's it.

A redness comes over my Noise, like nothing I ever felt before, sudden and raw, like a red-hot brand pressing into my own self, a burning
bright redness of everything that's made me hurt and keeps on hurting, a
roaring rage of the unfairness and the injustice and the lies.

Of everything coming back to *one* thing.

I raise my eyes up to the girl's and she steps back from the force of it.

"*You*," I say and there ain't gonna be no stopping me. "This is all *you*!
If you hadn't shown up in that ruddy swamp, none of this woulda happened! I'd be home RIGHT NOW! I'd be tending my effing sheep and
living in my effing house and sleeping in my own EFFING BED!"

Except I don't say "effing."

"But oh NO," I shout, getting louder. "Here's YOU! Here's YOU and
yer SILENCE! And the whole world gets SCREWED!"

I don't realize I'm walking toward her till I see her stepping back.
But she just looks back at me.

And I don't hear a goddam thing.

"You're NOTHING!" I scream, stepping forward some more. "NOTHING! You're nothing but EMPTINESS! There's nothing in you! You're EMPTY and NOTHING and we're gonna die FOR NOTHING!"

I have my fists clenched so hard my nails are cutting into my palms. I'm so furious, my Noise raging so loud, so *red,* that I have to raise my fists to her, I have to hit her, I have to beat her, I have to make her ruddy silence STOP before it SWALLOWS ME AND THE WHOLE EFFING WORLD!

I take my fist and punch myself hard in the face.

I do it again, hitting where my eye is swollen from Aaron.

And a third time, splitting open the cut on my lip from where Aaron hit me yesterday morning.

You *fool,* you *worthless, effing fool.*

I do it again, hard enough to knock me off balance. I fall and catch myself on my hands and spit out some blood onto the path.

I look up at the girl, breathing hard.

Nothing. Just looking back at me and nothing.

We both turn to look across the river. They've got to the place where they can see the bridge clearly. See *us* clearly on the other side. We can see the faces of the men as they ride. Hear the chatter of their Noise as it flies up the river at us. Mr. MacInerny, the Mayor's best horseman, is in the lead, the Mayor riding behind, looking as calm as if it was nothing more than a Sunday ride.

We got maybe a minute, probably less.

I turn back to the girl, trying to stand, but I'm so tired. So, so tired. "We might as well run," I say, spitting out more blood. "We might as well try."

And I see her face change.

Her mouth opens wide, her eyes, too, and suddenly she yanks her bag out in front of her and shoves her hand in it.

"What're you doing?" I say.

She takes out the campfire box, looking all around her till she sees a good-sized rock. She sets the box down and raises up the rock.

"No, wait, we could use—"

She brings down the rock and the box cracks. She picks it up and twists it hard, making it crack some more. It starts to leak some kind of fluid. She moves to the bridge and starts flinging fluid all over the knots on the closest stake, shaking out the last drops into a puddle at the base.

The riders are coming up to the bridge, coming up, coming up, coming up—

"Hurry!" I say.

The girl turns to me, telling me with her hands to get back. I scrabble back a little ways, grabbing Manchee by his scruff and taking him with me. She steps back as far as she can, holding out the remains of the box at arm's length and pressing a button on it. I hear a clicking sound. She tosses the box in the air and jumps back toward me.

The horses reach the bridge—

The girl lands almost on top of me and we watch as the campfire box falls—

Falls—

Falls—

Toward the little puddle of liquid, clicking as it goes—

Mr. MacInerny's horse puts a hoof on the bridge to cross it—

The campfire box lands in the puddle—

Clicks one more time—

Then—

WHOOOOMP!!!!

The air is sucked outta my lungs as a fireball WAY bigger than what you'd think for that little amount of fluid makes the world quiet for a second and then—

BOOM!!!!!

It blasts away the ropes and the stake, spraying fiery splinters all over us and obliterating all thought, Noise, and sound.

When we can look up again, the bridge is already so much on fire it's starting to lean to one side and we see Mr. MacInerny's horse rear up and stumble, trying to back up into four or five more oncoming horses.

The flames roar a weird bright green and the sudden heat's incredible, like the worst sunburn ever and I think we're gonna catch fire ourselves when this end of the bridge just falls right away, taking Mr. MacInerny and his horse with it. We sit up and watch them fall and fall and fall into the river below, way too far to ever live thru it. The bridge is still attached at their end and it slaps the facing cliff but it's burning so fierce it won't be no time at all before the whole thing is just ash. The Mayor and Mr. Prentiss Jr. and the others all have to back their horses away from it.

The girl crawls away from me and we lay there a second, just breathing and coughing, trying to stop being dazed.

Holy crap.

"Y'all right?" I say to Manchee, still held by my hand.

"Fire, Todd!" he barks.

"Yeah," I cough. "Big fire. *You* all right?" I say to the girl, who's still crouching, still coughing. "Man, what was in that thing?"

But of course she don't say nothing.

"TODD HEWITT!" I hear from across the canyon.

I look up. It's the Mayor, shouting his first words ever to me in person, thru sheets of smoke and heat that make him look all wavy.

"We're not finished, young Todd," he calls, over the crackle of the burning bridge and the roar of the water below. "Not by a long way."

And he's calm and still ruddy clean and looking like there's no way he's not gonna get what he wants.

I stand up, hold out my arm and give him two fingers but he's already disappearing behind big clouds of smoke.

I cough and spit blood again. "We gotta keep moving," I say, coughing some more. "Maybe they'll turn back, maybe there's no other way across, but we shouldn't wait to find out."

I see the knife in the dust. Shame comes real quick, like a new pain all its own. The things I said. I reach down and pick it up and put it back in its sheath.

The girl's still got her head down, coughing to herself. I pick up her bag and hold it out for her to take.

"Come on," I say. "We can at least get away from the smoke."

She looks up at me.

I look back at her.

My face burns and not from the heat.

"I'm sorry." I look away from her, from her eyes and face, blank and quiet as ever.

I turn back up the path.

"Viola," I hear.

I spin around, look at her.

"What?" I say.

She's looking back at me.

She's opening her mouth.

She's talking.

"My name," she says. "It's Viola."

PART III

13

ACROSS THE BRIDGE

I DON'T SAY NOTHING to this for a minute. Neither does she. The fire burns, the smoke rises, Manchee's tongue hangs out in a stunned pant, till finally I say, "Viola."

She nods.

"Viola," I say again.

She don't nod this time.

"I'm Todd," I say.

"I know," she says.

She's not quite meeting my eye.

"So you can talk then?" I say, but all she does is look at me again quickly and then away. I turn to the still burning bridge, to the smoke turning into a fog bank twixt us and the other side of the river, which I don't know if it makes me feel safer or not, if not seeing the Mayor and his men is better than seeing them. "That was–" I start to say, but she's getting up and holding out her hand for her bag.

I realize I'm still holding it. I hand it to her and she takes it.

"We should go on," she says. "Away from here."

Her accent's funny, different from mine, different from anyone in Prentisstown's. Her lips make different kinds of outlines for the letters, like they're swooping down on them from above, pushing them into shape, telling them what to say. In Prentisstown, everyone talks like they're sneaking up on their words, ready to club them from behind.

Manchee's just in awe of her. "Away," he says lowly, staring up at her like she's made of food.

There's this moment now where it feels like I could start asking her stuff, like now that she's talking, I could just hit her with every asking I can think of about who she is, where she's from, what happened, and them askings are all over my Noise, flying at her like pellets, but there's so much stuff wanting to come outta my mouth that nothing is and so my mouth don't move and she's holding her bag over her shoulder and looking at the ground and then she's walking past me, past Manchee, on up the trail.

"Hey," I say.

She stops and turns back.

"Wait for me," I say.

I pick up my rucksack, hooking it back over my shoulders. I press my hand against the knife in its sheath against my lower back. I make the rucksack comfortable with a shrug, say "C'mon, Manchee," and off we go up the trail, following the girl.

On this side of the river the path makes a slow turn away from the cliff side, heading into what looks like a landscape of scrub and brush, making its way around and away from the larger mountain, looming up at us on the left.

At the place where the trail turns, we both stop and look back without saying that we're gonna. The bridge is still burning like you wouldn't believe, hanging on the opposite cliff like a waterfall on fire, flames having leaped up the entire length of it, angry and greenish yellow. The smoke's so thick, it's still impossible to tell what the Mayor and his men are doing, have done, if they're gone or waiting or what. There could be a whisper of Noise coming thru but there could also *not* be a whisper of Noise, what with the fire blazing and the wood popping and the white water below. As we watch, the fire finishes its business on the stakes on the other side of the river and with a great *snap,* the burning bridge falls, falls, falls, clattering against the cliff side, splashing into the river, sending up more clouds of smoke and steam, making everything even foggier.

"What was in that box?" I say to the girl.

She looks at me, opens her mouth, but then closes it again, turning away.

"It's okay," I say. "I'm not gonna hurt ya."

She looks at me again and my Noise is full of just a few minutes ago when I *was* just about to hurt her, when I was just about to—

Anyway.

We don't say no more. She turns back onto the path and me and Manchee follow her into the scrub.

Knowing she can speak don't help with the silence none. Knowing she's got words in her head don't mean nothing if you can only hear 'em when she talks. Looking at the back of her head as she's walking, I still feel my heart pull toward her silence, still feel like I've lost something terrible, something so sad I want to weep.

"Weep," Manchee barks.

The back of her head just keeps on walking.

The path is still pretty wide, wide enough for horses, but the terrain around us is getting rockier, the path twistier. We can hear the river down below us to our right now but it feels like we're tending away from it a bit, getting ourselves deep into an area that feels almost walled, rock face sometimes coming up on both sides, like we're walking at the bottom of a box. Little prickly firs grow out of every crevice and yellow vines with thorns wrapping themselves around the firs' trunks and you can see and hear yellow razor lizards hissing at us as we pass. **Pite!** they say, as a threat. **Pite! Pite!**

Anything you might want to touch here would cut you.

After maybe twenty, thirty minutes the path gets to a place where it widens out, where a few real trees start growing again, where the forest looks like it might be about to restart, where there's grass and stones low enough for sitting on. Which is what we do. Sit.

I take some dried mutton outta my rucksack and use the knife to cut strips for me, for Manchee, and for the girl. She takes them without saying anything and we sit quietly apart and eat for a minute.

I am Todd Hewitt, I think, closing my eyes and chewing, embarrassed for my Noise now, now that I know she can hear it, now that I know she can think about it.

Think about it in secret.

I am Todd Hewitt.

I will be a man in twenty-nine days' time.

Which is true, I realize, opening my eyes. Time goes on, even when yer not looking.

I take another bite. "I ain't never heard the name Viola before," I say after a while, looking only at the ground, only at my strip of mutton. She don't say nothing so I glance up in spite of myself.

To find her looking back at me.

"What?" I say.

"Your face," she says.

I frown. "What about my face?"

She makes both of her hands into fists and mimes punching herself with them.

I feel myself redden. "Yeah, well."

"And from before," she says. "From—" She stops.

"Aaron," I say.

"Aaron," Manchee barks and the girl flinches a little.

"That was his name," she says. "Wasn't it?"

I nod, chewing on my mutton. "Yep," I say. "That's his name."

"He never said it out loud. But I knew what it was."

"Welcome to New World." I take another bite, having to tear an extra-chewy bit off with my teeth, which catches one sore spot among many in my mouth. "Ow." I spit out the bit of mutton and a whole lot of extra blood.

The girl watches me spit and then sets down her food. She picks up her bag, opens it, and finds a little blue box, slightly larger than the green campfire one. She presses a button on the front to open it and takes out what looks like a white plastic cloth and a little metal scalpel. She gets up from her rock and walks over to me with them.

I'm still sitting but I lean back when she brings her hands to my face.

"Bandages," she says.

"I've got my own."

"These are better."

I lean back farther. "Yer . . ." I say, blowing out air thru my nose. "Yer quiet kinda . . ." I shake my head a little.

"Bothers you?"

"Yes."

"I know," she says. "Hold still."

She looks closer at the area around my swollen eye and then cuts off a piece of bandage with the little scalpel. She's about to put it over my eye but I can't help it and I move back from her touch. She don't say nothing, just keeps her hands up, like she's waiting. I take a deep breath, close my eyes, and offer up my face.

I feel the bandage touch the swollen area and immediately it gets cooler, immediately the pain starts to edge back, like it's all being swept away by feathers. She puts another one on a cut I have at my hairline and her fingers brush my face as she puts another one just below my lower lip. It all feels so good I haven't even opened my eyes yet.

"I don't have anything for your teeth," she says.

"'S okay," I say, almost whispering it. "Man, these *are* better than mine."

"They're partially alive," she says. "Synthetic human tissue. When you're healed, they die."

"Uh-huh," I say, acting like I might know what that means.

There's a longer silence, long enough to make me open my eyes again. She's stepped back, back to a rock she can sit down on, watching me, watching my face.

We wait. Cuz it seems like we should.

And we should cuz after a little bit of waiting, she begins to talk.

"We crashed," she starts quietly, looking away. Then she clears her throat and says it again. "We crashed. There was a fire and we were flying low and we thought we'd be okay but something went wrong with the safety flumes and–" She holds open her hands to explain what follows the *and*. "We crashed."

She stops.

"Was that yer ma and pa?" I ask, after a bit.

But she just looks up into the sky, blue and spare, with clouds that look like bones. "And when the sun came up," she says, "that man came."

"Aaron."

"And it was so weird. He would shout and he would scream and then he'd *leave*. And I'd try to run away." She folds her arms. "I *kept* trying so he wouldn't find me, but I was going in circles and wherever I hid, there he'd be, I don't know how, until I found these sort of hut things."

"The Spackle buildings," I say but she ain't really listening. She looks at me. "Then you came." She looks at Manchee. "You and your dog that talks."

"Manchee!" Manchee barks.

Her face is pale and when she meets my eyes again, her own have gone wet. "What is this place?" she asks, her voice kinda thick. "Why do the animals talk? Why do I hear your voice when your mouth isn't moving? Why do I hear your voice a whole bunch over, piled on top of each other like there's nine million of you talking at once? Why do I see pictures of other things when I look at you? Why could I see what that man . . ."

She fades off. She draws her knees up to her chest and hugs them. I feel like I better start talking real quick or she's gonna start rocking again.

"We're settlers," I say. She looks up at this, still hugging her knees but at least not rocking. "We *were* settlers," I continue. "Landed here to found New World about twenty years ago or so. But there were aliens here. The Spackle. And they . . . didn't want us." I'm telling her what every boy in Prentisstown knows, the history even the dumbest farm boy like yours truly knows by heart. "Men tried for years to make peace but the Spackle weren't having it. And so war started."

She looks down again at the word *war*. I keep talking.

"And the way the Spackle fought, see, was with germs, with diseases. That was their weapons. They released germs that did things. One of them we think was meant to kill all our livestock but instead it just made every animal able to talk." I look at Manchee. "Which ain't as much fun as it sounds." I look back at the girl. "And another was the Noise."

I wait. She don't say nothing. But we both sorta know what's coming cuz we been here before, ain't we?

I take a deep breath. "And that one killed half the men and all the women, including my ma, and it made the thoughts of the men who survived no longer secret to the rest of the world."

She hides her chin behind her knees. "Sometimes I can hear it clearly," she says. "Sometimes I can tell exactly what you're thinking. But only sometimes. Most of the time it's just—"

"Noise," I say.

She nods. "And the aliens?"

"There ain't no more aliens."

She nods again. We sit for a minute, ignoring the obvious till it can't be ignored no longer.

"Am I going to die?" she asks quietly. "Is it going to kill me?"

The words sound different in her accent but they mean the same damn thing and my Noise can only say *probably* but I make it so my mouth says, "I don't know."

She watches me for more.

"I really *don't* know," I say, kinda meaning it. "If you'd asked me last week, I'd have been sure, but today—" I look down at my rucksack, at the book hiding inside. "I don't know." I look back at her. "I hope not."

But probably, says my Noise. *Probably yer gonna die,* and tho I try to cover it up with other Noise it's such an unfair thing it's hard not to have it right at the front.

"I'm sorry," I say.

She don't say nothing.

"But maybe if we get to the next settlement—" I say, but I don't finish cuz I don't know the answer. "You ain't sick yet. That's something."

"You must warn them," she says, down into her knees.

I look up sharply. "What?"

"Earlier, when you were trying to read that book—"

"I wasn't *trying*," I say, my voice a little bit louder all of a sudden.

"I could see the words in your whatever," she says, "and it's 'You must warn them.'"

"I know that! I know what it says."

Of course it's ruddy *You must warn them.* Course it is. Idiot.

The girl says, "It seemed like you were—"

"I know how to read."

She holds up her hands. "Okay."

"I do!"

"I'm just saying—"

"Well, *stop* just saying," I frown, my Noise roiling enough to get Manchee on his feet. I get to my feet as well. I pick up the rucksack and put it back on. "We should get moving."

"Warn who?" asks the girl, still sitting. "About what?"

I don't get to answer (even tho I don't *know* the answer) cuz there's a loud click above us, a loud clangy click that in Prentisstown would mean one thing:

A rifle being cocked.

And standing on a rock above us, there's someone with a freshly cocked rifle in both hands, looking down the sight, pointing it right at us.

"What's foremost in my mind at this partickalar juncture," says a voice rising from behind the gun, "is what do two little pups think they're doing a-burning down my bridge?"

14

THE WRONG END OF A GUN

GUN! GUN! GUN!" Manchee starts barking, hopping back and forth in the dust.

"I'd quiet down yer beastie there," says the rifle, his face obscured by looking down the sight straight at us. "Wouldn't want anything to happen to it, now wouldja?"

"Quiet, Manchee!" I say.

He turns to me. "Gun, Todd?" he barks. "Bang, bang!"

"I know. Shut up."

He stops barking and it's quiet.

Aside from my Noise, it's *quiet*.

"I do believe I sent out an asking to a partickalar pair of pups," says the voice, "and I am a-waiting on my answer."

I look back at the girl. She shrugs her shoulders, tho I notice we both have our hands up. "What?" I say back up to the rifle.

The rifle gives an angry grunt. "I'm asking," it says, "what exactly gives ye permisshun to go a-burning down other people's bridges?"

I don't say nothing. Neither does the girl.

"D'ye think this is a *stick* I'm a-pointing at ye?" The rifle bobs up and down once.

"We were being chased," I say, for lack of nothing else.

"Chased, were ye?" says the rifle. "Who was a-chasing ye?"

And I don't know how to answer this. Would the truth be more dangerous than a lie? Is the rifle on the side of the Mayor? Would we be bounty? Or would the rifle have even *heard* of Prentisstown?

The world's a dangerous place when you don't know enough.

Like why is it so quiet?

"Oh, I heard of Prentisstown, all right," says the rifle, reading my Noise with unnerving clarity and cocking the gun again, making it ready to shoot. "And if that's where yer from—"

Then the girl speaks up and says that thing that suddenly makes me think of her as *Viola* and not *the girl* anymore.

"He saved my life."

I saved her life.

Says Viola.

Funny how that works.

"Did he now?" says the rifle. "And how do you know he don't aim to just be a-saving it for himself?"

The girl, Viola, looks at me, her forehead creased. It's my turn to shrug.

"But no." The rifle's voice changes. "No, uh-uh, no, I'm not a-seeing that in ye, am I, boy? Cuz yer just a boy pup still, ain't ye?"

I swallow. "I'll be a man in 29 days."

"Not something to be proud of, pup. Not where yer from."

And then he lowers the gun away from his face.

And that's why it's so quiet.

He's a woman.

He's a grown woman.

He's an *old* woman.

"I'll thank ye kindly to call me *she*," the woman says, still pointing the rifle at us from chest level. "And not so old I won't still shoot ye."

She's looking at us more closely now, reading me up and down, seeing right into my Noise with a skill I've only ever felt in Ben. Her face is making all kindsa shapes, like she's considering me, like Cillian's face does when he tries to read me to see if I'm lying. Tho this woman ain't got no Noise at all so she might be singing a song in there for all I know.

She turns to Viola and pauses for another long look.

"As pups go," she says, looking back at me, "ye are as easy to read as a newborn, m'boy." She turns her face to Viola. "But ye, wee girl, yer story's not a usual one, is it?"

"I'd be happy to tell you all about it if you'd stop pointing a gun at us," Viola says.

This is so surprising even Manchee looks up. I turn to Viola with my mouth open.

We hear a chuckle from up on the rock. The old woman is laughing to herself. Her clothes seem like real dusty leather, worn and creased for years and years with a rimmed hat and boots for ignoring mud. Like she ain't nothing more than a farmer, really.

She's still pointing the gun at us, tho.

"Ye were a-running from Prentisstown, were ye?" she asks, looking into my Noise again. There's no point in hiding it so I go ahead and put forward what we were running from, what happened at the bridge, who was chasing us. She sees all of it, I know she does, but all I see her do is wrinkle up her lips and squint her eyes a bit.

"Well, now," she says, crooking the rifle in her arm and starting to make her way down from the rocks to where we're standing. "I can't rightly say that I'm not peeved bout ye blowing up my bridge. Heard the boom all the way back at the farm, oh, yeah." She steps off the last rock and stands a little ways away from us, the force of her grown-up quiet so large I feel myself stepping back without even knowing I decided to do it. "But the only place it led to ain't been worth a-going to for a decade nor more. Only left it up outta hope." She looks us over again. "Who's to say I weren't right?"

We still have our hands in the air cuz she ain't making much sense, is she?

"I'll ask ye this once," the woman says, lifting the rifle again. "Am I gonna need this?"

I exchange a glance with Viola.

"No," I say.

"No, mam," Viola says.

Mam? I think.

"It's like *sir,* bonny boy." The woman slings the rifle over her shoulder by its strap. "For if yer a-talking to a lady." She squats down to Manchee's level. "And who might ye be, pup?"

"Manchee!" he barks.

"Oh, yeah, that's definitely who ye be, innit?" says the woman, giving him a vigorous rubbing. "And ye two pups?" she asks, not looking up. "What might yer good mothers have dubbed ye?"

Me and Viola exchange another glance. It seems like a price, giving up our names, but maybe it's a fair exchange for the gun being lowered.

"I'm Todd. That's Viola."

"As surely true as the sun a-coming up," says the woman, having succeeded in getting Manchee on his back for a tummy rub.

"Is there another way over that river?" I ask. "Another bridge? Cuz those men—"

"I'm Mathilde," the old woman interrupts, "but people who call me that don't know me, so you can call me Hildy and one day ye may even earn the right to shake my hand."

I look at Viola again. How can you tell if someone with no Noise is crazy?

The old woman cackles. "Yer a funny one there, boy." She stands up from Manchee who rolls back over and stares at her, already a worshipper. "And to answer yer asking, there's shallow crossings a couple days' traveling upstream but there ain't no bridges for a good distance more either way."

She turns her gaze back to me, steady and clear, a small smile on her lips. She's gotta be reading my Noise again but I can't feel no prodding like I do when men try it.

And the way she keeps on looking I start to realize a few things, put a few things together. It must be right that Prentisstown was quarantined cuz of the Noise germ, huh? Cuz here's a grown-up woman who ain't dead from it, who's looking at me friendly but keeping her distance, a woman ready to greet strangers from my direkshun with a rifle.

And if I'm contagious that means Viola's probably definitely caught it by now, could be dying as we speak, and that I'm probably definitely not gonna be welcome in the settlement, probably definitely gonna be told to keep way way out and that's probably the end of that, ain't it? My journey ended before I even found anywhere to go.

"Oh, ye won't be welcome in the settlement," the woman says. "No probably about it." – She winks at me, actually winks –"But, what ye don't know won't kill ye."

"Wanna bet?" I say.

She turns back and steps up the rocks the way she came. We just watch her go till she gets to the top and turns around again.

"Ye all a-coming?" she says, as if she's invited us along and we're keeping her waiting.

I look at Viola. She calls up to the woman, "We're meant to be heading for the settlement." Viola looks at me again. "Welcome or not."

"Oh, ye'll get there," says the woman, "but what ye two pups need first is a good sleeping and a good feeding. Any blind man could see that."

The idea of sleep and hot food is so tempting, I forget for a second that she ever pointed a gun at us. But only for a second. Cuz there's other things to think about. I make the decision for us. "We should keep on the road," I say to Viola quietly.

"I don't even know where we're going," she says, also quietly. "Do you? Honestly?"

"Ben said–"

"Ye two pups come to my farm, get some good eatings in ye, sleep on a bed – tho it ain't soft, I grant ye that – and in the morning, we'll go to the *settlement*." And that's how she says it, opening her eyes wide on it, like a word to make fun of us for calling it that.

We still don't move.

"Look at it thusly," the old woman says. "I got me a gun." She waves it. "But I'm *asking* ye to come."

"Why don't we go with her?" Viola whispers. "Just to see."

My Noise rises a little in surprise. "See what?"

"I could use a bath," she says. "I could use some sleep."

"So could I," I say, "but there's men who're after us who probably ain't gonna let one fallen bridge stop them. And besides, we don't know nothing about her. She could be a killer for all we know."

"She seems okay." Viola glances up at the woman. "A little crazy, but she doesn't seem *dangerous* crazy."

"She don't *seem* anything." I feel a little vexed, if I'm honest. "People without Noise don't seem like nothing at all."

Viola looks at me, her brows suddenly creased and her jaw set a little.

"Well, not *you*, obviously," I say.

"Every time . . ." she starts to say but then she just shakes her head.

"Every time what?" I whisper, but Viola just scrunches her eyes and turns to the woman.

"Hold on," she says, her voice sounding annoyed. "Let me get my stuff."

"Hey!" I say. What happened to her remembering I saved her life? "Wait a minute. We gotta follow the road. We gotta get to the settlement."

"Roads is never the fastest way to get nowhere," the woman says. "Don't ye know that?"

Viola don't say nothing, just picks up her bag, frowning all over the place. She's ready to go, ready to head off with the first quiet person she sees, ready to leave me behind at the first sweet beckoning.

And she's missing the thing I don't wanna say.

"I *can't* go, Viola," I say, low, thru clenched teeth, hating myself a little as I say it, my face turning hot, which weirdly makes a bandage fall off. "I carry the germ. I'm dangerous."

She turns to me and there's a sting in her voice. "Then maybe you shouldn't come."

My jaw drops open. "You'd do that? You'd just *leave*?"

Viola looks away from my eyes but before she can answer, the old woman speaks. "Boy pup," she says, "if it's being infeckshus yer worried about, then yer girl mate can come a-walking up ahead with ol' Hildy while ye stay back a little ways with the puppup to guard ye."

"Manchee!" Manchee barks.

"Whatever," Viola says, turning and starting to climb the rocks to where the old woman stands.

"And I told ye," the woman says, "it's *Hildy*, not *old woman*."

Viola reaches her and they walk off outta sight without another word. Just like that.

"Hildy," Manchee says to me.

"Shut up," I say.

And I don't got no choice but to climb the rocks after 'em, do I?

So that's how we make our way, along a much narrower path thru rocks and scrub, Viola and old Hildy keeping close together when they can, me and Manchee miles back, tripping our way toward who knows what further danger and the whole time I'm looking back over my shoulder, expecting to see the Mayor and Mr. Prentiss Jr. and Aaron all coming after us.

I don't know. How can you know? How can Ben and Cillian have expected me to be prepared for this? Sure, the idea of a bed and hot food sounds like something worth getting shot for but maybe it's a trick and we're being so stupid we deserve to get caught.

And there's people after us and we should be running.

But maybe there really ain't another way over that river.

And Hildy could have forced us and she didn't. And Viola said she seems okay and maybe one Noise-less person can read another.

You see? How can you know?

And who cares what Viola says?

"Look at 'em up there," I say to Manchee. "They fell together pretty quick. Like they're long lost family or something."

"Hildy," Manchee says again. I swat after his rump but he runs on ahead.

Viola and Hildy are talking together but I can only hear the murmurings of words here and there. I don't know what they're saying at all. If they were normal Noisy people, it wouldn't matter how far back on the trail I was, we could all talk together and nobody'd have no automatic secrets. Everybody'd be jabbering, whether they wanted to or not.

And nobody'd be left out. Nobody'd be left on his own at the first chance you had.

We all walk on.

And I'm starting to think some more.

And I'm starting to let them get a little farther ahead, too.

And I'm thinking more.

Cuz as time passes, it's all starting to sink in.

Cuz maybe now we found Hildy, maybe she *can* take care of Viola.

They're clearly peas in a pod, ain't they? Different from me, anyway. And so maybe Hildy could help her get back to wherever she's from cuz obviously I can't. Obviously I ain't got nowhere I can be except Prentisstown, do I? Cuz I'm carrying a germ that'll kill her, may kill her still, may kill everybody else I meet, a germ that'll forever keep me outta that settlement, that'll probably even leave me sleeping in Hildy's barn with the sheep and the russets.

"That's it, ain't it, Manchee?" I stop walking, my chest starting to feel heavy. "There ain't no Noise out here, less I'm the one who brings it." I rub some sweat off my forehead. "We got nowhere to go. We can't go forward. We can't go back."

I sit down on a rock, realizing the truth of it all.

"We got nowhere," I say. "We got nothing."

"Got Todd," Manchee says, wagging his tail.

It ain't fair.

It just ain't fair.

The only place you belong is the place you can never go back to.

And so yer always alone, forever and always.

Why'd you do it, Ben? What'd I do that was so bad?

I wipe my eyes with my arm.

I wish Aaron and the Mayor *would* come and get me.

I wish it would just be over already.

"Todd?" Manchee barks, coming up to my face and trying to sniff it.

"Leave me alone," I say, pushing him away.

Hildy and Viola are getting still farther away and if I don't get up, I'll lose the trail.

I don't get up.

I can still hear them talking, tho it gets steadily quieter, no one looking back to see if I'm still following.

Hildy, I hear, and ɟirl pup and blasted leaky pipe and Hildy again and burning bridge.

And I lift my head.

Cuz it's a new voice.

And I ain't hearing it. Not with my ears.

Hildy and Viola are getting farther away, but there's someone coming toward them, someone raising a hand in greeting.

Someone whose Noise is saying Hello.

15

BROTHERS IN SUFFERING

IT'S AN OLD MAN, also carrying a rifle but way down at his side, pointing to the ground. His Noise rises as he approaches Hildy, it stays raised as he puts an arm around her and kisses her in greeting, it buzzes as he turns and is introduced to Viola who stands back a little at being greeted so friendly.

Hildy is married to a man with Noise.

A full grown man, walking around Noisy as anything.

But how–?

"Hey, boy pup!" Hildy shouts back at me. "Ye going to sit there all day picking yer nose or are ye going to join us for supper?"

"Supper, Todd!" Manchee barks and takes off running toward them.

I don't think nothing. I don't know *what* to think.

"Another Noisy fella!" shouts the old man, stepping past Viola and Hildy and coming toward me. He's got Noise pouring outta him like a bright parade, all full of unwelcome welcome and pushy good feeling. Boy pup and bridges falling and leaky pipe and brother in suffering and Hildy, my Hildy. He's still carrying his rifle but as he reaches me, his hand's out for me to shake.

I'm so stunned that I actually shake it.

"Tam's my name!" the old man more or less shouts. "And who might ye be, pup?"

"Todd," I say.

"Pleasedtameetya, Todd!" He puts an arm around my shoulders and pretty much drags me forward up the path. I stumble along, barely keeping my balance as he pulls us to Hildy and Viola, talking all the way. "We haven't had guests for dinner in many a moon, so ye'll have to be a-scusing our humble shack. Ain't been no travelers thisaway for nigh on ten years nor more but yer welcome! Yer all welcome!"

We get to the others and I still don't know what to say and I look from Hildy to Viola to Tam and back again.

I just want the world to make sense now and then, is that so wrong?

"Not wrong at all, Todd pup," Hildy says kindly.

"How can you not have caught the Noise?" I ask, words finally making their way outta my head via my mouth. Then my heart suddenly rises, rises so high I can feel my eyes popping open and my throat starting to clench, my own Noise coming all high hopeful white.

"Do you have a cure?" I say, my voice almost breaking. "Is there a cure?"

"Now if there were a cure," Tam says, still pretty much shouting, "d'ye honestly think I'd be subjecting ye to all this here rubbish a-floating outta my brain?"

"Heaven help ye if ye did," Hildy says, smiling.

"And heaven help *ye* if ye couldn't tell me what I was meant to be thinking." Tam smiles back, love fuzzing all over his Noise. "Nope, boy pup," he says to me. "No cure that I know of."

"Well, now," Hildy says, "Haven's meant to be a-working on one. So people say."

"Which people?" Tam asks, sceptical.

"Talia," Hildy says. "Susan F. My sister."

Tam makes a *pssht* sound with his lips. "I rest my case. Rumors of rumors of rumors. Can't trust yer sister to get her own name right much less any useful info."

"But—" I say, looking back and forth again and again, not wanting to let it go. "But how can you be alive then?" I say to Hildy. "The Noise kills women. *All* women."

Hildy and Tam exchange a look and I hear, no, I *feel* Tam squash something in his Noise.

"No, it don't, Todd pup," Hildy says, a little too gently. "Like I been telling yer girl mate Viola here. She's safe."

"Safe? How can she be safe?"

"Women are immune," Tam says. "Lucky buggers."

"No, they're not!" I say, my voice getting louder. "No, they're *not*! Every woman in Prentisstown caught the Noise and every single one of them *died* from it! My *ma* died from it! Maybe the version the Spackle released on us was stronger than yers but—"

"Todd pup." Tam puts a hand on my shoulder to stop me.

I shake him off but I don't know what to say next. Viola hasn't said a word in all of this so I look at her. She don't look at me. "I know what I know," I say, even tho that's been half the trouble, ain't it?

How can this be true?

How can this be *true*?

Tam and Hildy exchange another glance. I look into Tam's Noise but he's as expert as anyone I've met at hiding stuff away when someone starts poking. What I see, tho, is all kind.

"Prentisstown's got a sad history, pup," he says. "A whole number of things went sour there."

"Yer wrong," I say, but even my voice says I ain't sure what I'm saying he's wrong about.

"This ain't the place for it, Todd," Hildy says, rubbing Viola on the shoulder, a rub that Viola don't resist. "Ye need to get some food in ye, some sleep in ye. Vi here says ye ain't slept hardly at all in many miles of traveling. Everything will be a-looking better when yer fed and rested."

"But she's safe from me?" I ask, making a point of not looking at Vi.

"Well, she's definitely safe from catching yer Noise," Hildy says, a smile breaking out. "What other safety she can get from ye is all down to a-knowing ye better."

I want her to be right but I also want to say she's wrong and so I don't say nothing at all.

"C'mon," Tam says, breaking the pause, "let's get to some feasting."

"No!" I say, remembering it all over again. "We ain't got time for *feasting*." I look at Viola. "There's men after us, in case you forgot. Men who ain't interested in our well-beings." I look up at Hildy. "Now, I'm sure yer feastings would be fine and all—"

"Todd pup—" Hildy starts.

"I ain't a pup!" I shout.

Hildy purses her lips and smiles with her eyebrows. "Todd pup," she says again, a little lower this time. "No man from any point beyond that river would ever set foot across it, do ye understand?"

"Yep," says Tam. "That's right."

I look from one to the other. "But—"

"I been guardian here of that bridge for ten plus years, pup," Hildy says, "and keeper of it for years before that. It's part of who I am to watch what comes." She looks over to Viola. "No one's coming. Ye all are safe."

"Yep," Tam says again, rocking back and forth on his heels.

"But—" I say again but Hildy don't let me finish.

"Time for feasting."

And that's that, it seems. Viola still don't look at me, still has her

arms crossed and is now under the arm of Hildy as they walk on again.
I'm stuck back with Tam who's waiting for me to start. I can't say as
I feel much like walking anymore but everyone else goes so I go, too. We
carry on up Tam and Hildy's private little path, Tam chattering away,
making enough Noise for a whole town.

"Hildy says ye blew up our bridge," he says.

"*My* bridge," Hildy says from in front of us.

"She did build it," Tam says to me. "Not that anyone's used it in forever."

· "No one?" I say, thinking for a second of all those men who disappeared outta Prentisstown, all the ones who vanished while I was growing up. Not one of them got this far.

"Nice bit of engineering, that bridge was," Tam's going on, like he
didn't hear me and maybe he didn't, what with how loud he's talking.
"Sad to hear it's gone."

"We had no choice," I say.

"Oh, there's always choices, pup, but from what I hear, ye made the
right one."

We walk on quietly for a bit. "Yer sure we're safe?" I ask.

"Well, ye can't never be sure," he says. "But Hildy's right." He grins,
a little sadly, I think. "There's more than bridges being out that'll keep
men that side of the river."

I try and read his Noise to see if he's telling the truth but it's almost
all shiny and clean, a bright, warm place where anything you want could
be true.

Nothing at all like a Prentisstown man.

"I don't understand this," I say, still gnawing on it. "It's gotta be a different kinda Noise germ."

"My Noise sound different from yers?" Tam asks, seeming genuinely
curious.

I look at him and just listen for a second. Hildy and Prentisstown and
russets and sheep and settlers and leaky pipe and Hildy.

"You sure think about yer wife a lot."

"She's my shining star, pup. Woulda lost myself in Noise if she
hadn't put a hand out to rescue me."

"How so?" I ask, wondering what he's talking about. "Did you fight in
the war?"

This stops him. His Noise goes as gray and featureless as a cloudy
day and I can't read a thing off him.

"I fought, young pup," he says. "But war's not something ye talk
about in the open air when the sun is shining."

"Why not?"

"I pray to all my gods ye never find out." He puts a hand on my shoulder. I don't shake it off this time.

"How do you do that?" I ask.

"Do what?"

"Make yer Noise so flat I can't read it."

He smiles. "Years of practice a-hiding things from the old woman."

"It's why I can read so good," Hildy calls back to us. "He gets better at hiding, I get better at *finding*."

They laugh together yet again. I find myself trying to send an eyeroll Viola's way about these two but Viola ain't looking at me and I stop myself from trying again.

We all come outta the rocky part of the path and around a low rise and suddenly there's a farm ahead of us, rolling up and down little hills but you can see fields of wheat, fields of cabbage, a field of grass with a few sheep on it.

"Hello, sheep!" Tam shouts.

"Sheep!" say the sheep.

First on the path is a big wooden barn, built as watertight and solid as the bridge, like it could last there forever if anyone asked it.

"Unless ye go a-blowing it up," Hildy says, laughing still.

"Like to see ye try." Tam laughs back.

I'm getting a little tired of 'em laughing about every damn thing.

Then we come around to the farmhouse, which is a totally different thing altogether. Metal, by the looks of it, like the gas stayshun and the Church back home but not nearly so banged up. Half of it shines and rolls on up to the sky like a sail and there's a chimney that curves up and out, folding down to a point, smoke coughing from its end. The other half of the house is wood built onto the metal, solid as the barn but cut and folded like—

"Wings," I say.

"Wings is right," Tam says. "And what kinda wings are they?"

I look again. The whole farmhouse looks like some kinda bird with the chimney as its head and neck and a shiny front and wooden wings stretching out behind, like a bird resting on the water or something.

"It's a swan, Todd pup," Tam says.

"A what?"

"A swan."

"What's a swan?" I say, still looking at the house.

His Noise is puzzled for a second, then I get a little pulse of sadness so I look at him. "What?"

"Nothing, pup," he says. "Memories of long ago."

Viola and Hildy are up ahead still, Viola's eyes wide and her mouth gulping like a fish.

"What did I tell ye?" Hildy asks.

Viola rushes up to the fence in front of the house. She stares at it, looking all over the metal part, up and down, side to side. I come up by her and look, too. It's hard for a minute to think of anything to say (shut up).

"Sposed to be a swan," I finally say. "Whatever that is."

She ignores me and turns to Hildy. "Is it an Expansion Three 500?"

"What?"

"Older than that, Vi pup," Hildy says. "X Three 200."

"We got up to X Sevens," Viola says.

"Not surprised," says Hildy.

"What the ruddy hell are you talking about?" I say. "Expanshun *whatsits*?"

"Sheep!" we hear Manchee bark in the distance.

"Our settler ship," Hildy says, sounding surprised that I don't know. "An Expansion Class Three, Series 200."

I look from face to face. Tam's Noise has a spaceship flying in it, one with a front hull that matches the upturned farmhouse.

"Oh, yeah," I say, remembering, trying to say it like I knew all along. "You build yer houses with the first tools at hand."

"Quite so, pup," Tam says. "Or ye make them works of art if yer so inclined."

"If yer wife is an engineer who can get yer damn fool sculptures to stay standing up," Hildy says.

"How do you know about all this?" I say to Viola.

She looks at the ground, away from my eyes.

"You don't mean—" I start to say but I stop.

I'm getting it.

Of *course* I'm getting it.

Way too late, like everything else, but I'm getting it.

"Yer a settler," I say. "Yer a new settler."

She looks away from me but shrugs her shoulders.

"But that ship you crashed in," I say, "that's way too tiny to be a set-tler ship."

"That was only a scout. My home ship is an Expansion Class Seven."

She looks at Hildy and Tam, who ain't saying nothing. Tam's Noise is bright and curious. I can't read nothing from Hildy. I get the feeling somehow, tho, that she knew and I didn't, that Viola told her and not me, and even if it's cuz I never asked, it's still as sour a feeling as it sounds.

I look up at the sky.

"It's up there, ain't it?" I say. "Yer Expanshun Class Seven."

Viola nods.

"Yer bringing more settlers in. More settlers are coming to New World."

"Everything was broken when we crashed," Viola says. "I don't have any way to contact them. Any way to warn them not to come." She looks up with a little gasp. *You must warn them.*

"That can't be what he meant," I say, fast. "No way."

Viola scrunches her face and eyebrows. "Why not?"

"What who meant?" Tam asks.

"How many?" I ask, still looking at Viola, feeling the world changing forever again. "How many settlers are coming?"

Viola takes a deep breath before she answers and I'll bet you she's not even told Hildy this part.

"Thousands," she says. "There's thousands."

16

THE NIGHT OF NO APOLOGIES

THEY WON'T be a-getting here for months," Hildy says, passing me another serving of mashed russets. Viola and I are stuffing our faces so much it's been Hildy and Tam doing all the talking.

All the *a*-talking.

"Space travel ain't like ye see it in vids," Tam says, a stream of mutton gravy tracking down his beard. "Takes years and years and years to get anywhere at all. Sixty-four to get from Old World to New World alone."

"*Sixty-four years?*" I say, spraying a few mashed blobs off my lips.

Tam nods. "Yer frozen for most of it, time passing you right on by, tho that's only if ye don't die on the way."

I turn to Viola. "Yer sixty-four years old?"

"Sixty-four Old World years," Tam says, tapping his fingers like he's adding something up. "Which'd be . . . what? Bout fifty-eight, fifty-nine New World—"

But Viola's shaking her head. "I was born on board. Never was asleep."

"So either yer ma or yer pa musta been a caretaker," Hildy says, snapping off a bite of a turnipy thing then giving me an explanashun. "One of the ones who stays awake and keeps track of the ship."

"Both of them were," Viola says. "And my dad's mother before him and granddad before that."

"Wait a minute," I say to her, two steps behind as ever. "So if we've been on New World twenty-odd years—"

"Twenty-three," says Tam. "Feels like longer."

"Then you left before we even *got* here," I say. "Or your pa or grandpa or whatever."

I look around to see if anyone's wondering what I'm wondering. "Why?" I say. "Why would you come without even knowing what's out here?"

"Why did the *first* settlers come?" Hildy asks me. "Why does anyone look for a new place to live?"

"Cuz the place yer a-leaving ain't worth staying for," Tam says. "Cuz the place yer a-leaving is so bad ye gotta leave."

"Old World's mucky, violent, and crowded," Hildy says, wiping her face with a napkin, "a-splitting right into bits with people a-hating each other and a-killing each other, no one happy till everyone's miserable. Least it was all those years ago."

"I wouldn't know," Viola says, "I've never seen it. My mother and father . . ." She drifts off.

But I'm still thinking about being born on a spaceship, an honest to badness *spaceship*. Growing up while flying along the stars, able to go wherever you wanted, not stuck on some hateful planet which clearly don't want you. You could go anywhere. If one place didn't suit, you'd find another. Full freedom in all direkshuns. Could there possibly be anything cooler in the whole world than that?

I don't notice that there's a silence fallen at the table. Hildy's rubbing Viola's back again and I see that Viola's eyes are wet and leaking and she's started to rock a little back and forth.

"What?" I say. "What's wrong now?"

Viola's forehead just creases at me.

"*What?*" I say.

"I think maybe we talked enough about Vi's ma and pa for now," Hildy says softly. "I think maybe it's time for boy and girl pups to get some shut-eye."

"But it's hardly late at all." I look out a window. The sun ain't even hardly set. "We need to be getting to the settlement—"

"The settlement is called Farbranch," Hildy says, "and we'll get ye there first thing in the morning."

"But those men—"

"I been a-keeping the peace here since before you were born, pup," Hildy says, kindly but firmly. "I can handle whatever is or ain't a-coming."

I don't say nothing to this and Hildy ignores my Noise on the subject.

"Can I ask what yer business in Farbranch might be?" Tam says, picking at his corncob, making his asking sound less curious than his Noise says it is.

"We just need to get there," I say.

"Both of ye?"

I look at Viola. She's stopped crying but her face is still puffy. I don't answer Tam's asking.

"Well, there's plenty of work going," Hildy says, standing and taking up her plate. "If that's what yer after. They can always use more hands in the orchards."

Tam stands and they clear the table, taking the dishes into their kitchen and leaving me and Viola sitting there by ourselves. We can hear them chatting in there, lightly enough and Noise-blocked enough for us not to be able to make it out.

"Do you really think we oughta stay the whole night?" I say, keeping my voice low.

But she answers in a violent whisper, like I didn't even send out an asking. "Just because my thoughts and feelings don't spill out into the world in a shout that never stops doesn't mean I don't have them."

I turn to her, surprised. *"Huh?"*

She keeps whispering something fierce. "Every time you think, *Oh, she's just emptiness,* or, *There's nothing going on inside her,* or, *Maybe I can dump her with these two,* I hear it, okay? I hear every stupid thing you think, all right? And I understand *way* more than I want to."

"Oh, yeah?" I whisper back, tho my Noise ain't a whisper at all. "Every time *you* think something or feel something or have some stupid thought, I *don't* hear it, so how am I sposed to know any effing thing about you, huh? How am I sposed to know what's going on if you keep it secret?"

"I'm *not* keeping it secret." She's clenching her teeth now. "I'm being *normal.*"

"Not normal for here, *Vi.*"

"And how would you know? I can hear you being surprised by just about everything they say. Didn't they have a school where you're from? Didn't you learn *anything?*"

"History ain't so important when yer just trying to survive," I say, spitting it out under my breath.

"That's actually when it's *most* important," Hildy says, standing at the end of the table. "And if this silly argument twixt ye two ain't enough to prove yer tired, then yer tired beyond all sense. C'mon."

Viola and I glare at each other but we get up and follow Hildy into a large common room.

"Todd!" Manchee barks from a corner, not getting up from the mutton bone Tam gave him earlier.

"We've long since took over our guest rooms for other purposes," Hildy says. "Ye'll have to make do on the settees."

We help her put down sheets, Viola still scowling, my Noise a buzzy red.

"Now," Hildy says when we're all done. "Apologize to each other."

"What?" Viola says. *"Why?"*

"I don't see how this is any of yer business," I say.

"Never go to sleep on an argument," Hildy says, hands on hips, looking like she ain't never gonna budge and would be pleased to see someone try and make her. "Not if ye want to stay friends."

Viola and I don't say nothing.

"He saved yer life?" Hildy says to Viola.

Viola looks down before finally saying, "Yeah."

"That's right, I did," I say.

"And she saved yers at the bridge, didn't she?" Hildy says.

Oh.

"Yes," Hildy says. *"Oh.* Don't ye both think that counts for something?"

We still don't say nothing.

Hildy sighs. "Fine. Any two pups so close to adulthood could maybe be left to their own apologies, I reckon." She makes her way out without even saying good night.

I turn my back on Viola and she turns her back on me. I take off my shoes and get myself under the sheet on one of Hildy's "settees" which seems to be just a fancy word for couch. Viola does the same. Manchee leaps up on my settee and curls himself by my feet.

There's no sound except my Noise and a few crackles from a fire it's too hot for. It can't be much later than dusk but the softness of the cushions and the softness of the sheet and the too-warm of the fire and I'm already pretty much closing my eyes.

"Todd?" Viola says from her settee across the room.

I swim up from sinking down to sleep. "What?"

She don't say nothing for a second and I guess she must be thinking of her apology.

But no.

"What does your book say you're supposed to do when you get to Farbranch?"

My Noise gets a bit redder. "Never you mind what my book says," I say. "That's my property, meant for me."

"You know when you showed me the map back in the woods," she says. "And you said we had to get to this settlement? You remember what was written underneath?"

"Course I do."

"What was it?"

There ain't no poking in her voice, not that I can hear, but that's gotta be what it is, ain't it? Poking?

"Just go to sleep, will ya?" I say.

"It was *Farbranch*," she says. "The name of the place we're meant to be heading."

"Shut up." My Noise is getting buzzy again.

"There's no shame in not being able to—"

"I said, *shut up!*"

"I could help you—"

I get up suddenly, dumping Manchee off the settee with a thump. I grab my sheets and blanket under my arm and I stomp off to the room where we ate. I throw them on the floor and lay down, a room away from Viola and all her meaningless, evil quiet.

Manchee stays in there with her. Typical.

I close my eyes but I don't sleep for ages and ages.

Till I finally do, I guess.

Cuz I'm on a path and it's the swamp but it's also the town and it's also my farm and Ben's there and Cillian's there and Viola's there and they're all saying, "What're you doing here, Todd?" and Manchee's barking "Todd! Todd!" and Ben's grabbing me by the arm to drag me out the door and Cillian's got his arm around my shoulders pushing me up the path and Viola's setting the campfire box by the front door of our farmhouse and the Mayor's horse rides right thru our front door and smashes her flat and a croc with the face of Aaron is rearing up behind Ben's shoulders and I'm yelling "No!" and—

And I'm sitting up and I'm sweating everywhere and my heart's racing like a horse and I'm expecting to see the Mayor and Aaron standing right over me.

But it's only Hildy and she's saying, "What the devil are ye a-doing in here?" She's standing in the doorway, morning sun flooding in behind her so bright I have to raise my hand to block it out.

"More comfortable," I mumble but my chest is thumping.

"I'll bet," she says, reading my just-waking Noise. "Breakfast is on."

The smell of the mutton-strip bacon frying wakes Viola and Manchee. I let Manchee out for his morning poo but Viola and I don't say nothing to each other. Tam comes in as we eat, having I guess been out feeding the sheep. That's what I'd be doing if I were home.

Home, I think.

Anyway.

"Buck up, pup," Tam says, plonking a cup of coffee down in front of me. I keep my face way down as I drink it.

"Anybody out there?" I say into my cup.

"Not a whisper," Tam says. "And it's a beautiful day."

I glance up at Viola but she ain't looking at me. In fact, we get all the way thru the food, thru washing our faces, thru changing our clothes and repacking our bags, all without saying nothing to each other.

"Good luck to ye both," Tam says, as we're about to leave with Hildy toward Farbranch. "It's always nice when two people who don't got no one else find each other as friends."

And we really don't say nothing to that.

"C'mon, pups," Hildy says. "Time's a-wasting."

We get back on the path, which before too long reconnects with the same road that musta gone across the bridge.

"Used to be the main road from Farbranch to Prentisstown," Hildy says, hoisting her own small pack. "Or New Elizabeth, as it was then."

"As what was then?" I ask.

"Prentisstown," she says. "Used to be called New Elizabeth."

"It never did," I say, raising my eyebrows.

Hildy looks at me, her own eyebrows mocking mine. "Was it never? I must be mistaken then."

"Must be," I say, watching her.

Viola makes a scoffing sound. I send her a look of death.

"Will there be somewhere we can stay?" she asks Hildy, ignoring me.

"I'll take ye to my sister," Hildy says. "Deputy Mayor this year, don't ye know?"

"What'll we do then?" I say, kicking at the dirt as we walk on.

"Reckon that's up to ye two," Hildy says. "Ye've gotta be the ones in charge of yer own destinies, don't ye?"

"Not so far," I hear Viola say under her breath and it's so exactly the words I have in my Noise that we both look up and catch each other's eyes.

We almost smile. But we don't.

And that's when we start hearing the Noise.

"Ah," Hildy says, hearing it too. "Farbranch."

The road comes out on the top of a little vale.

And there it is.

The other settlement. The other settlement that wasn't sposed to be.

Where Ben wanted us to go.

Where we might be safe.

The first thing I see is where the valley road winds down thru orchards, orderly rows of well-tended trees with paths and irrigashun systems, all carrying on down a hill toward buildings and a creek at the bottom, flat and easy and snaking its way back to meet the bigger river no doubt.

And all thruout are men and women.

Most are scattered working in the orchard, wearing heavy work aprons, all the men in long sleeves, the women in long skirts, cutting down pine-like fruits with machetes or carrying away baskets or working on the irri-gashun pipes and so on.

Men and women, women and men.

A coupla dozen men, maybe, is my general impression. Less than Prentisstown.

Who knows how many women.

Living in a whole other place.

The Noise (and silence) of them all floats up like a light fog.

Two, please and The way I see it is and Weedy waste and She might say yes, she might not and If service ends at one, then I can always and so on and so on, never ending, amen.

I just stop in the road and gape for a second, not ready to walk down into it yet.

Cuz it's weird.

It's more than weird, truth to tell.

It's all so, I don't know, *calm*. Like normal chatter you'd have with yer pals. Nothing accidental nor abusive.

And nobody's hardly longing for nothing.

No awful, awful, despairing longing nowhere I can hear or feel.

"We sure as ruddy heck ain't in Prentisstown no more," I say to Manchee under my breath.

Not a second later, I hear Prentisstown? float in from a field right next to us.

And then I hear it in a coupla different places. Prentisstown? and Prentisstown? and then I notice that the men in the orchards nearby ain't picking fruit or whatever anymore. They're standing up. They're looking at us.

"Come on," Hildy says. "Keep on a-walking. It's just curiosity."

The word Prentisstown multiplies along the fields like a crackling fire. Manchee brings hisself in closer to my legs. We're being stared at on all sides as we carry on. Even Viola steps in a bit so we're a tighter group.

"Not to worry," Hildy says. "There'll just be a lot of people who'll want to meet—"

She stops midsentence.

A man has stepped onto the path in front of us.

His face don't look at all like he wants to meet us.

"Prentisstown?" he says, his Noise getting uncomfortably red, uncomfortably fast.

"Morning, Matthew," Hildy says, "I was just a-bringing–"

"Prentisstown," the man says again, no longer an asking, and he's not looking at Hildy.

He's looking straight at me.

"Yer not welcome here," he says. "Not welcome at all."

And he's got the biggest machete in his hand you ever seen.

17

ENCOUNTER IN AN ORCHARD

MY HAND GOES right behind my rucksack to my own knife.

"Leave it, Todd pup," Hildy says, keeping her eyes on the man. "That's not how this is gonna go."

"What do ye think yer a-bringing into our village, Hildy?" the man says, hefting his machete in his hand, still looking at me and there's real surprise in his asking and—

And is that *hurt*?

"I'm a-bringing in a boy pup and a girl pup what's lost their way," Hildy says. "Stand aside, Matthew."

"I don't see a boy pup nowhere," Matthew says, his eyes starting to burn. He's massively tall, shoulders like an ox and a thickened brow with lots of bafflement but not much tenderness. He looks like a walking, talking thunderstorm. "I see me a Prentisstown man. I see me a Prentisstown man with Prentisstown filth all over his Prentisstown Noise."

"That's not what yer a-seeing," Hildy says. "Look close."

Matthew's Noise is already lurching on me like hands pressing in, forcing its way into my own thinking, trying to ransack the room. It's angry and asking and Noisy as a fire, so uneven I can't make hide nor hair of it.

"Ye know the law, Hildy," he says.

The law?

"The law is for men," Hildy says, her voice staying calm, like we were standing there talking bout the weather. Can't she see how red this

man's Noise is getting? Red ain't yer color if you wanna have a chat. "This
here pup ain't a man yet."

"I've still got twenty-eight days," I say, without thinking.

"Yer numbers don't mean nothing here, boy," Matthew spits. "I don't
care how many days away ye are."

"Calm yerself, Matthew," Hildy says, sterner than I'd want her to.
But to my surprise, Matthew looks at her all sore and steps back a step.
"He's a-fleeing Prentisstown," she says, a little softer. "He's a-running
away."

Matthew looks at her suspiciously and back to me but he's lowering
the machete. A little.

"Just like ye did yerself once," Hildy says to him.

What?

"Yer from Prentisstown?" I blurt out.

Up comes the machete and Matthew steps forward again, threatening enough to start Manchee barking, "Back! Back! Back!"

"I was from *New Elizabeth*," Matthew growls, twixt clenched teeth.
"I'm *never* from Prentisstown, boy, not never, and don't ye forget it."

I see clearer flashes in his Noise now. Of impossible things, of crazy
things, coming in a rush, like he can't help it, things worse than the worst
of the illegal vids Mr. Hammar used to let out on the sly to the oldest
and rowdiest of the boys in town, the kind where people seemed to die for
real but there was no way of ever knowing for sure. Images and words and
blood and screaming and—

"Stop that right this second!" Hildy shouts. "Control yerself,
Matthew Lyle. Control yerself *right now*."

Matthew's Noise subsides, suddenlike but still roiling, without quite
so much control as Tam but still more than any man in Prentisstown.

But as soon as I think it, his machete raises again. "Ye'll not say that
word in our town, boy," he says. "Not if ye know what's good for ye."

"There'll be no threats to guests of mine as long as I'm alive," Hildy
says, her voice strong and clear. "Is that understood?"

Matthew looks at her, he don't nod, he don't say yes, but we all understand that he understands. He ain't happy bout it, tho. His Noise still
pokes and presses at me, slapping me if it could. He finally looks over to
Viola.

"And who might this be then?" he says, pointing the machete at her.

And it happens before I even know I'm doing it, I swear.

One minute I'm standing there behind everyone and the next thing
I know, I'm between Matthew and Viola, my knife pointing at him, my own
Noise falling like an avalanche and my mouth saying, "You best take two
steps away from her and you best be taking 'em real quick."

"Todd!" Hildy shouts.

And "Todd!" Manchee barks.

And "Todd!" Viola shouts.

But there I am, knife out, my heart thumping fast like it's finally figured out what I'm doing.

But there ain't no stepping back.

Now how do you spose *that* happened?

"Give me a reason, Prentissboy," Matthew says, hoisting the machete. "Just give me one good reason."

"Enough!" Hildy says.

And her voice has got something in it this time, like the rule of law,
so much so that Matthew flinches a little. He's still holding up his machete, still glaring at me, glaring at Hildy, his Noise throbbing like a
wound.

And then his face twists a little.

And he begins, of all things, to cry.

Angrily, furiously trying not to, but standing there, big as a bull, machete in hand, crying.

Which ain't what I was expecting.

Hildy's voice pulls back a bit. "Put the knife away, Todd pup."

Matthew drops his machete to the ground and puts an arm across
his eyes as he snuffles and yowls and moans. I look over at Viola. She's
just staring at Matthew, probably as confused as I am.

I drop the knife to my side but I don't let it go. Not yet.

Matthew's taking deep breaths, pain Noise and grief Noise dripping
everywhere, and fury, too, at losing control so publicly. "It's meant to be
over," he coughs. "Long over."

"I know," Hildy says, going forward and putting a hand on his arm.

"What's going on?" I say.

"Never you mind, Todd pup," Hildy says. "Prentisstown has a sad
history."

"That's what Tam said," I say. "As if I don't know."

Matthew looks up. "Ye don't know the first bit of it, boy," he says,
teeth clenched again.

"That's enough now," Hildy says. "This boy ain't yer enemy." She
looks at me, eyes a bit wide. "And he's putting away his knife for that
very reason."

I twist the knife in my hand a time or two but then I reach behind
my rucksack and put it away. Matthew's glaring at me again but he's
starting to back off for real now and I'm wondering who Hildy is that
he's obeying her.

"They're both innocent as lambs, Matthew pup," Hildy says.

"Ain't nobody innocent," Matthew says bitterly, sniffing away his last bits of weepy snot and hefting up his machete again. "Nobody at all."

He turns his back and strides into the orchard, not looking back.

Everyone else is still staring at us.

"The day only ages," Hildy says to them, turning round in a circle. "There'll be time enough for a-meeting and a-greeting later on."

Me and Viola watch as the workers start returning to their trees and their baskets and their whatevers, some eyes still on us but most people getting back to work.

"Are you in charge here or something?" I ask.

"Or something, Todd pup. C'mon, ye haven't even seen the town yet."

"What law was he talking about?"

"Long story, pup," she says. "I'll tell ye later."

The path, still wide enough for men and vehicles and horses, tho I only see men, curves its way down thru more orchards on the hillsides of the little vale.

"What kind of fruit is that?" Viola asks, as two women cross the road in front of us with full baskets, watching us as they go.

"Crested pine," Hildy says. "Sweet as sugar, loaded with vitamins."

"Never heard of it," I say.

"No," Hildy says. "Ye wouldn't have."

I look at way too many trees for a settlement that can't have more than fifty people in it. "Is that all you eat here?"

"Course not," Hildy says. "We trade with the other settlements down the road."

The surprise is so clear in my Noise that even Viola laughs a little.

"Ye didn't think it was just two settlements on all of New World, did ye?" Hildy asks.

"No," I say, feeling my face turn red, "but all the other settlements were wiped out in the war."

"Mmm," Hildy says, biting her bottom lip, nodding but not saying nothing more.

"Is that Haven?" Viola says quietly.

"Is what Haven?" I ask.

"The other settlement," Viola says, not quite looking at me. "You said there was a cure for Noise in Haven."

"Ach!" Hildy psshts. "That's just rumours and speckalashuns."

"Is Haven a real place?" I ask.

"It's the biggest and first of the settlements," Hildy says. "Closest New World's got to a big city. Miles away. Not for peasants like us."

"I ain't never heard of it," I say again.

No one says nothing to this and I get the feeling they're being polite. Viola hasn't really looked at me since the weirdness back there with me and Matthew and the knife. To be honest, I don't know what to make of it neither.

So everyone just keeps walking.

There's maybe seven buildings total in Farbranch, smaller than Prentisstown and just buildings after all but somehow so different, too, it feels like I've wandered right off New World into some whole other place altogether.

The first building we pass is a tiny stone church, fresh and clean and open, not at all like the darkness Aaron preached in. Farther on is a general store with a mechanic's garage by it, tho I don't see much by way of heavy machinery around. Haven't even seen a fissionbike, not even a dead one. There's a building that looks like a meeting hall, another with a doctor's snakes carved into the front, and two barnlike buidings that look like storage.

"Not much," Hildy says. "But it's home."

"Not yer home," I say. "You live way outside."

"So do most people," Hildy says. "Even when yer used to it, it's nice to only have the Noise of yer most beloved a-hanging round yer house. Town gets a bit rackety."

I listen out for rackety but it still ain't *nothing* like Prentisstown. Sure there's Noise in Farbranch, men doing their usual boring daily business, chattering their thoughts that don't mean nothing, Chop, chop, chop and I'll only give seven for the dozen and Listen to her sing there, just listen and That coop needs fixing tonight and He's gonna fall right off of that and on and on and on, so heedless and safe-sounding to me it feels like taking a bath in comparison to the black Noise I'm used to.

"Oh, it gets black, Todd pup," Hildy says. "Men still have their tempers. Women, too."

"Some people would call it impolite to always be listening to a man's Noise," I say, looking around me.

"Too true, pup." She grins. "But ye aren't a man yet. Ye said so yerself."

We cross the central strip of the town. A few men and women walk to and fro, some tipping their hats to Hildy, most just staring at us.

I stare back.

If you listen close, you can hear where the women are in town almost as clear as the men. They're like rocks that the Noise washes over and once yer used to it you can feel where their silences are, dotted all about, Viola and Hildy ten times over and I'll bet if I stopped and stood here I could tell exactly how many women are in each building.

And mixed in with the sound of so many men, you know what? The silence don't feel half so lonesome.

And then I see some teeny, tiny people, watching us from behind a bush.

Kids.

Kids smaller than me, *younger* than me.

The first I ever seen.

A woman carrying a basket spies them and makes a shooing movement with her hands. She frowns and smiles at the same time and the kids all run off giggling round the back of the church.

I watch 'em go. I feel my chest pull a little.

"Ye coming?" Hildy calls after me.

"Yeah," I say, still watching where the kids went. I turn and keep on following, my head still twisted back.

Kids. Real kids. *Safe* enough for kids and I find myself wondering if Viola would be able to feel at home here with all these nice-seeming men, all these women and children. I find myself wondering if she'd be safe, even if I'm obviously not.

I'll bet she would.

I look at Viola and catch her looking away.

Hildy's led us to the house farthest along the buildings of Farbranch. It's got steps that go up the front and a little flag flying from a pole out front.

I stop.

"This is a mayor's house," I say. "Ain't it?"

"Deputy Mayor," Hildy says, walking up the steps, clomping her boots loud against the wood. "My sister."

"And *my* sister," says a woman opening the door, a plumper, younger, frownier version of Hildy.

"Francia," Hildy says.

"Hildy," Francia says.

They nod at each other, not hug or shake hands, just nod.

"What trouble d'ye think yer bringing into my town?" Francia says, eyeing us up.

"Yer town, is it now?" Hildy says, smiling, eyebrows up. She turns to us. "Like I told Matthew Lyle, it's just two pups a-fleeing for safety, seeking their refuge." She turns back to her sister. "And if Farbranch ain't a refuge, sister, then what is it?"

"It's not them I'm a-talking about," Francia says, looking at us, arms crossed. "It's the army that's a-following them."

18

FARBRANCH

ARMY?" I say, my stomach knotting right up. Viola says it at the same time I do but there's nothing funny bout it this time.

"What army?" Hildy frowns.

"Rumors a-floating down from the far fields of an army a-gathering on the other side of the river," Francia says. "Men on horseback. Prentisstown men."

Hildy purses her lips. "*Five* men on horseback," she says. "Not an army. Those were just the posse sent after our young pups here."

Francia don't look too convinced. I never seen arms so crossed.

"And the river gorge crossing is down anyhow," Hildy continues, "so there ain't gonna be anyone a-coming into Farbranch any time soon." She looks back at us. "An *army*," she says, shaking her head. "Honestly."

"If there's a threat, sister," Francia says, "it's my duty—"

Hildy rolls her eyes. "Don't be a-talking to me about yer duty, sister," she says, stepping past Francia and opening the front door to the house. "I *invented* yer duty. C'mon, pups, let's get ye inside."

Viola and I don't move. Francia don't invite us to neither. "Todd?" Manchee barks by my feet.

I take a deep breath and go up the front steps. "Howdy, mim," I say.

"*Mam,*" Viola whispers behind me.

"Howdy, mam," I say, trying not to miss a beat. "I'm Todd. That's Viola." Francia's arms are still crossed, like there's a prize for it. "There really were only five men," I say, tho the word *army* is echoing round my Noise.

"And I should just trust ye?" Francia says. "A boy who's a-being chased?" She looks down to Viola, still waiting on the bottom step. "I can just imagine why *ye* were running."

"Oh, stuff it, Francia," Hildy says, still holding the door open for us.

Francia turns and shooshes Hildy outta the way. "I'll be in charge of entry into my own house, thank ye very much," Francia says, then to us, "Well, c'mon if yer coming."

And that's how we first see the hospitality of Farbranch. We go inside. Francia and Hildy bickering twixt themselves about whether Francia's got a place to put us in for however long we might wanna stay. Hildy wins the bickering and Francia shows me and Viola to separate small rooms next to each other one floor up.

"Yer dog has to sleep outside," Francia says.

"But he's—"

"That wasn't an asking," Francia says, leaving the room.

I follow her out to the landing. She don't turn back as she goes downstairs. In less than a minute, I can hear her and Hildy arguing again, trying to keep their voices down. Viola comes outta her room to listen, too. We stand there for a second, wondering.

"Whaddya think?" I say.

She don't look at me. Then it's like she decides to look at me and does.

"I don't know," she says. "What do *you* think?"

I shrug my shoulders. "She don't seem too happy to see us," I say, "but it's still safer than I've felt in a while. Behind walls and such." I shrug again. "And Ben wanted us to get here and all."

Which is true but I still ain't sure if it feels right.

Viola's clutching her arms to herself, just like Francia but not like Francia at all. "I know what you mean."

"So I guess it'll do for now."

"Yes," Viola says. "For now."

We listen to a bit more arguing.

"What you did back there—" Viola says.

"It was stupid," I say, real fast. "I don't wanna talk about it."

My face is starting to burn so I step back in my little room. I stand there and chew my lip. The room looks like it used to belong to an old person. Kinda smells that way, too, but at least it's got a real bed.

I go to my rucksack and open it.

I look round to make sure no one's followed me in and I pull out the book. I open it to the map, to the arrows that point down thru the swamp, to the river on the other side. No bridge on the map but there's the settlement. With a word underneath it.

"Fayre," I say, to myself. "Fayre braw nk."

Which I guess is Farbranch.

I breathe loud thru my nose as I look at the page of writing on the back of the map. *You must warn them* (of course, of *course*, shut up) still underlined at the bottom. Like Viola said, tho, warn who? Warn Farbranch? Warn Hildy?

"About what?" I say. I thumb thru the book and there's pages of stuff, pages and pages of it, words on words on words on words, like Noise shoved down onto paper till you can't make no sense from it. How can I warn anybody about all *this*?

"Aw, Ben," I say under my breath. "What were you thinking?"

"Todd?" Hildy calls from downstairs. "Vi?"

I close the book and look at its cover.

Later. I'll ask about it later.

I *will*.

Later.

I put it away and I go downstairs. Viola's already waiting there. Hildy and Francia, arms crossed again, waiting, too.

"I've got to get back to my farm, pups," Hildy says. "Work to do for the good of all but Francia's agreed to look after ye for today and I'll come back tonight to see how yer a-getting on."

Viola and I look at each other, suddenly not wanting Hildy to leave.

"Thank ye for that," Francia says, frowning. "Despite what my sister may have told ye two about me, I'm hardly an ogre."

"She didn't say—" I start to say before I stop myself, even tho my Noise finishes it up for me. *Anything about you.*

"Yeah, well, that's typical," Francia says, glaring at Hildy but not seeming too put out. "Ye can stay here for the time being. Pa and Auntie are long dead and there's not too much call for their rooms these days."

I was right. Old person's room.

"But we're a working town here in Farbranch." Francia looks from me to Viola and back again. "And ye'll be expected to earn yer keep, even if it's just for a day or two while ye make whatever plans yer going to make."

"We're still not sure," Viola says.

"*Hmmph*," Francia hmmphs. "And if ye two stay on past this first cresting of the orchards, there'll be a-schooling for ye to do."

"School?" I say.

"School and church," Hildy says. "That's if ye stay long enough." I'm guessing she's reading my Noise again. "Are ye going to stay long enough?"

I don't say nothing and Viola don't say nothing and Franica hmmphs again.

"Please, Mrs. Francia?" Viola says as Francia turns to talk to Hildy.

"Just Francia, child," Francia says, looking surprised. "What is it?"

"Is there somewhere I can send a message back to my ship?"

"Yer ship," Francia says. "This a-being that settler ship way out in the dark black yonder?" Her mouth draws thin. "With all them people on it?"

Viola nods. "We were supposed to report back. Let them know what we found."

Viola's voice is so quiet and her face so hopeful, so open and wide and ready for disappointment that I feel that familiar tug of sadness again, pulling all Noise into it like grief, like being lost. I put a hand on the back of a settee to steady myself.

"Ah, girl pup," Hildy says, her voice getting suspiciously gentle again. "I'm guessing ye tried to contact us folks down here on New World when ye were a-scouting the planet?"

"Yeah," Viola says. "No one answered."

Hildy and Francia exchange nods. "Yer a-forgetting we were church settlers," Francia says, "getting away from worldly things to set up our own little utopia, so we let that kinda machinery go to rack and ruin as we got on with the business of surviving."

Viola's eyes get a little wider. "You have no way of communicating with anyone?"

"We don't have communicators for other *settlements*," Francia says, "much less the beyond."

"We're farmers, pup," Hildy says. "Simple farmers, looking for a simpler way of life. That was the whole point in flying all this ridiculous way to get here. Setting down the things that caused such strife for people of old." She taps her fingers on a tabletop. "Didn't quite work out that way, tho."

"We weren't really expecting no others," Francia says. "Not the way Old World was when we left."

"So I'm stuck here?" Viola says, her voice a little shaky.

"Until yer ship arrives," Hildy says. "I'm afraid so."

"How far out are they?" Francia asks.

"System entry in twenty-four weeks," Viola says quietly. "Perihelion four weeks later. Orbital transfer two weeks after that."

"I'm sorry, child," Francia says. "Looks like yer ours for seven months."

Viola turns away from all of us, obviously taking this news in.

A lot can happen in seven months.

"Well, now," Hildy says, making her voice bright, "I hear tell they got all kindsa things in Haven. Fissioncars and city streets and more stores than ye can shake a stick at. Ye might try there before ye really start a-worrying, yes?"

Hildy looks toward Francia and Francia says, "Todd pup? Why don't we get you a-working in the barn? Yer a farm boy, ain't ye?"

"But—" I start to say.

"All kinds of work to be done on a farm," Francia says, "as I'm sure ye know all too well—"

Chattering away like this, Francia gets me out the back door. Looking over my shoulder, I can see Hildy comforting Viola in soft words, unhearable words, things being said that I don't know yet again.

Francia closes the door behind us and leads me and Manchee across the main road to one of the big storage houses I saw when we were walking in. I can see men pulling handcarts up to the main door and another man unloading the baskets of orchard fruit.

"This is east barn," Francia says, "where we store things ready to be traded. Wait here."

I wait and she walks up to the man unloading the baskets from the cart. They talk for a minute and I can hear **Prentisstown?** clear as day in his Noise and the sudden surge of feeling behind it. It's a slightly different feeling than before but it fades before I can read it and Francia comes back.

"Ivan says ye can work in the back a-sweeping up."

"*Sweeping up?*" I say, kinda appalled. "I know how farms work, mim, and I—"

"I'm sure ye do but ye may have noticed that Prentisstown ain't our most popular neighbor. Best to keep ye away from everyone till we've all had a chance to get used to ye. Fair enough?"

She's still stern, still arms crossed, but actually, yeah, this seems sensible and tho her face ain't kind exactly maybe it sorta is.

"Okay," I say.

Francia nods and takes me over to Ivan, who looks about Ben's age, but short, dark-haired, and with arms like effing tree trunks.

"Ivan, this is Todd," Francia says.

I hold out my hand to shake. Ivan doesn't take it. He just eyeballs me something fierce.

"You'll work in back," he says. "And you'll keep yerself and yer dog outta my way."

Francia leaves us and Ivan takes me inside, points out a broom, and I get to work. And that's how I start my first day in Farbranch: inside a dark barn, sweeping dust from one corner to another, seeing one single stitch of blue sky out a door at the far end.

Oh, the joy.

"Poo, Todd," Manchee says.

"Not in here, you don't."

It's a pretty big barn, 200 to 250 feet from end to end, maybe, and about half full of baskets of crested pine. There's a section with big rolls of silage, too, packed up to the ceiling with thin rope, and another section with huge sheaves of wheat ready to be ground into flour.

"You sell this stuff to other settlements?" I call out to Ivan.

"Time for chatter later," he calls back from the front.

I don't say nothing to this but something kinda rude shows up in my Noise before I can stop it. I hurry and get back to sweeping.

The morning waxes on. I think about Ben and Cillian. I think about Viola. I think about Aaron and the Mayor. I think about the word *army* and how it's making my stomach clench.

I don't know.

It don't feel right to be stopped. Not after all that running.

Everyone's acting like it's safe here but I don't know.

Manchee wanders in and out the back doors as I sweep, sometimes chasing the pink moths I stir from faint corners. Ivan keeps his distance, I keep mine, but I can see all the people who come to his door and drop off goods taking a deep, long look to the back of the barn, sometimes squinting into the darkness to see if they can find me there, the Prentisstown boy.

So they hate Prentisstown, I get that. *I* hate Prentisstown but I got more cause for grief than any of them.

I start noticing things, too, as the morning gets older. Like that tho men and women both do the heavy labor, women give more orders that more men follow. And with Francia being Deputy Mayor and Hildy being whoever she is in Farbranch, I'm beginning to think it's a town run by women. I can often hear their silences as they walk by outside and I can hear men's Noise responding to it, too, sometimes with chafing but usually in a way that just gets on with things.

Men's Noise here, too, is a *lot* more controlled than what I'm used to. With so many women around and from what I know of the Noise of Prentisstown, you'd think the sky would be full of Noisy women with no clothes doing the most remarkable things you could think of. And sure you hear that sometimes here, men are men after all, but more of the time the Noise is songs or it's prayers or it's directed to the work at hand.

They're calm here in Farbranch but they're a little spooky.

Once in a while, I see if I can not-hear Viola.

But no.

At lunchtime, Francia comes to the back of the barn with a sandwich and a jug of water.

"Where's Viola?" I ask.

"Yer welcome," Francia says.

"For what?"

Francia sighs and says, "Viola's in the orchards, gathering dropped fruits."

I want to ask how she is but I don't and Francia refuses to read it in my Noise.

"How ye getting on?" she asks.

"I know how to do a lot more than ruddy sweep."

"Mind yer language, pup. There'll be time enough to get ye to real work."

She don't stay, walking back toward the front, having another word with Ivan and then she's off to do whatever Deputy Mayors fill their days with.

Can I say? It makes no sense but I sorta like her. Probably cuz she reminds me of Cillian and all the things that used to drive me crazy bout him. Memory is stupid, ain't it?

I tear into my sandwich and I'm chewing my first bite when I hear Ivan's Noise approaching.

"I'll sweep up my crumbs," I say.

To my surprise, he laughs, kinda roughly. "I'm sure ye will." He takes a bite of his own sandwich. "Francia says there's a village meeting tonight," he says after a minute.

"Bout me?" I ask.

"Bout ye both. Ye and the girl. Ye and the girl what escaped Prentisstown."

His Noise is strange. It's cautious but strong, like he's checking me out. I don't read no hostility, not toward me, anyway, but *something's* percolating in it.

"We gonna meet everyone?" I say.

"Ye might. We'll all be a-talking bout ye first."

"If there's a vote," I say, chomping on the sandwich, "I think I lose."

"Ye've got Hildy a-speaking for yer side," he says. "That counts for more than aught in Farbranch." He swallows his own bite. "And the people here are kind people and good. We've taken in Prentisstown folk before. Not for a while but from way back in the bad times."

"The war?" I say.

He looks at me, his Noise sizing me up, what I know. "Yeah," he says, "the war." He turns his head round the barn, casual-like, but I get the feeling he's looking to see if we're alone. He turns back and fixes his eye on me. An eye that's really looking for something. "And then, too," he says, "not all of us feel the same."

"Bout what?" I say, not liking his look, not liking his buzz.

"Bout history." He's talking low, his eyes still poring into me, leaning a little closer.

I lean back a little. "I don't know what you mean."

"Prentisstown's still got allies," he whispers, "hidden away in surprising places."

His Noise gets pictures in it, small ones, like Noise speaking just to me and I'm starting to see them clearer and clearer, bright things, wet things, fast things, the sun shining down on red—

"Puppies! Puppies!" Manchee barks in the corner. I jump and even Ivan startles and his Noise pictures fade pretty quick. Manchee keeps barking and I hear a whole raft of giggling that ain't him at all. I look.

A group of kids is kneeling down, peeking in thru a torn-away board, smiling, laughing with daring, pushing each other closer to the hole.

Pointing at me.

And all so small.

So small.

I mean, *look* at 'em.

"Get outta here, ye rats!" Ivan calls but there's humor in his voice and Noise, all trace of what was before hidden. There's squeals of laughter outside the hole in the wall as the kids scatter.

And that's it, they're gone.

Like I mighta made 'em up.

"Puppies, Todd!" Manchee barks. "Puppies!"

"I know," I say, scratching his head when he comes over. "I know."

Ivan claps his hands together. "That's lunch then. Back to work." He gives me one more important look before he heads back to the front of the barn.

"What was that all about?" I say to Manchee.

"Puppies," he murmurs, digging his face into my hand.

And so there follows an afternoon pretty much exactly like my morning. Sweeping, folks stopping by, a break for water where Ivan don't say nothing to me, more sweeping.

I spend some time trying to think about what we might do next. If it's even *we* who's doing it. Farbranch'll have its meeting about us and they'll definitely keep Viola till her ship arrives, anyone can see that, but will they want me?

And if they do, do I stay?

And do I warn 'em?

I get a burning in my stomach every time I think about the book so I keep changing the subject.

After what seems like forever, the sun starts to set. There's no more damn sweeping I can do. I've already covered the whole barn more than once, counted the baskets, recounted them, made an attempt to fix the loose board in the wall even tho no one asked me to. There's only so much you can ruddy well do if no one lets you leave a barn.

"Ain't that the truth?" Hildy says, standing there suddenly.

"You shouldn't sneak up on people like that," I say. "All you quiet folk."

"There's some food over at Francia's house for ye and for Viola. Why don't ye go on there, get something to eat?"

"While you all have yer meeting?"

"While we all have our meeting, yes, pup," Hildy says. "Viola's already in the house, no doubt eating all yer dinner."

"Hungry, Todd!" Manchee barks.

"There's food for ye, too, puppup," Hildy says, leaning down to pet him. He flops right over on his back for her, no dignity whatsoever.

"What's this meeting really about?" I ask.

"Oh, the new settlers that are a-coming. That's big news." She looks up from Manchee to me. "And introducing ye around, of course. Getting the town used to the idea of a-welcoming ye."

"And are they gonna *a-welcome* us?"

"People are scared of what they don't know, Todd pup," she says, standing. "Once they know ye, the problem goes away."

"Will we be able to stay?"

"I reckon so," she says. "If ye want to."

I don't say nothing to that.

"Ye get on up to the house," she says. "I'll come collect ye both when the time's right."

I only nod in response and she gives a little wave and leaves, walking back across a barn that's growing ever darker. I take the broom back to where it was hanging, my steps echoing. I can hear the Noise of men and the silence of women gathering across town in the meeting hall. The word Prentisstown filters in most heavily and my name and Viola's name and Hildy's name.

And I gotta say, tho there's fear and suspishun in it, I don't get a feeling of overwhelming nonwelcome. There's more askings than there is anger of the Matthew Lyle sort.

Which, you know, maybe. Maybe that ain't so bad after all.

"C'mon, Manchee," I say, "let's go get some food."

"Food, Todd!" he barks along at my heels.

"I wonder how Viola's day was," I say.

And as I step toward the entrance to the barn I realize one bit of Noise is separating itself from the general murmuring outside.

One bit of Noise lifting from the stream.
And heading for the barn.
Coming up right outside it.
I stop, deep in the dark of the barn.
A shadow steps into the far doorway.
Matthew Lyle.
And his Noise is saying, Ye ain't going nowhere, boy.

19

FURTHER CHOICES OF A KNIFE

BACK! BACK! BACK!" Manchee immediately starts barking.

The moons glint off Matthew Lyle's machete.

I reach behind me. I'd hidden the sheath under my shirt while I worked but the knife is definitely still there. Definitely. I take it and hold it out at my side.

"No old mama to protect ye this time," Matthew says, swinging his machete back and forth, like he's trying to cut the air into slices. "No skirts to hide ye from what ye did."

"I didn't do nothing," I say, taking a step backward, trying to keep my Noise from showing the back door behind me.

"Don't matter," Matthew says, walking forward as I step back. "We got a law here in this town."

"I don't have no quarrel with you," I say.

"But I've got one with *ye*, boy," he says, his Noise starting to rear up and there's anger in it, sure, but that weird grief's in it, too, that raging hurt you can almost taste on yer tongue. There's also nervousness swirling about him, edgy as you please, much as he's trying to cover it.

I step back again, farther in the dark.

"I ain't a bad man, you know," he says, suddenly and kinda confusingly but swinging the machete. "I have a wife. I have a daughter."

"They wouldn't be wanting you to hurt no innocent boy, I'm sure—"

"Quiet!" he shouts and I can hear him swallow.

He ain't sure of this. He ain't sure of what he's about to do.

What's going on here?

"I don't know why yer angry," I say, "but I'm sorry. Whatever it is—"

"What I want you to know before you pay," he says over me, like he's forcing himself not to listen to me. "What you *need* to know, boy, is that my mother's name was Jessica."

I stop stepping back. "'Scuse me?"

"My mother's name," he growls, "was Jessica."

This don't make no sense at all.

"What?" I say. "I don't know what yer—"

"Listen, boy!" he yells. "Just listen."

And then his Noise is wide open.

And I see—

And I see—

And I see—

I see what he's showing.

"That's a lie," I whisper. "That's a ruddy lie."

Which is the wrong thing to say.

With a yell, Matthew leaps forward, running the length of the barn toward me.

"Run!" I shout to Manchee, turning and making a break for the back door. (Shut up, you honestly think a knife is a match for a machete?) I hear Matthew still yelling, his Noise exploding after me, and I reach the back door and fling it open before I realize.

Manchee's not with me.

I turn round. When I said "run", Manchee'd run the other way, flinging himself with all his unconvincing viciousness toward the charging Matthew.

"Manchee!" I yell.

It's ruddy dark in the barn now and I can hear grunts and barks and clanks and then I hear Matthew cry out in pain at what must surely be a bite.

Good dog, I think, *Good effing dog.*

And I can't leave him, can I?

I run back into the darkness, toward where I can see Matthew hopping around and the form of Manchee dancing twixt his legs and swipes of the machete, barking his little head off.

"Todd! Todd! Todd!" he's barking.

I'm five steps away and still running when Matthew makes a two-handed strike down at the ground, embedding the tip of the machete into the wooden floor. I hear a squeal from Manchee that don't have no words, just pain, and off he flies into a dark corner.

I let out a yell and crash right into Matthew. We both go flying, toppling to the floor in a tumble of elbows and kneecaps. It hurts but mostly I'm landing on Matthew so that's okay.

We roll apart and I hear him call out in pain. I get right back up to my feet, knife in hand, a few feet away from him, far from the back door now and with Matthew blocking the front. I hear Manchee whimpering in the dark.

I also hear some Noise rising from across the village road in the direkshun of the meeting hall but there ain't time to think about that now.

"I'm not afraid to kill you," I say, tho I totally am but I'm hoping my Noise and his Noise are now so rackety and revved up that he won't be able to make any sense of it.

"That makes two of us then," he says, lunging for his machete. It don't come out the first tug, or the second. I take the chance to jump back into the dark, looking for Manchee.

"Manchee?" I say, frantically looking behind the sheaves and the piles of fruit baskets. I can still hear Matthew grunting to get his machete outta the floor and the ruckus from the town is growing louder.

"Todd?" I hear from deep in the darkness.

It's coming from beside the silage rolls, down a little nook that opens up next to them back to the wall. "Manchee?" I call, sticking my head down it.

I look back real quick.

With a heave, Matthew gets his machete outta the floor.

"Todd?" Manchee says, confused and scared. "Todd?"

And here comes Matthew, coming on in slow steps, like he no longer has to hurry, his Noise reaching forward in a wave that don't brook no argument.

I have no choice. I wedge myself back into the nook and hold out my knife.

"I'll leave," I say, my voice rising. "Just let me get my dog and we'll leave."

"Too late for that," Matthew says, getting closer.

"You don't wanna do this. I can tell."

"Shut yer mouth."

"Please," I say, waving the knife. "I don't wanna hurt you."

"Do I look concerned, boy?"

Closer, closer, step by step.

There's a bang outside somewhere, off in the distance. People really are running and shouting now but neither of us look.

I press myself back into the little nook but it's really not wide enough for me. I glance round, seeing where escape might lie.

I don't find nothing much.

My knife's gonna have to do it. It's gonna have to act, even if it is against a machete.

"Todd?" I hear behind me.

"Don't worry, Manchee," I say. "It's gonna be all right."

And who knows what a dog believes?

Matthew's almost on us now.

I grip my knife.

Matthew stops a few feet from me, so close I can see his eyes glinting in the dark.

"Jessica," he says.

He raises his machete above his head.

I flinch, knife up, steeling myself—

But he pauses—

He pauses—

In a way I reckernize—

And that's enough—

With a quick prayer that they ain't covered with the same stuff from the bridge, I swing my knife in an arc to my side, slicing right thru (thank you thank you) the ropes holding up the silage rolls, cutting the first lot clean away. The other ropes snap pretty quick from the sudden shift in weight and I cover my head and press myself away as the silage rolls start to tumble.

I hear thumps and clumps and an *oof* from Matthew and I look up and he's buried in silage rolls, his arm out to one side, the machete dropped. I step forward and kick it away, then turn to find Manchee.

He's back in a dark corner behind the now fallen rolls. I race over to him.

"Todd?" he says when I get close. "Tail, Todd?"

"Manchee?" It's dark so I have to squat down next to him to see. His tail's two thirds shorter than it used to be, blood everywhere, but, God bless him, he's still trying to wag.

"Ow, Todd?"

"It's okay, Manchee," I say, my voice and Noise near crying from relief that it's just his tail. "We'll get you fixed right up."

"Okay, Todd?"

"I'm okay," I say, rubbing his head. He nips my hand but I know he can't help it cuz he's in pain. He licks me in apology then nips me again. "Ow, Todd," he says.

"Todd Hewitt!" I hear shouted from the front of the barn.

Francia.

"I'm here!" I call, standing up. "I'm all right. Matthew went crazy—"

But I stop cuz she ain't listening to me.

"Ye gotta get yerself indoors, Todd pup," Francia says in a rush. "Ye gotta—"

She stops when she sees Matthew under the silage.

"What happened?" she says, already starting to tug away the rolls, getting one off his face and leaning down to see if he's still breathing.

I point to the machete. "*That* happened."

Francia looks at it, then a long look up at me, her face saying something I can't read nor even begin to figure out. I don't know if Matthew's alive nor dead and I ain't never gonna find out.

"We're under attack, pup," she says, standing.

"Yer *what*?"

"Men," she says, rising. "Prentisstown men. That posse that's after ye. They're attacking the whole town."

My stomach falls right outta my shoes.

"Oh, no," I say. And then I say it again, "Oh, no."

Francia's still looking at me, her brain thinking who knows what.

"Don't give us to them," I say, backing away again. "They'll kill us."

Francia frowns at this. "What kinda woman do ye think I am?"

"I don't know," I say, "that's the whole problem."

"I'm not gonna *give* ye to them. Nor Viola. Honestly, now. In fact the feeling of the town meeting, as far along as it got, was how we were a-deciding to protect ye both from what was almost certainly a-coming." She looks down at Matthew. "Tho maybe that's a promise we couldn't keep."

"Where's Viola?"

"Back at my house," Francia says, suddenly all active again. "C'mon. We gotta get ye inside."

"Wait." I squeeze back behind the silage rolls and find Manchee still in his corner, licking his tail. He looks up at me and barks, just a little bark that's not even a word. "I'm gonna pick you up now," I say to him. "Try not to bite me too hard, okay?"

"Okay, Todd," he whimpers, yelping each time he wags his stumpy tail.

I reach down, put my arms under his tummy and hoist him up to my chest. He yelps and bites hard at my wrist, then licks it.

"It's okay, buddy," I say, holding him as best I can.

Francia's waiting for me at the door to the barn and I follow her out into the main road.

There are people running about everywhere. I see men and women with rifles running up toward the orchards and other men and women scooting kids (there they are again) into houses and such. In the distance I can hear bangs and shouts and yelling.

"Where's Hildy?" I yell.

Francia don't say nothing. We reach her front steps.

"What about Hildy?" I ask again as we climb up.

"She went off to fight," Francia says, not looking at me, opening the door. "They would have reached her farm first. Tam was still there."

"Oh, no," I say again stupidly, like my *oh nos* will do any good.

Viola comes flying down from the upper floor as we enter.

"What took you so long?" she says, her voice kinda loud, and I don't know which one of us she's talking to. She gasps when she sees Manchee.

"Bandages," I say. "Some of those fancy ones."

She nods and races back up the stairs.

"Ye two stay here," Francia says to me. "Don't come out, whatever ye hear."

"But we need to run!" I say, not understanding this at all. "We need to get outta here!"

"No, Todd pup," she says. "If Prentisstown wants ye, then that's reason enough for us to keep ye from them."

"But they've got guns—"

"So do we," Francia says. "No posse of Prentisstown men is going to take *this* town."

Viola's back down the stairs now, digging thru her bag for bandages.

"Francia—" I say.

"Stay right here," she says. "We'll protect ye. Both of ye."

She looks at both of us, hard, like seeing if we agree, then she turns and is out the door to protect her town, I guess.

We stare at the closed door for a second, then Manchee whimpers again and I have to set him down. Viola gets out a square bandage and her little scalpel.

"I don't know if these'll work on dogs," she says.

"Better than nothing," I say.

She cuts off a little strip and I have to hold Manchee's head down while she loops it around the mess of his tail. He growls and apologizes and growls and apologizes until Viola's covered the whole wound up tight. He immediately sets to licking it when I let him go.

"Stop that," I say.

"Itches," Manchee says.

"Stupid dog." I scratch his ears. "Stupid ruddy dog."

Viola pets him, too, trying to keep him from licking off the bandage.

"Do you think we're safe?" she asks quietly, after a long minute.

"I don't know."

There's more bangs out in the distance. We both jump. More people shouting. More Noise.

"No sign of Hildy since this started," Viola says.

"I know."

Another bit of silence as we overpet Manchee. More ruckus from up in the orchards above town.

It all seems so far away, as if it's not even happening.

"Francia told me that you can find Haven if you keep following the main river," Viola says.

I look at her. I wonder if I know what this means.

I think I do.

"You wanna leave," I say.

"They'll keep coming," she says. "We're putting the people around us in danger. Don't you think they'll keep coming if they've already come this far?"

I do. I do think this. I don't say it but I do.

"But they said they could protect us," I say.

"Do you believe that?"

I don't say nothing to this neither. I think of Matthew Lyle.

"I don't think we're safe here anymore," she says.

"I don't think we're safe *anywhere*," I say. "Not on this whole planet."

"I need to contact my ship, Todd," she says, almost pleading. "They're waiting to hear from me."

"And you wanna run off into the unknown to do it?"

"You do, too," she says. "I can tell." She looks away. "If we went to-gether . . ."

I look up at her at this, trying to see, trying to *know*, to know real and true.

All she does is look back.

Which is enough.

"Let's go," I say.

We pack fast without any more words. I get my rucksack on, she gets her bag around her shoulders, Manchee's on his feet again and walking, and out the back door we go. As simple as that, we're going. Safer for Farbranch, definitely, safer for us, who knows? Who knows if this is the right thing to do? After what Hildy and Francia seemed to promise, it's hard leaving.

But we're leaving. And that's what we're doing.

Cuz at least it's *us* who decided it. I'd rather not have no one else tell me what they'll do for me, even when they mean well.

It's full dark night outside now, tho both moons are shining bright. Everyone in town's attenshun is behind us so there's no one to stop us from running. There's a little bridge that crosses the creek that runs thru town. "How far is this Haven?" I ask, whispering as we cross.

"Kinda far," Viola whispers back.

"How far is kinda far?"

She don't say nothing for a second.

"How *far*?" I say again.

"Coupla weeks' walk," she says, not looking back.

"Coupla *weeks!*"

"Where else do we have?" she says.

And I don't have an answer so we keep on walking.

Across the creek, the road heads up the far hill of the valley. We decide to take it as the fastest way outta town then find our way back south to the river and follow that. Ben's map ends at Farbranch so the river's all we got for direkshuns from here on out.

There's so many askings that come with us as we run outta Farbranch, askings that we'll never know the answers to: Why would the Mayor and a few men go miles outta their way to attack a whole ruddy town on their own? Why are they still after us? Why are we so important? And what happened to Hildy?

And did I kill Matthew Lyle?

And was what he showed me in his Noise right there at the end a true thing?

Was that the real history of Prentisstown?

"Was what the real history?" Viola asks as we hurry on up the path.

"Nothing," I say. "And quit reading me."

We get to the top of the far hill of the valley just as another rattle of gunfire echoes across it. We stop and look.

And then we see.

Boy, do we see.

"Oh, my God," Viola says.

Under the light of the two moons, the whole valley kinda shines, across the Farbranch buildings and back up into the hills where the orchards are.

We can see the men and women of Farbranch running back down that hill.

In retreat.

And marching over the top, are five, ten, fifteen men on horseback.

Followed by rows of men five across, carrying guns, marching in a line behind what has to be the Mayor's horses in front.

Not a posse. Not a posse at all.

It's Prentisstown. I feel like the world's crumbling at my feet. It's every ruddy man in Prentisstown.

They have three times as many people as even live in Farbranch.

Three times as many guns.

We hear gunshots and we see the men and women of Farbranch fall as they run back to their houses.

They'll take the town easily. They'll take it before the hour is thru.

Cuz the rumors were true, the rumors that Francia heard.

The word was true.

It's an army.

A whole army.

There's a whole army coming after me and Viola.

PART IV

20

ARMY OF MEN

WE DUCK BEHIND SOME BUSHES, even tho it's dark, even tho the army is across the valley, even tho they don't know we're up here and there's no way they could hear my Noise amidst all the ruckus going on down there, we duck anyway.

"Can yer binocs see in the dark?" I whisper.

By way of answer Viola digs 'em outta her bag and holds 'em up to her own eyes. "What's happening?" she says, looking thru 'em, pressing more buttons. "Who are all those men?"

"It's Prentisstown," I say, holding out my hand. "It looks like every man in the whole effing town."

"How can it be the whole town?" She looks for a second or two more then hands the binocs to me. "What kind of sense does that make?"

"You got me." The night setting on the binocs turns the valley and all that's in it a bright green. I see horses galloping down the hill into the main part of town, the riders shooting their rifles on the way, I see the people of Farbranch shooting back but mostly running, mostly falling, mostly dying. The Prentisstown army don't seem interested in taking prisoners.

"We have to get out of here, Todd," Viola says.

"Yeah," I say, but I'm still looking thru the binocs.

With everything green, it's hard to make out faces. I press a few more buttons on the binocs till I find the ones that take me in closer.

The first person I see for sure is Mr. Prentiss Jr., in the lead, firing his rifle into the air when he don't have nothing else to shoot at. Then there's

Mr. Morgan and Mr. Collins chasing some Farbranch men into the storage barns, firing their rifles after them. Mr. O'Hare's there, too, and more of the Mayor's usual suspects on horseback, Mr. Edwin, Mr. Henratty, Mr. Sullivan. And there's Mr. Hammar, the smile on his face showing up green and evil even from this distance as he fires his rifle into the backs of fleeing women hustling away small children and I have to look away or throw up the nothing I had for dinner.

The men on foot march their way into town. The first one I reckernize is, of all people, Mr. Phelps the storekeeper. Which is weird cuz he never seemed armylike at all. And there's Dr. Baldwin. And Mr. Fox. And Mr. Cardiff who was our best milker. And Mr. Tate who had the most books to burn when the Mayor outlawed them. And Mr. Kearney who milled the town's wheat and who always spoke softly and who made wooden toys for each Prentisstown boy's birthday.

What are these men doing in an army?

"Todd," Viola says, pulling at my arm.

The men marching don't look none too happy, I spose. Grim and cold and scary in a different way from Mr. Hammar, like they're lacking all feeling.

But they're still marching. They're still shooting. They're still kicking down doors.

"That's Mr. Gillooly," I say, binocs pressed to my eyes. "He can't even butcher his own meat."

"*Todd,*" Viola says and I feel her backing away from the bushes. "Let's *go.*"

What's going on? Sure, Prentisstown was as awful a place as you could ever not wanna paint it but how can it suddenly be an army? There's plenty of Prentisstown men who're bad thru and thru but not all of them. Not *all*. And Mr. Gillooly with a rifle is a sight so wrong it almost hurts my eyes just to look at it.

And then of course I see the answer.

Mayor Prentiss, not even holding a gun, just one hand on his horse's reins, the other at his side, riding into town like he's out for an evening canter. He's watching the rout of Farbranch as if it was a vid and not a very interesting one at that, letting everyone else do the work but so obviously in charge no one would even think of asking him to break a sweat.

How can he make so many men do what he wants?

And is he bulletproof that he can ride so fearlessly?

"Todd," Viola says behind me. "I swear, I'll leave without you."

"No, you won't," I say. "One more second."

Cuz I'm looking from face to face now, ain't I? I'm going from

Prentisstown man to Prentisstown man cuz even if they're marching into town and are gonna find out soon enough that neither me nor Viola is there and are gonna have to come this way after us, I gotta know.

I gotta know.

Face to face to face as they march and shoot and burn. Mr. Wallace, Mr. Asbjornsen, Mr. St. James, Mr. Belgraves, Mr. Smith the Older, Mr. Smith the Younger, Mr. Smith With Nine Fingers, even Mr. Marjoribanks, wobbling and teetering but marching marching marching. Prentisstown man after Prentisstown man after Prentisstown man, my heart clenching and burning at each one I can identify.

"They ain't there," I say, almost to myself.

"Who isn't?" Viola says.

"Ain't!" Manchee barks, licking at his tail.

They ain't there.

Ben and Cillian ain't there.

Which, of course, is grand, ain't it? Of course they ain't part of an army of killers. Of *course* they ain't, even when every other Prentisstown man is. They wouldn't be. Not never, not no how, no matter what.

Good men, *great* men, both, even Cillian.

But if that's true, then that means the other is true, too, don't it?

If they ain't there, then that means once and for all.

And there's yer lesson.

There ain't nothing good that don't got real bad waiting to follow it.

I hope they put up the best fight ever.

I take the binocs from my face and I look down and I wipe my eyes with my sleeve and I turn and I hand Viola back the binocs and I say, "Let's go."

She takes them from me, squirming a little like she's itching to leave, but then she says, "I'm sorry," so she musta seen it in my Noise.

"Nothing that ain't already happened," I say, talking to the ground and readjusting the rucksack. "C'mon, before I put us in danger any worse."

I take off up the path toward the top of the hill, keeping my head down, motoring fast, Viola after me, Manchee trying to keep himself from biting at his tail as we run.

Viola matches my speed before we get far at all. "Did you see . . . him?" she says, between breaths.

"Aaron?"

She nods.

"No," I say. "Come to think of it, no, I didn't. And you'd think he'd be out in front."

We're quiet for a minute as we hurry on our way and wonder what that means.

The road on this side of the valley is wider and we're doing our best to keep to the darker side of it as it twists and turns up the hill. Our only lights are the moons but they're bright enough to cast our shadows running along the road which is too bright when yer running away. I never seen no night vision binocs in Prentisstown but I didn't see no army neither so we're both crouching as we run. Manchee's running on ahead of us, his nose to the ground, barking, "This way! This way!" as if he knows any better than us where we're going.

Then at the top of the hill, the road forks.

Which just figures.

"You gotta be kidding," I say.

One part of the road goes left, the other goes right.

(Well, it's a *fork*, ain't it?)

"The creek in Farbranch was flowing to the right," Viola says, "and the main river was always to our right once we crossed the bridge, so it's got to be the right fork if we want to get back there."

"But the left looks more traveled," I say. And it does. The left fork looks smoother, flatter, like the kinda thing you should be rolling carts over. The right fork is narrower with higher bushes on each side and even tho it's night you can just tell it's dusty. "Did Francia say anything about a fork?" I look back over my shoulder at the valley still erupting behind us.

"No," Viola says, also looking back. "She just said Haven was the first settlement and new settlements sprang up down the river as people moved west. Prentisstown was the farthest out. Farbranch was second farthest."

"That one probably goes to the river," I say, pointing right, then left, "that one probably goes to Haven in a straight line."

"Which one will they think we took?"

"We need to decide," I say. "Quickly now."

"To the right," she says, then turns it into an asking. "To the right?"

We hear a *BOOM* that makes us jump. A mushroom of smoke is rising in the air over Farbranch. The barn where I worked all day is on fire.

Maybe our story will turn out differently if we take the left fork, maybe the bad things that are waiting to happen to us won't happen, maybe there's happiness at the end of the left fork and warm places with the people who love us and no Noise but no silence neither and there's plenty of food and no one dies and no one dies and no one never never dies.

Maybe.

But I doubt it.

I ain't what you call a lucky person.

"Right," I decide. "Might as well be right."

We run down the right fork, Manchee at our heels, the night and a dusty road stretching out in front of us, an army and a disaster behind us, me and Viola, running side by side.

We run till we can't run and then we walk fast till we can run again. The sounds of Farbranch disappear behind us pretty quick and all we can hear are our footsteps beating on the path and my Noise and Manchee's barking. If there are night creachers out there, we're scaring 'em away.

Which is probably good.

"What's the next settlement?" I gasp after a good half hour's run-walking. "Did Francia say?"

"Shining Beacon," Viola says, gasping herself. "Or Shining Light." She scrunches her face. "*Blazing* Light. Blazing Beacon?"

"That's helpful."

"Wait." She stops in the path, bending at the waist to catch her breath. I stop, too. "I need water."

I hold up my hands in a way that says *And?* "So do I," I say. "You got some?"

She looks at me, her eyebrows up. "Oh."

"There was always a river."

"I guess we'd better find it then."

"I guess so." I take a deep breath to start running again.

"Todd," she says, stopping me. "I've been thinking."

"Yeah?" I say.

"Blazing Lights or whatever?"

"Yeah?"

"If you look at it one way," she lowers her voice to a sad and uncomfortable sound and says it again, "if you look at it one way, we led an army into Farbranch."

I lick the dryness of my lips. I taste dust. And I know what she's saying.

"*You must warn them,*" she says quietly, into the dark. "I'm sorry, but—"

"We can't go into any other settlements," I say.

"I don't think we can."

"Not till Haven."

"Not until Haven," she says, "which we have to hope is big enough to handle an army."

So, that's that then. In case we needed any further reminding, we're really on our own. Really and truly. Me and Viola and Manchee and the darkness for company. No one on the road to help us till the end, if even there, which knowing our luck so far—

I close my eyes.

I am Todd Hewitt, I think. *When it gets to be midnight I will be a man in twenty-seven days. I am the son of my ma and pa, may they rest in peace. I am the son of Ben and Cillian, may they—*

I am Todd Hewitt.

"I'm Viola Eade," Viola says.

I open my eyes. She has her hand out, palm down, held toward me.

"That's my surname," she says. "Eade. E-A-D-E."

I look at her for a second and then down at her outstretched hand and I reach out and I take it and press it inside my own and a second later I let go.

I shrug my shoulders to reset my rucksack. I put my hand behind my back to feel the knife and make sure it's still there. I give poor, panting, half-tail Manchee a look and then match eyes with Viola.

"Viola Eade," I say, and she nods.

And off we run into further night.

21

THE WIDER WORLD

HOW CAN IT BE THIS FAR?" Viola asks. "It doesn't make any logical sense."

"Is there another kind of sense it does make?"

She frowns. So do I. We're tired and getting tireder and trying not to think of what we saw at Farbranch and we've walked and run what feels like half the night and still no river. I'm starting to get afraid we've taken a seriously wrong turn which we can't do nothing about cuz there ain't no turning back.

"*Isn't any* turning back," I hear Viola say behind me, under her breath.

I turn to her, eyes wide. "That's wrong on two counts," I say. "Number one, constantly reading people's Noise ain't gonna get you much welcome here."

She crosses her arms and sets her shoulders. "And the second?"

"The second is I talk how I please."

"Yes," Viola says. "That you do."

My Noise starts to rise a bit and I take a deep breath but then she says *Shhh,* and her eyes glint in the moonlight as she looks beyond me.

The sound of running water.

"River!" Manchee barks.

We take off down the road and round a corner and down a slope and round another corner and there's the river, wider, flatter, and slower than when we saw it last but just as wet. We don't say nothing, just drop to our knees on the rocks at water's edge and drink, Manchee wading in up to his belly to start lapping.

Viola's next to me and as I slurp away, there's her silence again. It's a two-way thing, this is. However clear she can hear my Noise, well, out here alone, away from the chatter of others or the Noise of a settlement, there's her silence, loud as a roar, pulling at me like the greatest sadness ever, like I want to take it and press myself into it and just disappear forever down into nothing.

What a relief that would feel like right now. What a blessed relief.

"I can't avoid hearing you, you know," she says, standing up and opening her bag. "When it's quiet and just the two of us."

"And I can't avoid not hearing you," I say. "No matter what it's like." I whistle for Manchee. "Outta the water. There might be snakes."

He's ducking his rump under the current, swishing back and forth until the bandage comes off and floats away. Then he leaps out and immediately sets to licking his tail.

"Let me see," I say. He barks "Todd!" in agreement but when I come near he curls his tail as far under his belly as the new length will go. I uncurl it gently, Manchee murmuring "Tail, tail" to himself all the while.

"Whaddyaknow?" I say. "Those bandages work on dogs."

Viola's fished out two discs from her bag. She presses her thumbs inside them and they expand right up into water bottles. She kneels by the river, fills both, and tosses one to me.

"Thanks," I say, not really looking at her.

She wipes some water from her bottle. We stand on the riverbank for a second and she's putting her water bottle back into her bag and she's quiet in a way that I'm learning means she's trying to say something difficult.

"I don't mean any offense by it," she says, looking up to me, "but I think maybe it's time I read the note on the map."

I can feel myself redden, even in the dark, and I can also feel myself get ready to argue.

But then I just sigh. I'm tired and it's late and we're running *again* and she's right, ain't she? There's nothing but spitefulness that'll argue she's wrong.

I drop my rucksack and take out the book, unfolding the map from inside the front cover. I hand it to her without looking at her. She takes out her flashlight and shines it on the paper, turning it over to Ben's message. To my surprise, she starts reading it out loud and all of sudden, even with her own voice, it's like Ben's is ringing down the river, echoing from Prentisstown and hitting my chest like a punch.

"Go to the settlement down the river and across the bridge," she reads. *"It's called Farbranch and the people there should welcome you."*

"And they did," I say. "Some of them."

Viola continues, *"There are things you don't know about our history, Todd, and I'm sorry for that but if you knew them you would be in great danger. The only chance you have of a welcome is yer innocence."*

I feel myself redden even more but fortunately it's too dark to see.

"Yer ma's book will tell you more but in the meantime, the wider world has to be warned, Todd. Prentisstown is on the move. The plan has been in the works for years, only waiting for the last boy in Prentisstown to become a man." She looks up. *"Is that you?"*

"That's me," I say, "I was the youngest boy. I turn thirteen in twenty-seven days and officially become a man according to Prentisstown law."

And I can't help but think for a minute about what Ben showed me–

About how a boy becomes–

I cover it up and say quickly, "But I got no idea what he means about them waiting for me."

"The Mayor plans to take Farbranch and who knows what else beyond. Sillian and I–"

"Cillian," I correct her. "With a K sound."

"Cillian and I will try to delay it as long as we can but we won't be able to stop it. Farbranch will be in danger and you have to warn them. Always, always, always remember that we love you like our own son and sending you away is the hardest thing we'll ever have to do. If it's at all possible, we'll see you again, but first you must get to Farbranch as fast as you can and when you get there, you must warn them. Ben." Viola looks up. "That last part's underlined."

"I know."

And then we don't say nothing for a minute. There's blame in the air but maybe it's all coming from me.

Who can tell with a silent girl?

"My fault," I say. "It's all my fault."

Viola rereads the note to herself. "They should have *told* you," she says. "Not expected you to read it if you can't–"

"If they'd told me, Prentisstown would've heard it in my Noise and known that I knew. We wouldn't've even got the head start we got." I glance at her eyes and look away. "I shoulda given it to someone to read and that's all there is to it. Ben's a good man." I lower my voice. "Was."

She refolds the map and hands it back to me. It's useless to us now but I put it back carefully inside the front cover of the book.

"I could read that for you," Viola says. "Your mother's book. If you wanted."

I keep my back to her and put the book in my rucksack. "We need to go," I say. "We've wasted too much time here."

"Todd–"

"There's an army after us," I say. "No more time for reading."

So we set off again and do our best to run for as much and as long as we can but as the sun rises, all slow and lazy and cold, we've had no sleep and that's no sleep after a full day's work and so even with that army on our tails, we're barely able to even keep up a fast walk.

But we do, thru that next morning. The road keeps following the river as we hoped and the land starts to flatten out around us, great natural plains of grass stretching out to low hills and to higher hills beyond and, to the north at least, mountains beyond that.

It's all wild, tho. No fences, no fields of crops, and no signs of any kind of settlement or people except for the dusty road itself. Which is good in one way but weird in another.

If New World isn't sposed to have been wiped out, where is everybody?

"You think this is right?" I say, as we come round yet another dusty corner of the road with nothing beyond it but more dusty corners. "You think we're going the right way?"

Viola blows out thoughtful air. "My dad used to say, 'There's only forward, Vi, only outward and up.'"

"There's only forward," I repeat.

"Outward and up," she says.

"What was he like?" I ask. "Yer pa?"

She looks down at the road and from the side I can see half a smile on her face. "He smelled like fresh bread," she says and then she moves on ahead and don't say nothing more.

Morning turns to afternoon with more of the same. We hurry when we can, walk fast when we can't hurry, and only rest when we can't help it. The river remains flat and steady, like the brown and green land around it. I can see bluehawks way up high, hovering and scouting for prey, but that's about it for signs of life.

"This is one empty planet," Viola says as we stop for a quick lunch, leaning on some rocks overlooking a natural weir.

"Oh, it's full enough," I say, munching on some cheese. "Believe me."

"I do believe you. I just meant I can see why people would want to settle here. Lots of fertile farmland, lots of potential for people to make new lives."

I chew. "People would be mistaken."

She rubs her neck and looks at Manchee, sniffing round the edges of the weir, probably smelling the wood weavers who made it living underneath.

"Why do you become a man here at thirteen?" she asks.

I look over at her, surprised. "What?"

"That note," she says. "The town waiting for the last boy to become a man." She looks at me. "Why wait?"

"That's how New World's always done it. It's sposed to be scriptural. Aaron always went on about it symbolizing the day you eat from the Tree of Knowledge and go from innocence into sin."

She gives me a funny look. "That sounds pretty heavy."

I shrug. "Ben said that the real reason was cuz a small group of people on an isolated planet need all the adults they can get so thirteen is the day you start getting real responsibilities." I throw a stray stone into the river. "Don't ask me. All I know is it's thirteen years. Thirteen cycles of thirteen months."

"*Thirteen* months?" she asks, her eyebrows up.

I nod.

"There are only twelve months in a year," she says.

"No, there ain't. There's thirteen."

"Maybe not here," she says, "but where I come from there's twelve."

I blink. "Thirteen months in a New World year," I say, feeling dumb for some reason.

She looks up like she's figuring something out. "I mean, depending on how long a day or a month is on this planet, you might be . . . fourteen years old already."

"That's not how it works here," I say, kinda stern, not really liking this much. "I turn thirteen in twenty-seven days."

"Fourteen and a *month*, actually," she says, still figuring it out. "Which makes you wonder how you tell how old anybody—"

"It's twenty-seven days till my birthday," I say firmly. I stand and put the rucksack back on. "Come on. We've wasted too much time talking."

It ain't till the sun's finally started to dip below the tops of the trees that we see our first sign of civilizayshun: an abandoned water mill at the river's edge, its roof burned off who knows how many years ago. We've been walking so long we don't even talk, don't even look around much for danger, just go inside, throw our bags down against the walls and flop to the ground like it's the softest bed ever. Manchee, who don't seem to ever get tired, is busy running around, lifting his leg on all the plants that have grown up thru the cracked floorboards.

"My feet," I say, peeling off my shoes, counting five, no, *six* different blisters.

Viola lets out a weary sigh from the opposite wall. "We have to sleep," she says. "Even if."

"I know."

She looks at me. "You'll hear them coming," she says, "if they come?"

"Oh, I'll hear them," I say. "I'll definitely hear them."

We decide to take turns sleeping. I say I'll wait up first and Viola can barely say good night before she's out. I watch her sleep as the light fades. The little bit of clean we got at Hildy's house is already long gone. She looks like I must, face smudged with dust, dark circles under her eyes, dirt under her nails.

And I start to think.

I've only known her for three days, you know? Three effing days outta my whole entire life but it's like nothing that happened before really happened, like that was all a big lie just waiting for me to find out. No, not *like,* it *was* a big lie waiting for me to find out and this is the real life now, running without safety or answer, only moving, only ever moving.

I take a sip of water and I listen to the crickets chirping *sex sex sex* and I wonder what *her* life was like before these last three days. Like, what's it like growing up on a spaceship? A place where there's never any new people, a place you can never get beyond the borders of.

A place like Prentisstown, come to think of it, where if you disappeared, you ain't never coming back.

I look back over to her. But she did get out, didn't she? She got seven *months* out with her ma and her pa on the little ship that crashed. How's that work, I wonder?

"You need to send scout ships out ahead to make local field surveys and find the best landing sites," she says, without sitting up or even moving her head. "How does anyone ever sleep in a world with Noise?"

"You get used to it," I say. "But why so long? Why seven months?"

"That's how long it takes to set up first camp." She covers her eyes with her hand in an exhausted way. "My mother and father and I were supposed to find the best place for the ships to land and build the first encampment and then we'd start building the first things that would be needed for settlers just landing. A control tower, a food store, a clinic." She looks at me twixt her fingers. "It's standard procedure."

"I never seen no control tower on New World," I say.

This makes her sit up. "I *know.* I can't believe you guys don't even have communicators between settlements."

"So yer not church settlers then," I say, sounding wise.

"What does that have to do with anything?" she says. "Why would any reasonable church want to be cut off from itself?"

"Ben said that they came to this world for the simpler life, said that there was even a fight in the early days whether to destroy the fission generators."

Viola looks horrified. "You would have all died."

"That's why they weren't destroyed," I shrug. "Not even after Mayor Prentiss decided to get rid of most everything else."

Viola rubs her shins and looks up into the stars coming out thru the hole that was the roof. "My mother and father were so excited," she says. "A whole new world, a whole new beginning, all these plans of peace and happiness." She stops.

"I'm sorry it ain't that way," I say.

She looks down at her feet. "Would you mind waiting outside for a little while until I fall asleep?"

"Yeah," I say, "no problem."

I take my rucksack and go out the opening where the front door used to be. Manchee gets up from where he's curled and follows me. When I sit down, he recurls by my legs and falls asleep, farting happily and giving a doggy sigh. Simple to be a dog.

I watch the moons rise, the stars following 'em, the same moons and the same stars as were in Prentisstown, still out here past the end of the world. I take out the book again, the oil in the cover shining from the moonlight. I flip thru the pages.

I wonder if my ma was excited to land here, if her head was full of peace and good hope and joy everlasting.

I wonder if she found any before she died.

This makes my chest heavy so I put the book back in the rucksack and lean my head against the boards of the mill. I listen to the river flow past and the leaves shushing to themselves in the few trees around us and I look at the shadows of far distant hills on the horizon and the rustling forests on them.

I'll wait for a few minutes, then go back inside and make sure Viola's okay.

The next thing I know she's waking me up and it's hours later and my head is completely confused till I hear her saying, "Noise, Todd, I can hear Noise."

I'm on my feet before I'm fully awake, quieting Viola and a groggy Manchee barking his complaints. They get quiet and I put my ear into the night.

Whisper whisper whisper there, like a breeze whisper whisper whisper no words and far away but hovering, a storm cloud behind a mountain whisper whisper whisper.

"We gotta go," I say, already reaching for my rucksack.

"Is it the army?" Viola calls, running thru the door of the mill as she grabs her own bag.

"Army!" Manchee barks.

"Don't know," I say. "Probably."

"Could it be the next settlement?" Viola comes back, bag around her shoulders. "We can't be too far from it."

"Then why didn't we hear it when we got here?"

She bites her lip. "Damn."

"Yeah," I say. "Damn."

And so the second night after Farbranch passes like the first, running in darkness, using flashlights when we need 'em, trying not to think. Just before the sun comes up, the river moves outta the flats and into another small valley like the one by Farbranch and sure enough, there's Blazing Beacons or whatever so maybe there really are people living out this way.

They've got orchards, too, and fields of wheat, tho nothing looks near as well tended as Farbranch. Lucky for us, the main part of town is on top of the hill with what looks like a bigger road going thru it, the left fork, maybe, and five or six buildings, most of which could use a coat of paint. Down on our dirt road by the river there are just boats and wormy-looking docks and dock houses and whatever else you build on a flowing river.

We can't ask anyone for help. Even if we got it, the army's coming, ain't it? We should warn them but what if they're Matthew Lyles rather than Hildys? And what if by warning them we draw the army right *to* them cuz then we're in everyone's Noise? And what if the settlement knows we're the reason the army's coming and they decide to turn us over to them?

But they deserve to be warned, don't they?

But what if that endangers *us*?

You see? What's the right answer?

And so we sneak thru the settlement like thieves, running from dock house to dock house, hiding from sight of the town up the hill, waiting as quiet as we can when we see a skinny woman taking a basket into a henhouse up by some trees. It's small enough that we get thru it before the sun even fully rises and we're out the other side and back on the road like it never existed, like it never happened, even to us.

"So that's that settlement then," Viola whispers as we take a look behind us and watch it disappear behind a bend. "We'll never even know what it was actually called."

"And now we *really* don't know what's ahead of us," I whisper back.

"We keep going until we get to Haven."

"And then what?"

She don't say nothing to that.

"That's a lotta faith we're putting in a word," I say.

"There's got to be something, Todd," she says, her face kinda grim. "There has to be *something* there."

I don't say nothing for a second and then I say, "I guess we'll see."

And so starts another morning. Twice on the road we see men with horse-drawn carts. Both times we hie off into the woods, Viola with her hand round Manchee's snout and me trying to keep my Noise as Prentisstown-free as possible till they pass.

Nothing much changes as the hours go by. We don't hear no more whispers from the army, if that's what it even was, but there ain't no point in finding out for sure, is there? Morning's turned into afternoon again when we see a settlement high up on a far hill. We're coming up a little hill ourselves, the river dropping down a bit, tho we can see it spreading out in the distance, what looks like the start of a plain we're gonna have to cross.

Viola points her binocs at the settlement for a minute, then hands them to me. It's ten or fifteen buildings this time but even from a distance it looks scrubby and run-down.

"I don't get it," Viola says. "Going by a regular schedule of settlement, subsistence farming should be years over by now. And there's obviously trade, so why is there still this much struggle?"

"You don't really know nothing about settlers' lives, do you?" I say, chafing just a little.

She purses her lips. "It was required in school. I've been learning about how to set up a successful colony since I was five."

"Schooling ain't life."

"*Ain't* it?" she says, her eyebrows raising in mock surprise.

"*What did I say before?*" I snap back. "Some of us were busy surviving and couldn't learn about subdivided farming."

"*Subsistence.*"

"Don't care." I get myself moving again on the road.

Viola stomps after me. "We're going to be teaching you all a thing or two when my ship arrives," she says. "You can be sure of that."

"Well, won't we dumb hicks be lining up to kiss yer behinds in thankfulness?" I say, my Noise buzzing and not saying "behinds."

"Yes, you *will* be." She's raising her voice. "Trying to turn back the clock to the dark ages has really worked out for you, hasn't it? When we get here, you'll see how people are *supposed* to settle."

"That's *seven months* from now," I seethe at her. "You'll have plenty of time to see how the other half live."

"Todd!" Manchee barks, making us jump again, and suddenly he takes off down the road ahead of us.

"Manchee!" I yell after him. "Get back here!"

And then we both hear it.

22

WILF AND
THE SEA OF THINGS

IT'S WEIRD, Noise, but almost wordless, cresting the hill in front of us and rolling down, single-minded but talking in legions, like a thousand voices singing the same thing.

Yeah.

Singing.

"What is it?" Viola asks, spooked as I am. "It's not the army, is it? How could they be in front of us?"

"Todd!" Manchee barks from the top of the small hill. "Cows, Todd! Giant cows!"

Viola's mouth twists. "Giant cows?"

"No idea," I say and I'm already heading up the little hill.

Cuz the sound—

How can I describe it?

Like how stars might sound. Or moons. But not mountains. Too floaty for mountains. It's a sound like one planet singing to another, high and stretched and full of different voices starting at different notes and sloping down to other different notes but all weaving together in a rope of sound that's sad but not sad and slow but not slow and all singing one word.

One word.

We reach the top of the hill and another plain unrolls below us, the river tumbling down to meet it and then running thru it like a vein of silver thru a rock and all over the plain, walking their way from one side of the river to the other, are creachers.

Creachers I never seen the like of in my life.

Massive, they are, twelve feet tall if they're an inch, covered in a shaggy, silvery fur with a thick, fluffed tail at one end and a pair of curved white horns at the other reaching right outta their brows and long necks that stretch down from wide shoulders to the grass of the plain below and these wide lips that mow it up as they trudge on dry ground and drink water as they cross the river and there's *thousands* of 'em, thousands stretching from the horizon on our right to the horizon on our left and the Noise of 'em all is singing one word, at different times in different notes, but one word binding 'em all together, knitting 'em as a group as they cross the plain.

"*Here,*" Viola says from somewhere off to my side. "They're singing *here.*"

They're singing **Here**. Calling it from one to another in their Noise.

Here I am.

Here we are.

Here we go.

Here is all that matters.

Here.

It's—

Can I say?

It's like the song of a family where everything's always all right, it's a song of belonging that makes you belong just by hearing it, it's a song that'll always take care of you and never leave you. If you have a heart, it breaks, if you have a heart that's broken, it fixes.

It's—

Wow.

I look at Viola and she has her hand over her mouth and her eyes are wet but I can see a smile thru her fingers and I open my mouth to speak.

"Ya won't get ver far on foot," says a completely other voice to our left.

We spin round to look, my hand going right to my knife. A man driving an empty cart pulled by a pair of oxen regards us from a little side path, his mouth left hanging open like he forgot to close it.

There's a shotgun on the seat next to him, like he just put it there.

From a distance, Manchee barks "Cow!"

"They's all go round carts," says the man, "but not safe on foot, no. They's squish ya right up."

And again leaves his mouth open. His Noise, buried under all the **Here**s from the herd, seems to pretty much be saying exactly what his mouth is. I'm trying so hard not to think of certain words I'm already getting a headache.

"Ah kin give y'all a ride thrus," he says. "If ya want."

He raises an arm and points down the road, which disappears under the feet of the herd crossing it. I hadn't even thought about how the creachers'd be blocking our way but you can see how you wouldn't wanna try walking thru 'em.

I turn and I start to say something, *anything*, that'll be the fastest way to get away.

But instead the most amazing thing happens.

Viola looks at the man and says, "Ah'm Hildy." She points at me. "At's Ben."

"What?" I say, barking it almost like Manchee.

"Wilf," says the man to Viola and it takes a second to realize he's saying his name.

"Hiya, Wilf," Viola says and her voice ain't her own, ain't her own at all, there's a whole new voice coming outta her mouth, stretching and shortening itself, twisting and unraveling and the more she talks the more different she sounds.

The more she sounds like Wilf.

"We're all fra Farbranch. Where yoo from?"

Wilf hangs his thumb back over his shoulder. "Bar Vista," he says. "I'm gone Brockley Falls, pick up s'plies."

"Well, at's lucky," Viola says. "We're gone Brockley Falls, too."

This is making my headache worse. I put my hands up to my temples, like I'm trying to keep my Noise inside, trying to keep all the wrong things from spilling out into the world. Luckily, the song of **нєʀє** has made it like we're already swimming in sound.

"Hop on," Wilf says with a shrug.

"C'mon, Ben," Viola says, walking to the back of the cart and hoisting her bag on top. "Wilf's gone give us a ride."

She jumps on the cart and Wilf snaps the reins on his oxes. They take off slowly and Wilf don't even look at me as he passes. I'm still standing there in amazement when Viola goes by, waving her hand frantically to me to get on beside her. I don't got no choice, do I? I catch up and pull myself up into the cart.

I sit down next to her and stare at her with my jaw down around my ankles. *"What are you doing?"* I finally hiss in what's sposed to be a whisper.

"Shh!" she shushes, looking back over her shoulder at Wilf, but he could've already forgotten he picked us up for all that's going on in his Noise. "I don't know," she whispers by my ear, "just play along."

"Play along with what?"

"If we can get to the other side of the herd, then it's between us and the army, isn't it?"

I hadn't thought about that. "But what are you doing? What do Ben and Hildy gotta do with it?"

"He has a gun," she whispers, checking on Wilf again. "And you said yourself how people might react about you being from a certain place. So, it just sort of popped out."

"But you were talking in his *voice*."

"Not very well."

"Good enough!" I say, my voice going a little loud with amazement.

"*Shh*," she says a second time but with the combo of the herd of creachers getting closer by the second and Wilf's obvious not-too-brightness, we might as well be having a normal conversayshun.

"How do you do it?" I say, still pouring surprise out all over her.

"It's just lying, Todd," she says, trying to shush me again with her hands. "Don't you have lying here?"

Well of course we have lying here. New World and the town where I'm from (avoiding saying the name, avoiding *thinking* the name) seem to be nothing *but* lies. But that's different. I said it before, men lie all the time, to theirselves, to other men, to the world at large, but who can tell when the lie's a strand in all the other lies and truths floating round outta yer head? Everyone knows yer lying but everyone else is lying, too, so how can it matter? What does it change? It's just part of the river of a man, part of his Noise, and sometimes you can pick it out, sometimes you can't.

But he never stops being himself when he does it.

Cuz all I know about Viola is what she says. The only truth I got is what comes outta her mouth and so for a second back there, when she said she was Hildy and I was Ben and we were from Farbranch and she spoke just like Wilf (even tho he ain't from Farbranch) it was like all those things *became* true, just for an instant the world changed, just for a second it became made of Viola's voice and it wasn't describing a thing, it was *making* a thing, it was making us different just by saying it.

Oh, my head.

"Todd! Todd!" Manchee barks, popping up at the end of the cart, looking up thru our feet. "Todd!"

"Crap," Viola says.

I hop off the cart and sweep him up in my arms, putting one hand round his muzzle and using the to other to get back on the cart. "Td?" he puffs thru closed lips.

"Quiet, Manchee," I say.

"I'm not even sure it matters," Viola says, her voice stretching out.

I look up.

"Cw," Manchee says.

A creacher is walking right past us.

We've entered the herd.

Entered the song.

And for a little while, I forget all about any kinda lies.

I've never seen the sea, only in vids. No lakes where I grew up neither, just the river and the swamp. There may have been boats once but
not in my lifetime.

But if I had to imagine being on the sea, this is what I'd imagine.
The herd surrounds us and takes up everything, leaving just the sky and
us. It cuts around us like a current, sometimes noticing us but more
usually noticing only itself and the song of **Here,** which in the midst
of it is so loud it's like it's taken over the running of yer body for a while,
providing the energy to make yer heart beat and yer lungs breathe.

After a while, I find myself forgetting all about Wilf and the – the
other things I could think about and I'm just lying back on the cart,
watching it all go by, individual creachers snuffling around, feeding,
bumping each other now and again with their horns, and there's baby
ones, too, and old bulls and taller ones and shorter ones and some with
scars and some with scruffier fur.

Viola's laying down next to me and Manchee's little doggie brain is
overwhelmed by it all and he's just watching the herd go by with his
tongue hanging out and for a while, for a little while, as Wilf drives us over
the plain, this is all there is in the world.

This is all there is.

I look over at Viola and she looks back at me and just smiles and
shakes her head and wipes away the wet from her eyes.

Here.

Here.

We're **Here** and nowhere else.

Cuz there's nowhere else but **Here.**

"So this . . . Aaron," Viola says after a while in a low voice and I know
exactly why it's now that she brings him up.

It's so safe inside the **Here** we can talk about any dangers we like.

"Yeah?" I say, also keeping my voice low, watching a little family of
creachers waltz by the end of the cart, the ma creacher nuzzling forward
a curious baby creacher who's staring at us.

Viola turns to me from where she's laying down. "Aaron was your
holy man?"

I nod. "Our one and only."

"What kind of things did he preach?"

"The usual," I say. "Hellfire. Damnayshun. Judgment."

She eyes me up. "I'm not sure that's the usual, Todd."

I shrug. "He believed we were living thru the end of the world," I say. "Who's to say he was wrong?"

She shakes her head. "That's not what the preacher we had on the ship was like. Pastor Marc. He was kind and friendly and made every-thing seem like it was going to be okay."

I snort. "No, that don't sound like Aaron at all. He was always say-ing, 'God hears' and 'If one of us falls, we all fall.' Like he was looking forward to it."

"I heard him say that, too." She crosses her arms over herself.

The **Here** wraps us still, flowing everywhere.

I turn to her. "Did he . . . Did he hurt you? Back in the swamp?"

She shakes her head again and lets out a sigh. "He ranted and raved at me, and I guess it might have been preaching, but if I ran, he'd run after me and rant some more and I'd cry and ask him for help but he'd ignore me and preach some more and I'd see pictures of myself in his Noise when I didn't even know what Noise was. I've never been so scared in my life, not even when our ship was crashing."

We both look up into the sun.

"*If one of us falls, we all fall,*" she says. "What does that even mean?"

Which, when I really think about it, I realize I don't know and so I don't say nothing and we just sink back into the **Here** and let it take us a little further.

Here we are.

Not nowhere else.

After an hour or a week or a second, the creachers start thinning and we come out the other side of the herd. Manchee jumps down off the cart. We're going slow enough that there's no danger of him getting left behind so I let him. We're not thru laying there on the cart just yet.

"That was amazing," Viola says quietly, cuz the song is already start-ing to disappear. "I forgot all about how much my feet hurt."

"Yeah," I say.

"What *were* those?"

"'Em big thangs," Wilf says, not turning round. "Jus thangs, thass all."

Viola and I look at each other, like we forgot he was even there.

How much have we given away?

"'Em thangs got a name?" Viola asks, sitting up, acting her lie again.

"Oh, sure," Wilf says, giving the oxen freer rein now that we're outta the herd. "Packy Vines or Field Baysts or Anta Fants." We see him shrug from behind. "I just call 'em thangs, thass all."

"Thangs," Viola says.

"Things," I try.

Wilf looks back over his shoulder at us. "Say what, y'all from Farbranch?" he asks.

"Yessir," Viola says with a look at me.

Wilf nods at her. "Y'all bin seen that there army?"

My Noise spikes real loud before I can quiet it but again Wilf don't seem to notice. Viola looks at me, worry on her forehead.

"And what army's that, Wilf?" she says, the voice missing a little.

"That there army from cursed town," he says, still driving along like we're talking about vegetables. "That there army come outta swamp, come takin settlements, growin as it comes? Y'all bin seen that?"

"Where'd yoo hear bout an army, Wilf?"

"Stories," Wilf says. "Stories a-come chatterin down the river. People talkin. Ya know. Stories. Y'all bin seen that?"

I shake my head at Viola but she says, "Yeah, we seen it."

Wilf looks back over his shoulder again. "Zit big?"

"Very big," Viola says, looking at him seriously. "Ya gotta prepare yerself, Wilf. There's danger comin. Yoo need to warn Brockley Hills."

"Brockley Falls," Wilf corrects her.

"Ya gotta warn 'em, Wilf."

We hear Wilf grunt and then we realize it's a laugh. "Ain't nobody lissnen to Wilf, I tell ya what," he says, almost to himself, then strikes the reins on the oxen again.

It takes most of the rest of the afternoon to get to the other side of the plain. Thru Viola's binocs we can see the herd of things still crossing in the distance, from south to north, like they're never gonna run out. Wilf don't say nothing more about the army. Viola and I keep our talking to a bare minimum so we don't give any more away. Plus, it's so hard to keep my Noise clear it's taking mosta my concentrayshun. Manchee follows along on the road, doing his business and sniffing every flower.

When the sun is low in the sky, the cart finally creaks to a halt.

"Brockley Falls," Wilf says, nodding his head to where we can see in the distance the river tumbling off a low cliff. There's fifteen or twenty buildings gathered round the pond at the bottom of the falls before the river starts up again. A smaller road turns off from this one and leads down to it.

"We're getting off here," Viola says and we hop down, taking our bags from the cart.

"Thought ya mite," Wilf says, looking back over his shoulder at us again.

"Thank ya, Wilf," she says.

"Welcome," he says, staring off into the distance. "Best take shelter 'fore too long. Gone rain."

Both Viola and me automatically look straight up. There ain't a cloud in the sky.

"Mmm," Wilf says. "No one lissnen to Wilf."

Viola looks back at him, her voice returning to itself, trying to get the point to him clearly. "You have to warn them, Wilf. Please. If you're hearing that an army's coming, then you're right and people have to be ready."

All Wilf says is "Mmm" again before snapping the reins and turning the oxen down the split road toward Brockley Falls. He don't even look back once.

We watch him go for a while and then turn back to our own road.

"Ow," Viola says, stretching out her legs as she steps forward.

"I know," I say. "Mine too."

"You think he was right?" Viola says.

"Bout what?"

"About the army getting bigger as it marches." She imitates his voice again. "Growin as it comes."

"How do you *do* that?" I ask. "Yer not even from here."

She shrugs. "A game I used to play with my mother," she says. "Telling a story, using different voices for every character."

"Can you do my voice?" I ask, kinda tentative.

She grins. *"So you can have a conversayshun with yerself?"*

I frown. "That don't sound nothing like me."

We head back down the road, Brockley Falls disappearing behind us. The time on the cart was nice but it weren't sleep. We try to go as fast as we can but most times that ain't much more than a walk. Plus maybe the army really is caught far behind, really will have to wait behind the creachers.

Maybe. Maybe not. But within the half hour, you know what?

It's raining.

"People should listen to Wilf," Viola says, looking up.

The road's found its way back down near the river and we find a reasonably sheltered spot twixt the two. We'll eat our dinner, see if the rain stops. If it don't we got no choice but to walk in it anyway. I haven't even checked to see if Ben packed me a slicker.

"What's a slicker?" Viola asks as we sit down against different trees.

"A raincoat," I say, looking thru my rucksack. Nope, no slicker. Great. "And what did I say bout listening too close?"

I still feel a little calm, if you wanna know the truth, tho I probably shouldn't. The song of **Here** still feels like it's being sung, even if I can't hear it, even if it's miles away back on the plain. I find myself humming

it, even tho it don't have a tune, trying to get that feeling of connected-
ness, of *belonging*, of having someone there to say that you're **Here**.

I look over at Viola, eating outta one of her packets of fruit.

I think about my ma's book, still in my rucksack.

Stories in voices, I think.

Could I stand to hear my ma's voice spoken?

Viola crinkles the fruit packet she's just finished. "That's the last of
them."

"I got some of this cheese left," I say, "and some dried mutton, but
we're gonna have to start finding some of our own on the way."

"You mean like stealing?" she asks.

"I mean like hunting," I say. "But maybe stealing, too, if we have to.
And there's wild fruit and I know some roots we can eat if you boil 'em
first."

"Mmm." Viola frowns. "There's not much call for hunting on a
spaceship."

"I could show you."

"Okay," she says, trying to sound cheerful. "Don't you need a gun?"

"Not if yer a good hunter. Rabbits are easy with snares. Fish with
lines. You can catch squirrels with yer knife but there ain't much meat."

"Horse, Todd," Manchee barks, quietly.

I laugh, for the first time in what seems like forever. Viola laughs,
too. "We ain't hunting *horses*, Manchee." I reach out to pet him. "Stupid
dog."

"Horse," he barks again, standing up and looking down the road
from the direkshun we just came.

We stop laughing.

23

A KNIFE IS ONLY AS GOOD AS THE ONE WHO WIELDS IT

THERE'S HOOFBEATS ON THE ROAD, distant but approaching at full gallop.

"Someone from Brockley Hills?" Viola says, hope and doubt both in her voice.

"Brockley *Falls*," I say, standing. "We need to hide."

We repack our bags in a hurry. It's a narrow strip of trees we've managed to get ourselves stuck in twixt the road and the river. We don't dare cross the road and with the river at our backs, a fallen log is the best we're gonna get. We gather the last of our things and crouch down behind it, Manchee held twixt my knees, rain splashing everywhere.

I take out my knife.

The hoofbeats keep coming, louder and louder.

"Only one horse," Viola whispers. "It's not the army."

"Yeah," I say, "but listen how fast he's riding."

Thump budda-thump budda-thump we hear. Thru the trees we can see the dot of him approaching. He's coming full out down the road, even tho it's raining and night's falling. No one'd ride like that with good news, would they?

Viola looks behind us at the river. "Can you swim?"

"Yeah."

"Good," she says. "Because I can't."

Thump budda-thump budda-thump.

I can hear the buzz of the rider's Noise starting but for a time the galloping is louder and I can't hear it clearly.

"Horse," Manchee says from down below.

It's there. Static twixt the hoofbeats. Flashes of it. Parts of words caught. **Rid** – and **Pa** – and **Dark** – and **Stup** – and more and more.

I clench the knife harder. Viola's not saying nothing now.

Thump budda-thump budda-thump budda–

Faster and **Nightfall** and **Shot** and **What-ever it** –

And he's coming down the road, round a little curve we took just a hundred metres back, leaning forward–

Thump budda–

The knife turns in my hand cuz–

Shot 'em all and **She was tasty** and **Dark here** –

Thump BUDDA–

I think I reckernize–

THUMP BUDDA-THUMP BUDDA–

And he's nearer and nearer till he's almost–

And then **Todd Hewitt?** rings out as clear as day thru the rain and the galloping and the river.

Viola gasps.

And I can see who it is.

"Junior," Manchee barks.

It's Mr. Prentiss Jr.

We try to duck down farther below the log but it ain't no use cuz we already see him pulling back hard on the reins to stop his horse, causing it to rear up and nearly throw him.

But only nearly.

And not enough to make him drop the rifle he's got under one arm.

Todd EFFING HEWITT! screams his Noise.

"Oh, shit," I hear Viola say and I know what she means.

"Well, HOOO-EEE!" Mr. Prentiss Jr. yells and we're close enough to see the smile on his face and hear amazement in his voice. "Yer taking the *ROAD?!* You ain't even going *OFF TRAIL?!*"

My eyes meet Viola's. What choice did we have?

"I been hearing yer Noise for almost yer whole stupid life, boy!" He turns his horse this way and that, trying to find where exactly we are in our little strip of woods. "You think I'm not gonna hear it if ya just *HIDE?*"

There's joy in his Noise. Real joy, like he can't believe his luck.

"And wait a minute," he says and we can hear him edging his horse off the road and into the woods. "Wait just a minute. What's that beside you? That empty space of *nothing.*"

He says it so nasty Viola flinches. I got the knife in my hand but he's on horseback and we know he's got a gun.

"Too effing right I've got a gun, Todd boy," he calls, no longer searching round but coming straight for us, getting his horse to step over bushes and round trees. "And I got another gun, too, another one special, just for yer little lady there, Todd."

I look at Viola. I know she sees what he's thinking, what's in his Noise, the pictures that ooze out of it. I know she does cuz I can see her face closing right up. I bump her arm and I flash my eyes over to our right, just about the only possibility we have for an escape.

"Oh, *please* run, boy," Mr. Prentiss Jr. calls. "Please give me a reason to hurt you."

The horse is so close we can hear its Noise, too, jittery and crazy. There's no farther down we can crouch.

He's nearly on top of us.

I grip the knife and squeeze Viola's hand once, hard, for luck.

It's now or never.

And—

"NOW!" I yell.

We jump up and a gun blast rings out, splintering the branches over our heads, but we run anyway.

"GET!" Mr. Prentiss Jr. shouts to his horse and here they come.

In two bounds, his horse turns and jumps back to the road, following along it as we run. The strip twixt the road and the river ain't getting any thicker and we can see each other as we go. Branches snap and puddles splash and feet slip and he pounds along the road matching our every step.

We ain't gonna get away from him. We just ain't.

But we try, each of us taking a twisty path up and over logs and thru bushes and Manchee's panting and barking at our heels and the rain's splashing down on us and the road's getting closer and then it suddenly veers sharply toward the river and we got no choice but to cross it in front of him to get to the deeper woods on the other side and I can see Viola leaping over the boundary and onto the road with her arms pumping and Mr. Prentiss Jr. rounding the bend and he's twirling something in his hand and we make a dash for the other side but the horse is roaring down on us and suddenly I feel something grab my legs, binding 'em so fast and so tight I fall right off my feet.

"*Aaagh!*" I yell and I hit my face into muck and fallen leaves and the rucksack goes over my head and nearly rips my arms off as it flies off my back and Viola sees me fall and she's nearly across the road but I see mud curling up from where her feet are digging in to stop herself and I shout, "NO! RUN! RUN!" and she locks my eyes and I see something change on her face but who knows what it means and as the horse bears down she turns and disappears into the woods and Manchee runs back to me and barks "Todd! Todd!" and I'm caught I'm caught I'm caught.

Cuz Mr. Prentiss Jr. is standing over me, breathing hard, high on his white horse, rifle cocked and pointed. I know what's happened. He's thrown a rope with weights at cither end right at my legs and they've twisted round and caught me, expert, just like a hunter after swamp deer. I'm stuck down here in the mud on my belly, caught like an animal.

"My pa sure is gonna be glad to see you," he says, his horse nervy and stepping side to side. **Rain,** I can hear it thinking, and **Is it a snake?**

"I was just sposed to see if there were rumors of you on the road ahead," Mr. Prentiss Jr. sneers, "but here you are, in the real honest-to-God flesh."

"Eff you," I say and do you think I say eff?

I've still got the knife in my hand.

"And it sure is making me quake with fear," he says, moving the rifle so I'm looking right down the barrel. "Drop it."

I hold my arm out away from me and drop the knife. It splashes in the mud and I'm still on my belly.

"Yer little lady sure didn't show you no loyalty, now did she?" he says, hopping off his horse, calming it with his free hand. Manchee growls at him but Mr. Prentiss Jr. just laughs. "What happened to its tail?"

Manchee jumps, his teeth bared, but Mr. Prentiss Jr. is faster, kicking him away with a vicious boot to the face. Manchee yelps and cowers in the bushes.

"Friends abandoning you right and left, Todd." He walks over to me. "But that's the lesson you learn, eh? Dogs is dogs and women turn out to be dogs, too."

"You *shut* up," I say, clenching my teeth.

His Noise goes all fake sympathy and triumph. "Poor, poor Toddy. All this time traveling with a woman and I'm guessing you never figured out what to do with one."

"You stop talking bout her," I spit. I'm still on my belly and my legs are still tied.

But I find I can bend my knees.

His Noise gets uglier, louder, but his face is all blank like a terror from a dream. "What you do, Todd," he says, squatting down to get closer to me, "is you keep the ones that're whores and you shoot the ones that're not."

He leans even closer. I can see the pathetic hairs on his upper lip, not even made darker by the rain coming down. He's only two years older than me. Only two years bigger.

Snake? thinks the horse.

I put my hands slowly down on the ground.

I push a little into the mud.

"After I tie you up," he says, turning it into a whispering taunt, "I'll go find yer little lady and let you know which kind she is."

Which is when I jump.

I push up with my hands and kick forward hard with my legs, launching myself right at his face. The top of my head hits his nose with a crunch and he falls backward, me coming down right on top of him. I hit him hard in the face with each fist while he's still too surprised to re-act and then ram my knees into the man's place twixt his legs.

He curls up like a bug and lets out a low, angry moan and I roll off him back over to my knife, picking it up, cutting the rope round my legs and getting to my feet and I kick the gun away and I jump in front of the horse screaming "Snake! Snake!" and waving my arms which does the trick instantly and it turns and runs back down the road with a terrified whinny, riderless into the rain.

I look round and *BAM!* Mr. Prentiss Jr. hits me across the bridge of the nose with his fist but I don't fall and he yells "You piece of –" and I swing my arm out with the knife in it and I make him jump back and I swing it again, water pouring outta my eyes from both the punch and the rain and he steps away from me, looking for his gun and limping a little and he sees it in the mud and he turns his body to fetch it and I'm not thinking at all and I jump on him, knocking him back down and he hits me with his elbow but I don't fall off and my Noise is screaming and his Noise is screaming.

And I don't even know how but I've got him on his back and the point of my knife held up under his chin.

We both stop struggling.

"Why are you after us?!" I shout into his face. "Why are you chasing us?!"

And him and his stupid pathetic nonmustache *smile.*

I knee him again twixt his legs.

He groans again and spits at me but I've still got the knife which has now made a little cut.

"My father wants you," he finally says.

"Why?" I say. "Why does he want us?"

"Us?" His eyes go wide. "There's no effing *us.* He wants you, Todd. Just you."

I can't believe this. "What?" I say. *"Why?"*

But he's not answering. He's looking into my Noise. He's looking and searching.

"Hey!" I say, slapping him cross the face with the back of my hand. "Hey! I'm asking you an asking!"

But the smile's back. I can't effing believe it but the smile's back.

"You know what my father always says, Todd Hewitt?" he leers up at me. "He says a knife is only as good as the one who wields it."

"Shut up," I say.

"Yer a fighter, I'll give you that." Still smiling, still bleeding a little below his chin. "But you ain't no killer."

"Shut *up!*" I yell but I know he can see in my Noise that I heard those exact words from Aaron.

"Oh, yeah?" he says. "Whaddya gonna do about it? *Kill* me?"

"I WILL," I shout. "I'll *KILL* you!"

He just licks some rain from his lips and laughs. I have him pinned to the ground with a knife up under his chin and he's *laughing*.

"STOP IT!" I scream at him and I raise the knife.

He keeps on laughing and then he looks at me and he says—

He says—

He says *this*—

"You wanna hear how Ben and Cillian screamed for mercy before I shot 'em twixt the eyes?"

And my Noise buzzes red.

And I clench the knife to strike at him.

And I'm going to kill him.

I'm going to *kill* him.

And—

And—

And—

And right at the top of my swing—

Right at the moment when I start to bring it down—

Right at the moment when the power is mine to command and do with as I please—

I hesitate—

Again—

I hesitate—

Only for a second—

But goddam me—

Goddam me forever and forever—

Cuz in that second he kicks up his legs, throws me off him, and elbows me in the throat. I lean over choking and I can only feel his hand wrench the knife away from my own.

As easy as candy from a baby.

"Now, Todd," he says, standing over me, "let me show you a thing or two about wielding."

24

THE DEATH OF THE WORTHLESS COWARD

I DESERVE IT. I've done everything wrong. I deserve it. If I had the knife back I'd kill myself with it. Except I'd probably be too much of a coward to do that, too.

"Yer some piece of work, Todd Hewitt," Mr. Prentiss Jr. says, examining my knife.

I'm kneeling now, knees in the mud, hand at my throat, still trying to get my breath.

"You had this fight won and then you went and just threw it away." He runs a finger up the blade. "Stupid as well as yella."

"Just finish it," I mumble into the mud.

"What was that?" Mr. Prentiss Jr. says, the smile back, his Noise bright.

"Just FINISH IT!" I shout up to him.

"Oh, I'm not gonna kill you," he says, his eyes flashing. "My pa wouldn't be too happy with that, now would he?"

He steps up to me and holds the knife near my face. He puts the tip of it into my nose so I have to hold my head back farther and farther.

"But there's lots of things you can do with a knife," he says, "without killing a man."

I'm not even looking round no more for ways to get away.

I'm looking right into his eyes which are awake and alive and about to win, his Noise the same, pictures of him in Farbranch, pictures from back at my farm, pictures of me kneeling in front of him.

There ain't nothing in my Noise but a pit full of my stupidity and worthlessness and hate.

I'm sorry, Ben.

I'm so, so sorry.

"But then again," he says, "you *ain't* a man, are ya?" He lowers his voice. "And you never will be."

He moves the knife in his hand, turning the blade toward my cheek.

I close my eyes.

And I feel a wash of silence flow over me from behind.

My eyes snap open.

"Well, looky here," Mr. Prentiss Jr. says, glancing up over the top of my head. My back is to the deeper woods opposite the river and I can feel the quiet of Viola standing there as clearly as if I could see her.

"Run!" I yell, without turning around. "Get away from here."

She ignores me. "Step back," I hear her say to Mr. Prentiss Jr. "I'm warning you."

"Yer warning *me*?" he says, pointing to himself with the knife, the smile back on his face.

Then he jumps a little as something smacks him in the chest and sticks there. It looks like a bunch of little wires with a plastic bulb on the end. Mr. Prentiss Jr. puts the knife underneath it and tries to flick it off but it stays stuck. He looks up at Viola, smirking. "Whatever this is sposed to be, sister," he says, "it didn't work."

And *SMACKFLASH!!*

There's a huge blast of light and I feel a hand on my collar yank me back to the point of choking. I fall back and away as Mr. Prentiss Jr.'s body jerks into a spasm, flinging the knife out to one side, sparks and little flashes of lightning flying out of the wires and into his body. Smoke and steam come from everywhere, his sleeves, his collar, his pant legs. Viola's still pulling me back outta the way by my neck when he falls to the ground, face first in the muck, right on top of his rifle.

She lets go and we tumble together on a little bank by the side of the road. I grab my neck again and we lay there breathing heavily for a second. The sparks and flashes stop and Mr. Prentiss Jr. twitches in the mud.

"I was afraid –" Viola says twixt deep breaths "– all this water around –" breath "– that I might take you and me with him –" breath "– but he was about to cut–"

I stand without saying nothing, my Noise focused, my eyes on the knife. I go right to it.

"Todd–" Viola says.

I pick it up and stand over him. "Is he dead?" I ask without looking at Viola.

"Shouldn't be," she says. "It was just the voltage from a—"

I raise the knife.

"Todd, no!"

"Give me one good reason," I say, knife still hovering, eyes still on him.

"You're not a killer, Todd," she says.

I spin round to her, my Noise roaring up like a beast. "Don't SAY THAT!! Don't you EVER SAY THAT!!"

"Todd," she says, her hands out, her voice calming.

"I'M why we're in this mess! They're not looking for YOU! They're looking for *ME*!" I turn back to Mr. Prentiss Jr. "And if I could kill one of them, then maybe we—"

"Todd, no, listen to me," she says, coming closer. "Listen to me!" I look at her. My Noise is so ugly and my face so twisted she hesitates a little but then she takes another step forward. "Listen to me while I tell you something."

And then out pour more words from her than I ever heard before.

"When you found me, back there in the swamp, I had been running from that man, from Aaron, for four days, and you were only the second person I'd ever seen on this planet and you came at me with that same knife and for all I knew you were exactly like him."

Her hands are still up, like I'm Mr. Prentiss Jr.'s long-gone horse in need of calming.

"But before I even understood what was going on with the Noise and with Prentisstown and with whatever your story was, I could tell about you. People can tell, Todd. We can see that you won't hurt us. That's not you."

"You hit me in the face with a branch," I say.

She puts her hands on her hips. "Well, what did you expect? You came at me with a knife. But I didn't hit you hard enough to hurt you badly, did I?"

I don't say nothing.

"And I was right," she says. "You bandaged my arm. You rescued me from Aaron when you didn't have to. You took me out of the swamp where I would have been killed. You stood up for me to that man in the orchard. You came with me when we needed to leave Farbranch."

"No," I say, my voice low, "no, ycr not reading the story right. We're only having to run cuz I couldn't—"

"I think I'm finally *understanding* the story, Todd," she says. "Why are they coming after you so fiercely? Why is a whole army chasing you across towns and rivers and plains and the whole stupid planet?" She points to Mr. Prentiss Jr. "I heard what he said. Don't you wonder why they want you so badly?"

The pit in me is just getting blacker and darker. "Cuz I'm the one who don't fit."

"Exactly!"

My eyes go wide. "Why is that good news? I have an army who wants to kill me cuz I'm not a killer."

"Wrong," she says. "You have an army who wants to *make* you a killer."

I blink. "Huh?"

She takes another step forward. "If they can turn you into the kind of man they want—"

"Boy," I say. "Not a man yet."

She waves this away. "If they can snuff out that part of you that's good, the part of you that won't kill, then they win, don't you see? If they can do it to you, they can do it to anyone. And they win. They *win!*"

She's near me now and she reaches out her hand and puts it on my arm, the one still holding the knife.

"We beat them," she says, "*you* beat them by not becoming what they want."

I clench my teeth. "He killed Ben and Cillian."

She shakes her head. "No, he *said* he did. And you believed him."

We look down at him. He's not twitching no more and the steam is starting to blow away.

"I know this kind of boy," she says. "We have this kind of boy even on spaceships. He's a liar."

"He's a man."

"How can you keep *saying that?*" she asks, her voice finally snappy. "How can you keep saying that he's a man and you're not? Just because of some stupid *birthday*? If you were where I came from you'd already be fourteen and a month!"

"I'm not where yer from!" I shout. "I'm from *here* and that's how it works here!"

"Well, how it works here is *wrong*." She lets go of my arm and kneels down by Mr. Prentiss Jr. "We'll tie him up. We'll tie him up good and tight and we'll get the heck out of here, all right?"

I don't let go of the knife.

I will never let go of this knife, no matter what she says, no matter how she says it.

She looks up and around. "Where's Manchee?"

Oh, no.

We find him in the bushes. He growls at us without words, just animal growls. He's holding his left eye shut and there's blood around his mouth. It takes a bunch of tries but I finally catch him while Viola takes out her medipak-of-wonders. I hold him down as she forces him to swallow a pill that makes him go floppy and then she cleans out his broken teeth and puts a cream in his eye. She tapes a bandage to it and he looks so small and beaten that when he says "Thawd?" thru one-eyed grogginess I just hug him to me and sit for a bit, under the bushes, outta the rain, while Viola repacks everything and gets my rucksack outta the mud.

"Your clothes are all wet," she says after a while. "And the food is smashed. But the book's still in the plastic. The book's all right."

And the thought of my ma knowing what a coward her son would be one day makes me want to throw the book in the river.

But I don't.

We go to tie up Mr. Prentiss Jr. with his own rope and find that the electric shock has blown the wooden stock right off of his rifle. Which is a shame cuz it coulda come in handy.

"What was that you shocked him with?" I ask, huffing and puffing as we drag him to the side of the road. Knocked-out people are *heavy*.

"A device for telling the ship in space where I am on the planet," she says. "It took forever to pull apart."

I stand up. "How will yer ship know where you are now?"

She shrugs. "We just have to hope that Haven'll have something."

I watch her go to her own bag and pick it up. I sure hope Haven has half what she's expecting.

We leave. Mr. Prentiss Jr. was right about the stupidity of staying on the road, so we keep a hundred or so feet away from it on the nonriver side, trying to keep it in sight as best we can. We take turns carrying Manchee as the night passes.

We don't talk much neither.

Cuz she might have a point, right? Yeah, okay, maybe that's what the army's after, maybe if they can make me join, they can make anyone join. Maybe I'm their test, who knows, the whole town's crazy enough to believe something like that.

If one of us falls, we all fall.

But for one that don't explain why Aaron's after us and for two I've heard her lie now, ain't I? Her words sound good but who's to know if she's making truth up rather than just saying it?

Cuz I'm *never* going to join the army and Mayor Prentiss must know that, not after what they did to Ben and Cillian, whether Mr. Prentiss Jr.'s Noise was true or not, so that's where she's dead wrong. Whatever they want, whatever the weakness is in me that I can't kill a man even when he deserves it, it's got to change for me to be a man. It's *got* to or how can I hold my head up?

Midnight passes and I'm twenty-five days and a million years from becoming a man.

Cuz if I'd killed Aaron, he couldn't've told Mayor Prentiss where he'd seen me last.

If I coulda killed Mr. Prentiss Jr. back at the farm, he wouldn't've led the Mayor's men to Ben and Cillian and wouldn't've lived to harm Manchee.

If I'd been any kinda killer, I could've stayed and helped Ben and Cillian defend themselves.

Maybe if I was a killer, they wouldn't be dead.

And that's a trade I'd make any day.

I'll be a killer, if that's what it takes.

Watch me.

The terrain's getting rougher and steeper as the river starts making canyons again. We rest for a while under a rocky outcropping and eat the last of the food that didn't get ruined by the fight with Mr. Prentiss Jr.

I lay Manchee across my lap. "What was in that pill?"

"It was just a little crumb of a human painkiller," she says. "I hope it's not too much."

I run my hand over his fur. He's warm and asleep so at least still living.

"Todd—" she says, but I stop her.

"I wanna keep moving as long as we can," I say. "I know we should sleep but let's go till we can't go no more."

She waits a minute and then she says, "Okay," and we don't say nothing more, just finish the last of the food.

The rain keeps up all night as we go and there's no racket like rainfall in the woods, a billion drops pattering down a billion leaves, the river swelling and roaring, the squish of the mud under our feet. I hear Noise now and again in the distance, probably from woodland creachers but always outta sight, always gone when we get near.

"Is there anything out here that could harm us?" Viola asks me, having to raise her voice over the rain.

"Too many to count," I say. I gesture to Manchee in her arms. "He awake yet?"

"Not yet," she says, worry in her voice. "I hope I—"

And that's how unprepared we are when we step round another rocky outcropping and into the campsite.

We both stop immediately and take in what's in front of our eyes, all in a flash.

A fire burning.

Freshly caught fish hanging from a spit over it.

A man leaning over a stone, scraping scales from another fish.

That man looking up as we step into his campsite.

In an *instant,* like knowing Viola was a girl even tho I'd never seen one, I know in the second it takes me to reach for my knife, I know that he's not a man at all.

He's a Spackle.

25

KILLER

THE WORLD STOPS SPINNING.

The rain stops falling, the fire stops burning, my heart stops beating.

A Spackle.

There ain't no more Spackle.

They all died in the war.

There ain't no more Spackle.

And here's one standing right in front of me.

He's tall and thin like in the vids I remember, white skin, long fingers and arms, the mouth midface where it ain't sposed to be, the ear flaps down by the jaw, eyes blacker than swamp stones, lichen and moss growing where clothes should be.

Alien. As alien as you can be.

Holy crap.

You might as well just crumple up the world I know and throw it away.

"Todd?" Viola says.

"Don't move," I say.

Cuz thru the sound of the rain I can hear the Spackle's *Noise.*

No words come out clear, just pictures, skewed up strange and with all the wrong colors, but pictures of me and Viola standing in front of him, looking shocked.

Pictures of the knife now outstretched in my hand.

"Todd," Viola says, a small warning in her voice.

Cuz his Noise has more in it. It's got feelings, washing up in a buzz.

Feelings of fear.

I feel his fear.

Good.

My Noise turns red.

"Todd," Viola says again.

"Quit saying my name," I say.

The Spackle pulls himself slowly upright from where he's skinning the fish. He's made his camp underneath another rocky outcropping down the slope of a small hill. A good part of it's dry and I see bags and a roll of moss that might be a bed.

There's also something shiny and long resting against the rock.

I can see the Spackle picture it in his Noise.

It's the spear he's been using to catch fish in the river.

"Don't," I say to him.

I think for a second, but *only* for a second, how clear I understand all this, how clear I can see him standing in the river, how easy he is to read, even tho it's all pictures.

But the second passes in a flash.

Cuz I see him thinking about making a leap for the spear.

"Todd?" she says. "Put the knife down."

And he makes his leap.

I leap at the same time.

(Watch me.)

"No!" I hear Viola scream but my Noise is roaring way too loud for me to hear it as more than a whisper.

Cuz all I'm thinking as I take running steps across the campsite, knife up and ready, bearing down on the Spackle, all skinny knees and elbows as he stumbles heading for his spear, all I'm thinking and sending forward to him in my red, red Noise are images and words and feelings, of all I know, all that's happened to me, all the times I failed to use the knife, every bit of me screaming—

I'll show you who's a killer.

I get to him before he gets to the spear, barreling into him with my shoulder. We fall to the less muddy dirt with a thud and his arms and legs are all over me, long, like wrestling with a spider, and he's striking me on the head but they're little more than slaps really and I realize and I realize and I realize—

I realize he's weaker than me.

"Todd, stop it!" I hear Viola call.

He scrabbles away from me and I thump him on the side of his head with a fist and he's so light it topples him over onto a pile of rocks and he looks back up at me and his mouth is making a hissing sound and there's terror and panic flying outta his Noise.

"STOP IT!" Viola screams. "Can't you see how scared he is?"

"And well he should be!" I yell back.

Cuz there ain't no stopping my Noise now.

I step toward him and he tries to crawl away but I grab him by his long white ankle and drag him off the rocks back onto the ground and he's making this horrible *keening* sound and I ready my knife.

And Viola must've put Manchee down somewhere cuz she grabs my arm and she pulls it back to stop me cutting down the spack and I push into her with my body to shake her off but she won't let go and we go stumbling away from the Spackle who cowers down by a rock, his hands in front of his face.

"Let go of me!" I yell.

"Please, Todd!" she yells back, pulling and twisting my arm. "Stop this, please!"

I twist my arm around and use my free one to push her away and when I turn the Spackle's skittered along the ground—

Heading for his spear—

Has his fingers on the end—

And all my hate erupts into me like a volcano at full bright red—

And I fall on him—

And I punch the knife into his chest.

It crunches as it goes in, turning to the side as it hits a bone and the Spackle screams the most terrible, terrible sound and dark red blood (red, it's red, they bleed *red*) sprays outta the wound and he brings a long arm up and scratches across my face and I pull back my arm and I stab him again and a long screeching breath comes outta his mouth with a loud gurgle and his arms and legs still scramble around him and he looks at me with his black, black eyes and his Noise filled with pain and bafflement and fear—

And I twist the knife—

And he won't die and he won't die and he won't die—

And in a moan and a shudder he dies.

And his Noise stops altogether.

I gag and I yank out the knife and paddle my way back along the mud.

I look at my hands, at the knife. There's blood all over everything. The knife is covered with it, even all over the handle, and both my hands and arms and the front of my clothes and a splash on my face that I wipe away mingling with my own blood from the scratch.

Even with the rain coming down on me now there's more of it than seems possible.

The Spackle lays where I—

Where I killed him.

I hear Viola make a choking and gasping sound and I look up to her and when I do she shrinks from me.

"You don't know!" I shout at her. "You don't know anything! They started the war. They killed my ma! All of it, everything that's happened, is their fault!"

And then I throw up.

And I keep throwing up.

And when my Noise starts to calm I throw up all over again.

I keep my head to the ground.

The world has stopped.

The world is still stopped.

I don't hear nothing from Viola but her silence. I feel my rucksack digging into the back of my neck as I lean forward. I don't look over at the Spackle.

"He woulda killed us," I finally say, talking into the ground.

Viola don't say nothing.

"He woulda killed us," I say again.

"He was *terrified*!" Viola cries, her voice breaking. "Even I could see how scared he was."

"He went for his spear," I say, lifting my head.

"Because you came after him with a knife!" I can see her now. Her eyes are wide and growing more blank, like they did when she closed up on herself and started rocking.

"They killed everyone on New World," I say.

She shakes her head, fiercely. "You idiot! You stupid fucking IDIOT!"

She don't say effing.

"How many times have you found out that what you've been told isn't true?" she says, backing away from me even farther, her face twisting. "How many times?"

"Viola—"

"Weren't all the Spackle killed in the war?" she says and my God how I hate how frightened her voice sounds. "Huh? *Weren't they?*"

And the last of my anger drops outta my Noise as I realize how I've been the fool again—

And I turn around to the Spackle—

And I see the campsite—

And I see the fish on the lines—

And (no no no no no) I see the fear that was coming from his Noise—
(No no no, please no.)
And there's nothing left for me to throw up but I heave anyway—
And I'm a killer—
I'm a killer—
I'm a killer—
(Oh, please no) I'm a killer.
I start to shake. I start to shake so bad I can't stand up. I find I'm
saying "No" over and over again and the fear in his Noise keeps echoing
around mine and there's nowhere to run from it, it's just there and there
and there and I'm shaking so bad I can't even stay on my hands and
knees and I fall into the mud and I can still see the blood everywhere
and the rain's not washing it off.
I squeeze my eyes shut tight.
And there's only blackness.
Only blackness and nothing.
One more time, I've ruined everything. One more time, I've done
everything wrong.
From a long way away I can hear Viola saying my name.
But it's so far away.
And I'm alone. Here and always, alone.
I hear my name again.
From a far, far distance I feel a pull on my arm.
It's only when I hear a squib of Noise not my own that I open my
eyes.
"I think there's more of them out there," Viola whispers down near
my ear.
I raise my head. My own Noise is so filled with junk and horror that
it's hard to hear clearly and the rain is still falling, heavy as ever, and I
take a stupid moment to wonder if we'll ever get dry again and then I
hear it, murmuring and indistinct in the trees, impossible to pin down
but definitely out there.
"If they didn't want to kill us before," Viola says, "they'll sure want to
now."
"We need to go." I try to get to my feet. I'm still shaking and it takes
a try or two, but I do.
I'm still holding the knife. It's sticky with blood.
I throw it to the ground.
Viola's face is a terrible thing, grieving and scared and horrified, all
at me, all at me, but as ever we ain't got no choice so I just say again,
"We need to go," and I go to pick up Manchee from where she'd set him
down in the dry lee of the Spackle's outcropping.

He's still sleeping and shivering from the cold when I pick him up and I bury my face in his fur and breathe in his familiar doggy stink.

"*Hurry,*" Viola says.

And I turn back to her to see her looking all around, the Noise still whispering all around thru the woods and the rain, the fear still on her face.

She returns her gaze to me and I find it impossible to hold and so I look away.

But as I'm looking away, I see movement behind her.

I see the bushes part behind where she's standing.

And I see her see my face changing.

And she turns in time to see Aaron coming outta the woods behind her.

And he's grabbing her by the neck with one hand and smashing a cloth over her nose and mouth with the other and as I call out and take a step forward I hear her scream from beneath it and she tries to fight with her hands but Aaron's holding her tight and by the time I've taken my second and third steps she's already swooning from whatever's on the cloth and on my fourth and fifth steps he's dropping her to the ground and Manchee is still in my arms and on my sixth step he's reaching behind his back and I don't have my knife and I have Manchee with me and I can only run toward him and on my seventh step I see him bring around a wooden staff that's been strapped to his back and it swings thru the air and strikes me full on the side of my head with a

CRACK

and I fall and Manchee tumbles from my arms and I crash into the ground on my belly and my head is ringing so hard I can't even catch myself and the world goes wobbly and gray and full of only pain and I'm on the ground and everything is tilting and sliding and my arms and legs weigh too much to lift and my face is half in the mud but half turned up and I can see Aaron watching me on the ground and I see his Noise and Viola in it and I see him see my knife shining red in the mud and he picks it up and I try to crawl away but the weight of my body sticks me to the spot and I can only watch as he stands over me.

"I have no further use for you, boy," he says and he raises the knife over his head and the last thing I see is him bringing it down with the full force of his arm.

PART V

26

THE END OF ALL THINGS

FALLING NO FALLING no please *help me Falling* The Knife *The Knife* Spackle spacks are dead, all spacks dead VIOLA sorry, please, sorry *he's got a spear* FALLING Please please *Aaron, behind you! He's coming!* no further use for you, boy *Viola falling*, Viola Eade Spackle *the screaming and the blood and no* WATCH ME watch me no *please* watch me he woulda killed us *Ben* please I'm sorry *Aaron! Run!* E-A-D-E More of them *we have to get outta here* FALLING falling dark blood *The Knife* dead run *I'm a killer please no* SPACKLE *Viola Viola Viola—*

"Viola!" I try to scream but it's blackness, it's blackness with no sound, blackness and I've fallen and I have no voice—

"Viola," I try again and there's water in my lungs and an ache in my gut and pain, pain in my—

"Aaron," I whisper to myself and no one. "Run, it's Aaron."

And then I fall again and it's blackness . . .

. . .

. . .

"Todd?"

. . .

"Todd?"

Manchee.

"Todd?"

I can feel a dog's tongue on my face which means I can feel my face which means I can tell where it is and with a rush of air clanging into me, I open my eyes.

Manchee's standing right by my head, shifting from foot to foot, licking his lips and nose nervously, the bandage still over his eye, but he's all blurry and it's hard to—

"Todd?"

I try to say his name to calm him but all I do is cough and a sharp pain soars thru my back. I'm still down on my belly in the muck, where I fell when Aaron—

Aaron.

When Aaron hit me in the head with his staff. I try to raise my head and a blinding ache stretches over the right side of my skull all the way down to my jaw and I have to lie there gritting my teeth for a minute just letting it hurt and blaze before I can even try speaking again.

"Todd?" Manchee whimpers.

"I'm here, Manchee," I finally mutter but it comes up outta my chest like a growl held back by goo and it sets off more coughing—

Which I have to cut short cuz of the sharp pain in my back.

My back.

I stifle another cough and a horror feeling spreads out from my gut into the rest of me.

The last thing I saw before—

No.

Oh, no.

I cough a little in my throat, trying not to move any muscle at all, failing at it and surviving the pain till it ebbs as far as it's gonna and then I work on making my mouth move without killing me.

"Is there a knife in me, Manchee?" I rasp.

"Knife, Todd," he barks and there's worry all over him. "Back, Todd."

He comes forward to lick my face again, the dog way of trying to make it better. All I do is breathe and not move for a minute. I close my eyes and pull air inside, despite how my lungs are complaining and already seem full.

I am Todd Hewitt, I think, which is a mistake, cuz here comes all of it back, falling on me, dragging me down and the Spackle's blood and Viola's face frightened of me and Aaron coming outta the woods and taking her—

I start to weep but the pain from the grip of the weep is so bad that for a minute I feel paralyzed and a fire burns thru my arms and back and there's nothing to do but suffer till it goes.

Slowly, slowly, slowly, I start to uncurl one arm from beneath me. My head and back hurt so bad I think I pass out for a minute but I wake again and slowly, slowly, slowly reach my hand up and behind me, crawling my fingers up my wet filthy shirt and up the wet filthy rucksack which unbelievably I'm still wearing and up and back till there it is under my fingertips.

The handle of the knife. Sticking outta my back.

But I'd be dead.

I'd be *dead*.

Am I dead?

"Not dead, Todd," Manchee barks. "Sack! Sack!"

The knife is sticking in me, up high twixt my shoulder blades, the pain's telling me all about it very specifically, but the knife's gone thru the rucksack first, something in the rucksack's stopped the knife from going all the way in—

The book.

My ma's book.

I feel with my fingers again, slowly as I can, but yes, Aaron raised his arm and brought it down thru the book in the rucksack and it's stopped it from going all the way thru my body.

(Like it did thru the Spackle.)

I close my eyes again and try to take as deep a breath as possible which ain't too deep and then I hold it till I can get my fingers round the knife and then I have to breathe and wait till the pain passes and then I try to pull but it's the heaviest thing in the world and I have to wait and breathe and try again and I pull and the pain in my back increases like a gun firing and I scream out uncontrollably as I feel the knife come outta my back.

I gasp and pant for a minute and try to stop from weeping again, all the while holding the knife away from me, still stuck thru the book and the rucksack.

Manchee licks my face once more.

"Good boy," I say, tho I don't know why.

It takes what feels like a lifetime to get the rucksack straps off my arms and finally be able to cast the knife and the whole mess aside. Even then, I can't come near standing up and I must pass out again cuz Manchee's licking my face and I'm having to open my eyes and cough in my breath all over again.

As I lay there, still in the muck, I wish to myself more than anything in the whole world that Aaron's knife had gone thru me, that I was as dead as the Spackle, that I could finish falling down that pit, down down down till there's only blackness, down into the nowhere where there's no more Todd to blame or screw things up or fail Ben or fail Viola, and I could fall away forever into nothingness and never have to worry no more.

But here's Manchee, licking away.

"Get off." I reach up an arm to push him away.

Aaron coulda killed me, coulda killed me so easy.

The knife thru my neck, the knife in my eye, the knife across my throat. I was his for the killing and he didn't kill me. He musta known what he was doing. He *musta*.

Was he leaving me for the Mayor to find? But why was he so far ahead of the army? How could he have come all this way without a horse like Mr. Prentiss Jr.? How long had he been following us?

How long before he stepped outta the bushes and took Viola away?

I let out a little moan.

That's why he left me alive. So I could live knowing that he took Viola. That's how he wins, ain't it? That's how he makes me suffer. Living and having the sight of him taking her forever in my Noise.

A new kinda energy runs thru me and I make myself sit up, ignoring the pain and bringing myself forward and breathing till I can think about standing. The rattle in my lungs and the pain in my back make me cough more but I grit my teeth and get thru it.

Cuz I have to find her.

"Viola," Manchee barks.

"Viola," I say and I grit my teeth even harder and try to get to my feet.

But it's too much, the pain takes my legs from me and I topple back in the mud and I just lay there pulled tight from it all and struggling to breathe and my mind goes all woozy and hot and in my Noise I'm running and I'm running and I'm running toward nothing and I'm hot all over and I'm sweating and I'm running in my Noise and I can hear Ben from behind the trees and I'm running toward him and he's singing the song, he's singing the song from my bedtimes, the song that's for boys and not men but when I hear it my heart stretches and it's *early one morning just as the sun was rising.*

I come back to myself. The song comes with me.

Cuz the song goes:

> *Early one morning just as the sun was rising,*
> *I heard a maiden call from the valley below.*
> *"Oh don't deceive me, oh never leave me."*

I open my eyes.

Don't deceive me. Never leave me.

I have to find her.

I have to find her.

I look up. The sun is in the sky but I have no idea how much time has passed since Aaron took Viola. That was just before dawn. It's cloudy but bright now and so it could be late morning or early afternoon.

It might not even be the same day, a thought I try to push away. I close my eyes and I try to listen. The rain's stopped so there's none of that clatter but the only Noise I can hear belongs to me and to Manchee and the distant wordless chatter of woodland creachers getting on with their lives that ain't got nothing to do with mine.

No sound of Aaron. No space of silence for Viola.

I open my eyes and I see her bag.

Dropped in the struggle with Aaron, of no use or interest to him and just left on the ground like it don't belong to no one, like it don't matter that it's Viola's.

That bag so full of stupid and useful things.

My chest clenches and I cough painfully.

I can't seem to stand so I crawl forward, gasping at the pain in my back and head but still crawling, Manchee barking, worried, "Todd, Todd," all the time, and it takes forever, it takes *too effing long* but I get to the bag and I have to lean hunched with the pain for a minute before I can do anything with it. When I can breathe again I open it and fish around till I find the box with the bandages. There's only one left but it'll have to do. Then I start on the process of taking off my shirt which requires more stopping, more breathing, inch by inch, but finally it's off my burning back and over my burning head and I can see blood and mud everywhere on it.

I find the scalpel in her medipak and cut the bandage in two. I put one part on my head, holding it till it sticks, and reach around slowly and put the other on my back. For a minute it hurts even more as the bandage material, the human cell whatever the hell she talked about, crawls into the wounds and makes a bind. I clench my teeth thru it but then the medicine starts to work and a flush of cool flows into my bloodstream. I wait for it to work enough till I can stand up. I'm wobbly when I first get to my feet but I can manage to just stand for a minute.

After another I can take a step. And then another.

But where do I go?

I've no idea where he took her. I've no idea how much time has passed. He could already be all the way back to the army by now.

"Viola?" Manchee barks, whimpering.

"I don't know, fella," I say. "Let me think."

Even with the bandages doing their thing I can't stand up straight all the way but I do my best and look around. The Spackle's body is on the edge of my vision but I turn myself so I can't see it.

Oh don't deceive me. Oh never leave me.

I sigh and I know what I have to do.

"There ain't nothing for it," I say to Manchee. "We have to go back to the army."

"Todd?" he whines.

"There ain't nothing for it," I say again and I put everything outta my head but moving.

First things first. I need a new shirt.

I keep the Spackle to my back and turn to the rucksack.

The knife is still thru the cloth of the rucksack and the book inside. I don't really wanna touch it and even in my haze I don't wanna see what's become of the book but I have to get the knife out so I brace the sack with my foot and pull hard. It takes a few tugs but it comes out and I drop it to the ground.

I look at it on the wet moss. There's blood all over it still. Spackle blood mostly but my blood brighter red at the tip. I wonder if that means that Spackle blood got into my blood when Aaron stabbed me. I wonder if there are extra special viruses you can catch directly from Spackle.

But there's no time for further wondering.

I open the rucksack and take out the book.

There's a knife-shaped hole all the way thru and out the other side. The knife is so sharp and Aaron must be so strong that it's hardly ruined the book at all. The pages have a slit running thru 'em all the way thru the book, my blood and Spackle blood staining the edges just a little, but it's still readable.

I could still read it, still have it read.

If I ever deserve to.

I push that thought away too and take out a clean shirt. I cough as I do and even with the bandages it hurts so I have to wait till I stop. My lungs feel filled with water, like I'm carrying a pile of river stones in my chest, but I put the shirt on, I gather what usable things I can still get from my rucksack, some clothes, my own medipak, what ain't been ruined by Mr. Prentiss Jr. or the rain and I take 'em and my ma's book over to Viola's bag and put 'em inside cuz there's no way I can carry a rucksack on my back no more.

And then there's still the asking, ain't there?

Where do I go?

I follow the road back to the army, that's where I go.

I go to the army and somehow I save her, even if it's changing my place for hers.

And for that I can't go unarmed, can I?

No, I can't.

I look at the knife again, sitting there on the moss like a thing without properties, a thing made of metal as separate from a boy as can be, a thing which casts all blame from itself to the boy who uses it.

I don't wanna touch it. Not at all. Not never again. But I have to go over and I have to clean off the blood as best I can on some wet leaves and I have to sheath it behind me in the belt that's still around my waist.

I have to do these things. There ain't no choice.

The Spackle hovers on the edge of my vision but I do not look at it as I handle the knife.

"C'mon, Manchee." I loop Viola's bag as gingerly as I can over one shoulder.

Don't deceive me. Never leave me.

Time to go.

"We're gonna find her," I say.

I keep the campsite behind me and head off in the direkshun of the road. Best to just get on it and walk back toward 'em as fast as I can. I'll hear 'em coming and can get outta the way and then I guess I'll see if there's any way I can save her.

Which might mean meeting them head-on.

I push my way thru a row of bushes when I hear Manchee bark, "Todd?"

I turn, trying to keep from seeing the campsite. "C'mon, boy."

"Todd!"

"I said c'mon, now. I mean it."

"This way, Todd," he barks and wags his half-tail.

I turn more fully to him. "What'd you say?"

He's pointing his nose in another direkshun altogether from the one I'm going. "This way," he barks. He rubs at the bandage over his eye with a paw, knocking it off and squinting at me with the injured eye.

"What do you mean 'This way'?" I ask, a feeling in my chest.

He's nodding his head and pushing his front feet in a direkshun not only away from the road but in the opposite direkshun from the army. "Viola," he barks, turning round in a circle and then facing that way again.

"You can smell her?" I ask, my chest rising.

He barks a bark of yes.

"You can *smell* her?"

"This way, Todd!"

"Not back to the road?" I say. "Not back to the army?"

"Todd!" he barks, feeling the rise in my Noise and getting excited himself.

"Yer sure?" I say. "You gotta be sure, Manchee. You gotta be."

"This way!" and off he runs, thru the bushes and off on a track parallel to the river, away from the army.

And toward Haven.

Who knows why and who cares cuz in the moment I'm running after him as best as my injuries will let me, in the moment I see him bounding away and ahead, I think to myself, *Good dog, ruddy good dog.*

27

ON WE GO

THIS WAY, TODD," Manchee barks, taking us round another out-cropping.

Ever since we left the Spackle campsite, the terrain's been getting more and more rugged. The woods've been rising up into hills for an hour or two now and we rush up 'em and down 'em and up 'em again and sometimes it's more like hiking than running. When we get up to the top of one, I see more and more rolling away in front of me, hills under trees, a few so steep you have to go around rather than over. The road and the river twist thru 'em on snaky paths off to my right and sometimes it's all I can do to keep them in sight.

Even with the bandages doing their best to hold me together, every step I take jars my back and my head and every once in a while I can't help but stop and sometimes throw up my empty stomach.

But on we go.

Faster, I think to myself. *Go faster, Todd Hewitt.*

They've got at least half a day's march on us, maybe even a *day* and a half, and I don't know where they're going or what Aaron plans on doing when he gets there and so on we go.

"Yer sure?" I keep asking Manchee.

"This way," he keeps barking.

The thing that makes no sense is that we're pretty much on the path that Viola and I would've taken anyway, following the river, keeping back from the road, and heading east toward Haven. I don't know why Aaron's going there, I don't know why he'd head away from the army, but that's where Manchee's smelling their scents and so that's the way we go.

We keep on thru the middle of the day, up hills, down hills, and onward, thru trees that turn from the broad-leafed trees on the plains to more needly kinds, taller and more arrowlike. The trees even smell different, sending a sharp tang in the air I can taste on my tongue. Manchee and I hop over all manner of streams and creeks that feed the river and I stop now and then to refill the water bottles and on we go.

I try not to think at all. I try to keep my mind pointed ahead, pointed toward Viola and finding her. I try not to think about how she looked after I killed the Spackle. I try not to think about how afraid she was of me or how she backed away like I might hurt her. I try not to think about how scared she musta been when Aaron came after her and I was no use.

And I try not to think about the Spackle's Noise and the fear that was in it or how surprised he musta been being killed for nothing more than being a fisherman or how the crunch felt up my arm when the knife went in him or how dark red his blood was flowing out onto me or the bafflement pouring outta him and into my Noise as he died as he died as he died as he—

I don't think about it.

On we go, on we go.

Afternoon passes into early evening, the forest and the hills seem never-ending, and there comes another problem.

"Food, Todd?"

"There ain't none left," I say, dirt giving way under my feet as we make our way down a slope. "I don't got nothing for myself neither."

"Food?"

I don't know how long it is since I ate last, don't know how long since I really slept, for that matter, since passing out ain't sleeping.

And I've lost track of how many days till I become a man but I can tell you it's never felt farther away.

"Squirrel!" Manchee suddenly barks and tears around the trunk of a needly tree and into a mess of ferns beyond. I didn't even see the squirrel but I can hear **Whirler dog** and "Squirrel!" and **Whirler-whirler-whirler—** and then it stops short.

Manchee jumps out with a waxy squirrel drooping in his mouth, bigger and browner than the ones from the swamp. He drops it on the ground in front of me, a gristly, bloody plop, and I ain't so hungry no more.

"Food?" he barks.

"That's all right, boy." I look anywhere but the mess. "You can have it."

I'm sweating more than normal and I take big drinks of water as Manchee finishes his meal. Little gnats cloud round us in near invisible swarms and I keep having to bat 'em away. I cough again, ignoring the pain in my back, the pain in my head, and when he's done and ready to go, I wobble just a little but on we go again.

Keep moving, Todd Hewitt. Keep going.

I don't dare sleep. Aaron may not so I can't. On and on, the clouds passing sometimes without me noticing, the moons rising, stars peeping. I come down to the bottom of a low hill and scare my way thru a whole herd of what look like deer but their horns are all different than the deer I know from Prentisstown and anyway they're off flying thru the trees away from me and a barking Manchee before I hardly register they're even there.

On we go still thru midnight (twenty-four days left? twenty-three?). We've come the whole day without hearing no more sounds of Noise or other settlements, not that I could see anyway, even when I was close enough to see brief snatches of the river and the road. But as we reach the top of another wooded hill and the moons are directly overhead, I finally hear the Noise of men, clear as a crash.

We stop, crouching down even tho it's night.

I look out from our hilltop. The moons are high and I can see two long huts in two separate clearings on hillsides across the way. From one I can hear the murmuring ruckus of sleeping men's Noise. *Julia?* and on *horseback* and *tell him it ain't so* and *up the river past morning* and lots of things that make no sense cuz dreaming Noise is the weirdest of all. From the other hut, there's silence, the aching silence of women, I can feel it even from here, men in one hut, women in another, which I guess is one way of solving the problem of sleeping, and the touch of the silence from the women's side makes me think of Viola and I have to keep my balance against a tree trunk for a minute.

But where there's people, there's food.

"Can you find yer way back to the trail if we leave it?" I whisper to my dog, stifling a cough.

"Find trail," Manchee barks, seriously.

"Yer sure?"

"Todd smell," he barks. "Manchee smell."

"Keep quiet as we go then." We start creeping our way down the hill, moving softly as we can thru the trees and brush till we get to the bottom of a little dale with the huts above us, sleeping on hillsides.

I can hear my own Noise spreading out into the world, hot and fusty, like the sweat that keeps pouring down my sides, and I try to keep it

quiet and gray and flat, like Tam did, Tam who controlled his Noise better than any man in Prentisstown—

And there's yer proof.

Prentisstown? I hear from the men's hut almost immediately.

We stop dead. My shoulders slump. It's still dream Noise I'm hearing but the word repeats thru the sleeping men like echoes down a valley. Prentisstown? and Prentisstown? and Prentisstown? like they don't
know what the word means yet.

But they will when they wake.

Idiot.

"Let's go," I say, turning and scurrying back the way we came, back
to our trail.

"Food?" Manchee barks.

"Come *on.*"

And so, still no food for me but on we go, thru the night, rushing the
best we can.

Faster, Todd. Get yer damn self moving.

On we go, on we go, up hills, grabbing onto plants sometimes to pull
myself up, and down hills, holding on to rocks to keep my balance now
and then, the scent keeping well clear of anywhere easy it might be to
walk, like the flatter parts down by the road or riverbank, and I'm coughing and sometimes stumbling and as the sun starts to show itself there
comes a time when I can't, when I just can't, when my legs crumple beneath me and I have to sit down.

I just have to.

(I'm sorry.)

My back is aching and my head is aching and I'm sweating so stinking much and I'm so hungry and I just have to sit down at the base of a
tree, just for a minute, I just have to and I'm sorry, I'm sorry, I'm sorry.

"Todd?" Manchee mumbles, coming up to me.

"I'm fine, boy."

"Hot, Todd," he says, meaning me.

I cough, my lungs rattling like rocks falling down a hill.

Get up, Todd Hewitt. Get off yer goddam butt and get going.

My mind drifts, I can't help it, I try to hold on to Viola but there my
mind goes and I'm little and I'm sick in bed and I'm *real* sick and Ben's
staying in my room with me cuz the fever is making me see things, horrible things, shimmering walls, people who ain't there, Ben growing fangs
and extra arms, all kindsa stuff and I'm screaming and pulling away but
Ben is there with me and he's singing the song and he's giving me cool
water and he's taking out tabs of medicine—

Medicine.

Ben giving me medicine.

I come back to myself.

I lift my head and go thru Viola's bag, taking out her medipak again. It's got all kindsa pills in it, too many. There's writing on the little packets but the words make no sense to me and I can't risk taking the tranquilizer that knocked out Manchee. I open my own medipak, nowhere near as good as hers, but there's white tabs in it that I know are at least pain relievers, however cruddy and homemade. I chew up two and then two more.

Get up, you worthless piece of crap.

I sit and breathe for a while and fight, fight, fight against falling asleep, waiting for the pills to work and as the sun starts to peek up over the top of a far hill I reckon I'm feeling a little better.

Don't know if I actually am but there ain't no choice.

Get up, Todd Hewitt. Get an effing MOVE ON!

"Okay," I say, breathing heavy and rubbing my knees with my hands. "Which way, Manchee?"

On we go.

The scent carries like it did before, avoiding the road, avoiding any buildings we might see at a distance, but always onward, always toward Haven, only Aaron knows why. Midmorning we find another small creek heading down to the river. I check for crocs, tho it's really too small a place, and refill the water bottles. Manchee wades in, lapping it up, snapping unsuccessfully at these little brass-colored fish that swim by, nibbling at his fur.

I sit on my knees and wash some of the sweat from my face. The water is cold as a slap and it wakes me up a little. I wish I knew if we were even gaining on 'em. I wish I knew how far they were ahead.

And I wish he'd never found us.

And I wish he'd never found Viola in the first place.

And I wish Ben and Cillian hadn't lied to me.

And I wish Ben was here right now.

And I wish I was back in Prentisstown.

I rest back on my heels, looking up into the sun.

No. No, I don't. I don't wish I was back in Prentisstown. Not no more, I don't.

And if Aaron hadn't found her then *I* might not have found her and that's no good neither.

"C'mon, Manchee," I say, turning round to pick up the bag again.

Which is when I see the turtle, sunning itself on a rock.

I freeze.

I never seen this kinda turtle before. Its shell is craggy and sharp, with a dark red streak going down either side. The turtle's got its shell all the way open to catch as much warmth as possible, its soft back fully exposed.

You can eat a turtle.

Its Noise ain't nothing but a long **ahhhhhh** sound, exhaling under sunlight. It don't seem too concerned about us, probably thinking it can snap its shell shut and dive underwater faster than we could get to it. And even if we did get to it, we wouldn't be able to get the shell back open to eat it.

Unless you had a knife to kill it with.

"Turtle!" Manchee barks, seeing it. He keeps back cuz the swamp turtles we know have more than enough snap to get after a dog. The turtle just sits there, not taking us seriously.

I reach behind my back for the knife.

I'm halfway there when I feel the pain twixt my shoulder blades.

I stop. I swallow.

(Spackle and pain and bafflement.)

I glance down into the water, seeing myself, my hair a bird's nest, bandage across half my head, dirtier than an old ewe.

One hand reaching for my knife.

(Red blood and fear and fear and fear.)

I stop reaching.

I take my hand away.

I stand. "C'mon, Manchee," I say. I don't look at the turtle, don't even listen for its Noise. Manchee barks at it a few more times but I'm already crossing the creek and on we go, on we go, on we go.

So I can't hunt.

And I can't get near settlements.

And so if I don't find Viola and Aaron soon I'll starve to death if this coughing don't kill me first.

"Great," I say to myself and there's nothing to do but keep going as fast as I can.

Not fast enough, Todd. Move yer effing feet, you gonk.

Morning turns to another midday, midday turns to another afternoon. I take more tabs, we keep on going, no food, no rest, just forward, forward, forward. The path is starting to tend downhill again, so at least that's a blessing. Aaron's scent moves closer to the road but I'm feeling so poor I don't even look up when I hear distant Noise now and then.

It ain't his and there's no silence that's hers so why bother?

Afternoon turns into another evening and it's when we're coming down a steep hillside that I fall.

My legs slip out from under me and I'm not quick enough to catch myself and I fall down and keep falling, sliding down the hill, bumping into bushes, picking up speed, feeling a tearing in my back, and I reach out to stop myself but my hands are too slow to catch anything and I judder judder judder along the leaves and grass and then I hit a bump and skip up into the air, tumbling over onto my shoulders, pain searing thru them, and I call out loud and I don't stop falling till I come to a thicket of brambles at the bottom of the hill and ram into 'em with a thump.

"Todd! Todd! Todd!" I hear Manchee, running down after me, but all I can do is try and withstand the pain again and the tired again and the gunk in my lungs and the hunger gnawing in my belly and bramble scratches all over me and I think I'd be crying if I had any energy left at all.

"Todd?" Manchee barks, circling round me, trying to find a way into the brambles.

"Gimme a minute," I say and push myself up a little. Then I lean forward and fall right over on my face.

Get up, I think. *Get up, you piece of filth, GET UP!*

"Hungry, Todd," Manchee says, meaning me that's hungry. "Eat. Eat, Todd."

I push with hands on the ground, coughing as I come up, spitting up handfuls of gunk from my lungs. I get to my knees at least.

"Food, Todd."

"I know," I say. "I know."

I feel so dizzy I have to put my head back down on the ground. "Just gimme a sec," I say, whispering it into the leaves on the ground. "Just a quick sec."

And I fall again into blackness.

I don't know how long I'm out but I wake to Manchee barking. "People!" he's barking. "People! Todd, Todd, Todd! People!"

I open my eyes. "What people?" I say.

"This way," he barks. "People. Food, Todd. Food!"

I take shallow breaths, coughing all the way, my body weighing ninety million pounds, and I push my way out the other side of the bramble. I look up and over.

I'm in a ditch right by the road.

I can see carts up ahead on the left, a whole string of 'em, pulled by oxen and by horses, disappearing round a bend.

"Help," I say, but my voice comes out like a gasp with not near enough volume.

Get up.

"Help," I call again, but it's only to myself.

Get up.

It's over. I can't stand no more. I can't move no more. It's over.
Get up.
But it's over.
The last cart disappears round the bend and it's over.
. . . give up.
I put my head down, right down, on the roadside, grit and pebbles digging into my cheek. A shiver shakes me and I roll to my side and pull myself to myself, curling my legs to my chest, and I close my eyes and I've failed and I've failed and please won't the darkness just take me please please please—

"That you, Ben?"

I open my eyes.

It's Wilf.

28

THE SMELL OF ROOTS

Y'ALL RIGHT, BEN?" he asks, putting a hand under my armpit to help me up but even with that I can't barely stand nor even raise my head much and so I feel his other hand under my other armpit. That don't work neither so he goes even further than that and lifts me over his shoulder. I stare down at the back of his legs as he carries me to his cart.

"Hoo is it, Wilf?" I hear a woman's voice ask.

"'s Ben," Wilf says. "Lookin poorly."

Next thing I know he's setting me down on the back of his cart. It's piled ragtag with parcels and boxes covered in leather skins, bits of furniture and large baskets, all tumbled together, almost overflowing with itself.

"It's too late," I say. "It's over."

The woman's walked over the back of the cart from the seat and hops down to face me. She's broad with a worn dress and flyaway hair and lines at the corners of her eyes and her voice is quick, like a mouse. "What's over, young'un?"

"She's gone." I feel my chin crumpling and my throat pulling. "I lost her."

I feel a cool hand on my forehead and it feels so good I press into it. She takes it away and says, "Fever," to Wilf.

"Yup," Wilf says.

"Best make a poultice," the woman says and I think she heads off into the ditch but that don't make no sense.

"Where's Hildy, Ben?" Wilf says, trying to get his eyes to meet mine. Mine are so watery it's hard to even see him.

"Her name ain't Hildy," I say.

"Ah know," Wilf says, "but at's whatcha call her."

"She's gone," I say, my eyes filling. My head falls forward again. I feel Wilf put a hand on my shoulder and he squeezes it.

"Todd?" I hear Manchee bark, unsure, a ways off the road.

"I ain't called Ben," I say to Wilf, still not looking up.

"Ah know," Wilf says again. "But at's what we're callin ya."

I look up to him. His face and his Noise are as blank as I remember but the lesson of forever and ever is that knowing a man's mind ain't knowing the man.

Wilf don't say nothing more and goes back to the front of the cart. The woman comes back with a seriously foul-smelling rag in her hands. It stinks of roots and mud and ugly herbs but I'm so tired I let her tie it round my forehead, right over the bandage that's still stuck on the side of my head.

"At should work onna fever," she says, hopping back up. We both lurch forward a little bit as Wilf snaps the rein on his oxen. The woman's eyes are wide open, looking into mine like searching for exciting news. "Yoo runnin from the army, too?"

Her quiet next to me reminds me so much of Viola it's all I can do not to just lean against her. "Kinda," I say.

"Yoo's what told Wilf about it, huh?" she says. "Yoo's and a girl told Wilf bout the army, told him to tell people, tell people they had to gett-away, dincha?"

I look up at her, smelly brown root water dripping down my face, and I turn back to look at Wilf, up there driving his cart. He hears me looking. "They lissened to Wilf," he says.

I look up and past him to the road ahead. As we go round a bend, I can hear not only the rush of the river to my right again, like an old friend, an old foe, I can also see a line of carts stretching on up ahead of us on the road at least as far as the next bend, carts packed with belongings just like Wilf's and all kindsa people straggled along the tops, holding on to anything that won't knock 'em off.

It's a caravan. Wilf is taking the rear of a long caravan. Men and women and I think even children, too, if I can see clearly thru the stink of the thing tied round my head, their Noise and silence floating up and back like a great, clattery thing all its own.

Army I hear a lot. Army and army and army.

And cursed town.

"Brockley Falls?" I ask.

"Bar Vista, too," the woman says, nodding her head fast. "And others. Rumor's been flyin up the river and road. Army from cursed town comin and comin, growin as it comes, with men pickin up arms to join in."

Growing as it comes, I think.

"Thousands strong, they say," says the woman.

Wilf makes a scoffing sound. "Ain't no thousand people 'tween here and cursed town."

The woman twists her lips. "Ah'm only sayin what people are sayin."

I look back at the empty road behind us, Manchee panting along a little distance away, and I remember Ivan, the man in the barn at Farbranch, who told me that not everyone felt the same about history, that Pren – that my town had allies still. Maybe not thousands, but still maybe growing. Getting bigger and bigger as it marches on till it's so big how can anyone stand against it?

"We're going to Haven," the woman says. "They'll pruhtekt us there."

"Haven," I mumble to myself.

"Say they even got a cure for Noise in them there parts," the woman says. "Now there's a thing Ah'd like to see." She laughs out loud at herself. "Or *hear,* Ah guess." She slaps her thigh.

"They got Spackle there?" I ask.

The woman turns to me surprised. "Spackle don't come near people," she says. "Not no more, not since the war. They's keep to theirselves and we's keep to ourselves and such is the peace kept." It sounds like she's reciting the last part. "Tain't hardly none left anyway."

"I gotta go." I put my hands down and try to lift myself up. "I gotta find her."

All that happens is that I lose my balance and fall off the end of the cart. The woman calls to Wilf to stop and they both lift me back up on it, the woman getting Manchee up top, too. She clears a few boxes away to lay me down and Wilf gets the cart going again. He snaps the oxen a bit harder this time and I can feel us moving along faster – faster than I could walk at least.

"Eat," the woman says, holding up some bread to my face. "Yoo can't go nowhere till yoo eat."

I take the bread from her and eat a bite, then tear into the rest so hungrily I forget to give some to Manchee. The woman just takes out some more and gives some to both of us, watching wide-eyed at every move I make.

"Thanks," I say.

"Ah'm Jane," she says. Her eyes are still way open, like she's just bursting to say stuff. "Didja see the army?" she asks. "With yer own eyes?"

"I did," I say. "In Farbranch."

She sucks in her breath. "So it's true." Not an asking, just saying it.

"*Told* yoo it were true," Wilf says from up front.

"Ah hear they're cuttin off people's heads and boilin their eyes," Jane says.

"Jane!" Wilf snaps.

"Ah'm just *sayin.*"

"They're killing folk," I say, low. "Killing's enough."

Jane's eyes dart all over my face and Noise but all she says after a bit is, "Wilf told me all bout yoo," and I can't figure out at all what her smile means.

A drip from the rag makes it to my mouth and I gag and spit and cough some more. "What *is* this?" I say, pressing the rag with my fingers and wincing from the smell.

"Poultice," Jane says. "For fevers and ague."

"It *stinks.*"

"Evil smell draws out evil fever," she says, as if telling me a lesson everyone knows.

"Evil?" I say. "Fever ain't evil. It's *fever.*"

"Yeah, and this poultice treats fever."

I stare at her. Her eyes never leave me and the wide open part of them is starting to make me uncomfortable. It's how Aaron looks when he's pinning you down, how he looks when he's imparting a sermon with his fists, when he's preaching you into a hole you might never come out of.

It's a mad look, I realize.

I try to check the thought but Jane don't give no sign she heard.

"I gotta go," I say again. "Thank you kindly for the food and the poultry but I gotta go."

"Yoo can't go off in these woods here, nosirree," she says, still staring, still not blinking. "Them's dangerous woods, them is."

"What do you mean, dangerous?" I push myself away from her a little.

"Settlements up the way," she says, her eyes even wider and a smile now, like she can't wait to tell me. "Crazy as anything. Noise sent 'em wild. Hear tell of one where everyone wears masks so's no one kin see their faces. There's another where no one don't do nothing but sing all day long they gone so crazy. And one where everyone's walls are made a glass and no one wears no clothes cuz no one's got secrets in Noise, do they?"

She's closer to me now. I can smell her breath, which is worse than the rag, and I feel the silence behind all these words. How can that be so? How can silence contain so much racket?

"People can keep secrets in Noise," I say. "People can keep all kindsa secrets."

"Leave a boy alone," Wilf says from his seat.

Jane's face goes slack. "Sorry," she says, a little grudgingly.

I raise up a little, feeling the benefit of food in my belly whatever the stinking rag may or may not be doing.

We've pulled closer to the rest of the caravan, close enough for me to see the backs of a few heads and hear more closely the Noise of men chattering up and down and the silence of women twixt them, like stones in a creek.

Every now and then one of 'em, usually a man, glances back at us, and I feel like they're seeking me out, seeing what I'm made of.

"I need to find her," I say.

"Yer girl?" Jane asks.

"Yeah," I say. "Thank you, but I need to go."

"But yer fever! And the other settlements!"

"I'll take my chances." I untie the dirty rag. "C'mon, Manchee."

"Yoo can't go," Jane says, eyes wider than ever, worry on her face. "The army—"

"I'll worry about the army." I pull myself up, readying to jump down off the cart. I'm still pretty unsteady so I have to take a cloudy breath or two before I do anything.

"But they'll get yoo!" Jane says, her voice rising. "Yer from Prentisstown—"

I look up, sharp.

Jane slaps a hand over her mouth.

"*Wife!*" Wilf yells, turning his head round from the front of the cart.

"Ah didn't mean it," she whispers to me.

But it's too late. Already the word is bouncing up and down the caravan in a way that's become too familiar, not just the word, but what pins it to me, what everyone knows or thinks they know about me, already faces turning round to look deeper at the last cart in the caravan, oxen and horses drawing to a stop as people turn more fully to examine us.

Faces and Noise aimed right back down the road at us.

"Who yoo got back there, Wilf?" a man's voice says from just one cart up.

"Feverish boy," Wilf shouts back. "Crazy with sickness. Don't know what he's sayin."

"Yoo entirely sure about that?"

"Yessir," Wilf says. "Sick boy."

"Bring him out," a woman's voice calls. "Let's see him."

"What if he's a spy?" another woman's voice calls, rising in pitch. "Leadin the army right to us?"

"We don't want no spies!" cries a different man.

"He's Ben," Wilf says. "He's from Farbranch. Got nightmares of cursed town army killin what he loves. I vouch for him."

No one shouts nothing for a minute but the Noise of the men buzzes in the air like a swarm. Everyone's face is still on us. I try to make my own look more feverish and put the invasion of Farbranch first and foremost. It ain't hard and it makes my heart sick.

And there's a long moment where nobody says nothing and it's as loud as a screaming crowd.

And then it's enough.

Slowly but surely the oxen and horses start moving forward again, pulling away from us, people still looking back but at least getting farther away. Wilf snaps the reins on his oxen but keeps them slower than the rest, letting a distance open between us and everyone else.

"Ah'm *sorry*," Jane says again, breathless. "Wilf told me not to say. He told me but—"

"That's okay," I say, just wanting her to stop talking already.

"Ah'm so so sorry."

There's a lurch and Wilf's stopped the cart. He waits till the caravan's off a good distance then hops down and comes back.

"No one lissens to Wilf," he says, maybe with a small smile. "But when they do, they believe him."

"I need to go," I say.

"Yup," he says. "T'ain't safe."

"Ah'm sorry," Jane keeps saying.

I jump off the cart, Manchee following me. Wilf reaches for Viola's bag and holds it open. He looks at Jane, who understands him. She takes an armful of fruits and breads and puts them in the bag, then another armful of dried meats.

"Thanks," I say.

"Hope yoo find her," Wilf says as I close the bag.

"I hope so, too."

With a nod, Wilf goes and reseats himself on the cart and snaps the reins on his oxen.

"Be careful," Jane calls after me, in the loudest whisper you ever heard. "Watch out for the crazies."

I stand for a minute and watch 'em pull away, coughing still, feverish still, but feeling better for the food if not the smell of roots and I'm hoping Manchee can find the trail again and I'm also wondering just exactly what kinda welcome I'm gonna get if I ever do get to Haven.

29

AARON IN A THOUSAND WAYS

IT TAKES A LITTLE WHILE, a horrible little while, for Manchee to find the scent again once we're back in the woods but then he barks, "This way," and we're off again.

He's a good ruddy dog, have I said that?

Night's fully fallen by now and I'm still sweating and I'm still coughing enough to win a contest and my feet ain't made of nothing but blisters and my head's still buzzy with feverish Noise but I've got food in my belly and more in the bag to see me thru a coupla days and so all that matters is still ahead of us.

"Can you smell her, Manchee?" I ask, as we balance on a log across a stream. "Is she still alive?"

"Smell Viola," he barks, jumping off the other side. "Viola fear."

Which hits me a little and I quicken my step. Another midnight (twenty-two days? twenty-one?) and my flashlight battery gives out. I take out Viola's but it's the last we got. More hills and steeper, too, as we go on thru the night, harder to climb up, dangerous to climb down but we go and go and go, Manchee sniffing away, eating Wilf's dried meat as we stumble forward, me coughing away, taking the shortest rests possible, usually bent double against trees, and the sun starts coming up over a hill so it's like we're walking up into the sunrise.

And it's when light hits us full that I see the world start to shimmer.

I stop, hanging on to a fern to keep my balance against the steepness of the hill. Everything's woozy for a second and I close my eyes but it don't help as there's just a wash of colors and sparkles behind my eyelids and my body is jellylike and waving in the breeze that I can feel coming off the hilltop and when it passes, it don't really pass altogether, the world keeping its weird brightness, like I've woke up in a dream.

"Todd?" Manchee barks, worry there, no doubt from seeing who knows what in my Noise.

"The fever," I say, coughing again. "I shouldn't've thrown away that filthy rag."

Ain't nothing for it.

I take the last of the pain tabs from my medipak and we gotta keep going.

We get to the top of the hill and for a minute all the other hills in front of us and the river and the road down below rumble up and down like they're on a blanket someone's shaking and I do my best to blink it away till it calms down enough for me to keep walking. Manchee whines by my feet. I nearly tip over when I try to scratch him so instead I focus on getting down the hill without falling.

I think again of the knife at my back, of the blood that was on it when it went into my body and my blood mixed with the Spackle's and who knows what now spinning round my insides since Aaron stabbed me.

"I wonder if he knew," I say, to Manchee, to myself, to no one, as we get to the bottom of the hill and I lean against a tree to make the world stop moving. "I wonder if he killed me slow."

"Course I did," Aaron says, leaning out from behind the tree.

I yell out and fall back away from him and fling my arms in front of me trying to slap him away and I hit the ground on my butt and start scampering back before I look up–

And he's gone.

Manchee's got his head cocked at me. "Todd?"

"Aaron," I say, my heart thundering, my breath catching and turning into meatier and meatier coughs.

Manchee sniffs the air again, sniffs the ground around him. "Trail this way," he barks, shifting from foot to foot.

I look around me, coughing away, the world spotty and wavy.

No sign of him, no Noise other than mine, no silence of Viola. I close my eyes again.

I am Todd Hewitt, I think against the swirling. *I am Todd Hewitt.*

Keeping my eyes shut, I feel for the water bottle and take a swig and I tear a piece from Wilf's bread and chew it down. Only then do I open my eyes again.

Nothing.

Nothing but woods and another hill to climb.

And sunlight that shimmers.

The morning passes and at the bottom of yet another hill there's yet another creek. I refill the water bottles and take a few drinks from the cold water with my hands.

I feel *bad,* ain't no two ways about it, my skin's tingling and sometimes I'm shivering and sometimes I'm sweating and sometimes my head weighs a million pounds. I lean into the creek and splash myself with the cold.

I sit up and Aaron is reflected in the water.

"Killer," he says, a smile across his torn-up face.

I jump back, scrabbling away for my knife (and feeling the pain shoot thru my shoulders again) but when I look up he ain't there and Manchee's made no sign of stopping his fish chasing.

"I'm coming to find you," I say to the air, air that's started to move more and more with the wind.

Manchee's head pops up from the water. "Todd?"

"I'll find you if it's the last thing I do."

"Killer," I hear again, whispered along the wind.

I lay for a second, breathing heavy, coughing but keeping my eyes peeled. I go back to the creek and I splash so much cold water on myself it makes my chest hurt.

I pick myself up and we carry on.

The cold water does the trick for a little while and we manage a few more hills as the sun gets to midday in the sky with minimal shimmer. When things do start to wobble again I stop us and we eat.

"Killer," I hear from the bushes around us and then again from another part of the forest. *"Killer."* And again from somewhere else. *"Killer."*

I don't look up, just eat my food.

It's just the Spackle blood, I tell myself. Just the fever and the sickness and that's all.

"Is that all?" Aaron says from across the clearing. *"If that's all I am, why you chasing me so bad?"*

He's wearing his Sunday robes and his face is all healed up like he's back in Prentisstown, his hands clasped in front of him like he's ready to lead us in prayer and he's glowing in the sun and he's smiling down at me.

The smiling fist I remember so well.

"The Noise binds us all, young Todd," he says, his voice slithering and shiny like a snake. *"If one of us falls, we all fall."*

"You ain't here," I say, clenching my teeth.

"Here, Todd," Manchee barks.

"Ain't I?" Aaron says and disappears in a shimmer.

My brain knows this Aaron ain't real but my heart don't care and it's beating in my chest like a race. It's hard to catch my breath and I waste more time waiting just to be able to stand up and move on into the afternoon.

The food's helping, God bless Wilf and his crazy wife, but sometimes we can't go much faster than a stumble. I start to see Aaron outta the corner of my eye pretty much all the time, hiding behind trees, leaning against rocks, standing on top of woodfall, but I just turn my head away and keep stumbling.

And then, from a hilltop, I see the road cross the river again down below. The landscape's moving in a way that turns my stomach but I can definitely see a bridge down there, taking the road to the other side so there's nothing now twixt me and the river.

I wonder for a minute about that other fork we never took back in Farbranch. I wonder where *that* road is in the middle of all this wilderness. I look from the hilltop to my left but there's just woods as far as I can see and more hills that move like hills shouldn't. I have to close my eyes for a minute.

We make our way down, too slow, too *slow,* the scent taking us close to the road and toward the bridge, a high rickety one with rails. Water's gathered where the road turns into it, filling it with puddles and muck.

"Did he cross the river, Manchee?" I put my hands on my knees to catch my breath and cough.

Manchee sniffs the ground like a maniac, crossing the road, recrossing it, going to the bridge and back to where we stand. "Wilf smell," he barks. "Cart smell."

"I can see the tracks," I say, rubbing my face with my hands. "What about Viola?"

"Viola!" Manchee barks. "This way."

He heads away from the road, keeping to this side of the river and following it. "Good dog," I say twixt raggedy breaths. "Good dog."

I follow him thru branches and bushes, the river rushing closer to my right than it's been in days.

And I step right into a settlement.

I stand up straight and cough in surprise.

It's been destroyed.

The buildings, eight or ten of them, are charcoal and ash and there ain't a whisper of Noise nowhere.

For a second I think the army's been here but then I see plants growing up in the burned-out buildings and no smoke is rising from any fire and the wind just blows thru it like only the dead live here. I look round and there's a few decrepit docks on the river, just down from the bridge, a lonely old boat knocking against one in the current and a few more half-sunk boats piled halfway up the riverbank along from what may have been a mill before it became a pile of burned wood.

It's cold and it's long dead and here's another place on New World that never made it to subdivided farming.

And I turn back round and in the center of it stands Aaron.

His face is back to how it was when the crocs tore it open, peeled half away, his tongue lolling out the side of the gash in his cheek.

And he's still smiling.

"Join us, young Todd," he says. *"The church is always open."*

"I'll kill you," I say, the wind stealing my words but I know he can hear me cuz I can hear every last thing he's saying.

"You won't," he says, stepping forward, his fists clenched by his sides. *"Cuz I says you ain't a real killer, Todd Hewitt."*

"Try me," I say, my voice sounding strange and metallic.

He smiles again, his teeth poking out the side of his face, and in a wash of shimmer he's right in front of me. He puts his cut-up hands to the opening of his robe and pulls it apart enough to show his bare chest.

"Here's yer chance, Todd Hewitt, to eat from the Tree of Knowledge." His voice is deep in my head. *"Kill me."*

The wind's making me shiver but I feel hot and sweaty at the same time and I can't get no more than a third of a breath down my lungs and my head is starting to ache in a way that food ain't helping and whenever I look anywhere fast everything I see has to slide into place to catch up.

I clench my teeth.

I'm probably dying.

But he's going first.

I reach behind me, ignoring the pain twixt my shoulders, and I grab the knife outta the sheath. I hold it in front of me. It's shiny with fresh blood and glinting in sunlight even tho I'm standing in shadow.

Aaron pulls his smile wider than his face can really go and he pushes his chest out to me.

I raise the knife.

"Todd?" Manchee barks. "Knife, Todd?"

"Go ahead, Todd," Aaron says and I swear I smell the dankness of him. *"Cross over from innocence to sin. If you can."*

"I've done it," I say. "I've already killed."

"Killing a Spackle ain't killing a man," he says, grinning away at how stupid I am. *"Spackles are devils put here to test us. Killing one's like killing a turtle."* He widens his eyes. *"'Cept you can't do that neither now, can you?"*

I grip the knife hard and I make a snarling sound and the world wavers.

But the knife still ain't falling.

There's a bubbling sound and gooey blood pours outta the gash in Aaron's face and I realize he's laughing.

"It took a long, long time for her to die," he whispers.

And I call out from the pain—

And I raise the knife higher—

And I aim it at his heart—

And he's still smiling—

And I bring the knife down—

And stab it right into Viola's chest.

"No!" I say, in the second that it's too late.

She looks up from the knife and right at me. Her face is filled with pain and confused Noise spills from her just like the Spackle that I—

(That I killed.)

And she looks at me with tears in her eyes and she opens her mouth and she says, *"Killer."*

And as I reach out for her, she's gone in a shimmer.

And the knife, clean of all blood, is still in my hand.

I fall onto my knees and then pitch forward and lie on the ground in the burned-out settlement, breathing and coughing and weeping and wailing as the world melts around me so bad I don't feel like it's even solid no more.

I can't kill him.

I want to. I want to *so bad.* But I can't.

Cuz it ain't me and cuz I lose her.

I can't. I can't, I can't, I can't.

I give in to the shimmering and I disappear for a while.

It's good old Manchee, the friend who's proved truest, who wakes me up with licks to my face and a worried murmured word coming thru his Noise and his whines.

"Aaron," he's yelping, quiet and tense. "Aaron."

"Buzz off, Manchee."

"Aaron," he whimpers, licking away.

"He ain't really there," I say, trying to sit up. "It's just something—"

It's just something Manchee can't see.

"Where is he?" I say, getting up too fast, causing everything to swirl bright pink and orange. I reel back from what's waiting for me.

There are a hundred Aarons at a hundred different places, all standing round me. There are Violas, too, frightened and looking to me for help, and Spackles with my knife sticking outta their chests and there're all talking at once, all talking to me in a roar of voices.

"Coward," they're saying. All of 'em. "Coward" over and over again.

But I wouldn't be a Prentisstown boy if I couldn't ignore Noise.

"Where, Manchee?" I say, getting to my feet, trying not to see how everything's pitching and sliding.

"This way," he barks. "Down the river."

I follow him thru the burned-out settlement.

He leads me past what must've been the church and I don't look at it as we go by and he runs up a small bluff and the wind's getting howlier and the trees are bending and I think it's not just how I'm seeing 'em and Manchee has to bark louder to let me know.

Coward Coward Coward COWARD Coward Coward Coward Coward Coward Coward Coward Coward Coward war Coward Coward

"Aaron!" he barks, sticking his nose in the air. "Upwind."

Coward Coward COWARD Cow oward Coward Coward Coward Coward Coward Coward Coward Coward Coward Coward Cowa Coward

Thru the trees on the little bluff I can see downriver. I can see a thousand Violas looking frightened of me.

Coward Coward Coward Cow COWARD Coward Coward Coward Cow Coward Coward oward oward Coward Cow oward Coward Coward oward Coward COWA oward Coward

I can see a thousand Spackle with my knife killing 'em.

Coward Coward oward Coward oward Coward oward Coward Coward Coward oward Coward

I can see a thousand Aarons looking back at me and calling me "coward" with the worst smile you ever seen.

Coward Coward Coward Coward Coward
Coward Coward Coward Coward Coward
oward Coward Coward Coward Coward
oward

And beyond 'em, in a camp by the side of the river, I see an Aaron who ain't looking back at me at all.

COWARD Coward Coward Coward
Coward Coward Coward Coward Coward
oward Coward Coward Coward
Coward

I see an Aaron kneeling down in prayer.

Coward Coward Coward Coward
Coward Coward Coward Coward
Coward Coward Coward Coward Coward

And I see Viola on the ground in front of him.

Coward Coward Coward Coward
Coward Coward Coward Coward Coward
Coward

Coward "Aaron," Manchee barks. Coward Coward
Coward Coward Coward Coward
Coward Coward Coward Coward

"Aaron," I say.
Coward.

10

A BOY CALLED TODD

WHAT ARE WE GONNA DO?" says the boy, creeping up to my shoulder.

I stumble back down from the bluff, elbowing my way thru crowds all calling me coward, and I get to the riverbank and I plunge my head straight in. I raise my head from the cold river water and let it splash down my back. Now the cold is making me shake violently but it's also calming the world down. I know it won't last, I know the fever and spack blood infection will win in the end, but for now, I'm gonna need to see as clearly as possible.

"How are we gonna get to them?" the boy asks, moving round to my other side. "He'll hear our Noise."

The shivering makes me cough, everything makes me cough, and I spit out handfuls of green goo from my lungs, but then I hold my breath and plunge in my head again.

The cold of the water feels like a vise but I hold it there, hearing the bubbling of the water rushing by and the wordless barks of a worried Manchee hopping around my feet. I can feel the bandage on my head detach and wash away in the current. I think of Manchee wriggling the bandage off his tail in a different part of the river and I forget and I laugh underwater.

I lift my head up, choking and gasping and coughing more.

I open my eyes. The world shines like it shouldn't and there are all kindsa stars out even tho the sun is still up but at least the ground has stopped floating and all the excess Aarons and Violas and Spackles are gone.

"Can we really do it alone?" asks the boy.

"Ain't no choice," I say to myself.

And I turn to look at him.

He's got a brown shirt like mine, no scars on his head, a book in one hand, and a knife in the other. I'm shaking from the cold still and it's all I can do to stand but I breathe and cough and shake and look at him.

"C'mon, Manchee," I say and I head back across the burned-out settlement, back to the bluff. Just walking is tough, like the ground could cave away at any minute, cuz I weigh more than a mountain but less than a feather, but I'm walking, I'm still walking, I'm keeping the bluff in sight, I'm reaching it, I'm taking the first steps up it, I'm taking the next steps, I'm grabbing on to branches to pull myself along, I'm reaching the top, I'm leaning against a tree at the top, and I'm looking out.

"Is it really him?" says the boy behind my ear.

I squint out across the trees, tracing the way down the river.

And there's still a campsite, still at the river's edge, so far away they're just specks against other specks. I still have Viola's bag around my shoulders and I reach for her binocs, holding 'em up to my eyes but shaking so much it's hard to get a clear image. They're far enough away that the wind's covering up his Noise but I'm sure I feel her silence out there.

I'm sure of it.

"Aaron," Manchee says. "Viola."

So I know it's not a shimmer and in the shakiness I can just about catch him still kneeling, praying some prayer, and Viola laid out on the ground in front of him.

I don't know what's happening. I don't know what he's doing.

But it's really them.

All this walking and stumbling and coughing and dying and it's really, really them, by God it's really them.

I may not be too late and it's only how my chest rises and my throat grips that makes me realize all along I've thought I *was* too late.

But I'm not.

I lean down again and (shut up) I cry, I cry, I'm *crying* but it has to pass cuz I have to figure it out, I have to figure it out, it's down to me, there's only me, I have to find a way, I have to save her, I have to save—

"What are we gonna do?" the boy asks again, standing a little ways away, book still in one hand, knife in the other.

I put my palms into my eyes and rub hard, trying to think straight, trying to concentrate, trying not to listen—

"What if this is the sacrifice?" says the boy.

I look up. "What sacrifice?"

"The sacrifice you saw in his Noise," he says. *"The sacrifice of—"*

"Why would he do it here?" I say. "Why would he come all this way and stop in the middle of a stupid forest and do it here?"

The boy's expression doesn't change. *"Maybe he has to,"* he says, *"before she dies."*

I step forward and have to catch my balance. "Dies of what?" I say, my voice snappy, my head aching and buzzy again.

"Fear," says the boy, taking a step backwards. *"Disappointment."*

I turn away. "I ain't listening to this."

"Listening, Todd?" Manchee barks. "Viola, Todd. This way."

I lean back again against the tree. I've got to think. I've got to ruddy *think.*

"We can't approach," I say, my voice thick. "He'll hear us coming."

"He'll kill her if he hears us," says the boy.

"Ain't talking to you." I cough up more gunk, which makes my head spin, which makes me cough more. "Talking to my dog," I finally choke out.

"Manchee," Manchee says, licking my hand.

"And I can't kill him," I say.

"You can't kill him," says the boy.

"Even if I want to."

"Even if he deserves it."

"And so there has to be another way."

"If she's not too scared to see you."

I look at him again. Still there, still book and knife and rucksack.

"You need to leave," I say. "You need to go away from me and never come back."

"Yer probably too late to save her."

"Yer of no use to me at all," I say, raising my voice.

"But I'm a killer," he says and the knife has blood on it.

I close my eyes and grit my teeth. "You stay behind," I say. "You stay *behind."*

"Manchee?" Manchee barks.

I open my eyes. The boy isn't there. "Not you, Manchee," I say, reaching out and rubbing his ears.

Then I regard him, Manchee. "Not you," I say again.

And I'm thinking. In the clouds and the swirls and the shimmers and the lights and the ache and the buzz and the shaking and the coughing, I'm thinking.

And I'm thinking.

I rub the ears of my dog, my stupid goddam ruddy *great* dog that I never wanted but who hung around anyway and who followed me thru the swamp and who bit Aaron when he was trying to choke me and who found Viola when she was lost and who's licking my hand with his little pink tongue and whose eye is still mostly squinted shut from where Mr. Prentiss Jr. kicked him and whose tail is way way shorter from when Matthew Lyle cut it off when my dog – *my dog* – went after a man with a machete to save me and who's right there when I need pulling back from the darkness I fall into and who tells me who I am whenever I forget.

"Todd," he murmurs, rubbing his face into my hand and thumping his back leg against the ground.

"I got an idea," I say.

"What if it don't work?" says the boy from behind the tree.

I ignore him and I pick up the binocs again. Shaking still, I find Aaron's campsite one more time and look at the area around it. They're near the river's edge and there's a forked tree just this side of them along the riverbank, bleached and leafless, like it maybe once got struck by lightning.

It'll do.

I put down the binocs and take Manchee's head in both hands. "We're gonna save her," I say, right to my dog. "Both of us."

"Save her, Todd," he barks, wagging his little stump.

"It won't work," says the boy, still outta sight.

"Then you should stay behind," I say to the air, riding thru a cough while I send pictures of Noise to my dog to tell him what he needs to do. "It's simple, Manchee. Run and run."

"Run and run!" he barks.

"Good boy." I rub his ears again. "Good boy."

I pull myself to my feet and half-stumble, half-slide my way back down the little bluff into the burned-out settlement. There's a thump in my head now, like I can hear my poisoned blood pumping, and everything in the world throbs with it. If I squeeze my eyes nearly shut, the swirling lights ain't so bad and everything sort of stays in its place.

The first thing I need is a stick. Manchee and I tear thru the burned-out buildings, looking for one the right size. Pretty much everything is black and crumbly but that suits me fine.

"Thith one, Thawd?" Manchee says, using his mouth to pull one about half the length of himself out from under what looks like a burned-up pile of stacked chairs. What happened in this place?

"Perfect." I take it from him.

"This won't work," the boy says, hiding in a dark corner. I can see the glint of the knife in one of his hands. *"You won't save her."*

"I will." I break off some larger splinters from the stick. Only one end is blackened charcoal but that's exactly what I want. "Can you carry this?" I say to Manchee, holding it out.

He takes it in his mouth, tosses it a little to get it comfortable, but then it rests just fine. "Yeth!" he barks.

"Great." I stand up straight and nearly fall over. "Now we need a fire."

"*You can't make a fire,*" the boy says, already outside waiting for us. "*Her fire-making box is broken.*"

"You don't know nothing," I say, not looking at him. "Ben taught me."

"*Ben's dead,*" says the boy.

"Early one mor-r-ning," I sing, loud and clear, making the whirly shapes of the world go spangly and weird, but I keep on singing. "Just as the sun was ri-i-sing."

"*Yer not strong enough to make a fire.*"

"I heard a maiden call from the val-l-ley below." I find a long, flat piece of wood and use the knife to carve a little hollow in it. "Oh, don't dece-e-ive me." I carve a rounded end on another smaller stick. "Oh, never le-e-ave me."

"*How could you use a poor maiden so?*" the boy finishes.

I ignore him. I put the rounded end of the stick into the little hollow and start spinning it twixt my hands, pressing hard into the wood. The rhythm of it matches the thumping in my head and I start to see me in the woods with Ben, him and me racing to see who could get the first smoke. He always won and half the time I could never get any sorta fire at all. But there were times.

There were times.

"C'mon," I say to myself. I'm sweating and coughing and woozy but I'm making my hands keep on spinning. Manchee's barking at the wood to try to help it along.

And then a little finger of smoke rises from the hollow.

"Ha!" I cry out. I protect it from the wind with my hand and blow on it to make it catch. I use some dried moss as kindling and when the first little flame shoots out it's as near as I've come to joy since I don't know when. I throw some small sticks on it, wait for them to catch, too, then some larger ones, and pretty soon there's a real fire burning in front of me. A real one.

I leave it to burn for a minute. I'm counting on us being downwind to keep the smoke from Aaron.

And I'm counting on that wind for other reasons, too.

I lurch my way toward the riverbank, using tree trunks to keep me upright, till I make it to the dock. "C'mon, c'mon," I say under my breath as I steady myself to walk down it. It creaks under my feet and once I nearly pitch over into the river but I do finally make it to the boat still tied there.

"*It'll sink,*" says the boy, standing knee-high in the river.

I hop in the little boat and after a lot of wobbling and coughing, I stand up in it. It's rickety and narrow and warping.

But it floats.

"*You don't know how to steer a boat.*"

I get out and cross the dock and make my way back to the settlement and search around till I find a piece of wood flat enough to use as an oar.

And that's all I need.

We're ready.

The boy's standing there, holding the things of mine in each hand, rucksack on his back, no real nothing on his face, no Noise that I can hear.

I stare him down. He don't say nothing.

"Manchee?" I call but he's already at my feet.

"Here, Todd!"

"Good boy." We go to the fire. I take the stick he found and put the already burned end into it. After a minute, the end is red hot and smoky, with flames catching on the new wood. "You sure you can hold this?" I say.

He takes the nonburning end into his mouth and there he is, best ruddy dog in the universe, ready to carry fire to the enemy.

"Ready, friend?" I say.

"Weddy, Thawd!" he says, mouth full, tail wagging so fast I see it as a blur.

"*He'll kill Manchee,*" the boy says.

I stand, world spinning and shining, my body barely my own, my lungs coughing up bits of themselves, my head thumping, my legs shaking, my blood boiling, but I stand.

I ruddy well stand.

"I am Todd Hewitt," I say to the boy. "And I am leaving you here."

"*You can't never do that,*" he says, but I'm already turning to Manchee and saying "Go on, boy," and he takes off back up the bluff and down the other side, burning stick in his mouth, and I count to a hundred, loud, so's I can't hear no one say nothing and then I make myself count to a hundred again and that's enough and I lurch as fast as I can back to the dock and the boat and I get myself in and I take the oar onto my lap and I use the knife to cut away the last of the raggedy rope tying the little boat in place.

"You can't never leave me behind," the boy says, standing on the dock, book in one hand, knife in the other.

"Watch me," I say and he gets smaller and smaller in the shimmering and fading light as the boat pulls away from the dock and starts making its way downstream.

Toward Aaron.

Toward Viola.

Toward whatever waits for me down the river.

31

THE WICKED ARE PUNISHED

THERE'S BOATS IN PRENTISSTOWN but no one's used 'em since I can remember. We got the river, sure, this same one that's sloshing me back and forth, but our stretch is rocky and fast and when it does slow down and spread out, the only peaceful area is a marsh full of crocs. After that, it's all wooded swamp. So I ain't never been on a boat and even tho it looks like it should be easy to steer one down a river, it ain't.

The one bit of luck I got is that the river here is pretty calm, despite some splashing from the wind. The boat drifts out into the current and is taken and moves its way downriver whether I do anything or not so I can put all my coughing energy into trying to keep the boat from spinning around as it goes.

It takes a minute or two before I'm successful.

"Dammit," I say under my breath. "Effing thing."

But after some splashing with the oar (and one or two full spins, shut up) I'm figuring out how to keep it more or less pointed the right way and when I look up, I realize I'm probably already halfway there.

I swallow and shake and cough.

This is the plan. It's probably not a very good one but it's all that my shimmering, flickering brain's gonna let me have.

Manchee'll take the burning stick upwind of Aaron and drop it somewhere to catch fire and make Aaron think I've lit up my own campsite. Then Manchee'll run back to *Aaron's* campsite, barking up a storm, pretending he's trying to tell me he's found Aaron. This is simple since all he has to do is bark my name, which is what he does all the time anyway.

Aaron'll chase him. Aaron'll try to kill him. Manchee'll be faster (Run and run, Manchee, run and run). Aaron'll see the smoke. Aaron, who fears me not one little bit, will go off into the woods toward the smoke to finish me off once and for all.

I'll float downstream, come upon his campsite from the riverside while he's out in the woods looking for me, and I'll rescue Viola. I'll pick up Manchee there, too, when he circles back round ahead of a chasing Aaron (run and run).

Yeah, okay, that's the plan.

I know.

I *know*, but if it don't work, then I'll have to kill him.

And if it comes to that, it can't matter what I become and it can't matter what Viola thinks.

It can't.

It'll have to be done and so I'll have to do it.

I take out the knife.

The blade still has dried blood smeared on it here and there, my blood, Spackle blood, but the rest of it still shines, shimmering and flickering, flickering and shimmering. The tip of it juts out and up like an ugly thumb and the serrashuns along one side spring up like gnashing teeth and the blade edge pulses like a vein full of blood.

The knife is alive.

As long as I hold it, as long as I use it, the knife lives, lives in order to take life, but it has to be commanded, it has to have me to tell it to kill, and it wants to, it wants to plunge and thrust and cut and stab and gouge, but I have to want it to as well, my will has to join with its will.

I'm the one who allows it and I'm the one responsible.

But the knife wanting it makes it easier.

If it comes to it, will I fail?

"*No,*" whispers the knife.

"*Yes,*" whispers the wind down the river.

A drop of sweat from my forehead splashes on the blade and the knife is just a knife again, just a tool, just a piece of metal in my hand.

Just a knife.

I lay it on the floor of the boat.

I'm shaking again. I cough up more goo. I look up and around me, ignoring the waviness of the world and letting the wind cool me down. The river's starting to bend and I keep on floating down it.

Here it comes, I think. Ain't no stopping it.

I look up and over the trees to my left.

My teeth are chattering.

I don't see no smoke yet.

C'mon, boy, it's the next thing that has to happen.

And no smoke.

And no smoke.

And the river's bending more.

C'mon, Manchee.

And no smoke.

And *chatter, chatter, chatter* go my teeth. I huddle my arms to myself—

And *smoke*! The first small puffs of it, coming up like cotton balls farther down the river.

Good dog, I think, holding my teeth together. *Good dog*.

The boat's tending slightly midriver so I row as best I can and guide it back to the river's edge.

I'm shaking so bad I can barely hang on to the oar.

The river's bending more.

And there's the forked tree, the tree struck by lightning, coming up on my left.

The sign that I'm almost there.

Aaron'll be just beyond it.

Here it comes.

I cough and sweat and tremble but I'm not letting go of the oar. I row some more, closer to the edge. If Viola can't run for any reason, I'm gonna have to beach it to go get her.

I keep my Noise as blank as I can but the world's closing up in folds of light and shimmer so there's no chance of that. I'll just have to hope the wind's loud enough and that Manchee—

"Todd! Todd! Todd!" I hear from a distance. My dog, barking my name to lure Aaron away. "Todd! Todd! Todd!"

The wind's keeping me from hearing Aaron's Noise so I don't even know if this is working but I'm moving past the forked tree so there's nothing for it now—

"Todd! Todd!"

C'mon, *c'mon*—

The forked tree passing by—

I crouch down in the boat—

"Todd! Todd!" getting fainter, moving back—

Snappings of branches—

And then I hear "TODD HEWITT!!" roared loud as a lion—

As a lion *moving away*—

"C'mon," I whisper to myself, "c'mon, c'mon, c'mon—"

My clenched fists trembling around the oar and—

Round the bend and—

Past the tree and—

The campsite comes and—

There she is.

There she is.

Aaron's gone and there she is.

Lying on the ground in the middle of his campsite.

Not moving.

My heart ratchets up and I cough without even noticing and I say, "Please, please, please," under my breath and I paddle the board furiously and get the boat closer and closer to the river's edge and I stand and leap out into the water and I fall on my rump but I still catch the front of the boat in my hands and "please, please, please" and I get up and I drag the boat far enough up the riverbank and I let go and I run and stumble and run to Viola, Viola, Viola—

"Please," I say as I run, my chest clenching and coughing and hurting, *"Please."*

I get to her and there she is. Her eyes are closed and her mouth is open a little and I put my head to her chest, shutting out the buzz of my Noise and the shouting of the wind and the barking and yelling versions of my name coming outta the woods around me.

"Please," I whisper.

And *thump, thump.*

She's alive.

"Viola," I whisper fiercely. I'm starting to see little flashing spots before my eyes but I ignore them. "Viola!"

I shake her shoulders and take her face in my hand and shake that, too.

"Wake up," I whisper. "Wake up, wake up, wake up!"

I can't carry her. I'm too shaky and lopsided and weak.

But I'll ruddy well carry her if I have to.

"Todd! Todd! Todd!" I hear Manchee barking from deep in the woods.

"Todd Hewitt!" I hear Aaron yell as he chases my dog.

And then, from below me, I hear, "Todd?"

"Viola?" I say and my throat is clenching and my eyes are blurring.

But she's looking back at me.

"You don't look too good," she says, her voice slurring and her eyes sleepy. I notice some bruising underneath her eyes and my stomach clenches in anger.

"Ya gotta get up," I whisper.

"He drugged . . ." she says, closing her eyes.

"Viola?" I say, shaking her again. "He's coming back, Viola. We gotta get outta here."

I can't hear no more barking.

"We gotta go," I say. "Now!"

"I weigh too much," she says, her words melting together.

"Please, Viola," I say and I'm practically *weeping* it. *"Please."*

She blinks open her eyes.

She looks into mine.

"You came for me," she says.

"I did," I say, coughing.

"You came for me," she says again, her face crumpling a little.

Which is when Manchee comes flying outta the bushes, barking my name like his life depends on it.

"TODD! TODD! TODD!" he yelps, running toward us and past. "Aaron! Coming! Aaron!"

Viola lets out a little cry and with a push that nearly knocks me over she gets to her feet and catches me as I fall and we steady ourselves against each other and I manage to point to the boat.

"There!" I say, trying hard to catch my breath.

And we run for it—

Across the campsite—

Toward the boat and the river—

Manchee bounding on ahead and clearing the front of the boat with a leap—

Viola stumbling ahead of me—

And we're five—

Four—

Three steps away—

And Aaron comes pounding outta the woods behind us—

His Noise so loud I don't even need to look—

"TODD HEWITT!!"

And Viola's reached the front of the boat and is falling in—

And two steps—

And one—

And I reach it and push with all my strength to get it back into the river—

And "TODD HEWITT!!"

And he's closer—

And the boat don't move—

"I WILL PUNISH THE WICKED!"

And closer still—

And the boat don't move—

And his Noise is hitting me as hard as a punch—

And the boat *moves*—

Step and step and my feet are in the water and the boat's moving—

And I'm falling—

And I don't have the strength to get in the boat—

And I'm falling into the water as the boat moves away—

And Viola grabs my shirt and yanks me up till my head and shoulders are over the front—

"NO, YOU DON'T!" Aaron roars—

And Viola calls out as she pulls me again and my front's in the boat—

And Aaron's in the water—

And he's grabbing my feet—

"No!" Viola screams and grips me harder, pulling with all her strength—

And I'm lifted in the air—

And the boat stops—

And Viola's face is twisted in the effort—

But it's a tug of war which only Aaron's ever gonna win—

And then I hear "TODD!" barked in a voice so ferocious I wonder for a minute if a croc's raised outta the water—

But it's Manchee—

It's Manchee—

It's my dog my dog my dog and he's leaping past Viola and I feel his feet hit my back and leave it again as he launches himself at Aaron with a snarl and a howl and a "TODD!" and Aaron calls out in anger—

And he lets go of my feet.

Viola lurches back but she don't let go and I go tumbling into the boat on top of her.

The lurch pushes us farther out into the river.

The boat is starting to pull away.

My head tips and whirls as I spin round and I have to stay on my hands and knees for balance but I'm up as much as I can and leaning out the boat and I'm calling, "Manchee!"

Aaron's fallen back into the soft sand at the river's edge, his robe getting tangled up in his legs. Manchee's going for his face, all teeth and claws, growls and roars. Aaron tries to shake him off but Manchee gets a bite either side of Aaron's nose and gives his head a twist.

He rips Aaron's nose clean away from his face.

Aaron yells out in pain, blood shooting everywhere.

"Manchee!" I scream. "Hurry, Manchee!"

"Manchee!" Viola yells.

"C'mon, boy!"

And Manchee looks up from Aaron to see me calling him—

And that's where Aaron takes his chance.

"No!" I scream.

He grabs Manchee violently by his scruff, lifting him off the ground and up in one motion.

"Manchee!"

I hear splashing and I'm dimly aware that Viola's got the oar and is trying to stop us going any farther into the river and the world is shimmering and throbbing and—

And Aaron has my dog.

"GET BACK HERE!" Aaron yells, holding Manchee out at arm's length. He's too heavy to be picked up by his scruff and he's yelping from the pain but he can't quite get his head round to bite Aaron's arm.

"Let him go!" I yell.

Aaron lowers his face—

There's blood pouring outta the hole where his nose used to be and tho the gash in his cheek is healed you can still see his teeth and it's this mess that repeats, almost calmly this time, burbling thru the blood and gore, "Come back to me, Todd Hewitt."

"Todd?" Manchee yelps.

Viola's rowing furiously to keep us outta the current but she's weak from the drugs and we're getting farther and farther away. "No," I can hear her saying. "No."

"Let him go!" I scream.

"The girl or the dog, Todd," Aaron calls, still with the calm that's so much scarier than when he was shouting. "The choice is yers."

I reach for the knife and I hold it out in front of me but my head spins too much and I fall and smack my teeth on the boat seat.

"Todd?" Viola says, still rowing against the current, the boat twisting and turning.

I sit up tasting blood and the world waves so much it nearly knocks me over again.

"I'll kill you," I say, but so quietly I might as well be talking to myself.

"Last chance, Todd," Aaron says, no longer sounding so calm.

"Todd?" Manchee's still yelping. "Todd?"

And no—

"I'll kill you," but my voice is a whisper—

And no—

And there ain't no choice—

And the boat's out in the current—

And I look at Viola, still rowing against it, tears dripping off her chin—

She looks back at me—

And there ain't no choice—

"No," she says, her voice choking. "Oh, no, Todd—"

And I put my hand on her arm to stop her rowing.

Aaron's Noise roars up in red and black.

The current takes us.

"I'm sorry!" I cry as the river takes us away, my words ragged things torn from me, my chest pulled so tight I can't barely breathe. "I'm sorry, Manchee!"

"Todd?" he barks, confused and scared and watching me leave him behind. *"Todd?"*

"Manchee!" I scream.

Aaron brings his free hand toward my dog.

"MANCHEE!"

"Todd?"

And Aaron wrenches his arms and there's a CRACK and a scream and a cut-off yelp that tears my heart in two forever and forever.

And the pain is too much it's too much it's too much and my hands are on my head and I'm rearing back and my mouth is open in a never-ending wordless wail of all the blackness that's inside me.

And I fall back into it.

And I know nothing more as the river takes us away and away and away.

PART VI

32

DOWNRIVER

THE SOUND OF WATER.

And bird noise.

Where's my safety? they sing. **Where's my safety?**

Behind it, there's music.

I swear there's music.

Layers of it, flutey and strange and familiar—

And there's light against the darkness, sheets of it, white and yellow.

And warmth.

And softness on my skin.

And a silence there next to me, pulling against me as strong as it ever did.

I open my eyes.

I'm in a bed, under a cover, in a small square room with white walls and sunlight pouring in at least two open windows with the sound of the river rushing by outside and birds flitting in the trees (and music, is that music?) and for a minute it's not just that I don't know where I am, I also don't know *who* I am or what's happened or why there's an ache in my—

I see Viola, curled up asleep on a chair next to the bed, breathing thru her mouth, her hands pressed twixt her thighs.

I'm still too groggy to make my own mouth move and say her name just yet but my Noise must say it loud enough cuz her eyes flutter open and catch mine and she's outta her seat in a flash with her arms wrapped around me and squishing my nose against her collarbone.

"Oh, Jesus, *Todd,*" she says, holding so tight it kinda hurts.

I put one hand on her back and I inhale her scent.

Flowers.

"I thought you were never coming back," she says, squeezing tight. "I thought you were dead."

"Wasn't I?" I croak, trying to remember.

"You were sick," Viola says, sitting back, knees still on my bed. "*Really* sick. Doctor Snow wasn't sure you'd ever wake up and when a doctor admits *that* much—"

"Who's Doctor Snow?" I ask, looking round the little room. "Where are we? Are we in Haven? And what's that music?"

"We're in a settlement called Carbonel Downs," she says. "We floated down the river and—"

She stops cuz she sees me looking at the foot of the bed.

At the space where Manchee ain't.

I remember.

My chest closes up. My throat clenches shut. I can hear him barking in my Noise. "*Todd?*" he's saying, wondering why I'm leaving him behind. "*Todd?*" with an asking mark, just like that, forever asking where I'm going without him.

"He's gone," I say, like I'm saying it to myself.

Viola seems like she's about to say something but when I glance up at her, her eyes are shiny and all she does is nod, which is the right thing, the thing I'd want.

He's gone.

He's gone.

And I don't know what to say about that.

"Is that Noise I hear?" says a loud voice, preceded by its own Noise thru a door opening itself at the foot of the bed. A man enters, a *big* man, tall and broad with glasses that make his eyes bug out and a flip in his hair and a crooked smile and Noise coming at me so filled with relief and joy it's all I can do not to crawl out the window behind me.

"Doctor Snow," Viola says to me, scooting off the bed to make way.

"Pleased to finally meet you, Todd," Doctor Snow says, smiling big and sitting down on the bed and taking a device outta his front shirt pocket. He sticks two ends of it into his ears and places the other end on my chest without asking. "Could you take a deep breath for me?"

I don't do nothing, just look at him.

"I'm checking if your lungs are clear," he says and I realize what it is I'm noticing. His accent's the closest to Viola's I ever heard on New World. "Not exactly the same," he says, "but close."

"He's the one who made you well," Viola says.

I don't say nothing but I take a deep breath.

"Good," Doctor Snow says, placing the end of the device on another part of my chest. "Once more." I breathe in and out. I find that I *can* breathe in and out, all the way down to the bottom of my lungs.

"You were a very sick boy," he says. "I wasn't sure we were going to be able to beat it. You weren't even giving off Noise until yesterday." He looks me in the eye. "Haven't seen that sort of sickness for a long time."

"Yeah, well," I say.

"Haven't heard of a Spackle attack for a *very* long time," he says. I don't say nothing to this, just breathe deep. "That's great, Todd," the doctor says. "Could you take off your shirt, please?"

I look at him, then over to Viola.

"I'll wait outside," she says and out she goes.

I reach behind me to pull my shirt over my head and as I do I realize there's no pain twixt my shoulder blades.

"Took some stitches, that one," Doctor Snow says, moving around behind me. He puts the device against my back.

I flinch. "That's cold."

"She wouldn't leave your side," he says, ignoring me and checking different places for my breath. "Not even to sleep."

"How long I been here?"

"This is the fifth morning."

"Five days?" I say and he barely has a chance to say yes before I'm pulling back the covers and getting outta the bed. "We gotta get outta here," I say, a little unsteady on my feet but standing nonetheless.

Viola leans back in the doorway. "I've been trying to tell them that."

"You're safe here," Doctor Snow says.

"We've heard that before," I say. I look to Viola for support but all she does is stifle a smile and I realize I'm standing there in just a pair of holey and seriously worn-out underpants that ain't covering as much as they should. "Hey!" I say, moving my hands down to the important bits.

"You're safe as you're going to be anywhere," Doctor Snow says behind me, handing me a pair of my pants from a neatly washed pile by the bed. "We were one of the main fronts in the war. We know how to defend ourselves."

"That was Spackle." I turn my back to Viola and shove my legs in the pants. "This is men. A *thousand* men."

"So the rumors say," Doctor Snow says. "Even though it's not actually numerically possible."

"I don't know nothing from numerickly," I say, "but they got guns."

"We have guns."

"And horses."

"We've got horses."

"Do you have men who'll join them?" I say, challenging him.

He don't say nothing to that, which is satisfying. Then again, it ain't satisfying at all. I button up my pants. "We need to go."

"You need to rest," the doctor says.

"We ain't staying and waiting for the army to show up." I turn to include Viola, turn without thinking to the space where my dog'd be waiting for me to include him too.

There's a quiet moment when my Noise fills the room with Manchee, just fills it with him, side to side, barking and barking and needing a poo and barking some more.

And dying.

I don't know what to say about that neither.

(He's gone, he's gone.)

I feel empty. All over empty.

"No one's going to make you do anything you don't want to, Todd," Doctor Snow says gently. "But the eldermen of the village would like to talk to you before you leave us."

I tighten my mouth. "'Bout what?"

"About anything that might help."

"How can I *help*?" I say, grabbing a washed shirt to put on. "The army will come here and kill everyone who don't join it. That's it."

"This is our home, Todd," he says. "We're going to defend it. We have no choice."

"Then count me out—" I start to say.

"Daddy?" we hear.

There's a little boy standing in the doorway next to Viola.

An actual boy.

He's looking up at me, eyes wide open, his Noise a funny, bright, roomy thing and I can hear myself described as *skinny* and *scar* and *sleeping boy* and at the same time there are all kindsa warm thoughts toward his pa with just the word *daddy* repeated over and over again, meaning everything you'd want it to: askings about me, identifying his daddy, telling him he loves him, all in one word, repeated forever.

"Hey, fella," Doctor Snow says. "Jacob, this is Todd. All woke up."

Jacob looks at me solemnly, a finger in his mouth, and gives a little nod. "Goat's not milking," he says quietly.

"She isn't?" Doctor Snow says, standing up. "Well, we'd better go see if we can talk her into it, hadn't we?"

Daddy, daddy, daddy says Jacob's Noise.

"I'll see to the goat," Doctor Snow is saying to me, "and then I'll go round up the rest of the eldermen."

I can't stop staring at Jacob. Who can't stop staring at me.

He's so much closer than the kids I saw at Farbranch.

And he's so *small*.

Was I that small?

Doctor Snow's still talking. "I'll bring the eldermen back here, see if you can't help us." He leans down till I'm looking at him. "And if we can't help you."

His Noise is sincere, truthful. I believe he means what he says. I also believe he's mistaken.

"Maybe," he says, with a smile. "Maybe not. You haven't even seen the place yet. Come on, Jake." He takes his son's hand. "There's food in the kitchen. I'll bet you're starved. Be back within the hour."

I go to the door to watch them leave. Jacob, finger still in his mouth, looks back at me till he and his pa disappear outta the house.

"How old is that?" I ask Viola, still looking down the hallway. "I don't even know how old that is."

"He's four," she says. "He's told me about eight hundred times. Which seems kind of young to be milking goats."

"Not on New World, it ain't," I say. I turn back to her and her hands are on her hips and she's giving me a serious look.

"Come and eat," she says. "We need to talk."

))

CARBONEL DOWNS

SHE LEADS ME TO A KITCHEN as clean and bright as the bedroom. River still rushing by outside, birds still Noisy, music still—

"What *is* that music?" I say, going to the window to look out. Sometimes it seems like I reckernize it but when I listen close, it's voices changing over voices, running around itself.

"It's from loudspeakers up in the main settlement," Viola says, taking a plate of cold meat outta the fridge.

I sit down at the table. "Is there some kinda festival going on?"

"No," she says, in a way that means *just wait*. "Not a festival." She gets out bread and some orange fruit I ain't never seen before and then some red-colored drink that tastes of berries and sugar.

I dig into the food. "Tell me."

"Doctor Snow is a good man," she says, like I need to know this first. "Everything about him is good and kind and he worked so hard to save you, Todd, I mean it."

"Okay. So what's up?"

"That music plays all day and all night," she says, watching me eat. "It's faint here at the house, but in the settlement, you can't hear yourself think."

I pause with a mouthful of bread. "Like the bar."

"What bar?"

"The bar in Prent—" I stop. "Where do they think we're from?"

"Farbranch."

I sigh. "I'll do my best." I take a bite of the fruit. "The bar where I come from played music all the time to try and drown out the Noise."

She nods. "I asked Doctor Snow why they did it here, and he said, 'To keep men's thoughts private.'"

I shrug. "It makes an awful racket, but it kinda makes sense, don't it? One way to deal with the Noise."

"*Men's* thoughts, Todd," she says. "*Men*. And you notice he said he was going to ask the elder*men* to come seek out your advice?"

I get a horrible thought. "Did the women all die here, too?"

"Oh, there's women," she says, fiddling with a butter knife. "They clean and they cook and they make babies and they all live in a big dormitory outside of town where they can't interfere in men's business."

I put down a forkful of meat. "I saw a place like that when I was coming to find you. Men sleeping in one place, women in another."

"Todd," she says, looking at me. "They wouldn't listen to me. Not one thing. Not a word I said about the army. They kept calling me *little girl* and practically patting me on the damn head." She crosses her arms. "The only reason they want to talk to you about it now is because caravans of refugees started showing up on the river road."

"Wilf," I say.

Her eyes scan over me, reading my Noise. "Oh," she says. "No, I haven't seen him."

"Wait a minute." I swallow some more drink. It feels like I haven't drunk anything for years. "How did we get so far ahead of the army? How come if I've been here five days we ain't been overrun yet?"

"We were in that boat for a day and a half," she says, running her nail at something stuck on the table.

"A day and a half," I repeat, thinking about this. "We must've come miles."

"Miles and miles," she says. "I just let us float and float and float. I was too afraid to stop at the places I passed. You wouldn't believe some of the things . . ." She drifts off, shaking her head.

I remember Jane's warnings. "Naked people and glass houses?" I ask.

Viola looks at me strange. "No," she says, curling her lip. "Just poverty. Just horrible, horrible poverty. Some of those places looked like they would have eaten us so I just kept on and on and you got sicker and sicker and then on the second morning I saw Doctor Snow and Jacob out fishing and I could see in his Noise he was a doctor and as weird as this place is about women, it's at least clean."

I look around the clean, clean kitchen. "We can't stay," I say.

"No, we can't." She puts her head in her hands. "I was so worried about you." There's feeling in her voice. "I was so worried about the army coming and nobody *listening* to me." She smacks the table in frustration. "And I was feeling so bad about—"

She stops. Her face creases and she looks away.

"Manchee," I say, out loud, for the first time since—

"I'm so sorry, Todd," she says, her eyes watery.

"Ain't yer fault." I stand up fast, scooting my chair back.

"He would have killed you," she says, "and then he would have killed Manchee just because he could."

"Stop talking about it, please," I say, leaving the kitchen and going back to the bedroom. Viola follows me. "I'll talk to these elder folks," I say, picking up Viola's bag from the floor and stuffing the rest of the washed clothes in it. "And then we'll go. How far are we from Haven, do you know?"

Viola makes a tiny smile. "Two days."

I stand up straight. "We came that far downriver?"

"We came that far."

I whistle quietly to myself. Two days. Just two days. Till whatever there is in Haven.

"Todd?"

"Yeah?" I say, putting her bag round my shoulders.

"Thank you," she says.

"For what?"

"For coming after me."

Everything's gone still.

"Ain't nothing," I say, feeling my face get hot and looking away. She don't say nothing more. "You all right?" I ask, still not looking at her. "From when he took you?"

"I don't really—" she starts to say but we hear a door close and a singsong daddy, daddy, daddy floating down the hall toward us. Jacob hugs the door frame of the room rather than coming in.

"Daddy sent me to fetch you," he says.

"Oh?" I raise my eyebrows. "I'm sposed to come to *them* now, am I?"

Jacob nods, very serious.

"Well, in that case, we're coming," I rearrange the sack and look at Viola. "And then we're going."

"Too right," Viola says and the way she says it makes me glad. We head out into the hallway after Jacob but he stops us at the door.

"Just you," he says, looking at me.

"Just me what?"

Viola crosses her arms. "He means just you to talk to the eldermen."

Jacob nods, again very serious. I look at Viola and back to Jacob. "Well now," I say, squatting down to his level. "Why don't you just go tell yer daddy that both me and Viola will be along in a minute. Okay?"

Jacob opens his mouth. "But he said—"

"I don't really care what he said," I say gently. "Go."

He gives a little gasp and runs out the door.

"I think I'm maybe thru with men telling me what to do," I say and I'm surprised at the weariness in my voice and suddenly I feel like I wanna get back in that bed and sleep for another five days.

"You going to be all right to walk to Haven?" Viola says.

"Try and stop me," I say and she smiles again.

I head on out the front door.

And for a third time I'm expecting Manchee to come bounding out with us.

His absence is so big it's like he's there and all the air goes outta my lungs again and I have to wait and breathe deep and swallow.

"Oh, man," I say to myself.

His last *Todd?* hangs in my Noise like a wound.

That's another thing about Noise. Everything that's ever happened to you just keeps right on talking, for ever and ever.

I see the last of Jacob's dust as he runs on up the trail thru some trees toward the rest of the settlement. I look round. Doctor Snow's house ain't too big but it stretches out to a deck overlooking the river. There's a small dock and a really low bridge connecting the wide path that comes from the center of Carbonel Downs to the river road that goes along on the other side. The road across the river, the one we spent so much time coming down, is almost hidden behind a row of trees as it goes on past the settlement on the final two days toward Haven.

"God," I say. "It's like paradise compared to the rest of New World."

"There's more to paradise than nice buildings," Viola says.

I look round some more. Doctor Snow's got a well-kept front garden on the path to the settlement. Looking up the path, I can see more buildings thru the trees and hear that music playing.

That weird music. Constantly changing to keep you from getting used to it, I guess. It's nothing I reckernize but it's louder out here and I guess on one level you ain't *sposed* to reckernize it but I swear I heard something in it when I was waking up—

"It's almost unbearable in the middle of the settlement," Viola says. "Most of the women don't even bother coming in from the dormitory." She frowns. "Which I guess is the whole point."

"Wilf's wife told me bout a settlement where everyone—"

I stop cuz the music changes.

Except it don't change.

The music from the settlement stays the same, messy and wordy and bending around itself like a monkey.

But there's more.

There's more music than just it.

And it's getting louder.

"Do you hear that?" I say.

I turn.

And turn again. Viola, too.

Trying to figure out what we're hearing.

"Maybe someone's set up another loudspeaker across the river," she says. "Just in case the women were getting any uppity ideas about leaving."

But I ain't listening to her.

"No," I whisper. "No, it can't be."

"What?" Viola says, her voice changing.

"*Shh.*" I listen close again, trying to calm my Noise so I can hear it.

"It's coming from the river," she whispers.

"*Shh,*" I say again, cuz my chest is starting to rise, my Noise starting to buzz too loud to be of any use at all.

Out there, against the rush of the water and the Noise of the bird-song, there's—

"A song," Viola says, real quiet. "Someone's singing."

Someone's singing.

And what they're singing is:

Early one mor-r-ning, just as the sun was ri-i-sing . . .

And my Noise surges louder as I say it.

"Ben."

34

OH NEVER LEAVE ME

I RUN DOWN TO THE RIVER'S EDGE and stop and listen again.

Oh don't deceive me.

"Ben?" I say, trying to shout and whisper at the same time.

Viola comes thumping up behind me. "Not *your* Ben?" she says. "Is it your Ben?"

I shush her with my hand and listen and try to pick away the river and the birds and my own Noise and there, just there under it all—

Oh never leave me.

"Other side of the river," Viola says and takes off across the bridge, feet smacking against the wood. I'm right behind her, passing her, listening and looking and listening and looking and there and there and there—

There in the leafy shrubs on the other side of the water—

It's Ben.

It really is Ben.

He's crouched down behind leafy greenery, hand against a tree trunk, watching me come to him, watching me run across the bridge, and as I near him, his face relaxes and his Noise opens up as wide as his arms and I'm flying into 'em both, leaping off the bridge and into the bushes and nearly knocking him over and my heart is busting open and my Noise is as bright as the whole blue sky and—

And everything's gonna be all right.

Everything's gonna be all right.

Everything's gonna be all right.

It's Ben.

And he's gripping me tight and he's saying, "Todd," and Viola's standing back a ways, letting me greet him, and I'm hugging him and hugging him and it's Ben, oh Christ Almighty, it's Ben, Ben, Ben.

"It's me," he says, laughing a little cuz I'm crushing the air outta his lungs. "Oh, it's good to see you, Todd."

"Ben," I say, leaning back from him and I don't know what to do with my hands so I just grab his shirt front in my fists and shake him in a way that's gotta mean love. "Ben," I say again.

He nods and smiles.

But there's creases round his eyes and already I can see the beginnings of it, so soon it's gotta be right up front in his Noise, and I have to ask, "Cillian?"

He don't say nothing but he shows it to me, Ben running back to a farmhouse already in flames, already burning down, with some of the Mayor's men inside but with Cillian, too, and Ben grieving, grieving still.

"Aw, no," I say, my stomach sinking, tho I'd long guessed it to be true.

But guessing a thing ain't knowing a thing.

Ben nods again, slow and sad, and I notice now that he's dirty and there's blood clotted on his nose and he looks like he ain't eaten for a week but it's still Ben and he can still read me like no other cuz his Noise is already asking me bout Manchee and I'm already showing him and here at last my eyes properly fill and rush over and he takes me in his arms again and I cry for real over the loss of my dog and of Cillian and of the life that was.

"I left him," I say and keep saying, snot-filled and coughing. "I left him."

"I know," he says and I can tell it's true cuz I hear the same words in his Noise. **I left him**, he thinks.

But after only a minute I feel him gently pushing me back and he says, "Listen, Todd, there ain't much time."

"Ain't much time for what?" I sniffle but I see he's looking over at Viola.

"Hi," she says, eyes all alert.

"Hi," Ben says. "You must be her."

"I must be," she says.

"You been taking care of Todd?"

"We've been taking care of each other."

"Good," Ben says, and his Noise goes warm and sad. "Good."

"C'mon," I say, taking his arm and trying to pull him back toward the footbridge. "We can get you something to eat. And there's a doctor—"

But Ben ain't moving. "Can you keep an eye out for us?" he asks Viola. "Let us know if you see anything, anything at all. Either from the settlement or the road."

Viola nods and catches my eye as she steps outta the green and back to the path.

"Things have escalated," Ben says to me, low, serious as a heart attack. "You gotta get to a place called Haven. Fast as you can."

"I *know* that, Ben." I say, "Why do you—?"

"There's an army after you."

"I know that, *too. And* Aaron. But now that yer here we can—"

"I can't come with you," he says.

My mouth hangs open. "What? *Course* you can—"

But he's shaking his head. "You know I can't."

"We can find a way," I say, but already my Noise is whirling, thinking, remembering.

"Prentisstown men ain't welcome anywhere on New World," he says.

I nod. "They ain't too happy bout Prentisstown *boys,* neither."

He takes my arm again. "Has anyone hurt you?"

I look at him quietly. "Lots of people," I say.

He bites his lip and his Noise gets even sadder.

"I looked for you," he says. "Day and night, following the army, getting round it, ahead of it, listening for rumors of a boy and a girl traveling alone. And here you are and yer okay and I knew you would be. I knew it." He sighs and there's so much love and sadness in it I know he's about to say the truth. "But I'm a danger to you in New World." He gestures at the bush we're hiding in, hiding in like thieves. "Yer gonna have to make it the rest of the way alone."

"I ain't alone," I say, without thinking.

He smiles, but it's still sad. "No," he says. "No, yer not, are you?" He looks around us again, peering thru the leaves and over the river to Doctor Snow's house. "Were you sick?" he asks. "I heard yer Noise yesterday morning coming down the river but it was feverish and sleeping. I been waiting here ever since. I was worried something was really wrong."

"I was sick," I say and shame starts to cloud my Noise like a slow fog.

Ben looks at me close again. "What happened, Todd?" he says, gently reading into my Noise like he always could. "What's happened?"

I open up my Noise for him, all of it from the beginning, the crocs that attacked Aaron, the race thru the swamp, Viola's ship, being chased by the Mayor on horseback, the bridge, Hildy and Tam, Farbranch and what happened there, the fork in the road, Wilf and the things that sang *Here,* Mr. Prentiss Jr., and Viola saving me.

And the Spackle.

And what I did.

I can't look at Ben.

"Todd," he says.

I'm still looking at the ground.

"Todd," he says again. "Look at me."

I look up at him. His eyes, blue as ever, catching mine and holding 'em. "We've all made mistakes, Todd. All of us."

"I killed it," I say. I swallow. "I killed *him*. It was a him."

"You were acting on what you knew. You were acting on what you thought best."

"And that *excuses* it?"

But there's something in his Noise. Something off and telling.

"What is it, Ben?"

He lets out a breath. "It's time you knew, Todd," he says. "Time you knew the truth."

There's a snap of branches as Viola comes rushing back to us.

"Horse on the road," she says, outta breath.

We listen. Hoofbeats, down the river road, coming fast. Ben slinks back a little farther into the bushes. We go with him but the horseman is coming so quick he ain't interested in us at all. We hear him thunder by on the road and turn up the bridge that heads straight into Carbonel Downs, hooves clattering on boards and then on dirt till they're swallowed up by the loudspeaker sounds.

"That can't be good news," Viola says.

"It'll be the army," Ben says. "By now they're probably not more than a few hours from here."

"What?" I say, rearing back. Viola jumps, too.

"I told you we don't have much time," Ben says.

"Then we gotta *go!*" I say. "You gotta come with us. We'll tell people—"

"No," he says. "No. You get yerselves to Haven. That's all there is to it. It's yer best chance."

We pelt him with sudden askings.

"Is Haven safe then?" Viola asks. "From an army?"

"Is it true they have a cure for the Noise?" I ask.

"Will they have communicators? Will I be able to contact my ship?"

"Are you sure it's safe? Are you *sure?*"

Ben raises his hands to stop us. "I don't know," he says. "I haven't been there in twenty years."

Viola stands up straight.

"Twenty years?" she says. "Twenty *years?*" Her voice is rising. "Then how can we know what we'll find when we get there? How do we know it's even still *there*?"

I rub my hand across my face and I think it's the emptiness where Manchee used to be that makes me realize, realize what we never wanted to know.

"We don't," I say, only saying the truth. "We never did."

Viola lets out a little sound and her shoulders slump down. "No," she says. "I guess we didn't."

"But there's always hope," Ben says. "You always have to hope."

We both look at him and there must be a word for how we're doing it but I don't know what it is. We're looking at him like he's speaking a foreign language, like he just said he was moving to one of the moons, like he's telling us it's all just been a bad dream and there's candy for everybody.

"There ain't a whole lotta hope out here, Ben," I say.

He shakes his head. "What d'you think's been driving you on? What d'you think's got you this far?"

"Fear," Viola says.

"Desperayshun," I say.

"No," he says, taking us both in. "No, no, no. You've come farther than most people on this planet will in their lifetimes. You've overcome obstacles and dangers and things that should've killed you. You've outrun an army and a madman and deadly illness and seen things most people will never see. How do you think you could have possibly come this far if you didn't have hope?"

Viola and I exchange a glance.

"I see what yer trying to say, Ben—" I start.

"Hope," he says, squeezing my arm on the word. "It's hope. I am looking into yer eyes right now and I am telling you that there's hope for you, hope for you both." He looks up at Viola and back at me. "There's hope waiting for you at the end of the road."

"You don't know that," Viola says and my Noise, as much as I don't want it to, agrees with her.

"No," Ben says, "but I believe it. I believe it for you. And that's why it's hope."

"Ben—"

"Even if you don't believe it," he says, "believe that I do."

"I'd believe it more if you were coming with us," I say.

"He ain't coming?" Viola says, surprised, then corrects herself. "*Isn't* coming?"

Ben looks at her, opens his mouth, and closes it again.

"What's the truth, Ben?" I ask. "What's the truth we need to know?"

Ben takes a long slow breath thru his nose. "Okay," he says.

But then a loud and clear "Todd?" comes calling from across the river.

And that's when we notice the music of Carbonel Downs is competing with the Noise of men now crossing the bridge.

Many men.

That's the other purpose of the music, I guess. So you can't hear men coming.

"Viola?" Doctor Snow is calling. "What are you two doing over there?"

I stand up straight and look over. Doctor Snow is crossing the bridge, little Jacob's hand in his, leading a group of men who look like less friendly versions of himself and they're eyeing us up and they're seeing Ben and seeing me and Viola talking to him.

And their Noise is starting to turn different colors as what they're seeing starts making sense to them.

And I see that some of 'em have rifles.

"Ben?" I say quietly.

"You need to run," he says, under his breath. "You need to run *now*."

"I ain't leaving you. Not again."

"Todd—"

"Too late," Viola says.

Cuz they're on us now, past the end of the bridge and heading toward the bushes where we're not really hiding no more.

Doctor Snow reaches us first. He looks Ben up and down. "And who might this be then?"

And the sound of his Noise ain't happy at all.

15

THE LAW

"THIS IS BEN," I say, trying to raise my Noise to block all the askings coming from the men.

"And who's Ben when he's at home?" Doctor Snow asks, his eyes alert and looking.

"Ben's my pa," I say. Cuz it's true, ain't it? In all that's important. "My father."

"Todd," I hear Ben say behind me, all kindsa feelings in his Noise, but warning most of all.

"Your father?" says a bearded man behind Doctor Snow, his fingers flexing along the stock of his rifle, tho not lifting it.

Not yet.

"You might want to be careful who you start claiming as a parent, Todd," Doctor Snow says slowly, pulling Jacob closer to him.

"You said the boy was from Farbranch," says a third man with a purple birthmark under his eye.

"That's what the girl told us." Doctor Snow looks at Viola. "Didn't you, Vi?"

Viola holds his look but don't say nothing.

"Can't trust the word of a woman," says the beard. "This is a Prentisstown man if I ever saw one."

"Leading the army right to us," says the birthmark.

"The boy is innocent," says Ben and when I turn I can see his hands are in the air. "I'm the one you want."

"Correction," says the beard, his voice angry and getting angrier. "You're the one we *don't* want."

"Hold on a minute, Fergal," Doctor Snow says. "Something's not right here."

"You know the law," says the birthmark.

The law.

Farbranch talked about the law, too.

"I also know these aren't normal circumstances," Doctor Snow says, then turns back to us. "We should at least give them a chance to explain themselves."

I hear Ben take a breath. "Well, I—"

"Not you," the beard interrupts.

"What's the story, Todd?" Doctor Snow says. "And it's become really important you tell us the truth."

I look from Viola to Ben and back again.

Which side of the truth do I tell?

I hear the cock of a rifle. The beard's raised his gun. And so have one or two of the men behind him.

"The longer you wait," the beard says, "the more you look like spies."

"We ain't spies," I say in a hurry.

"The army your girl's been talking about has been spotted marching down the river road," Doctor Snow says. "One of our scouts just reported them as less than an hour away."

"Oh, no," I hear Viola whisper.

"She ain't my girl," I say, low.

"What?" Doctor Snow says.

"What?" Viola says.

"She's her own girl," I say. "She don't belong to anyone."

And does Viola ever *look* at me.

"Whichever," the birthmark says. "We've got a Prentisstown army marching on us and a Prentisstown man hiding in our bushes and a Prentisstown boy who's been in our midst for the last week. Looks mighty fishy if you ask me."

"He was sick," Doctor Snow says. "He was out cold."

"So you say," says the birthmark.

Doctor Snow turns to him real slow. "Are you calling me a liar now, Duncan? Remember, please, that you're talking to the head of the council of eldermen."

"You telling me you're not seeing a plot here, Jackson?" says the birthmark, not backing down and raising his own rifle. "We're sitting ducks. Who knows what they've told their army?" He aims his rifle at Ben. "But we'll be putting an end to that right now."

"We ain't *spies*," I say again. "We're running from the army just as hard as you should be."

And the men look at each other.

In their Noise, I can hear just these thoughts about the army, about running from it instead of defending the town. I can also see anger bubbling, anger at having to make this choice, anger at not knowing the best way to protect their families. And I can see the anger focusing itself, not on the army, not on themselves for being unprepared despite Viola warning 'em for days, not at the world for the state it's in.

They're focusing their anger on Ben.

They're focusing their anger on Prentisstown in the form of one man.

Doctor Snow kneels down to get to Jacob's level. "Hey, fella," he says to his son. "Why don't you run on back to the house now, okay?"

Daddy daddy daddy I hear in Jacob's Noise. "Why, Daddy?" he says, staring at me.

"Well, I'll betcha the goat's getting lonely," Doctor Snow says. "And who wants a lonely goat, huh?"

Jacob looks at his father, back at me and Ben, then to the men around him. "Why is everyone so upset?" he says.

"Oh," Doctor Snow says, "we're just figuring some things out, is all. It'll all be right soon enough. You just run on back home, make sure the goat's okay."

Jacob thinks about this for a second, then says, "Okay, Daddy."

Doctor Snow kisses him on the top of the head and ruffles his hair. Jacob goes running back over the bridge toward Doctor Snow's house. When Doctor Snow turns back to us, a whole raft of pointed guns accompany him.

"You can see how this doesn't look good, Todd," he says, and there's real sadness in his voice.

"He doesn't know," Ben says.

"Shut your hole, murderer!" says the beard, gesturing with his rifle.

Murderer?

"Tell me true," Doctor Snow says to me. "Are you from Prentisstown?"

"He *saved* me from Prentisstown," Viola speaks up. "If it hadn't been for him—"

"Shut up, girl," says the beard.

"Now's not really the time for women to be talking, Vi," Doctor Snow says.

"But—" Viola says, her face getting red.

"Please," Doctor Snow says. Then he looks at Ben. "What have you told your army? How many men we have? What our fortifications are like—"

"I've been *running* from the army," Ben says, hands still in the air. "Look at me. Do I look like a well-tended soldier? I haven't told them anything. I've been on the run, looking for my . . ." He pauses and I know the reason. "For my son," he says.

"You did this knowing the law?" Doctor Snow asks.

"I know the law," Ben says. "How could I possibly not know the law?"

"What ruddy LAW?" I yell. "What the hell is everyone talking about?"

"Todd is innocent," Ben says. "You can search his Noise for as long as you like and you won't find anything to say I'm lying."

"You can't trust them," says the beard, still looking down his gun. "You know you can't."

"We don't know anything," Doctor Snow says. "Not for ten years or more."

"We know they've raised themselves into an army," says the birthmark.

"Yes, but I don't see any crime in this boy," Doctor Snow says. "Do you?"

A dozen different Noises come poking at me like sticks.

He turns to Viola. "And all the girl is guilty of is a lie that saved her friend's life."

Viola looks away from me, face still red with anger.

"And we've got bigger problems," Doctor Snow continues. "An army coming that may or may not know all about how we're preparing to meet them."

"We ain't SPIES!" I shout.

But Doctor Snow is turning to the other men. "Take the boy and the girl back into town. The girl can go with the women and the boy is well enough to fight alongside us."

"Wait a minute!" I yell.

Doctor Snow turns to Ben. "And though I do believe you're just a man out looking for his son, the law's the law."

"Is that your final ruling?" the beard says.

"If the eldermen agree," Doctor Snow says. There's a general but re-luctant nodding of heads, all serious and curt. Doctor Snow looks at me. "I'm sorry, Todd."

"Hold on!" I say, but the birthmark's already stepping forward and grabbing my arm. "Let go of me!"

Another man's grabbing on to Viola and she's resisting just as much as I am.

"Ben!" I call, looking back at him. "*Ben!*"

"Go, Todd," he says.

"No, Ben!"

"Remember I love you."

"What're they gonna do?" I say, still pulling away from the birthmark's hand. I turn to Doctor Snow. "What're you gonna do?"

He don't say nothing but I can see it in his Noise.

What the law demands.

"The HELL you are!" I yell and with my free arm I'm already reaching for my knife and bringing it round toward the birthmark's hand, slicing it across the top. He yelps and lets go.

"Run!" I say to Ben. "Run, already!"

I see Viola biting the hand of the man who's grabbing her. He calls out and she stumbles back.

"You, too!" I say to her. "Get outta here!"

"I wouldn't," says the beard and there are rifles cocking all over the place.

The birthmark is cursing and he raises his arm to strike but I've got my knife out in front of me. "Try it," I say thru my teeth. "*Come on!*"

"ENOUGH!" Doctor Snow yells.

And in the sudden silence that follows, we hear the hoofbeats.

Thump budda-thump budda-thump.

Horses. Five of 'em. Ten. Maybe even fifteen.

Roaring down the road like the devil hisself is on their tail.

"Scouts?" I say to Ben tho I know they ain't.

He shakes his head. "Advance party."

"They'll be armed," I say to Doctor Snow and the men, thinking fast. "They'll have as many guns as you."

Doctor Snow's thinking, too. I can see his Noise whirring, see him thinking how much time they've got before the horses get here, how much trouble me and Ben and Viola are going to cause, how much time we'll waste.

I see him decide.

"Let them go."

"What?" says the beard, his Noise itching to shoot *something*. "He's a traitor and a murderer."

"And we've got a town to protect," Doctor Snow says firmly. "I've got a son to keep safe. So do you, Fergal."

The beard frowns but says nothing more.

Thump budda-thump budda-thump comes the sound from the road.

Doctor Snow turns to us. "Go," he says. "I can only hope you haven't sealed our fate."

"We haven't," I say, "and that's the truth."

Doctor Snow purses his lips. "I'd like to believe you." He turns to the men. "Come on!" he shouts. "Get to your posts! Hurry!"

The group of men breaks up, scurrying back to Carbonel Downs, the beard and the birthmark still seething at us as they go, looking for a reason to use their guns, but we don't give 'em one. We just watch 'em go.

I find I'm shaking a little.

"Holy crap," Viola says, bending at the waist.

"We gotta get outta here," I say. "The army's gonna be more interested in us than it is in them."

I still have Viola's bag with me, tho all it's got in it anymore are a few clothes, the water bottles, the binocs and my ma's book, still in its plastic bag.

All the things we got in the world.

Which means we're ready to go.

"This is only gonna keep happening," Ben says. "I can't come with you."

"Yes, you can," I say. "You can leave later but we're going now and yer coming with us. We ain't leaving you to be caught by no army." I look over to Viola. "Right?"

She puts her shoulders back and looks decisive. "Right," she says.

"That's settled then," I say.

Ben looks back and forth twixt the two of us. He furrows his brow. "Only till I know yer safe."

"Too much talking," I say. "Not enough running."

36

ANSWERS TO ASKINGS

WE STAY OFF THE RIVER ROAD for obvious reasons and tear thru the trees, heading, as always, toward Haven, snapping thru twigs and branches, getting away from Carbonel Downs as fast as our legs can carry us.

It's not ten minutes before we hear the first gunshots.

We don't look back. We don't look back.

We run and the sounds fade.

We keep running.

Me and Viola are both faster than Ben and sometimes we have to slow down to let him catch up.

We run past one, then two small, empty settlements, places that obviously heeded the rumors about the army better than Carbonel Downs did. We keep to the woods twixt the river and the road but we don't even see any caravans. They must be hightailing it to Haven.

On we run.

Night falls and we keep on running.

"You all right?" I ask Ben, when we stop by the river to refill the bottles.

"Keep on going," he says, gasping. "Keep on going."

Viola sends me a worried look.

"I'm sorry we don't got food," I say, but he just shakes his head and says, "Keep going."

So we keep going.

Midnight comes and we run thru that, too.

(Who knows how many days? Who cares anymore?)

Till finally, Ben says, "Wait," and stops, hands on his knees, breathing hard in a real unhealthy way.

I look around us by the light of the moons. Viola's looking, too. She points. "There."

"Up there, Ben," I say, pointing up the small hill Viola's seen. "We'll be able to get a view."

Ben don't say nothing, just gasps and nods his head and follows us. There's trees all the way up the side but a well-tended path and a wide clearing at the top.

When we get there, we see why.

"A sematary," I say.

"A what?" Viola says, looking round at all the square stones marking out their graves. Must be a hundred, maybe two, in orderly rows and well-kept grass. Settler life is hard and it's short and lotsa New World people have lost the battle.

"It's a place for burying dead folk," I say.

Her eyes widen. "A place for doing *what*?"

"Don't people die in space?" I ask.

"Yeah," she says. "But we burn them. We don't put them in *holes*." She crosses her arms around herself, mouth and forehead frowning, peering around at the graves. "How can this be sanitary?"

Ben still hasn't said anything, just flopped down by a gravestone and leaned against it, catching his breath. I take a swig from a water bottle and then hand it to Ben. I look out around us. You can see down the road for a piece and there's a view of the river, too, rushing by us on the left now. It's a clear sky, the stars out, the moons starting to crescent in the sky above us.

"Ben?" I say, looking up into the night.

"Yeah?" he says, drinking down his water.

"You all right?"

"Yeah." His breath's getting back to normal. "I'm built for farm labor. Not sprinting."

I look at the moons one more time, the smaller one chasing the larger one, two brightnesses up there, still light enough to cast shadows, ignorant of the troubles of men.

I look into myself. I look deep into my Noise.

And I realize I'm ready.

This is the last chance.

And I'm ready.

"I think it's time," I say. I look back at him. "I think now's the time, if it's ever gonna be."

He licks his lips and swallows his water. He puts the cap back on the bottle. "I know," he says.

"Time for what?" Viola asks.

"Where should I start?" Ben asks.

I shrug. "Anywhere," I say, "as long as it's true."

I can hear Ben's Noise gathering, gathering up the whole story, taking one stream out of the river, finally, the one that tells what really happened, the one hidden for so long and so deep I didn't even know it was there for my whole up-growing life.

Viola's silence has gone more silent than usual, as still as the night, waiting to hear what he might say.

Ben takes a deep breath.

"The Noise germ wasn't Spackle warfare," he says. "That's the first thing. The germ was here when we landed. A naturally occurring phenomenon, in the air, always had been, always will be. We got outta our ships and within a day everyone could hear everyone's thoughts. Imagine our surprise."

He pauses, remembering.

"Except it *wasn't* everyone," Viola says.

"It was just the men," I say.

Ben nods. "No one knows why. Still don't. Our scientists were mainly agriculturalists and the doctors couldn't find a reason and so for a while, there was chaos. Just . . . *chaos,* like you wouldn't believe. Chaos and confusion and Noise, Noise, Noise." He scratches underneath his chin. "A lotta men scattered theirselves into far communities, getting away from Haven as fast as roads could be cut. But soon folk realized there was nothing to be done about it so for a while we all tried to live with it the best we could, found different ways to deal with it, different communities taking their own paths. Same as we did when we realized all our livestock were talking, too, and pets and local creachers."

He looks up into the sky and to the sematary around us and the river and road below.

"Everything on this planet talks to each other," he says. "Everything. That's what New World is. Informayshun, all the time, never stopping, whether you want it or not. The Spackle knew it, evolved to live with it, but we weren't equipped for it. Not even close. And too much informayshun can drive a man mad. Too much informayshun becomes just Noise. And it never, never stops."

He pauses and the Noise is there, of course, like it always is, his and mine and Viola's silence only making it louder.

"As the years went by," he goes on, "times were hard all over New World and getting harder. Crops failing and sickness and no prosperity and no Eden. Definitely no Eden. And a preaching started spreading in the land, a poisonous preaching, a preaching that started to blame."

"They blamed the aliens," Viola says.

"The Spackle," I say and the shame returns.

"They blamed the Spackle," Ben confirms. "And somehow preaching became a movement and a movement became a war." He shakes his head. "They didn't stand a chance. We had guns, they didn't, and that was the end of the Spackle."

"Not all," I say.

"No," he says. "Not all. But they learned better than to come too near men again, I tell you that."

A brief wind blows across the hilltop. When it stops, it's like we're the only three people left on New World. Us and the sematary ghosts.

"But the war's not the end of the story," Viola says quietly.

"No," Ben says. "The story ain't finished, ain't even *half* finished."

And I know it ain't. And I know where it's heading.

And I changed my mind. I don't want it to finish.

But I do, too.

I look into Ben's eyes, into his Noise.

"The war didn't stop with the Spackle," I say. "Not in Prentisstown."

Ben licks his lips and I can feel unsteadiness in his Noise and hunger and grief at what he's already imagining is our next parting.

"War is a monster," he says, almost to himself. "War is the devil. It starts and it consumes and it grows and grows and grows." He's looking at me now. "And otherwise normal men become monsters, too."

"They couldn't stand the silence," Viola says, her voice still. "They couldn't stand women knowing everything about them and them knowing nothing about women."

"*Some* men thought that," Ben says. "Not all. Not me, not Cillian. There were good men in Prentisstown."

"But enough thought it," I say.

"Yes," he nods.

There's another pause as the truth starts to show itself.

Finally. And forever.

Viola is shaking her head. "Are you saying . . . ?" she says. "Are you really saying . . . ?"

And here it is.

Here's the thing that's the center of it all.

Here's the thing that's been growing in my head since I left the swamp, seen in flashes of men along the way, most clearly in Matthew Lyle's but also in the reakshuns of everyone who even hears the word Prentisstown.

Here it is.

The truth.

And I don't want it.

But I say it anyway.

"After they killed the Spackle," I say, "the men of Prentisstown killed the women of Prentisstown."

Viola gasps even tho she's got to have guessed it, too.

"Not *all* the men," Ben says. "But many. Allowing themselves to be swayed by Mayor Prentiss and the preachings of Aaron, who used to say that what was hidden must be evil. They killed all the women and all the men who tried to protect them."

"My ma," I say.

Ben just nods in confirmayshun.

I feel a sickness in my stomach.

My ma dying, being killed by men I probably saw every day.

I have to sit down on a gravestone.

I have to think of something else, I just do. I have to put something else in my Noise so I can stand it.

"Who was Jessica?" I say, remembering Matthew Lyle's Noise back in Farbranch, remembering the violence in it, the Noise that now makes sense even tho it don't make no sense at all.

"Some people could see what was coming," Ben says. "Jessica Elizabeth was our Mayor and she could see the way the wind was blowing."

Jessica Elizabeth, I think. New Elizabeth.

"She organized some of the girls and younger boys to flee across the swamp," Ben continues. "But before she could go herself with the women and the men who hadn't lost their minds, the Mayor's men attacked."

"And that was that," I say, feeling numb all over. "New Elizabeth becomes Prentisstown."

"Yer ma never thought it would happen," Ben says, smiling sadly to himself at some memory. "So full of love that woman, so full of hope in the goodness of others." He stops smiling. "And then there came a moment when it was too late to flee and you were way too young to be sent away and so she gave you to us, told us to keep you safe, no matter what."

I look up. "How was staying in Prentisstown keeping me safe?"

Ben's staring right at me, sadness everywhere around him, his Noise so weighted with it, it's a wonder he can stay upright.

"Why didn't you leave?" I ask.

He rubs his face. "Cuz we didn't think the attack would really happen either. Or *I* didn't, anyway, and we had put the farm together and I thought it would blow over before anything really bad happened.

I thought it was just rumors and paranoia, including on the part of yer ma, right up to the last." He frowns. "I was wrong. I was stupid." He looks away. "I was willfully blind."

I remember his words comforting me about the Spackle.

We've all made mistakes, Todd. All of us.

"And then it was too late," Ben says. "The deed was done and word of what Prentisstown had done spread like wildfire, starting with the few who'd managed to escape. All men from Prentisstown were declared criminals. We couldn't leave."

Viola's arms are still crossed. "Why didn't someone come and get you? Why didn't the rest of New World come after you?"

"And do what?" Ben says, sounding tired. "Fight another war but this time with heavily armed men? Lock us up in a giant prison? They laid down the law that if any man from Prentisstown crossed the swamp, he'd be executed. And then they left us to it."

"But they could have . . ." Viola says, holding her palms to the air. "Something. I don't know."

"If it ain't happening on yer doorstep," Ben says, "it's easier to think, Why go out and *find* trouble? We had the whole of the swamp twixt us and New World. The Mayor sent word that Prentisstown would be a town in exile. Doomed, of course, to a slow death. We'd agree never to leave and if we ever did, he'd hunt us down and kill us hisself."

"Didn't people try?" Viola says. "Didn't they try to get away?"

"They *tried*," Ben says, full of meaning. "It wasn't uncommon for people to disappear."

"But if you and Cillian were innocent–" I start.

"We *weren't* innocent," Ben says strongly, and suddenly his Noise tastes bitter. He sighs. "We weren't."

"What do you mean?" I ask, raising my head. The sickness in my stomach ain't leaving. "What do you mean you weren't innocent?"

"You let it happen," Viola says. "You didn't die with the other men who were protecting the women."

"We didn't fight," he says, "and we didn't die." He shakes his head. "Not innocent at all."

"Why didn't you fight?" I ask.

"Cillian wanted to," Ben says quickly. "I want you to know that. He wanted to do whatever he could to stop them. He would have given his life." He looks away once more. "But I wouldn't let him."

"Why not?"

"I get it," Viola whispers.

I look at her, cuz I sure don't. "Get what?"

Viola keeps looking at Ben. "They either die fighting for what's right and leave you an unprotected baby," she says, "or they become complicit with what's wrong and keep you alive."

I don't know what complicit means but I can guess.

They did it for me. All that horror. They did it for me.

Ben and Cillian. Cillian and Ben.

They did it so I could live.

I don't know how I feel about any of this.

Doing what's right should be easy.

It shouldn't be just another big mess like everything else.

"So we waited," Ben says. "In a town-sized prison. Full of the ugliest Noise you ever heard before men started denying their own pasts, before the Mayor came up with his grand plans. And so we waited for the day you were old enough to get away on yer own, innocent as we could keep you." He rubs a hand over his head. "But the Mayor was waiting, too."

"For me?" I ask, tho I know it's true.

"For the last boy to become a man," Ben says. "When boys became men, they were told the truth. Or a version of it, anyway. And then they were made complicit themselves."

I remember his Noise from back on the farm, about my birthday, about how a boy becomes a man.

About what complicity really means and how it can be passed on.

How it was waiting to be passed on to me.

And about the men who—

I put it outta my head.

"That don't make no sense," I say.

"You were the last," Ben says. "If he could make every single boy in Prentisstown a man by his own meaning, then he's God, ain't he? He's created all of us and is in complete control."

"*If one us falls,*" I say.

"*We all fall,*" Ben finishes. "That's why he wants you. Yer a symbol. Yer the last innocent boy of Prentisstown. If he can make you fall, then his army is complete and of his own perfect making."

"And if not?" I say, tho I'm wondering if I've already fallen.

"If not," Ben says, "he'll kill you."

"So Mayor Prentiss is as crazy as Aaron, then," Viola says.

"Not quite," Ben says. "Aaron is crazy. But the Mayor knows enough to use craziness to achieve his ends."

"Which are what?" Viola says.

"This world," Ben says calmly. "He wants all of it."

I open my mouth to ask more stuff I don't wanna know but then, as if there was never gonna be anything else that could ever happen, we hear it.

Thump budda-thump budda-thump. Coming down the road, relentless, like a joke that ain't ever gonna be funny.

"You've *got* to be kidding," Viola says.

Ben's already back on his feet, listening. "It sounds like just one horse."

We all look down the road, shining a little in the moonlight.

"Binocs," Viola says, now right by my side. I fish 'em out without another word, click on the night setting and look, searching out the sound as it rings thru the night air.

Budda-thump budda-thump.

I search down the road farther and farther back till—

There it is.

There *he* is.

Who else?

Mr. Prentiss Jr., alive and well and untied and back on his horse.

"Damn," I hear from Viola, reading my Noise as I hand her the binocs.

"Davy Prentiss?" Ben says, also reading my Noise.

"The one and only." I put the water bottles back in Viola's bag. "We gotta go."

Viola hands the binocs to Ben and he looks for himself. He takes them away from his eyes and gives the binocs a quick once over. "Nifty," he says.

"We need to go," Viola says. "As always."

Ben turns to us, binocs still in his hand. He's looking from one of us to the other and I see what's forming in his Noise.

"Ben—" I start.

"No," he says. "This is where I leave you."

"Ben—"

"I can handle Davy Prentiss."

"He has a gun," I say. "You don't."

Ben comes up to me. "Todd," he says.

"No, Ben," I say, my voice getting louder. "I ain't listening."

He looks me in the eye and I notice he don't seem to be having to bend down anymore to do it.

"Todd," he says again. "I atone for the wrong I've done by keeping you safe."

"You can't leave me, Ben," I say, my voice getting wet (shut up). "Not again."

He's shaking his head. "I can't come to Haven with you. You know I can't. I'm the enemy."

"We can *explain* what happened."

But he's still shaking his head.

"The horse is getting closer," Viola says.

Thump budda-thump budda-thump.

"The only thing that makes me a man," Ben says, his voice steady as a rock, "is seeing you safely into becoming a man yerself."

"I ain't a man yet, Ben," I say, my throat catching (shut *up*). "I don't even know how many days I got left."

And then he smiles and it's the smile that tells me it's over.

"Sixteen," he says. "Sixteen days till yer birthday." He takes my chin and lifts it. "But you've been a man for a good while now. Don't let *no one* tell you otherwise."

"Ben—"

"Go," he says and he comes up to me and hands Viola the binocs behind my back and takes me in his arms. "No father could be prouder," I hear him say by my ear.

"No," I say, my words slurring. "It ain't fair."

"It ain't." He pulls himself away. "But there's hope at the end of the road. You remember that."

"Don't go," I say.

"I have to. Danger's coming."

"Closer and closer," Viola says, binocs to her eyes.

Budda-thump budda-THUMP.

"I'll stop him. I'll buy you time." Ben looks at Viola. "You take care of Todd," he says. "I have yer word?"

"You have my word," Viola says.

"Ben, please," I whisper. "Please."

He grips my shoulders for a last time. "Remember," he says. "*Hope.*"

And he don't say nothing more and he turns and runs down the hill from the sematary to the road. When he gets to the bottom, he looks back and sees us still watching him.

"What are you waiting for?" he shouts. "Run!"

37

WHAT'S THE POINT?

I WON'T SAY WHAT I FEEL when we run down the other side
of the hill and away from Ben, for ever this time cuz how is there any life
after this?

Life equals running and when we stop running maybe that's how
we'll know life is finally finished.

"Come on, Todd," Viola calls, looking back over her shoulder.
"Please, hurry."

I don't say nothing.

I run.

We get down the hill and back by the river. Again. With the road on
our other side. *Again.*

Always the same.

The river's louder than it was, rushing by with some force, but who
cares? What does it matter?

- Life ain't fair.

It ain't.

Not never.

It's pointless and stupid and there's only suffering and pain and
people who want to hurt you. You can't love nothing or no one cuz it'll all
be taken away or ruined and you'll be left alone and constantly having to
fight, constantly having to run just to stay alive.

There's nothing good in this life. Not nothing good nowhere.

What's the effing point?

"The point is," Viola says, stopping halfway thru a dense patch of scrub to hit me *really hard* on the shoulder, "he cared enough about you to maybe sacrifice himself and if you just GIVE UP" – she shouts that part – "then you're saying that the sacrifice is worth *nothing!*"

"Ow," I say, rubbing my shoulder. "But why should he have to sacrifice himself? Why should I have to lose him *again?*"

She steps up close to me. "Do you think you're the only person who's lost someone?" she says in a dangerous whisper. "Do you forget that my parents are dead, too?"

I did.

I did forget.

I don't say nothing.

"All I've got now is you," she says, her voice still angry. "And all you've got now is *me*. And I'm mad Ben left, too, and I'm mad my parents died and I'm mad we ever thought of coming to this planet in the first place but that's how it is and it sucks that it's just us but we can't do anything about it."

I still don't say nothing.

But there she is and I look at her, *really* look at her, for probably the first time since I saw her cowering next to a log back in the swamp when I thought she was a Spackle.

A lifetime ago.

She's still kinda cleaned up from the days in Carbonel Downs (only yesterday, only just yesterday) but there's dirt on her cheeks and she's skinnier than she used to be and there are dark patches under her eyes and her hair is messy and tangled and her hands are covered in sooty blackness and her shirt has a green stain of grass across the front from when she once fell and there's a cut on her lip from when a branch smacked her when we were running with Ben (and no bandages left to stitch it up) and she's looking at me.

And she's telling me she's all I've got.

And that I'm all *she's* got.

And I feel a little bit how that feels.

The colors in my Noise go different.

Her voice softens but only a little. "Ben's gone and Manchee's gone and my mother and father are gone," she says. "And I hate all of that. I *hate* it. But we're almost at the end of the road. We're almost there. And if you don't give up, I don't give up."

"Do you believe there's hope at the end?" I ask.

"No," she says simply, looking away. "No, I don't, but I'm still going." She eyes me. "You coming with?"

I don't have to answer.

We go on running.

But.

"We should just take the road," I say, holding back yet another branch.

"But the army," she says. "And the horses."

"They know where we're going. We know where they're going. We all seem to have taken the same route to get to Haven."

"And we'll hear them coming," she agrees. "And the road's fastest.

"The road's fastest."

And she says, "Then let's just take the effing road and get ourselves to Haven."

I smile, a little. "You said *effing*," I say. "You actually said the word *effing*."

So we take the effing road, as fast as our tiredness will let us. It's still the same dusty, twisty, sometimes muddy river road that it was all those miles and miles ago and the same leafy, tree-filled New World all around us.

If you were just landing here and didn't know nothing about nothing you really might think it was Eden after all.

A wide valley is opening up around us, flat at the bottom where the river is but distant hills beginning to climb up on either side. The hills are lit only by moonlight, no sign of distant settlements or, anyway, of ones with lights still burning.

No sign of Haven ahead neither but we're at the flattest point of the valley and can't see much past the twists in the road either before us or back. Forest still covers both sides of the river and you'd be tempted to think that all of New World had closed up and everyone left, leaving just this road behind 'em.

We go on.

And on.

Not till the first stripes of dawn start appearing down the valley in front of us do we stop to take on more water.

We drink. There's only my Noise and the river rushing by.

No hoofbeats. No other Noise.

"You know this means he succeeded," Viola says, not meeting my eye. "Whatever he did, he stopped the man on the horse."

I just *mmm* and nod.

"And we never heard gunshots."

I *mmm* and nod again.

"I'm sorry for shouting at you before," she says. "I just wanted you to keep going. I didn't want you to stop."

"I know."

We're leaning against a pair of trees by the riverbank. The road is to our backs and across the river is just trees and the far side of the valley rises up and then only the sky above, getting lighter and more blue and bigger and emptier till even the stars start leaving it.

"When we left on the scout ship," Viola says, looking up across the river with me, "I was really upset leaving my friends behind. Just a few kids from the other caretaker families, but still. I thought I'd be the only one my age on this planet for seven whole months."

I drink some water. "I didn't have friends back in Prentisstown."

She turns to me. "What do you mean, no friends? You had to have friends."

"I had a few for a while, boys a coupla months older than me. But when boys become men they stop talking to boys," I shrug. "I was the last boy. In the end there was just me and Manchee."

She gazes up into the fading stars. "It's a stupid rule."

"It is."

We don't say nothing more, just me and Viola by the riverside, resting ourselves as another dawn comes.

Just me and her.

We stir after a minute, get ourselves ready to go again.

"We could reach Haven by tomorrow," I say. "If we keep on going."

"Tomorrow," Viola nods. "I hope there's food."

It's her turn to carry the bag so I hand it to her and the sun is peeking up over the end of the valley where it looks like the river's running right into it and as the light hits the hills across the river from us, something catches my eye.

Viola turns immediately at the spark in my Noise. "What?"

I shield my eyes from the new sun. There's a little trail of dust rising from the top of the far hills.

And it's moving.

"What is that?" I say.

Viola fishes out the binocs and looks thru 'em. "I can't see clearly," she says. "Trees in the way."

"Someone traveling?"

"Maybe that's the other road. The fork we didn't take."

We watch for a minute or two as the dust trail keeps rising, heading toward Haven at the slow speed of a distant cloud. It's weird seeing it without any sound.

"I wish I knew where the army was," I say. "How far they were behind us."

"Maybe Carbonel Downs put up too good a fight." Viola points the binocs upriver to see the way we came but it's too flat, too twisty. All there is to be seen is trees. Trees and sky and quiet and a silent trail of dust making its way along the far hilltops.

"We should go," I say. "I'm starting to feel a little spooked."

"Let's go then," Viola says, quietlike.

Back on the road.

Back to the life of running.

We have no food with us so breakfast is a yellow fruit that Viola spies on some trees we pass that she swears she ate in Carbonel Downs. They become lunch, too, but it's better than nothing.

I think again of the knife at my back.

Could I hunt, if there was time?

But there ain't no time.

We run past midday and into afternoon. The world is still abandoned and spooky. Just me and Viola running along the valley bottom, no settlements to be seen, no caravans or carts, no other sound loud enough to be heard over the rushing of the river, getting bigger by the hour, to the point where it's hard even to hear my Noise, where even if we want to talk, we have to raise our voices.

But we're too hungry to talk. And too tired to talk. And running too much to talk.

And so on we go.

And I find myself watching Viola.

The trail of dust on the far hilltop follows us as we run, pulling ahead slowly as the day gets older and finally disappearing in the distance and I watch her checking it as we hurry on. I watch her run next to me, flinching at the aches in her legs. I watch her rub them when we rest and watch her when she drinks from the water bottles.

Now that I've seen her, I can't stop seeing her.

She catches me. "What?"

"Nothing," I say and look away cuz I don't know either.

The river and the road have straightened out as the valley gets steeper and closer on both sides. We can see a little bit back the way we came. No army yet, no horsemen neither. The quiet is almost scarier than if there was Noise everywhere.

Dusk comes, the sun setting in the valley behind us, setting over wherever the army might be and whatever's left of New World back there, whatever's happened to the men who fought against the army and the men who joined.

Whatever's happened to the women.

Viola runs in front of me.

I watch her run.

Just after nightfall we finally come to another settlement, another one with docks on the river, another one abandoned. There are only five houses in total along a little strip of the road, one with what looks like a small general store tacked onto the front.

"Hold on," Viola says, stopping.

"Dinner?" I say, catching my breath.

She nods.

It takes about six kicks to open the door of the general store and tho there clearly ain't no one here at all, I still look round expecting to be punished. Inside, it's mostly cans but we find a dry loaf of bread, some bruised fruit and a few strips of dried meat.

"These aren't more than a day or two old," Viola says, twixt mouthfuls. "They must have fled to Haven yesterday or the day before."

"Rumors of an army are a powerful thing," I say, not chewing my dried meat well enough before I swallow and coughing up a little bit of it.

We fill our bellies as best we can and I shove the rest of the food into Viola's bag, now hanging round my shoulders. I see the book when I do. Still there, still wrapped in its plastic bag, still with the knife-shaped slash all the way thru it.

I reach in thru the plastic bag, rubbing my fingers across the cover. It's soft to the touch and the binding still gives off a faint whiff of leather.

The book. My ma's book. It's come all the way with us. Survived its own injury. Just like us.

I look up at Viola.

She catches me again.

"What?" she says.

"Nothing." I put the book back in the bag with the food. "Let's go."

Back on the road, back down the river, back toward Haven.

"This should be our last night, you know," Viola says. "If Doctor Snow was right, we'll be there tomorrow."

"Yeah," I say, "and the world will change."

"Again."

"Again," I agree.

We go on a few more paces.

"You starting to feel hope?" Viola asks, her voice curious.

"No," I say, fuddling my Noise. "You?"

Her eyebrows are up but she shakes her head. "No, no."

"But we're going anyway."

"Oh, yeah," Viola says. "Hell or high water."

"It'll probably be both," I say.

The sun sets, the moons rise again, smaller crescents than the night before. The sky is still clear, the stars still up, the world still quiet, just the rush of the river, getting steadily louder.

Midnight comes.

Fifteen days.

Fifteen days till—

Till what?

We carry on thru the night, the sky falling slowly past us, our words stopping a little as dinner wears off and tiredness takes hold again. Just before dawn we find two overturned carts in the road, grains of wheat spilled everywhere and a few empty baskets rolled on their sides across the road.

"They didn't even take the time to save everything," Viola says. "They left half of it on the ground."

"Good a place as any for breakfast." I flip over one of the baskets, drag it over to where the road overlooks the river, and sit down on it.

Viola picks up another basket, brings it over right next to me, and sits down. There are glimmers of light in the sky as the sun gets set to rise, the road pointing right toward it, the river, too, rushing toward the dawn. I open up the bag and take out the general store food, handing some to Viola and eating what I've got. We drink from the water bottles.

The bag is open on my lap. There are our remaining clothes and there are the binocs.

And there's the book again.

I feel her silence next to me, feel the pull of it on me and the hollows in my chest and stomach and head and I remember the ache I used to feel when she got too close, how it felt like grief, how it felt like a loss, like I was falling, falling into nothing, how it clenched me up and made me want to weep, made me actually *weep*.

But now—

Now, not so much.

I look over to her.

She's gotta know what's in my Noise. I'm the only one around and she's got better and better at reading it despite how loud the river's getting.

But she sits there, quietly eating, waiting for me to say.

Waiting for me to ask.

Cuz this is what I'm thinking.

When the sun comes up, it'll be the day we get to Haven, the day we get to a place filled with more people than I've ever seen together in my life, a place filled with so much Noise you can't never be alone, unless they found a cure, in which case I'll be the only Noisy one which would actually be worse.

We get to Haven, we'll be part of a city.

It won't just be Todd and Viola, sitting by a river as the sun comes up, eating our breakfast, the only two people on the face of the planet.

It'll be everyone, all together.

This might be our last chance.

I look away from her to speak. "You know that thing with voices that you do?"

"Yeah," she says, quiet.

I take out the book.

"D'you think you could do a Prentisstown voice?"

18

I HEARD A MAIDEN CALL

MY DEAREST TODD," Viola reads, copying Ben's accent as best she can. Which is pretty ruddy good. *"My dearest son."*

My ma's voice. My ma speaking.

I cross my arms and look down into the wheat spilled across the ground.

"I begin this journal on the day of yer birth, the day I first held you in my arms rather than in my belly. You kick just as much outside as in! And yer the most beautiful thing that's ever happened in the whole entire universe. Yer easily the most beautiful thing on New World and there's no contest in New Elizabeth, that's for sure."

I feel my face getting red but the sun's still not high enough for anyone to see.

"I wish yer pa were here to see you, Todd, but New World and the Lord above saw fit to take him with the sickness five months ago and we'll both just have to wait to see him in the next world.

"You look like him. Well, babies don't look much like anything but babies but I'm telling you, you look like him. Yer going to be tall, Todd, cuz yer pa was tall. Yer going to be strong, cuz yer pa was strong. And yer going to be handsome, oh, are you ever going to be handsome. The ladies of New World won't know what hit them."

Viola turns a page and I don't look at her. I sense she's not looking at me neither and I wouldn't wanna see a smile on her face right about now.

Cuz that weird thing's happening too.

Her words are not her words and they're coming outta her mouth sounding like a lie but making a new truth, creating a different world where my ma is talking directly to me, Viola speaking with a voice not her own and the world, for a little while at least, the world is all for me, the world's being made just for me.

"*Let me tell you bout the place you've been born into, son. It's called New World and it's a whole planet made entirely of hope—*"

Viola stops, just for a second, then carries on.

"*We landed here almost exactly ten years ago looking for a new way of life, one clean and simple and honest and good, one different from Old World in all respects, where people could live in safety and peace with God as our guide and with love for our fellow man.*

"*There've been struggles. I won't begin this story to you with a lie, Todd. It ain't been easy here—*

"*Oooh, listen to me, writing down 'ain't' when addressing my son. That's settler life for you, I spose, not much time for niceties and it's easy to sink to the level of people who revel in squandering their manners. But there's not much harm in 'ain't,' surely? Okay, that's decided then. My first bad choice as a mother. Say 'ain't' all you like, Todd. I promise not to correct you.*"

Viola purses her lips but I don't say nothing so she continues.

"*So there's been hardship and sickness on New World and in New Elizabeth. There's something called the Noise here on this planet that men have been struggling with since we landed but the strange thing is you'll be one of the boys in the settlement who won't know any different and so it'll be hard to explain to you what life was like before and why it's so difficult now but we're managing the best we can.*

"*A man called David Prentiss, who's got a son just a bit older than you, Todd, and who's one of our better organizers — I believe he was a caretaker on the ship over, if memory serves me correct—*"

Viola pauses at this, too, but this time it's me who waits for her to say something. She don't.

"*He convinced Jessica Elizabeth, our Mayor, to found this little settlement on the far side of an enormous swamp so that the Noise of the rest of New World can't never reach us unless we allow it to. It's still Noisy as anything here in New Elizabeth but at least it's people we know, at least it's people we trust. For the most part.*

"*My role here is that I farm several fields of wheat up north of the settlement. Since yer pa passed, our close friends Ben and Cillian have been helping me out since theirs is the next farm over. I can't wait for you to meet them. Well wait, you already have! They've already held you and said hello so look at that, one day in the world and you've already made two friends. It's a good way to start, son.*

"*In fact, I'm sure you'll do fine cuz you came out two weeks early.*

Clearly you'd decided you'd had enough and wanted to see what this world had to offer you. I can't blame you. The sky is so big and blue and the trees so green and this is a world where the animals talk to you, really talk, and you can even talk back and there's so much wonder to be had, so much just waiting for you, Todd, that I almost can't stand that it's not happening for you right now, that yer going to have to wait to see all that's possible, all the things you might do."

Viola takes a breath and says, "There's a break in the page here and a little space and then it says *Later* like she got interrupted." She looks up at me. "You okay?"

"Yeah, yeah," I nod real fast, my arms still crossed. "Go on."

It's getting lighter, the sun truly coming up. I turn away from her a little.

She reads.

"Later.

"Sorry, son, had to stop for a minute for a visit from our holy man, Aaron."

Another pause, another lick of the lips.

"We've been lucky to have him, tho I must admit of late he's not been saying things I exactly agree with about the natives of New World. Which are called the Spackle, by the way, and which were a BIG surprise, since they were so shy at first neither the original planners back on Old World or our first scout ships even knew they were here!

"They're very sweet creachers. Different and maybe primitive and no spoken or written language that we can really find but I don't agree with some of the thinking of the people here that the Spackle are animals rather than intelligent beings. And Aaron's been preaching lately about how God has made a dividing line twixt us and them and—

"Well that's not really something to discuss on yer first day, is it? Aaron believes what he believes devoutly, has been a pillar of faith for all of us these long years and should anyone find this journal and read it, let me say here for the record that it was a privilege to have him come by and bless you on yer first day of life. Okay?

"But I will say also on yer first day that the attractiveness of power is something you should learn about before you get too much older, it's the thing that separates men from boys, tho not in the way most men think.

"And that's all I'll say. Prying eyes and all that.

"Oh, son, there's so much wonder in the world. Don't let no one tell you otherwise. Yes, life has been hard here on New World and I'll even admit to you here, cuz if I'm going to start out at all it has to be an honest start, I'll tell you that I was nearly given to despair. Things in the settlement are maybe more complicated than I can quite explain right now and there's things you'll learn for yerself before too long whether I like it or not and there've been difficulties

with food and with sickness and it was hard enough even before I lost yer pa and I nearly gave up.

"*But I didn't give up. I didn't give up cuz of you, my beautiful, beautiful boy, my wondrous son who might make something better of this world, who I promise to raise only with love and hope and who I swear will see this world come good. I swear it.*

"*Cuz when I held you for the first time this morning and fed you from my own body, I felt so much love for you it was almost like pain, almost like I couldn't stand it one second longer.*

"*But only almost.*

"*And I sang to you a song that my mother sang to me and her mother sang to her and it goes,*"

And here, amazingly, Viola sings.

Actually *sings*.

My skin goes goosepimply, my chest crushes. She musta heard the whole tune in my Noise and of course Ben singing it cuz here it comes, rolling outta her mouth like the peal of a bell.

The voice of Viola making the world into the voice of my ma, singing the song.

"*Early one morning, just as the sun was rising,*
I heard a maiden call from the valley below,
'Oh don't deceive me, oh never leave me,
How could you use a poor maiden so?'"

I can't look at her.

I can't look at her.

I put my hands to my head.

"*And it's a sad song, Todd, but it's also a promise. I'll never deceive you and I'll never leave you and I promise you this so you can one day promise it to others and know that it's true.*

"*Oh, ha, Todd! That's you crying. That's you crying from yer cot, waking up from yer first sleep on yer first day, waking up and asking the world to come to you.*

"*And so for today I have to put this aside.*

"*Yer calling for me, son, and I will answer.*"

Viola stops and there's only the river and my Noise.

"There's more," Viola says after a while when I don't raise my head. She flips thru the pages. "There's a lot more." She looks at me. "Do you want me to read more?" She looks back at the book. "Do you want me to read the end?"

The end.

Read the last thing my ma wrote in the last days before—

"No," I say quickly.

Yer calling for me, son, and I will answer.

In my Noise forever.

"No," I say again. "Let's leave it there for now."

I glance over at Viola and I see that her face is pulled as sad as my Noise feels. Her eyes are wet and her chin shakes, just barely, just a tremble in the dawn sunlight. She sees me watching, feels my Noise watching her, and she turns away to face the river.

And there, in that morning, in that new sunrise, I realize something.

I realize something important.

So important that as it dawns fully I have to stand up.

I know what she's thinking.

I *know* what she's thinking.

Even looking at her back, I know what she's thinking and feeling and what's going on inside her.

The way she's turned her body, the way she's holding her head and her hands and the book in her lap, the way she's stiffening a little in her back as she hears all this in my Noise.

I can read it.

I can read *her*.

Cuz she's thinking about how her own parents also came here with hope like my ma. She's wondering if the hope at the end of our road is just as false as the one that was at the end of my ma's. And she's taking the words of my ma and putting them into the mouths of her own ma and pa and hearing them say that they love her and they miss her and they wish her the world. And she's taking the song of my ma and she's weaving it into everything else till it becomes a sad thing all her own.

And it hurts her, but it's an okay hurt, but it hurts still, but it's good, but it hurts.

She hurts.

I know all this.

I *know* it's true.

Cuz I can read her.

I can read her Noise even tho she ain't got none.

I know who she is.

I know Viola Eade.

I raise my hands to the side of my head to hold it all in.

"Viola," I whisper, my voice shaking.

"I know," she says quietly, pulling her arms tight around her, still facing away from me.

And I look at her sitting there and she looks across the river and we wait as the dawn fully arrives, each of us knowing.

Each of us knowing the other.

39

THE FALLS

THE SUN CREEPS UP into the sky and the river is loud as we look across it and we can now see it rushing fast down toward the valley's end, throwing up white water and rapids.

It's Viola who breaks the spell that's fallen twixt us. "You know what it has to be, don't you?" she says. She takes out the binocs and looks downriver. The sun is rising at the end of the valley. She has to shield the lenses with her hand.

"What is it?" I say.

She presses a button or two and looks again.

"What do you see?" I ask.

She hands the binocs to me.

I look downriver, following the rapids, the foam, right to—

Right to the end.

A few miles away, the river ends in midair.

"Another falls," I say.

"Looks way bigger than the one we saw with Wilf," she says.

"The road'll find a way past it," I say. "Shouldn't bother us."

"That's not what I mean."

"What then?"

"I mean," she says, frowning a bit at my denseness, "that falls that big're bound to have a city at the bottom of them. That if you had to choose a place anywhere on a planet for a first settlement, then a valley at the base of a waterfall with rich farmland and ready water might just look perfect from space."

My Noise rises a little but only a little.

Cuz who would dare to think?

"Haven," I say.

"I'll bet you anything we've found it," she says. "I'll bet you when we get to that waterfall we'll be able to see it below us."

"If we run," I say, "we could be there in an hour. Less than."

She looks me in the eye for the first time since my ma's book.

And she says, "*If* we run?"

And then she smiles.

A genuine smile.

And I know what that means, too.

We grab our few things and go.

Faster than before.

My feet are tired and sore. Hers must be, too. I've got blisters and aches and my heart hurts from all I miss and all that's gone. And hers does, too.

But we run.

Boy, do we run.

Cuz maybe (shut up)–

Just maybe (don't think it)–

Maybe there really *is* hope at the end of the road.

The river grows wider and straighter as we rush on and the walls of the valley move in closer and closer, the one on our side getting so close the edge of the road starts to slope up. Spray from the rapids is floating in the air. Our clothes get wet, our faces, too, and hands. The roar becomes thunderous, filling up the world with itself, almost like a physical thing, but not in a bad way. Like it's washing you, like it's washing the Noise away.

And I think, *Please let Haven be at the bottom of the falls.*

Please.

Cuz I see Viola looking back at me as we run and there's brightness on her face and she keeps urging me on with tilts of her head and smiles and I think how hope may be the thing that pulls you forward, may be the thing that keeps you going, but that it's dangerous, too, that it's painful and risky, that it's making a dare to the world and when has the world ever let us win a dare?

Please let Haven be there.

Oh please, oh please, oh please.

The road finally starts rising a bit, pulling up above the river slightly as the water starts really crashing thru rocky rapids. There ain't no more wooded parts twixt us and it now at all, just a hill climbing up steeper and steeper on our right side as the valley closes in and then nothing but river and the falls ahead.

"Almost there," Viola calls from ahead of me, running, her hair bouncing off the back of her neck, the sun shining down on everything.

And then.

And then, at the edge of the cliff, the road comes to a lip and takes a sudden angle down and to the right.

And that's where we stop.

The falls are huge, half a mile cross easy. The water roars over the cliff in a violent white foam, sending spray hundreds of feet out into the sheer drop and above and all around, soaking us in our clothes and throwing rainbows all over the place as the rising sun lights it.

"Todd," Viola says, so faintly I can barely hear it.

But I don't need to.

I know what she means.

As soon as the falls start falling, the valley opens up, wide as the sky itself, taking the river that starts again at the base of the falls. It crashes forward with white water before it pools and calms down and becomes a river again.

And flows into Haven.

Haven.

Gotta be.

Spread out below us like a table full of food.

"There it is," Viola says.

And I feel her fingers wrap around my own.

The falls to our left, spray and rainbows in the sky, the sun rising ahead of us, the valley below.

And Haven, sitting waiting.

It's three, maybe four miles away down the farther valley.

But there it is.

There it ruddy well is.

I look round us, round to where the road has taken a sharp turn at our feet, sloping down and cutting into the valley wall to our right but then zigzagging its way steeply down in a twisty pattern so even it's like a zipper running down the hillside to where it picks up the river again.

And follows it right into Haven.

"I want to see it," Viola says, letting go of my hand and taking out the binocs. She looks thru them, wipes spray off the lenses, and looks some more. "It's beautiful," she says and that's all she says and she just looks and wipes off more spray.

After a minute and without saying nothing more, she hands me the binocs and I get my first look at Haven.

The spray is so thick, even wiping it down you can't see details like people or anything but there are all kindsa different buildings, mostly surrounding what looks like a big church at the center, but other big buildings, too, and real roads curling outta the middle thru trees to more groups of buildings.

There's gotta be at least fifty buildings in all.

Maybe a *hundred*.

It's the biggest thing I've ever seen in my entire life.

"I've got to say," Viola shouts, "it's kind of smaller than I expected."

But I don't really hear her.

With the binocs, I follow the river road back from it and I see what's probably a roadblock with what might be a fortified fence running away from it and to either side.

"They're getting ready," I say. "They're getting ready to fight."

Viola looks at me, worried. "You think it's big enough? You think we're safe?"

"Depends on if the rumors of the army are true or not."

I look behind us, by instinct, as if the army was just waiting there for us to move on. I look up the valley hill next to us. Could be a good view.

"Let's find out," I say.

We run back down the road a ways, looking for a good climbing spot, find one, and make our way up. My legs feel light as I climb, my Noise clearer than it's been in days. I'm sad for Ben, I'm sad for Cillian, I'm sad for Manchee, I'm sad for what's happened to me and Viola.

But Ben was right.

There's hope at the bottom of the biggest waterfall.

And maybe it don't hurt so much after all.

We climb up thru the trees. The hill is steep above the river and we have to pull on vines and hang on to rocks to make our way up high enough to look back down the road, till the valley is stretching out beneath us.

I still have the binocs and I look downriver and down the road and over the treetops. I keep having to wipe spray away.

I look.

"Can you see them?" Viola asks.

I look, the river getting smaller into the far distance, back and back and back.

"No," I say.

I look.

And again.

And–

There.

Down in the deepest curve of the road in the deepest part of the valley, in farthest shadow against the rising sun, there they are.

A mass that's gotta be the army, marching its way forward, so far away I can only tell it's them at all cuz it looks like dark water flowing into a dry riverbed. It's hard to get detail at this distance so I can't see individual men and I don't think I can see horses.

Just a mass, a mass pouring itself down the road.

"How big is it?" she asks. "How big has it grown?"

"I don't know," I say. "Three hundred? Four? I don't know. We're too far to really—"

I stop.

"We're too far to really tell." I crack a smile. "Miles and miles."

"We beat them," Viola says, a smile coming, too. "We ran and they chased us and we beat them."

"We'll get to Haven and we'll warn whoever's in charge," I say, talking faster, my Noise rising with excitement. "But they've got battle lines and the approach is real narrow and the army's at *least* the rest of the day away, maybe even tonight, too, and I swear that can't be a thousand men."

I swear it.

(But.)

Viola's smiling the tiredest, happiest smile I ever saw. She takes my hand again. "We beat them."

But then the risks of hope rise again and my Noise grays a little. "Well, we ain't there yet and we don't know if Haven can—"

But she's shaking her head. "Nuh-uh," she says. "We beat them. You listen to me and you be happy, Todd Hewitt. We've spent all this time outrunning an army and guess what? We outran them."

She looks at me, smiling, expecting something from me.

My Noise is buzzing and happy and warm and tired and relieved and a little bit worried still but I'm thinking that maybe she's right, maybe we did win and maybe I should put my arms round her if it didn't feel weird and I find that in the middle of it all I do actually agree with her.

"We beat 'em," I say.

And then she does stick her arms round me and pulls tight, like we might fall down, and we just stand there on the wet hillside and breathe for a little bit.

She smells a little less like flowers but it's okay.

And I look out and the falls are below us, charging away, and Haven glitters thru the sunlit spray and the sun is shining down the length of the river above the falls, lighting it up like a snake made of metal.

And I let my Noise bubble with little sparks of happy and my gaze
flow back along the length of the river and—

No.

Every muscle in my body jolts.

"What?" Viola says, jumping back.

She whips her head round to where I'm looking.

"What?" she says again.

And then she sees.

"No," she says. "No, it can't be."

Coming down the river is a boat.

Close enough to see without binocs.

Close enough to see the rifle and the robe.

Close enough to see the scars and the righteous anger.

Rowing his way furiously toward us, coming like judgment itself.

Aaron.

40

THE SACRIFICE

HAS HE SEEN US?" Viola asks, her voice pulled taut.

I point the binocs. Aaron rears up in them, huge and terrifying. I press a few buttons to push him back. He's not looking at us, just rowing like an engine to get the boat to the side of the river and the road.

His face is torn and horrible, clotted and bloody, the hole in his cheek, the new hole where his nose used to be, and still, underneath all that, a look feroshus and devouring, a look without mercy, a look that won't stop, that won't never, never stop.

War makes monsters of men, I hear Ben saying.

There's a monster coming toward us.

"I don't think he's seen us," I say. "Not yet."

"Can we outrun him?"

"He's got a gun," I say, "and you can see all the way down that road to Haven."

"Off the road then. Through the trees."

"There ain't that many twixt us and the road down. We'll have to be fast."

"I can be fast," she says.

And we jump on down the hill, skidding on leaves and wet vines, using rocks as handholds as best we can. The tree cover is light and we can still see down the river, see Aaron as he rows.

Which means he can see us if he looks in the right place.

"Hurry!" Viola says.

Down—

And down—
And sliding to the road—
And squelching in the mud at the roadside—
And as we get to the road he's outta sight again, still up the river—
But only for a second—
Cuz there he is—
The current bringing him fast—
Coming down the river—
In full view—
Looking right at us.
The roar of the falls is loud enough to eat you, but I still hear it.
I'd hear it if I was on the other side of the planet.
"TODD HEWITT!"
And he's reaching for his rifle.
"Go!" I shout.
Viola's feet hit the ground running and I'm right behind her, heading for the lip of the road that goes down to the zigzags.
It's fifteen steps, maybe twenty till we can disappear over the edge—
We run like we've spent the last two weeks resting—
Pound, pound, pound against the road—
I check back over my shoulder—
To see Aaron try to take the rifle in one hand—
Try to balance it while keeping the boat steady—
It's bouncing in the rapids, knocking him back and forth—
"He won't be able to," I yell to Viola. "He can't row and fire at the same—"
CRACK!
A pop of mud flies up outta the road next to Viola's feet ahead of me—
I cry out and Viola cries out and we both instinctively flinch down—
Running faster and faster—
Pound, pound, pound—
Run, run, run, run, run my Noise chugs like a rocket—
Not looking back—
Five steps—
Run, run—
Three—
CRACK!
And Viola falls—
"NO!" I shout—
And she's falling over the lip of the road, tripping down the other side and crashing down in a roll—
"NO!" I shout again and leap after her—

Stumbling down the steep incline—
Pounding down to where she's rolling—
No—
Not this—
Not now—
Not when we're—
Please no—
And she tumbles to some low shrubs at the side of the road and keeps going into them—

And stops facedown.

And I'm racing toward her and I'm barely in control of my own standing up and I'm kneeling down already in the brush and I'm grabbing her and rolling her over and I'm looking for the blood and the shot and I'm saying, "*No, no, no, no, no—*"

And I'm almost blinded by rage and despair and the false promise of hope and no, no, no—

And she opens her eyes—

She's opening her eyes and she's grabbing me and she's saying, "I'm not hit, I'm not hit."

"Yer not?" I say, shaking her a little. "Yer sure?"

"I just fell," she says. "I swear I felt the bullet fly right by my eyes and I fell. I'm not hurt."

And I'm breathing heavy and heavy and heavy

"Thank God," I say. "Thank God."

And the world spins and my Noise whirls.

And she's already getting to her feet and I'm up after her standing in the scrub and looking at the road around and below us.

The falls are crashing over the cliff to our left and the twisting road is both behind us and in front of us as it starts doubling back on itself and making the steep zipper down to the bottom of the falls.

It's a clear shot all the way.

No trees, just low scrub.

"He'll pick us off," Viola says, looking back up to the top of the road, to where we can't see Aaron no doubt making his way to the river's edge, stomping thru roaring water, *walking* on it for all I know.

"TODD HEWITT!" we hear again, faint over the roar of the water but loud as the whole entire universe.

"There's nowhere to hide," Viola says, looking around us and down. "Not till we get to the bottom."

I'm looking round, too. The hillsides are too steep, the road too open, the areas between the road's double-backs too shallow with shrubs.

Nowhere to hide.

"TODD HEWITT!"

Viola points up. "We could get up to those trees on top of the hill."

But it's so steep, I can already hear the hope failing in her voice.

And I spin round, looking still—

And then I see.

A little faint trail, skinny as anything, hardly even there, leading away from the first turn of the road and toward the falls. It disappears after a few feet but I follow it to where it might have gone.

Right to the cliff side.

Right down sharp to a place almost below the falls.

Right to a ledge that's almost hidden.

A ledge underneath the waterfall itself.

I take a few steps outta the scrub and back onto the road. The little trail disappears.

So does the ledge.

"What is it?" Viola asks.

I go back into the scrub again.

"There," I say, pointing. "Can you see it?"

She squints where I'm pointing. The falls are casting a little shadow on the ledge, darkening where the little trail ends.

"You can see it from here," I say, "but you can't see it from the road." I look at her. "We'll hide."

"He'll hear you," she says. "He'll come after us."

"Not over this roar, not if I don't shout in my Noise."

Her forehead creases and she looks down at the road to Haven and up to where Aaron's gotta be coming any second.

"We're so close," she says.

I take her arm and start pulling on it. "Come on. Just till he passes. Just till dark. With luck he'll think we doubled back into the trees above."

"If he finds us, we're trapped."

"And if we run for the city, he shoots us." I look in her eyes. "It's a chance. It gives us a *chance*."

"Todd—"

"Come with me," I say, looking right into her as hard as I can, pouring out as much hope as I can muster. *Oh, never leave me.* "I promise I'll get you to Haven tonight." I squeeze her arm. *Oh, don't deceive me.* "I promise you."

She looks right back at me, listening to it all, and then gives a single, sharp nod and we run to the little trail and down to where it ends and jump over the scrub to where it should continue and—

"TODD HEWITT!"

He's almost to the falls—

And we scrabble down a steep embankment next to the edge of the water, the steepness of the hill rearing above us—

And slide down and over to the edge of the cliff—

The falls straight ahead—

And I get to the edge and I suddenly have to lean back into Viola cuz the drop goes straight down—

She grabs onto my shirt and holds me up—

And the water is smashing down right in front of us to the rocks below—

And the ledge leading under it all is just there—

Needing a jump over emptiness to get to it—

"I didn't see this part," I say, Viola grabbing at my waist to keep us from tumbling over.

"TODD HEWITT!"

He's close, he's so close—

"Now or never, Todd," she says in my ear—

And she lets go of me—

And I jump across—

And I'm in the air—

And the edge of the falls is shooting over my head—

And I land—

And I turn—

And she's jumping after me—

And I grab her and we fall backward onto the ledge together—

And we lay there breathing

And listening—

And all we hear for a second is the roar of the water over us now—

And then, faint, against it all—

"TODD HEWITT!"

And he suddenly sounds miles away.

And Viola's on top of me and I'm breathing heavy into her face and she's breathing heavy into mine.

And we're looking in each other's eyes.

And it's too loud to hear my Noise.

After a second, she puts her hands on either side of me and pushes herself away. She looks up as she does and her eyes go wide.

I can just hear her say, "Wow."

I roll away and look up.

Wow.

The ledge is more than just a little ledge. It carries on till it's back, *way* back under the waterfall. We're standing at the beginning of a tunnel with one wall made of rock and another made of pure falling water, roaring past white and clean and so fast it looks almost solid.

"Come on," I say and head on down the ledge, my shoes slipping and sliding under me. It's rocky and wet and slimy and we lean as close as we can to the rock side, away from the thundering water.

The noise is just tremendous. All-consuming, like a real thing you could taste and touch.

So loud, Noise is obliterated.

So loud, it's the quietest I've ever felt.

We scramble on down the ledge, under the falls, making our way over rocky bumps and little pools with green goop growing in them. There are roots, too, hanging down from the rocks above, belonging to who knows what kinda plant.

"Do these look like steps to you?" Viola shouts, her voice small in the roar.

"TODD HEWITT!!" we hear from what sounds like a million miles away.

"Is he finding us?" Viola asks.

"I don't know," I say. "I don't think so."

The cliff face isn't even and the ledge curves round it as it stretches forward. We're both soaking wet and the water is cold and it's not easy grabbing onto the roots to keep our balance.

Then the ledge suddenly drops down and widens out, carved steps becoming more obvious. It's almost a stairway down.

Someone's been here before.

We descend, the water thundering inches away from us.

We get to the bottom.

"Whoa," Viola says behind me and I just know she's looking up.

The tunnel opens up abruptly and the ledge widens at the same time to become a cavern made of water, the rocks stretching up way over our heads, the falls slamming down past them in a wall curving way out like a moving, living sail, enclosing the wall and the shelf under our feet.

But that's not the *whoa*.

"It's a church," I say.

It's a church. Someone has moved or carved rocks into four rows of simple pews with an aisle down the middle, all facing a taller rock, a pulpit, a pulpit with a flat surface which a preacher could stand on and preach with a blazing white wall of water crashing down behind him, the morning sun lighting it up like a sheet of stars, filling the room with shimmering sparkles on every shiny wet surface, all the way back to a carved circle in the stone with two smaller carved circles orbiting it to one side, New World and its moons, the settler's new home of hope and

God's promise somehow painted a waterproof white and practically *glowing* on the rock wall, looking down and lighting up the church.

The church underneath a waterfall.

"It's beautiful," Viola says.

"It's abandoned," I say, cuz after the first shock of finding a church I see where a few of the pews have been knocked from their places and not replaced and there's writing all over the walls, some of it carved in with tools, some of it written in the same waterproof paint as the New World carving, most of it nonsense. *P.M.+M.A.* and *Willz & Chillz 4Ever* and *Abandon All Hope Ye Who* something something.

"It's kids," Viola says. "Sneaking in here, making it their own place."

"Yeah? Do kids do that?"

"Back on the ship we had an unused venting duct that we snuck into," she says, looking around. "Marked it up worse than this."

We wander in, looking round us, mouths open. The point of the roof where the water leaves the cliff must be a good thirty feet above us and the ledge fifteen feet wide easy.

"It musta been a natural cavern," I say. "They musta found it and thought it was some kinda miracle."

Viola crosses her arms against herself. "And then they found it wasn't very practical as a church."

"Too wet," I say. "Too cold."

"I'll bet it was when they first landed," she says, looking up at the white New World. "I'll bet it was in the first year. Everything hopeful and new." She turns around, taking it all in. "Before reality set in."

I turn slowly, too. I can see exactly what they were thinking. The way the sun hits the falls, turning everything bright white, and it's so loud and so silent at the same time that even without the pulpit and the pews it would have felt like we'd somehow walked into a church anyway, like it'd be holy even if no man had ever seen it.

And then I notice that at the end of the pews, there's nothing beyond. It stops and it's a 150-foot drop to the rocks below.

So this is where we're gonna have to wait.

This is where we're gonna have to hope.

In the church underwater.

"Todd Hewitt!" barely drifts in down the tunnel to us.

Viola visibly shivers. "What do we do now?"

"We wait till nightfall," I say. "Sneak out and hope he don't see us."

I sit down on one of the stone benches. Viola sits down next to me. She lifts the bag over her head and sets it on the stone floor.

"What if he finds the trail?" she asks.

"We hope he don't."

"But what if he does?"

I reach behind me and take out the knife.

The knife.

Both of us look at it, the white water reflecting off of it, droplets of spray already catching and pooling on its blade, making it shine like a little flashlight.

The knife.

We don't say nothing about it, just watch it gleam in the middle of the church.

"Todd Hewitt!"

Viola looks up to the entrance and puts her hands to her face and I can see her clench her teeth. "What does he even *want*?" she suddenly rages. "If the army's all about you, what does he want with me? Why was he shooting at me? I don't understand it."

"Crazy people don't need an explanayshun for nothing," I say.

But my Noise is remembering the sacrifice that I saw him making of her way back in the swamp.

The sign, he called her.

A gift from God.

I don't know if Viola hears this or if she remembers it herself cuz she says, "I don't think I'm the sacrifice."

"What?"

She turns to me, her face perplexed. "I don't think it's me," she says. "He kept me asleep almost the entire time I was with him and when I did wake up, I kept seeing confusing things in his Noise, things that didn't make sense."

"He's crazy," I say. "Crazier than most."

She don't say nothing more, just looks out into the waterfall.

And reaches over and takes my hand.

"TODD HEWITT!"

I feel her hand jump right as my heart leaps.

"That's closer," she says. "He's getting closer."

"He won't find us."

"He will."

"Then we'll deal with it."

We both look at the knife.

"TODD HEWITT!"

"He's found it," she says, grabbing my arm and squeezing into me.

"Not yet."

"We were almost there," she says, her voice high and breaking a little. "Almost there."

"We'll get there."

"TODD HEWITT!"

And it's definitely louder.

He's found the tunnel.

I grip my knife and I look over at Viola, her face looking straight back up the tunnel, so much fear on it my chest begins to hurt.

I grip the knife harder.

If he *touches* her—

And my Noise reels back to the start of our journey, to Viola before she said anything, to Viola when she told me her name, to Viola when she talked to Hildy and Tam, to when she took on Wilf's accent, to when Aaron grabbed her and stole her away, to waking up to her in Doctor Snow's house, to her promise to Ben, to when she took on my ma's voice and made the whole world change, just for a little while.

All the things we've been thru.

How she cried when we left Manchee behind.

Telling me I was all she had.

When I found out I could read her, silence or not.

When I thought Aaron had shot her on the road.

How I felt in those few terrible seconds.

How it would feel to lose her.

The pain and the unfairness and the injustice.

The rage.

And how I wished it was me.

I look at the knife in my hand.

And I realize she's right.

I realize what's been right all along, as insane as it is.

She's not the sacrifice.

She's not.

If one of us falls, we all fall.

"I know what he wants," I say, standing up.

"What?" Viola says.

"TODD HEWITT!"

Definitely coming down the tunnel now.

Nowhere to run.

He's coming.

She stands, too, and I move myself twixt her and the tunnel.

"Get down behind one of the pews," I say. "Hide."

"Todd—"

I move away from her, my hand staying on her arm till I'm too far away.

"Where are you going?" she says, her voice tightening.

I look back the way we came, up the tunnel of water.

He'll be here any second.

"TODD HEWITT!"

"He'll *see* you!" she says.

I hold up the knife in front of me.

The knife that's caused so much trouble.

The knife that holds so much power.

"Todd!" Viola says. "What are you *doing*?"

I turn to her. "He won't hurt you," I say. "Not when he knows I know what he wants."

"What does he want?"

I search her out, standing among the pews, the white planet and moons glowing down on her, the water shining watery light over her, I search out her face and the language of her body as she stands there watching me, and I find I still know who she is, that she's still Viola Eade, that silent don't mean empty, that it *never* meant empty.

I look right into her eyes.

"I'm gonna greet him like a man," I say.

And even tho it's too loud for her to hear my Noise, even tho she can't read my thoughts, she looks back at me.

And I see her understand.

She pulls herself up a little taller.

"I'm not hiding," she says. "If you're not, I'm not."

And that's all I need.

I nod.

"Ready?" I ask.

She looks at me.

She nods once, firmly.

I turn back to the tunnel.

I close my eyes.

I take a deep breath.

And with every bit of air in my lungs and every last note of Noise in my head, I rear up—

And I shout, as loud as I can—

"AARON!!!!!!"

And I open my eyes and I wait for him to come.

41

IF ONE OF US FALLS

I SEE HIS FEET FIRST, slipping down the steps some but not hurrying, taking his time now that he knows we're here.

I hold the knife in my right hand, my left hand out and ready, too. I stand in the aisle of the little pews, as much in the center of the church as I can get, Viola's back behind me a bit, down one of the rows.

I'm ready.

I realize I *am* ready.

Everything that's happened has brought me here, to this place, with this knife in my hand, and something worth saving.

Someone.

And if it's a choice twixt her and him, there is no choice, and the army can go eff itself.

And so I'm ready.

As I'll ever be.

Cuz I know what he wants.

"Come on," I say, under my breath.

Aaron's legs appear, then his arms, one carrying the rifle, the other holding his balance against the wall.

And then his face.

His terrible, terrible face.

Half torn away, the gash in his cheek showing his teeth, the hole where his nose used to be open and gaping, making him look barely human.

And he's smiling.

Which is when I feel all the fear.

"Todd Hewitt," he says, almost as a greeting.

I raise my voice over the water, willing it not to shake. "You can put the rifle down, Aaron."

"Oh, can I, now?" he says, eyes widening, taking in Viola behind me. I don't look back at her but I know she's facing Aaron, I know she's giving him all the bravery she's got.

And that makes me stronger.

"I know what you want," I say. "I figured it out."

"Have you, young Todd?" Aaron says and I see he can't help himself, he looks into my Noise, the little he can hear over the roar.

"She's not the sacrifice," I say.

He says nothing, just takes the first steps into the church, eyes glancing up at the cross and the pews and the pulpit.

"And I'm not the sacrifice neither," I say.

His evil smile draws wider. A new tear opens up at the edge of his gash, blood waving down it in the spray. "A clever mind is a friend of the devil," he says, which I think is his way of saying I'm right.

I steady my feet and turn with him as he steps round toward the pulpit half of the church, the half nearer the edge.

"It's you," I say. "The sacrifice is you."

And I open my Noise as loud as it'll go so that both he and Viola can see I'm telling the truth.

Cuz the thing Ben showed me back when I left our farm, the way that a boy in Prentisstown becomes a man, the reason that boys who've become men don't talk to boys who are still boys, the reason that boys who've become men are *complicit* in the crimes of Prentisstown is—

It's—

And I make myself say it—

It's by killing another man.

All by theirselves.

All those men who disappeared, who *tried* to disappear.

They didn't disappear after all.

Mr. Royal, my old schoolteacher, who took to whisky and shot himself, *didn't* shoot himself. He was shot by Seb Mundy on his thirteenth birthday, made to stand alone and pull the trigger as the rest of the men of Prentisstown watched. Mr. Gault, whose sheep flock we took over when he disappeared two winters ago, only *tried* to disappear. He was found by Mayor Prentiss running away thru the swamp and Mayor Prentiss was true to his agreement with the law of New World and executed him, only he did it by waiting till Mr. Prentiss Jr.'s thirteenth birthday and having his son torture Mr. Gault to death without the help of no one else.

And so on and so on. Men I knew killed by boys I knew to become men theirselves. If the Mayor's men had a captured escapee hidden away for a boy's thirteenth, then fine. If not, they'd just take someone from Prentisstown who they didn't like and *say* he disappeared.

One man's life was given over to a boy to end, all on his own.

A man dies, a man is born.

Everyone complicit. Everyone guilty.

Except me.

"Oh my God," I hear Viola say.

"But I was gonna be different, wasn't I?" I say.

"You were the last, Todd Hewitt," Aaron says. "The final soldier in God's perfect army."

"I don't think God's got nothing to do with yer army," I say. "Put down the rifle. I know what I have to do."

"But are you a messenger, Todd?" he asks, cocking his head, pulling his impossible smile wider. "Or are you a deceiver?"

"Read me," I say. "Read me if you don't believe I can do it."

He's at the pulpit now, facing me down the center aisle, reaching out his Noise over the sound of the falls, pushing it toward me, grabbing at what he can, and the sacrifice and God's perfect work and the martyrdom of the saint I hear.

"Perhaps, young Todd," he says.

And he sets the rifle down on the pulpit.

I swallow and grip the knife harder.

But he looks over at Viola and laughs a little laugh. "No," he says. "Little girls will try to take advantage, won't they?"

And, almost casually, he tosses the rifle off the ledge into the waterfall.

It goes so fast, we don't even see it disappear.

But it's gone.

And so there's just me and Aaron.

And the knife.

He opens his arms and I realize he's assuming his preacher's pose, the one from his own pulpit, back in Prentisstown. He leans against the pulpit stone here and holds his palms up and raises his eyes to the white shining roof of water above us.

His lips move silently.

He's *praying*.

"Yer crazy," I say.

He looks at me. "I'm blessed."

"You want me to kill you."

"Wrong, Todd Hewitt," he says, taking a step forward down the aisle toward me. "Hate is the key. Hate is the driver. Hate is the fire that purifies the soldier. The soldier must *hate*."

He takes another step.

"I don't want you to kill me," he says. "I want you to *murder* me."

I take a step back.

The smile flickers. "Perhaps the boy promises bigger than he can deliver."

"Why?" I say, stepping back some more. Viola moves back, too, behind and around me, underneath the carving of New World. "Why are you doing this? What possible sense does this make?"

"God has told me my path," he says.

"I been here for almost thirteen years," I say, "and the only thing I ever heard was *men*."

"God works thru men," Aaron says.

"So does evil," Viola says.

"Ah," Aaron says. "It speaks. Words of temptayshun to lull—"

"Shut up," I say. "Don't you talk to her."

I'm past the back row of pews now. I move to my right, Aaron follows till we're moving in a slow circle, Aaron's hands still out, my knife still up, Viola keeping behind me, the spray covering everything. The room slowly turns around us, the ledge still slippery, the wall of water shining white with the sun.

And the roar, the constant roar.

"You were the final test," Aaron says. "The last boy. The one that completes us. With you in the army, there's no weak link. We would be truly blessed. If one of us falls, we all fall, Todd. And all of us have to fall." He clenches his fists and looks up again. "So we can be reborn! So we can take this cursed world and remake it in—"

"I wouldn't've done it," I say and he scowls at the interrupshun. "I wouldn't've killed anyone."

"Ah, yes, Todd Hewitt," Aaron says. "And that's why yer so very very special, ain't you? The boy who can't kill."

I sneak a glance back at Viola, off to my side a little. We're still going round in the little circle.

And Viola and I are reaching the side with the tunnel in it.

"But God demands a sacrifice," Aaron's saying. "God demands a martyr. And who better for the special boy to kill than God's very own mouthpiece?"

"I don't think God tells you nothing," I say. "Tho I can believe he wants you dead."

Aaron's eyes go so crazy and empty I get a chill. "I'll be a saint," he says, a small fire burning in his voice. "It is my destiny."

He's reached the end of the aisle and is following us past the last row of benches.

Viola and I are backing up still.

Almost to the tunnel.

"But how to motivate the boy?" Aaron continues, eyes like holes. "How to bring him into manhood?"

And his Noise opens up to me, loud as thunder.

My eyes widen.

My stomach sinks to my feet.

My shoulders hunch down as I feel weakness on me.

I can see it. It's a fantasy, a lie, but the lies of men are as vivid as their truths and I can see every bit of it.

He was going to murder Ben.

That's how he was going to force me to kill him. That's how they woulda done it. To perfect their army and make me a killer, they were going to murder Ben.

And make me watch.

Make me hate enough to kill Aaron.

My Noise starts to rumble, loud enough to hear. *"You effing piece of—"*

"But then God sent a sign," Aaron says, looking at Viola, his eyes even wider now, the blood pouring from the gash, the hole where his nose used to be stretching taut. "The girl," he says. "A gift from the heavens."

"Don't you look at her!" I yell. "Don't you even *look at her!*"

Aaron turns back to me, the smile still there. "Yes, Todd, yes," he says. "That's yer path, that's the path you'll take. The boy with the soft heart, the boy who couldn't kill. What would he kill for? Who would he protect?"

Another step back, another step nearer the tunnel.

"And when her cursed, evil silence polluted our swamp, I thought God had sent me a sacrifice to make myself, one last example of the evil that hides itself which I could destroy and purify." He cocks his head. "But then her true purpose was revealed." He looks at her and back at me. "Todd Hewitt would protect the helpless."

"She ain't helpless," I say.

"And then you *ran.*" Aaron's eyes widen, as if in false amazement. "You ran rather than fulfill yer destiny." He lifts his eyes to the church again. "Thereby making victory over you all the sweeter."

"You ain't won yet," I say.

"Haven't I?" He smiles again. "Come, Todd. Come to me with hate in yer heart."

"I *will*," I say. "I'll do it."

But another step back.

"You've been near before, young Todd," Aaron says. "In the swamp, the knife raised, me killing the girl, but no. You hesitate. You injure but you do not kill. And then I steal her from you and you hunt her down, as I knew you would, suffering from the wound I gave you, but again, not enough. You sacrifice yer beloved dog rather than see her come to harm, you let me break his very body rather than serve yer true purpose."

"You shut up!" I say.

He holds his palms up to me.

"Here I am, Todd," he says. "Fulfil yer purpose. Become a man." He lowers his head till his eyes are looking up at me. *"Fall."*

I curl my lip.

I stand up straighter.

"I already *am* a man," I say.

And my Noise says it, too.

He stares at me. As if staring thru me.

And then he *sighs*.

Like he's *disappointed*.

"Not yet a man," he says, his face changing. "Perhaps not ever."

I don't step back.

"Pity," he says.

And he leaps at me—

"Todd!" Viola yells—

"Run!" I scream—

But I'm not stepping back—

I'm moving forward—

And the fight is on.

I'm charging at him and he's throwing himself at me and I'm holding the knife but at the last second, I leap to the side, letting him slam hard into the wall—

He whirls around, face in a snarl, swinging an arm round to hit me and I duck and slash at it with the knife, cutting across his forearm, and it don't even slow him down—

And he's swinging at me with his other arm and he's catching me just under the jaw—

Knocking me back—

"Todd!" Viola calls again—

I tumble backward onto the last pew, falling hard—

But I'm looking up—

Aaron's turning to Viola—

She's at the bottom of the stairs—

"Go!" I yell—

But she's got a big flat stone in her hands and launches it at Aaron with a grimace and an angry grunt and he ducks and tries to deflect it with one hand but it catches him across the forehead, causing him to stumble away from both her and me, toward the ledge, toward the front of the church—

"Come on!" Viola yells at me—

I scramble to my feet—

But Aaron's turned, too—

Blood running down his face—

His mouth open in a yell—

He jumps forward like a spider, grabbing Viola's right arm—

She punches fiercely with her left hand, bloodying it on his face—

But he don't let go—

I'm yelling as I fly at them—

Knife out—

But again I turn it at the last minute—

And I just knock into him—

We land on the upslope of the stairs, Viola falling back, me on top of Aaron, his arms boxing my head and he reaches forward with his horrible face and *takes a bite* out of an exposed area of my neck—

I yell and jerk back, punching him with a backhand as I go—

Scooting away from him back into the church, holding my neck—

He comes at me again, his fist flying forward—

Catching me on the eye—

My head jerks back—

I stumble thru the rows of pews, back to the center of the church—

Another punch—

I raise my knife hand to block it—

But keep the knife edge sideways—

And he hits me again—

I scrabble away from him on the wet stone—

Up the aisle toward the pulpit—

And a third time his fist reaches my face—

And I feel two teeth tear outta their roots—

And I nearly fall—

And then I do fall—

My back and head hitting the pulpit stone—

And I drop the knife.

It clatters away toward the edge.

Useless as ever.

"Yer Noise reveals you!" Aaron screams. *"Yer Noise reveals you!"* He's stepping forward to me now, standing over me. *"From the moment I stepped into this sacred place, I knew it would be thus!"* He stops at my feet, staring down at me, his fists clenched and bloody with my blood, his face bloody with his own. "You will *never* be a man, Todd Hewitt! *Never!"*

I see Viola outta the corner of my eye frantically looking for more rocks–

"I'm already a man," I say, but I've fallen, I've dropped the knife, my voice is faltering, my hand over the bleeding from my neck.

"You rob me of my sacrifice!" His eyes have turned to burning diamonds, his Noise blazing a red so fierce it's practically steaming the water away from him. "I will kill you." He bows his head to me. "And you will die knowing that I killed her slowly."

I clench my teeth.

I start to pull myself to my ruddy feet.

"Come on if yer coming," I growl.

Aaron yells and takes a step toward me–

Hands reaching out for me–

My face rising to meet him–

And Viola CLUMPS him on the side of the head with a rock she can barely lift–

He stumbles–

Leaning toward the pews and catching himself–

And he stumbles again–

But he doesn't fall.

He *doesn't ruddy fall.*

He staggers but he stands, twixt me and Viola, uncurling himself, his back to Viola but towering over her, a whole rivulet of blood spouting from the side of his head now, but he's effing well tall as a nightmare–

He really is a monster.

"You ain't human," I say.

"I have told you, young Todd," he says, his voice low and monstrous, his Noise glowering at me with a fury so pure it nearly knocks me back. "I am a saint."

He lashes his arm out in Viola's direkshun without even looking her way, catching her square on the eye, knocking her back as she calls out and falls, falls, falls, tripping over a pew, hitting her head hard on the rocks–

And not rising.

"Viola!" I yell–

And I leap past him–

He lets me go–

I reach her—
Her legs are up on the stone bench—
Her head's on the stone floor—
A little stream of blood running from it—
"Viola!" I say and I lift her—
And her head falls back—
"VIOLA!" I yell—
And I hear a low rumble from behind me—
Laughter.
He's laughing.
"You were always going to betray her," he says. "It was foreseen."
"You SHUT UP!"
"And do you know *why*?"
"I'll KILL YOU!"
He lowers his voice to a whisper—
But a whisper I can feel shiver thru my entire body—
"You've already fallen."
And my Noise blazes red.
Redder than it's ever been.
Murderous red.
"Yes, Todd," Aaron hisses. "Yes, that's the way."
I lay Viola gently down and I stand and face him.
And my hate is so big, it fills the cavern.
"Come on, boy," he says. "Purify yerself."
I look at the knife—
Resting in a puddle of water—
Near the ledge by the pulpit behind Aaron—
Where I dropped it—
And I hear it calling to me—
Take me, it says—
Take me and use me, it says—
Aaron holds open his arms.
"Murder me," he says. "Become a man."
Never let me go, says the knife—
"I'm sorry," I whisper under my breath tho I don't know who to or
what for—
I'm sorry—
And I leap—
Aaron doesn't move, arms open as if to embrace me—
I barrel into him with my shoulder—
He doesn't resist—
My Noise screams red—

We fall past the pulpit to the ledge—
I'm on top of him—
He still doesn't resist—
I punch his face—
Over—
And over—
And over—
Breaking it further—
Breaking it into bloody messy pieces—
Hate pouring outta me thru my fists—
And still I pound him—
Still I hit—
Thru the breaking of bone—
And the snapping of gristle—
And an eye crushed under my knuckles—
Till I can no longer feel my hands—
And still I hit—
And his blood spills on me and over—
And the red of it matches the red of my Noise—
And then I lean back, still on him, covered in his blood—
And he's laughing, he's laughing *still*—
And he's gurgling "Yes" thru broken teeth, "Yes—"
And the red rises in me—
And I can't hold it back—
And the hate—
And I look over—
At the knife—
Just a few feet away—
On the ledge—
By the pulpit—
Calling for me—
Calling—
And this time I know—
This time I know—

I'm going to use it.

And I jump for it—
My hand outstretched—
My Noise so red I can barely see—
Yes, says the knife—

*   *   *

Yes.

Take me.
Take the power in yer hand—

But another hand is there first—

Viola.

And as I fall toward it there's a rush in me—
A rush in my Noise—
A rush from seeing her there—
From seeing her alive—
A rush that rises higher than the red—
And "Viola," I say—
Just "Viola."

And she picks up the knife.

My momentum is tumbling me toward the edge and I'm turning to try and catch myself and I can see her lifting the knife and I can see her stepping forward and I'm falling into the ledge and my fingers are slipping on wet stone and I can see Aaron sitting up and he's only got one eye now and it's staring at Viola as she's raising the knife and she's bringing it forward and I can't stop her and Aaron is trying to rise and Viola's moving toward him and I'm hitting the ledge with my shoulder and stopping just short of falling over and I'm watching and what's left of Aaron's Noise is radiating anger and fear and it's saying *No*—
It's saying *Not you*—
And Viola's raising her arm—
Raising the knife—
And bringing it down—
And down—
And down—
And plunging it straight into the side of Aaron's neck—
So hard the point comes out the other side—
And there's a crunch, a crunch I remember—
Aaron falls over from the force of it—
And Viola lets go of the knife—
She steps back.
Her face is white.
I can hear her breathing over the roar.

I lift myself with my hands—

And we watch.

Aaron's pushing himself up.

He's pushing himself up, one hand clawing at the knife, but it stays in his neck. His remaining eye is wide open, his tongue lolling outta his mouth.

He gets to his knees.

And then to his feet.

Viola cries out a little and steps back.

Steps back till she's next to me.

We can hear him trying to swallow.

Trying to breathe.

He steps forward but stumbles against the pulpit.

He looks our way.

His tongue swells and writhes.

He's trying to say something.

He's trying to say something to me.

He's trying to make a word.

But he can't.

He can't.

His Noise is just wild colors and pictures and things I won't ever be able to say.

He catches my eye.

And his Noise stops.

Completely stops.

At last.

And gravity takes his body and he slumps sideways.

Away from the pulpit.

And over the edge.

And disappears under the wall of water.

Taking the knife with him.

42

LAST ROAD TO HAVEN

VIOLA SITS DOWN NEXT TO ME so hard and fast it's like she fell there.

She's breathing heavy and staring into the space where Aaron was. The sunlight thru the falls casts waves of watery light over her face but that's the only thing on it that moves.

"Viola?" I say, leaping up into a squat next to her.

"He's gone," she says.

"Yeah," I say. "He's gone."

And she just breathes.

My Noise is rattling like a crashing spaceship full of reds and whites and things so different it's like my head is being pulled apart.

I woulda done it.

I woulda done it for her.

But instead—

"I woulda done it," I say. "I was ready to do it."

She looks at me, her eyes wide. "Todd?"

"I woulda killed him myself." I find my voice rising a little. "I was ready to do it!"

And then her chin starts shaking, not as if she's going to cry, but actually *shaking* and then her shoulders, too, and her eyes are getting wider and she's shaking harder and nothing leaves my Noise and it's all still there but something else enters it and it's for her and I grab her and hold her to me and we rock back and forth for a while so she can just shake all she wants to.

She don't speak for a long time, just makes little moaning sounds in her throat, and I remember just after I killed the Spackle, how I could feel the crunch running down my arm, how I could keep seeing his blood, how I saw him die again and again.

How I do still.

(But I woulda.)

(I was ready.)

(But the knife is gone.)

"Killing someone ain't nothing like it is in stories," I say into the top of her head. "Ain't nothing at all."

(But I woulda.)

She's still shaking and we're still right next to a raging, roaring water-fall and the sun's higher in the sky and there's less light in the church and we're wet and bloody and bloody and wet.

And cold and shaking.

"Come on," I say, making to stand. "First thing we need to do is get dry, okay?"

I get her to her feet. I go get the bag, still on the floor twixt two pews and go back to her and hold out my hand.

"The sun is up," I say. "It'll be warm outside."

She looks at my hand for a minute before taking it.

But she takes it.

We make our way round the pulpit, unable to keep from looking where Aaron was, his blood already washed away by the spray.

(I woulda done it.)

(But the knife.)

I can feel my hand shaking in hers and I don't know which one of us it is.

We get to the steps and it's halfway up that she first speaks.

"I feel sick," she says.

"I know," I say.

And we stop and she leans closer to the waterfall and is sick.

A lot.

I guess this is what happens when you kill someone in real life.

She leans forward, her hair wet and tangled down. She spits.

But she don't look up.

"I couldn't let you," she says. "He would have won."

"I woulda done it," I say.

"I know," she says, into her hair, into the falls. "That's why I did it."

I let out a breath. "You shoulda let me."

"No." She looks up from being crouched over. "I *couldn't* let you." She wipes her mouth and coughs again. "But it's not just that."

"What then?" I say.

She looks into my eyes. Her own are wide and they're bloodshot from the barfing.

And they're older than they used to be.

"I *wanted* to, Todd," she says, her forehead creasing. "I *wanted* to do it. I *wanted* to kill him." She puts her hands to her face. "Oh my God," she breathes. "Oh my God, oh my God, oh my God."

"Stop it," I say, taking her arms and pulling her hands away. "Stop it. He was evil. He was *crazy* evil—"

"I know!" she shouts. "But I keep seeing him. I keep seeing the knife going into his—"

"Yeah, okay, you wanted to," I stop her before she gets worse. "So what? So did *I*. But he *made* you want to. He made it so it was him or us. That's why he was evil. Not what you did or what I did, what *he* did, okay?"

She looks up at me. "He did just what he promised," she says, her voice a little quieter. "He made me fall."

She moans again and clamps her hands over her mouth, her eyes welling up.

"No," I say strongly. "No, see, here's the thing, here's what I think, okay?"

I look up to the water and the tunnel and I don't know what I think but she's there and I can see it and I don't know what she's thinking but I *know what she's thinking* and I can see her and she's teetering on the edge and she's looking at me and she's asking me to save her.

Save her like she saved me.

"Here's what I think," I say and my voice is stronger and thoughts are coming, thoughts that trickle into my Noise like whispers of the truth. "I think maybe *everybody* falls," I say. "I think maybe we all do. And I don't think that's the asking."

I pull on her arms gently to make sure she's listening.

"I think the asking is whether we get back up again."

And the water's rushing by and we're shaking from the cold and everything else and she stares at me and I wait and I hope.

And I see her step back from the edge.

I see her come back to me.

"Todd," she says and it ain't an asking.

It's just my name.

It's who I am.

"Come on," I say. "Haven's waiting."

I take her hand again and we make our way up the rest of the steps and back to the flatter part of the ledge, following the curves out from the center, steadying ourselves again on the slippery stones. The jump back to the embankment is harder this time cuz we're so wet and weak but I take a running shot at it and then catch Viola as she comes tumbling after me.

And we're in sunlight.

We breathe it in for a good long while, getting the wettest of the wet off of us before we gather up and climb the little embankment, pushing ourselves thru the scrub to the trail and back to the road.

We look down the hill, down the zigzag trail.

It's still there. Haven's still there.

"Last bit," I say.

Viola rubs her arms to dry herself a little more. She squints at me, looking close. "You get hit in the face a lot, you know that?"

I bring my fingers up. My eye is starting to swell some and I notice a gap on the side of my mouth where I lost a few teeth.

"Thanks," I say. "It wasn't hurting till you said that."

"Sorry." She smiles a little and puts her hand up to the back of her own head and winces.

"How's yers?" I ask.

"Sore," she says, "but I'll live."

"Yer indestructible, you," I say.

She smiles again.

And then there's a weird *zipSNICK* sound in the air and Viola lets out a little gasp, a little *oh* sound.

We look at each other for a second, in the sunshine, both of us surprised but not sure why.

And then I follow her glance down her front.

There's blood on her shirt.

Her own blood.

New blood.

Pouring out a little hole just to the right of her belly button.

She touches the blood and holds up her fingers.

"Todd?" she says.

And then she falls forward.

I catch her, stumbling back a bit from the weight.

And I look up behind her.

Up to the cliff top, right where the road begins.

Mr. Prentiss Jr.

On horseback.

Hand outstretched.

Holding a pistol.

"Todd?" Viola says against my chest. "I think someone *shot* me, Todd."

There are no words.

No words in my head or my Noise.

Mr. Prentiss Jr. kicks his horse and edges him down the road toward us.

Pistol still pointed.

There's nowhere to run.

And I don't got my knife.

The world unfolds as clear and as slow as the worst pain, Viola starting to pant heavy against me, Mr. Prentiss Jr. riding down the road, and my Noise rising with the knowledge that we're finished, that there's no way out this time, that if the world wants you, it's gonna keep on coming till it gets you.

And who am I that can fix it? Who am I that can change this if the world wants it so badly? Who am I to stop the end of the world if it keeps on coming?

"I think she wants you *bad,* Todd," Mr. Prentiss Jr. sneers.

I clench my teeth.

My Noise rises red and purple.

I'm Todd effing Hewitt.

That's who I effing well am.

I look him right in the eye, sending my Noise straight for him, and I spit out in a rasp, "I'll thank you to call me *Mr. Hewitt.*"

Mr. Prentiss Jr. flinches, actually *flinches* a little and pulls his reins involuntarily, making his horse rear up for a second.

"Come on, now," he says, his voice slightly less sure.

And he knows we both can hear it.

"Hands up," he says. "I'm taking you to my father."

And I do the most amazing thing.

The most amazing thing I ever did.

I ignore him.

I kneel Viola down to the dirt road.

"It burns, Todd," she says, her voice low.

I set her down and drop the bag and slip my shirt off my back, crumpling it up and holding it against the bullet hole. "You hold that tight, you hear me?" I say, my anger rising like lava. "This won't take a second."

I look up at *Davy* Prentiss.

"Get up," he says, his horse still jumpy and edgy from the heat coming off me. "I ain't telling you twice, Todd."

I stand.

I step forward.

"I said put yer hands up," Davy says, his horse whinnying and bluffing and clopping from foot to foot.

I march toward him.

Faster.

Till I'm running.

"I'll shoot you!" Davy shouts, waving the gun, trying to control his horse which is sending **Charge! Charge!** all over the place in its Noise.

"No, you won't!" I yell, running right up to the horse's head and sending a crash of Noise right at it.

SNAKE!

The horse rears up on its back legs.

"Goddammit, Todd!" Davy yells, wheeling and whirling, trying to control his horse with the one hand that's not holding the pistol.

I jump in, slap the horse's front quarters and jump back. The horse whinnies and rears up again.

"Yer a dead man!" Davy shouts, going in a full circle with the horse jumping and rearing.

"Yer *half* right," I say.

And I'm seeing my chance—

The horse neighs loudly and shakes its head back and forth—

I wait—

Davy pulls on the reins—

I dodge—

I wait—

"Effing horse!" Davy shouts—

He tries to jerk the reins again—

The horse is twisting round one more time—

I wait—

The horse brings Davy round to me, careening him low in the saddle—

And there's my chance—

My fist is back and waiting—

BOOM!

I catch him across the face like a hammer falling—

I swear I feel his nose break under my fist—

He calls out in pain and falls from the saddle—

Dropping the pistol in the dust—

I jump back—

Davy's foot catches in the stirrup—

The horse rears round again—

I smack its hindquarters as hard as I can—

And the horse has had enough.

It charges back up the hill, back up the road, Davy's foot still caught, making him bounce hard against rocks and dirt as he's dragged, fast, up the incline—

The pistol's in the dust—

I move for it—

"Todd?" I hear.

And there's no time.

There's no time at all.

Without hardly thinking, I leave the pistol and I run back down to Viola at the edge of the scrub.

"I think I'm dying, Todd," she says.

"Yer not dying," I say, getting an arm under her shoulders and another under her knees.

"I'm cold."

"Yer *not effing dying!*" I say. "Not today!"

And I stand, with her in my arms, and I'm at the top of the zigzag that goes down into Haven.

And that's not going to be fast enough.

I plunge straight down. Straight down thru the scrub.

"Come on!" I say out loud as my Noise forgets itself and all there is in the universe is my legs moving.

Come on!

I run.

Thru scrub—

And across road—

Thru more scrub—

Across road again as it doubles back—

Down and down—

Kicking up clods of earth and jumping over bushes—

Stumbling over roots—

Come on.

"Hang on," I say to Viola. "You hang on, you hear me?"

Viola grunts every time we land hard—

But that means she's still breathing.

Down—

And down—

Come on.

Please.

I skid on some bracken—

But I do not fall—

Road and scrub—

My legs aching at the steepness—

Scrub and road—

Down—

Please—

"Todd?"

"Hang on!"

I reach the bottom of the hill and I hit it running.

She's so light in my arms.

So light.

I run to where the road rejoins the river, the road into Haven, trees springing up again all around us, the river rushing on.

"Hang on!" I say again, running down the road, fast as my feet will carry me.

Come on.

Please.

Round curves and corners—

Under trees and by the riverbank—

Up ahead I see the battlement I spotted with the binocs from the hill above, huge wooden Xs piled up in a long row out to either side with an opening across the road.

"HELP!" I'm shouting as we come to it. "HELP US!"

I run.

Come on.

"I don't think I can—" Viola says, her voice breathless.

"Yes you CAN!" I shout. "Don't you DARE give up!"

I run.

The battlement's coming—

But there's no one.

There's no one there.

I run thru the opening on the road and to the other side.

I stop long enough to take a turn around.

There's *no one.*

"Todd?"

"We're almost there," I say.

"I'm losing it, Todd—"

And her head rolls back.

"No yer NOT!" I shout at her face. "You WAKE UP, Viola Eade! You keep yer ruddy eyes open."

And she tries. I see her try.

And her eyes open, only a little, but open.

And I run again as fast as I can.

And I'm shouting "HELP!" as I go.

"HELP!"

Please.

"HELP!"

And her breath is starting to gasp.

"HELP US!"

Please no.

And I'm not seeing NO ONE.

The houses I pass are shut up and empty. The road turns from dirt to paved and still no one out and about.

"HELP!"

My feet slam against the pavement—

The road is leading to the big church up ahead, a clearing of the trees, the steeple shining down onto a town square in front of it.

And no one's there neither.

No.

"HELP!"

I race on to the square, crossing it, looking all around, listening out—

No.

No.

It's empty.

Viola's breathing heavy in my arms.

And Haven is empty.

I reach the middle of the square.

I don't see nor hear a soul.

I spin around again.

"HELP!" I cry.

But there's no one.

Haven is completely empty.

There ain't no hope here at all.

Viola slips a little from my grasp and I have to kneel to catch her. My shirt has dropped from her wound and I use one hand to hold it in place.

There ain't nothing left. The bag, the binocs, my ma's book, I'm realizing it's all left up on the hillside.

Me and Viola are all we got, everything we have in the world.

And she's bleeding *so much—*

"Todd?" she says, her voice low and slurring.

"Please," I say, my eyes welling, my voice cracking. "Please."

Please please please please please—

"Well, since you asked so nicely," comes a voice across the square, hardly even raising itself to a shout.

I look up.

Coming round the side of the church is a single horse.

With a single rider.

"No," I whisper.

No.

No.

"Yes, Todd," says Mayor Prentiss. "I'm afraid so."

He rides his horse almost lazily across the square toward me. He looks as cool and unruffled as ever, no sweat marking his clothes, even wearing riding gloves, even clean boots.

This ain't possible.

This ain't possible at all.

"How can you be here?" I say, my voice rising. "How?"

"Even a simpleton knows there's two roads to Haven," he says, his voice calm and silky, almost smirking but not quite.

The dust we saw. The dust we saw moving toward Haven yesterday.

"But *how*?" I say, so stunned I can barely get the words out. "The army's a day away at least—"

"Sometimes the rumor of an army is just as effective as the army itself, my boy," he says. "The terms of surrender were most favorable. One of which was clearing the streets so I could welcome you here myself." He looks back up toward the falls. "Tho I was of course expecting my son to bring you."

I look around the square and now I can see faces, faces peering outta windows, outta doors.

I can see four more men on horseback coming round the church.

I look back at Mayor Prentiss.

"Oh, it's *President* Prentiss now," he says. "You'll do well to remember that."

And then I realize.

I can't hear his Noise.

I can't hear *anyone's*.

"No," he says. "I imagine you can't, tho that's an interesting story and not what you might—"

Viola slips a little more from my hands, the shift of it making her give a pained gasp. "Please!" I say. "Save her! I'll do anything you say! I'll join the army! I'll—"

"All good things to those who wait," the Mayor says, finally looking a little annoyed.

He dismounts in one easy movement and starts taking off his gloves one finger at a time.

And I know we've lost.

Everything is lost.

Everything is over.

"As the newly appointed President of this fair planet of ours," the Mayor says, holding out his hand as if to show me the world for the first time, "let me be the very first to welcome you to its new capital city."

"Todd?" Viola whispers, her eyes closed.

I hold her tightly to me.

"I'm sorry," I whisper to her. "I'm so sorry."

We've run right into a trap.

We've run right off the end of the world.

"Welcome," says the Mayor, "to New Prentisstown."

END OF BOCK ONE

THE ASK

AND THE

ANSWER

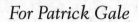
For Patrick Gale

Battle not with monsters
lest you become a monster
and if you gaze into the abyss
the abyss gazes into you.

Friedrich Nietzsche

THE END

"YOUR NOISE REVEALS YOU, TODD HEWITT."

A voice–

In the darkness–

I blink open my eyes. Everything is shadows and blur and it feels like the world's spinning and my blood is too hot and my brain is clogged and I can't think and it's dark–

I blink again.

Wait–

No, *wait*–

Just now, just *now* we were in the square–

Just now she was in my arms–

She was *dying* in my arms–

"Where is she?" I spit into the dark, tasting blood, my voice croaking, my Noise rising like a sudden hurricane, high and red and furious. *"WHERE IS SHE?"*

"I will be the one doing the asking here, Todd."

That voice.

His voice.

Somewhere in the dark.

Somewhere behind me, somewhere unseen.

Mayor Prentiss.

I blink again and the murk starts to turn into a vast room, the only light coming from a single window, a wide circle up high and far away, its glass not clear but colored into shapes of New World and its two circling moons, the light from it slanting down onto me and nothing else.

"*What have you done with her?*" I say, loud, blinking against fresh blood trickling into my eyes. I try to reach up to clear it away but I find my hands are tied behind my back and panic rises in me and I struggle against the binds and my breathing speeds up and I shout again, "*WHERE IS SHE?*"

A fist comes from nowhere and punches me in the stomach.

I lean forward into the shock of it and realize I'm tied to a wooden chair, my feet bound to its legs, my shirt gone somewhere up on a dusty hillside and as I'm throwing up my empty stomach I notice there's carpet beneath me, repeating the same pattern of New World and its moons, over and over and over, stretching out forever.

And I'm remembering we were in the square, in the square where I'd run, holding her, carrying her, telling her to stay alive, stay alive till we got safe, till we got to Haven so I could save her–

But there *weren't* no safety, no safety at all, there was just *him* and his men and they took her from me, they *took* her from my arms–

"You notice that he does not ask, *Where am I?*" says the Mayor's voice, moving out there, somewhere. "His first words are, *Where is she?*, and his Noise says the same. Interesting."

My head's throbbing along with my stomach and I'm waking up some more and I'm remembering I *fought* them, I fought them when they took her till the butt of a gun smashed against my temple and knocked me into blackness–

I swallow away the tightness in my throat, swallow away the panic and the fear–

Cuz this is the end, ain't it?

The end of it all.

The Mayor has me.

The Mayor has her.

"If you hurt her–" I say, the punch still aching in my belly. Mr. Collins stands in front of me, half in shadow, Mr. Collins who farmed corn and cauliflower and who tended the Mayor's horses and who stands over me now with a pistol in a holster, a rifle slung round his back and a fist rearing up to punch me again.

"She seemed quite hurt enough already, Todd," the Mayor says, stopping Mr. Collins. "The poor thing."

My fists clench in their bindings. My Noise feels lumpy and half-battered but it still rises with the memory of Davy Prentiss's gun pointed at us, of her falling into my arms, of her bleeding and gasping–

And then I make it go even redder with the feel of my own fist landing on Davy Prentiss's face, of Davy Prentiss falling from his horse, his foot caught in the stirrup, dragged away like so much trash.

"Well," the Mayor says, "that explains the mysterious whereabouts of my *son.*"

And if I didn't know better, I'd say he sounded almost *amused.*

But I notice the only way I can tell this is from the sound of his voice, a voice sharper and smarter than any old Prentisstown voice he might once have had, and that the nothing I heard coming from him when I ran into Haven is still a big nothing in whatever room this is and it's matched by a big nothing from Mr. Collins.

They ain't got Noise.

Neither of 'em.

The only Noise here is mine, bellering like an injured calf.

I twist my neck to find the Mayor but it hurts too much to turn very far and all I can tell is that I'm sitting in the single beam of dusty, colored sunlight in the middle of a room so big I can barely make out the walls in the far distance.

And then I do see a little table in the darkness, set back just far enough so I can't make out what's on it.

Just the shine of metal, glinting and promising things I don't wanna think about.

"He still thinks of me as Mayor," his voice says, sounding light and amused again.

"It's President Prentiss now, boy," grunts Mr. Collins. "You'd do well to remember that."

"What have you done with her?" I say, trying to turn again, this way and that, wincing at the pain in my neck. "If you *touch* her, I'll—"

"You arrive in my town this very morning," interrupts the Mayor, "with nothing in your possession, not even the shirt on your back, just a girl in your arms who has suffered a terrible accident—"

My Noise surges. "It was no *accident—*"

"A very bad accident indeed," continues the Mayor, his voice giving the first hint of the impayshunce I heard when we met in the square. "So very bad that she is near death and here is the boy who we have spent so much of our time and energy trying to find, the boy who has caused us so much trouble, offering himself up to us *willingly,* offering to do anything we wish if we just *save the girl* and yet when we try to do just that—"

"Is she all right? Is she safe?"

The Mayor stops and Mr. Collins steps forward and backhands me across the face. There's a long moment as the sting spreads across my cheek and I sit there, panting.

Then the Mayor steps into the circle of light, right in front of me.

He's still in his good clothes, crisp and clean as ever, as if there ain't a man underneath there at all, just a walking talking block of ice. Even Mr. Collins has sweat marks and dirt and the smell you'd expect but not the Mayor, no.

The Mayor makes you look like yer nothing but a mess that needs cleaning up.

He faces me, leans down so he's looking into my eyes.

And then he gives me an asking, like he's only curious.

"What is her name, Todd?"

I blink, surprised. "What?"

"What is her name?" he repeats.

Surely he must know her name. Surely it must be in my Noise–

"You know her name," I say.

"I want you to tell me."

I look from him to Mr. Collins, standing there with his arms crossed, his silence doing nothing to hide a look on his face that would happily pound me into the ground.

"One more time, Todd," says the Mayor lightly, "and I would very much like for you to answer. What is her name? This girl from across the worlds."

"If you know she's from across the worlds," I say, "then you must know her name."

And then the Mayor smiles, actually *smiles*.

And I feel more afraid than ever.

"That's not how this works, Todd. How this works is that I ask and you answer. Now. What is her name?"

"Where is she?"

"What's her name?"

"Tell me where she is and I'll tell you her name."

He sighs, as if I've let him down. He nods once to Mr. Collins, who steps forward and punches me again in the stomach.

"This is a simple transaction, Todd," the Mayor says, as I gag onto the carpet. "All you have to do is tell me what I want to know and this ends. The choice is yours. Genuinely, I have no wish to harm you further."

I'm breathing heavy, bent forward, the ache in my gut making it difficult to get enough air in me. I can feel my weight pulling at the bonds on my wrists and I can feel the blood on my face, sticky and drying, and I look out bleary eyed from my little prison of light in the middle of this room, this room with no exits–

This room where I'm gonna die–

This room—

This room where she ain't.

And something in me chooses.

If this is it, then something in me decides.

Decides not to say.

"You know her name," I say. "Kill me if you want but you know her name already."

And the Mayor just watches me.

The longest minute of my life passes with him watching me, reading me, seeing that I mean it.

And then he steps to the little wooden table.

I look to see but his back's hiding what he's doing. I hear him fiddling with things on top of it, a *thunk* of metal scraping against wood.

"*I'll do anything you want*," he says and I reckernize he's aping my own words back at me. "*Just save her and I'll do anything you want.*"

"I ain't afraid of you," I say, tho my Noise says otherwise, thinking of all the things that could be on that table. "I ain't afraid to die."

And I wonder if I mean it.

He turns to me, keeping his hands behind his back so I can't see what he's picked up. "Because you're a man, Todd? Because a man isn't afraid to die?"

"Yeah," I say. "Cuz I'm a man."

"If I'm correct, your birthday is not for another fourteen days."

"That's just a number." I'm breathing heavy, my stomach flip-flopping from talking like this. "It don't mean *nothing*. If I was on Old World, I'd be—"

"You ain't on Old World, *boy*," Mr. Collins says.

"I don't believe that's what he means, Mr. Collins," the Mayor says, still looking at me. "Is it, Todd?"

I look back and forth twixt the two of 'em. "I've killed," I say. "I've killed."

"Yes, I believe you've killed," says the Mayor. "I can see the shame of it all over you. But the asking is who? *Who* did you kill?" He steps into the darkness outside the circle of light, whatever he picked up from the table still hidden as he walks behind me. "Or should I say *what*?"

"I killed Aaron," I say, trying to follow him, failing.

"Did you, now?" His lack of Noise is an awful thing, especially when you can't see him. It's not like the silence of a girl, a girl's silence is still active, still a living thing that makes a shape in all the Noise that clatters round it.

(I think of her, I think of her silence, the ache of it)

(I don't think of her name)

But with the Mayor, however he's done it, however he's made it so
he and Mr. Collins don't got Noise, it's like it's nothing, like a dead thing,
no more shape nor Noise nor life in the world than a stone or a wall,
a fortress you ain't never gonna conquer. I'm guessing he's reading my
Noise but how can you tell with a man who's made himself of stone?

I show him what he wants anyway. I put the church under the waterfall at the front of my Noise. I put up all the truthful fight with Aaron,
all the struggle and the blood, I put me fighting him and beating him
and knocking him to the ground, I put me taking out my knife.

I put me stabbing Aaron in the neck.

"There's truth there," says the Mayor. "But is it the whole truth?"

"It is," I say, raising my Noise loud and high to block out anything
else he might hear. "It's the truth."

His voice is still amused. "I think you're lying to me, Todd."

"I ain't!" I practically shout. "I done what Aaron wanted! I murdered
him! I became a man by yer own laws and you can have me in yer army
and I'll do whatever you want, just tell me what you've done with her!"

I see Mr. Collins notice a sign from behind me and he steps forward
again, fist back and—

(I can't help it)

I jerk away from him so hard I drag the chair a few inches to the
side—

(shut up)

And the punch never falls.

"Good," says the Mayor, sounding quietly pleased. "Good." He
begins to move again in the darkness. "Let me explain a few things to
you, Todd," he says. "You are in the main office of what was formerly the
Cathedral of Haven and what yesterday became the Presidential Palace.
I have brought you into my home in the hope of helping you. Helping
you see that you are mistaken in this hopeless fight you put up against
me, against us."

His voice moves behind Mr. Collins—

His voice—

For a second it feels like he's not talking out loud—

Like he's talking right in my head—

Then it passes.

"My soldiers should arrive here tomorrow afternoon," he says, still
moving. "You, Todd Hewitt, will first tell me what I ask of you and then
you will be true to your word and you will assist me in our creation of a
new society."

He steps into the light again, stopping in front of me, his hands still
behind his back, whatever he picked up still hidden.

"But the process I want to begin here, Todd," he says, "is the one where you learn that I am not your enemy."

I'm so surprised I stop being afraid for a second.

Not my enemy?

I open my eyes wide.

Not my enemy?

"No, Todd," he says. "Not your enemy."

"Yer a murderer," I say, without thinking.

"I am a general," he says. "Nothing more, nothing less."

I stare at him. "You killed people on yer march here. You killed the people of Farbranch."

"Regrettable things happen in wartime, but that war is now over."

"I saw you shoot them," I say, hating how the words of a man without Noise sound so solid, so much like unmovable stone.

"Me personally, Todd?"

I swallow away a sour taste. "No, but it was a war *you started!*"

"It was necessary," he says. "To save a sick and dying planet."

My breathing is getting faster, my mind getting cloudier, my head heavier than ever. But my Noise is redder, too. "You murdered Cillian."

"Deeply regrettable," he says. "He would have made a fine soldier."

"You killed my mother," I say, my voice catching (shut up), my Noise filling with rage and grief, my eyes screwing up with tears (shut up, shut up, shut up). "You killed all the women of Prentisstown."

"Do you believe everything you hear, Todd?"

There's a silence, a real one, as even my own Noise takes this in. "I have no desire to kill women," he adds. "I never did."

My mouth drops open. "Yes, you *did–*"

"Now is not the time for a history lesson."

"Yer a *liar!*"

"And you presume to know everything, do you?" His voice goes cold and he steps away from me and Mr. Collins strikes me so hard on the side of the head I nearly fall over onto the floor.

"Yer a LIAR AND A MURDERER!" I shout, my ears still ringing from the punch.

Mr. Collins hits me again the other way, hard as a block of wood.

"I am *not* your enemy, Todd," the Mayor says again. "Please stop making me do this to you."

My head is hurting so bad I don't say nothing. I *can't* say nothing. I can't say the word he wants. I can't say nothing else without getting beaten senseless.

This is the end. It's gotta be the end. They won't let me live. They won't let *her* live.

It's gotta be the end.

"I hope it *is* the end," the Mayor says, his voice actually making the sounds of truth. "I hope you'll tell me what I want to know so we can stop all this."

And then he says—

Then he says—

He says, "Please."

I look up, blinking thru the swelling coming up round my eyes.

His face has a look of concern on it, a look of almost *pleading*.

What the hell? What the ruddy hell?

And I hear the buzz of it inside my head again—

Different than just hearing someone's Noise—

PLEASE like it's said in my own voice—

PLEASE like it's coming from me—

Pressing on me—

On my insides—

Making me feel like I wanna say it—

PLEASE—

"The things you think you know, Todd," the Mayor says, his voice still twining around inside my own head. "Those things aren't true."

And then I remember—

I remember Ben—

I remember Ben saying the same thing to me—

Ben who I lost—

And my Noise hardens, right there.

Cutting him off.

The Mayor's face loses the look of pleading.

"All right," he says, frowning a little. "But remember that it is your choice." He stands up straight. "What is her name?"

"You know her name."

Mr. Collins strikes me across the head, careening me sideways.

"What is her name?"

"You already know it—"

Boom, another blow, this time the other way.

"What is her name?"

"No."

Boom.

"Tell me her name."

"No!"

BOOM!

"What is her *name*, Todd?"

"EFF YOU!"

Except I don't say "eff" and Mr. Collins hits me so hard my head whips back and the chair overbalances and I do topple sideways to the floor, taking the chair with me. I slam into the carpet, hands tied so I can't catch myself, my eyes filling up with little New Worlds till there ain't nothing else to see.

I breathe into the carpet.

The toes of the Mayor's boots approach my face.

"I am not your enemy, Todd Hewitt," he says one more time. "Just tell me her name and this will all stop."

I take in a breath and have to cough it away.

I take in another and say what I have to say.

"Yer a murderer."

Another silence.

"So be it," says the Mayor.

His feet move away and I feel Mr. Collins pull my chair up from the floor, taking me up with it, my body groaning against its own weight, till I'm sat up again in the circle of colored light. My eyes are so swollen now I can't hardly see Mr. Collins at all even tho he's right in front of me.

I hear the Mayor at the small table again. I hear him moving things round on the top. I hear again the scrape of metal.

I hear him step up beside me.

And after all that promising, here it really, finally is.

My end.

I'm sorry, I think. *I'm so, so sorry.*

The Mayor puts a hand on my shoulder and I flinch away from it but he keeps it there, pressing down steadily. I can't see what he's holding, but he's bringing something toward me, toward my face, something hard and metal and filled with pain and ready to make me suffer and end my life and there's a hole inside me that I need to crawl into, away from all this, down deep and black, and I know this is the end, the end of all things, I can never escape from here and he'll kill me and kill her and there's no chance, no life, no hope, nothing.

I'm sorry.

And the Mayor lays a bandage across my face.

I gasp from the coolness of it and jerk away from his hands but he keeps pressing it gently into the lump on my forehead and onto the wounds on my face and chin, his body so close I can smell it, the cleanliness of it, the woody odor of his soap, the breath from his nose brushing over my cheek, his fingers touching my cuts almost tenderly, dressing the swelling round my eyes, the splits on my lip, and I can feel the bandages get to work almost instantly, feel the swelling going right down, the painkillers flooding into my system, and I think for a second how *good* the bandages are in Haven, how much like *her* bandages, and the relief comes so quick, so unexpected that my throat clenches and I have to swallow it away.

"I am not the man you think I am, Todd," the Mayor says quietly, almost right into my ear, putting another bandage on my neck. "I did not do the things you think I did. I asked my son to bring you back. I did not ask him to shoot anyone. I did not ask Aaron to kill you."

"Yer a liar," I say but my voice is weak and I'm shaking from the effort of keeping the weep out of it (shut up).

The Mayor puts more bandages across the bruises on my chest and stomach, so gentle I can barely stand it, so gentle it's almost like he cares how it feels.

"I *do* care, Todd," he says. "There will be time for you to learn the truth of that."

He moves behind me and puts another bandage around the bindings on my wrists, taking my hands and rubbing feeling back into them with his thumbs.

"There will be time," he says, "for you to come to trust me. For you, perhaps, to come to even *like* me. To even think of me, one day, as a kind of father to you, Todd."

It feels like my Noise is melting away with all the drugs, with all the pain disappearing, with me disappearing along with it, like he's killing me after all, but with the cure instead of the punishment.

I can't keep the weep from my throat, my eyes, my voice.

"Please," I say. "Please."

But I don't know what I mean.

"The war is over, Todd," the Mayor says again. "We are making a new world. This planet finally and truly living up to its name. Believe me when I say, once you see it, you'll *want* to be part of it."

I breathe into the darkness.

"You could be a leader of men, Todd. You have proven yourself very special."

I keep breathing, trying to hold on to it but feeling myself slip away.

"How can I know?" I finally say, my voice a croak, a slur, a thing not quite real. "How can I know she's even still alive?"

"You can't," says the Mayor. "You only have my word."

And waits again.

"And if I do it," I say. "If I do what you say, you'll save her?"

"We will do whatever's necessary," he says.

Without pain, it feels almost like I don't have a body at all, almost like I'm a ghost, sitting in a chair, blinded and eternal.

Like I'm dead already.

Cuz how do you know yer alive if you don't hurt?

"We are the choices we make, Todd," the Mayor says. "Nothing more, nothing less. I'd like you to choose to tell me. I would like that very much indeed."

Under the bandages is just further darkness.

Just me, alone in the black.

Alone with his voice.

I don't know what to do.

I don't know anything.

(what do I do?)

But if there's a chance, if there's even a *chance*–

"Is it really such a sacrifice, Todd?" the Mayor says, listening to me think. "Here, at the end of the past? At the beginning of the future?"

No. No, I can't. He's a liar and a murderer, no matter what he says–

"I'm waiting, Todd."

But she might be alive, he might keep her alive–

"We are nearing your last opportunity, Todd."

I raise my head. The movement opens the bandages some and I squint up into the light, up toward the Mayor's face.

It's blank as ever.

It's the empty, lifeless wall.

I might as well be talking into a bottomless pit.

I might as well *be* the bottomless pit.

I look away. I look down.

"Viola," I say into the carpet. "Her name's Viola."

The Mayor lets out a long, pleased-sounding breath. "Good, Todd," he says. "I thank you."

He turns to Mr. Collins.

"Lock him up."

PART I

TODD IN THE TOWER

1

THE OLD MAYOR

[TODD]

MR. COLLINS PUSHES ME up a narrow, windowless staircase, up and up and up, turning on sharp landings but always straight up. Just when I think my legs can't take no more, we reach a door. He opens it and shoves me hard and I go tumbling into the room and down onto a wooden floor, my arms so stiff I can't even catch myself and I groan and roll to one side.

And look down over a hundred-foot drop.

Mr. Collins laughs as I scrabble back away from it. I'm on a ledge not more than five boards wide that runs round the walls of a square room. In the middle is just an enormous hole with some ropes dangling down thru the center. I follow 'em up thru a tall shaft to the biggest set of bells I ever saw, two of 'em hanging from a single wooden beam, huge things, big as a room you could live in, archways cut into the sides of the tower so the bell-ringing can be heard.

I jump when Mr. Collins slams the door, locking it with a *ker-thunk* sound that don't brook no thoughts of escape.

I get myself up and lean against the wall till I can breathe again.

I close my eyes.

I am Todd Hewitt, I think. *I am the son of Cillian Boyd and Ben Moore. My birthday is in fourteen days but I am a man.*

I am Todd Hewitt and I am a man.

(a man who told the Mayor her name)
"I'm sorry," I whisper. "I'm so sorry."

After a while, I open my eyes and look up and around. There are small rectangular openings at eye level all around this floor of the tower, three on each wall, fading light shining in thru the dust.

I go to the nearest opening. I'm in the bell tower of the cathedral, obviously, way up high, looking out the front, down onto the square where I first entered the town, only this morning but it already feels like a lifetime ago. Dusk is falling, so I musta been out cold for a bit before the Mayor woke me, time where he coulda done anything to her, time where he coulda–

(shut up, just shut up)

I look out over the square. It's still empty, still the quiet of a silent town, a town with no Noise, a town waiting for an army to come and conquer it.

A town that didn't even try to fight.

The Mayor just turned up and they handed it right over to him. *Sometimes the rumor of an army is just as effective as the army itself*, he told me and wasn't he right?

All that time, running here as fast as we could, not thinking bout what Haven'd be like once we got here, not saying it out loud but hoping it'd be safe, hoping it'd be paradise.

I'm telling you there's hope, Ben said.

But he was wrong. It wasn't Haven at all.

It was New Prentisstown.

I frown, feeling my chest tighten and I look out west across the square, across the treetops that spread out into the farther silent houses and streets and on up to the waterfall, smashing down from the rim of the valley in the near distance, the zigzag road zipping up the hill beside it, the road where I fought Davy Prentiss Jr., the road where Viola–

I turn back into the room.

My eyes are adjusting to the fading light but there don't seem to be nothing here anyway but boards and a faint stink. The bell ropes dangle about six feet from any side. I look up to see where they're tied fast to the bells to make 'em chime. I squint down into the hole but it's too dark to see clearly what might be at the bottom. Probably just hard brick.

Six feet ain't that much at all, tho. You could jump it easy and grab onto a rope to climb yer way down.

But then–

"It's quite ingenious, really," says a voice from the far corner.

I jerk back, fists up, my Noise spiking. A man is standing up from where he was sitting, another Noiseless man.

Except–

"If you try to escape by climbing down the ropes left so temptingly available," he continues, "every person in town is going to know about it."

"Who are you?" I say, my stomach high and light but my fists clenching.

"Yes," he says. "I could tell you weren't from Haven." He steps away from the corner, letting light catch his face. I see a blackened eye and a cut lip that looks like it's only just scabbed over. No bandages spared for him, obviously. "Funny how quickly one forgets the *loudness* of it," he says, almost to himself.

He's a small man, shorter than me, wider, too, older than Ben tho not by much, but I can also see he's soft all over, soft even in his face. A softness I could beat if I had to.

"Yes," he says, "I imagine you could."

"Who are you?" I say again.

"Who am I?" repeats the man softly, then raises his voice like he's playing at something. "I am Con Ledger, my boy. Mayor of Haven." He smiles in a dazed way. "But not Mayor of New Prentisstown." He shakes his head a little as he looks at me. "We even gave the refugees the cure when they started pouring in."

And then I see that his smile ain't a smile, it's a *wince*.

"Good God, boy," he says. "How Noisy you are."

"I ain't a boy," I say, my fists still up.

"I completely fail to see how that's any sort of point."

I got ten million things I wanna say but my curiosity wins out first. "So there *is* a cure then? For the Noise?"

"Oh, yes," he says, his face twitching a bit at me, like he's tasting something bad. "Native plant with a natural neurochemical mixed with a few things we could synthesize and there you go. Quiet falls at last on New World."

"Not *all* of New World."

"No, well," he says, turning to look out the rectangle with his hands clasped behind his back. "It's very hard to make, isn't it? A long and slow process. We only got it right late last year and that was after twenty years of trying. We made enough for ourselves and were just on the point of starting to export it when . . ."

He trails off, looking firmly out onto the town below.

"When you surrendered," I say, my Noise rumbling, low and red. "Like cowards."

He turns back to me, the wincing smile gone, *way* gone. "And why should the opinion of a boy matter to me?"

"I *ain't* a boy," I say again and are my fists still clenched? Yes, they are.

"Clearly you are," he says, "for a *man* would know the necessary choices that have to be made when one is facing one's oblivion."

I narrow my eyes. "You ain't got nothing you can teach me bout oblivion."

He blinks a little, seeing the truth of it in my Noise as if it were bright flashes trying to blind him, and then his stance slumps. "Forgive me," he says. "This isn't me." He puts a hand up to his face and rubs it, smarting at the bruise around his eye. "Yesterday, I was the benevolent Mayor of a beautiful town." He seems to laugh at some private joke. "But that was yesterday."

"How many people in Haven?" I say, not quite ready to let it go.

He looks over at me. "Boy—"

"My name is Todd Hewitt," I say. "You can call me Mr. Hewitt."

"He promised us a new beginning—"

"Even *I* know he's a liar. *How many people?*"

He sighs. "Including refugees, three thousand, three hundred."

"The army ain't a third that size," I say. "You coulda fought."

"Women and children," he says. "Farmers."

"Women and children fought in other towns. Women and children *died*."

He steps forward, his face getting stormy. "Yes, and now the women and children of this city will *not* die! Because *I* reached a peace!"

"A peace that blacked yer eye," I say. "A peace that split yer lip."

He looks at me for another second and then gives a sad snort. "The words of a sage," he says, "in the voice of a hick."

And he turns back to look out the opening.

Which is when I notice the low *buzz*.

Asking marks fill my Noise but before I can open my mouth, the Mayor, the *old* Mayor, says, "Yes, that's me you hear."

"You?" I say. "What about the cure?"

"Would you give your conquered enemy his favorite medicine?"

I lick my upper lip. "It comes back? The Noise?"

"Oh, yes." He turns to me again. "If you don't take your daily dose, it most definitely comes back." He returns to his corner and slowly sits himself down. "You'll notice there are no toilets," he says. "I apologize in advance for the unpleasantness."

I watch him sit, my Noise still rattling red and sore and full of askings.

"It *was* you, if I'm not mistaken?" he says. "This morning? The one who the town was cleared for, the one the new President greeted himself on horseback?"

I don't answer him. But my Noise does.

"So, who are you then, Todd Hewitt?" he says. "What makes you so special?"

Now *that*, I think, is a very good asking.

Night falls quick and full, Mayor Ledger saying less and less and fidgeting more and more till he finally can't stand it and starts to pace. All the while, his *buzz* gets louder till even if we wanted to talk, we'd have to shout to do it.

I stand at the front of the tower and watch the stars come out, night covering the valley below.

And I'm thinking and I'm trying not to think cuz when I do, my stomach turns and I feel sick, or my throat clenches and I feel sick, or my eyes wet and I feel sick.

Cuz she's out there somewhere.

(*please* be out there somewhere)

(*please* be okay)

(*please*)

"Do you always have to be so bloody *loud*?" Mayor Ledger snaps. I turn to him, ready to snap back, and he holds up his hands in apology. "I'm sorry. I'm not like this." He starts fidgeting his fingers again. "It's difficult having one's cure taken away so abruptly."

I look back out over New Prentisstown as lights start coming on in people's houses. I ain't hardly seen no one out there the whole day, everyone staying indoors, probably under the Mayor's orders.

"They all going thru this out there, then?" I say.

"Oh, everyone will have their little stockpile at home," Mayor Ledger says. "They'll have to have it pried out of their hands, I imagine."

"I don't reckon that'll be a problem when the army gets here," I say.

The moons rise, crawling up the sky as if there was nothing to hurry about. They shine bright enough to light up New Prentisstown and I see how the river cuts thru town but that there ain't nothing much north of it except fields, empty in the moonlight, then a sharp rise of rocky cliffs that make up the north wall of the valley. To the north, you can also see a thin road coming outta the hills before cutting its way back into town, the other road that Viola and I didn't take after Farbranch, the other road the Mayor *did* take and got here first.

To the east, the river and the main road just carry on, going God knows where, round corners and farther hills, the town petering out as it goes. There's another road, not much paved, that heads south from the square and past more buildings and houses and into a wood and up a hill with a notch on the top.

And that's all there is of New Prentisstown.

Home to three thousand, three hundred people, all hiding in their houses, so quiet they might be dead.

Not one of them lifting a hand to save theirselves from what's coming, hoping if they're meek enough, if they're *weak* enough, then the monster won't eat 'em.

This is where we spent all our time running to.

I see movement down on the square, a shadow flitting, but it's only a dog. **Home, home, home,** I can just about hear him think. **Home, home, home.**

Dogs don't got the problems of people.

Dogs can be happy any old time.

I take a minute to breathe away the tightness that comes over my chest, the water in my eyes.

Take a minute to stop thinking bout my own dog.

When I can look out again, I see someone not a dog at all.

He's got his head slumped forward and he's walking his horse slow across the town square, the hoofs clopping against the brick and, as he approaches, even tho Mayor Ledger's **buzz** has started to become such a nuisance I don't know how I'm ever gonna sleep, I can still hear it out there.

Noise.

Across the quiet of a waiting city, I can hear the man's Noise.

And he can hear mine.

Todd Hewitt? he thinks.

And I can hear the smile growing on his face, too.

Found something, Todd, he says, across the square, up the tower, seeking me out in the moonlight. **Found something of yers.**

I don't say nothing. I don't *think* nothing.

I just watch as he reaches behind him and holds something up toward me.

Even this far away, even by the light of the moons, I know what it is.

My ma's book.

Davy Prentiss has my ma's book.

2

THE FOOT UPON THE NECK

[TODD]

EARLY NEXT MORNING, a platform with a microphone on it gets built noisily and quickly near the base of the bell tower and, as the morning turns to afternoon, the men of New Prentisstown gather in front of it.

"Why?" I say, looking out over 'em.

"Why do you think?" Mayor Ledger says, sitting in a darkened corner, rubbing his temples, his Noise *buzz* sawing away, hot and metallic. "To meet the new man in charge."

The men don't say much, their faces pale and grim, tho who can know what they're thinking when you can't hear their Noise? But they look cleaner than the men in my town used to, shorter hair, shaved faces, better clothes. A good number of 'em are rounded and soft like Mayor Ledger.

Haven musta been a comfortable place, a place where men weren't fighting every day just to survive.

Maybe too much comfort was the problem.

Mayor Ledger snorts to himself but don't say nothing.

Mayor Prentiss's men are on horseback at strategic spots across the square, ten or twelve of 'em, rifles ready, to make sure everyone behaves tho the threat of an army coming seems to have done most of the work. I see Mr. Tate and Mr. Morgan and Mr. O'Hare, men I grew up with, men I used to see every day being farmers, men who were just men till suddenly they became something else.

I don't see Davy Prentiss nowhere and my Noise starts rumbling again at the thought of him.

He musta come back down the hillside from wherever his horse dragged him and found the rucksack. All it had in it anymore was a bunch of ruined clothes and the book.

My ma's book.

My ma's words to me.

Written when I was born. Written till just before she died.

Before she was murdered.

My wondrous son who I swear will see this world come good.

Words read to me by Viola cuz I couldn't–

And now *Davy bloody Prentiss–*

"Can you please," Mayor Ledger says thru gritted teeth, "at least *try–*" He stops himself and looks at me apologetically. "I'm sorry," he says, for the millionth time since Mr. Collins woke us up with breakfast.

Before I can say anything back I feel the hardest, sudden tug on my heart, so surprising I nearly gasp.

I look out again.

The women of New Prentisstown are coming.

They start to appear farther away, in groups down side streets away from the main body of men, kept there by the Mayor's men patrolling on horseback.

I feel their silence in a way I can't feel the men's. It's like a loss, like great groupings of sorrow against the sound of the world and I have to wipe my eyes again but I press myself closer to the opening, trying to see 'em, trying to see every single one of 'em.

Trying to see if she's there.

But she ain't.

She ain't.

They look like the men, most of 'em wearing trousers and shirts of different cuts, some of 'em wearing long skirts, but most looking clean and comfortable and well fed. Their hair has more variety, pulled back or up or over or short or long and not nearly as many of 'em are blonde as they are in the Noise of the menfolk where I come from.

And I see that more of their arms are crossed, more of their faces looking doubtful.

More anger there than on the faces of the men.

"Did anyone fight you?" I ask Mayor Ledger while I keep on looking. "Did anyone not wanna give up?"

"This is a democracy, Todd," he sighs. "Do you know what that is?"

"No idea," I say, still looking, still not finding.

"It means the minority is listened to," he says, "but the majority rules."

I look at him. "All these people wanted to surrender?"

"The President made a *proposal*," he says, touching his split lip, "to the elected Council, promising that the city would be unharmed if we agreed to this."

"And you believed him?"

His eyes flash at me. "You are either forgetting or do not know that we already fought a great war, a war to end *all* wars, at just about the time you would have been born. If any repeat of that can be avoided—"

"Then yer willing to hand yerselves over to a murderer."

He sighs again. "The majority of the Council, led by myself, decided this was the best way to save the most lives." He rests his head against the brick. "Not everything is black and white, Todd. In fact, almost nothing is."

"But what if—"

Ker-thunk. The lock on the door slides back and Mr. Collins enters, pistol pointed.

He looks straight at Mayor Ledger. "Get up," he says.

I look back and forth twixt 'em both. "What's going on?" I say.

Mayor Ledger stands from his corner. "It seems the piper must be paid, Todd," he says, his voice trying to sound light but I hear his buzz rev up with fear. "This was a beautiful town," he says to me. "And I was a better man. Remember that, please."

"What are you talking about?" I say.

Mr. Collins takes him by the arm and shoves him out the door.

"Hey!" I shout, coming after them. "Where are you taking him?"

Mr. Collins raises a fist to punch me—

And I flinch away.

(shut *up*)

He laughs and locks the door behind him.

Ker-thunk.

And I'm left alone in the tower.

And as Mayor Ledger's buzz disappears down the stairs, that's when I hear it.

March march march, way in the distance.

I go to an opening.

They're here.

The conquering army, marching into Haven.

*   *   *

They flow down the zigzag road like a black river, dusty and dirty and coming like a dam's burst. They march four or five across and the first of them disappear into the far trees at the base of the hill as the last finally crest the top. The crowd watches them, the men turning back from the platform, the women looking out from the side streets.

The *march march march* grows louder, echoing down the city streets. Like a clock ticking its way down.

The crowd waits. I wait with them.

And then, thru the trees, at the turning of the road–

Here they are.

The army.

Mr. Hammar at their front.

Mr. Hammar who lived in the petrol stayshun back home, Mr. Hammar who thought vile, violent things no boy should ever hear, Mr. Hammar who shot the people of Farbranch in the back as they fled.

Mr. Hammar leads the army.

I can hear him now, calling out marching words to keep everyone in time together. *The foot*, he's yelling to the rhythm of the march.

The foot.

The foot.

The foot upon the neck.

They march into the square and turn down its side, cutting twixt the men and the women like an unstoppable force. Mr. Hammar's close enough so I can see the smile, a smile I know full well, a smile that clubs, a smile that beats, a smile that dominates.

And as he gets closer, I grow more sure.

It's a smile without Noise.

Someone, one of those men on horseback maybe, has gone out to meet the army on the road. Someone carrying the cure with him. The army ain't making a sound except with its feet and with its chant.

The foot, the foot, the foot upon the neck.

They march round the side of the square to the platform. Mr. Hammar stops at a corner, letting the men start to make up formayshuns behind the platform, lining up with their backs to me, facing the crowd now turned to watch them.

I start to reckernize the soldiers as they line up. Mr. Wallace. Mr. Smith the younger. Mr. Phelps the storekeeper. Men from Prentisstown and many, many more men besides.

The army that grew as it came.

I see Ivan, the man from the barn at Farbranch, the man who

secretly told me there were men in sympathy. He stands at the head of one of the formayshuns and everything that proves him right is standing behind him, arms at attenshun, rifles at the ready.

The last soldier marches into place with a final chant.

The foot upon the NECK!

And then there ain't nothing but silence, blowing over New Prentisstown like a wind.

Till I hear the doors of the cathedral open down below me.

And Mayor Prentiss steps out to address his new city.

"Right now," he says into the microphone, having saluted Mr. Hammar and climbed his way up the platform steps, "you are afraid."

The men of the town look back up at him, saying nothing, making no sound of Noise nor buzzing.

The women stay in the side streets, also silent.

The army stands at attenshun, ready for anything.

I realize I'm holding my breath.

"Right now," he continues, "you think you are conquered. You think there is no hope. You think I come up here to read out your doom."

His back is to me but from speakers hidden in the four corners, his voice booms clear over the square, over the city, probably over the whole valley and beyond. Cuz who else is there to hear him talk? Who else is there on all of New World that ain't either gathered here or under the ground?

Mayor Prentiss is talking to the whole planet.

"And you're right," he says and I tell you I'm certain I hear the smile. "You *are* conquered. You *are* defeated. And I read to you your doom."

He lets this sink in for a moment. My Noise rumbles and I see a few of the men look up to the top of the tower. I try to keep it quiet but who are these people? Who are these clean and comfortable and not-at-all-hungry people who just handed theirselves over?

"But it is not I who conquered you," the Mayor says. "It is not I who has beaten you or defeated you or enslaved you."

He pauses, looking out over the crowd. He's dressed all in white, white hat, white boots, and with the white cloths covering the platform and the afternoon sun shining on down, he's practically blinding.

"You are enslaved by your idleness," says the Mayor. "You are defeated by your complacency. You are *doomed*"—and here his voice rises suddenly, hitting *doomed* so hard half the crowd jumps—"by your good intentions!"

He's working himself up now, heavy breaths into the microphone.

"You have allowed yourselves to become so *weak*, so *feeble* in the face of the challenges of this world that in a single generation you have become a people who would surrender to *RUMOR!*"

He starts to pace the stage, microphone in hand. Every frightened face in the crowd, every face in the army, turns to watch him move back and forth, back and forth.

I'm watching, too.

"You let an army *walk* into your town and instead of making them *take* it, you *offer it willingly!*"

He's still pacing, his voice still rising.

"And so you know what I did. I *took*. I took *you*. I took your freedom. I took your town. I took your future."

He laughs, like he can't believe his luck.

"I expected a war," he says.

Some of the crowd look at their feet, away from each other's eyes.

I wonder if they're ashamed.

I hope so.

"But instead of a war," the Mayor says, "I got a conversation. A conversation that began, *Please don't hurt us* and ended with *Please take anything you want.*"

He stops in the middle of the platform.

"I expected a WAR!" he shouts again, thrusting his fist at them.

And they flinch.

If a crowd can flinch, they flinch.

More than a thousand men flinch under the fist of just one.

I don't see what the women do.

"And because you did not give me a war," the Mayor says, his voice light, "you will face the consequences."

I hear the doors to the cathedral open again and Mr. Collins comes out pushing Mayor Ledger forward thru the ranks of the army, hands tied behind his back.

Mayor Prentiss watches him come, arms crossed. Murmurs finally start in the crowd of men, louder in the crowds of women, and the men on horseback do some waving of their rifles to stop it. The Mayor don't even look back at the sound, like it's beneath his notice. He just watches Mr. Collins push Mayor Ledger up the stairs at the back of the platform.

Mayor Ledger stops at the top of the steps, looking out over the crowd. They stare back at him, some of them squinting at the shrillness of his Noise *buzz*, a *buzz* I realize is now starting to shout some real words, words of fear, *pictures* of fear, pictures of Mr. Collins giving him the bruised eye and the split lip, pictures of him agreeing to surrender and being locked in the tower.

"Kneel," Mayor Prentiss says and tho he says it quietly, tho he says it away from the microphone, somehow I hear it clear as a bell chime in the middle of my head, and from the intake of breath in the crowd, I wonder if that's how they heard it, too.

And before it looks like he even knows what he's doing, Mayor Ledger is kneeling on the platform, looking surprised that he's down there.

The whole town watches him do it.

Mayor Prentiss waits a moment.

And then he steps over to him.

And takes out a knife.

It's a big, no-kidding, death of a thing, shining in the sun.

The Mayor holds it up high over his head.

He turns slowly, so everyone can see what's about to happen.

So that everyone can see the knife.

My gut falls and for a second I think—

But it ain't mine—

It ain't—

And then someone calls, "Murderer!" from across the square.

A single voice, carrying above the silence.

It came from the women.

My heart jumps for a second—

But of course it can't be her—

But at least there's someone. At least there's *someone*.

Mayor Prentiss walks calmly to the microphone. "Your victorious enemy addresses you," he says, almost politely, as if the person who shouted was simply not understanding. "Your leaders are to be executed as the inevitable result of your defeat."

He turns to look at Mayor Ledger, kneeling there on the platform. His face is trying to look calm but everyone can hear how badly he don't wanna die, how childlike his wishes are sounding, how loud his newly uncured Noise is spilling out all over the place.

"And now you will learn," Mayor Prentiss says, turning back to the crowd, "what kind of man your new President is. And what he will demand from you."

Silence, still silence, save for Mayor Ledger's mewling.

Mayor Prentiss walks over to him, knife glinting. Another murmur starts spreading thru the crowd as they finally get what they're about to see. Mayor Prentiss steps behind Mayor Ledger and holds up the knife again. He stands there, watching the crowd watch him, watching their faces as they look and listen to their former Mayor try and fail to contain his Noise.

"BEHOLD!" Mayor Prentiss shouts. "YOUR FUTURE!".

He turns the knife to a stabbing angle, as if to say again, *behold*–

The murmuring of the crowd rises–

Mayor Prentiss raises his arm–

A voice, a female one, maybe the same one, cries out, "No!"

And then suddenly I realize I know exactly what's gonna happen.

In the chair, in the room with the circle of colored glass, he brought me to defeat, he brought me to the edge of death, he made me *know* that it would come–

And then he put a bandage on me.

And *that's* when I did what he wanted.

The knife swishes thru the air and slices thru the binds on Mayor Ledger's hands.

There's a town-sized gasp, a *planet*-sized one.

Mayor Prentiss waits for a moment, then says once more, "Behold your future," quietly, not even into the microphone.

But there it is again, right inside yer mind.

He puts the knife away in a belt behind his back and returns to the microphone.

And starts to put bandages on the crowd.

"I am not the man you think I am," he says. "I am not a tyrant come to slaughter his enemies. I am not a madman come to destroy even that which would save himself. I am *not*"–he looks over at Mayor Ledger– "your executioner."

The crowds, men and women, are so quiet now the square might as well be empty.

"The war is *over*," the Mayor continues. "And a new peace will take its place."

He points to the sky. People look up, like he might be conjuring something up there to fall on them.

"You may have heard a rumor," he says. "That there are new settlers coming."

My stomach twists again.

"I tell you as your President," he says. "The rumor is true."

How does he know? How does he ruddy *know*?

The crowd starts to murmur at this news, men and women. The Mayor lets them, happily talking over them.

"We will be ready to greet them!" he says. "We will be a proud society ready to welcome them into a new Eden!" His voice is rising again. "We will show them that they have left Old World and entered PARADISE!"

Lots more murmuring now, talking everywhere.

"I am going to take your cure away from you," the Mayor says.

And boy, does the murmuring *stop*.

The Mayor lets it, lets the silence build up, and then he says, "For now."

The men look at one another and back to the Mayor.

"We are entering a new era," Mayor Prentiss says. "You will earn my trust by joining me in creating a new society. As that new society is built and as we meet our first challenges and celebrate our first successes, you will earn the right to be called men again. You will earn the right to have your cure returned to you and that will be the moment all men truly will be brothers."

He's not looking at the women. Neither are the men in the crowd. Women got no use for the reward of a cure, do they?

"It will be difficult," he continues. "I don't pretend otherwise. But it *will* be rewarding." He gestures toward the army. "My deputies have already begun to organize you. You will continue to follow their instructions but I assure you they will never be too onerous and you will soon see that I am not your conqueror. I am not your doom. I am not," he pauses again, "your enemy."

He turns his head across the crowd of men one last time.

"I am your savior," he says.

And even without hearing their Noise, I watch the crowd wonder if there's a chance he's telling the truth, if maybe things'll be okay after all, if maybe, despite what they feared, they've been let off the hook.

You ain't, I think. *Not by a long shot.*

Even before the crowds have started to properly leave after the Mayor's finished, there's a *ker-thunk* at my door.

"Good evening, Todd," the Mayor says, stepping into the bell-ringing jail and looking around him, wrinkling his nose a little at the smell. "Did you like my speech?"

"How do you know there are settlers coming?" I say. "Have you been talking to her? Is she all right?"

He don't answer this but he don't hit me for it neither. He just smiles and says, "All in good time, Todd."

We hear Noise coming up the stairs outside the door. Alive, I'm alive it says alive alive alive and into the room comes Mayor Ledger, pushed by Mr. Collins.

He pulls up his step when he sees Mayor Prentiss standing there.

"New bedding will arrive tomorrow," Mayor Prentiss says, still looking at me. "As will toilet privileges."

Mayor Ledger's moving his jaw but it takes a few tries before any words come out. "Mr. President–"

Mayor Prentiss ignores him. "Your first job will also begin tomorrow, Todd."

"*Job?*" I say.

"Everyone has to work, Todd," he says. "Work is the path to freedom. I will be working. So will Mr. Ledger."

"I will?" Mayor Ledger says.

"But we're in jail," I say.

He smiles again and there's more amusement in it and I wonder how I'm about to be stung.

"Get some sleep," he says, stepping to the door and looking me in the eye. "My son will pick you up first thing in the morning."

3

THE NEW LIFE

[TODD]

BUT IT TURNS OUT IT ain't Davy that worries me when I get dragged into the cold of the next morning in front of the cathedral. It ain't even Davy I look at.

It's the horse.

BOY COLT, it says, shifting from hoof to hoof, looking down at me, eyes wide in that horse craziness, like I need a good stomping.

"I don't know nothing bout horses," I say.

"She's from my private herd," Mayor Prentiss says atop his own horse, Morpeth. "Her name is Angharrad and she will treat you well, Todd."

Morpeth is looking at my horse and all he's thinking is **Submit, submit, submit,** making my horse even more nervous and that's a ton of nervous animal I'm sposed to ride.

"Whatsa matter?" Davy Prentiss sneers from the saddle of a third horse. "You scared?"

"Whatsa matter?" I say. "Daddy not give you the cure yet?"

His Noise immediately rises. "You little piece of–"

"My, my," says the Mayor. "Not ten words in and the fight's already begun."

"He started it," Davy says.

"And he would finish it, too, I wager," says the Mayor, looking at me, reading the red, jittery state of my Noise, filled with urgent red askings about Viola, with more askings I wanna take outta Davy Prentiss's hide. "Come, Todd," the Mayor says, reining his horse. "Ready to be a leader of men?"

"It's a simple division," he says as we trot thru the early morning, way faster than I'd like. "The men will move to the west end of the valley in front of the cathedral and the women to the east behind it."

We're riding east down the main street of New Prentisstown, the one that starts at the zigzag road by the falls, carries thru to the town square and around the cathedral and now out the back into the farther valley. Small squads of soldiers march up and down side roads and the men of New Prentisstown come past us the other way on foot, carrying rucksacks and other luggage.

"I don't see no women," Davy says.

"*Any* women," corrects the Mayor. "And no, Captain Morgan and Captain Tate supervised the transfer of the rest of the women last night."

"What are you gonna do with 'em?" I say, my knuckles gripping so hard on the saddle horn they're turning white.

He looks back at me. "Nothing, Todd. They will be treated with the care and dignity that befits their importance to the future of New World." He turns away. "But for now, separate is best."

"You put the bitches in their place," Davy sneers.

"You will not speak that way in front of me, David," the Mayor says, calmly but in a voice that ain't joking. "Women will be respected at all times and given every comfort. Though in a nonvulgar sense you are correct. We all have places. New World made men forget theirs, and that means men must be away from women until we all remember who we are, who we were meant to be."

His voice brightens a little. "The people will welcome this. I offer clarity where before there was only chaos."

"Is Viola with the women?" I ask. "Is she okay?"

He looks back at me again. "You made a promise, Todd Hewitt," he says. "Need I remind you once more? *Just save her and I'll do anything you want,* I believe were your exact words."

I lick my lips nervously. "How do I know yer keeping yer end of the bargain?"

"You don't," he says, his eyes on mine, like he's peering right past every lie I could tell him. "I want your faith in me, Todd, and faith with proof is no faith at all."

He turns back down the road and I'm left with Davy snickering to my side so I just whisper "Whoa, girl," to my horse. Her coat is dark brown with a white stripe down her nose and a mane brushed so nice I'm trying not to grab onto it less it make her mad. **Boy colt,** she thinks.

She, I think. *She*. Then I think an asking I ain't never had a chance to ask before. Cuz the ewes I had back on the farm had Noise, too, and if women ain't got Noise–

"Because women are not animals," the Mayor says, reading me. "No matter what anyone claims I believe. They are merely naturally Noise-less."

He lowers his voice. "Which makes them different."

It's mostly shops that line this part of the road, dotted twixt all the trees, closed, reopening who knows when, with houses stretching back from side streets both toward the river on the left and the hill of the valley on the right. Most of the buildings, if not all, are built a fair distance from one another, which I spose is how you'd plan a big town before you found a cure for the Noise.

We pass more soldiers marching in groups of five or ten, more men heading west with their belongings, still no women. I look at the faces of the men going by, most of them pointed to the road at their feet, none of them looking ready to fight.

"Whoa, girl," I whisper again cuz riding a horse is turning out to be powerfully uncomfortable on yer private parts.

"And there's Todd," Davy says, pulling up next to me. "Moaning already."

"Shut it, Davy," I say.

"You will address each other as Mr. Prentiss Jr. and Mr. Hewitt," the Mayor calls back to us.

"*What?*" Davy says, his Noise rising. "He ain't a man yet! He's just–"

The Mayor silences him with a look. "A body was discovered in the river in the early hours of this morning," he says. "A body with many terrible wounds to its flesh and a large knife sticking out of its neck, a body dead not more than two days."

He stares at me, looking into my Noise again. I put up the pictures he wants to see, making my imaginings seem like the real thing, cuz that's what Noise is, it's everything you think, not just the truth, and if you think hard enough that you did something, well, then, maybe you actually did.

Davy scoffs. "*You* killed Preacher Aaron? I don't believe it."

The Mayor don't say nothing, just moves Morpeth along a little faster. Davy sneers at me, then kicks his own horse to follow.

"Follow," Morpeth nickers.

"Follow," Davy's horse whinnies back.

Follow, thinks my own horse, taking off after them, bouncing me even worse.

As we go, I'm on the constant lookout for her, even tho there's no chance of seeing her. Even if she's still alive, she'd still be too sick to walk, and if she weren't too sick to walk, she'd be locked up with the rest of the women.

But I keep looking–

(cuz maybe she escaped–)

(maybe she's looking for me–)

(maybe she's–)

And then I hear it.

I AM THE CIRCLE AND THE CIRCLE IS ME.

Clear as a bell, right inside my head, the voice of the Mayor, twining around my own voice, like it's speaking direktly into my Noise, so sudden and real I sit up and nearly fall off my horse. Davy looks surprised, his Noise wondering what I'm reacting to.

But the Mayor just rides on down the road, like nothing happened at all.

The town gets less shiny the farther east we get from the cathedral and soon we're riding on gravel. The buildings get plainer, too, long wooden houses set at distances from each other like bricks dropped into clearings of trees.

Houses that radiate the silence of women.

"Quite correct," the Mayor says. "We're entering the new Women's Quarter."

My heart starts to clench as we go past, the silence rising up like a grasping hand.

I try to sit up higher on my horse.

Cuz this is where she'd be, this is where she'd be healing.

Davy rides up next to me again, his pathetic, half-there mustache bending into an ugly smile. **I'll tell you where yer whore is,** his Noise says.

Mayor Prentiss spins round in his saddle.

And there's the weirdest flash of sound from him, like a shout but quiet and away from me, not in the world at all, like a million words all said together, so fast I swear I feel my hair brush back like in a wind.

But it's Davy who reacts—

His head jerks back like he's been hit, and he has to catch his horse's reins so he don't fall off, spinning the horse round, his eyes wide and dazed, his mouth open, some drool dripping out.

What the hell—?

"He doesn't know, Todd," the Mayor says. "Anything his Noise tells you about her is a lie."

I look at Davy, still dazed and blinking with pain, then back to the Mayor. "Does that mean she's safe?"

"It means he doesn't know. Do you, David?"

No, Pa, says Davy's Noise, still shaky.

Mayor Prentiss raises his eyebrows.

I see Davy clench his teeth. "No, Pa," he says out loud.

"I know my son is a liar," the Mayor says. "I know he is a bully and a brute and ignorant of the things I hold dear. But he is my son." He turns back down the road. "And I believe in redemption."

Davy's Noise is quiet as we follow on but there's a dark red seething in it.

New Prentisstown fades in the distance and the road becomes almost free of buildings. Farm fields start showing up red and green thru the trees and up the hills, with crops I reckernize and others I don't. The silence of the women starts to ease a little and the valley becomes a wilder place, flowers growing in the ditches and waxy squirrels chattering insults to each other and the sun shining clear and cool like nothing else was going on.

At a bend in the river, we curve round a hill and I see a large metal tower poking out the top of it, stretching up into the sky.

"What's that?" I say.

"Wouldn't you like to know?" Davy says, tho it's obvious he don't know neither. The Mayor don't answer.

Just past the tower, the road bends again and follows a long stone wall emerging outta the trees. Down a little farther, the wall connects to a big arched gate with a huge set of wooden doors. It's the only opening in the long, long wall I see. The road beyond is dirt, like we've come to the end.

"New World's first and last monastery," the Mayor says, stopping at the gate. "Built as a refuge of quiet contemplation for our holiest of men. Built when there was still faith we could beat the Noise germ through self-denial and discipline." His voice goes hard. "Abandoned before it was even properly finished."

He turns to face us. I hear a strange spark of happiness rising in Davy's Noise. Mayor Prentiss gives him a warning look.

"You are wondering," he says to me, "why I appointed my son as your overseer."

I cast a look over to Davy, still smiling away.

"You need a firm hand, Todd," the Mayor says. "Your thoughts even now are of how you might escape at the first opportunity and try to find your precious Viola."

"Where is she?" I say, knowing I won't get no answer.

"And I have no doubt," the Mayor continues, "that David here will be quite a firm hand for you indeed."

Davy's face and Noise both smirk.

"And in return, David will learn what real courage looks like." Davy's smirk vanishes. "He will learn what it's like to act with honor, what it's like to act like a real man. What it's like, in short, to act like you, Todd Hewitt." He gives his son a last glance and then turns Morpeth in the road. "I shall be exceedingly eager to hear how your first day together went."

Without another word, he sets off back to New Prentisstown. I wonder now why he came in the first place. Surely he's got more important things to do.

"Surely I do," the Mayor calls, not turning back. "But don't underestimate yourself, Todd."

He rides off. Davy and I wait till he's well outta hearing distance.

I'm the one who speaks first.

"Tell me what happened to Ben or I'll rip yer effing throat out."

"I'm yer boss, boyo," Davy says, smirking again, jumping off his horse and throwing his rucksack to the ground. "Best treat me with respect or Pa ain't gonna—"

But I'm already off Angharrad and hitting him as hard as I can in the face, aiming right for that sad excuse for a mustache. He takes the punch but comes back fast with his own. I ignore the pain, he does, too, and we fall to the ground in a heap of fists and kicks and elbows and knees. He's still bigger than me but only just, only in a way that don't feel like much of a difference no more, but still enough so that after a bit he's got me on my back with his forearm pressed into my throat.

His lip's bleeding, so's his nose, the same as my own poor face but that ain't concerning me now. Davy reaches behind him and pulls a pistol from a holster strapped to his back.

"Ain't no way yer pa's gonna let you shoot me," I say.

"Yeah," he says, "but I still got a gun and you don't."

"Ben beat you," I grunt, underneath his arm. "He stopped you on the road. We got away from you."

"He didn't stop me," Davy sneers. "I took him prisoner, didn't I? And I took him back to Pa and Pa let me torture him. Let me torture him right to *death*."

And Davy's Noise–

I–

I can't say what's in Davy's Noise (he's a liar, he's a *liar*) but it makes me strong enough to push him away. We fight more, Davy fending me off with the butt of the gun till finally, with an elbow to his throat, I knock him down.

"You remember *that*, boy," Davy says, coughing, gun still gripped. "When my pa says all those nice things about you. He's the one who had me torture yer Ben."

"Yer a liar," I say. "Ben beat you."

"Oh, yeah?" Davy says. "Where is he now then? Coming to rescue you?"

I step forward, my fists up, cuz of course he's right, ain't he? My Noise surges with the loss of Ben, like it's happening all over again right here.

Davy's laughing, scrambling back away from me till he's against the huge wooden door. "My pa can read you," he says, then his eyes widen into a taunt. "Read you like a *book*."

My Noise gets even louder. "You *give* me that book! Or I swear, I'll kill you!"

"You ain't gonna do nothing to me, *Mr. Hewitt*," Davy says, rising, his back still against the door. "You wouldn't wanna put yer beloved bitch at risk now, would you?"

And there it is.

They know they got me.

Cuz I won't put her in no more danger.

My hands are ready to do more damage to Davy Prentiss, like they did before when he hurt her, when he *shot* her–

But they won't now–

Even tho they *could*–

Cuz he's weak.

And we both know it.

Davy's smile drops. "Think yer special, do you?" he spits. "Think Pa's got a treat for you?"

I clench my fists, unclench them.

But I keep my place.

"Pa knows you," Davy says. "Pa's *read* you."

"He don't know," I say. "You don't neither."

Davy sneers again. "That so?" His hand reaches for the cast-iron handle of the door. "Come and meet yer new flock then, Todd Hewitt."

His weight opens the door behind him and he steps into the paddock and outta the way, giving me a clear view.

Of a hundred or more Spackle staring right back at me.

4

THE MAKING OF A NEW WORLD

[TODD]

MY FIRST THOUGHT is to turn and run. Run and run and run and never stop.

"I'd like to see *that*," Davy says, standing inside the gate, smiling like he just won a prize.

There's so many of 'em, so many long white faces looking back at me, their eyes too big, their mouths too small and toothy and high on their faces, their ears looking nothing like a man's.

But you can still see a man's face in there, can't you? Still see a face that feels and fears–

And suffers.

It's hard to tell which are male and which are female cuz they all got the same lichen and moss growing right on their skins for clothing but there seem to be whole Spackle *families* in there, larger spacks protecting their spack children and what must be spack husbands protecting spack wives, arms wrapped round each other, heads pressed close together. All of them silently–

Silently.

"I *know*!" Davy says. "Can you believe they gave the cure to these *animals*?"

They look at Davy now and a weird clicking starts passing twixt 'em all with glances and nods moving along the crowd. Davy raises his pistol

and steps farther into the monastery grounds. "Thinking of trying something?" he yells. "Give me a reason! Go on! GIVE ME A REASON!"

The Spackle huddle closer together in their little groups, backing
away from him where they can.

"Get in here, Todd," Davy says. "We got work to do."

I don't move.

"I said, get in here! They're animals. They ain't gonna do *nothing*."

I still don't move.

"He murdered one of y'all," Davy says to the Spackle.

"*Davy!*" I shout.

"Cut its head right off with a knife. Sawed and sawed–"

"Stop it!" I run at him to get him to shut his effing mouth. I don't
know how he knows but he knows and he's gotta shut up right *effing
now*.

The Spackle nearest the gate scoot way back at my approach, getting
outta my way as fast as they can, looking at me with frightened faces,
parents getting their children behind them. I push Davy hard but he just
laughs and I realize I'm inside the monastery walls now.

And I see just how many Spackle there are.

The stone wall of the monastery surrounds a *huge* bit of land but only
one little building, some kind of storehouse. The rest is divided up into
smaller fields, separated by old wooden fences with low gates. Most
of 'em are badly overgrown and you can see heavy grass and brambles
stretching all the way to the back walls a good hundred yards away.

But mostly you can see Spackle.

Hundreds and hundreds of 'em spread out over the grounds.

Maybe even more than a thousand.

They're pushing themselves against the monastery wall, huddling
behind the rotting fences, sitting in groups or standing in rows.

But all watching me, silent as the grave, as my Noise spills out all
over the place.

"He's a liar!" I say. "It weren't like that! It weren't like that at all!"

But what was it like? What was it like that I can explain?

Cuz I *did* do it, didn't I?

Not how Davy said but nearly as bad and completely as big in my
Noise, too big to cover with all their eyes looking back at me, too big to
surround with lies and confuse the truth, too big to not think about as a
crowd of Spackle faces just stare.

"It was an accident," I say, my voice trailing off, looking from face
to weird face, not seeing no pictures of Spackle Noise, not understand-

ing the clicking they make, so doubly not knowing what's happening. "I didn't mean it."

But not one of 'em says a thing back. They don't do nothing but stare.

There's a creak as the gate behind us opens up again. We turn to look.

It's Ivan from Farbranch, the one who joined the army rather than fight it.

And look how right he was. He's wearing an officer's uniform and he's got a group of soldiers with him.

"Mr. Prentiss Jr.," he says, nodding at Davy, who nods back. Ivan turns to me, a look in his eye I can't read and no Noise to be heard. "It's good to see you well, Mr. Hewitt."

"You two *know* each other?" Davy says, sharplike.

"We've had past acquaintance," Ivan says, still looking at me.

But I ain't saying a word to him.

I'm too busy putting up pictures in my Noise.

Pictures of Farbranch. Pictures of Hildy and Tam and Francia. Pictures of the massacre that happened there. The massacre that didn't include him.

A look of annoyance crosses his face. "You go where the power is," he says. "That's how you stay alive."

I put up a picture of his town burning, men and women and children burning with it.

He frowns harder. "These men will stay here as guards. Your orders are to set the Spackle a-clearing the fields and make sure they're fed and watered."

Davy rolls his eyes. "Well, we know *that*—"

But Ivan's already turning and heading out the gate, leaving behind ten men with rifles. They take up stayshuns standing on top of the monastery wall, already getting to work unrolling coils of barbed wire along its edge.

"Ten men with rifles and us against all these Spackle," I say, under my breath but all over my Noise.

"Ah, we'll be okay," Davy says. He raises his pistol at the Spackle nearest him, maybe a female, holding a Spackle baby. She turns the baby away so her body's protecting it. "They ain't got no fight in 'em anyway."

I see the face of the Spackle protecting her baby.

It's defeated, I think. They all are. And they know it.

I know how they feel.

"Hey, pigpiss, check it out," Davy says. He raises his arms in the air, getting all the Spackle eyes on him. "People of New Prentisstown!" he shouts, waving his arms about. "I read to you yer *dooooooom!*"

And he just laughs and laughs and laughs.

Davy decides to oversee the Spackle clearing the fields of scrub but that's only cuz that means I'm the one who'll have to shovel out the fodder from the storehouse for all of 'em to eat and then fill troughs for 'em to drink from.

But it's farmwork. I'm used to it. All the chores Ben and Cillian set me to doing every day. All the chores I used to complain about.

I wipe my eyes and get on with it.

The Spackle keep their distance from me as best they can while I work. Which, I gotta say, is okay by me.

Cuz I find I can't really look 'em in the eyes.

I keep my head down and carry on shoveling.

Davy says his pa told him the Spackle worked as servants or cooks but one of the Mayor's first orders was for everyone to keep 'em locked away in their homes till the army picked 'em up last night while I slept.

"People had 'em living in their back *gardens*," Davy says, watching me shovel as the morning turns to afternoon, eating what's sposed to be lunch for both of us. "Can you believe that? Like they're effing members of the *family*."

"Maybe they were," I say.

"Well they ain't no more," Davy says, rising and taking out his pistol. He grins at me. "Back to work."

I empty most of the storehouse of fodder but it still don't look like nearly enough. Plus, three of the five water pumps ain't working and by sunset, I've only managed to fix one.

"Time to go," Davy says.

"I ain't done," I say.

"Fine," he says, walking toward the gate. "Stay here on yer own then."

I look back at the Spackle. Now that the work day's thru, they've pushed themselves as far away from the soldiers and the front gates as possible.

As far away from me and Davy as possible, too.

I look back and forth twixt them and Davy leaving. They ain't got enough food. They ain't got enough water. There ain't no place to go to the toilet and no shelter of any kind at all.

I hold out my empty hands toward 'em but that don't do no kind of explaining that'll make anything okay. They just stare at me as I drop my hands and follow Davy out the gate.

"So much for being a man of courage, eh, pigpiss?" Davy says, untying his horse, which he calls Deadfall but which only seems to answer to Acorn.

I ignore him cuz I'm thinking bout the Spackle. How I'll treat them well. I will. I'll see that they get enough water and food and I'll do everything I can to protect 'em.

I *will*.

I promise that to myself.

Cuz that's what she'd want.

"Oh, I'll tell you what she *really* wants," Davy sneers.

And we fight again.

New bedding's been put in the tower when I get back, a mattress and a sheet spread out on one side for me and another on the other side for Mayor Ledger, already sitting on his, Noise jangling, eating a bowl of stew.

The bad smell's gone, too.

"Yes," says Mayor Ledger. "And guess who had to clean it up?"

It turns out he's been put to work as a rubbish man.

"Honest labor," he says to me, shrugging, but there are other sounds in his grayish Noise that make me think he don't believe it's very honest at all. "Symbolic, I suppose. I go from the top of the heap to the bottom. It'd be poetic if it weren't so obvious."

There's stew for me by my bed, too, and I take it to the window to look out over the town.

Which is starting to buɀɀ.

As the cure leaves the systems of the men of the town, you begin to hear it. From inside the houses and buildings, from down the side streets and behind the trees.

Noise is returning to New Prentisstown.

It was hard for me to even walk thru *old* Prentisstown and that only ever had one hundred forty-six men in it. New Prentisstown's gotta have ten times that many. And boys, too.

I don't know how I'm gonna be able to bear it.

"You'll get used to it," Mayor Ledger says, finishing his stew. "Remember, I lived here for twenty years before we found a cure."

I close my eyes but all I see is a herd of Spackle, looking back at me.

Judging me.

Mayor Ledger taps me on the shoulder and points at my bowl of stew. "Are you going to eat that?"

That night I dream—

About her—

The sun's shining behind her and I can't see her face and we're on a hillside and she's saying something but the roar of the falls behind us is too loud and I say "What?" and when I reach for her, I don't touch her but my hand comes back covered in blood—

"Viola!" I say, sitting up on my mattress in the dark, breathing heavy.

I look over to Mayor Ledger on his mattress, facing away from me, but his Noise ain't sleeping Noise, it's the gray-type Noise he has when he's awake.

"I know yer up," I say.

"You dream quite loud," he says, not looking back. "She someone important?"

"Never you mind."

"We just have to get through it, Todd," he says. "That's all any of us has to do now. Just stay alive and get through it."

I turn to the wall.

There ain't nothing I can do. Not while they got her.

Not while I don't know.

Not while they could still hurt her.

Stay alive and get thru it, I think.

And I think of her out there.

And I whisper it, whisper it to her, wherever she is. "Stay alive and get thru it."

Stay alive.

PART
II

HOUSE OF
HEALING

5

VIOLA WAKES

(VIOLA)

"CALM YOURSELF, MY GIRL."

A voice–

In the brightness–

I blink open my eyes. Everything is a pure white so bright it's almost a sound and there's a voice out there in it and my head is groggy and there's a pain in my side and it's too bright and I can't think–

Wait–

Wait–

He was carrying me down the hill–

Just *now* he was carrying me down the hill into Haven after–

"Todd?" I say, my voice a rasp, full of cotton and spit, but I run at it as hard as I can, forcing it out into the bright lights blinding my eyes. "*TODD?*"

"I said to calm yourself, now."

I don't recognize the voice, the voice of a woman–

A woman.

"Who are you?" I ask, trying to sit up, pushing out my hands to feel what's around me, feeling the coolness of the air, the softness of–

A bed?

I feel panic begin to rise.

"*Where is he?*" I shout. "*TODD?*"

"I don't know any Todd, my girl," the voice says as shapes start to come together, as the brightness separates into lesser brightnesses, "but I do know you're in no shape to be demanding information."

"You were *shot*," says another voice, another woman, younger than the first, off to my right.

"Hush your mouth, Madeleine Poole," says the first woman.

"Yes, Mistress Coyle."

I keep on blinking and I start to see what's right in front of me. I'm in a narrow white bed in a narrow white room. I'm wearing a thin white gown, tied at the back. A woman both tall and plump stands in front of me, a white coat with a blue outstretched hand stitched into it draped over her shoulders, her mouth set in a line, her expression solid. Mistress Coyle. Behind her at the door holding a bowl of steaming water is a girl not much older than me.

"I'm Maddy," says the girl, sneaking a smile.

"Out," says Mistress Coyle, without even turning her head. Maddy catches my eye as she leaves, another smile sent my way.

"Where am I?" I ask Mistress Coyle, my breath still fast.

"Do you mean the room, my girl? Or the *town*?" She holds my eyes. "Or indeed the planet?"

"Please," I say and my eyes suddenly start to fill with water and I'm angry about that but I keep talking. "I was with a boy."

She sighs and looks away for a second, then she purses her lips and sits down in a chair next to the bed. Her face is stern, her hair pulled back in plaits so tight you could probably climb them, her body solid and big and not at all someone who you'd mess around with.

"I'm sorry," she says, almost tenderly. Almost. "I don't know anything about a boy." She frowns. "I'm afraid I don't know anything about anything except that you were brought to this house of healing yesterday morning so close to death I wasn't at all sure we would be able to bring you back. Except that we were informed in no uncertain terms that *our* survival rather depended upon *yours*."

She waits to see how I take this.

I have no idea how I take this.

Where *is* he? What have they done with him?

I turn away from her to try and *think* but I'm wrapped so tight in bandages around my middle I can't properly sit up.

Mistress Coyle runs a couple of fingers across her brow. "And now that you're back," she says, "I'm not at all sure you're going to thank us for the world to which we've returned you."

She tells me of Mayor Prentiss arriving in Haven in front of the rumor of an army, a big one, big enough to crush the town without effort, big enough to set the whole world ablaze. She tells me of the surrender of someone called Mayor Ledger, of how he shouted down the few people who wanted to fight, of how most people agreed to let him "hand over the town on a plate with a bow tied round it."

"And then the houses of healing," she says, real anger coming off her voice, "suddenly became prisons for the women inside."

"So you're a doctor, then?" I ask, but all I can feel is my chest pulling in on itself, sinking as if under an enormous weight, sinking because we failed, sinking because outrunning the army proved to be of no use at all.

Her mouth curls in a small smile, a secret one, like I just let something go. But it's not cruel and I'm finding myself less afraid of her, of what this room might mean, less afraid for myself, more afraid for *him*.

"No, my girl," she says, cocking her head. "As I'm sure you know, there are no women doctors on New World. I'm a healer."

"What's the difference?"

She runs her fingers across her brow again. "What's the difference indeed?" She drops her hands in her lap and looks at them. "Even though we're locked up," she says, "we still hear rumors, you see. Rumors of men and women being separated all over town, rumors of the army arriving perhaps this very day, rumors of slaughter coming over the hill to vanquish us all no matter how well we *surrendered*."

She's looking at me hard now. "And then there's you."

I look away from her. "I'm not anyone special."

"Are you not?" She looks unconvinced. "A girl whose arrival the whole town has to be cleared for? A girl whose life I am ordered to save on pain of my own? A girl"–she leans forward to make sure I'm listening–"fresh from the great black beyond?"

I stop breathing for a second and hope she doesn't notice. "Where'd you get an idea like that?"

She grins again, not unkindly. "I'm a healer. The first thing I ever see is skin and so I know it well. Skin tells the story of a person, where they've been, what they've eaten, who they are. You've got some surface wear, my girl, but the rest of your skin is the softest and whitest I've seen in my twenty years of doing the good work. Too soft and white for a planet of farmers."

I'm still not looking at her.

"And then there are the rumors, of course, brought in by the refugees, of more settlers on the way. Thousands of them."

"Please," I say quietly, my eyes welling up again. I try to force them to stop.

"And no girl from New World would ever ask a woman if she was a doctor," she finishes.

I swallow. I put a hand to my mouth. Where is he? I don't care about any of this because *where is he?*

"I know you're frightened," Mistress Coyle says. "But we're suffering from an *excess* of fright here in this town and there's nothing I can do about that." She reaches out a rough hand to touch my arm. "But maybe you can do something to help *us*."

I swallow but I don't say anything.

There's only one person I can trust.

And he's not here.

Mistress Coyle leans back in her chair. "We did save your life," she says. "A little knowledge could be a large comfort."

I breathe in deep, looking around the room, around at the sunlight streaming in from a window looking out onto trees and a river, *the* river, the one we followed into what was supposed to be safety. It seems impossible that anything bad could be happening anywhere on a day so bright, that there's any danger on the doorstep, that there's an army coming.

But there *is* an army coming.

There *is*.

And it won't be any friend to Mistress Coyle, no matter what's happened to–

I feel a little pain in my chest.

But I take a breath.

And I start to talk.

"My name," I say, "is Viola Eade."

"More settlers, huh?" Maddy says with a smile. I'm lying on my side as she unwraps the long bandage around my middle. The underside is covered in blood, my skin dusty and rust colored where it's dried. There's a little hole in my stomach, tied up with fine string.

"Why doesn't this hurt?" I say.

"Jeffers root on the bandages," Maddy says. "Natural opiate.

You won't feel any pain but you won't be able to go to the toilet for a month either. Plus, you'll be sound asleep in about five minutes."

I touch the skin around the bullet wound, gently, gently. There's another on my back where the bullet went in. "Why aren't I dead?"

"Would you rather be dead?" She smiles again, which changes to the smiliest frown I've ever seen. "I shouldn't joke. Mistress Coyle's always saying I lack the *proper seriousness* to be a healer." She dips a cloth in a basin of hot water and starts washing the wounds. "You aren't dead because Mistress Coyle is the best healer in all of Haven, better than any of those so-called *doctors* they've got in this town. Even the bad guys know that. Why do you think they brought you here instead of a clinic?"

She's wearing the same long white coat as Mistress Coyle but she's also got on a short white cap with the blue outstretched hand stitched on it, which she told me is something apprentices wear. She can't be more than a year or two older than me, whatever way they measure age on this planet, but her hands are sure, gentle, and firm all around the wounds.

"So," she says, her voice deceptively light. "How bad *are* these bad guys?"

The door opens. A short girl in another apprentice cap leans in, young as Maddy but with dark brown skin and a storm cloud hanging over her head. "Mistress Coyle says you need to finish up right now."

Maddy doesn't look up from taping new bandages to my front. "Mistress Coyle knows I've only had time to get halfway done."

"We've been summoned," says the girl.

"You say that like we get *summoned* all the time, Corinne." The bandages are almost as good as the ones I had from my ship, the medicine on them already cooling my torso, already making my eyelids heavy. Maddy finishes on the front and turns to cut another set for my back. "I am in the middle of a healing."

"A man came by with a gun," Corinne says.

Maddy stops bandaging.

"Everyone's been called to the town square," Corinne continues. "Which includes you, Maddy Poole, healing or not." She crosses her arms hard. "I'll bet it's the army coming."

Maddy looks me in the eyes. I look away.

"We'll finally see what our end looks like," Corinne says.

Maddy rolls her eyes. "Always so cheerful, you," she says. "Tell Mistress Coyle I'll be out in two ticks."

Corinne gives her a sour look but leaves. Maddy finishes up the bandages on my back, by which time I can barely stay awake.

"You sleep now," Maddy says. "It'll be all right, you just watch. Why would they save you if they were going to . . ." She doesn't finish the thought, just scrunches her lips and then smiles. "I'm always *saying* Corinne's got enough proper seriousness in her for all of us put together."

Her smile is the last thing I see before I sleep.

"*TODD!*"

I jolt awake again, the nightmare dashing away, Todd slipping from me–

I hear a clunk and I see a book drop from Maddy's lap as she blinks herself awake in the chair by the bed. Night's fallen, and the room is dark, just a little lamp on where Maddy was meant to have been reading.

"Who's Todd?" she asks, yawning, already smiling through it. "Your *boyfriend?*" The look on my face makes her drop the tease immediately. "Someone important?"

I nod, still breathing heavily from the nightmare, my hair plastered to my forehead with sweat. "Someone important."

She pours me a glass of water from a pitcher on the bedside table. "What happened?" I say, taking a drink. "You were summoned."

"Ah, yes, that," Maddy says, sitting back. "*That* was interesting."

She tells me about how everyone in the entire town–not Haven anymore, New Prentisstown, a name that makes my stomach sink–gathered to watch the army march in and watch the new Mayor execute the old one.

"Except he didn't," Maddy says. "He spared him. Said he would spare all of us, too. That he was taking away the Noise cure, which the men weren't too happy about and good Lord it's been nice not to hear it yammering for the past six months, but that we should all know our place and remember who we were and that we would make a new home together in preparation for all the settlers that were coming."

She widens her eyes, waits for me to say something.

"I didn't understand half of that," I say. "There's a cure?"

She shakes her head but not to say no. "Boy, you really aren't from around here, are you?"

I set down the glass of water, leaning forward and lowering my voice to a whisper. "Maddy, is there a communications hub near here?"

She looks at me like I just asked her if she'd like to move with me to one of the moons. "So I can contact the ships," I say. "It might be a big, curved dish? Or a tower, maybe?"

She looks thoughtful. "There's an old metal tower up in the hills," she says, also whispering, "but I'm not even sure it *is* a communications tower. It's been abandoned for ages. Besides, you won't be able to get to it. There's a whole army out there, Vi."

"How big?"

"Big enough." We're both still whispering. "People are saying they're separating out the last of the women tonight."

"To do what?"

Maddy shrugs. "Corinne said a woman in the crowd told her they rounded up the Spackle, too."

I sit up, pressing against the bandages. "Spackle?"

"They're the native species here."

"I know who they are." I sit up even more, straining against the bandage. "Todd told me things, told me what happened before. Maddy, if the Mayor's separating out women and Spackle, then we're in danger. We're in the *worst kind* of danger."

I push back my sheets to get up but a sudden bolt of lightning rips through my stomach. I call out and fall back.

"Pulled a stitch," Maddy tuts, standing right up.

"Please." I grit my teeth against the pain. "We have to get out of here. We have to *run*."

"You're in no position to run anywhere," she says, reaching for my bandage.

Which is when the Mayor walks in the door.

6

SIDES OF THE STORY

{VIOLA}

MISTRESS COYLE LEADS HIM IN. Her face is sterner than
ever, her forehead creased, her jaw set. Even having only met her
once I can tell she's not happy.

He stands behind her. Tall, thin but broad shouldered, all in
white with a hat he hasn't taken off.

I've never properly seen him. I was bleeding, dying when he ap-
proached us in the town square.

But it's him.

It can only be him.

"Good evening, Viola," he says. "I've been wanting to meet you
for a very long time."

Mistress Coyle sees me struggling with the sheet, sees Maddy
reaching for me. "Is there a problem, Madeleine?"

"Nightmare," Maddy says, catching my eye. "I think she pulled
a stitch."

"We'll deal with that later," Mistress Coyle says and the calm
and serious way she says it gets Maddy's full attention. "Get her
400 units of Jeffers root in the meantime."

"400?" Maddy says, sounding surprised, but seeing the look on

Mistress Coyle's face, all she says is, "Yes, Mistress." She gives my hand a last squeeze and leaves the room.

They both watch me for a long moment, then the Mayor says, "That'll be all, Mistress."

Mistress Coyle gives me a silent look as she leaves, maybe to reassure me, maybe to ask me something or *tell* me something, but I'm too frightened to figure it out before she backs out of the room, closing the door behind her.

And then I'm alone with him.

He lets the silence build until it's clear I'm meant to say something. I'm gripping the sheet to my chest with a fist, still feeling the lightning pain fire up my side if I move.

"You're Mayor Prentiss," I say. My voice shakes when I say it but I say it.

"*President* Prentiss," he says, "but you would know me as Mayor, of course."

"Where's Todd?" I look into his eyes. I do not blink. "What have you done with him?"

He smiles again. "Smart in your first sentence, courageous in your second. We may be friends yet."

"Is he hurt?" I swallow away the burn rising in my chest. "Is he alive?"

For a second, it looks like he's not going to tell me, not even going to acknowledge that I asked, but then he says, "Todd is well. Todd is alive and well and asking about you every chance he gets."

I realize I've held my breath for his answer. "Is that true?"

"Of course it's true."

"I want to see him."

"And he wants to see you," says Mayor Prentiss. "But all things in their proper order."

He keeps his smile. It's almost friendly.

Here is the man we spent all those weeks running from, here he is, standing in my very own room, where I can barely move from the pain.

And he's *smiling*.

And it's almost friendly.

If he's hurt Todd, if he's laid a *finger* on him–

"Mayor Prentiss–"

"*President* Prentiss," he says again, then his voice brightens. "But you may call me David."

I don't say anything, just press down harder onto my bandage against the pain.

There's something about him. Something I can't quite place–

"That is," he says, "if I may call you Viola."

There's a knock on the door. Maddy opens it, a phial in her hand. "Jeffers," she says, keeping her eyes firmly on the floor. "For her pain."

"Yes, of course," the Mayor says, moving away from my bed, hands behind his back. "Proceed."

Maddy pours me a glass of water and watches me swallow four yellow gel caps, two more than I've taken before. She takes the glass from me and, with her back to the Mayor, gives me a firm look, a solid one, no smile but all kinds of bravery, and it makes me feel a little bit good, a little bit stronger.

"She'll grow tired very quickly," Maddy says to the Mayor, still not looking at him.

"I understand," the Mayor says. Maddy leaves, closing the door behind her. My stomach immediately starts to grow warm but it'll take a minute just yet to make the pain start to go or take away the quivering running all through me.

"So," the Mayor says. "May I?"

"May you what?"

"Call you Viola?"

"I can't stop you," I say. "If you want."

"Good," he says, not sitting, not moving, the smile still fixed. "When you are feeling better, Viola, I would very much like to have a talk with you."

"About what?"

"Why, your ships, of course," he says. "Coming closer by the moment."

I swallow. "What ships?"

"Oh, no, no, no." He shakes his head but still smiles. "You started out with intelligence and with courage. You are frightened but that has not stopped you from addressing me with calmness and clarity. All most admirable." He bends his head down. "But to that we must add honesty. We *must* start out honestly with each other, Viola, or how may we proceed at all?"

Proceed to where? I think.

"I have told you that Todd is alive and well," he says, "and what I tell you is true." He places a hand on the rail at the end of the bed. "And he will *stay* safe." He pauses. "And you will give me your honesty."

And I understand without having to be told that one depends on the other.

The warmth is starting to spread up from my stomach, making everything seem slower, softer. The lightning in my side is fading, but it's taking wakefulness along with it. Why *two* doses when that would put me to sleep so fast? So fast I won't even be able to talk to–

Oh.

Oh.

"I need to see him to believe you," I say.

"Soon," he says. "There is much to be done in New Prentisstown first. Much to be *un*done."

"Whether anyone wants it or not." My eyelids are getting heavy. I force them up. Only then do I realize I said it out loud.

He smiles again. "I find myself saying this with great frequency, Viola. The war is over. I am not your enemy."

I lift my groggy eyes to him in surprise.

I'm afraid of him. I am.

But–

"You were the enemy of the women of Prentisstown," I say. "You were the enemy of everyone in Farbranch."

He stiffens a little, though he tries not to let me see it. "A body was found in the river this morning," he says. "A body with a knife in its throat."

I try to keep my eyes from widening, even under the Jeffers. He's looking at me close now. "Perhaps the man's death was justified," he says. "Perhaps the man had *enemies*."

I see myself doing it–

I see myself plunging the knife–

I close my eyes.

"As for me," the Mayor says, "the war is over. My days of soldiering are at an end. Now come the days of leadership, of bringing people together."

By separating them, I think, but my breathing is slowing. The whiteness of the room is growing brighter but only in a soft way that makes me want to fall down into it and sleep and sleep and sleep. I press farther into the pillow.

"I'll leave you now," he says. "We will meet again."

I begin to breathe through my mouth. Sleep is becoming impossible to avoid.

He sees me starting to drift off.

And he does the most surprising thing.

He steps forward and pulls the sheet straight across me, almost like he's tucking me in.

"Before I go," he says. "I have one request."

"What?" I say, fighting to keep awake.

"I'd like you to call me David."

"*What?*" I say, my voice heavy.

"I'd like you to say, *Good night, David.*"

The Jeffers has so disconnected me that the words come out before I know I'm even saying them. "Good night, David."

Through the haze of the drug, I see him look a little surprised, even a little disappointed.

But he recovers quickly. "And to you, Viola." He nods at me and steps toward the door to leave.

And I realize what it is, what's so different about him.

"I can't hear you," I whisper from my bed.

He stops and turns. "I said, *And to–*"

"No," I say, my tongue barely able to move. "I mean I can't *hear* you. I can't hear you think."

He raises his eyebrows. "I should hope not."

And I think I'm asleep before he can even leave.

I don't wake for a long, long time, finally blinking again into the sunshine, wondering what was real and what was a dream.

(. . . my father, holding out his hand to help me up the ladder into the hatch, smiling, saying, "Welcome aboard, skipper . . .")

"You snore," says a voice.

Corinne is seated in the chair, her fingers flying a threaded needle through a piece of fabric so fast it's like it's not her doing it, like someone else's angry hands are using her lap.

"I do not," I say.

"Like a cow in estrus."

I push back the covers. My bandages have been changed and the lightning pain is gone so the stitch must be repaired. "How long have I been asleep?"

"More than a day." She sounds disapproving. "The President's already sent men by twice to check on your condition."

I put a hand on my side, tentatively pushing on the wound. The pain is almost nonexistent.

"Nothing to say to that then, my girl?" Corinne says, needle thrashing ferociously.

I furrow my forehead. "What's there to say? I'd never met him before."

"He was sure keen to know *you* though, wasn't he? Ow!" She breathes in a sharp hiss and sticks a fingertip in her mouth. "All the while he's got us trapped," she says around her finger. "All the while we can't even leave this building."

"I don't see how that's my fault."

"It isn't your fault, my girl," Mistress Coyle says, coming into the room. She looks sternly at Corinne. "And no one here thinks it is."

Corinne stands, bows slightly to Mistress Coyle, and leaves without another word.

"How are you feeling?" Mistress Coyle asks.

"Groggy." I sit up more, finding it much easier to do so this time. I also notice my bladder is uncomfortably full. I tell Mistress Coyle.

"Well, then," she says, "let's see if you can stand on your own to help with that."

I take in a breath and turn to put my feet on the floor. My legs don't want to bend very fast but eventually they get there and eventually I can stand up and even walk to the door.

"Maddy *said* you were the best healer in town," I marvel.

"Maddy tells no lies."

She accompanies me down a long white hallway to a toilet. When I've finished and washed and opened the door again, Mistress Coyle is holding a heavier white gown for me to wear, longer and much nicer than the backwards robe I have on. I slip it over my head and we walk back up the hallway, a little wobbly, but walking all the same.

"The President has been asking after your health," she says, steadying me with her hand.

"Corinne told me." I look up at her out of the corner of my eye. "It's only because of the settler ships. I don't know him. I'm not on his side."

"Ah," Mistress Coyle says, getting me back through the door to my room and onto my bed. "You do recognize there are sides then?"

I lie back, my tongue pressed against the back of my teeth. "Did you give me two doses of Jeffers so I wouldn't have to speak to him for very long?" I say. "Or so I wouldn't be able to tell him very much?"

She gives a nod as if to say how clever I am. "Would it be the worst thing in the world if it was a little of both?"

"You could have asked."

"Wasn't time," she says, sitting down in the chair next to the bed. "We only know him by his history, my girl, and his history is bad, bad, bad. Whatever he might say about a new society, there is good reason to want to be better prepared if he starts a conversation."

"I don't know him," I say again. "I don't know anything."

"But, done rightly," she says, with a little smile, "you might *learn* things from a man who takes an interest."

I try to read her, read what she's trying to tell me, but of course women here don't have Noise either, do they?

"What are you saying?" I ask.

"I'm saying it's time for you to get something solid into your stomach." She stands, brushing invisible threads off her white coat. "I'll have Madeleine bring in some breakfast for you."

She walks to the door, taking hold of the handle but not turning it yet. "But know this," she says, without turning around. "If there *are* sides and our President is on one. . . ." She glances back at me over her shoulder. "Then I am most definitely on the other."

7

MISTRESS COYLE

{VIOLA}

"THERE ARE SIX SHIPS," I say from my bed, for the third time in as many days, days where Todd is still out there somewhere, days where I don't know what's happening to him or to anyone else outside.

From the windows of my room, I see soldiers marching by all the time, but all they do is march. Everyone here at the house of healing half expected them to come bursting through the doors at any moment, ready to do terrible things, ready to assert their victory.

But they haven't. They just march by. Other men bring us deliveries of food to the back doors, and the healers are left to their work.

We still can't leave, but the world outside doesn't seem to be ending. Which isn't what anyone expected, not least, it seems, Mistress Coyle, who's convinced it only means something worse is waiting to happen.

I can't help but think that she's probably right.

She frowns into her notes. "Just six?"

"Eight hundred sleeping settlers and three caretaker families in each," I say. I'm getting hungry, but I know by now there's no eating until she says the consultation is finished. "Mistress Coyle–"

"And you're sure there are eighty-one members total of the caretaker families?"

"I should know," I say. "I was in school with their children."

She looks up. "I know this is tedious, Viola, but information is power. The information we give him. The information we learn *from* him."

I sigh impatiently. "I don't know anything *about* spying."

"It's not spying," she says, returning to her notes. "It's just finding things out." She writes something more in her pad. "Four thousand, eight hundred and eighty-one people," she says, almost to herself.

I know what she means. More people than the entire population of this planet. Enough to change everything.

But change it how?

"When he speaks with you again," she says, "you can't tell him about the ships. Keep him guessing. Keep him off the right number."

"While I'm also supposed to be finding out what I can," I say.

She closes her pad, consultation over. "Information is power," she repeats.

I sit up in the bed, pretty much sick to death of being a patient. "Can I ask you something?"

She stands and reaches for her cloak. "Certainly."

"Why do you trust me?"

"Your face when he walked into your room," she says without hesitating. "You looked as if you'd just met your worst enemy."

She snaps the buttons of the cloak under her chin. I watch her carefully. "If I could just find Todd or get to that communications tower . . ."

"And be taken by the army?" She's not frowning but her eyes are bright. "Lose us our one advantage?" She opens the door. "No, my girl, the President will come a-calling and when he does, what you find out from him will help us."

I call out after her as she goes, "Who do you mean by *us*?"

But she's gone.

". . . and the last thing I really remember is him picking me up and carrying me down a long, long hill, and telling me that I wasn't going to die, that he'd save me."

"Wow," breathes Maddy softly, wisps of hair sneaking out from under her cap as we walk slowly up one hallway and down another to build my strength. "And he did save you."

"But he can't kill," I say, "not even to save himself. That's the thing about him, why they wanted him so bad. He isn't like them. He killed a Spackle once and you should have seen how he suffered for it. And now they've *got* him–"

I have to stop and blink a lot and look at the floor.

"I need to get *out* of here," I say, clenching my teeth. "I'm no spy. I need to find him and I need to get to that tower and *warn* them. Maybe they can send help. They have more scout ships that could reach here. They've got weapons . . ."

Maddy's face looks tense, like it always does when I talk this way. "We're not even allowed outside yet."

"You can't just accept what people tell you, Maddy. You can't just *do* that if they're wrong."

"And *you* can't fight an army on your own." She turns me gently back down the hallway, giving me a smile. "Not even the great and brave Viola Eade."

"I did it before," I say. "I did with *him*."

She lowers her voice. "Vi–"

"I lost my parents," I say and my voice is husky. "And there's no way I can get them back. And now I've lost him. And if there's a chance, if there's even a chance–"

"Mistress Coyle won't allow it," she says, but there's something in her voice that makes me look up.

"But?" I say.

Maddy says no more, just walks us over to the hall window that looks out onto the road. A troop of soldiers passes by in the bright sunlight, a cart full of dusty purple grain passing by the other way, the Noise we can hear from the town coming down the road like an army all on its own.

At first it was like no Noise I'd ever heard, this weird buzzing sound of metal grinding against metal. Then it got even louder than that, like a thousand men shouting at once, which I guess is pretty much what it is, too loud and messy to be able to pick out any individual person.

Too loud to pick out one boy.

"Maybe it's not as bad as we all think." Maddy's voice is slow, weighing every word as if she's testing them out for herself. "I mean, the town looks peaceful. *Loud,* but the men who deliver the food say the stores are about to reopen. I'll bet your Todd is out there working away at a job, safe and alive and waiting to see you."

I can't tell if she's saying this because she believes it or because she's trying to get *me* to believe it. I wipe my nose with my sleeve. "That could be true."

She looks at me for a long time, obviously thinking something but not saying it. Then she turns back to the glass.

"Just listen to them roar," she says.

There are three other healers here besides Mistress Coyle. Mistress Waggoner, a short round puff of a woman with wrinkles and a mustache, Mistress Nadari, who treats cancers and who I've only seen once closing a door behind her, and Mistress Lawson, who treats children in another house of healing but who was trapped here while having a consultation with Mistress Coyle when the surrender happened and who's been fretting ever since about the ill children she left behind.

There are more apprentices, too, a dozen besides Maddy and Corinne, who–because they work with Mistress Coyle–seem to be the top two apprentices out of the whole house, maybe even all of Haven. I rarely see the others except when they're trailing behind one of the healers, stethoscopes bouncing, white coats flapping behind them, off to find something to do.

Because the truth of it is, as the days go by and the town gets on with whatever it's doing beyond our doors, most of us patients are getting better and new ones aren't arriving. All the male patients were taken out of here the first night, Maddy told me, whether they could travel or not, and no new women have been brought here even though invasion and surrender aren't bars to getting sick.

Mistress Coyle worries about this.

"Well, if she can't heal, then who is she?" Corinne says, snapping the elastic band around my arm a little too tight. "She used to run all of the houses of healing, not just this one. Everyone knew her, everyone respected her. For a while, she was even Chair of the Town Council."

I blink. "She used to be in charge?"

"Years ago. Quit moving around." She jabs the needle into my arm harder than she needs to. "She's always saying that being a leader is making the people you love hate you a little more each day." She catches my eye. "Which is something I believe, too."

"So what happened?" I ask. "Why isn't she still in charge?"

"She made a mistake," Corinne says primly. "People who didn't like her took advantage of it."

"What kind of mistake?"

Her permanent frown gets bigger. "She saved a life," she says and snaps loose the elastic band so hard it leaves a mark.

* * *

Another day passes, and another, and nothing changes. We're still not allowed out, our food still comes, and the Mayor still hasn't asked for me. His men check on my condition but the promised talk never happens. He's just leaving me here, so far.

Who knows why?

He's all anyone ever talks about, though.

"And do you know what he's done?" Mistress Coyle says over dinner, my first one where I'm allowed out of bed and in the canteen. "The cathedral isn't just his base of operations. He's made it into his *home*."

There's a general clucking of disgust from the women around her. Mistress Waggoner even pushes her plate away. "He fancies himself *God* now," she says.

"He hasn't burned the town down, though," I say, wondering aloud from the other end of the table. Maddy and Corinne both look up from their plates with wide eyes. I carry on anyway. "We all thought he would, but he hasn't."

Mistresses Waggoner and Lawson give Mistress Coyle a meaningful look.

"You show your youth, Viola," Mistress Coyle says. "And you shouldn't challenge your superiors."

I blink, surprised. "That's not what I meant," I say. "I'm only saying it's not what we expected."

Mistress Coyle takes another bite while eyeing me. "He killed every woman in his town because he couldn't hear them, because he couldn't *know* them in the way that men could be known before the cure."

The other mistresses nod. I open my mouth to speak but she overrides me.

"What's also true, my girl," she says, "is that everything we've been through since landing on this planet—the surprise of the Noise, the chaos that followed—all of that remains unknown to your friends up there." She's watching me closely now. "Everything that happened to us is waiting to happen to them."

I don't reply, I just watch her.

"And who do you want in charge of that process?" she asks. "Him?"

She's done talking to me and returns to quieter conference with the mistresses. Corinne starts eating again, a smug grin on her face.

Maddy's still staring at me wide-eyed, but all I can think of is the word left hanging in the air.

When she said *Him?*, did she also mean, *Or her?*

On our ninth day locked indoors, I'm no longer a patient. Mistress Coyle summons me to her office.

"Your clothes," she says, handing me a package over her desk. "You can put them on now, if you like. Make you feel like a real person again."

"Thank you," I say genuinely, heading behind the screen she's pointed out. I lift off the patient's robe and look for a second at my wound, almost healed both front and back.

"You really are the most amazing healer," I say.

"I do try," she says from her desk.

I unwrap the package and find all of my own clothes, freshly laundered, smelling so clean and crisp I feel a strange pull on my face and discover I'm smiling.

"You know, you're a brave girl, Viola," Mistress Coyle is saying, as I start to dress. "Despite not knowing when to keep quiet."

"Thank you," I say, a little annoyed.

"The crashing of your ship, the deaths of your parents, the amazing journey here. All faced with intelligence and resourcefulness."

"I had help," I say, sitting down to put on clean socks.

I notice Mistress Coyle's pad on a little side table, the one so full of notes from our little consultations. I look up but she's still on the other side of the screen. I reach over and flip open the cover.

"I sense big things in you, my girl," she says. "Leadership potential."

The notebook is upside down and I don't want to make a noise by moving it so I try to twist round to see what it says.

"I see a lot of myself in you."

On the first page, before her notes start, there's only a single letter, written in blue.

A.

Nothing else.

"We are the choices we make, Viola," Mistress Coyle is still talking. "And you can be so valuable to us. If you choose."

I lift up my head from the pad. "Us who?"

The door bursts open so loud and sudden I jump up and look

around the screen. It's Maddy. "There was a messenger," she says, breathless. "Women can start leaving their houses."

"It's so loud out here," I say, wincing into the ROAR of all the New Prentisstown Noise twining together.

"You get used to it," Maddy says. We're sitting on a bench outside a store while Corinne and another apprentice named Thea buy supplies for the house of healing, stocking up for the expected flood of new patients.

I look around the streets. Stores are open, people pass by, mostly on foot but on fissionbikes and horses, too. If you don't look too closely, you'd almost think nothing was even wrong.

But then you see that the men who move down the road never talk to each other. And women are allowed out only in groups of four and only in daylight and only for an hour at a time. And the groups of four never interact. Even the men of Haven don't approach us.

And there are soldiers on every corner, rifles in hand.

A bell chimes as the door of the store opens. Corinne storms out, arms full of bags, face full of thunder, Thea struggling behind her. "The storekeeper says no one's heard from the Spackle since they were taken," Corinne says, practically dropping a bag in my lap.

"Corinne and her spacks," Thea says, rolling her eyes and handing me another bag.

"Don't call them that," Corinne says. "If *we* could never treat them right, what do you think *he's* going to be doing to them?"

"I'm sorry, Corinne," Maddy says before I can ask what Corinne means, "but don't you think it makes more sense to worry about us right now?" Her eyes are watching some soldiers who've noticed Corinne's raised voice. They aren't moving, haven't even shifted from the veranda of a feed store.

But they're looking.

"It was inhuman, what we did to them," Corinne says.

"Yes, but they *aren't* human," Thea says, under her breath, looking at the soldiers, too.

"*Thea Reese!*" A vein bulges out of Corinne's forehead. "How can you call yourself a healer and say–"

"Yes, yes, all right," Maddy says, trying to calm her down. "It was awful. I agree. You know we *all* agree, but what could we have done about it?"

"What are you talking about?" I say. "Did *what* to them?"

"The *cure*," Corinne says, saying it like a curse.

Maddy turns to me with a frustrated sigh. "They found out that the cure worked on the Spackle."

"By *testing* it on them," Corinne says.

"But it does more than that," Maddy says. "The Spackle don't *speak*, you see. They can click their mouths a little but it's hardly more than like when we snap our fingers."

"The Noise was the only way they communicated," Thea says.

"And it turned out we didn't really need them to talk to us to tell them what to do," Corinne says, her voice rising even more. "So who cares if they needed to talk to each *other*?"

I'm beginning to see. "And the cure . . ."

Thea nods. "It makes them docile."

"Better slaves," Corinne says bitterly.

My mouth drops open. "They were *slaves*?"

"Shhhh," Maddy shushes harshly, jerking her head toward the soldiers watching us, their lack of Noise among all the ROAR of the other men making them seem ominously blank.

"It's like we cut out their tongues," Corinne says, lowering her voice but still burning.

But Maddy is already getting us on our way, looking back over her shoulder at the soldiers.

Who watch us go.

We walk the short distance back to the house of healing in silence, entering the front door under the blue outstretched hand painted over the door frame. After Corinne and Thea go inside, Maddy takes my arm lightly to hold me back.

She looks at the ground for a minute, a dimple forming in the middle of her eyebrows. "The way those soldiers looked at us," she says.

"Yeah?"

She crosses her arms and shivers. "I don't know if I like this version of peace very much."

"I know," I say softly.

She waits a moment, then she looks at me square. "Could your people help us? Could they stop this?"

"I don't know," I say, "but finding out would be better than just sitting here, waiting for the worst to happen."

She looks around to see if we're being overheard. "Mistress

Coyle is brilliant," she says, "but sometimes she can only hear her own opinion."

She waits, biting her upper lip.

"Maddy?"

"We'll watch out," she says.

"For what?"

"*If* the right moment arrives, and *only if*," she looks around again, "we'll see what we can do about contacting your ships."

8

THE NEWEST APPRENTICE

{VIOLA}

"BUT SLAVERY IS WRONG," I say, rolling up another bandage.

"The healers were always opposed to it." Mistress Coyle ticks off another box on her inventory. "Even after the Spackle War, we thought it inhuman."

"Then why didn't you stop it?"

"If you ever see a war," she says, not looking up from her clipboard, "you'll learn that war only destroys. No one escapes from a war. No one. Not even the survivors. You accept things that would appall you at any other time because life has temporarily lost all meaning."

"*War makes monsters of men*," I say, quoting Ben from that night in the weird place where New World buried its dead.

"And women," Mistress Coyle says. She taps her fingers on boxes of syringes to count them.

"But the Spackle War was over a long time ago, wasn't it?"

"Thirteen years now."

"Thirteen years where you could have righted a wrong."

She finally looks at me. "Life is only that simple when you're young, my girl."

"But you were in charge," I say. "You could have done something."

"And who told you I was in charge?"

"Corinne said–"

"Ah, Corinne," she says, turning back to her clipboard, "doing her best to love me no matter what the facts."

I open up another bag of supplies. "But if you were head of this Council thing," I press on, "surely you could have done *something* about the Spackle."

"Sometimes, my girl," she says, giving me a displeased look, "you can lead people where they don't want to go, but most of the time you *can't*. The Spackle weren't going to be freed, not after we'd just beaten them in an awful and vicious war, not when we needed so much labor to rebuild. But they could be treated better, couldn't they? They could be fed properly and set to work humane hours and allowed to live together with their families. All victories *I* won for them, Viola."

Her writing on the clipboard is a lot more forceful than it was. I watch her for a second. "Corinne says you were thrown off the Council for saving a life."

She doesn't answer me, just sets down her clipboard and looks on one of the higher shelves. She reaches up and takes down an apprentice hat and a folded apprentice cloak. She turns and tosses them to me.

"Who are these for?" I say, catching them.

"You want to find out about being a leader?" she says. "Then let's put you on the path."

I look at her face.

I look down at the cloak and the cap.

From then on, I barely have time to eat.

The day after women were allowed to move again, there were eighteen new patients, all female, who'd been suffering all kinds of things–appendicitis, heart problems, lapsed cancer treatments, broken bones–all trapped in houses where they'd been stuck after being separated from husbands and sons. The next day, there were eleven more. Mistress Lawson went back to the children's house of healing the second she was able, but Mistresses Coyle, Waggoner, and Nadari were suddenly rushing from room to room, shouting orders and saving lives. I don't think anyone's been to sleep since.

There's certainly no time for me and Maddy to look for our moment, no time to even notice that the Mayor still hasn't come to see me. Instead, I run around a lot, getting in the way, helping out where I can, and squeezing apprentice lessons in.

I turn out not to be a natural healer.

"I don't think I'm ever going to get this," I say, failing yet again to tell the blood pressure of a sweet old patient called Mrs. Fox.

"It sure feels that way," Corinne says, glancing up at the clock.

"Patience, pretty girl," Mrs. Fox says, her face wrinkling up in a smile. "A thing worth learning is worth learning well."

"You're right there, Mrs. Fox," Corinne says, looking back at me. "Try it again."

I pump up the armband to inflate it, listen through the stethoscope for the right kind of *whoosh, whoosh* in Mrs. Fox's blood and match that up to the little dial. "Sixty over twenty?" I guess weakly.

"Well, let's find out," Corinne says. "Have you died this morning, Mrs. Fox?"

"Oh, dearie me, no," Mrs. Fox says.

"Probably not sixty over twenty then," Corinne says.

"I've only been doing this for three days," I say.

"I've been doing it for six years," Corinne says, "since I was *way* younger than you, my girl. And here you are, can't even work a blood pressure sleeve, yet suddenly an apprentice just like me. Funny how life works, huh?"

"You're doing fine, sweetheart," Mrs. Fox says to me.

"No, she isn't, Mrs. Fox," Corinne says. "I'm sorry to contradict you, but some of us regard healing as a sacred duty."

"I regard it as a sacred duty," I say, almost as a reflex.

This is a mistake.

"Healing is more than a *job*, my girl," Corinne says, making *my girl* sound like the worst insult. "There is nothing more important in this life than the preservation of it. We're God's hands on this world. We are the opposite of your friend the tyrant."

"He's not my–"

"To allow someone, *anyone*, to suffer is the greatest sin there is."

"Corinne–"

"You don't understand anything," she says, her voice low and fierce. "Quit pretending that you do."

Mrs. Fox has shrunk down nearly as far as I have.

Corinne glances at her and back at me, then she straightens her cap and tugs the lapels on her cloak, stretching out her neck from right to left. She closes her eyes and lets out a long, long breath.

Without looking at me, she says, "Try it again."

*   *   *

"The difference between a clinic and a house of healing?" Mistress Coyle asks, ticking off boxes on a sheet.

"The main difference is that clinics are run by male doctors, houses of healing by female healers," I recite, as I count out the day's pills into separate little cups for each patient.

"And why is that?"

"So that a patient, male or female, can have a choice between knowing the thoughts of their doctor or not."

She raises an eyebrow. "And the real reason?"

"Politics," I say, returning her word.

"Correct." She finishes the paperwork and hands it to me. "Take these and the medicines to Madeleine, please."

She leaves and I finish filling up the tray of medicines. When I come out with it in my hands, I see Mistress Coyle down at the end of the hallway, passing by Mistress Nadari.

And I swear I see her slip Mistress Nadari a note, without either of them pausing.

We can still only go out for an hour at a time, still only in groups of four, but that's enough to see how New Prentisstown is putting itself together. As my first week as an apprentice comes to an end, we hear tell that some women are even being sent out into fields to work in women-only groups.

We hear tell that the Spackle are being kept somewhere on the edge of town, all together as one group, awaiting "processing," whatever that might mean.

We hear tell the old Mayor is working as a dustman.

We hear nothing about a boy.

"I missed his birthday," I tell Maddy, as I practice tying bandages around a rubber leg so ridiculously realistic everyone calls it Ruby. "It was four days ago. I lost track of how long I was asleep and–"

I can't say any more, just pull the bandage tight–

And think of when he put a bandage on me–

And when I put bandages on him.

"I'm sure he's fine, Vi," Maddy says.

"No, you're not."

"No," she says, looking back out the window to the road, "but against all odds the city's not at war. Against all odds, we're still alive and still working. So, against all odds, Todd could be alive and well."

I pull tighter on the bandage. "Do you know anything about a blue *A*?"

She turns to me. "A what?"

I shrug. "Something I saw in Mistress Coyle's notebook."

"No idea." She looks back out the window.

"What are you looking for?"

"I'm counting soldiers," she says. She looks back again at me and Ruby. "It's a good bandage." Her smile makes it almost seem true.

I head down the main hallway, Ruby kicking from one hand. I have to practice injecting shots into her thigh. I already feel sorry for the poor woman whose thigh gets my first real jab.

I come round a corner as the hallway reaches the center of the building, where it turns ninety degrees down the other wing, and I nearly collide with a group of mistresses, who stop when they see me.

Mistress Coyle and four, five, *six* other healers behind her. I recognize Mistress Nadari and Mistress Waggoner, and there's Mistress Lawson, too, but I've never seen the other three before and didn't even see them come into the house of healing.

"Have you no work, my girl?" Mistress Coyle says, some edge in her voice.

"Ruby," I stammer, holding out the leg.

"Is this her?" asks one of the healers I don't recognize.

Mistress Coyle doesn't introduce me.

She just says, "Yes, this is the girl."

I have to wait all day to see Maddy again, but before I can ask her about it, she says, "I've figured it out."

"Did one of them have a scar on her upper lip?" Maddy whispers in the dark. It's well past midnight, well past lights-out, well past when she should be in her own room.

"I think so," I whisper back. "They left really quickly."

We watch another pair of soldiers march down the road. By Maddy's reckoning, we've got three minutes.

"That would have been Mistress Barker," she says. "Which means the others were probably Mistress Braithwaite and Mistress Forth." She looks back out the window. "This is crazy, you know. If she catches us, we'll get it good."

"I hardly think she's going to fire you under the circumstances."

Her face goes thoughtful. "Did you hear what the mistresses were saying?"

"No, they shut up the second they saw me."

"But you were *the girl*?"

"Yeah," I say. "And Mistress Coyle avoided me the rest of today."

"Mistress Barker . . ." Maddy says, still thinking. "But how could that accomplish anything?"

"How could what accomplish what?"

"Those three were on the Council with Mistress Coyle. Mistress Barker still *is*. Or was, before all this. But why would they be–" She stops and leans closer to the window. "That's the last foursome."

I look out and see four soldiers marching up the road.

If the pattern Maddy's spotted is right, the time is now.

If the pattern's right.

"You ready?" I whisper.

"Of *course* I'm not ready," Maddy says, with a terrified smile. "But I'm going."

I see how she's flexing her hands to keep them from shaking. "We're just going to look," I say. "That's all. Out and back again before you know it."

Maddy still looks terrified but nods her head. "I've never done anything like this before in my whole life."

"Don't worry," I say, lifting the sash on my window all the way up. "I'm an expert."

The ROAR of the town, even when it's sleeping, covers our footsteps pretty well as we sneak across the dark lawn. The only light is from the two moons, shining down on us, half circles in the sky.

We make it to the ditch at the side of the road, crouching in the bushes.

"What now?" Maddy whispers.

"You said two minutes, then another pair."

Maddy nods in the shadows. "Then another break of seven minutes."

In that break, Maddy and I will start moving down the road, sticking to the trees, staying undercover, and see if we can get to the communications tower, if that's even what it *is*.

See what's there when we do.

"You all right?" I whisper.

"Yeah," she whispers back. "Scared but excited, too."

I know what she means. Out here, crouching in a ditch under the cover of night, it's crazy, it's dangerous, but I finally feel like I'm *doing* something, finally feel like I'm taking charge of my own life for the first time since being stuck in that bed.

Finally feel like I'm doing something for Todd.

We hear the crunch of gravel on the road and crouch a little lower as the expected pair of soldiers march past us and away.

"Here we go," I say.

We stand up as much as we dare and move quickly down the ditch, away from the town.

"Do you still have family on the ships?" Maddy whispers. "Someone besides your mother and father?"

I wince a little at the sound she's making but I know she's only talking to cover her nerves. "No, but I know everyone else. Bradley Tench, he's lead caretaker on the *Beta*, and Simone Watkin on the *Gamma* is really smart."

The ditch bends with the road and there's a crossroads coming up that we'll have to negotiate.

Maddy starts up again. "So Simone's the one you'd–"

"Shh," I say because I think I heard something.

Maddy comes close enough to press against me. Her whole body is shaking and her breath is coming in short little puffs. She has to come this time because she knows where the tower is, but I can't ask her to do it again. When I come back, I'll come on my own.

Because if anything goes wrong–

"I think we're okay," I say.

We step slowly out from the ditch to cross the crossroads, looking all around us, stepping lightly in the gravel.

"Going somewhere?" says a voice.

Maddy takes in a sharp breath behind me. There's a soldier leaning against a tree, his legs crossed like he couldn't be more relaxed.

Even in the moonlight I can see the rifle hanging lazily from his hand.

"Little late to be out, innit?"

"We got lost," I sputter. "We were separated from–"

"Yeah," he interrupts. "I'll bet."

He strikes a match against the zip of his uniform jacket. In the flare of light, I see SERGEANT HAMMAR written across his pocket. He uses the match to light a cigarette in his mouth.

Cigarettes were banned by the Mayor.

But I guess if you're an officer.

An officer without Noise who can hide in the dark.

He takes a step forward and we see his face. He's got a smile on over the cigarette, an ugly one, the ugliest I've ever seen.

"You?" he says, recognition in his voice as he gets nearer.

As he raises his rifle.

"Yer the girl," he says, looking at me.

"Viola?" Maddy whispers, a step behind me and to my right.

"Mayor Prentiss knows me," I say. "You won't harm me."

He inhales on the cigarette, flashing the ember, making a streak against my vision. "*President* Prentiss knows you."

Then he looks at Maddy, pointing at her with the rifle.

"I don't reckon he knows you, tho."

And before I can say anything–

Without giving any kind of warning–

As if it was as natural to him as taking his next breath–

Sergeant Hammar pulls the trigger.

9

WAR IS OVER

"YOUR TURN TO DO THE BOG," Davy says, throwing me the canister of lime.

We never see the Spackle use the corner where they've dug a bog to do their business but every morning it's a little bit bigger and stinks a little bit more and it needs lime powdered over it to cut down on the smell and the danger of infeckshun.

I hope it works better on infeckshun than it does on smell.

"Why ain't it never *yer* turn?" I say.

"Cuz Pa may think yer the *better man*, pigpiss," Davy says, "but he still put me in charge."

And he grins at me.

I start walking to the bog.

The days passed and they kept passing, till there was two full weeks of 'em gone and more.

I stayed alive and got thru.

(did she?)

(*did* she?)

Davy and I ride to the monastery every morning and he "oversees" the Spackle tearing down fences and pulling up brambles and I spend the day shoveling out not enough fodder and trying and failing to fix the last two water pumps and taking every turn to do the bog.

The Spackle've stayed silent, still not doing nothing that could save themselves, fifteen hundred of 'em when we finally got 'em counted, crammed into an area where I wouldn't herd two hundred sheep. More guards came, standing along the top of the stone wall, rifles pointed twixt rows of barbed wire, but the Spackle don't do nothing that even comes close to threatening.

They've stayed alive. They've got thru it.

And so has New Prentisstown.

Every day, Mayor Ledger tells me what he sees out on his rubbish rounds. Men and women are still separated and there are more taxes, more rules about dress, a list of books to be surrendered and burned, and compulsory church attendance, tho not in the cathedral, of course.

But it's also started to act like a real town again. The stores are back open, carts and fissionbikes and even a fissioncar or two are back on the roads. Men've gone back to work. Repairmen returned to repairing, bakers returned to baking, farmers returned to farming, loggers returned to logging, some of 'em even signing up to join the army itself, tho you can tell who the new soldiers are cuz they ain't been given the cure yet.

"You know," Mayor Ledger said one night and I could see it in his Noise before he said it, see the thought forming, the thought I hadn't thought myself, the thought I hadn't *let* myself think. "It's not nearly as bad as I thought," he said. "I expected slaughter. I expected my own death, certainly, and perhaps the burning of the entire town. The surrender was a fool's chance at best, but maybe he's not lying."

He got up and looked out over New Prentisstown. "Maybe," he said, "the war really is over."

"Oi!" I hear Davy call as I'm halfway to the bog. I turn round. A Spackle has come up to him.

It's holding its long white arms up and out in what may be a peaceful way and then it starts clicking, pointing to where a group of Spackle have finished tearing down a fence. It's clicking and clicking, pointing to one of the empty water troughs, but there ain't no way of understanding it, not if you can't hear its Noise.

Davy steps closer to it, his eyes wide, his head nodding in sympathy, his smile dangerous. "Yeah, yeah, yer thirsty from the hard work," he says. "Course you are, course you are, thank you for bringing that to my attenshun, thank you very much. And in reply, let me just say this."

He smashes the butt of his pistol into the Spackle's face. You can hear the crack of bone and the Spackle falls to the ground clutching at its jaw, long legs twisting in the air.

There's a wave of clicking around us and Davy lifts his pistol again, bullet end facing the crowd. Rifles cock on the fence top, too, soldiers pointing their weapons. The Spackle slink back, the broken-jawed one still writhing and writhing in the grass.

"Know what, pigpiss?" Davy says.

"What?" I say, my eyes still on the Spackle on the ground, my Noise shaky as a leaf about to fall.

He turns to me, pistol still out. "It's *good* to be in charge."

Every minute I've expected life to blow apart.

But every minute, it don't.

And every day I've looked for her.

I've looked for her from the openings outta the top of the bell tower but all I ever see is the army marching and men working. Never a face I reckernize, never a silence I can feel as hers.

I've looked for her when Davy and I ride back and forth to the monastery, seeking her out in the windows of the Women's Quarter, but I never see her looking back.

I've even half looked for her in the crowds of Spackle, wondering if she's hiding behind one, ready to pop out and yell at Davy for beating on 'em and then saying to me, like everything's okay, "Hey, I'm here, it's me."

But she ain't there.

She ain't there.

I've asked Mayor Prentiss bout her every time I've seen him and he's said I need to trust him, said he's not my enemy, said if I put my faith in him that everything will be all right.

But I've looked.

And she ain't there.

"Hey, girl," I whisper to Angharrad as I saddle her up at the end of our day. I've gotten way better at riding her, better at talking to her, better at reading her moods. I'm less nervous about being on her back and she's less nervous about being underneath me. This morning after I gave her an apple to eat, she clipped her teeth thru my hair once, like I was just another horse.

Boy colt, she says, as I climb on her back and me and Davy set off back into town.

"Angharrad," I say, leaning forward twixt her ears, cuz this is what horses like, it seems, constant reminders that everyone's there, constant reminders that they're still in the herd.

Above anything else, a horse hates to be alone.

Boy colt, Angharrad says again.

"Angharrad," I say.

"Jesus, pigpiss," Davy moans, "why don't you marry the effing–" He stops. "Well, goddam," he says, his voice suddenly a whisper, "would you look at this?"

I look up.

There are women coming out of a store.

Four of 'em, together in a group. We knew they were being let out but it's always daylight hours, always while me and Davy are at the monastery, so we always return to a city of men, like the women are just phantoms and rumor.

It's been ages since I even seen one more than just thru a window or from up top of the tower.

They're wearing longer sleeves and longer skirts than I saw before and they each got their hair tied behind their heads the same way. They look nervously at the soldiers that line the streets, at me and Davy, too, all of us watching 'em come down the store's front steps.

And there's still the silence, still the pull at my chest and I have to wipe my eyes when I'm sure Davy ain't looking.

Cuz none of 'em is her.

"They're late," Davy says, his voice so quiet I guess he ain't seen a woman for weeks neither. "They're all sposed to be in way before sundown."

Our heads turn as we watch 'em pass by, parcels held close, and they carry on down the road back to the Women's Quarter and my chest tightens and my throat clenches.

Cuz *none* of 'em is *her.*

And I realize–

I realize all over again how much–

And my Noise goes all muddy.

Mayor Prentiss has used her to control me.

Duh.

Any effing idiot would know it. If I don't do what they say, they kill her. If I try to escape, they kill her. If I do anything to Davy, they kill her.

If she ain't dead already.

My Noise gets blacker.

No.

No, I think.

Cuz she might not be.

She mighta been out here, on this very street, in another group of four.

Stay alive, I think. *Please please please stay alive.*

(*please be alive*)

I stand at an opening as me and Mayor Ledger eat our dinners, looking for her again, trying to close my ears against the ROAR..

Cuz Mayor Ledger was right. There's so many men that once the cure left their systems, you stopped being able to hear individual Noise. It'd be like trying to hear one drop of water in the middle of a river. Their Noise became a single loud wall, all mushed together so much it don't say nothing but ROAR

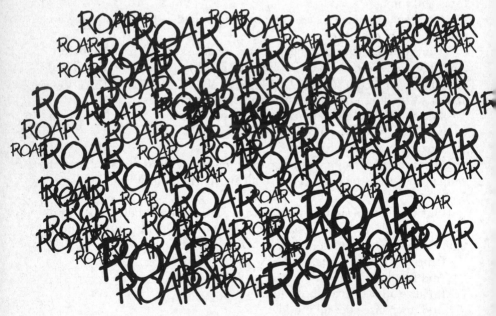

But it's actually something you can sorta get used to. In a way, Mayor Ledger's words and thoughts and feelings bubbling round his own personal gray Noise are more distracting.

"Quite correct," he says, patting his stomach. "A man is capable of thought. A crowd is not."

"An army is," I say.

"Only if it has a general for a brain."

He looks out the opening next to mine as he says it. Mayor Prentiss is riding across the square, Mr. Hammar, Mr. Tate, Mr. Morgan, and Mr. O'Hare riding behind him, listening to the orders he's giving.

"The inner circle," Mayor Ledger says.

And for a second, I wonder if his Noise sounds jealous.

We watch the Mayor dismount, hand his reins to Mr. Tate, and disappear into the cathedral.

Not two minutes later, *ker-thunk*, Mr. Collins opens our door.

"The President wants you," he says to me.

"One moment, Todd," the Mayor says, opening up one of the crates and looking inside.

We're in the cellar of the cathedral, Mr. Collins having pushed me down the stairs at the back of the main lobby. I stand there waiting, wondering how much of my dinner Mayor Ledger will eat before I can get back.

I watch Mayor Prentiss look thru another crate.

"*President* Prentiss," he says, without looking up. "Do try to remember that." He stands up straight. "Used to be wine stored down here. Far more than was ever needed for communion."

I don't say nothing. He looks at me, curious. "You aren't going to ask, are you?"

"Bout what?" I say.

"The cure, Todd," he says, thumping one of the crates with his fist. "My men have retrieved every last trace of it from every home in New Prentisstown and here it all is."

He reaches in and takes out a phial of the cure pills. He pops the lid off and takes out a small white pill twixt his finger and thumb. "Do you never wonder why I haven't given the cure to you or David?"

I shift from foot to foot. "Punishment?"

He shakes his head. "Does Mr. Ledger still fidget?"

I shrug. "Sometimes. A little."

"They made the cure," the Mayor says. "And then they made themselves *need* it." He indicates row after row of crates and boxes. "And if I have *all* of what they need . . ."

He puts the pill back in the phial and turns more fully to me, smiling wider.

"You wanted something?" I mumble.

"You really don't know, do you?" he asks.

"Know what?"

He pauses again, and then he says, "Happy birthday, Todd."

I open my mouth. Then I open it wider.

"It was four days ago," he says. "I'm surprised you didn't mention it."

I don't believe it. I completely forgot.

"No celebrations," the Mayor says, "because of course we both know you are *already* a man, now, aren't you?"

And again I raise the pictures of Aaron.

"You have been very impressive these past two weeks," he says, ignoring them. "I know it's been a great struggle for you, not knowing what to believe about Viola, not knowing exactly how you should behave to keep her safe." I can feel his voice buzzing in my head, searching around. "But you have worked hard nonetheless. You have even been a good influence on David."

I can't help but think of the ways I'd like to beat Davy Prentiss into a bloody pulp but Mayor Prentiss just says, "As a reward, I bring you two belated birthday presents."

My Noise rises. "Can I see her?"

He smiles like he expected it. "You may not," he says, "but I will promise you this. On the day that you can bring yourself to trust me, Todd, truly bring yourself to understand that I mean good for this town and good for you, then on that day, you will see that I am indeed trustworthy."

I can hear myself breathing. It's the closest he's come to saying she's all right.

"No, your first birthday present is one you've earned," he says. "You'll have a new job starting tomorrow. Still with our Spackle friends, but added responsibility and an important part of our new process." He looks me hard in the eye again. "It's a job that could take you far, Todd Hewitt."

"All the way up to be a leader of men?" I say, my voice a bit more sarcastic than he'd probably like.

"Indeed," he says.

"And the second present?" I say, still hoping it might be her.

"My second present to you, Todd, surrounded by all this cure"—he gestures at the crates again—"is not to give you any at all."

I screw up my mouth. "Huh?"

But he's already walking toward me as if we're thru talking.

And as he passes me—

I AM THE CIRCLE AND THE CIRCLE IS ME.

Rings thru my head, just the once, coming right from the center of me, of who I am.

I jump from the surprise of it.

"Why can I hear it if yer taking the cure?" I say.

But he just gives me a sly smile and disappears up the staircase, leaving me there.

Happy late birthday to me.

I am Todd Hewitt, I think, as I lie in bed, staring up into the dark. *I am Todd Hewitt and four days ago I was a man.*

Sure don't feel no different, tho.

All that reaching for it, all that importance on the date, and I'm still the same ol' stupid effing Todd Hewitt, powerless to do anything, powerless to save myself, much less her.

Todd effing Hewitt.

And lying here in the dark, Mayor Ledger snoring away over on his mattress, I hear a faint *pop* outside, somewhere in the distance, some stupid soldier firing off his gun at who knows what (or who knows who) and that's when I think it.

That's when I think getting thru it ain't enough.

Staying alive ain't enough if yer barely living.

They'll play me as long as I let 'em.

And she coulda been out there.

She coulda been out there *today*.

I'm gonna find her—

First chance I get, I'm gonna take it and I'm gonna find her—

And when I do—

And then I notice Mayor Ledger ain't snoring no more.

I raise my voice into the dark. "You got something to say?"

But then he's snoring again and his Noise is gray and muzzy and I wonder if I imagined it.

10

IN GOD'S HOUSE

{VIOLA}

"I CAN'T TELL YOU HOW SORRY I AM."

I don't take the cup of root coffee he offers.

"Please, Viola," he says, holding it out toward me.

I take it. My hands are still shaking.

They haven't stopped since last night.

Since I watched her fall.

First to her knees, then onto her side down to the gravel, her eyes still open.

Open, but already unseeing.

I watched her fall.

"Sergeant Hammar will be punished." The Mayor takes a seat across from me. "He was by no means and under no circumstances following my orders."

"He killed her," I say, hardly any sound to my voice. Sergeant Hammar dragged me back to the house of healing, pounding on the door with the butt of his rifle, waking everyone up, sending them out after Maddy's body.

I couldn't speak, I could barely even cry.

They wouldn't look at me, the mistresses, the other apprentices. Even Mistress Coyle refused to meet my eye.

What did you think you were doing? Where did you think you were taking her?

And then Mayor Prentiss summoned me here this morning to his cathedral, to his home, to God's house.

And then they *really* wouldn't look at me.

"I'm sorry, Viola," he says. "Some of the men of Prentisstown, *old* Prentisstown, still bear grudges against women over what happened all those years ago."

He sees my look of horror. "The story you think you know," he says, "is not the story that's true."

I'm still gaping at him. He sighs. "The Spackle War was in Prentisstown, too, Viola, and it was a terrible thing, but women and men fought side by side to save themselves." He puts his fingertips together in a triangle, his voice still calm, still gentle. "But there was division in our little outpost even as we were victorious. Division between men and women."

"I'll say there was."

"They made their own army, Viola. They splintered off, not trusting men whose thoughts they could read. We tried to reason with them, but eventually, they wanted war. And I'm afraid they got it."

He sits up, looking at me sadly. "An army of women is still an army with guns, still an army that can defeat you."

I can hear myself breathing. "You killed every single one."

"I did not," he says. "Many of them died in battle, but when they saw the war was lost, they spread the word that we were their murderers and then they killed themselves so that the remaining men would be doomed either way."

"I don't believe you," I say, remembering that Ben told us a different version. "That's not how it happened."

"I was there, Viola. I remember it all far more clearly than I want to." He catches my eye. "I am also the one most keen that history doesn't repeat itself. Do you understand me?"

I think I do understand him and my stomach sinks and I can't help it–I start to cry, thinking of how they brought Maddy's body back, how Mistress Coyle insisted I be the one to help her prepare the body for burial, how she wanted me to see up close the cost of trying to find the tower.

"Mistress Coyle," I say, fighting to control myself. "Mistress Coyle wanted me to ask if we can bury her this afternoon."

"I've already sent word that she can," the Mayor says. "Everything Mistress Coyle requires is being delivered to her as we speak."

I set the coffee down on a little table next to my chair. We're in a huge room, bigger than any place indoors I've ever seen except for the launch hangars of my ship. Too large for just a pair of comfortable chairs and a wooden table. The only light shines down through a round window of colored glass showing this world and its two moons.

Everything else is in shadow.

"How are you finding her?" the Mayor asks. "Mistress Coyle."

The weight on my shoulders, the weight of Maddy being gone, the weight of Todd still out there, sits so heavily I'd forgotten for a minute he was even there. "What do you mean?"

He shrugs a little. "How is she to work with? How is she as a teacher?"

I swallow. "She's the best healer in Haven."

"And now the best healer in New Prentisstown," he corrects. "People tell me she used to be quite powerful around here. A force to be reckoned with."

I bite my lip and look back at the carpet. "She couldn't save Maddy."

"Well, let's forgive her for that, shall we?" His voice is low, soft, almost kind. "Nobody's perfect."

He sets down his cup. "I'm sorry about your friend," he says again. "And I'm sorry it has taken this long for us to speak again. There has been much work to do. I look to *stop* the suffering on this planet, which is why your friend's death grieves me so. That's been my whole mission. The war is over, Viola, it truly is. Now is the time for healing."

I don't say anything to that.

"But your mistress doesn't see it that way, does she?" he asks. "She sees me as the enemy."

In the early hours of this morning, as we dressed Maddy in her white burial cloths, she said, *If he wants a war, he's got a war. We haven't even* started *fighting.*

But then when I was summoned here, she said to tell him no such thing, to ask only about the funeral.

And to find out what I could.

"You see me as the enemy, too," he says, "and I truly wish that weren't the case. I am so disappointed that this terrible incident has made you even more suspicious of me."

I feel Maddy rising again in my chest. I feel Todd rising, too. I have to breathe through my mouth for a minute.

"I know how appealing it seems that there should be sides, that you should be on *her* side," he says. "I don't blame you. I haven't even asked you about your ships because I know you would lie to me. I know she would have asked you to. If I were in Mistress Coyle's position, I would do exactly the same thing. Push you to help me. Use an asset that's fallen into my lap."

"She's not using me," I say quietly.

You can be so valuable to us, I remember, *if you choose.*

He leans forward. "Can I tell you something, Viola?"

"What?" I ask.

He cocks his head. "I really do wish you would call me David."

I look back down to the carpet. "What is it, David?"

"Thank you, Viola," he says. "It really does mean something to me." He waits until I look up again. "I've met the Council that ran Haven as was. I've met the former Mayor of Haven. I've met the former police chief and the chief medical officer and the head of education. I've met everyone of any importance in this town. Some of them now work for me. Some of them don't fit into the new administration and that's fine, there's plenty of work to be done rebuilding this city, making it ready for *your* people, Viola, making it the proper paradise that they need and want and expect."

He's still looking right into my eyes. I notice how dark blue his own are, like water running over a slate.

"And of all the people I've met in New Prentisstown, your Mistress Coyle is the only one who truly knows what leading is like. Leadership isn't grown, Viola. It's *taken,* and she may be the only person on this entire planet besides myself who has enough strength, enough *will* to take it."

I keep looking at his eyes and a thought comes.

His Noise is still silent as the black beyond and his face and eyes give away nothing either.

But I do begin to wonder–

Right there, just at the back of my thinking–

Is he *afraid* of her?

"Why do you think I had you taken to her for your gunshot wound?" he asks.

"She's the best healer. You said it yourself."

"Yes, but she's far from the only one. Bandages and medicine do most of the work. Mistress Coyle just applies them especially skillfully."

My hand goes unconsciously to my front scar. "It's not just that."

"It is not, you're correct." He leans even farther forward. "I want her on my side, Viola. I *need* her on my side if I'm going to make this new society any kind of success. If we worked together, Mistress Coyle and I"–he leans back–"well, what a world we could make."

"You locked her up."

"But I wasn't going to *keep* her locked up. The borders between men and women had become blurred, and the reintroduction of those borders is a slow and painful process. The formation of mutual trust takes time, but the important thing to remember is, as I've said, the war is *over*, Viola. It truly is. I want no more fighting, no more bloodshed."

For something to do, I pick up the cooling cup of coffee. I put it to my lips but I don't drink it.

"Is Todd okay?" I ask, not looking at him.

"Happy and healthy and working in the sun," the Mayor says.

"Can I see him?"

He's silent, as if he's considering it. "Will you do something for me?" he asks.

"What?" Another idea begins to form in my head. "You want me to spy on her for you."

"No," he says. "Not *spying*, not at all. I just want your help in convincing her that I'm not the tyrant she thinks, that history isn't as she knows it, that if we work together, we can make this place into the home we *both* wanted when our people left Old World all those many years ago. I am not her enemy. And I am not yours."

He seems so sincere. He really does.

"I'm asking for your help," he says.

"You're in complete control," I say. "You don't need my help."

"I do," he says insistently. "You've grown closer to her than I ever possibly could."

Have I? I think.

This is the girl, I remember.

"I also know that she drugged you that first night so you would fall asleep before you told me anything."

I sip my cold coffee. "Wouldn't you have done the same?"

He smiles. "So you agree we're not that different, she and I?"

"How can I trust you?"

"How can you trust her if she drugged you?"

"She saved my life."

"After I delivered you to her."

"She's not keeping me locked up in the house of healing."

"You came here unchaperoned, didn't you? The restrictions are being lessened this very day."

"She's training me as a healer."

"And who are all those other healers she's been meeting with?"

He folds his fingers back into a tent. "What are they up to, do you suppose?"

I look down into the coffee cup and swallow, wondering how he knows.

"And what do they have planned for *you*?" he asks.

I still don't look at him.

He stands. "Come with me, please."

He leads me out of the huge room and across the short lobby at the front of the cathedral. The doors are wide open onto the town square. The army is doing marching exercises out there and the *pound pound pound* of their feet pours in and the ROAR of the men who no longer have the cure floods in right behind it.

I wince a little.

"Look there," says the Mayor.

Past the army, in the center of the square, some men are assembling a small platform of plain wood, a bent pole up on the top.

"What's that?"

"It's where Sergeant Hammar is going to be hanged tomorrow afternoon for his terrible, terrible crime."

The memory of Maddy, of her lifeless eyes, rises in my chest again. I have to press my hand to my mouth to hold it back.

"I spared the old Mayor of this town," he says, "but I will not spare one of my most loyal and long-standing sergeants." He looks at me. "Do you honestly think I would go to such lengths just to please one girl who has information I could use? Do you honestly think I would go to that much trouble when, as you say, I'm in complete control?"

"Why are you doing it then?" I ask.

"Because he broke the law. Because this is a civilized world and acts of barbarity will not be tolerated. Because the *war* is *over*." He turns to me. "I would very much like you to convince Mistress Coyle of that." He steps closer. "Will you do that? Will you at least tell her the things I'm doing to remedy this tragic situation?"

I look down at my feet. My mind is whirling, spinning like a meteor.

The things he says could be true.

But Maddy is dead.

And it's my fault.

And Todd's still gone.

What do I do?

(what do I do?)

"Will you, Viola?"

At least, I think, *it's Information to give to Mistress Coyle.*

I swallow. "I'll try?"

He smiles again. "Wonderful." He touches me gently on the arm. "Run along back now. They'll be needing you for the funeral service."

I nod and step out onto the front steps and away from him, moving into the square a little bit, the ROAR of it all beating down on me as hard as the sun. I stop and try to catch the breath that seems to have run away from me.

"Viola." He's still watching me, watching me from the steps of his house, the cathedral. "Why don't you have dinner with me here tomorrow night?"

He grins, seeing how I try to hide how much I don't want to come.

"Todd will be there, of course," he says.

I open my eyes wide. Another wave rises from my chest, bringing the tears again and surprising me so much I hiccup. "Really?"

"Really," he says.

"You mean it?"

"I mean it," he says.

And then he opens his arms to me for an embrace.

11

SAVED YER LIFE

[TODD]

"WE GOTTA NUMBER 'EM," Davy says, getting out a heavy canvas bag that's been left in the monastery storeroom and dropping it loudly to the grass. "That's our new job."

It's the morning after the Mayor wished me a late happy birthday, the morning after I vowed I'd find her.

But ain't nothing's changed.

"Number 'em?" I ask, looking out at the Spackle, still staring back at us in the silence that don't make no sense. Surely the cure shoulda worn off by now? "Why?"

"Don't you *never* listen to Pa?" Davy says, getting out some of the tools. "Everyone's gotta know their place. Besides, we gotta keep track of the animals somehow."

"They ain't animals, Davy," I say, not too heated cuz we've had this fight before a coupla times. "They're just aliens."

"Whatever, pigpiss," he says and pulls out a pair of bolt cutters from the bag, setting them on the grass. He reaches in the bag again. "Take these," he says, holding out a handful of metal bands, strapped together with a longer one. I take them from him.

Then I reckernize what I'm holding.

"We're not," I say.

"Oh, yes, we are." He holds up another tool, which I also reckernize. It's how we marked sheep back in Prentisstown. You·take the tool

Davy's holding and you wrap a metal band around a sheep's leg. The tool bolts the ends together tight, too tight, so tight it cuts into the skin, so tight it starts an infeckshun. But the metal's coated with a medicine to fight it so what happens is that the infeckted skin starts to heal around the band, grow *into* it, replacing that bit of skin with the metal band itself.

I look up again at the Spackle, looking back at us.

Cuz the catch is, it don't heal if you take it off. The sheep'll bleed to death if you do. You put on a band and it's yers till the sheep dies. There ain't no going back from it.

"Then all you gotta do is think of 'em as sheep," Davy says, standing up with the bolting tool and looking out over the Spackle. "Line up!"

"We'll do one field at a time," he shouts, gesturing at the Spackle with the bolting tool in one hand and the pistol in the other. The soldiers on the stone walls keep their rifles pointed into the herd. "Once you get yer number, you stay in that field and you don't leave it, unnerstand?"

And they seem to unnerstand.

That's the thing.

They unnerstand way more than a sheep would.

I look at the packet of metal bands I'm holding. "Davy, this is–"

"Just get a move on, pigpiss," he says impayshuntly. "We're meant to get thru two hundred today."

I swallow. The first Spackle in line is watching the metal bands as well. I think it's female cuz sometimes you can tell by the color of the lichen they've got growing for their clothes. She's shorter than usual, too, for a Spackle. My height or less.

And I'm thinking, if I don't do it, if I'm not the one who does this, then they'll just get someone else who won't care if it hurts. Better they have me who'll treat 'em right. Better than just Davy on his own.

Right?

(right?)

"Just wrap the effing band round its arm or we'll be here all effing morning," Davy says.

I gesture for her to hold out her arm. She does, staring at my eyes, not blinking. I swallow again. I unwrap the packet of bands and peel off the one marked 0001. She's still staring, still not blinking.

I take hold of her outstretched hand.

The flesh is warm, warmer than I expected, they look so white and cold.

I wrap the band round her wrist.

I can feel her pulse beating under my fingertips.

She still looks into my eyes.

"I'm sorry," I whisper.

Davy steps up, takes the loose ends of the bands in the bolting tool, gives it a twist so sharp and hard the Spackle lets out a pained hiss, and then he slams the bolting tool together, locking the metal strip into her wrist, making her 0001 forever and ever.

She bleeds from under the band. 0001 bleeds red.

(which I already knew)

Holding her wrist with her other hand, she moves away from us, still staring, still unblinking, silent as a curse.

None of 'em fight. They just line up and stare and stare and stare. Once in a while they make their clicking sounds to one another but no Noise, no struggles, no resistance.

Which makes Davy angrier and angrier.

"Damn things," he says, holding the twist for a second before he bolts it off just to see how long he can make 'em hiss. And a second or two longer than that.

"How d'you like *that*, huh?" he yells at a Spackle as it walks away, holding its wrist, staring back at us.

0038 is next in line. It's a tall one, probably male, skinny as anything and getting skinnier cuz even a fool can see that the fodder we put out every morning ain't enough for fifteen hundred Spackle.

"Put the band round its neck," Davy says.

"What?" I say, my eyes widening. *"No!"*

"Put it round its effing neck!"

"I'm not—"

He lunges forward suddenly, clonking me on the head with the bolting tool and ripping the metal bands outta my hand. I fall to one knee, clutching at my skull and the pain keeps me from looking up for a few seconds.

And when I do, it's too late.

Davy's got the Spackle kneeling in front of him, the 0038 band twisted tight around its neck, and is using the bolting tool to twist it tighter. The soldiers on the top of the wall are laughing and the Spackle's gasping for air, clawing at the band with its fingers, blood coming from round its neck.

"Stop it!" I shout, struggling to get to my feet.

But Davy slams the bolting tool shut and the Spackle tumbles over into the grass, making loud gagging sounds, its head starting to turn a cruel-looking pink. Davy stands above it, not moving, just watching it choke to death.

I see the bolt cutters Davy set on the grass and I stumble to 'em, grabbing 'em and rushing back over to 0038. Davy tries to stop me but I swing the bolt cutters at him and he jumps back and I kneel beside 0038 and try to get to the metal band but Davy's twisted it so tight and the Spackle's thrashing so much from suffocating that I finally have to force him down with one fist.

I cut the band free. It flies off in a mess of blood and skin. The Spackle takes in a rake of air so loud it hurts yer ears and I lean back away from him, bolt cutters still in my hand.

And as I watch the Spackle struggle to breathe again and possibly fail and as Davy hovers behind me, bolting tool in his hand, I realize how much *clicking* I'm hearing running thru the Spackle and it's now, of all times, of all moments, of all reasons–

It's *right now* they decide to attack.

The first punch glances lightly off the crown of my head. They're thin and they're light so there's not much weight behind the punch.

But there are fifteen hundred of 'em.

And they come in a wave, so thick it's like being plunged underwater–

More fists, more punching, scratches across my face and the back of my neck and I'm knocked farther to the ground and the weight of 'em presses down on me, grabbing at my arms and legs, grabbing at my clothes and hair, and I'm calling out and yelling and one of 'em's taken the bolt cutters from my hand and swings it hard into my elbow and the pain of it is more than I can actually stand–

And my only thought, my only stupid thought is–

Why are they attacking *me*? I tried to *save* 0038.

(but they know, they know–)

(they know I'm a killer–)

Davy cries out as I hear the first gunshots from the top of the stone walls. More punches and more scratches but more gunshots, too, and the Spackle start to scatter which is something I can hear more than see cuz of the pain radiating up from my elbow.

And there's still one on top of me, scratching at me from behind as I lie facedown on the grass and I manage to turn myself over and tho the guns are still firing and the smell of cordite is filling the air and Spackle are running and running, this one stays on me, scratching and slapping away.

And the same second I realize it's 0001, the first one in line, the first one I touched, there's a bang and she spins and falls to the grass beside me. Dead.

Davy's standing over me with his pistol, smoke still coming from its barrel. His nose and lip are bleeding, he's got as many scratches as I do, and he's leaning heavily to one side.

But he's smiling.

"Saved yer life, didn't I?"

The firing of rifles carries on. The Spackle keep running but there's nowhere to go. They fall and they fall and they fall.

I look down at my elbow. "I think my arm's broke."

"I think my *leg's* broke," Davy says, "but you go back to Pa. Tell him what's happened. Tell him I *saved yer life*."

Davy's not looking at me, still raising his pistol, firing it, keeping his weight all weird on his legs.

"Davy—"

"Go!" he says and there's a grim kinda joy coming from him. "I got me a job to finish here." He fires the gun again. Another Spackle falls. They're falling all over the place.

I take a step toward the gate. And another.

And then I'm running.

My arm throbs with every step but Angharrad says **bQy cQlt** when I get to her and snuffles my face with a wet nose. She kneels down so I can flop forward onto her saddle. When she takes off down the road, she waits till I'm upright before she hits the fastest gallop I ever seen from her. I'm hanging onto her mane with one hand, my hurt arm curled under me, and I'm trying not to throw up from the pain.

I look up now and then to see women, quiet and distant, watch me ride past from their windows. I see men watch the horse run by, looking at my face all bloody and injured.

And I wonder who they think they're seeing.

Are they seeing one of them?

Or are they seeing their enemy?

Who do they think I am?

I close my eyes but I nearly lose my balance so I open them again.

Angharrad takes me down the road on the side of the cathedral, her shoes striking sparks on the cobbles as she turns the corner to go round to the entrance. The army's in the square doing marching exercises. Most of them still ain't got Noise but the pounding of their feet is loud enough to bend the air.

I wince at it all and look up to where we're going, to the front door of the cathedral—

* * *

And my Noise gives such a shock, Angharrad stops up short, scrabbling on the cobbles, flanks foaming from getting me here so fast.
 I barely notice–
 My heart has stopped beating–
 I've stopped breathing–

Cuz there she is.

In front of my eyes, walking up the steps of the cathedral–
 There she *is*.

And my heart jump-starts again and my Noise is ready to scream her name and my pain is disappearing–
 Cuz she's alive–
 She's *alive*–
 But then I'm seeing more–
 I'm seeing her walking up the steps–
 Toward Mayor Prentiss–

Into his open arms–

And he's *embracing* her–

And she's *letting* him–

And all I can think–
 All I can say–
 Is–

"Viola?"

PART III

WAR IS OVER

12

BETRAYAL

(VIOLA)

MAYOR PRENTISS STANDS THERE.
The leader of this town, this world.
Arms wide.
As if this is the price.
Do I pay it?
It's just one hug, I think.
(isn't it?)
One hug to see Todd.
I step forward–
(just one hug)
– and he puts his arms around me.
I try not to go rigid at his touch.

"I never told you," he says into my ear. "We found your ship in the swamp as we marched here. We found your parents."

I let out a little gasp of tears and try to swallow them back.

"We gave them a decent burial. I'm so sorry, Viola. I know how lonely you must be, and nothing would please me more than if, one day, maybe, you could consider me as your–"

There's a sudden sound above the *ROAR* –

One bit of Noise flying higher than the rest, clear as an arrow–

An arrow fired directly at me–

Viola! it screams, knocking the words right out of the Mayor's mouth–

I step back from his embrace, his arms falling away–

I turn–

And there, in the afternoon sunshine, in the square, on the back of a horse not ten yards away–

There he is.

It's him.
It's *him*.

"TODD!" I yell and I'm already running.

He's standing where he slid off the horse, holding his arm at a bad angle, and I hear Viola! roaring through his Noise but I can also hear the pain in his arm and confusion lacing through everything but my own mind is racing too fast and my heart is pounding too loud for me to hear any of it clearly.

"TODD!" I yell again and I reach him and his Noise opens even farther and wraps around me like a blanket and I'm grabbing him to me, grabbing him to me like I'll never let him go and he calls out in pain but his other arm is grabbing me back, it's grabbing me back, it's grabbing me back–

"I thought you were dead," he's saying, his breath on my neck. "I thought you were dead."

"Todd," I say and I'm crying and the only thing I can say is his name. "*Todd*."

He gasps sharply again and the pain flashes so loud in his Noise I'm almost blinded by it. "Your arm," I say, pulling back.

"Broken," he pants, "broken by–"

"Todd?" the Mayor says, right behind us, staring hard into him. "You're back early."

"My arm," Todd says. "The Spackle–"

"The *Spackle*?" I say.

"That looks bad, Todd," the Mayor says, talking over us. "We need to get you healed right away."

"He can come to Mistress Coyle!"

"Viola," the Mayor says and I hear Todd think "Viola"?, wondering

all over how the Mayor speaks to me like this. "Your house of healing is too far for Todd to walk with an injury this bad."

"I'll come with you!" I say. "I'm training as an apprentice!"

"Yer what?" Todd says. His pain is wailing like a siren but he's
still looking back and forth between me and the Mayor. "What's
going on? How do you know–"

"I'll explain everything," the Mayor says, taking Todd's free arm,
"after we get you healed." He turns to me. "The invitation is still on
for tomorrow. You have a funeral to get to just now."

"Funeral?" Todd says. "What funeral?"

"Tomorrow," the Mayor says to me again firmly, pulling Todd
away.

"Wait–" I say.

"Viola!" Todd shouts, jerking away from the Mayor's grasp but
the movement shakes his broken arm and he falls to one knee with
the pain of it, pain so sharp, so loud and clear in his Noise that soldiers from the army stop to hear it. I jump forward to help but the
Mayor holds out a hand to stop me.

"Go," he says and it's not a voice that's asking for discussion.
"I'll help Todd. You go to your funeral and mourn your friend. You'll
see Todd tomorrow night, good as new."

Viola? Todd's Noise says again, choking back a weep from pain
so heavy now I don't think he can speak.

"Tomorrow, Todd," I say loudly, trying to get through his Noise.
"I'll see you tomorrow."

Viola! he calls again but the Mayor is already leading him away.

"You promised!" I call after them. "Remember that you promised!"

The Mayor gives me a smile. "Remember you promised, too."

Did I? I think.

And then I'm watching them go, so fast it's like it didn't even
happen.

But Todd–

Todd is alive.

I have to bend down close to the ground for a minute and just
let it be true.

"And with burdened hearts, we commit you to the earth."

"Here." Mistress Coyle takes my hand after the priestess finishes
speaking and puts some loose dirt into it. "We sprinkle it over the
coffin."

I stare at the dirt in my hand. "Why?"

"So that she's been buried by the efforts of all of us." She directs me to a place with her in the line of healers gathering by the graveside. We pass by the hole one by one, each of us throwing our handful of dry soil onto the wooden box where Maddy now rests. Everyone stands as far away from me as they can.

No one but Mistress Coyle will even speak to me.

They blame me.

I blame me, too.

There are more than fifty women here, healers, apprentices, patients. Soldiers are spread out in a circle around us, more than you'd think necessary for a funeral. Men, including Maddy's father, are kept separate on the other side of the grave. Maddy's father's weeping Noise is the saddest thing I think I've ever heard.

And in the middle of everything, I can only feel even more guilty because what I'm mostly thinking about is Todd.

Now that I'm away from it, I can see the confusion in his Noise more clearly, see how it must have looked to find me in the arms of the Mayor, how friendly we must have seemed together.

Even though I can explain it all, I still feel ashamed.

And then he was gone.

I throw my dirt on Maddy's coffin, then Mistress Coyle takes me by the arm. "We need to talk."

"He wants to *work* with me?" Mistress Coyle says, over a cup of tea in my small bedroom.

"He says he admires you."

Her eyebrows raise. "Does he now?"

"I know," I say. "I know how it sounds, but maybe if you *heard* him–"

"Oh, I think I've heard enough from our President to last me a good while."

I lean back on my bed. "But he could have, I don't know, *forced* me to tell him about the ships. And he's not forcing me to do anything." I look away. "He's even letting me see my friend tomorrow."

"Your Todd?"

I nod. Her expression is solid as stone.

"And I suppose that makes you grateful to him, does it?"

"No," I say, rubbing my face with my hands. "I saw what his army did as they marched. I saw it with my own two eyes."

There's a long silence.

"But?" Mistress Coyle finally says.

I don't look at her. "But he's hanging the man who shot Maddy. He's executing him tomorrow."

She makes a dismissive sound with her lips. "What's one more killing to a man like him? What's one more life to take? Typical that he should think that solves the problem."

"He seemed genuinely sorry."

She looks at me sideways. "I'm sure he did. I'm sure that's exactly how he *seemed*." She lowers her voice. "He's the President of Lies, my girl. He will lie so well you'll believe it's the truth. The Devil tells the best stories. Didn't your mama teach you that?"

"He doesn't think he's the Devil," I say. "He thinks he's just a soldier who won a war."

She looks at me carefully. "Appeasement," she says. "That's what it's called. Appeasement. It's a slippery slope."

"What does it mean?"

"It means you want to work with the enemy. It means you'd rather join him than beat him, and it's a surefire way to stay beaten."

"I don't want *that*!" I yell. "I just want this all to *stop*! I want this to be a home for all the people on their way, the home that we were all looking forward to. I want there to be peace and happiness." My voice starts to thicken. "I don't want anyone else to die."

She sets down her teacup, puts her hands on her knees and looks hard at me. "Are you sure that's what you want?" she says. "Or is it your boy you'll do anything for?"

And I wonder for a minute if she can read my mind.

(because, yes, I want to see Todd-)

(I want to *explain* to him-)

"Clearly your loyalty doesn't lie with *us*," Mistress Coyle says. "After your little stunt with Maddy, there are those of us who aren't so sure you're not more of a danger than an asset."

Asset, I think.

She sighs, long and hard. "For the record," she says, "I don't blame you for Maddy's death. She was old enough to make her own decisions and if she chose to help you, well, then." She runs her fingers across her forehead. "I see so much of myself in you, Viola. Even when I'd rather not." She stands to leave. "So please know, I don't blame you. Whatever happens."

"What do you mean, *whatever happens*?"

But she doesn't say anything more.

* * *

That night, they have something called a wake, where everyone at the house of healing drinks lots of weak beer and sings songs that Maddy liked and tells stories about her. There are tears, including my own, and they're not happy tears but they're not as sad as they could be.

And I'm going to see Todd again tomorrow.

And that's as close as I can feel to all right about anything just now.

I wander around the house of healing, around the other healers and apprentices and patients talking to one another. None of them will talk to me. I see Corinne sitting by herself in a chair by the window, looking especially stormy. She's refused to speak to anyone since Maddy's death, even declining to say something over the grave. You'd have to have been sitting right next to her to see how many tear tracks were on her cheeks.

It must be the beer working in me, but she looks so upset I go over and sit down next to her.

"I'm sorry–" I start to say but she stands up before I can even finish and walks away, leaving me there.

Mistress Coyle comes over, two glasses of beer in her hands. She hands one to me. We both watch Corinne as she leaves the room. "Don't be too bothered about her," Mistress Coyle says, sitting down.

"She's always hated me."

"She hasn't. She's just had a hard time of it, that's all."

"How hard?"

"It's her place to tell you, not mine. Drink up."

I take a drink. It's sweet and wheaty-tasting, the bubbles sharp against the roof of my mouth but not in a bad way. We sit and drink for a minute or two.

"Have you ever seen an ocean, Viola?" Mistress Coyle asks.

I cough away a little of the beer. "An ocean?"

"There's oceans on New World," she says, "big as anything."

"I was born on the settler ship," I say, "but I saw them from orbit as we flew in on the scout."

"Ah, well, then you've never stood on a beach as the waves came crashing in, the water stretching out from you until it's beyond sight, moving and blue and alive and so much bigger than even the black beyond seems because the ocean hides what it contains." She shakes her head in a happy way. "If you ever want to see how small you are in the plan of God, just stand at the edge of an ocean."

"I've only ever been to a river."

She puffs out her bottom lip, regarding me. "This river goes to the ocean, you know. It's not even all that far. Two days on horseback at most. A long morning in a fissioncar, though the road's not that great."

"There's a road?"

"Not much left of it anymore."

"Is there something there?"

"Used to be my home," she says, shifting in her chair. "When we first landed, going on twenty-three years ago now. Meant to be a fishing settlement, boats and everything. In a hundred years' time, it might have even been a port."

"What happened?"

"What happened all over this planet, all our grand plans just sort of falling by the wayside in the first couple of years in the face of difficulty. It was harder to start a new civilization than we thought. You have to crawl before you can walk." She takes a sip of her beer. "And then sometimes you go back to crawling." She smiles to herself. "Probably for the best, though. Turns out New World's oceans aren't really for fishing."

"Why not?"

"Oh, the fish are the size of your boat and they swim up alongside and look you in the eye and tell you how they're going to eat you." She laughs a little. "And then they eat you."

I laugh a little, too. And then I remember all that's happened.

She looks at me again, catching my eye. "It's beautiful, though, the ocean. Like nothing you've ever seen."

"You miss it." I drink the last of my beer.

"To see the ocean once is to learn how to miss it," she says, taking my glass. "Let me get you another."

That night, I dream.

I dream of oceans and of fish that will eat me. I dream of armies that swim by and of Mistress Coyle leading them. I dream of Maddy taking my hand and holding me up from the water.

I dream of thunder making a single loud *BOOM!* that almost breaks the sky in two.

Maddy smiles when I jump at the sound of it. "I'm going to see him," I tell her.

She glances over my shoulder and says, "There he is."

I turn to look.

*   *   *

I wake but the sun's all wrong. I sit up, my head feeling like it's a boulder, and I have to close my eyes to make everything stop spinning.

"Is this what a hangover feels like?" I say out loud.

"There was no alcohol in that beer," Corinne says.

I snap my eyes open, which is a mistake as black spots form everywhere in my vision. "What are you doing here?"

"Waiting for you to wake up so the President's men can take you."

"What?" I say, as she stands. "What's going on?"

"She drugged you. Jeffers in your beer, plus bandy root to disguise the taste. She left you this." She holds out a small piece of paper. "You're to destroy it after you read it."

I take the paper. It's a note from Mistress Coyle.

Forgive me, my girl, it says, *but the President is wrong. The war is* not *over. Keep to the side of right, keep gathering information, keep leading him astray. You'll be contacted.*

"They blew up a storefront and left in the confusion," Corinne says.

"They did *what*?" My voice starts to rise. "Corinne, *what's going on*?"

But she's not even looking at me. "I told them they were abandoning their sacred trust, that *nothing* was more important than saving lives."

"Who else is here?"

"Just you and me," she says. "And the soldiers waiting outside to take you to your President." She looks down at her shoes and for the first time I notice the anger, the *rage* burning off her. "I expect I'll be interrogated by someone less *handsome*."

"Corinne–"

"You'll have to start calling me Mistress Wyatt now," she says, turning toward the door. "That is, in the unlikely event that both of us get back here alive."

"They're gone?" I say, still not believing it.

Corinne just glares at me, waiting for me to rise.

They're gone.

She left me here alone with Corinne.

She *left* me here.

To go off and start a war.

13

SPLINTERS

"FISSION FUEL, SIR, soaked into clay powder to make a paste—"

"I know how to make a bush bomb, Corporal Parker," says the Mayor, surveying the damage from his saddle. "What I do not know is how a group of unarmed women managed to *plant* one in full view of soldiers under your command."

We see Corporal Parker swallow, actually see it move in his throat. He's not a man from old Prentisstown, so he musta been picked up along the way. *You go where the power is*, Ivan said. But what about when the power wants answers you ain't got? "It may not have been just women, sir," Parker says. "People are talking about something called—"

"Look at this, pigpiss," Davy says to me. He's ridden Deadfall/Acorn over to a tree trunk, near where we've stopped across the road from the blown-out storefront.

I chirrup to Angharrad, using my one good hand to tap the reins. She picks her feet lightly over the bits of wood and plaster and glass and foodstuffs that are scattered everywhere, like the store finally let go of a sneeze it was holding in. We get over to Davy, who's pointing at a bunch of light-colored splinters sticking straight outta the tree trunk.

"Explozhun so big it rammed 'em straight into the tree," he says. "Those bitches."

"It was late at night," I say, readjusting my arm in the sling. "They didn't hurt no one."

"Bitches," Davy repeats, shaking his head.

"You'll turn in your supply of cure, Corporal," we hear the Mayor say, loud enough so Corporal Parker's men hear the punishment, too. "All of you will. Privacy is a privilege for those who've earned it."

The Mayor ignores Corporal Parker's mumbled, "Yes, sir," and turns to have a short, quiet word with Mr. O'Hare and Mr. Morgan, who then ride off in different direkshuns. The Mayor comes over to us next, not saying nothing, face frowning like a slap. Morpeth stares viciously at our mounts, too. **Submit,** says his Noise. **Submit. Submit.** Deadfall and Angharrad both lower their heads and step back.

All horses are a little bit crazy.

"Want me to go hunting for 'em, Pa?" Davy says. "The bitches who did this?"

"Mind your language," the Mayor says. "You both have work to be getting on with."

Davy gives me a sideways glance and holds out his left leg. The whole bottom half is covered in a cast. "Pa?" he says. "If you ain't noticed, I can barely walk and pigpiss here's in a sling and–"

He don't even finish the sentence before there's that *whoosh* of sound; flying from the Mayor faster than thought, like a bullet made of Noise. Davy flinches back in his saddle, yanking the reins so hard Deadfall rears up, nearly dumping Davy to the ground. Davy recovers, breathing heavy, eyes unfocused.

What the hell *is* that?

"Does this look like a day you can take off?" the Mayor says, indicating all the wreckage of the store stretched around us, the husk of the building still smoking in some parts.

Blown up.

(I've been hiding it in my Noise, doing my best to keep it down–)

(but it's there, hidden away, bubbling below the surface–)

(the thought of a bridge that blew up once–)

I look back to see the Mayor staring at me so hard I'm blurting it out before I can barely think. "It wasn't her," I say. "I'm sure it wasn't."

He keeps on staring. "I never thought it might be, Todd."

Fixing my arm didn't take very long yesterday once he'd dragged me cross the square to a clinic where men in white coats set it and gave me two injeckshuns of bone-mending that hurt more than the break but by then he was already gone, promising I'd see Viola the next night (tonight, tonight) and already outta reach of a million and one askings about how he came to be embracing her and calling her all friendly-like by her first name and how she's working as a doctor or something and how she had to leave to go to a funeral and–

(and how my heart just exploded from my chest when I saw her–)

(and how it hurt all over again when she left–)

And then off she went somehow to a life of her own already being lived out there somewhere without me in it and then there was just me and my arm going back to the cathedral with the painkillers making me so sleepy I barely had time to fall on my mattress before blinking right out.

I didn't wake when Mayor Ledger came back in with his gray day-of-rubbish-collecting Noise complaints. I didn't wake when dinner came and Mayor Ledger ate both servings. I didn't wake when we were locked inside for the night *ker-thunk*.

But I surely did wake when a *BOOM!* shook the entire city.

And even as I sat up in the darkness and felt the queasy of the painkillers in my stomach, even without knowing what the *BOOM* was or where it had come from or what it meant, even then I knew things had changed again, that the world had suddenly become different one more time.

And sure enough, out we came with the Mayor and his men at first light, injuries or no, straight to the bombsite. I look at him on Morpeth. The morning sun's shining behind him, casting his shadow over everything.

"Will I still see her tonight?" I ask.

There's a long, quiet moment where he just stares.

"Mr. President?" calls Corporal Parker, as his men take away a long plank of wood that was blown against another tree.

Something's been drawn on the trunk underneath.

Even with not knowing how to–

Well, even with not knowing much, I can tell what it is.

A single letter, smeared on the trunk in blue.

A, it says. Just the letter **A.**

"I can't believe he's making us effing go back there one day after we fought off the attack," Davy grumbles as we make our way down the long road to the monastery.

I can't believe it neither, frankly. Davy can barely walk and even with the bone-mending doing its work on my arm, it'll be a coupla days before everything's back to normal. I can start to bend it already but I sure as hell can't fight off a Spackle army with it.

"Did you tell him I saved yer life?" Davy asks, looking both angry and shy.

"Didn't *you* tell him?" I say.

Davy's mouth flattens, pulling his sad little mustache fluff even thinner. "He don't believe me when I tell him stuff like that."

I sigh. "I told him. He saw it in my Noise anyway."

We ride in silence for a bit before Davy finally says, "Did he say anything?"

I hesitate. "He said, *Good for him*."

"That all?"

"He said it was good for me, too."

Davy bites his lip. "That's it?"

"That's it."

"I see." He don't say no more, just jigs Deadfall along a bit faster.

Even tho it was only one building that got blown up in the night, the whole city looks different as we ride. The patrols of soldiers are suddenly larger and there's more of 'em, marching up and down the roads and side streets so fast it's like they're running. There are soldiers on rooftops now, too, here and there, holding rifles, watching watching watching.

The only nonsoldier men out are hustling as fast as they can from place to place, staying outta the way, not looking up.

I ain't seen no women this morning. Not one.

(not her)

(what was she *doing* with him?)

(is she lying to him?)

(is he believing her?)

(did she have something to do with the explozhun?)

"Did *who* have something to do with it?" Davy asks.

"Shut up."

"Make me," he says. But his heart ain't in it.

We ride past a group of soldiers escorting a beat-up–looking man with his wrists bound. I press my slinged arm closer to my chest and we keep on riding. The morning sun's high in the sky by the time we pass the hill with the metal tower and come round the final bend to the monastery.

Ain't no putting off getting there any longer.

"What happened after I left?" I say.

"We beat 'em," Davy says, huffing a little with the rising pain in his leg, pain I can see in his Noise. "We beat 'em back good and proper."

Something lands on Angharrad's mane. I brush it away and something else lands on my arm. I look up.

"What the hell?" Davy says.

It's snowing.

* * *

I only ever seen snow once in my whole life, back when I was too young to really know that I'd hardly never see it again.

Flakes of white fall thru the trees and onto the road, catching on our clothes and hair. It's a silent fall and it's weird how it makes everything else seem quiet, too, like it's trying to tell you a secret, a terrible, terrible secret.

But the sun is blazing.

And this ain't snow.

"Ash," Davy spits when a flake lands near his mouth. "They're burning the bodies."

They're burning the bodies. The men are still on the tops of the stone walls with their rifles, making the Spackle that lived pile up the bodies of the ones that died. The burning pile is huge, taller than the tallest living Spackle, and more bodies are being brought to it by Spackle with their heads down and their mouths shut.

I watch a body get thrown up to the top of the pile. It lands askew and tumbles down the side, rolling over other bodies, thru the flames, till it reaches the mud below and comes to a stop facing straight up, holes in its chest, blood dried on its wounds–

(a dead-eyed Spackle, faceup in a campsite–)

(a Spackle with a knife in its chest–)

I breathe a heavy breath and I look away.

Apart from some of the clicking, the living Spackle still ain't got no Noise. No sounds of mourning nor anger nor nothing at all bout the mess they're having to clean up.

It's like someone cut out their tongues.

Ivan's there waiting for us, rifle in the crook of his arm. He's quieter this morning and his face ain't happy.

"You're to be a-carrying on with the numbers," he says, kicking over the bag with the numbering bands and tools. "Though there's less to do now."

"How many'd we get?" Davy says, smiling.

Ivan shrugs, annoyed. "Three hundred, three fifty, can't say for sure."

I feel another greasy twist in my stomach at that but Davy's grin gets even higher. "That's hot stuff, right there."

"I'm to give you this," Ivan says, holding out the rifle to me.

"Yer *arming* him?" Davy says, his Noise rising right up.

"President's orders," Ivan snaps. He's still holding out the rifle. "You're to give it to the night watch when you leave. It's only for your protection while you're in here." He looks at me, frowning. "The President says to tell you he knows you'll do the right thing."

I'm just staring at the rifle.

"I don't effing believe this," Davy says, under his breath and shaking his head.

I know how to use a rifle. Ben and Cillian taught me how to use one so I didn't blow my own head off, how to hunt safely with it, how to use it only when necessary.

The right thing.

I look up. Most of the Spackle are back and away in the far fields, as far as they can get from the entrance. The rest are dragging broken and torn bodies to the fire that's burning in the middle of the next field over.

But the ones that can see me are watching me.

And they're watching me watch the rifle.

And they ain't thinking nothing I can hear.

So who knows what they're planning?

I take the rifle.

It don't mean nothing. I won't use it. I just take it.

Ivan turns and walks back to the gate to leave and as he goes, I notice it.

A low *buzz*, just barely beyond hearing, but there. And growing.

No wonder he looked so pissed off.

The Mayor took away *his* cure, too.

We spend the rest of the morning shoveling out the fodder, refilling the troughs, and putting lime on the bogs, me one-handed, Davy one-legged, but taking more time than even that would allow for cuz brag tho he may I don't think Davy wants to get back to the numbering just yet either. We may both have guns now but touching an enemy that almost killed you, well, that takes a bit of leading up to.

Morning turns to early afternoon. For the first time, instead of taking both our lunches for himself, Davy throws a sandwich at me, hitting me in the chest with it.

So we eat and watch the Spackle watching us, watch the pile of bodies burn, watch the eleven hundred fifty Spackle left over from the attack that went wrong, wrong, wrong. They're gathered round the edges of the fields we opened up and along the wall of the monastery, as far from us and from the burning pile as they can be.

"The bodies should go in a swamp," I say, eating my sandwich with one tired arm. "That's what Spackle bodies are for. You put 'em in water and then–"

"Fire's good enough for 'em," Davy says, leaning against the bag of numbering tools.

"Yeah, but–"

"There's no buts here, pigpiss." He frowns. "And what're you moaning for their sakes anyway? All yer blessed kindness didn't stop 'em from trying to rip yer arm off, now did it?"

He's right but I don't say nothing to that, just keep on watching them, feeling the rifle at my back.

I could take it. I could shoot Davy. I could run from here.

"You'd be dead before you got to the gate," Davy mumbles, looking at his sandwich. "And so would yer precious girl."

I don't say nothing to that neither, just finish my lunch. Every pile of food is out, every trough has been refilled, every bog has been limed up. There ain't nothing left to do except the thing we gotta do.

Davy sits up from where he was leaning against the bag. "Where were we?" he says, opening it up.

"0038," I say, keeping my gaze on the Spackle.

He sees from the metal bands that I'm right. "How'd you remember that?" he says, amazed.

"I just do."

They're looking back at us now, all of 'em. Their faces are hollowed out, bruised, blank. They know what we're doing. They know what's coming. They know what's in the bag. They know there ain't nothing they can do about it except die if they resist us.

Cuz I got a rifle on my back to make that happen.

(what's the right thing?)

"Davy," I start to say but it's all that comes out cuz–

BOOM!

– in the distance, almost not a sound at all, more like the faraway thunder of a storm you know is gonna get here quick and do its best to knock yer house down.

We turn, as if we could see over the walls, as if the smoke's already rising over the treetops outside the gates.

We can't and it ain't yet.

"Those bitches," Davy whispers.

But I'm thinking–

(is it her?)

(is it her?)

(what is she *doing*?)

14

THE SECOND BOMB

{VIOLA}

THE SOLDIERS WAIT until midday to take me and Corinne. They practically have to tear her away from treating the remaining patients and they march us down the road, eight soldiers to guard two small girls. They won't even look at us, the one next to me so young he's barely older than Todd, so young he's got a large angry spot on his neck that for some stupid reason I can't keep my eyes off.

Then I hear Corinne gasp. They've marched us past the storefront where the bomb went off, the front of the building collapsed on itself, soldiers guarding what's left of it. Our escort slows to take a look.

And that's when it happens.

BOOM!

A sound so big it makes the air as solid as a fist, as a wave of bricks, as if the world's dropped out beneath you and you're falling sideways and up and down all at once, like the weightlessness of the black beyond.

There's a blankness where I can't remember anything and then I open my eyes to find myself lying on the ground with smoke twirling around me in spinning, floating ribbons and bits of fire drifting down from the sky here and there and for a minute it seems almost peaceful, almost beautiful, and then I realize I can't hear anything except a high-pitched whine that's drowning out all the sounds the people around me are making as they stagger to their feet or open their mouths in what must be shouting and I sit up slowly, the world still gone in whining silence and there's the soldier with the spot on his neck, there he is on the ground next to me, covered in wooden splinters, and he must have shielded me from the blast because I'm mostly okay but he's not moving.

He's not moving.

And sound begins to return and I start to hear the screaming.

"This is exactly the kind of history I did *not* want to repeat," the Mayor says, staring up thoughtfully into the shaft of light coming down from the colored-glass window.

"I didn't know anything about a bomb," I say for a second time, my hands still shaking and my ears ringing so loud it's hard to hear what he's saying. "Neither one."

"I believe you," he says. "You were very nearly killed yourself."

"A soldier blocked most of it for me," I stutter out, remembering his body, remembering the blood from it, the splinters that were stuck in nearly every part of him–

"She drugged you again, didn't she?" he asks, staring back up into the colored window, as if the answers might be there. "She drugged you and abandoned you."

This hits me like a punch.

She did abandon me.

And set off a bomb that killed a young soldier.

"Yes," I finally say. "She left. They all did."

"Not all." He walks behind me, becoming just a voice in the room, talking loud and clear enough so I can hear. "There are five houses of healing in this city. One remains fully staffed, three others are partially depleted of their healers and apprentices. It's only yours where there's been complete desertion."

"Corinne stayed," I whisper and then I'm suddenly pleading. "She tended the soldiers who were hurt in the second bomb. She didn't hesitate. She went right to the worst injured and tied tourniquets and cleared airways and–"

"Duly noted," he interrupts, even though it's true, even though she called me over to help her and we did the best we could until other stupid soldiers who couldn't or *wouldn't* see what we were doing grabbed us and dragged us away. Corinne struggled against them but they hit her in the face and she stopped.

"Please don't hurt her," I say again. "She has nothing to do with this. She stayed behind out of choice. She tried to help those–"

"I'm not going to *hurt* her!" he shouts suddenly. "Enough of this *cowering*! There will be no harm to women as long as I am President! Why is that so difficult for you to understand?"

I think of the soldiers hitting Corinne. I think of Maddy falling to the ground.

"Please don't hurt her," I whisper again.

He sighs and lowers his voice. "We just need answers from her, that's all. The same answers I'll be needing from you."

"I don't know where they went," I say. "She didn't tell me. She didn't mention anything."

And I stop myself and he notices. Because she did mention something, didn't she?

She told me a story about–

"Something you'd like to share, Viola?" the Mayor asks, coming around to face me, looking suddenly interested.

"Nothing," I say quickly. "Nothing, just . . ."

"Just what?" His eyes are keen on me, flitting over my face, trying to read me, even though I have no Noise, and I realize briefly how much he must *hate* that.

"Just that she spent her first years on New World in the hills," I lie, swallowing. "Out west of town past the waterfall. I thought it was just idle talk."

He's still staring deep into me and there's a long silence while he looks and looks before starting his walk again.

"The most important issue," he says, "is whether the second bomb was a mistake, part of the first bomb that went off later by accident?" He comes round again to read my face. "Or was it on purpose? Was it set to go off later deliberately so that my men would be surrounding a crime scene, so that there would be maximum loss of life?"

"No," I say, shaking my head. "She wouldn't. She's a healer. She wouldn't kill–"

"A general would do anything to win a war," he says. "That's why it's war."

"No," I keep saying. "No, I don't believe–"

"I know you don't believe it." He steps away from me again, turning his back. "That's why you were left behind."

He goes to the small table next to his chair and picks up a piece of paper. He holds it up so I can see it.

There's a blue *A* written across it.

"Does this mean anything to you, Viola?"

I try to keep any look off my face.

"I've never seen that before." I swallow again, cursing myself as I do. "What is it?"

He looks at me long and hard again, then he puts the paper back down on the table. "She will contact you." He watches my face. I try to give him nothing. "Yes," he says, as if to himself. "She will, and when she does, pass along one message in particular, please."

"I don't–"

"Tell her that we can stop this bloodshed at once, that we can end all this before it even begins, before more people die and peace is forever put aside. Tell her that, Viola."

He's staring so hard at me, I say, "Okay."

He's not blinking, his eyes black holes I can't turn away from. "But also tell her that if she wants war, she can have her war."

"Please–" I start to say.

"That'll be all," he says, gesturing me to my feet and toward the door. "Go back to your house of healing. Treat what patients you can."

"But–"

He opens the door for me. "There'll be no hanging this afternoon," he says. "Some civic functions will have to be curtailed in light of recent terrorist activities."

"*Terrorist*–?"

"And I'm afraid I'll be far too busy sweeping up the mess your mistress has made to host the dinner I promised you tonight."

I open my mouth but nothing comes out.

He closes the door on me.

My head spins as I stagger back down the main road. Todd is out here somewhere and all I can think of is how I can't see him and won't be able to tell him anything about what's happened or explain myself or anything.

And it's her fault.

It is. I hate to say it but it's her fault. All of this. Even if it was for reasons she thought were right, it's all her fault. Her fault that I won't see Todd tonight. Her fault that war is coming. Her fault–

I come upon the wreckage again.

There are four bodies lying in the road, covered in white sheets that don't quite conceal the pools of blood beneath them. Nearest to me but behind a cordon of soldiers guarding the site is the sheet covering the soldier who accidentally saved me.

I didn't even know his name.

And then all of a sudden he was dead.

If she'd just waited, if she'd just seen what the Mayor wanted her to do–

But then I think *Appeasement, my girl, it's a slippery slope*–

But the bodies here in the road–

But Maddy dying–

But the boy soldier who saved me–

But Corinne being hit to stop her from helping–

(oh, Todd, where are you?)

(what do I do? what's the right thing?)

"Move along there," a soldier barks at me, making me jump.

I hurry along the road and before I even realize it, I'm running.

I return to the nearly empty house of healing out of breath and slam the front door behind me. There were yet more soldiers on the road, more patrols, men on rooftops with rifles who watched me run very closely, one of them even whistling rudely as I went by.

There'll be no getting to the communications tower now, not anymore.

Another thing she screwed up.

As I catch my breath, it sinks in that I'm the only thing even resembling a healer here now. Many of the patients were well enough to follow Mistress Coyle out to wherever she's gone and, who knows, might have even been the ones to plant the bombs, but there's still at least two dozen in beds here, with more coming in every day.

And I'm just about the worst healer New Prentisstown has ever seen.

"Oh, help," I whisper to myself.

"Where'd everybody go?" Mrs. Fox asks as soon as I open the door to her room. "There's been no food, no medicine–"

"I'm sorry," I say, bustling up her bedpan. "I'll get you food as soon as I can."

"Good heavens, dear!" she says as I turn, her eyes widening.

I look at the back of my white coat where her eyes have gone. There's a dirty smear of the young soldier's blood all the way down to the hem.

"Are you all right?" Mrs. Fox asks.

I look at the blood, and all I can say is, "I'll get your food."

The next hours pass in a blur. The help staff are all gone, too, and I do my best to cook for the remaining patients, serving them and asking at the same time which medicines they take and when and how much and though they're all wondering what's going on, they see how I must look and try to be as helpful as they can.

It's well past nightfall when I come round a corner with a tray full of dirty dinner dishes and there's Corinne, just inside the entrance, pressing on the wall with one hand to hold herself up.

I throw the tray on the floor and run to her. She holds up her other hand to stop me before I reach her. She winces as I get close.

And I see the swelling around her eyes.

And the swelling in her lower lip.

And the way she's holding her body up too straight, like it hurts, like it really hurts.

"Oh, Corinne," I say.

"Just," she says, taking a breath. "Just help me to my room."

I take her hand to help her along and feel something hidden in her palm, pressed into mine. She holds up a finger to her lips to shush the wonderings about to come from my open mouth.

"A girl," she whispers. "Hidden in the bushes by the road." She shakes her head angrily. "No more than a girl."

I don't look at it until I've got Corinne to her room and left again to get bandages for her face and compresses for her ribs. I wait until I'm alone in the supply room and open my palm.

It's a note, folded, with V written on the outside. Inside, it's only a few lines, saying almost nothing at all.

My girl, it says. *Now is the time you must choose.*

And then there's a single asking.

Can we count on you?

I look up.

I swallow.

Can we count on you?

I fold the note into my pocket and I take up the bandages and compresses and I go to help Corinne.

Who was beaten by the Mayor's men.

But who wouldn't have been beaten if she hadn't had to speak for Mistress Coyle.

But who was beaten even though the Mayor said she wouldn't
be hurt.

Can we count on you?

And it wasn't signed with a name.

It just said, The Answer.

And Answer was spelled with a bright blue *A*.

15

LOCKED IN

BOOM!

–and the sky tears open behind us and a rush of wind comes up the road and Angharrad rears back in terror and I tumble off her to the ground and there's dust and screaming and a throbbing in my ears as I lay there and wait to see if I'm dead or not.

Another bomb. The third this week since the first two. Not two hundred yards away from us this time.

"Bitches," I hear Davy spit, getting to his own feet and looking back down the road.

My ears are ringing and my body's shaking as I get to my feet. The bombs've come at different times of day and night, at different spots in the city. Once it was an aqueduct that fed water to the western part of town, once it was the two main bridges to the farmlands north of the river. Today, it's–

"That's that café," Davy says, trying to stop Deadfall/Acorn from bolting. "Where the soldiers eat."

He gets Deadfall to heel and climbs back up on the saddle. "Come on!" he barks. "We'll go see if they need help."

I put my hands on Angharrad who's still frightened, still saying **boy colt boy colt** over and over again. I say her name a buncha times and finally get back up on her.

"Don't you go getting no funny ideas," Davy says. He takes out his pistol and points it at me. "You ain't sposed to leave my sight."

Cuz that's also how life's gone since the bombs started.

Davy with a gun on me, every waking minute of every waking day.

So I can't never go looking for her.

"The women certainly aren't helping their own cause any," says Mayor Ledger, mouth filled with chicken.

I don't say nothing, just eat my own dinner and field off the asking marks coming from his Noise. The café was bombed at a time when it was closed, like everything else this Answer thing bombs, but just cuz it's sposed to be empty don't mean it always is. Davy and I found two dead soldiers when we got there and one other dead guy who probably mopped the floors or something. Three more soldiers have died in the other bombs.

It's all really pissing off Mayor Prentiss.

I don't hardly see him no more, not since the day of my arm break, not since the day I sorta got to see Viola again. Mayor Ledger says he's arresting people and stuffing 'em in prisons west of town but not getting the knowledge he wants out of 'em. Mr. Morgan, Mr. O'Hare, and Mr. Tate are leading parts of the army off into the hills west of town looking for the camps of the bomb-planters, who are all these women who disappeared the night of the first bombs.

But the army ain't finding nothing and the Mayor just gets madder and madder, making more and more curfews, taking away more and more cure from his soldiers.

New Prentisstown gets louder by the day.

"The Mayor's denying the Answer even exists," I say.

"Well, the *President* can say anything he likes." Mayor Ledger pokes at his dinner with a fork. "But people talk." He takes another bite. "Oh, yes, they do."

In addishun to the mattresses wedged in on the tower ledges, they've put in a basin with fresh water every morning and a little chemical toilet back in the darkest corner. We're also getting better food, brought to us by Mr. Collins, who then locks us back inside.

Ker-thunk.

That's where I am, locked up here every minute I'm not with Davy. The Mayor obviously don't want me out looking for Viola, despite what he says about *trust*.

"We don't know it's just women," I say, trying to keep her outta my Noise. "We don't know for sure."

The Ask and the Answer463

"A group calling themselves the Answer played a role in the Spackle War, Todd. Covert bombing, nighttime operations, that sort of thing."

"And?"

"And it was all women. No Noise to be heard by the enemy, you see." He shakes his head. "But they got out of hand at the end, became a law unto themselves. After the peace, they even attacked our own city. We were finally forced to execute some of them. A nasty business."

"But if you executed them, how can it be them?"

"Because an idea lives on after the death of the person." He burps quietly. "I don't know what they think they're going to accomplish, though. It's only a matter of time before the President finds them."

"Men have gone missing, too," I say, cuz it's true but what I'm thinking is—

(did she go with 'em?)

I lick my lips. "These healing houses where women work," I say, "are they marked somehow? Some way to tell what they are?"

He takes a sip of his water, watching me over his cup. "Why do you want to know a thing like that?"

I rustle my Noise a little to hide anything that might give me away. "No reason," I say. "Never mind." I set my dinner on the little table they've given us, our agreed sign that he can eat the rest of mine. "I'm gonna sleep."

I lay back on my bed and face the wall. The last of the setting sun's coming thru the openings in the tower. There ain't no glass in the openings and winter's coming. I don't know how we're gonna get thru the cold. I put my arm under my pillow and pull my legs up to me, trying not to think too loud. I can hear Mayor Ledger eating the rest of my dinner.

But then a picture comes floating from his Noise, floating right over to me, a picture of an outstretched hand, painted in blue.

I turn to look at him. I've seen the hand on at least two different buildings on the way to the monastery.

"There are five of them," he says, his voice low. "I can tell you where they are. If you want."

I look into his Noise. He looks into mine. We're both covering something, hiding something beneath all the other strands of our thoughts. All these days locked together and we're still wondering if we can trust each other.

"Tell me," I say.

"1017," I read out to Davy as he spins the bolting tool around, latching the band to a Spackle who instantly becomes 1017.

"That's enough for today," Davy says, tossing the bolting tool in the bag.

"We've still got—"

"I said that's enough." He limps back over to our bottle of water and takes a swig. His leg should be healed by now. My *arm* is, but he still limps.

"We were sposed to be done with this in a week," I say. "We're going on *two* now."

"I don't see no one hurrying us along." He spits out some water. "Do you?"

"No, but—"

"And no further instruckshuns and no new jobs . . ." He trails off, takes another swig of water, and spits some more. He glares to my left. "What're you looking at?"

1017 is still standing there, holding the band with one hand and staring at us. I think it's a male and I think it's young, not quite an adult. It clicks at us once and then once again and even tho it ain't got Noise the click sure sounds like something rude.

Davy thinks so, too. "Oh, yeah?" He reaches for the rifle slung on his back, his Noise firing it again and again at fleeing Spackle.

1017 stands his ground. He looks me in the eye and clicks again.

Yeah, definitely rude.

He backs off, walking away but still staring at us, one hand rubbing his metal band. I turn to Davy, who's got his rifle up and pointed at 1017 as he goes.

"Don't," I say.

"Why not?" Davy says. "Who's gonna stop us?"

I don't got the answer, cuz it seems there's nobody.

The bombs have come every third or fourth day. No one knows where they'll be or how they're planted, but *BOOM! BOOM! BOOM!* The evening of the sixth bomb, a small fission reactor this time, Mayor Ledger comes in with a blackened eye and a swollen nose.

"What happened?" I ask.

"Soldiers." He spits. He takes up his dinner plate, stew again, and winces as he takes the first bite.

"What did you do?"

His Noise rises a little and he turns an angry eye on me. "I didn't *do* anything."

"You know what I mean."

He grumbles some, eats some more stew, then says, "Some of them got the brilliant idea that *I* was the Answer. *Me*."

"You?" I say, maybe a bit too surprised.

He stands, setting down his stew, mostly uneaten, so I know he must be *really* sore. "They can't find the women responsible and the soldiers are looking for someone to blame." He stares outta one of the openings, watching night fall across the town that was once his home. "And did our President do anything to stop my beating?" he says, almost to himself. "No, he did not."

I keep eating, trying to keep my Noise quiet of things I don't wanna think.

"People are talking," Mayor Ledger says, keeping his voice low, "about a new healer, a young one no one's ever seen before, going in and out of this very cathedral a while back, now working at the house of healing Mistress Coyle used to run."

Viola, I think, loud and clear before I can cover it.

Mayor Ledger turns to me. "That's one you won't have seen. It's off the main road and down a little hill toward the river about halfway to the monastery. There are two barns together on the road where you need to turn." He looks out the opening again. "You can't miss it."

"I can't get away from Davy," I say.

"I'm sure I don't know what you're talking about," Mayor Ledger says, lying back down on his bed. "I'm merely telling you idle facts about our fair city."

My breathing gets heavier, my mind and Noise racing thru possibilities about how I can get there, how I can get away from Davy to find the house of healing.

(to find her)

It isn't till later that I think to ask, "Who's Mistress Coyle?"

Even tho it's dark, I can feel Mayor Ledger's Noise get a little redder. "Ah, well," he says, into the night. "She'd be your Answer, wouldn't she?"

"That's the last of 'em," I say, watching Spackle 1182 slink away, rubbing her wrist.

"About effing time," Davy says, flopping down onto the grass. There's a crispness to the air but the sun is out and the sky is mostly clear.

"What are we sposed to do now?" I say.

"No effing idea."

I stand there and watch the Spackle. If you didn't know no better, you really wouldn't think they were much smarter than sheep.

"They *ain't*," Davy says, closing his eyes to the sun.

"Shut up," I say.

But I mean, *look* at 'em, tho.

They just sit on the grass, still no Noise, not saying nothing, half of 'em staring at us, half of 'em staring at each other, clicking now and then but hardly ever moving, not doing nothing with their hands or their time. All these white faces, looking drained of life, just sitting by the walls, waiting and waiting for *something*, whatever that something's gonna be.

"And the time for that something is now, Todd," booms a voice behind us. Davy scrambles to his feet as the Mayor comes in thru the main opening, his horse tied up outside.

But he looks at me, only me. "Ready for your new job?"

"Ain't barely talked to me for weeks," Davy's fuming as we ride home. Things didn't go so well twixt him and his pa. "Just *keep watch on Todd* this and *hurry up with the Spackle* that." His hands're gripped tightly round the reins. "Do I even get a *thank you*? Do I even get a *nice job, David*?"

"We were sposed to band the Spackle in a week," I say, repeating what the Mayor told him. "It took us more'n twice that."

He turns to me, his Noise really rising red. "We got *attacked*! How's that sposed to be *my* fault?"

"I ain't saying it was," I say back but my Noise is remembering the band around 0038's neck.

"So you blame me, *too*, do you?" He's stopped his horse and is glaring at me, leaning forward in the saddle, ready to jump off.

I open my mouth to answer but then I glance down the road behind him.

There's two barns by a turning in the road, a turning that heads down to the river.

I look back to Davy quickly.

He's got an evil smile. "What's down there?"

"Nothing."

"Yer girl, ain't it?" he sneers.

"Eff you, Davy."

"No, pigpiss," he says, sliding off his saddle to the ground, his Noise rising even redder. "Eff *you*."

There ain't nothing to do but fight.

"Soldiers?" Mayor Ledger asks, seeing my bruises and blood as I come into the tower for dinner.

"Never you mind," I growl. It was me and Davy's worst fight in ages. I'm so sore I can barely reach my bed.

"You going to eat that?" Mayor Ledger asks.

A certain word in my Noise lets him know that no, I ain't gonna eat that. He picks it up and starts chomping away without even a thank you.

"You trying to eat yer way to freedom?" I say.

"Says a boy who's always had food provided for him."

"I ain't a boy."

"The supplies we brought when we landed only lasted a year," he says, twixt mouthfuls, "by which time our hunting and farming wasn't quite up to where it should have been." He takes another bite. "Lean times make you appreciate a hot meal, Todd."

"What is it about men that makes them need to turn everything into a lesson?" I cover my face with my arm, then take it away cuz of how much my blackening eye hurts.

Night falls again. The air is even cooler and I leave most of my clothes on as I get under the blanket. Mayor Ledger starts to snore, dreaming about walking in a house with endless rooms and not being able to find the exit.

This is the safest time I got to think about her.

Cuz is she really out there?

And is she part of this Answer thing?

And other things, too

Like what would she say if she saw me?

If she saw what I did every day?

And with *who*?

I swallow the cool night air and blink away the wet in my eyes.

(are you still with me, Viola?)

(are you?)

An hour later and I'm still not asleep. Something's nagging at me and I'm turning in my sheets, trying to clear my Noise of whatever it is, trying to calm down enough so I can be ready for the new job the Mayor's got planned for us tomorrow, one which don't sound all that bad, if I'm honest.

But it's like I'm missing something, something obvious, right in front of my face.

Something–

I sit up, listening to the snoring Noise of Mayor Ledger, the sleeping roar of New Prentisstown outside, the night birds chirping, even the river rushing by in the distance.

There was no *ker-thunk* sound after Mr. Collins let me in.
I think back.
Definitely not.
I look thru the darkness toward the door.
He forgot to lock it.
Right now, right this second.
It's unlocked.

16

WHO YOU ARE

(VIOLA)

"I HEAR NOISE OUTSIDE," Mrs. Fox says as I refill her water jug for the night.

"It'd only be remarkable if you *didn't*, Mrs. Fox."

"Just by the window–"

"Soldiers smoking their cigarettes."

"No, I'm sure it was–"

"I'm really very busy, Mrs. Fox, if you don't mind."

I replace her pillows and empty her bedpan. She doesn't speak again until I'm almost ready to go.

"Things aren't like they used to be," she says quietly.

"You can say that again."

"Haven used to be better," she says. "Not perfect. But better than this."

And she just looks out of her window.

I'm dying with tiredness at the end of my rounds but I sit down on my bed and take out the note that hasn't left my pocket. I read it for the hundredth, thousandth time.

My girl,
Now is the time you must choose.

Can we count on you?
The Answer

Not even a name, not even *her* name.

Almost three weeks I've had this note. Three weeks and nothing, so maybe that's how much they think they can count on me. Not another note, not another sign, just stuck here in this house with Corinne–or Mistress Wyatt, as I have to call her now–and the patients. Women who've fallen sick in the normal course of things, yes, but also women who've returned from "interviews" with the Mayor's men about the Answer, women with bruises and cuts, women with broken ribs, broken fingers, broken arms. Women with burns.

And those are the lucky ones, the ones who aren't in prison.

And every third or fourth day, *BOOM! BOOM! BOOM!*

And more are arrested and more are sent here.

And there's no word from Mistress Coyle.

And no word from the Mayor.

No word about why I'm being left alone. You'd think I'd be the one who'd be taken in first, the one who'd have interview after interview, the one who'd be sitting rotting in a prison cell.

"But nothing," I whisper. "Nothing at all."

And no word from Todd.

I close my eyes. I'm too tired to feel anything. Every day, I look for ways to get to the communications tower but there are soldiers *everywhere* now, way too many to find a pattern, and it only gets worse with each new bomb.

"I've got to do *something,*" I say out loud. "I have to or I'll go crazy." I laugh. "I'll go crazy and start talking to myself."

I laugh some more, a lot more than how funny it actually is.

And there's a knock at my window.

I sit up, my heart pumping.

"Mistress Coyle?" I say.

Is this it? Is it now?

Is this where I have to choose?

Can they count on me?

(but is that *Noise* I can hear . . .?)

I get to my knees on the bed and pull the curtains back just far enough to look through a slit outside, expecting that frown, those fingers going over her forehead–

But it's not her.

It's not her at all.

"Todd!"

And I'm throwing back the sash and lifting up the glass and he's leaning in and his Noise is saying my name and I'm putting my arms around him and dragging him inside, actually *lifting* him off the ground and pulling him through my window and he's climbing up and we fall onto my bed and I'm on my back and he's lying on top of me and my face is close to his and I remember how we were like this after we'd jumped under the waterfall with Aaron right behind us and I looked right into his eyes.

And I knew we'd be safe.

"*Todd.*"

In the light of my room, I see his eye is blackened and there's blood on his nose and I'm saying, "What happened? Are you hurt? I can–"

But he just says, "It's you."

I don't know how much time passes with us just lying there, just feeling that the other is really there, really true, really *alive*, feeling the safety of him, his weight against mine, the roughness of his fingers touching my face, his warmth and his smell and the dustiness of his clothes, and we barely speak and his Noise is roiling with feeling, with complicated things, with memories of me being shot, of how he felt when he thought I was dying, of how I feel now at his fingertips, but at the front of it all, he's just saying, Viola, Viola, Viola.

And it's Todd.

Bloody hell, it's *Todd*.

And everything's all right.

And then there are footsteps in the hall.

Footsteps that stop right outside my room.

We both look toward the door. A shadow is cast underneath it, two legs of someone standing just on the other side.

I wait for the knock.

I wait for the order to get him out of here.

I wait for the fight I'll put up.

But then the feet walk away.

"Who was that?" Todd asks.

"Mistress Wyatt," I say, and I can hear the surprise in my own voice.

*   *   *

"And then the bombs started going off," I finish, "and he only called for me twice, early on, to ask me if I knew anything and I didn't, I truly didn't, and then that was it. Nothing. That's all I know about him, I swear."

"He ain't barely spoken to me since the bombs neither," Todd says, looking down at his feet. "I was worried it was you setting 'em off."

I see the bridge blowing up in his Noise. I see me being the one to do it. "No," I say, thinking of the note in my pocket. "It wasn't me."

Todd swallows, then he says simply, clearly, "Should we run?"

"Yes," I say, betraying Corinne so fast I feel a red blush of shame already coming over me, but yes, we should run, we should run and run.

"Where, tho?" he asks. "Where is there to go?"

I open my mouth to answer–

But I hesitate.

"Where are the Answer hiding?" he asks. "Can we go there?"

And I notice some tension in his Noise, disapproval and reluctance.

The bombs. He doesn't like the bombs either.

I see a picture of some dead soldiers in the wreckage of a café.

But there's more, too, isn't there?

I hesitate again.

I'm wondering, just for the briefest moment, just as if it's a fly I'm brushing away, I'm wondering–

I'm wondering if I can tell him.

"I don't know," I say. "I really don't. They didn't tell me in case I couldn't be trusted."

Todd looks up at me.

And for a second, I see the doubt on his face, too.

"You don't trust me," I say, before I think to stop.

"You don't trust me neither," he says. "Yer wondering if I'm working for the Mayor right now. And yer wondering what took me so long to find you." He looks down sadly at the floor again. "I can still read you," he says. "Nearly as well as my own self."

I look at him, into his Noise. "*You* wonder if I'm part of the Answer. You think it's something I'd do."

He doesn't look at me, but he nods. "I was just trying to stay alive, looking for ways to find you, hoping you hadn't left me behind."

"Never," I say. "Not ever."

He looks back up at me. "I'd never leave you neither."

"You promise?"

"Cross my heart, hope to die," he says, grinning shyly.

"I promise, too," I say and I smile at him. "I ain't never leaving you, Todd Hewitt, not never again."

He smiles harder when I say *ain't* but it fades and then I see him gathering his Noise to tell me something, something difficult, something he's ashamed of, but before he does, I want him to *know*, I want him to know for *sure*.

"I think they're at the ocean," I say. "Mistress Coyle told me a story about it before she left. I think she was trying to tell me that's where they were going."

He looks back up at me.

"Now tell me I don't trust you, Todd Hewitt."

And then I see my mistake.

"What?" he says, seeing the look on my face.

"It's in your Noise," I say, standing up. "Todd, it's all *over* your Noise. *Ocean*, over and over and over again."

"It ain't on purpose," he says but his eyes are widening and I see the door of his cell left unlocked and I see a man in the cell with him telling him where I am and I see asking marks rising–

"I'm so *stupid*," Todd says, standing, too. "Such an effing *idiot*! We need to go. Now!"

"Todd–"

"How far away is the ocean?"

"Two days' ride–"

"Four days' walk then." He's pacing now. His Noise says *Ocean* again, clear as a bomb itself. He sees me looking at him, sees me seeing it. "I'm not spying on you," he says. "I'm *not*, but he musta left the door open so I'd–" He pulls his hair in frustration. "I'll hide it. I hid the truth about Aaron and I can hide this."

My stomach flutters, remembering what the Mayor said to me about Aaron.

"But we have to go," Todd's saying. "Do you have any food we can take?"

"I can get some," I say.

"*Hurry.*"

As I turn to leave, I hear my name in his Noise. *Viola*, it says, and it's covered in worry, worry that we've been set up, worry that

I think he was sent here on purpose, worry that I think he's lying, and all I can do is just look at him and think his name.

Todd.

And hope he knows what I mean.

I burst into the canteen and run to the cabinets. I leave most of the lights off, trying to keep quiet as I grab meal-packs and loaves of bread.

"That fast, huh?" Corinne says.

She's sitting at a table far back in the darkness, cup of coffee in front of her. "Your friend shows up and you just leave." She stands and walks over to me.

"I have to," I say. "I'm sorry."

"You're sorry?" she says, eyebrows raised. "And what happens here, then? What happens to all the patients who need you?"

"I'm a *terrible* healer, Corinne, all I do is wash and feed them–"

"So that I can have time to do the very little healing that I'm capable of."

"Corinne–"

Her eyes flash. "*Mistress Wyatt.*"

I sigh. "Mistress Wyatt," I say and then I think and say it at the same time. "Come with us!"

She looks startled, threatened almost. "What?"

"Can't you see where this is all headed? Women in prison, women with injuries. Can't you see this isn't going to get any better?"

"Not with bombs going off every day, it isn't."

"It's the President who's the enemy," I say.

She crosses her arms. "You think you can have just one enemy?"

"Corinne–"

"A healer doesn't take life," she says. "A healer *never* takes life. Our first oath is to do no harm."

"The bombs are set for empty targets."

"Which aren't always empty, are they?" She shakes her head, her face looking suddenly sad, sadder than I've ever seen it. "I know who I am, Viola. In my *soul*, I know it. I heal the sick, I heal the wounded, that's who I am."

"If we stay here, they'll eventually come for us."

"If we leave, patients will die." She doesn't even sound angry anymore, which is scarier than before.

"And if you're taken in?" I say, my voice getting challenging. "Who'll heal them then?"

"I was hoping you would."

I just breathe for a second. "It's not that simple."

"It is to me."

"Corinne, if I can get away, if I can contact my people–"

"Then what? They're still five months away, you said. Five months is a long time."

I turn back to the cabinets, continue filling the sack with food. "I have to try," I say. "I have to do *something*." I turn back to her, bag full. "That's who *I* am." I think of Todd, waiting for me, and my heart races faster. "That's who I've become, anyway."

She regards me quietly and then she quotes something Mistress Coyle once said to me. "We are the choices we make."

It takes me a second to realize she's just said good-bye.

"What took so long?" Todd says, anxiously looking out of the window.

"Nothing," I say. "I'll tell you later."

"You got the food?"

I hold up the bag.

"And I'm guessing we just follow the river again?" he says.

"I guess so."

He takes a second to look at me awkwardly, trying not to smile. "Here we go again."

And I feel this funny rush and I know that however much danger we're in, the rush is *happiness* and he feels it, too, and we clasp hands hard for just a second and then he stands on the bed, puts a leg on the sill and jumps through.

I pass the bag of food to him and climb out, my shoes thudding on the hard mud. "Todd," I whisper.

"Yeah?"

"Someone told me there's a communications tower somewhere outside of town," I say. "It's probably surrounded by soldiers but I was thinking if we could find it–"

"Big metal tower?" he interrupts. "Higher than the trees?"

I blink. "Probably," I say and my eyes open wide. "You know where it is?"

He nods. "I pass it every day."

"*Really?*"

"Yes, really," he says and I see it in his Noise, I see the road–

"And I think finally that's enough," says a voice from the darkness.

A voice we both recognize.

The Mayor steps out of the blackness, a row of soldiers behind him.

"Good evening to you both," he says.

And I hear a flash of Noise from the Mayor.

And Todd collapses.

17

HARD LABOR

[TODD]

IT'S A SOUND but it's not a sound and it's louder than anything possible and it would burst yer eardrums if you were hearing it with yer ears rather than the inside of yer head and everything goes white and it's not just like I'm blind but deaf and dumb and frozen, too, and the pain of it comes from right deep down within so there's no part of yerself you can grab to protect it, just a stinging, burning slap right into the middle of who you are.

This is what Davy felt, every time he got hit with the Mayor's Noise.

And it's words—

All it is is *words*—

But it's *every* word, crammed into yer head all at once, and the whole world is shouting at you that YER NOTHING YER NOTHING YER NOTHING and it rips away every word of yer own, like pulling yer hair out at the roots and taking skin with it—

A flash of words and I'm nothing—

I'm nothing—

YER NOTHING—

And I fall to the ground and the Mayor can do whatever he wants with me.

* * *

I don't wanna talk about what happens next.

The Mayor leaves some soldiers behind to guard the house of heal-ing and the others drag me back to the cathedral and he don't say noth-ing as we go, not a word as I beg him not to hurt her, as I promise and scream and cry (shut up) that I'll do anything he wants as long as he don't hurt her.

(shut up, shut up)

When we get back, he ties me to the chair again.

And lets Mr. Collins go to town.

And–

And I don't wanna talk about it.

Cuz I cry and I throw up and I beg and I call out her name and I beg some more and it all shames me so much I can't even say it.

. And all thru it, the Mayor says nothing. He just walks round me, over and over again, listening to me yell, listening to me plead.

Listening to my Noise beneath it all.

And I tell myself that I'm doing all this yelling, all this begging, to hide in my Noise what she told me, to keep her safe, to keep him from knowing. I tell myself I have to cry and beg as loud as I can so he won't hear.

(shut up)

That's what I tell myself.

And I don't wanna say no more about it.

(just effing shut the hell up)

By the time I get back in the tower, it's nearly morning and Mayor Ledger's waiting up for me and even tho I'm in no fitness to do anything, I'm wondering if maybe he played a part in all this somehow but his in-stant concern for me, his horror at the shape I'm in, it all sounds true in his Noise, so true that I just lie slowly down on the mattress and don't know what to think.

"They barely even came in," he says, standing behind me. "Collins just opened the door, took a look, then locked me in again. It's like they knew."

"Yeah," I say into my pillow. "It sure is like they knew."

"I had nothing to do with it, Todd," he says, reading me. "I swear to you. I'd never help that man."

"Just leave me be," I say.

And he does.

I don't sleep.

I burn.

I burn with the stupidity of how easy they trapped me, how easy it was to use her against me. I burn with the shame of crying at the beating (shut *up*). I burn with the ache of being taken from her again, the ache of her promise to me, the ache of not knowing what's going to happen to her now.

I don't care nothing bout what they do to me.

Eventually, the sun rises and I find out my punishment.

"Put yer back into it, pigpiss."

"Shut it, Davy."

Our new job is putting the Spackle to work in groups, digging up foundayshuns for new buildings in the monastery grounds, new buildings that'll house the Spackle for the coming winter.

My punishment is, I'm working right down there with 'em.

My punishment is, Davy's in complete charge.

My punishment is, he's got a new whip.

"C'mon," he says, slashing it against my shoulders. "Work!"

I spin round, every bit of me sore and aching. "You hit me with that again, I'll tear yer effing throat out."

He smiles, all teeth, his Noise a joyous shout of triumph. "Like to see you try, *Mr. Hewitt*."

And he just *laughs*.

I turn back to my shovel. The Spackle in my group are all staring at me. I ain't had no sleep and my fingers are cold in the sharp, morning sun and I can't help myself and I shout at 'em. "Get back to work!"

They make a few clicking sounds one to another and start digging at the ground again with their hands.

All except one, who looks at me a minute longer.

I stare at him, seething, my Noise riled and raging right at him. He just takes it silently, his breath steaming from his mouth, his eyes daring me to do something. He holds up his wrist, like he's identifying himself, as if I don't know which one he is, then he returns to working the cold earth as slowly as he can.

1017 is the only one who ain't afraid of us.

I take my shovel and stab it hard into the ground.

"Enjoying yerself?" Davy calls.

I put something in my Noise, rude as I can think of.

"Oh, my mother's long dead," he says. "Just like yers." Then he laughs. "I wonder if she talked as much in real life as she wrote in her little book."

I straighten up, my Noise rising red. "Davy–"

"Cuz boy, don't she go on for *pages*."

"One of these days, Davy," I say, my Noise so fierce I can almost see it bending the air like a heat shimmer. "One of these days, I'm gonna—"

"You're going to what, dear boy?" the Mayor says, riding thru the entrance on Morpeth. "I can hear you two arguing from out on the road." He turns his gaze to Davy. "And arguing is not working."

"Oh, I got 'em working, Pa," Davy says, nodding out to the fields.

.And it's true. Me and the Spackle are all separated into teams of ten or twenty, spread out among the whole enclosed bit of the monastery, removing stones from the low internal walls and pulling up the sod in the fields. Others are piling the dug-up dirt in other fields and my group here near the front have already dug parts of the trenches for the foundayshuns of the first building. I've got a shovel. The Spackle have to use their hands.

"Not bad," the Mayor says. "Not bad at all."

Davy's Noise is so pleased it's embarrassing. Nobody looks at him.

"And you, Todd?" The Mayor turns to me. "How is your morning progressing?"

"Please don't hurt her," I say.

"*Please don't hurt her*," Davy mocks.

"For the last time, Todd," the Mayor says, "I'm not going to hurt her. I'm just going to *talk* with her. In fact, I'm on my way to speak with her right now."

My heart jumps and my Noise raises.

"Oh, he don't like *that*, Pa," Davy says.

"Hush," the Mayor says. "Todd, is there anything you'd like to tell me that might make my visit with her go more quickly, more pleasantly for everyone?"

I swallow.

And the Mayor's just *staring* at me, staring into my Noise, and words form in my brain, PLEASE DON'T HURT HER said in my voice and his voice all twisted together, pressing down on the things I think, the things I know and it's different from the Noise slap, this voice pokes around where I don't want him, trying to open locked doors and turn over stones and shine lights where they shouldn't never be shone and all the while saying PLEASE DON'T HURT HER and I can feel myself starting to *want* to tell (*ocean*), starting to *want* to unlock those doors (*the ocean*), starting to *want* to do just exactly what he says, cuz he's right, he's right about everything and who am I to resist—

"She don't know nothing," I say, my voice wobbly, almost gasping.

He arches an eyebrow. "You seem distressed, Todd." He angles Morpeth to approach. **Submit,** Morpeth says. Davy watches the Mayor's attenshuns on me and even from here I can hear him getting jealous.

"Whenever my passions need calming, Todd, there's something I like to do."

He looks into my eyes.

I AM THE CIRCLE AND THE CIRCLE IS ME.

Hatched right in the middle of my brain, like a worm in an apple.

"Reminds me who I am," the Mayor says. "Reminds me of how I can control myself."

"What does?" Davy says and I realize he's not hearing it.

I AM THE CIRCLE AND THE CIRCLE IS ME.

Again, right on the inside of me.

"What does it mean?" I almost gasp cuz it's sitting so heavy in my brain I'm finding it hard to speak.

And then we hear it.

A whining in the air, a buzzing that ain't Noise, a buzz more like a fat purple bee coming in to sting you.

"What the ?" Davy says.

And then we're all turning, looking at the far end of the monastery, looking up over the heads of the soldiers along the top of the wall.

Buzzzz–

It's in the sky, a shape making an arc, high and sharp, coming up thru some trees behind the monastery, trailing smoke behind it, but the buzzing is getting louder and the smoke is starting to thicken into black.

And then the Mayor pulls Viola's binocs out of his shirt pocket to get a closer look.

I stare at them, my Noise churning, slopping out with asking marks that he ignores.

Davy musta brought them back down the hill, too.

I clench my fists.

"Whatever it is," Davy says, "it's coming this way."

I look back round. The thing has reached the high point of its arc and is heading back down to earth.

Down toward the monastery where we're all standing.

Buzzzz–

"I'd get out of the way if I were you," the Mayor says. "That's a bomb."

Davy runs so fast back to the gate he drops the whip. The soldiers on the wall start jumping off to the outside. The Mayor readies his horse but he don't move yet, waiting to see where the bomb's gonna land.

"Tracer," he's saying, his voice full of interest. "Antiquated, practically useless. We used them in the Spackle War."

The *buzzzzzz* is getting louder. The bomb's still falling, but picking up speed.

"Mayor Prentiss?"

"President," he corrects but he's still looking thru the binocs almost like he's hypnotized. "The sound and the smoke," he says. "Far too obvious for covert use."

"Mayor Prentiss!" My Noise is getting higher with nerves.

"The city's all been bush bombs, so why—"

"RUN!" I yell.

Morpeth starts and the Mayor looks at me.

But I ain't talking to him.

"RUN!" I'm yelling and waving my hands and the shovel at the Spackle nearest me, the Spackle in my field.

The field the bomb is heading right for.

Buzzzzz—

They don't understand. Most of 'em are just watching the bomb coming right for them. "RUN!" I keep shouting and I'm sending explozhuns out in my Noise, showing 'em what'll happen when that bomb lands, imagining blood and guts and the **BOOM** that's on its way. "*RUN*, GODDAMMIT!"

It finally gets thru and some start to scatter, maybe just to get away from me screaming and waving my shovel, but they run and I chase them farther up the field. I look back. The Mayor's moved to the entrance of the monastery, ready to ride farther if necessary.

But he's watching me.

"RUN!" I keep yelling, getting the Spackle to move up and away, fleeing from the center of this field. The last few hop over the nearest internal wall and I hop over with 'em, gasping for breath and turning round again to watch it land—

And I see 1017, still there in the middle of the field, just staring up at the sky.

At the bomb that's gonna kill him where he stands.

I'm jumping back over the internal wall before I even know it—

My feet pounding over the grass—

Leaping over the trenches we've dug—

Running so hard there ain't nothing in my Noise—

Just the *BUZZ* of the bomb—

Getting louder and lower—

And 1017 raising up his hand to shield his eyes from the sun—
Why ain't he running?
And *pound pound* go my feet—
And I'm chanting *"Damn you, damn you"* —
BUZZZZZZZZZZZZZZZZZZZZ—
And 1017 don't see me coming—

I slam into him hard enough to lift him off his feet, feeling the air punched from his lungs as we fly across the grass, as we hit the ground rolling, as we go end over end across the dirt and into a shallow trench, as one titanic—

BOOM

eats the entire planet in a single bite of sound

blasting away every thought and bit of Noise

picking up yer brain and shattering it into pieces

and every bit of air is sucked up and blown past us
and dirt and grass hits us in hard, heavy clods
and smoke fills our lungs

And then there's silence.

Loud silence.

"Are you hurt?" I hear the Mayor shout, as if he's miles and miles away and deep underwater.

I sit back up in the trench, see the huge smoking crater in the middle of the field, smoke already thinning cuz there's nothing to burn, row upon row of Spackle watching huddled from the far fields.

I'm breathing but I can't hear it.

I turn back to 1017, still mostly under me in the trench, scrabbling to get up, and I'm opening my mouth to ask him if he's all right even tho there's no way for him to answer—

And he hits me in a hard slap that leaves a rake of scratches across my face.

"Hey!" I shout, tho I can barely hear myself–

He's twisting out from under me and I reach out a hand to hold him there-

And he bites it hard with his rows of little sharp teeth–

And I pull it back, already bleeding–

And I'm ready to punch him, ready to *pound* him–

And he's out from under me, running away across the crater, back toward the other Spackle–

"Hey!" I shout again, my Noise rising into red.

He's just running and staring back and the rows of Spackle are all looking back at me, too, their stupid silent faces with less expresshun than the dumbest sheep I ever had back on the farm and my hand is bleeding and my ears are ringing and my face is stinging from the scratches and I saved his stupid life and this is the thanks I get?

Animals, I think. *Stupid, worthless, effing animals.*

"Todd?" says the Mayor again, riding over to me. "Are you hurt?"

I turn my face up toward him, not even sure if I'm calm enough to answer, but when I open my mouth–

The ground heaves.

My hearing's still gone so I feel it more than hear it, feel the rumble thru the dirt, feel the air pulse with three hard vibrayshuns, one right after the other, and I see the Mayor turn his head suddenly back toward town, see Davy and all the Spackle do the same.

More bombs.

In the distance, toward the city, the biggest bombs that've ever exploded in the history of this world.

18

TO LIVE IS TO FIGHT

{VIOLA}

I'M SO STUPIDLY UNDONE after the Mayor and his soldiers take Todd away that Corinne finally has to give me something for it, though I feel the prick of the needle in my arm as little as I feel her hand on my back, not moving, not caressing, not doing anything to make it feel better, just holding me there, keeping me to earth.

I'm sorry to say, I'm not grateful.

When I wake in my bed, it's only just dawn, the sun so low it's not quite over the horizon yet, everything else in morning shadow.

Corinne is in the chair next to me.

"As much as it would do you good to sleep longer," she says, "I'm afraid you can't."

I lean forward in the bed until I'm almost bent in half. There's a weight in my chest so heavy, it's like I'm being pulled into the ground. "I know," I whisper. "I know."

I don't even know why he collapsed. He was dazed, nearly unconscious, foam coming from his mouth, and then the soldiers lifted him to his feet and dragged him away.

"They'll come for me," I say, having to swallow away the tightness in my throat. "After they're done with Todd."

"Yes, I expect they will," Corinne says simply, looking at her hands, at the cream-colored calluses raised on her fingertips, at the ash-colored skin that flakes off the top of her hands because of so much time under hot water.

The morning is cold, surprisingly, harshly so. Even with my window closed, I can feel a shiver coming. I wrap my arms around my middle.

He's gone.

He's gone.

And I don't know what'll happen now.

"I grew up in a settlement called the Kentish Gate," Corinne suddenly says, keeping her eyes off mine, "on the edge of a great forest."

I look up. "Corinne?"

"My father died in the Spackle War," she presses on, "but my mother was a survivor. From the time I could stand, I worked with her in our orchards, picking apples and crested pine and roisin fruit."

I stare at her, wondering why now, why this story now?

"My reward for all that hard work," she continues, "was a camping trip every year after final harvest, just me and my mother, as deep in the forest as we dared to go." She looks out into the dark dawn. "There's so much life here, Viola. So much, in every corner of every forest and stream and river and mountain. This planet just *hums* with it."

She runs a fingertip over her calluses. "The last time we went, I was eight. We walked south for three whole days, a present for how grown-up I was getting. God only knows how many miles away we were, but we were alone, just me and her and that was all that mattered."

She lets a long pause go by. I don't break it.

"She was bitten by a Banded Red, on her heel, as she cooled her feet in a stream." She's rubbing her hands again. "It's fatal, red snake venom, but slow."

"Oh, Corinne," I say, under my breath.

She stands suddenly, as if my sympathy is almost rude. She walks over to my window. "It took her seventeen hours to die," she says, still not looking at me. "And they were awful and painful and when she went blind, she grabbed onto me and begged me to save her, begged me over and over to save her life."

I remain silent.

"What we know now, what the healers have discovered, is that I *could* have saved her life just by boiling up some Xanthus root." She crosses her arms. "Which was all around us. In abundance."

The ROAR of New Prentisstown is only just starting to rise with the sun. Light shoots in from the far horizon, but we stay silent for a moment longer.

"I'm sorry, Corinne," I finally say. "But why–?"

"Everyone here is someone's daughter," she says quietly. "Every soldier out there is someone's son. The only crime, the *only* crime is to take a life. There is nothing else."

"And that's why you don't fight," I say.

She turns to me sharply. "To live *is* to fight," she snaps. "To preserve life is to fight *everything* that man stands for." She takes an angry huff of air. "And now her, too, with all the bombs. I fight them every time I bandage the blackened eye of a woman, every time I remove shrapnel from a bomb victim."

Her voice has risen but she lowers it again. "That's my war," she says. "That's the war I'm fighting."

She walks back to her chair and picks up a bundle of cloth next to it. "And to that end," she says, "I need you to put these on."

She doesn't give me time to argue or even ask about her plan. She takes my apprentice robes and my own few much-washed clothes and has me put on poorer rags, a long-sleeved blouse, a long skirt, and a headscarf that completely covers my hair.

"Corinne," I say, tying up the scarf.

"Shut up and hurry."

When I'm dressed, she takes me down to the end of the long hallway leading out to the riverside by the house of healing. There's a heavy canvas bag of medicines and bandages loaded up by the door. She hands it to me and says, "Wait for the sound. You'll know it when you hear it."

"Corinne–"

"Your chances aren't very good, you have to know that." She's looking me in the eye now. "But if you get to wherever they're hiding, you put these supplies to use as a *healer*, do you hear me? You've got it in you whether you know it or not."

My breathing is heavy, nervous, but I look at her and I say, "Yes, Mistress."

"*Mistress* is right," she says and looks out of the window in the door. We can see a single bored soldier at the corner of the building, picking his nose. Corinne turns to me. "Now. Strike me, please."

I blink. "What?"

"Strike me," she says again. "I'll need a bloody nose or a split lip at least."

"Corinne–"

"Quickly or the streets will grow too crowded with soldiers."

"I'm not going to *hit* you!"

She grabs me by the arm, so fiercely I flinch back. "If the President comes for you, do you honestly think you'll return? He's tried to get the truth from you by asking and then by trapping your friend. Do you honestly think the patience of a man like that lasts forever?"

"Corinne–"

"He will eventually hurt you," she says. "If you refuse to help him, he will kill you."

"But I don't *know*–"

"He doesn't *care* what you don't know!" she hisses through her teeth. "If I can prevent the taking of a life, I will do so, even one as irritating as yours."

"You're hurting me," I say quietly, as her fingers dig into my arm.

"Good," she says. "Get angry enough to strike me."

"But why–"

"Just do it!" she shouts.

I take in a breath, then another, then I hit her across the face as hard as I can.

I wait, crouched by the window in the door, watching the soldier. Corinne's footsteps fade down the corridor as she runs to the reception room. I wait some more. The soldier is one of the many now who have had the cure taken from them and in the relative quiet of the morning I can hear what he thinks. Thoughts of boredom, thoughts of the village he lived in before the army invaded, thoughts of the army he was forced to join.

Thoughts of a girl he knew who died.

And then I hear the faint shout of Corinne coming from the front. She'll be screaming that the Answer snuck in during the night, beat her senseless, and kidnapped me under their very noses but that she saw us all flee in the opposite direction I'm going to be running.

It's a poor story; there's no way it's going to work. How could anyone sneak in with guards everywhere?

But I know what she's counting on. A legend that's been rising, a legend about the Answer.

How can the bombs be planted with no one seeing?

With no one being caught?

If the Answer can do that, could they sneak past armed guards?

Are they invisible?

I hear thoughts just like this as soon as I see the soldier's head snap up when he hears the ruckus. It grows louder in his Noise as he runs around the corner and out of view.

And as fast as that, it's time.

I hoist the bag of medicines up onto my shoulder.

I open the door.

I run.

I run toward a line of trees and down to the river. There's a path along the riverbank but I stick to the trees beside it and as the bag bashes my shoulders and back with heavy corners, I can't help but think of me and Todd running down this same river, this same riverbank, running from the army, running and running and running.

I have to get to the ocean.

As much as I want to save Todd, my only chance is to find her first.

And then I'll come back for him.

I will.

I ain't never leaving you, Todd Hewitt.

My heart aches as I remember saying it.

As I break my promise.

(you hold on, Todd)

(you stay alive)

I run.

I make my way downriver, avoiding patrols, cutting across back gardens, running behind back fences, staying as far clear of houses and housing blocks as I can.

The valley is narrowing again. The hills approach the road and the houses begin to thin out. Once, I hear marching and I have to dive deep into the undergrowth as soldiers pass, holding my breath, crouching as low to the ground as I can. I wait until there's only birdcall (Where's my safety?) and the now distant ROAR of the town, wait for a breath or two more, then I raise my head and look down the road.

The river bends in the distance and the road is lost from view behind farther rolling hills and forests. Across the road here, this far from town, there are mostly farms and farmhouses, working their way up sloping hillsides, back toward more forest. Directly across, there's a small drive leading to a farmhouse with a little stand of trees in the front garden. The farming fields spread out to the right, but above and beyond the farmhouse, thicker forest begins again. If I can get up the drive, that'll be the safest place for me. If I have to, I'll hide until nightfall and make my way in the dark.

I look up and down the road again and once more. I listen for marching, for stray Noise, for the rattle of a cart.

I take in a breath.

And I bolt across the road.

I keep my eyes on the farmhouse, the bag banging into my back, my arms pumping the air, my lungs gasping as I run faster and faster and faster–

Up the drive–

Nearly to the trees–

Nearly there–

And a farmer steps out from behind them.

I skid to a stop, sliding in the dirt and nearly falling. He jumps back, obviously surprised to see me appearing suddenly in front of him.

We stare at each other.

His Noise is quiet, disciplined, almost gentlemanly, which is why I didn't hear it from a distance. He's holding a basket under one arm and a red pear in his free hand.

He looks me up and down, sees the bag on my back, sees me alone out on the road in a break of the law, sees from the heaviness of my breath that I've obviously been running.

And it comes in his Noise, fast and clear as morning.

The Answer, he thinks.

"No," I say. "I'm not–"

But he holds a finger up to his lips.

He cocks his head in the direction of the road.

And I hear the distant sound of soldiers marching down it.

"That way," the farmer whispers. He points up a narrow path, a small entrance to the woods above that would be easy to miss if you didn't know it was there. "Quickly now."

I look at him again, trying to see a trap, trying to *tell* but there's no time. There's no time.

"Thank you," I say and I take off running.

*   *   *

The path leads almost immediately into thicker woods, all uphill. It's narrow and I have to push back vines and branches to make my way. The trees swallow me and I can only go forward and forward, hoping that I'm not being led into a trap. I get to the top of the hill only to find a small slope down and then another hill to climb. I run up that, too. I'm still heading east but I can't see enough over anything to tell where the road is or the river or which way I'm–

I nearly stumble out into a clearing.

Where there's a soldier not ten yards from me.

His back is to me (thank god, thank god) and it's not until my heart has leaped out of my chest and I've caught myself and fallen back into the bushes that I see what he's guarding.

There it is.

In the middle of a clearing cresting the hill, stretching up on three metal legs almost fifty yards into the sky. The trees around it have been felled, and across the clearing underneath it I can see a small building and a road that leads back down the other side of the hill to the river.

I've found the communications tower.

It's here.

And there aren't that many soldiers around it. I count five, no, six.

Just six. With big gaps.

My heart rises.

And rises.

I've found it.

And a *BOOM!* echoes in the distance beyond the tower.

I flinch, along with the soldiers. Another bomb. Another statement from the Answer. Another–

The soldiers are leaving.

They're running, running toward the sound of the explosion, running away from me and down the other side of the hill, toward where I can already see a white pillar of smoke rising.

The tower stands in front of me.

All of a sudden, it's completely unguarded.

I don't even wait to think how stupid I'm being–

I'm just running–

Running toward the tower–
If this is my chance to save us then–
I don't know–
I'm just running–
Across the open ground–
Toward the tower–
Toward the building underneath–
I can save us–
Somehow I can save all of us–

And out of the corner of my eye, I see someone else break cover
from the trees to my left–
Someone running straight toward me–
Someone–
Someone saying my name–

"Viola!" I hear. "Get back!"
"Viola, *NO!*" Mistress Coyle is screaming at me.

I don't stop–
Neither does she–
"GET BACK!" she's yelling–
And she's crossing the clearing in front of me–
Running and running and running–
And then I realize–
Like a blow to the stomach–
The reason why she's yelling–
No–
Even as I'm skidding to a stop–
No, I think–
No, you can't–
And Mistress Coyle reaches me–
You CAN'T–
And pushes us both to the ground–
NO!

And the legs of the tower explode in three blinding flashes of light.

PART
IV

NIGHT
FALLING

19

WHAT YOU DON'T KNOW

{VIOLA}

"GET OFF ME!"

She slaps her hand over my mouth, holding it there, holding *me* there with the weight of her body as clouds of dust billow around us from the rubble of the communications tower. "*Quit shouting,*" she hisses.

I bite her hand.

She makes a pained face, fierce and angry, but she doesn't let go, just takes the bite and doesn't move.

"You can scream and shout all you want later, my girl," she says, "but in two seconds, this place is going to be swarming with soldiers and do you honestly think they're going to believe you just *happened by?*"

She waits to see my reaction. I glare at her but finally nod. She takes away her hand.

"Don't you call me *my girl*," I say, keeping my voice low but just as fierce as hers. "Don't you call me that ever again."

I follow her down a steep slope, heading back toward the road, sliding on fallen leaves and gathered dew but always down and down. I hop over logs and roots, the canvas bag like a stone around my shoulders.

I have no choice but to go with her.

I'd be captured and God knows what else if I went back to town.

And she took my other choice away.

She reaches a stand of bushes at the bottom of a steepening in the slope. She ducks fast under them and beckons for me to follow. I slide down next to her, my breath almost gone, and she says, "Whatever you do, don't scream."

Before I can even open my mouth, she's jumped out through the bushes. They close up behind her and I have to fight my way through leaves and branches to follow. I'm still pushing them back when I practically tumble out the other side.

Onto the road.

Where two soldiers stand by a man with a cart, all of them looking straight at me and Mistress Coyle.

The soldiers look more astonished than angry, but they have no Noise, so there's no way to know.

But they're carrying rifles.

And they're raising them at us.

"And who the hell is *this*?" one barks, a middle-aged man with a shaved head and a scar down his jaw line.

"Don't shoot!" Mistress Coyle says, hands out and up.

"We heard the explosion," says the other soldier, a younger one, not much older than me, with blond, shoulder-length hair.

Then the older soldier says something else, something unexpected.

"You're *late*."

"That's enough, Magnus," Mistress Coyle says, lowering her hands and stepping forward to the cart. "And put your rifles down. She's with me."

"What?" I say, still frozen to my spot.

"The tracer malfunctioned completely," the younger soldier says to her. "We're not even sure where it came down."

"I told you they were too old," Magnus says.

"It did its job," Mistress Coyle says, bustling around the cart, "wherever it landed."

"Hey!" I say. "What's going on?"

And then I hear, "Hildy?"

Mistress Coyle stops in her tracks. The two soldiers do, too, and stare at the man driving the cart.

"Iss you, ain it?" he says. "Hildy hoo's also called Viola."

My mind's been racing so fast, so completely focused on the soldiers, that I barely took in the man driving the cart, the nearly expressionless face, the clothes, the hat, the voice, the Noise flat and calm as the far horizon.

The man that once drove me and Todd across a sea of things.

"*Wilf*," I gasp.

Now everyone looks at *me*, Mistress Coyle's eyebrows so high it's like they're trying to crawl into her hair.

"Hey," Wilf says, in greeting.

"Hey," I say back, too stunned to say any more.

He touches two fingers to the brim of his hat. "Ah'm glad to see yoo mayde it."

Mistress Coyle's mouth is moving but no sound comes out for a second or two. "There'll be time for that later," she finally says. "We have to go *now*."

"Will there be room for two?" the younger soldier asks.

"There'll have to be." She ducks down under the cart and removes a panel from the underside. She motions to me. "Get in."

"In where?" I bend down and see a compartment hidden like a trick of the eye in the width of the cart, narrow and thin as a cot above the rear axle.

"Pack won't fit," Wilf says, pointing at the bag on my back. "Ah'll take it."

I slip it off and hand it to him. "Thank you, Wilf."

"*Now*, Viola," Mistress Coyle says.

I give Wilf a last nod, duck under the cart and crawl in, forcing my way across the compartment until my head's nearly touching the far side. Mistress Coyle doesn't wait and forces herself in after me. The younger soldier was right. There isn't enough room. She's pressed right up against me, face-to-face, her knees digging into my thighs, our noses less than an inch apart. She's barely drawn her feet inside when the panel is replaced, plunging us into almost complete darkness.

"Where are we—" I start to say but she shushes me harshly.

And outside I hear soldiers marching fast up the road, led by the clopping of horse's hooves.

"Report!" one of them shouts as they stop by the cart.

His voice—

It's up high and I hear the horse whinnying beneath it—

But his voice–

"Heard the explosion, sir," the older of our soldiers replies. "This man says he saw women heading past him down the river road about an hour ago."

We hear the real soldier spit. "Bitches."

I recognize his voice–

It's Sergeant Hammar.

"Whose unit you two in?" he says.

"First, sir," says our younger soldier, after the briefest of pauses. "Captain O'Hare."

"*That* pansy?" Sergeant Hammar spits. "You wanna do some *real* soldiering, transfer to the Fourth. I'll show you what's what."

"Yes, sir," says our older soldier, sounding more nervous than I'd want him to.

I can hear the Noise of the soldiers in Sergeant Hammar's unit. They're thinking of the cart. They're thinking of the explosions. They're thinking about shooting women.

But there's no Noise coming from Sergeant Hammar.

"Arrest this man," Sergeant Hammar finally says, meaning Wilf.

"We were just doing that, sir."

"Bitches," Sergeant Hammar says again, and we hear him spur his horse (**Yield**, it thinks) and he and his men march off at full speed.

I let out the breath I didn't realize I was holding. "He wasn't even *punished*," I whisper, more to myself than to Mistress Coyle.

"Later," she whispers back.

I hear Wilf snap the reins and we rock as the cart plods slowly forward.

So the Mayor was a liar. All along.

Of course he was, you *idiot*.

And Maddy's killer walks free to kill again, his cure still in place.

And I'm bumping and shaking against the woman who destroyed the only hope of contacting the ships that might save us.

And Todd is out there. Somewhere. Being left behind.

I've never felt so lonely in my life.

The compartment is hellishly small. We share too much of each other's air, elbows and shoulders bruising away as we ride along, the heat soaking our clothes.

We don't speak.

Time passes. And then more. And more after that. I fall into a kind of doze, the close warmth sucking the life right out of me. The rocking of the cart eventually flattens all my worries and I close my eyes against it.

I'm awakened by the older soldier knocking on the wood and I think we're going to finally get out, but he just says, "We're at the rough bit. Hold on."

"To what?" I say, but I don't say any more as the cart feels like it drops off a cliff.

Mistress Coyle's forehead smacks into my nose and I smell blood almost at once. I hear her gasp and choke as my stray hand is shoved into her neck and still the cart tumbles and bumps and I wait for the moment where we topple end over end.

And then Mistress Coyle is working both arms around me, pulling me close to her and bracing us in the compartment with one hand and one foot pressed against the opposite side. I resist her, resist the implied comfort, but there's wisdom in it as almost immediately we stop knocking each other about, even though the cart lurches and stutters.

And so it's in Mistress Coyle's arms that the last bit of my journey is taken. And it's in Mistress Coyle's arms that I enter the camp of the Answer.

Finally the cart stops and the panel is removed almost immediately.

"We're here," says the younger soldier, the blond one. "Everyone okay?"

"Why wouldn't we be?" Mistress Coyle says sourly. She lets go of me and scoots her way out of the compartment, extending a hand to help me out, too. I ignore it, getting myself out and looking at my surroundings.

We've come down a steep rocky path that's barely fit for a cart and into what looks like a gash of rocks in the middle of a forest. Trees press in on every side, a row of them on the level ground in front of us.

The ocean must be beyond them. Either I dozed off for longer than I thought or she lied and it's closer than she said.

Which wouldn't surprise me.

The blond soldier whistles when he sees our faces, and I can feel caked blood under my nose. "I can get you something for that," he says.

"She's a healer," Mistress Coyle says. "She can do it herself."

"I'm Lee," he says to me, a grin on his face.

For a brief second, I'm completely aware of how terrible I must look with my bloody nose and this ridiculous outfit.

"I'm Viola," I say to the ground.

"'Ere's yer bag," Wilf says, suddenly next to me, holding out the canvas sack of medicines and bandages. I look at him for a second and then I pretty much throw myself at him in a hug, pulling him tight to me, feeling the big, safe bulk of him. "Ah'm glad to see yoo, Hildy," he says.

"You, too, Wilf," I say, my voice thick. I let him go and take the bag.

"Corinne pack that?" Mistress Coyle asks.

I fish out a bandage and start cleaning the blood from my nose. "What do you care?"

"You can accuse me of many things," she says, "but not caring isn't one of them, my girl."

"I told you," I say, catching her eye, "never call me that again."

Mistress Coyle licks her teeth. She makes a quick glance to Lee and to the other soldier, Magnus, and they leave, quickly, disappearing into the trees ahead of us. "You, too, Wilf."

Wilf looks at me. "Yoo gone be all right?"

"I think so, Wilf," I say, swallowing, "but don't you go far."

He nods, touching the brim of his hat again and walking after the soldiers. We watch him go.

"All right." Mistress Coyle turns to me, crossing her arms. "Let's hear it."

I look at her, at her face full of defiance, and I feel my breath quicken, the anger rising up again so fast, so easily, it feels like I might crack in two. "How *dare you*–"

But she's interrupting, *already*. "Whoever contacts your ships first has the advantage. If he's first, he tells them all about the nasty little terrorist organization he's got on his hands and can they please use their guidance equipment to track us down and blow us off the face of New World."

"Yes but if we–"

"If we got to them first, yes, of course, we could have told them all about our local tyrant, but that was never going to happen."

"We could have tried–"

"Did you know what you were doing when you ran toward that tower?"

I clench my fists. "*No*, but at least I could have–"

"Could have what?" Her eyes challenge me. "Sent out a message to the very coordinates the President's been searching for? Don't you think he was counting on you *trying*? Just why exactly do you think you haven't been arrested yet?"

I dig my nails into my palms, forcing myself not to hear what she's saying.

"We were running out of time," she says. "And if *we* can't use it to contact help, then at the very least we prevent him from doing the same."

"And when they land? What's your brilliant plan then?"

"Well," she says, uncrossing her arms and taking a step toward me, "if we haven't overthrown him, then there's a race to get to them first, isn't there? At least this way, it's a fair fight."

I shake my head. "You had no right."

"It's a war."

"That you started."

"*He* started it, my girl."

"And you escalated it."

"Hard decisions have to be made."

"And who put you in charge of making them?"

"Who put *him* in charge of locking away half the population of this planet?"

"You're blowing people up!"

"Accidents," she says. "Deeply regrettable."

Now it's my turn to take a step toward her. "That sounds exactly like something *he* would say."

Her shoulders rise and if she had Noise, it would be taking the top of my head off. "Have you *seen* the women's prisons, my girl? What you don't know could fill a *crater*–"

"Mistress Coyle!" A voice calls from the trees. Lee steps back into the rocky gash. "There's a report just come in."

"What is it?" Mistress Coyle says.

He looks from her to me. I look at the ground again.

"Three divisions of soldiers marching down the river road," he says, "dead set for the ocean."

I look up sharply. "They're coming *here*?"

Both Mistress Coyle and Lee look at me.

"No," Lee says. "They're going to the ocean."

I blink back and forth between them. "But aren't we–?"

"Of course not," Mistress Coyle says, her voice flat, mocking. "Whatever made you think we were? And whatever, I wonder, makes the *President* think we are?"

I feel an angry chill, despite the sun, and I notice I'm shaking inside these big stupid puffy sleeves.

She was *testing* me.

As if I would tell the Mayor where–

"How *dare* you–" I start to say again.

But the anger suddenly fades as it comes flooding back.

"Todd," I whisper.

Ocean all over his Noise.

How he promised to hide it.

And how I know he'd keep that promise–

If he could.

(oh, Todd, did he–?)

(are you–?)

Oh, *no*.

"I have to go back," I say. "I have to *save* him–"

She's already shaking her head. "There's nothing we can do for him right now–"

"He'll kill him."

She looks at me, not without pity. "He's probably dead already, my girl."

I feel my throat closing up but I fight it. "You don't know that."

"If he's not dead, then he must have told the President voluntarily." She cocks her head. "Which would you rather be true?"

"No," I say, shaking my head. "No–"

"I'm sorry, my girl." Her voice is a little calmer than before, a little softer, but still strong. "I truly am, but there are thousands of lives at stake. And like it or not, you've picked a side." She looks over to where Lee stands. "So why don't you let me show you your army?"

20

RUBBLE

"BITCHES," Mr. Hammar says from atop his horse.

"Your analysis was not asked for, Sergeant," says the Mayor, riding Morpeth thru the smoke and the twisted metal.

"They've left the mark, tho," Mr. Hammar says, pointing at the trunk of a large tree at the edge of the clearing.

The blue *A* of the Answer is smeared across it.

"Your concern for my eyesight does you credit," says the Mayor, sharply enough that even Mr. Hammar shuts up.

We rode up here straight from the monastery, meeting Mr. Hammar's squadron coming up the hill, looking ready for battle. When we got to the top, we found Ivan and the soldiers who were meant to be guarding the tower. Ivan got promoted here, I guess, after all the Spackle were rounded up, but now he's looking like he wishes he never *heard* of a tower.

Cuz it ain't here no more. It's just a heap of smoking metal, mostly in a long line where it fell, like a drunk man tipping forward onto the ground and deciding to just stay there and sleep.

(and I do my damnedest not to think about her asking me how to get here)

(saying we should go here first)

(oh, Viola, you didn't–)

"If they got enough to blow up something this big . . ." Davy says to

my right, looking across the field. He don't finish his sentence cuz it's
the same thing we're all thinking, the thing that's in everyone's Noise.

Everyone that's *got* Noise, that is, cuz Mr. Hammar seems to be one
of the lucky ones. "Hey, boy," he sneers at me. "You a man yet?"

"Don't you have somewhere you need to be heading, Sergeant?" the
Mayor asks, not looking at him.

"With haste, sir," Mr. Hammar says again, giving me an evil wink,
then spurring his horse and shouting for his men to follow. They speed
down the hill in the fastest march I've seen, leaving us with Ivan and his
soldiers, all of their Noise regretting to a man how they ran toward the
monastery after hearing the tracer bomb hit.

It's obvious, tho, when you look back. A smaller bomb in one place
to get people running away from where you want to plant yer bigger
bomb.

But what the hell were they doing bombing the monastery?

Why attack the Spackle?

Why attack *me*?

"Private Farrow," the Mayor says to Ivan.

"It's *Corporal* Farrow, actually—" Ivan says.

The Mayor turns his head slowly and Ivan stops talking as he comes
to understand. "Private Farrow," the Mayor says again. "You will salvage
what metal and scrap you can and then report to your commanding officer to relinquish your supply of cure—"

He stops. We can all hear Ivan's Noise clear as day. The Mayor looks
round. Every soldier in the squadron has Noise. Every one of 'em's already been punished for one thing or another.

"You will submit yourselves to your commanding officer for appropriate punishment."

Ivan don't reply but his Noise rumbles.

"Is something unclear, Private?" the Mayor says, his voice dangerously bright. He looks into Ivan's eyes, holding his gaze. "You will submit
yourselves to your commanding officer for appropriate punishment," he
says again, but there's something in his voice, some weird vibrayshun.

I look at Ivan. His eyes are going foggy, unfocused, his mouth a little
slack. "I will submit to my commanding officer for appropriate punishment," he says.

"Good," the Mayor says, looking back at the wreckage.

Ivan slumps a little when the eye contact is broken, blinking as if
he's just woken up, forehead furrowing.

"But, sir," he says to the Mayor's back.

The Mayor turns round again, looking *very* surprised at still being
spoken to.

Ivan presses on. "We were coming to your aid when—"

The Mayor's eyes flash. "When the Answer watched you do exactly what it wanted you to do and then blew up *my tower*."

"But, sir—"

Without changing his expresshun, the Mayor pulls out a pistol from his holster and shoots Ivan in the leg.

Ivan tumbles over, wailing. The Mayor looks at the other soldiers. "Anyone else care to contribute before you get to work?"

As the rest of the soldiers ignore Ivan's screams and start clearing up the wreckage, the Mayor moves Morpeth right in front of that **A,** loud and clear like the announcement it is. "The Answer," he says, in a low voice like he's talking to himself. "The Answer."

"Let *us* go after 'em, Pa," Davy says.

"Hmm?" The Mayor turns his head slowly, like he forgot we were there.

"We can fight," Davy says. "We proved that. And instead you got us babysitting animals that are already beat."

The Mayor considers us for a minute, tho I don't know how or when Davy turned him and me into an *us*. "If you think they're already beaten, David," he finally says, "then you know very little about the Spackle."

Davy's Noise ruffles a little. "I think I've learned a thing or two by now."

And as much as I hate to, I have to agree with him.

"Yes," says the Mayor. "I suppose you have. Both of you." He looks me in the eye and I can't help thinking of me saving 1017 from the bomb, risking my own life to get him outta the way.

And him biting and scratching me by way of thanks.

"Then how about a new project?" the Mayor says, steering Morpeth over to us. "One where you can put all your expertise to work."

Davy's Noise ain't sure of this. There's pride but doubt, too.

All I got in mine is dread.

"Are you ready to lead, Todd?" the Mayor asks lightly.

"*I'm* ready, Pa," Davy says.

The Mayor still looks only at me. He knows I'm thinking about her but he's ignoring all my askings.

"The Answer," he says, turning back to the **A.** "If that's who they want to be, then let them." He looks back at us. "But if there's an Answer, then someone must first . . ."

He lets his voice fade and he gets a faraway smile on his face, like he's laughing at his own private joke.

* * *

Davy unfolds the big white scroll onto the grass, not caring that it's getting wet in the cold morning dew. There's words written across the top and diagrams and squares and things drawn in below it.

"Measurements mostly," Davy reads. "Too effing many. I mean, *look* at that."

He holds the scroll up to me, trying to get me to agree.

And, well–

Yeah, okay, I–

Whatever.

"Too effing many," I say, feeling sweat come up under my arms.

It's the day after the tower fell and we're back at the monastery, back to putting teams of Spackle to work. My escape seems to be forgotten, like it was part of another life and now we've all got new things to think about. The Mayor won't talk to me about Viola and I'm back working for Davy, who ain't too happy.

So it's like old times.

"There's fighting to be done and he's got us building an effing *palace*." Davy frowns, looking over the plans.

It ain't a palace but he's got a point. Before it was just gonna be rough shacks to shelter the Spackle for the winter but this looks like a whole new building for men, taking up most of the inside of the monastery.

It's even got a name written across the top.

A name my eye stumbles over, trying to–

Davy turns to me, his eyes widening. I make my Noise as Noisy as possible.

"We should get started," I say, standing up.

But Davy's still looking at me. "What do you think about what it says right here?" he asks, putting his finger on a block of words. "Ain't that something amazing what it says?"

"Yeah," I shrug. "I guess."

His eyes get even wider with delight. "It's a list of materials, pigpiss!" His voice is practically celebrating. "You can't read, can you?"

"Shut up," I say, looking away.

"You can't even *read!*" Davy's smiling up into the cold sun and around at all the Spackle watching us. "What kinda idiot gets thru life–"

"I said, *shut up!*"

Davy's mouth drops open as he realizes.

And I know what he's gonna say before he says it.

"Yer ma's book," he says. "She wrote it for you and you can't even–"

And what can I do but hit him across his stupid mouth?

*   *   *

I'm getting taller and bigger and he comes off worst in the fight but he
don't seem to mind all that much. Even when we get back to work, he's
still giggling and making a big show outta reading the plans.

"Mighty complicated, these instruckshuns," he says, a big smile
across his bloody lips.

"Just effing get on with it!"

"Fine, fine," he says. "First step is what we were already doing. Tearing down all the internal walls." He looks up. "I could write it down for
you."

My Noise rages red at him but Noise is useless as a weapon.

Unless yer the Mayor.

I didn't think life could turn more to crap but it always does, don't it?
Bombs and towers falling and having to work with Davy and the Mayor
paying me special attenshun and–

(and I don't know where she is)

(and I don't know what the Mayor's gonna do to her)

(and did she plant the bombs?)

(did she?)

I turn back round to the work site.

1,150 pairs of Spackle eyes are watching us, watching *me*, like
they're just effing farm animals looking up from their grazing cuz they
heard a loud noise.

Stupid effing *sheep*.

"GET TO WORK!" I shout.

"You look like hell," Mayor Ledger says, as I fall onto my bed.

"Stuff it," I say.

"Working you hard, is he?" He brings me over the dinner that's already waiting for us. It don't even look like he ate too much of mine
before I got here.

"Ain't he working *you* hard?" I say, digging in to the food.

"I think he's forgotten about me, truth to tell." He sits back on his
own bed. "I haven't spoken to him in I don't know how long."

I look up at him. His Noise is gray, like he's hiding something, tho
that ain't unusual.

"I've just been doing my rubbish duties," he says, watching me eat.
"Listening to people talk."

"And what're they saying?" I ask, cuz it seems like he wants to talk.

"Well," he says. His Noise shifts uncomfortably.

"Well what?"

And then I see the reason his Noise is so flat is cuz there's something he don't wanna tell me but feels like he has to, so here it comes.

"That house of healing," he says. "That one in particular."

"What about it?" I say, trying not to make it sound important, failing.

"It's closed down," he says. "Empty."

I stop eating. "What do you mean, empty?"

"I mean *empty*," he says gently, cuz he knows it's bad news. "There's no one there, not even the patients. Everyone's gone."

"Gone?" I whisper.

Gone.

I stand up tho there ain't nowhere to go, my stupid plate of dinner still in my hand.

"Gone where? What's he done with her?"

"He hasn't done anything," Mayor Ledger says. "Your friend ran. That's what I heard. Ran off with the women just before the tower fell." He rubs his chin. "Everyone else was arrested and taken to the prisons. But your friend . . . got away."

He says *got away* like that's not what he means, like what he means is she was planning to get away all along.

"You can't know that," I say. "You can't know that's true about her."

He shrugs. "Maybe not," he says. "But I heard it from one of the soldiers who was guarding the house of healing."

"No," I say, but I don't know what I mean. "No."

"How well did you really know her?" Mayor Ledger says.

"You shut up."

I'm breathing hard, my chest rising and falling.

It's good that she ran, ain't it?

Ain't it?

She was in danger and now–

(but)

(but did she blow up the tower?)

(why didn't she tell me she was going to?)

(did she lie to me?)

And I shouldn't think it, I shouldn't think it, but here it comes–

She promised.

And she left.

She left *me*.

(Viola?)

(did you leave me?)

21

THE MINE

I OPEN MY EYES to the sound of wings flapping outside the door, something I already know in the few days I've been here means that the bats have returned to the caves after their night's hunting, that the sun is about to rise, that it's almost time to get myself out of bed.

Some women start to stir, stretching in their cots. Others are still dead to the world, still snoring, still farting, still drifting on in the empty nothing of sleep.

I spend a second wishing I was still there, too.

The sleeping quarters are basically just a long shack, swept earth floor, wood walls, wood door, barely any windows and only an iron stove in the center for not enough heat. The rest is just a row of cots stretched from one end to the other, full of sleeping women.

As the newest arrival, I'm at one end.

And I'm watching the occupant of the bed at the other end. She sits up straight, body fully under her command, like she never actually sleeps, just puts herself on pause until she can start work again.

Mistress Coyle turns in her cot, sets her feet on the floor, and looks over the other sleepers straight at me.

Checking on me first.

To see, no doubt, if I've run off sometime in the night to find Todd.

I don't believe he's dead. And I don't believe he told the Mayor on us, either.

There must be another answer.

I look back at Mistress Coyle, unmoving.

Not gone, I think. *Not yet.*

But mainly because I don't even know where we are.

We're not by the ocean. Not even close, as far as I can tell, though that's not saying much because secrecy is the watchword of the camp. No one gives information out unless it's absolutely necessary. That's in case anyone gets captured on a bombing raid or, now that the Answer have started running out of things like flour and medicine, raids for supplies as well.

Mistress Coyle guards information as her most valuable resource.

All I know is that the camp is at an old mine, started up–like so many other things seem to have been on this planet–with great optimism after the first landings but abandoned after just a few years. There are a number of shacks around the openings to a couple of deep caves. The shacks, some new, some from the mining days, serve as sleeping quarters and meeting rooms and dining halls and so on.

The caves–the ones where there aren't bats, anyway–are the food and supply stores, always worryingly low, always guarded fiercely by Mistress Lawson, still fretting over the children she left behind and taking out her fretting on anyone who requests another blanket for the cold.

Deeper in the caves are the mines, originally sunk to find coal or salt and then when none was found, diamonds and then gold, which weren't found either, as if they'd do anyone any good in this place anyway. The mines are now where the weapons and explosives are hidden. I don't know how they got here or where they came from, but if the camp is found, they'll be detonated, probably wiping us all off the map.

But for now it's a camp that's near a natural well and hidden by the forest around it. The only entrance is through the trees at the bottom of the path Mistress Coyle and I bumped our way down, and it's so steep and hard you'd hear intruders come from a long way away.

"And they'll come," Mistress Coyle said to me on my first day. "We'll just have to make sure we're ready to meet them."

"Why haven't they come already?" I asked. "People must know there's a mine here."

All she did was wink at me and touch the side of her nose.

"What's *that* supposed to mean?" I asked.

But that was all I got, because information is her most valuable resource, isn't it?

At breakfast, I get my usual snubbing by Thea and the other apprentices I recognize, none of whom will say a word to me, still blaming me for Maddy's death, blaming me for somehow being a traitor, blaming me for this whole damn war, for all I know.

Not that I care.

Because I don't.

I leave them to the dining hall, and I take my plate of gray porridge out in the cold morning to some rocks near the mouth of one of the caves. As I eat, I watch the camp start to wake itself, start to put itself together for the things that terrorists spend their days doing.

The biggest surprise is how few people there are. Maybe a hundred. That's all. That's the big Answer causing all the fuss in New Prentisstown by blowing things up. One hundred people. Mistresses and apprentices, former patients and others, too, disappearing in the night and returning in the morning, or keeping the camp running for those that come and go, tending to the few horses the Answer has and the oxes that pull the carts and the hens we get our eggs from and a million other things that need doing.

But only a hundred people. Not enough to have a whisper of a prayer if the Mayor's *real* army comes marching down toward us.

"All right, Hildy?"

"Hi, Wilf," I say, as he comes up to me, a plate of porridge in his hands, too. I scoot over so he can sit near me. He doesn't say anything, just eats his porridge and lets me eat mine.

"Wilf?" we both hear. Jane, Wilf's wife, is coming for us, two steaming mugs in her hands. She picks her way over the rocks toward us, stumbling once, spilling some coffee and causing Wilf to rise halfway up, but she recovers. "Here ya go!" she practically shouts, thrusting the mugs at us.

"Thank you," I say, taking mine.

She shoves her hands under her armpits against the cold and smiles, eyes wide and searching around, like she eats with them. "Awful cold to be eating outside," she says, like an overly friendly demand that we explain ourselves.

"Yup," Wilf says, going back to his porridge.

"It's not too bad," I say, also going back to eating.

"Didja hear they got a grain store last night?" she says, lowering her voice to a whisper but somehow making it louder at the same time. "We can have *bread* again!"

"Yup," Wilf says again.

"D'you like bread?" she asks me.

"I do."

"Ya gotta have bread," she says, to the ground, to the sky, to the rocks. "Ya gotta have bread."

And then she's back off to the dining hall, not another word, though Wilf doesn't seem to much mind or even notice. But I know, I *definitely* know that Wilf's clear and even Noise, his lack of words, his seeming blankness doesn't describe all of him, not even close.

Wilf and Jane were refugees, fleeing into Haven as the army swept behind them, passing us on the road as Todd slept off his fever in Carbonel Downs. Jane fell ill on the trip and, after asking directions, Wilf took her straight to Mistress Forth's house of healing, where Jane was still recovering when the army invaded. Wilf, whose Noise is as free of deception as anyone's on this planet, was assumed by the soldiers to be an idiot and so allowed to visit his wife when no other man was.

When the women ran, Wilf helped. When I asked him why, all he did was shrug and say, "They were gone take Jane." He hid the less able women on his cart as they fled, built a hidey-hole in it so others could return for missions, and for weeks on end has risked his life taking them to and fro because the soldiers have always assumed a man so transparent couldn't be hiding anything.

All of which has been a surprise to the leaders of the Answer.

But none of which is a surprise to me.

He saved me and Todd once when he didn't have to. He saved Todd again when there was even more danger. He was even ready the first night I was here to turn right back around to help me find him, but Sergeant Hammar knows Wilf's face now, knows that he should have been arrested, so any trip back is pretty much a death sentence.

I take a last spoonful of my porridge and sigh heavily as I pop it into my mouth. I could be sighing at the cold, sighing at the boring porridge, sighing at the lack of anything to do in camp.

But, somehow, Wilf knows. Somehow, Wilf always knows.

"Ah'm shur he's okay, Hildy," he says, finishing up his own porridge. "He survives, does our Todd."

I look up into the cold morning sun and I swallow again, though there's no porridge left in my throat.

"Keep yerself strong," Wilf stays, standing. "Strong for what's comin."

I blink. "What's coming?" I ask as he walks on toward the dining hall, drinking his mug of coffee.

He just keeps on going.

I finish my coffee, rubbing my arms to gather some heat, thinking I'll ask her again today, no, I'll *tell* her I'm coming on the next mission, that I need to find–

"You're sitting out here all by yourself?"

I look up. Lee, the blond soldier, is standing there, smiling all toothy.

I immediately feel my face go hot.

"No, no," I say, standing straight up, turning away from him, and picking up the plate.

"You don't have to leave–" he's saying.

"No, I'm finished–"

"Viola–"

"All yours–"

"That's not what I meant–"

But I'm already stomping back to the dining hall, cursing myself for the redness of my face.

Lee isn't the only man. Well, he's hardly a *man*, but like Wilf, he and Magnus can no longer pretend to be soldiers and go to the city, now that their faces are known.

But there are others who can. Because that's the biggest secret of all about the Answer.

At least a third of the people here are men, men who pretend to be soldiers to shuttle women in and out of the city, men who help Mistress Coyle with the planning and targets, men with expertise on handling explosives, men who believe in the cause and want to fight against the Mayor and all he stands for.

Men who've lost wives and daughters and mothers and who are fighting to save them or fighting to avenge their memories.

Mostly it's memories.

I suppose it's useful if everyone thinks it's only women; it allows men to come and go, even if the Mayor surely knows what's what, which is probably why he's denying the cure to so much of his own army, why the Answer's own supply of cure is becoming more burden than blessing.

I cast a glance quickly back to Lee behind me and forward again.

I'm not sure of his reason for being here.

I haven't been able–

I haven't had the *chance* to ask him yet.

I'm not paying attention as I reach the dining room door and don't really notice when it opens before I can take the handle.

I look up into Mistress Coyle's face.

I don't even greet her.

"Take me with you on the next raid," I say.

Her expression doesn't change. "You know why you can't."

"Todd would join us," I say. "In a *second*."

"Others aren't so sure about that, my girl." I open my mouth to reply but she interrupts. "If he's even still alive. Which matters not, because we can't afford to have you captured. You're the most valuable prize of all. The girl who can help the President when the ships land."

"I–"

She holds up her hand. "I won't have this fight with you again. There is too much important work to do."

The camp feels silent now. The people behind her have stopped moving as we stare at one another, no one willing to ask her to get out of the way, not even Mistresses Forth and Nadari, who wait there patiently. Like Thea, they've barely spoken to me since my arrival, all these acolytes of Mistress Coyle, all these people who wouldn't dare to dream of speaking to her the way I'm speaking to her now.

They treat me as if I'm a little dangerous.

I'm slightly surprised to find I kind of like it.

I look into her eyes, into the unyieldingness of them. "I won't forgive you," I say quietly, as if I'm only talking to her. "I won't. Not now, not ever."

"I don't want your forgiveness," she says, equally quietly. "But one day, you *will* understand."

And then her eyes glint and she pulls her mouth into a smile. "You know," she says, raising her voice. "I think it's time you had some employment."

22

1017

"CAN'T YOU EFFING THINGS move any faster?"

The four or five Spackle nearest to me flinch away, tho I ain't even spoken that loud.

"Get a *move* on!"

And as ever, no thoughts, no Noise, no nothing.

They can only be getting the cure in the fodder I still have to shovel out. But why? Why when no one else is? It makes them a sea of silent clicking and white backs bent into the cold and white mouths sending out puffs of steam and white arms pulling up handfuls of dirt and when yer looking out across the monastery grounds, all those white bodies working, well, they could be a herd of sheep, couldn't they?

Even tho if you look close you can see family groups and husbands and wives and fathers and sons. You can see older ones lifting smaller amounts more slowly. You can see younger ones helping 'em, trying to keep us from seeing that the older ones can't work too hard. You can see a baby strapped to its mother's chest with an old piece of cloth. You can see an especially tall one directing others along a faster work chain. You can see a small female packing mud around the infected number band of a larger female. You can see 'em working together, keeping their heads down, trying not to be the one who gets seen by me or Davy or the guards behind the barbed wire.

You can see all that if you look close.

But it's easier if you don't.

We can't give 'em shovels, of course. They could use 'em against us as weapons and the soldiers on the walls get twitchy if a Spackle even stretches its arms up too high. So there they all are, bending to the ground, digging, moving rocks, silent as clouds, suffering, and not doing nothing about it.

I got a weapon, tho. They gave me the rifle back.

Cuz where am I gonna go?

Now that she's gone.

"Hurry it *up!*" I shout at the Spackle, my Noise rising red at the thought of her.

I catch Davy looking over at me, a surprised grin on his face. I turn away and cross the field to another group. I'm halfway there when I hear a louder click.

I look round till I find the source.

But it's only ever the same one.

1017, staring at me again, with that look that ain't forgiveness. He moves his eyes to my hands.

It's only then I realize I've got them both clenched hard around my rifle.

I can't even remember taking it off my shoulder.

Even with all this Spackle labor, it's still gonna take a coupla months to even come close to finishing this building, whatever it is, and by that time it'll be midwinter and the Spackle won't have the shelter they were sposed to be building for themselves and I know they live outside more than men do but I don't think even they can live unsheltered in the winter frost and I ain't heard of nowhere else they're gonna be going yet.

Still, we had all the internal walls torn down in seven days, two ahead of schedule, and no Spackle even died, tho we did have a few with broken arms. Those Spackle were taken away by soldiers.

We ain't seen 'em since.

By the end of the second week after the tower bomb, we've nearly dug all the trenches and blocks for the foundayshuns to be poured, something Davy and I are sposed to supervize even tho it's gonna be the Spackle who know how to do it.

"Pa says they were the labor that rebuilt the city after the Spackle War," Davy says. "Tho you wouldn't know it from this bunch."

He spits out a shell from the seeds he's eating. Food's getting a bit scarce what with the Answer adding supply raids to the ongoing bombs but Davy always manages to scrounge up something. We're sitting on a pile of rocks, looking out over the one big field, now dug up with square holes and ditches and so full of rock piles there's barely any room for the Spackle to crowd into.

But they do, cramming onto the edges and huddling together in the cold. And they don't say nothing about it.

Davy spits out another shell. "You ever gonna talk again?"

"I talk," I say.

"No, you scream at yer workforce and you grunt at me. That ain't talking." He's spits out another shell, high and long, hitting the nearest Spackle in the head. It just brushes it away and keeps on digging out the last of a trench.

"She left ya," Davy says. "Get over it."

My Noise rises. "*Shut up.*"

"I don't mean it in a bad way."

I turn to look at him, eyes wide.

"*What?*" he says. "I'm just saying, you know? She left, don't mean she's dead or nothing." Spit. "From what I remember, that filly can take plenty care of herself."

There's a memory in his Noise of being electrocuted on the river road. It should make me smile, but it don't, cuz she's standing right there in his Noise, standing right there and taking him down.

Standing right there and not standing right here.

(where'd she go?)

(where'd she effing *go*?)

Mayor Ledger told me just after the tower bombs that the army had gone straight for the ocean cuz they'd got a tip-off that that's where the Answer were hiding–

(was it me? did he hear it in me? I burn at the thought–)

But when Mr. Hammar and his men got there, they didn't find nothing but long-abandoned buildings and half-sunken boats.

Cuz the informayshun turned out to be false.

And I burn at that, too.

(did she lie to me?)

(did she do it on purpose?)

"Jesus, pigpiss." Davy spits again. "It's not like any of the *rest* of us got girlfriends. They're all in ruddy *jail* or setting off bombs every week or walking around in groups so big you can't even talk to 'em."

"She ain't my girlfriend," I say.

"Not the point," he says. "All it means is that yer just as alone as the rest of us, so get over it."

There's a sudden, ugly strength of feeling in his Noise, which he wipes away in an instant when he sees me watching him. "What're you looking at?"

"Nothing," I say.

"Damn right." He stands, takes his rifle, and stomps back into the field.

Somehow 1017 keeps ending up in my part of the work. I'm mainly in the back part of the fields, finishing up digging the trenches. Davy's near the front, getting Spackle to snap together the preformed guide walls we'll be using once the concrete gets poured. 1017's sposed to be doing that, but every time I look up, there he is, nearest me again no matter how many times I send him back.

He's working, sure, digging up his handfuls of dirt or piling up the sod in even rows, but always looking for me, always trying to catch my eye.

Clicking at me.

I walk toward him, my hand up on the stock of my rifle, gray clouds starting to move in overhead. "I sent you over to Davy," I bark. "What're you doing here?"

Davy, hearing his name, calls from far across the field. "What?"

I call back, "Why do you keep letting this one back over here?"

"What the hell are you talking about?" Davy yells. "They all look the same!"

"It's 1017!"

Davy gives an exaggerated shrug. "*So?*"

I hear a click, a rude and sarcastic one, from behind me.

I turn and I swear 1017 is *smiling* at me.

"You little piece of–" I start to say, reaching my rifle round my front.

Which is when I see a flash of Noise.

Coming from 1017.

Quick as anything but clear, too, me standing in front of him, reaching for my rifle, nothing more than what he's seeing with his eyes–

Except a flash as he grabs the rifle from me–

And then it's gone.

I've still got the rifle in my hands, 1017 still knee-deep in the ditch. No Noise at all.

I look him up and down. He's skinnier than he used to be, but they *all* are, they never get quite enough fodder for a day, and I'm wondering if 1017's been skipping meals altogether.

So he don't take no cure.

"What're you playing at?" I ask him.

But he's back at work, arms and hands digging for more dirt, ribs showing thru the side of his white, white skin.

And he don't say nothing.

* * *

"Why do we keep giving 'em the cure if yer pa's taking it away from everyone else?"

Me and Davy are lunching the next day. The clouds are heavy in the sky and it'll probably start raining soon, the first rain in a good long while, and it'll be cold rain, too, but we've got orders to keep working no matter what so we're spending the day watching the Spackle pour out the first concrete from the mixer.

Ivan brought it in this morning, healed but limping, his Noise raging. I wonder where he thinks the power is *now*.

"Well, it keeps 'em from plotting, don't it?" Davy says. "Keeps 'em from passing along ideas to each other."

"But they can do that with the clicking." I think for a second. "Can't they?"

Davy just gives a *who cares, pigpiss* shrug. "Got any of that sandwich left?"

I hand him my sandwich, keeping an eye out over the Spackle. "Shouldn't we know what they're thinking?" I say. "Wouldn't that be a good thing to know?"

I look out over the field for 1017 who, sure enough, is looking back at me.

Plick. The first drop of rain hits me on the eyelash.

"Aw, crap," Davy says, looking up.

It don't let up for three days. The site gets muckier and muckier but the Mayor still wants us to keep on somehow so those three days are spent slipping and sliding thru mud and putting up huge tarpaulins on frames to cover big parts of the field.

Davy's got the inside work, bossing Spackle around to keep the tarpaulin frames in place. I spend most of my time out in the rain, trying to keep the edges of the tarpaulin pinned to the ground with heavy stones.

It's ruddy *stupid* work.

"Hurry up!" I shout to the Spackle helping me get one of the last edges pinned to the ground. My fingers are freezing cuz no one's given us gloves and there ain't been no Mayor round to ask. "Ow!" I put a bloodied knuckle up to my lips, having scraped my hand for the millionth time.

The Spackle keep at it with the rocks, seeming oblivious to the rain, which is good cuz there ain't room under the tarpaulins for all of 'em to shelter.

"Hey," I say, raising my voice. "Watch the edge! Watch that—"

A gust of wind rips away the whole sheet of tarpaulin we just pinned down. One of the Spackle keeps hold of it as it flies up, taking him with it and tumbling him hard down to the ground. I leap over him as I chase after the tarpaulin, twisting and rolling away across the muddy field and up a little slope, and I've just about got a hand on it–

And I slip badly, skidding right down the other side of the slope on my rump–

And I realize where I've run, where I've slipped–

I'm heading right down into the bog.

I grab at the mud to stop myself but there's nothing to hold on to and I drop right in with a *splat*.

"Gah!" I shout and try to stand. I'm up to my thighs in lime-covered Spackle shit, splattered all up my front and back, the stink of it making me retch–

And I see another flash of Noise.

Of me standing in the bog.

Of a Spackle standing right over me.

I look up.

There's a wall of Spackle staring.

And right in front of 'em all.

1017.

Above me.

With a huge stone in his hands.

He don't say nothing, just stands there with the stone, more'n big enough to do a lot of harm if thrown right.

"Yeah?" I say up to him. "That's what you want, ain't it?"

He just stares back.

I don't see the Noise again.

I reach up for my rifle, slowly.

"What's it gonna be?" I ask and he can see in my Noise just how ready I am, how ready I am to fight him.

How ready I am to–

I've got the rifle stock in my hand now.

But he's just staring at me.

And then he tosses the rock down on the ground and turns back toward the tarpaulin. I watch him go, five steps, then ten, and my body relaxes a bit.

It's when I'm pulling myself outta the bog that I hear it.

The click.

His rude click.

* * *

And I lose it.

I'm running toward him and I'm yelling but I don't know what I'm saying and Davy's turning round in shock as I reach the shelter of the tarpaulin just after 1017 and I'm running in with the rifle up above my head like I'm some stupid madman and 1017's turning to me but I don't give him a chance to do nothing and I knock him hard in the face with the butt of the rifle and he falls back on the ground and I lift the rifle again and bring it down and he raises his hands to protect himself and I hit him again and again and again–

In the hands–

And the face–

And in those skinny ribs–

And my Noise is raging–

And I hit–

And I hit–

And I hit–

And I'm screaming

I'm screaming out–

"WHY DID YOU LEAVE?"

"WHY DID YOU LEAVE ME?"

And I hear the cold, crisp *snick* of his arm breaking.

It fills the air, louder than the rain or the wind, turning my stomach upside down, making a thick lump in my throat.

I stop, midswing.

Davy's staring at me, his mouth open.

All the Spackle are edging back, terrified.

And from the ground, 1017 is looking back up at me, red blood pouring from his weird nose and the corner of his too-high eyes but there's no sound coming from him, no Noise, no thoughts, no clicks, no nothing–

(and we're in the campsite and there's a dead Spackle on the ground and Viola's looking so scared and she's backing away from me and there's blood everywhere and I've done it again I've done it again and why did you go oh jesus dammit Viola why did you *leave*–)

And 1017 just looks at me.

And I swear to God, it's a look of triumph.

23

SOMETHING'S COMING

{VIOLA}

"WATER PUMP'S workin agin, Hildy."

"Thank you, Wilf." I hand him a tray of bread, the heat still coming off it. "Could you take these to Jane, please? She's setting the tables for breakfast."

He takes the tray, a flat little tune coming from his Noise. As he leaves the kitchen shack, I hear him call out, "Wife!"

"Why does he call you Hildy?" Lee says, appearing at the back door with a basket of flour he just pounded. He's wearing a sleeveless shirt and the skin up to his elbows is dusty white.

I look at his bare arms for a second and look away quickly.

Mistress Coyle put us to work together since he can't go back to New Prentisstown anymore either.

No, I will certainly *not* forgive her.

"Hildy was the name of someone who helped us," I say. "Someone worth being called after."

"And by *us*, you mean–"

"Me and Todd, yes." I take the basket of flour from him and thump it down heavily on the table.

There's a silence, as there always seems to be when Todd's name comes up.

"No one's seen him, Viola," Lee says gently. "But they mostly go in at night so that doesn't–"

"She wouldn't tell me even if she did." I start separating the flour into bowls. "She thinks he's dead."

Lee shifts from foot to foot. "But you say different."

I look at him. He smiles and I can't help but smile back. "And you believe me, do you?"

He shrugs. "Wilf believes you. And you'd be surprised how far the word of Wilf goes around here."

"No." I look out the window to where Wilf disappeared. "No, actually I wouldn't."

That day passes like the others and still we cook. That's our new employment, Lee and me, cooking. All of it, for the entire camp. We've learned how to make bread from a starting point of *wheat*, not even flour. We've learned how to skin squirrels, de-shell turtles, and gut fish. We've learned how much base you need for soup to feed a hundred. We've learned how to peel potatoes and pears faster than possibly anyone on this whole stupid planet.

Mistress Coyle swears this is how wars are won.

"This isn't really why I signed up," Lee says, pulling another handful of feathers off the sixteenth forest fowl of the afternoon.

"At least signing up was your idea," I say, fingers cramping on my own fowl. The feathers hover in the air like a swarm of sticky flies, catching everywhere they touch. I've got little green puffs under my fingernails, in the crooks of my elbows, glopped in the corner of my eyes.

I know this because Lee's got them all over his face, too, all through his long golden hair and in the matching golden hair on his forearms.

I feel my face flush again and pull out a furious rip of feathers.

A day turned into two, turned into three, turned into a week, turned into the week after and the week after that, cooking with Lee, washing up with Lee, sitting out three days of solid rain stuck in this shack with Lee.

And still. And *still*.

Something's coming, something's being prepared for, no one's telling me anything.

And I'm still stuck *here*.

Lee tosses a plucked fowl onto the table and picks up another one. "We're going to make this species extinct if we're not careful."

"It's the only thing Magnus can shoot," I say. "Everything else is too fast."

"A whole animal lost," Lee says, "because the Answer lacked an optician."

I laugh, too loud. I roll my eyes at myself.

I finish my own fowl and pick up a new one. "I'm doing three of these for every two of yours," I say. "*And* I did more loaves this morning *and*–"

"You burned half of them."

"Because *you* stoked the oven too hot!"

"I'm not made for cooking," he says, smiling. "I'm made for soldiering."

I gasp. "And you think *I'm* made for cooking–"

But he's laughing and keeps laughing even when I throw a handful of wet feathers at him, smacking him straight on the eye. "Ow," he says, wiping it away. "You got some aim, Viola. We really need to get a gun in your hands."

I turn my face quickly back down to the millionth fowl in my lap.

"Or maybe not," he says, more quietly.

"Have you–?" I stop.

"Have I what?"

I lick my lips, which is a mistake because then I have to spit out a mouthful of feathery puffs, so when I do finally say it, it comes out more exasperated than I meant. "Have you ever shot someone?"

"No." He sits up straighter. "Have you?"

I shake my head and see him relax, which makes me immediately say, "But I've *been* shot."

He sits back up. "No way!"

I say it before I mean to, before I even know it's coming, and then I'm saying it and I realize I've never said it, not out loud, not to myself, not ever, not since it happened, and yet here it is, tumbling out in a room full of floating feathers.

"And I've stabbed someone." I stop plucking. "To death."

My body feels suddenly twice as heavy in the silence that follows.

When I start to cry, Lee just hands me a kitchen towel and lets me, not crowding me or saying anything stupid or even asking about it, though he must be dying of curiosity. He just lets me cry.

Which is exactly right.

"Yes, but we're gaining sympathy," Lee says near the end of dinner with Wilf and Jane. I'm putting off finishing because as soon as

I do, we have go back to the kitchens to start preparing the yeasts to cook *tomorrow's* bread. You wouldn't believe how much bloody bread a hundred people can eat.

I take half of my last bite. "I'm just saying there aren't very many of you."

"Of *us*," Lee says, looking at me seriously. "And we've got spies working throughout the city and people join us when they can. Things are only getting worse there. They're rationing *food* now and no one's getting the cure anymore. They're going to have to start turning against him."

"And so many in prisons," Jane adds. "Hundreds of women, all locked up, all chained together underground, starving and dying by the dozen."

"Wife!" Wilf snaps.

"Ah'm only sayin what Ah heard!"

"Yoo din't hear nothin of the sort."

Jane looks sullen. "Don't mean it's not true."

"There are a lot of people who'd support us in prison, though," Lee says. "And so that might turn out–"

He stops.

"What?" I ask, looking up. "Turn out what?"

He doesn't answer me, just looks over to another table where Mistress Coyle is sitting with Mistresses Braithwaite, Forth, Waggoner, Barker, and Thea, too, like they always do, discussing things, whispering in low voices, devising secret orders for other people to carry out.

"Nothing," Lee says, seeing Mistress Coyle stand and come toward us.

"I'm going to need the cart hitched up for tonight, Wilf, please," she says, approaching our table.

"Yes, Mistress," he says, getting to his feet.

"Eat a little longer," she says, stopping him. "This isn't forced labor."

"Ah'm happy to do it," Wilf says, brushing off his trousers and leaving us.

"Who are you blowing up tonight?" I ask.

Mistress Coyle pulls her lips tight. "I think that's enough for now, Viola."

"I want to come," I say. "If you're going back into the city tonight, I want to come with you."

"Patience, my girl," she says. "You'll have your day."

"Which day?" I ask as she walks off. "*When?*"

"Patience," she says again.

But she says it impatiently.

It gets dark earlier and earlier every day. I sit outside on a pile of rocks as night falls, watching tonight's mission-takers head on out to the carts, their bags packed with secret things. Some of the men have Noise now, taking reduced amounts of cure from our own dwindling supply stashed in the cave. They take enough to blend in with the city but not enough to give anything away. It's a tricky balance, and it's getting more and more dangerous for our men to be on city streets, but still they go.

And as the people of New Prentisstown sleep tonight, they'll be stolen from and bombed, all in the name of what's right.

"Hey," Lee says, hardly more than a shadow in the twilight as he sits down next to me.

"Hey," I say back.

"You okay?"

"Why wouldn't I be?"

"Yeah." He picks up a stone and tosses it into the night. "Why wouldn't you be?"

Stars start to appear in the sky. My ships are up there somewhere. People who might've been able to help us, no, who *would* have helped us if I could've contacted them. Simone Watkin and Bradley Tench, good people, *smart* people who would have stopped all this stupidity and the explosions and–

I feel my throat clench again.

"You really killed someone," Lee says, tossing another stone.

"Yeah," I say, pulling my knees up to my chest.

Lee waits a moment. "With Todd?"

"*For* Todd," I say. "To save him. To save *us*."

Now that the sun's gone, the real cold moves in swiftly. I hold my knees tighter.

"She's afraid of you, you know," he says. "Mistress Coyle. She thinks you're powerful."

I look over at him, trying to see him in the dark. "That's stupid."

"I heard her say it to Mistress Braithwaite. Said you could lead whole armies if you put your mind to it."

I shake my head but of course he can't see. "She doesn't even know me."

"Yeah, but she's smart."

"And everyone here follows her like little lambs."

"Everyone but you." He bumps me with his shoulder in a friendly way. "Maybe that's what she's talking about."

We start to hear the low rumble from the caves that means the bats are readying themselves.

"Why are *you* here?" I ask. "Why do you follow her?"

I've asked before but he's always changed the subject.

But maybe tonight's different. It sure *feels* different.

"My father died in the Spackle War," he says.

"Lots of fathers did," I say and I think of Corinne, wondering where she is, wondering if–

"I don't really remember him," Lee's saying. "It was just me and my mother and my older sister growing up, really. And my sister"–he laughs–"you'd like her. All mouth and fire and we had some fights you wouldn't believe."

He laughs again but more quietly. "When the army came, Siobhan wanted to fight but Mum didn't. I wanted to fight, too, but Siobhan and Mum really went at it, Siobhan ready to take up arms and Mum practically having to bar the door to keep her from running out into the streets when the army came marching in."

The rumbling is getting louder and the bats' Noise starts to echo through the cave opening. *Fly, fly,* they say. *Away, away.*

"And then it was out of our hands, wasn't it?" he says. "The army was here and that night they took all the women away to the houses east of town. Mum said to cooperate, you know, 'just for now, just to see where it goes, maybe he's not all that bad.' That sort of thing."

I don't respond and I'm glad it's dark so he can't see my face.

"But Siobhan wasn't going to go without a fight, was she? She shouted and screamed at the soldiers and refused to go along and Mum's just begging for her to stop, to not make them angry, but Siobhan–" He stops and makes a clicking sound with his tongue. "Siobhan punched the first soldier who tried to move her by force."

He takes a deep breath. "And then it was uproar. I tried to fight and the next thing I know I'm on the ground with my ears ringing and a soldier's knee in my back and Mum is screaming but there's nothing from Siobhan and I black out and when I wake up, I'm alone in my house."

Fly, fly, we hear, just inside the cave mouth. *Away, away, away.*

"I looked for them when the restrictions eased," he says, "but I never found them. I looked in every cabin and dormitory and at every house of healing. And finally, at the last one, Mistress Coyle answered."

He pauses and looks up. "Here they come."

The bats swarm out of the caves, like the world's been tipped on its side and they're being poured out over the top of us, a flood of greater darkness against the night sky. The sheer *whoosh* of them makes it impossible to talk for a minute so we just sit and watch them.

Each is at least six feet across, with furred wings and short stubby ears and a green glowing dot of phosphorus on each outstretched wingtip which they use somehow to confuse and stun the moths and bugs they eat. The dots glow in the night, making a blanket of temporary fluttering stars above us. We sit, surrounded by the slapping of wings, the cheeping of their Noise, the 𝕗𝕝𝕪 𝕗𝕝𝕪 𝖆𝖜𝖆𝖞 𝖆𝖜𝖆𝖞 𝖆𝖜𝖆𝖞.

And in five minutes they're gone, out into the surrounding forest, not to return until just before dawn.

"Something's coming," Lee says in the quiet that follows. "You know that. I can't say what but I'm going along because there's one more place to look for them."

"Then I'll go, too," I say.

"She won't let you." He turns to me. "But I promise you, I'll look for Todd. With the same eyes I look for Siobhan and my mother, I'll look for him."

A bell chimes out over the camp, signaling all raiding teams are off into town and all remaining people in camp are to go to bed. Lee and I sit in the dark for a while longer, his shoulder brushed up against mine, and mine brushed up against his.

24

PRISON WALLS

[TODD]

"NOT BAD," says the Mayor from atop Morpeth, "for an unskilled workforce."

"There'd be more," Davy says, "but it rained and then everything was just *mud*."

"No, no," the Mayor says, casting his eyes around the field. "You've done admirably, both of you, managing so much in just a month."

We all take a minute to look at what we've managed admirably. We've got all the concrete foundayshuns poured for a single long building. Every guide wall is up, some have even started to be filled in by the stones we took from the monastery's internal walls, and the tarpaulin makes a kind of roof. It already looks like a building.

He's right, we have done admirably.

Us and 1,150 Spackle.

"Yes," says the Mayor. "Very pleasing."

Davy's Noise is taking on a pinkish glow that's uncomfortable to look at.

"So what is it?" I ask.

The Mayor looks my way. "What's what?

"This." I gesture at the building. "What's it sposed to be?"

"You finish building it, Todd, and I promise to invite you to the grand opening."

"It's not for the Spackle, tho, is it?"

The Mayor frowns slightly. "No, Todd, it's not."

I rub the back of my neck with my hand and I can hear some clanking in Davy's Noise, clanks that are gonna get louder if he thinks I'm messing up his moment of praise. "It's just," I say, "there's been frost the past three nights and it's only getting colder."

The Mayor turns Morpeth to face me. **Bᴏʏ cᴏʟt,** he thinks. **Bᴏʏ cᴏʟt steps back.**

I step back without even thinking.

The Mayor's eyebrows raise. "Are you wanting heaters for your work-force?"

"Well," I look at the ground and at the building and at the Spackle who are doing their best to stay at the far end, as much away from the three of us as is possible to do when there are so many crowded into such a limited space. "Snow might come," I say. "I don't know that they'll survive."

"Oh, they're tougher than you think, Todd." The Mayor's voice is low and full of something I can't put my finger on. "A lot tougher."

I look down again. "Yeah," I say. "Okay."

"I'll have Private Farrow bring in some small fission heaters if that will make you feel better."

I blink. "Really?"

"*Really*?" Davy says.

"They've done good work," the Mayor says, "under your direction, and you've shown real dedication these past weeks, Todd. Real *leadership*."

He smiles, almost warmly.

"I know you're the kind of soul who hates to see others suffer." He keeps hold of my eye, almost daring me to break it. "Your tenderness does you credit."

"*Tenderness*," Davy snickers.

"I'm proud of you." The Mayor gathers up his reins. "*Both* of you. And you will be rewarded for your efforts."

Davy's Noise beams again as the Mayor rides outta the monastery gates. "Didja hear that?" he says, waggling his eyebrows. "Rewards, my tender pigpiss."

"Shut up, Davy." I'm already walking down the guide wall and toward the back of the building where there's the last of the clear ground and so that's where all the Spackle are having to crowd themselves. They get outta my way as I move thru them. "Heaters're coming," I say, putting it in my Noise, too. "Things'll be better."

But they just keep doing all they can not to touch me.

"I *said* things'll be better!"

Stupid ungrateful–
I stop. I take in a breath. I keep walking.

I get to the back of the building where we've leaned a few unused guide walls against the building frame, forming a nook. "You can come out now," I say.

There's no sound for a minute, then a bit of rustling and 1017 emerges, his arm in a sling made up from one of my few shirts. He's skinnier than ever, some redness still creeping up his arm from the break but it seems to be finally fading. "I managed to scrounge some painkillers," I say, taking 'em outta my pocket.

He snatches 'em from my hand with a slap, scratching my palm.

"Watch it," I say thru clenched teeth. "You wanna be taken away to whatever they do with lame Spackle?"

There's a burst of Noise from him, one I've grown to expect, and it's the usual thing, him standing over me with a rifle, him hitting me and hitting me, me pleading for him to stop, him breaking *my* arm.

"Yeah," I say. "Whatever."

"Playing with yer pet?" Davy's come round, too, leaning against the building with his arms crossed. "You know, when horses break their legs, they shoot 'em."

"He ain't a horse."

"Nah," Davy says. "He's a sheep."

I puff out my lips. "Thanks for not telling yer pa."

Davy shrugs. "Whatever, pigpiss, as long as it don't screw up our reward."

1017 makes his rude clicking at both of us, but mostly at me.

"He don't seem too grateful, tho," Davy says.

"Yeah, well, I saved him twice now." I look at 1017, look right into eyes that never leave mine. "I ain't doing it again."

"You say that," Davy says, "but everyone knows you will." He nods at 1017. "Even him." Davy's eyes widen in a mock. "It's cuz yer *tender*."

"Shut up."

But he's already laughing and leaving and 1017 just stares at me and stares at me.

And I stare back.

I saved him.

(I saved him for her)

(if she was here, she could see, see how I saved him)

(if she was here)

(but she ain't)
I clench my fists and then force myself to unclench them.

New Prentisstown has changed in the past month. I see it every day as we ride home.

Part of it's winter coming. The leaves on the trees have turned purple and red and dropped to the ground, leaving the tall winter skeletons behind them. The evergreens have kept their needles but dropped their cones and the reachers have pulled their branches tight into their trunks, leaving naked poles to sit out the cold. All of it plus the constant darker skies makes it look like the town's going hungry.

Which it is. The army invaded at the end of harvest, so there were food stocks, but there's no one left in the outer settlements to bring in food to trade and the Answer are keeping up their bombs and food raids. One night a whole storehouse of wheat was taken, so completely and successfully it's obvious now there's people in the town and the army who've been helping 'em.

Which is bad news for the town and the army.

The curfew got lowered two weeks ago and again last week till no one's allowed out after dark at all except for a few patrols. The square in front of the cathedral has become a place for bonfires, of books, of the wordly belongings of people found to have helped the Answer, of a bunch of healer uniforms from when the Mayor closed the last house of healing. And practically no one takes the cure no more, except some of the Mayor's closest men, Mr. Morgan, Mr. O'Hare, Mr. Tate, Mr. Hammar, men from old Prentisstown who've been with him for years. Loyalty, I guess.

Me and Davy ain't never been given it in the first place so there weren't never a chance for him to take it away.

"Maybe that's our reward," Davy says as we ride. "Maybe he'll get some outta the cellar and we'll finally see what it's like."

Our *reward*, I think. *We.*

I run my hand along Angharrad's flank, feeling the chill in her skin. "Almost home, girl," I whisper twixt her ears. "Nice warm barn."

Warm, she thinks. **Boy colt.**

"Angharrad," I say back.

Horses ain't pets and they're half crazy all the time but I've been learning if you treat 'em right, they get to know you.

Boy colt, she thinks again and it's like I'm part of her herd.

"Maybe the reward is women!" Davy says suddenly. "Yeah! Maybe he's gonna give us some women and finally make a real man outta you."

"Shut up," I say, but it don't turn into a fight. Come to think of it, we ain't had a fight in a good long while.

We're just used to each other, I guess.

We don't hardly see women no more neither. When the communicayshuns tower fell, they were all confined to their houses again, except when teams of 'em are working the fields, readying for next year's planting, under guard from armed soldiers. The visits from husbands and sons and fathers are now once a week at most.

We hear stories about soldiers and women, stories about soldiers getting into dormitories at night, stories about awful things going on that no one gets punished for.

And that don't even count the women in the prisons, prisons I've only seen from the cathedral tower, a group of converted buildings in the far west of town down near the foot of the waterfalls. Who knows what goes on inside? They're way far away, outta sight of everyone 'cept for those that guard 'em.

Kinda like the Spackle.

"Jesus, Todd," Davy says, "the racket you make by *thinking* all the time."

Which is exactly the kinda thing I've learned to ignore from Davy. Except this time, he called me *Todd*.

We leave our horses in the barn near the cathedral. Davy walks me back to the cathedral, tho I don't really need a guard no more.

Cuz where would I go?

I go in the front door and I hear, "Todd?"

The Mayor's waiting for me.

"Yes, sir?" I say.

"Always so polite," he smiles, walking toward me, boots clicking on the marble. "You seem better lately, calmer." He stops a yard away. "Have you been using the tool?"

Huh?

"What tool?" I ask.

He sighs a little. And then–

I AM THE CIRCLE AND THE CIRCLE IS ME.

I put a hand up to the side of my head. "How do you do that?"

"Noise can be used, Todd," he says. "If you're disciplined enough. And the first step is using the tool."

"I am the Circle and the Circle is me?"

"It's a way of centering yourself." He nods. "A way of aligning your

Noise, of reining it in, *controlling* it, and a man who can control his Noise is a man with an advantage."

I remember him chanting away back in his house in old Prentisstown, how sharp and scary his Noise sounded compared to other men's, how much it felt like–

Like a weapon.

"What's the Circle?" I ask.

"Your destiny, Todd Hewitt. A circle is a closed system. There's no way of getting out, so it's easier if you don't fight it."

. I AM THE CIRCLE AND THE CIRCLE IS ME.

But this time, my voice is in there, too.

"There's so much I look forward to teaching you," he says and leaves without saying good night.

I pace the walls of the bell tower, looking out toward the falls in the west, the hill with the notch on it in the south, and to the east, the hills that lead toward the monastery, tho you can't see it from here. All you can see is New Prentisstown, indoors and huddled together as a cold night settles in.

She's out there somewhere.

A month and she ain't come.

A month and–

(shut up)

(just effing shut up your effing whiny *mouth*)

I start pacing again.

We've got glass in the openings now and a heater to protect us from the autumn nights. More blankets, too, and a light and approved books for Mayor Ledger to read.

"Still a prison, though, isn't it?" he says behind me, mouth full. "You'd think he'd have at least found a better place for *you* by now."

"I sure wish everyone would stop thinking it's okay to read me all the damn time," I say, without turning around.

"He probably wants you out of the town," he says, finishing up his meal, which is just over half what we used to get. "Wants you away from all the rumors."

"What rumors?" I say, tho I'm barely interested.

"Oh, rumors of the great mind-control powers of our Mayor. Rumors of weapons made from Noise. Rumors he can fly, I don't doubt."

I don't look back at him and I keep my Noise quiet.

I am the Circle, I think.

And then I stop.

* * *

It's after midnight when the first one goes off.

Boom!

I jump a little on my mattress but that's all.

"Where do you think that was?" Mayor Ledger asks, also not rising from his bed.

"Sounded near east," I say, looking up into the dark of the tower bells. "Maybe a food store?"

We wait for the second. There's always a second now. As the soldiers rush to the first, the Answer take the chance for a second–

Boom!

"There it is," Mayor Ledger says, sitting up in bed and looking out of an opening. I get up, too.

"Damn," he says.

"What?" I say, moving next to him.

"I think that was the water plant down by the river."

"What does that mean?"

"It means we'll have to boil every stupid cup of–"

BOOM!

There's a huge flash that causes me and Mayor Ledger to flinch back from the window. The glass shakes in its frames.

And every light in New Prentisstown goes off.

"The power station," Mayor Ledger says, unbelieving. "But that's guarded every hour of the day. How could they possibly get to *that*?"

"I don't know," I say, my stomach sinking. "But there's gonna be hell to pay."

Mayor Ledger runs a tired hand over his face as we hear sirens and soldiers shouting down in the city below. He's shaking his head. "I don't know *what* they think they're accomp–"

BOOM!
BOOM!
BOOM!
BOOM!
BOOM!

Five huge explosions, one right after the other, shaking the tower so much that me and Mayor Ledger are thrown to the floor and a bunch of our windows shatter, busting inward, covering us in shards and powdery glass.

We see the sky light up.

The sky to the west.

A cloud of fire and smoke shooting so high above the prisons it's like a giant's flinging it there.

Mayor Ledger is breathing heavy beside me.

"They've done it," he says, gasping. "They've really done it."

They've really done it, I think.

They've started their war.

And I can't help it—

I can't help but think it—

Is she coming for me?

25

THE NIGHT IT HAPPENS

(VIOLA)

"I NEED YOUR HELP," Mistress Lawson says, standing in the doorway of the kitchen.

I hold up my hands, covered in flour. "I'm kind of in the middle of–"

"Mistress Coyle specifically asked me to fetch you."

I frown. I don't like the word *fetch*. "Then who's going to finish these loaves for tomorrow? Lee's out getting firewood–"

"Mistress Coyle said you had experience in medical supplies," Mistress Lawson interrupts. "We've brought a lot more in and the girl I have now is hopeless at sorting them out."

I sigh. It's better than cooking, at least.

I follow her out into the dusk, into the mouth of a cave and through a series of passages until we get to the large cavern where we keep our most valuable supplies.

"This might take a while," Mistress Lawson says.

We spend most of the evening and into the night counting just how many medicines, bandages, compresses, bed linens, ethers, tourniquets, diagnostic bands, blood pressure straps, stethoscopes, gowns, water purification tablets, splints, cotton swabs, clamps, Jeffers root pills, adhesives, and everything else we have, sorting them out into smaller piles and spreading them across the supply cavern, right up the lip of the main tunnel.

I wipe cold sweat from my forehead. "Shouldn't we be stacking these up already?"

"Not just yet," Mistress Lawson says. She looks around at the neat piles of everything we've done. She rubs her hands together, a worried frown creasing her face. "I hope it's enough."

"Enough for what?" I follow her with my eyes as she goes from pile to pile. "Enough for *what*, Mistress Lawson?"

She looks up at me, biting her lip. "How much of your healing do you remember?"

I stare at her for a second, suspicions rising and rising, then I take off running out of the cavern. "Wait!" she calls after me, but I'm already out into the central tunnel, running out of the main mouth of the cave and shooting into the camp.

Which is deserted.

"Don't be angry," Mistress Lawson says after I've searched every cabin.

I stand there, stupidly, hands on my hips, staring around at the empty camp. Having found a distraction for me, Mistress Coyle left, along with all the other mistresses except for Mistress Lawson. Thea and the apprentices are gone, too.

And everyone else. Every cart, horse, and ox.

And Lee.

Wilf's gone, too, though Jane is here, the only other one who stayed behind.

Tonight's the night.

Tonight's the night it happens.

"You know why she couldn't take you," Mistress Lawson says.

"She doesn't trust me," I say. "None of you do."

"That's neither here nor there right now," she says, her voice taking on that stern mistress tone I've grown to hate. "What matters is that when they come back, we're going to need all the healing hands we can get."

I'm about to argue but I see how much she's still wringing her hands, how worried her face looks, how much is going on beneath the surface.

And then she says, "If any of them make it back at all."

*　*　*

There's nothing left to do but wait. Jane makes us coffee, and we sit in the increasing cold, watching the path out of the woods, watching to see who returns down it.

"Frost," Jane says, digging her toe across the small breath of ice frozen on a stone near her foot.

"We should have done it earlier," Mistress Lawson says into her cup, face over the rising steam. "We should have done it before the weather turned."

"Done *what*?" I ask.

"Rescue," Jane says simply. "Wilf tole me when he was leavin."

"Rescue of who?" I say, though of course it can only be–

We hear rocks fall on the path. We're already on our feet when Magnus comes barreling over the hill. "Hurry!" he's shouting. "Come on!"

Mistress Lawson grabs some of the most urgent of the medical supplies and starts running after him up the path. Jane and I do the same.

We're halfway up when they start to come out of the forest.

On the backs of carts, across the shoulders of others, on stretchers, on horseback, with more people pouring down the path behind them and more cresting the hill behind *them*.

All the ones who needed rescuing.

The prisoners locked away by the Mayor and his army.

And the *state* of them–

"Oh, m'Gawd," Jane says, quietly, next to me, both of us stopped, stunned.

Oh, my God.

The next hours are a blur, as we rush to bring the wounded into camp, though some of them are hurt so bad we have to treat them where they are. I'm ordered from one healer to another and another, racing from wound to wound, running back for more supplies, going so fast it's only after a while that I start to realize that most of the wounds being treated aren't from fighting.

"They've been beaten," I say.

"And starved," Mistress Lawson says angrily, setting up a fluid injection into the arm of a woman we've carried into the cave. "And tortured."

The woman is just one of a growing number that threatens never to stop. Most of them too shocked to speak, staring at you in the most horrible silence or keening at you without words, burn scars on their arms and faces, old wounds left untreated, the sunken eyes of women who haven't eaten for days and days and days.

"He did this," I say to myself. "He did this."

"Hold it together, my girl," Mistress Lawson says. We rush back outside, arms full of bandages that don't begin to cover what's needed. Mistress Braithwaite waves me over with a frantic hand. She tears the bandages from me, furiously wrapping up the leg of a woman screaming beneath her. "Jeffers root!" Mistress Braithwaite snaps.

"I didn't bring any," I say.

"Then bloody well get some!"

I go back to the cave, twisting around healers and apprentices and fake soldiers crouched over patients everywhere, up the hillsides, on backs of carts, everywhere. It's not just women injured either. I see male prisoners, also starved, also beaten. I see people from the camp wounded in the fighting, including Wilf with a burn bandage up the side of his face, though he's still helping carry patients on stretchers into the camp.

I run into the cave, grab more bandages and Jeffers root, and run back to the gully for the dozenth time. I cross the open ground and look up the path, where a few more people are still arriving.

I stop a second and check the new faces before running back to Mistress Braithwaite.

Mistress Coyle hasn't returned yet.

Neither has Lee.

"He was right in the thick of it," Mistress Nadari says, as I help her get a freshly drugged woman to her feet. "Like he was looking for someone."

"His mother and sister," I say, taking the woman's weight against me.

"We didn't get everyone," Mistress Nadari says. "There was a whole other building where the bomb didn't go off–"

"Siobhan!" we hear someone shout in the distance.

I turn, my heart racing a lot faster and bigger than I expect, a smile breaking my cheeks. "He's found them!"

But you can see right away it's not true.

"Siobhan?" Lee is coming down the path from the forest, the arm and shoulder of his uniform blackened, his face covered in soot, his eyes looking everywhere, this way and that through all the people in the gully as he walks through them. "Mum?"

"Go," Mistress Nadari says to me. "See if he's hurt."

I let the woman lean onto Mistress Nadari and I run toward Lee, ignoring the other mistresses calling my name.

"Lee!" I call.

"Viola?" he says, seeing me. "Are they here? Do you know if they're here?"

"Are you hurt?" I reach him, taking the blackened sleeve and looking at his hands. "You're burned."

"There were fires," he says, and I look into his eyes. He's looking at me but he's not seeing me, he's seeing what he saw at the prisons, he's seeing the fires and what was behind them, he's seeing the prisoners they found, maybe he's seeing guards he had to kill.

He's not seeing his sister or his mother.

"Are they *here?*" he pleads. "Tell me they're here."

"I don't know what they look like," I say quietly.

Lee stares at me, his mouth open, his breath heavy and raspy, like he's breathed in a lot of smoke. "It was . . ." he says. "Oh, God, Viola, it was . . ." He looks up and past me, over my shoulder. "I've got to find them. They've got to be here."

He steps past me and down the gully. "Siobhan? *Mum?*"

I can't help it and I call after him. "Lee? Did you see Todd?"

But he keeps on walking, stumbling away.

"Viola!" I hear and at first I think it's just another mistress calling for my help.

But then a voice beside me says, "Mistress Coyle!"

I turn and look up. At the top of the path is Mistress Coyle, on horseback, clopping down the rocks of the path as fast as she can make the horse go. She's got someone in the saddle behind her, someone tied to her to keep them from falling off. I feel a jolt of hope. Maybe it's Siobhan. Or Lee's mum.

(or him, maybe it's him, maybe–)

"Help us, Viola!" Mistress Coyle shouts, working the reins.

And as I start to run up the hill toward them, the horse turns to find its footing and I see who it is, unconscious and leaning badly.

Corinne.

"No," I keep saying, under my breath, hardly realizing it. "No, no, no, no, no," as we get her down onto a flat of rock and as Mistress Lawson runs toward us with armfuls of bandages and medicines. "No, no, no," as I take her head in my hands to cradle it from the hard rock and Mistress Coyle tears off Corinne's sleeve to prepare for injections. "No," as Mistress Lawson reaches us and gasps as she sees who it is.

"You found her," Mistress Lawson says.

Mistress Coyle nods. "I found her."

I feel Corinne's skull under my hands, feel how the skin burns with fever. I see how sharp her cheeks look, how the bruising that discolors her eyes is against skin sagging and limp. And the collarbones that jut up from above the neckline of her torn and dirty mistress cloak. And the circles of burns against her neck. And the cuts on her forearms. And the tearing at her fingernails.

"Oh, Corinne," I whisper and wet from my eyes drops onto her forehead. "Oh, no."

"Stay with us, my girl," Mistress Coyle says, and I don't know whether she's talking to me or Corinne.

"Thea?" Mistress Lawson asks, not looking up.

Mistress Coyle shakes her head.

"Thea's dead?" I ask.

"And Mistress Waggoner," Mistress Coyle says, and I notice the smoke on her face, the red angry burns on her forehead. "And others." Her mouth draws thin. "But we got some of *them*, too."

"Come on, my girl," Mistress Lawson says to Corinne, still unconscious. "You were always the stubborn one. We need that now."

"Hold this," Mistress Coyle says, handing me a bag of fluid connected to a tube injected into Corinne's arm. I take it in one hand, keeping Corinne's head in my lap.

"Here it is," Mistress Lawson says, peeling away a strap of crusted cloth on Corinne's side. A terrible smell hits all of us at the same time.

It's worse than how sickening it stinks. It's worse because of what it means.

"Gangrene," Mistress Coyle says pointlessly, because we can all see that it's way past infection. The smell means the tissue's dead. It means it's started to eat her alive. Something I wish I didn't remember that Corinne taught me herself.

"They didn't even give her basic bloody treatment," grunts Mistress Lawson, getting to her feet and running back toward the cave to get the heaviest medicines we've got.

"Come on, my difficult girl," Mistress Coyle says quietly, stroking Corinne's forehead.

"You stayed until you found her," I say. "That's why you were last."

"She'd never yield, this one," Mistress Coyle says, her voice rough and not just because of smoke. "No matter what they did to her."

We look down at Corinne's face, her eyes still closed, her mouth dropped open, her breath faltering.

Mistress Coyle's right. Corinne would never yield, would never give names or information, would take the punishment to keep other daughters, other mothers, from feeling it themselves.

"The infection," I say, my throat swelling. "The smell, it means–"

Mistress Coyle just bites her lips hard and shakes her head.

"Oh, Corinne," I say. "Oh, no."

And right there, right there in my hands, in my lap, her face turned up to mine–

She dies.

There's only silence when it happens. It isn't loud or struggled against or violent or anything at all. She just falls quiet, a certain type of quiet you know is endless as soon as you hear it, a quiet that muffles everything around it, turning off the volume of the world.

The only thing I *can* hear, in fact, is my own breathing, wet and heavy and like I'll never feel lightness again. And in the silence of my breath I look down the hillside, I see the rest of the wounded around us, their mouths open to cry out in pain, their eyes blank with horrors still being seen even after rescue. I see Mistress Lawson, running toward us with medicine, too late, too late. I see Lee, coming back up the path, calling out for his mother and sister, not willing to believe yet that in all this mess, they're still not here.

I think of the Mayor in his cathedral, making promises, telling lies.

(I think of Todd in the Mayor's hands)

I look down at Corinne in my lap, Corinne who never liked me, not ever, but who gave her life for mine anyway.

We are the choices we make.

When I look up at Mistress Coyle, the wet in my eyes makes everything shine with pointed lights, makes the first peek of the rising sun a smear across the sky.

But I can see her clearly enough.

My teeth are clenched, my voice thick as mud.

"I'm ready," I say. "I'll do anything you want."

26

THE ANSWER

[TODD]

"OH, GOD," Mayor Ledger keeps saying under his breath. "Oh, God."

"What're *you* so upset about?" I finally snap at him.

The door ain't unlocked at its usual time. Morning's come and gone with no sign of anyone remembering that we're here. Outside the city burns and ROARs but a sour part of me can't help thinking he's moaning cuz they're late with our breakfast.

"The surrender was supposed to bring *peace*," he says. "And that bloody woman has ruined *everything*."

I look at him strangely. "It's not like it's paradise here or nothing. There's curfews and prisons and—"

But he's shaking his head. "Before she started her little *campaign*, the President was relaxing the laws. He was easing the restrictions. Things were going to be okay."

I stand and look out the windows to the west, where smoke still rises and fires still rage and the Noise of men don't show no sign of stopping.

"You've got to be *practical*," Mayor Ledger says, "even in the face of tyrants."

"Is that what you are then?" I say. "Practical?"

He narrows his eyes. "I don't know what you're getting at, *boy*."

I don't really know what I'm getting at neither but I'm frightened and I'm hungry and we're stuck in this stupid tower while the world falls to bits around us and we can *watch* it but we can't do nothing to *change* it and I don't know what Viola's part in all this is or *where* she is and I don't know where the future's heading and I don't know how any good can possibly come outta any of this but what I *do* know is that Mayor Ledger telling me how *practical* he's been is kinda pissing me off.

Oh, yeah, and one more thing.

"Don't you call me 'boy'."

He takes a step toward me. "A man would understand that things are more complicated than just right or wrong."

"A man trying to save his own skin surely would." And my Noise is saying *Try it, come on, try it.*

Mayor Ledger clenches his fists. "What you don't know, Todd," he says, nostrils flaring. "What you don't know."

"*What* don't I know?" I say but then the door goes *kerthunk*, making us both jump.

Davy comes busting in, rifles in hand. "Come on," he says, shoving one at me. "Pa wants us."

I go without another word, leaving Mayor Ledger shouting "Hey!" behind us as Davy locks the door.

"Fifty-six soldiers killed," Davy says as we trundle down the stairs on the inside of the tower. "We killed a dozen of 'em and captured a dozen more but they got away with almost two hundred prisoners."

"*Two hundred?*" I say, stopping for a second. "How many people were in prison?"

"Come on, pigpiss, Pa's waiting."

I run to catch up. We cross the lobby of the cathedral and head out the front door. "Those bitches," Davy's saying, shaking his head. "You wouldn't believe the things they're capable of. They blew up a bunkhouse. A *bunkhouse!* Where men were *sleeping!*"

We exit the cathedral to chaos in the square. Smoke is still blowing in from the west, making everything hazy. Soldiers, both by themselves and in squads, run this way and that, some of them pushing people before them, beating them with their rifles. Others are standing guard around groups of terrified-looking women and separate smaller groups of terrified-looking men.

"But we showed them, tho," Davy says, grimacing.

"You were there?"

"No." He looks down at his rifle. "But I will be next time."

"David!" we hear. "Todd!" The Mayor's riding toward us from across the square, moving so heavy and fast Morpeth's shoes are striking sparks from the bricks.

"Something's happened at the monastery," he's shouting. "Get there. *Now!*"

The chaos is citywide. We see soldiers everywhere as we ride, herding townspeople before them, forcing them into bucket-lines to help put out the smaller fires from the first three bombs of last night, the ones that *did* take out the power stayshun, the water plant, and a food store, all still burning cuz New Prentisstown's fire hoses are busy trying to put out the prisons.

"They won't know what hit 'em," Davy says as we ride, fast.

"Who won't?"

"The Answer and any man who helps them."

"There ain't gonna be no one *left*."

"There'll be us," Davy says, looking at me. "That'll be a start."

The road gets quieter as we get away from the city, till you can almost believe things are still normal, unless you look back and see the columns of smoke rising in the air. There ain't no one on the roads down this far and it starts to get so quiet it's like the world's ended.

We ride past the hill where the tower rubble lies but don't see no soldiers going up the path toward it. We turn the last corner and come round to the monastery.

And pull back hard on our reins.

"Holy shit," Davy says.

The whole front wall of the monastery has been blown open. There ain't any guards on the walls, just a gaping hole in the masonry where the gate used to be.

"Those bitches," Davy says. "They set them *free*."

I feel a weird smile in my stomach at the thought of it.

(is this what she did?)

"Now we're gonna have to bloody fight them, *too*," Davy whines.

But I'm hopping off Angharrad, my stomach all funny and light. *Free*, I think. *They're free.*

(is this why she joined them?)

I feel so—

So *relieved*.

I pick up the pace as I near the opening, my hands gripping my rifle but I have a feeling I ain't gonna need it.

(ah, Viola, I knew I could count–)
Then I reach the opening and stop.
Everything stops.
My stomach falls right thru my feet.
"They all gone?" Davy says, coming up beside me.
Then he sees what I see.
"What the–?" Davy says.
The Spackle ain't all gone.
They're still here.
Every single one.
All 1,150 of them.
Dead.

"I don't unnerstand this at all," Davy says, looking round.
  "Shut up," I whisper.
  The guide walls have all been knocked down till it's just a field
again and bodies are piled everywhere, thrown on top of each other and
tumbled across the grass, too, like someone tossed 'em away, males and
females and children and babies, tossed away like they were trash.
  Something's burning somewhere and white smoke twists thru the
field, circling the piles, pushing at them with smoky fingers, finding
nothing alive.
  And the quiet.
  No clicking, no shuffling, no *breathing*.
  "I gotta tell Pa," Davy says, already turning back. "I gotta tell Pa."
  And he's off back out the front, hopping on Deadfall and riding back
up the road.
  I don't follow.
  My feet will only go forward, thru them all, my rifle dragging be-
hind me.
  The piles of bodies are higher than my head. I have to look up to see
the dead faces flung back, the eyes still open, grassflies already picking
at the bullet wounds in their heads. Looks like all of 'em were shot, most
of 'em in the middle of their high foreheads, but some of the bodies look
slashed, too, cut across the throat or the chest and I start to see ripped-
off limbs and heads twisted all the way round and–
  I drop my rifle to the grass. I barely even notice.
  I keep walking, not blinking, mouth open, not believing what I'm
seeing, not taking in the scale of it–
  Cuz I have to step over bodies with arms flung out, arms with bands
round 'em that *I* put there, twisted mouths that I fed, broken backs that I–

That I–
Oh, God.
Oh, God, no, I hated 'em–
I tried not to but I couldn't help it–
(no, I could–)
I think of all the times I cursed 'em–
All the times I imagined 'em as sheep–
(a knife in my hand, plunging down–)
But I didn't want *this*–
Never, I–
And I come round the biggest pile of bodies, stacked near the east wall–
And I see it.
And I fall to my knees in the frozen grass.

Written on the wall, tall as a man–
The *A.*
The *A* of the Answer.
Written in blue.

I lean my head forward slowly till it's touching the ground, the cold sinking into my skull.
(no)
(no, it can't be her)
(it *can't* be)
My breath comes up around me as steam, melting a little spot of mud. I don't move.
(have they done this to you?)
(have they changed you?)
(Viola?)
(*Viola*?)
The blackness starts to overwhelm me, starts to fall over me like a blanket, like water rising above my head, no Viola no, it can't be you, it can't be you (can it?) no no no it can't–
No–
No–
And I sit up–
And I lean back–
And I strike myself in the face.
I punch myself hard.

Again.
And again.
Not feeling nothing as I hit.
As my lips crack open.
As my eyes swell.
No–
God no–
Please–
And I reach back to punch myself again–
But I switch off–
I feel it go cold inside me–
Deep down inside–
(where are you to save me?)
I switch off.
I go numb.
I look at the Spackle, dead, everywhere dead.
And Viola gone–
Gone in ways that I can't even say–
(you did *this*?)
(you did *this* instead of finding me?)
And inside I just *die*.

And a body tumbles from the pile, knocking right into me.

I scoot back fast, rolling over other bodies, scrambling to my feet, wiping my hands on my trousers, wiping the dead away.
    And then another body falls.
    I look up at the pile.
    1017 is working his way out.

He sees me and freezes, his head and arms sticking out from the rest of the bodies, bones showing thru his skin, thin as the dead.
    Course he survived. *Course* he did. If any of 'em is spiteful enough to find a way to live, it's him.
    I run to the pile and I start pulling on his shoulders to get him out, to get him out from under the dead, all the dead.
    We fall back as he pops free, tumbling to the ground, rolling apart and then staring at each other across the ground.
    Our breaths are heavy, clouds of steam huffing into the air.

He don't look injured, tho the sling's gone from his arm. He's just staring, eyes probably open as wide as mine.

"Yer alive," I say stupidly. "Yer alive."

He just stares back, no Noise this time, no clicking, nothing. Just the silence of us in the morning, the smoke sneaking thru the air like a vine.

"How?" I say. "How did–?"

But there ain't no answer from him, just staring and staring.

"Did you–?" I say, then I have to clear my throat. "Did you see a girl?"

And then I hear, *Thump budda-thump–*

Hoofbeats down the road. Davy musta caught his pa coming the other way.

I look hard at 1017.

"Run," I say. "You gotta get outta here."

Thump budda-thump–

"Please," I whisper. "Please, I'm so sorry, I'm *so* sorry, but please, just run, just run, just get outta here–"

I stop cuz he's getting to his feet. He's still eyeing me, not blinking, his face almost dead of expresshun.

Thump budda-THUMP–

He takes one step away, then two, then faster, heading for the blown open gate.

And then he stops and looks back.

Looks back at me.

A clear flash of Noise coming right at me.

Of me, alone.

Of 1017 with a gun.

Of him pulling the trigger.

Of me dying at his feet.

Then he turns and runs out the gate and into the woods beyond.

"I know how hard this must be for you, Todd," says the Mayor, looking at the blown-out gate. We've come outside. No one wanted to see the bodies anymore.

"But *why*?" I say, trying to keep the tightness outta my voice. "Why would they do it?"

The Mayor looks at the blood on my face from where I hit myself but he don't say nothing about it. "They thought we would have used them as soldiers, I expect."

"But to kill them *all*?" I look up at him on his horse. "The Answer never killed no one before except by accident."

"Fifty-six soldiers," Davy says.

"Seventy-five," the Mayor corrects. "And three hundred escaped prisoners."

"They tried to bomb us here before, remember?" Davy adds. "The bitches."

"The Answer have stepped up their campaign," the Mayor says, looking mainly at me. "And we will respond in kind."

"Damn right, we will," Davy says, cocking his rifle for no reason.

"I'm sorry about Viola," the Mayor says to me. "I'm as disappointed as you are that she's a part of this."

"We don't know that," I whisper.

(is she?)

(are you?)

"Regardless," the Mayor says. "The time for your boyhood is well and truly past. I need leaders now. I need *you* to be a leader. Are you ready to lead, Todd Hewitt?"

"*I'm* ready," Davy says, his Noise feeling like it's being left out.

"I already know I can count on you, son."

And there's the pink Noise again.

"It's Todd I need to hear from." He comes a bit closer to me. "You're no longer my prisoner, Todd Hewitt. We're beyond that now. But I need to know if you'll join *me*"—he nods his head toward the opening in the wall—"or them. There is no other choice."

I look into the monastery, at all those bodies, all those shocked and dead faces, all that pointless end.

"Will you help me, Todd?"

"Help you how?" I say to the ground.

But he just asks it again. "Will you help me?"

I think of 1017, alone now, alone in the entire world.

His friends, his family for all I know, piled like rubbish, left for the flies.

I can't stop seeing it, even when I close my eyes.

I can't stop seeing that bright blue **A.**

Oh don't deceive me, I think.

Oh never leave me.

(but she's gone)

(she's gone)

And I'm dead.

Inside, I'm dead dead dead.

There ain't nothing left.

"I will," I say. "I'll help."

"Excellent," the Mayor says, with feeling. "I knew you'd be special, Todd. I've known it all along."

Davy's Noise squeaks at this but the Mayor ignores it. He turns Morpeth to face the killing grounds of the monastery.

"As to how you'll help me," he says. "Well, we have met the Answer, have we not?" He turns back to look at us, his eyes glinting. "It is time for them to meet the Ask."

PART V

THE OFFICE OF THE ASK

27

THE WAY WE LIVE NOW

[TODD]

"DON'T LET THIS period of quiet fool you," says the Mayor, standing atop the platform, voice booming thru the square from speakers set at every corner, extra loud to be heard above the ROAR . The people of New Prentisstown stare up at him in the cold morning, the men gathered in front of the platform, surrounded by the army, with the women back on the side streets.

Here we all are again.

Davy and I are behind the platform on our horses, directly behind the Mayor.

Kinda like an honor guard.

Wearing our new uniforms.

I think, *I am the Circle and the Circle is me*.

Cuz when I think it, I don't gotta think about nothing else at all.

"Even now our enemies move against us. Even now they plot our destruction. Even now we have reason to believe an attack is imminent."

The Mayor takes a long sweeping look across the crowd. It's easy to forget how many people are still here, still working, still trying to eat, still getting on with their daily lives. They're tired looking, hungry, many of 'em dirty, but still staring, still listening.

"The Answer could strike in any place, at any time, against any-*one*," he says, tho the Answer ain't done no such thing, not for almost a month now. The prison break was the last we heard from 'em before they disappeared into the wild, the soldiers who woulda chased 'em killed while sleeping in their bunkers.

But that just means they're out there, gloating on their victory and planning the next.

"Three hundred escaped prisoners," the Mayor says. "Almost two hundred soldiers and civilians dead."

"Up they go again," Davy mutters under his breath, talking about the numbers. "Next time he gives this speech, the whole *city'll* be dead." He looks to me to see if I'll laugh. I don't. I don't even look at him. "Yeah, whatever," he says, turning back.

"And not to mention the genocide," says the Mayor.

The crowd murmurs at this and the ROAR gets a bit louder and redder.

"The very same Spackle who served in your homes so peacefully for the past decade, the ones we had all grown to admire for their pluck under duress, the ones we had come to regard as our partners on New World."

He pauses again. "All dead, all gone."

The crowd ROARs some more. The deaths of the Spackle really did affect the people, even more than the deaths of the soldiers or the townspeople caught up in the attack. Men even started joining the army again. Then the Mayor let some of the women who remained in prison out, some of 'em even back with their families and not even in dormitories. He upped everyone's food rashuns, too.

And he started holding these rallies. Explaining things.

"The Answer says it fights for freedom. But are these the people in whom you put your faith for salvation? The ones who would kill an entire *unarmed* population?"

I feel a choke rising and I make my Noise empty space, make it a wasteland, thinking nothing, *feeling* nothing, except–

I am the Circle and the Circle is me.

"I know these past weeks have been difficult. The food and water shortages, the necessary curfews, the power cuts, especially during the cold nights. I applaud your fortitude. The only way we're going to get thru this is by pulling together against those who would destroy us."

And people have pulled together, ain't they? They obey the curfew and take their assigned amounts of water and food without fuss and stay inside when they're sposed to and turn off their lights after a certain hour and generally keep getting on with things even as it gets colder. You ride thru the town, you even see stores open, big lines of people outside 'em, waiting to get what they need.

Their eyes looking at the ground, waiting it out.

At night, Mayor Ledger tells me the townsfolk still grumble against

Mayor Prentiss, but now there's even louder grumbles against the Answer, for blowing up the water plant, for blowing up the power stayshun, and specially for killing all the Spackle.

Better the devil you know, Mayor Ledger says.

We're still up in that tower, me and Mayor Ledger, for some reason best known to Mayor Prentiss, but I got a key now and I lock him in when I ain't there. He don't like it but what's he gonna do?

Better the devil you know.

I wonder why the only choice is twixt two devils, tho.

"I also want to express my thanks," says the Mayor to the people, "for your continued help in coming forward with information. It is only eternal vigilance that will lead us into the light. Let your neighbor know he is watched. Only then are we truly safe."

"How long is this gonna go *on*?" Davy says, accidentally spurring Deadfall/Acorn, who has to be reined back when he steps forward. "I'm effing freezing over here."

Angharrad moves from foot to foot below me. **Go?** her Noise asks, her breath heavy and white in the cold. "Almost," I say, rubbing my hand against her flank.

"Effective tonight," says the Mayor, "curfew is pushed back by two hours and visiting times for wives and mothers is extended by thirty minutes."

There's some nodding in the crowd of men, some relieved crying from the crowd of women.

They're grateful, I think. *Grateful* to the Mayor.

Ain't that something.

"Finally," says the Mayor. "It is my pleasure to announce that building work has been completed on a new Ministry, one that will keep us safe from the threat of the Answer, a building where no secret may be kept, where anyone who tries to undermine our way of life will be reeducated into understanding our ideals, where our future will be secured against those who would steal it from us."

The Mayor pauses, to give his words maximum impact.

"Today we launch the Office of the Ask."

Davy catches my eye and taps the sharp, silver *A* sewn on the shoulders of our new uniforms, the *A* that the Mayor picked special cuz it's got all kinda associashuns, don't it?

Me and Davy are now Officers of the Ask.

I don't share his excitement.

But that's cuz I don't feel nothing much at all no more.

I am the Circle and the Circle is me.

* * *

"Good speech, Pa," Davy says. "Long."

"It wasn't for you, David," the Mayor says, not looking at him.

The three of us are riding down the road to the monastery.

Tho it ain't the monastery no more.

"Everything *is* ready, I trust?" the Mayor says, barely turning his head. "I'd hate to be made a liar of."

"It ain't gonna get less ready if you keep asking," Davy mumbles.

The Mayor turns to him, a deep frown on his face, but I speak before anyone gets slapped with Noise.

"It's as ready as it can be," I say, my voice flat. "The walls and roof are up but the inside—"

"No need to sound so morose, Todd," the Mayor says. "The inside can follow in due course. The building is up, that's all that's important. They can look at the outside and they can tremble."

He's got his back to us now, riding on ahead, but I can *feel* him smile at *they can tremble*.

"Are we gonna have a part in it?" Davy asks, Noise still stormy. "Or are you just gonna find a way for us to be babysitters again?"

The Mayor turns Morpeth in the road, blocking our way. "Do you ever hear Todd complain this much?" he asks.

"No," Davy says, sullen. "But he's just, you know, *Todd*."

The Mayor raises his eyebrows. "And?"

"And I'm yer *son*."

The Mayor walks Morpeth toward us, making Angharrad step back. **Submit,** Morpeth says. **Lead,** Angharrad says in answer, lowering her head. I stroke her mane, untangling a bit with my fingers, trying to calm her down.

"Let me tell you something interesting, David," the Mayor says, looking hard at him. "The officers, the army, the townspeople, they see the two of you riding together, in your new uniforms, with all your new authority, and they know that *one* of you is my son." He's almost side by side with Davy now, pushing him back down the road. "And as they watch you ride by, as they watch you go about your business, do you know? They often guess wrong. They often guess wrong as to which one of you is my own flesh and blood."

The Mayor looks over to me. "They see Todd with his devotion to duty, with his modest brow and his serious face, with his calm exterior and mature handling of his Noise, and they never even consider that his loud, sloppy, *insolent* friend is the one who's actually my son."

Davy's looking at the ground, his teeth clenched, his Noise boiling. "He don't even *look* like you."

"I know," says the Mayor, turning Morpeth back down the road. "I just thought it was interesting. How often it happens."

We keep on riding, Davy in a silent, red storm of Noise, lagging behind. I keep Angharrad in the middle with the Mayor clopping on ahead.

"Good girl," I murmur to her.

Boy colt, she says back, and then she thinks **Todd.**

"Yeah, girl," I whisper twixt her ears. "I'm here."

I've taken to hanging round her stable at the end of the day, taken to unsaddling her myself and brushing her mane and bringing her apples to eat. The only thing she needs from me is assurance that I'm there, proof I haven't left the herd, and as long as that's true, she's happy and she calls me **Todd** and I don't have to explain myself to her and I don't have to ask her nothing and she don't need nothing from me.

Except that I don't leave her.

Except that I don't never *leave*.

My Noise starts getting cloudy and I think it again, *I am the Circle and the Circle is me.*

The Mayor looks back at me. And he smiles.

Even tho we got uniforms, we ain't in the army, the Mayor was particular about that. We don't got ranks except Officer but the uniform and the **A** on its sleeve is enough to keep people outta our way as we ride toward the monastery.

Our job till now has been guarding the men and women who're still in prison, tho it's mostly women. After the prisons were busted into and burned down, the prisoners left over were moved to a former house of healing down by the river.

Guess which one?

For the past month, Davy and I've been escorting work crews of prisoners back and forth from the house of healing to the monastery to finish the work the Spackle started, women and men working faster than Spackle, I guess. The Mayor didn't ask us to supervise the building this time, something I'm grateful for.

When everyone's in for the night back at the house of healing, Davy and I ain't got much to do except ride our horses round the building, doing what we can so as not to hear the screams coming from inside.

Some of the ones still in prison, see, are from the Answer, the ones the Mayor caught the night of the prison break. We don't never see them, they don't get sent out with the work parties, they just get Asked all day long till they answer with something. So far, all the Mayor's got from 'em is the locayshun of a camp around a mine, which was deserted by the time the soldiers got there. Anything else useful is slow in coming.

There are others in there, too, found guilty of helping the Answer or whatever, but the ones who said they saw the Answer kill the Spackle and saw women writing the *A* on the wall, those prisoners are the ones who've been set free and sent back to their families. Even tho there ain't really no way they coulda been there to see it.

The others, well, the others keep being Asked till they answer.

Davy talks loud to cover the sounds we hear while the Asking's going on inside, trying to pretend it don't bother him when any fool could see it does.

I just keep myself in myself, closing my eyes, waiting for the screaming to stop.

I have an easier time than Davy.

Cuz like I say, I don't feel nothing much, not no more.

I am the Circle and the Circle is me.

But today, everything's sposed to change. Today, the new building is ready, or ready enough, and Davy and I are gonna guard it instead of the house of healing, while sposedly learning the business of Asking.

Fine. It don't matter.

Nothing matters.

"The Office of the Ask," the Mayor says as we round the final corner.

The front wall of the monastery has been rebuilt and you can see the new building sticking over the top, a big stone block that looks like it'd happily knock yer brains out if you stood too close. And on the newly built gate, there's a great, shiny silver *A* to match the ones on our uniforms.

There are guards in army uniforms on either side of the door. One of them is Ivan, still a Private, still sour faced as anything. He tries to catch my eye as I ride up, his Noise clanging loud with things he don't want the Mayor to hear, I reckon.

I ignore him. So does the Mayor.

"Now we find out when the real war begins," the Mayor says.

The gate opens and out walks the man in charge of all the Asking, the man charged with finding out where the Answer are hiding and how best to track them down.

Our newly promoted boss.

"Mr. President," he says.

"Captain Hammar," says the Mayor.

SOLDIER

{VIOLA}

"QUIET," Mistress Coyle says, a finger to her lips.

The wind has died and you can hear our footsteps snapping the twigs on the ground at the foot of the trees. We stop, ears open for the sounds of soldiers marching.

Nothing.

More nothing.

Mistress Coyle nods and continues moving down the hill and through the trees. I follow her. It's just the two of us.

Me and her and the bomb strapped to my back.

The rescue saved one hundred thirty-two prisoners. Of these, twenty-nine died either on the way to or back in the camp. Corinne was number thirty. There are others unrescued, like poor old Mrs. Fox, whose fates I'm probably never going to know. But Mistress Coyle estimates we killed at least twenty of their soldiers. Miraculously, only six members of the Answer on the original raid were killed, including Thea and Mistress Waggoner, but another five were captured and there was no possibility they wouldn't be tortured for information about where the Answer was hiding.

So we moved. In a hurry.

Even before many of the injured could walk for themselves,

we loaded up supplies and weapons, anything and everything we could carry on carts, horses, the backs of the able-bodied, and we fled into the woods, keeping moving all through the night, the next day, and the night after that until we came to a lake at the base of a rock cliff, where at least we might have water and some shelter.

"It'll do," Mistress Coyle said.

We pitched camp along the shore.

And then we began our preparations for war.

She makes a movement with the palm of her hand and I instantly duck below some shrubs. We've reached a narrow drive up from the main road and I can hear a troop of soldiers Noisily moving away from us in the distance.

Our own supply of cure is getting lower by the day, and Mistress Coyle has set up a rationing system, but since the raid, it's too dangerous for any man, with or without Noise, to go into town anyway, which means they can no longer ferry us in hidden compartments to easy targets. We have to take a cart to a certain point outside of town and walk the rest of the way.

Escaping will be more difficult, so we'll just have to be more careful.

"Okay," Mistress Coyle whispers.

I stand. The moons are our only light.

We cross the road, keeping low.

After we moved to the lake, after the rescue of all those people, after the death of Corinne–

After I joined the Answer–

I began to learn things.

"Basic training," Mistress Coyle called it. Led by Mistress Braithwaite and done not only for me but for every patient who improved enough to join in, which was most of them, more than you'd think, we were taught how to load a rifle and fire it, basics of infiltration, nighttime maneuvers, tracking, hand communications, code words.

How to wire and set a bomb.

"How do you know how to do this?" I asked one night at dinner, my body weary and aching from the running and diving and carrying we'd done all throughout the day. "You're healers. How do you know how–"

"To run an army?" Mistress Coyle said. "You forget about the Spackle War."

"We were our own division," Mistress Forth said, down the table, snuffling up some broth.

The mistresses talked to me, now that they could see how hard I was training.

"We weren't very popular," giggled Mistress Lawson, across from her.

"We didn't like how some of the generals were waging the war," Mistress Coyle said to me. "We thought an underground approach would be more effective."

"And since we didn't have Noise," said Mistress Nadari, down the table, "we could sneak into places, couldn't we?"

"The men in charge didn't think we were the answer to their problem, though," Mistress Lawson said, still giggling.

"Hence the name," Mistress Coyle said.

"And when the new government was formed and the city rebuilt, well," Mistress Forth said, "it wouldn't have been sensible not to keep important materials available should the need ever arise."

"The explosives in the mine," I said, realizing. "You hid them there years ago."

"And what a good decision it turned out to be," Mistress Lawson said. "Nicola Coyle always was a woman of foresight."

I blinked at the name Nicola, as if it was hardly possible that Mistress Coyle had a first name.

"Yes, well," said Mistress Coyle. "Men are creatures of war. It's only prudent to remember that."

Our target is deserted, as we expect it to be. It's small, but symbolic, a well above a tract of farmland east of the city. The well and the apparatus above it only bring water for the field below, not any huge system or set of buildings. But if the city goes on allowing the Mayor to imprison, torture, and kill, then the city won't eat.

It's also a good way away from the city center, so no chance of me seeing Todd.

Which I won't argue about. For now.

We've come up the cut-off road, keeping to the ditch beside it, holding our breaths as we move past the sleeping farmhouse, a light still on in the upper floor but it's so late it can only be for security.

Mistress Coyle makes another hand signal and I move past her, ducking under a wire carriage of laundry, hung outside to dry. I trip on a child's toy scooter but manage to keep my balance.

The bomb's supposed to be safe, supposed to be impervious to any kind of jostling or shaking.

But.

I let out a breath and keep on toward the well.

Even in the weeks when we hid, when we didn't approach the city at all, the weeks when we laid low and kept quiet, training and preparing, even then a few escapees from the city found us.

"They're saying *what*?" Mistress Coyle said.

"That you killed all the Spackle," the woman said, pressing the poultice against her bleeding nose.

"Wait," I said. "*All* the Spackle are dead?"

The woman nodded.

"And they're saying we did it," Mistress Coyle repeated.

"Why would they say that?" I asked.

Mistress Coyle stood and looked out across the lake. "Turn the city against us. Make us look like the bad guys."

"That's exactly what he's saying," the woman said. I found her on a training run through the woods. She'd tripped down a rocky embankment, managing to break only her nose. "There's rallies every other day," she said. "People are listening."

"I'm not surprised," Mistress Coyle said.

I looked up at her. "You didn't do it, did you? You didn't kill them?"

Her face could've lit a match. "Exactly what sort of people do you think we are, my girl?"

I kept her gaze. "Well, I don't know, do I? You blew up a bunker. You killed soldiers."

But she just shook her head, though I didn't know if that was an answer.

"You're sure you weren't followed?" she asked the woman.

"I was wandering in the woods for three days," she said. "I didn't even find you." She pointed at me. "*She* found *me*."

"Yes," Mistress Coyle said, eyeing me. "Viola's useful that way."

There's a problem at the well.

"It's too close to the house," I whisper.

"It's not," Mistress Coyle whispers back, going behind me and unzipping my pack.

"Are you sure?" I say. "The bombs you blew up the tower with were–"

"There are bombs and there are bombs." She makes a few adjustments to the contents of my pack, then turns me around to face her. "Are you ready?"

I look over to the house, where anyone could be sleeping inside, women, innocent men, children. I won't kill anyone, not unless I have to. If I'm doing this for Todd and Corinne, well, then. "Are you sure?" I ask.

"Either you trust me, Viola, or you do not." She tilts her head. "Which will it be?"

The breeze has picked up again and it blows a bit of the sleeping Noise of New Prentisstown down the road. One indefinable, snuffling, snoring ROAR, almost quiet, if such a thing could be.

Todd somewhere in it all.

(not dead, no matter what she says)

"Let's get this done," I say, taking off the pack.

The rescue wasn't a rescue for Lee. His sister and his mother weren't among the prisoners saved or the prisoners who died. It's possible they were in the one prison the Answer didn't manage to break.

But.

"Even if they're dead," he said, one night as we sat on the shore of the lake, throwing in stones, aching again after yet another long day's training. "I just want to know."

I shook my head. "If you don't know, then there's still a chance."

"Knowing or not knowing doesn't keep them alive." He sat down, close to me again. "I think they're dead. I *feel* like they're dead."

"Lee–"

"I'm going to kill him." His voice was that of a man making a promise, not a threat. "If I get close enough, I swear to you."

The moons rose over us, making two more of themselves in the surface of the lake. I threw in another stone, watching it skip across the moons' reflections. The camp gave a low bustle in the trees behind us and up the bank. You could hear Noise here and there, including a growing buzz from Lee, not lucky enough to qualify for Mistress Coyle's ration.

"It's not what you think it's going to be like," I said quietly.

"Killing someone?"

I nodded. "Even if it's someone who deserves it, someone who will kill you if you don't kill them, even then it's not what you think."

There was more silence, until he finally said. "I know."

I looked over at him. "You killed a soldier."

He didn't answer, which was its own answer.

"Lee?" I said. "Why didn't you tell–?"

"Because it's not what you think it's going to be like, is it?" he said. "Even if it's someone who deserves it."

He threw another stone into the lake. We weren't resting our shoulders on each other. We were a space apart.

"I'm still going to kill him," he said.

I peel off the backing paper and press the bomb into the side of the well, sticking it there with a glue made from tree sap. I take two wires out of my pack and twist the ends on two more wires already sticking out of the bomb, hooking two together and leaving one end dangling.

The bomb is now armed.

I take a small green number pad from the front pocket of my pack and twist the end of the dangling wire around a point at the end of the pad. I press a red button on the pad and then a gray one. The green numbers light up.

The bomb is now ready for timing.

I click a silver button until the digits count up to 30:00. I press the red button again, flip over the green pad, slide one metal flap into another, then press the gray button one more time. The green numbers immediately change to 29:59, 29:58, 29:57.

The bomb is now live.

"Nicely done," Mistress Coyle whispers. "Time to go."

And then after almost a month of hiding in the forest, waiting for the prisoners to recuperate, waiting for the rest of us to train, waiting for a real army to have life breathed into it, there came a night when that waiting was over.

"Get up, my girl," Mistress Coyle said, kneeling at the foot of my cot.

I blinked myself awake. It was still pitch-black. Mistress Coyle's voice was low so as not to wake the others in the long tent.

"Why?" I whispered back.

"You said you'd do anything."

I got up and went out into the cold, hopping to get my boots on while Mistress Coyle readied a pack for me to wear.

"We're going into town, aren't we?" I said, tying my laces.

"She's a genius, this one," Mistress Coyle muttered into the pack.

"Why tonight? Why now?"

She looked up at me. "Because we need to remind them that we're still here."

The pack rests empty against my back. We cross the yard and sidle up to the house, stopping to listen for anyone stirring.

No one does.

I'm ready to go but Mistress Coyle is leaning back from the outer wall of the house, looking at the white expanse of it.

"This should do fine," she says.

"For what?" I look around us, spooked now that there's a timer running.

"Have you forgotten who we are?" She reaches into a pocket of her long healer's skirt, still worn even though trousers are so much more practical. She pulls out something and tosses it to me. I catch it without even thinking.

"Why don't you do the honors?" she says.

I look in my hand. It's a crumbling piece of blue charcoal, pulled from our wood fires, the remains of the reacher trees we burn to keep warm. It smears dusty blue across my hand, across my skin.

I look at it for a moment longer.

"Tick tock," says Mistress Coyle.

I swallow. Then I raise the charcoal and make three quick slashes against the white wall of the house.

A, looking back at me, by my hand.

I find myself breathing heavily.

When I look round, Mistress Coyle's already off down the ditches of the drive. I hurry after her, keeping my head low.

Twenty-eight minutes later, just as we reach our cart, deep in the woods, we hear the *Boom*.

"Congratulations, soldier," Mistress Coyle says, as we set off back to camp. "You have just fired the first shot of the final battle."

29

THE BUSINESS OF ASKING

[TODD]

THE WOMAN IS STRAPPED against a metal frame, her arms out behind her and up, each tied at the wrist to a bar of the frame.

It looks like she's diving into a lake.

Except for the watery blood on her face.

"She's gonna get it now," Davy says.

But his voice is oddly quiet.

"One more time, my female friend," Mr. Hammar says, walking behind her. "Who set the bomb?"

The first bomb since the prison break went off last night, taking out a well and pump on a farm.

It's begun.

"I don't know," says the woman, her voice strangled and coughing. "I haven't even left Haven since–"

"Haven't left *where*?" Mr. Hammar says. He grabs a handle on the frame and tips the whole thing forward, plunging the woman face-first into a tub of water, holding her there as she thrashes against her bindings.

I look down at my feet.

"Raise your head, please, Todd," the Mayor says, standing behind us. "How else will you learn?"

I raise my head.

We're on the other side of a two-way mirror, in a small room looking in on the Arena of the Ask, which is just a room with high concrete walls and similar mirrored rooms off of each side. Davy and I sit next to each other on a short bench.

Watching.

Mr. Hammar pulls up the frame. The woman rises outta the water, gasping for air, straining against where her arms are tied.

"*Where* do you live?" Mr. Hammar's got his smile on, that nasty thing that hardly ever leaves his face.

"New Prentisstown," the woman gasps. "New Prentisstown."

"Correct," says Mr. Hammar, then watches as the woman coughs so hard she throws up down her front. He takes a towel from a side table and gently wipes the woman's face, cleaning as much of the vomit off her as he can.

The woman's still gasping but her eyes don't leave Mr. Hammar as he cleans her.

She looks even more frightened than before.

"Why's he doing that?" Davy says.

"Doing what?" the Mayor says.

Davy shrugs. "Being, I don't know, *kind*."

I don't say nothing. I keep my Noise clear of the time the Mayor put bandages on me.

All those months ago.

I hear the Mayor shift his stance, rustling himself to cover up my Noise so Davy don't hear it. "We're not inhuman, David. We don't do this for our own joy."

I look out at Mr. Hammar, look at his smile.

"Yes, Todd," the Mayor says, "Captain Hammar does show a certain *glee* that is perhaps unseemly, but you have to admit, he does get results."

"Are you recovered?" Mr. Hammar asks the woman. We can hear his voice over a microphone system, pumped into the room. It separates it oddly from his mouth, making it seem like we're watching a vid rather than a real thing.

"I'm sorry to have to keep Asking you," Mr. Hammar says. "This can end as quick as you want."

"Please," says the woman in a whisper. "Please, I don't know anything."

And she starts to weep.

"Christ," Davy says, under his breath.

"The enemy will try many tricks to win our sympathy," says the Mayor.

Davy turns to him. "So this is a trick?"

"Almost certainly."

I keep watching the woman. It don't look like a trick.

I am the Circle and the Circle is me, I think.

"Just so," says the Mayor.

"Yer in control here," says Mr. Hammar, starting round the woman again. Her head turns to try and follow him but there ain't much movement from where she's strapped to the frame. He hovers just outside of her vision. To keep her off balance, I'm guessing.

Cuz of course Mr. Hammar ain't got no Noise.

Me and Davy do, tho.

"Only muffled sounds, Todd," the Mayor says, reading my asking. "Do you see the metal rods coming out of the frame by the sides of her head?"

He points. Davy and I see them.

"They play a whining buzz into her ears at all times," the Mayor says. "Muffles any Noise she might hear from the observation rooms. Keeps her focused on the Officer of the Ask."

"Wouldn't want 'em hearing what we already know," Davy says.

"Yes," the Mayor says, sounding a little surprised. "Yes, that's it exactly, David."

Davy smiles and his Noise glows a bit.

"We saw the **A** written in blue on the side of the farmhouse," Mr. Hammar says, still hovering behind the woman. "The bomb was the same as all the others planted by your organizayshun–"

"It's not *my* organization!" says the woman but Mr. Hammar continues like she didn't even speak.

"And we know you've worked in that field for the past month."

"So have other women!" she yells, sounding more and more desperate. "Milla Price, Cassia MacRae, Martha Sutpen–"

"So they were in on it, too?"

"No! No, just that–"

"Cuz Mrs. Price and Mrs. Sutpen have already been Asked."

The woman stops, her face suddenly even more frightened.

Davy chuckles next to me. "Got you," he whispers.

But I can hear a weird sense of relief in him.

I wonder if the Mayor hears it, too.

"What did–" the woman says, stopping and then having to go on. "What did they say?"

"They said you tried to get 'em to help," Mr. Hammar says calmly. "Said you tried to enlist 'em as terrorists and when they refused, you said you'd carry on alone."

The woman goes pale, her mouth falling open, her eyes wide in disbelief.

"That's not true, is it?" I say, my voice level. *I am the Circle and the Circle is me.* "He's trying to make her confess by pretending he don't need her to."

"Excellent, Todd," says the Mayor. "You may end up having a flair for this."

Davy looks first at me, then at his pa, then at me again, askings left unsaid.

"We already know yer responsible," Mr. Hammar says. "We already have enough to stick you in prison for the rest of yer life." He stops in front of her. "I stand before you as yer friend," he says. "I stand before you as the one who can save you from a fate worse than prison."

The woman swallows and looks like she's going to vomit again.

"But I don't *know* anything," she says weakly. "I just don't *know.*"

Mr. Hammar sighs. "Well, that's a real disappointment, I must say."

He walks behind her again, grabs the frame, and plunges her into the water.

And holds her there—

And holds her there—

He looks up to the mirror where he knows we're watching—

He smiles at us—

And still holds her there—

The water churns with the limited thrashing she can do—

I am the Circle and the Circle is me, I think, closing my eyes—

"Open them, Todd," the Mayor says—

I do—

And still Mr. Hammar holds her there—

The thrashing gets worse—

So hard the binds on her wrists start to bleed—

"Jesus," Davy says, under his breath—

"He's gonna kill her," I say, voice still low—

It's only a vid—

It's only a vid—

(except it ain't—)

(feeling nothing—)

(cuz I'm dead—)

(I'm dead—)

The Mayor leans past me and presses a button on the wall. "I should think that's enough, Captain," he says, his voice carrying into the Arena of the Ask.

Mr. Hammar raises the frame outta the water. But he does it slowly.

The woman hangs from it, chin down on her chest, water pouring from her mouth and nose.

"He killed her," Davy says.

"No," says the Mayor.

"Tell me," Mr. Hammar says to the woman, "and this will all stop."

There's a long silence, longer still.

And then a croaking sound from the woman.

"What was that?" Mr. Hammar says.

"I did it," croaks the woman.

"*No way!*" says Davy.

"What did you do?" Mr. Hammar asks.

"I set the bomb," the woman says, her head still down.

"And you tried to get yer worksisters to join you in a terrorist orga-nizayshun."

"Yes," the woman whispers. "Anything."

"Ha!" Davy says, and again there's relief, relief that he tries to cover. "She confessed! She did it!"

"No, she didn't," I say, still looking at her, still not moving on the bench.

"*What?*" Davy says to me.

"She's making it up," I say, still looking thru the mirror. "So he'll stop drowning her." I move my head just slightly to show I'm talking to the Mayor. "Ain't she?"

The Mayor waits before answering. Even without Noise, I can tell he's impressed. Ever since I started with *the Circle*, things have taken on the worst kinda clarity.

Maybe that's the point.

"Almost certainly she's making it up," he finally says. "But now we've got her confession, we can use it against her."

Davy's eyes are still rocketing back and forth twixt me and his pa. "You mean, yer gonna . . . Ask her some more?"

"All women are part of the Answer," the Mayor says, "if only in sym-pathy. We need to know what she thinks. We need to know what she *knows*."

Davy looks back at the woman, still panting against the frame.

"I don't get it," he says.

"When they send her back to prison," I say, "all the other women will know what happened to her."

"Quite," says the Mayor, putting a hand briefly on my shoulder. Al-most like affecshun. When I don't move, he takes it away. "They'll know what's in store for them if they don't answer. And that way, we'll find out what we need to know from whoever knows it. The bomb last night was a resumption of aggression, the start of something larger. We need to know what their next move is going to be."

Davy's still looking at the woman. "What about her?"

"She'll be punished for the crime she confessed to, of course," the Mayor says, carrying on talking when Davy tries to interrupt with the obvious. "And who knows? Maybe she really *does* know something." He looks back up thru the mirror. "There's only one way to find out."

"I want to thank you for yer help today," Mr. Hammar says, putting his hand under the woman's chin to lift it. "You've been very brave and can be proud of the fight you put up." He smiles at her but she won't meet his eye. "You've shown more spirit than many a man I've seen under Asking."

He steps away from her, going to a little side table and removing a cloth that's lying on top. Underneath are several shiny bits of metal. Mr. Hammar picks one up.

"And now for the second part of our interview," he says, approaching the woman.

Who starts to scream.

"That was," Davy says, pacing around as we wait outside but it's all he can get out. "That was." He turns to me. "Holy crap, Todd."

I don't say nothing, just take the apple I been saving outta my pocket. "Apple," I whisper to Angharrad, my head close to hers. **Apple,** she says back, clipping at it with her teeth, lips back. **Todd,** she says, munching it and then she makes an asking of it, **Todd?**

"Nothing to do with you, girl," I whisper, rubbing her nose.

We're down from the gate where Ivan's still guarding, still trying to catch my eye. I can hear him calling quietly to me in his Noise.

I still ignore him.

"That was effing intense," Davy says, trying to read my Noise, trying to see what I might think about it all, but I'm keeping it as flat as I can.

Feeling nothing.

Taking nothing in.

"Yer a cool customer these days," Davy says, voice scornful, ignoring Deadfall, who's wanting an apple, too. "You didn't even flinch when he—"

"Gentlemen," the Mayor says, coming outta the gate, a long, heavy sack in one hand.

Ivan stands up straight as a board, back at attenshun.

"Pa," Davy says in greeting.

"Is she dead?" I say, looking into Angharrad's eyes.

"She's no use to us dead, Todd," the Mayor says.

"She sure *looked* dead," Davy says.

"Only when she lost consciousness," the Mayor says. "Now, I've got a new job for the two of you."

There's a beat as we take in the words, *a new job*.

I close my eyes. *I am the Circle and the Circle is me*.

"Would you quit effing *saying* that?" Davy shouts at me.

But we can all hear the horror in his own Noise, the anxiety that's rising, the fear of his pa, of the *new job*, fear he won't be able to—

"You won't be leading the Askings, if that's what you're afraid of," says the Mayor.

"I ain't afraid," Davy says, too loud. "Who's saying I'm afraid?"

The Mayor drops the bag at our feet.

I reckernize its shape.

Feeling nothing, taking nothing in.

Davy's looking down at the bag, too. Even *he's* shocked.

"Just the prisoners," says the Mayor. "So we can fight against enemy infiltration on the inside."

"You want us to—?" Davy looks up at his pa. "On *people*?"

"Not people," says the Mayor. "Enemies of the state."

I'm still looking at the bag.

The bag that we all know carries a bolting tool and a supply of numbered bands.

30

THE BAND

(VIOLA)

I'VE JUST SET THE TIMER running and turned to Mistress Braithwaite to tell her we can leave when a woman comes tumbling out of the bushes behind us.

"Help me," she says, so gently it's almost as if she doesn't know we're there and is just asking the universe to help her somehow.

Then she collapses.

"What *is* this thing?" I say, taking another bandage from the too-small first aid kit we keep hidden in the cart, trying to tend her wound as we rock back and forth. There's a metal band encircling the middle of her forearm, so tight it seems like the skin around it is trying to grow *into* it. It's also so red with infection I can almost feel the heat coming off it.

"It's for branding livestock," Mistress Braithwaite says, angrily snapping the reins on the oxes, bumping us along paths that we aren't meant to take this fast. "That vicious *bastard*."

"Help me," the woman whispers.

"I'm helping you," I say. Her head is in my lap to cushion it from the bumps in the road. I wrap a bandage around the metal band but not before I see a number etched into the side.

1391.

"What's your name?" I ask.

But her eyes are half closed and all she says is, "Help me."

"And we're sure she's not a spy?" Mistress Coyle says, arms crossed.

"Good *God*," I snap. "Is there a stone where your heart should be?"

Her brow darkens. "We have to consider all manner of tricks–"

"The infection is so bad we're not going to be able to save her arm," Mistress Braithwaite says. "If she's a spy, she's in no position to return with information."

Mistress Coyle sighs. "Where was she?"

"Near that new Office of the Ask we've been hearing about," Mistress Braithwaite says, frowning even harder.

"We planted a device on a small storehouse nearby," I say. "It was as close as we could get."

"*Branding* strips, Nicola," Mistress Braithwaite says, anger puffing out of her like the steam of her breath.

Mistress Coyle rubs her fingers along her forehead. "I know."

"Can't we just cut it off?" I ask. "Heal the wound?"

Mistress Braithwaite shakes her head. "Chemicals make it so the banded skin never heals, that's the point. You can never remove it unless you want to bleed to death. They're permanent. *Forever*."

"Oh, my God."

"I need to talk to her," Mistress Coyle says.

"Nadari's treating her," Mistress Braithwaite says. "She might be lucid before the surgery."

"Let's go then," Mistress Coyle says and they head off toward the healing tent. I move to follow, but Mistress Coyle stops me with a look. "Not you, my girl."

"Why not?"

But off they keep walking, leaving me standing in the cold.

"Y'all right, Hildy?" Wilf asks as I wander among the oxes. He's brushing them down where they strained against the harnesses. **Wilf**, they say.

That's pretty much all they ever say.

"Rough night," I say. "We rescued a woman who'd been branded with some kind of metal band."

Wilf looks thoughtful for a minute. He points to a metal band around the right front leg of each ox. "Like these 'ere?"

I nod.

"On a person?" He whistles in amazement.

"Things are turning, Wilf," I say. "Turning for the worse."

"Ah know," he says. "We'll make a move soon and that'll be it, one way or t'other."

I look up at him. "Do you know exactly what she's planning?"

He shakes his head and runs his hand around the metal band on one of the oxes. **Wilf,** says the ox.

"Viola!" I hear, called across the camp.

Wilf and I both see Mistress Coyle treading through the darkened camp toward us. "She's gone wake everyone up," Wilf says.

"She's a little delirious," Mistress Nadari says as I kneel down by the cot of the rescued woman. "You've got a minute, tops."

"Tell her what you told us, my girl," Mistress Coyle says to the woman. "Just once more and we'll let you sleep."

"My arm?" says the woman, her eyes cloudy. "It don't hurt no more."

"Just tell her what you said, my love," Mistress Coyle says, her voice as warm as it ever gets. "And everything'll be all right."

The woman's eyes focus briefly on mine and widen slightly. "You," she says. "The girl who was there."

"Viola," I say, touching her nonbanded arm.

"We haven't got much time, Jess." Mistress Coyle's voice gets a little sterner, even as she says what must be the woman's name. "Tell her."

"Tell me what?" I say, getting a little annoyed. It's cruel to keep her awake like this and I'm about to say as much when Mistress Coyle says, "Tell her who did this to you."

Jess's eyes grow frightened. "Oh," she says. "Oh, oh."

"Just this one thing and we'll leave you be," Mistress Coyle says.

"Mistress Coyle–" I start to say, getting angry.

"*Boys,*" the woman says. "Boys. Not even men."

I take in a breath.

"Which boys?" Mistress Coyle asks. "What were their names?"

"Davy," says the woman, her eyes not seeing the inside of the tent anymore. "Davy was the older one."

Mistress Coyle catches my eye. "And the other?"

"The quiet one," the woman says. "Didn't say nothing. Just did his job and didn't say nothing."

"What was his name?" Mistress Coyle insists.

"I need to go," I say, standing up, not wanting to hear. Mistress Coyle grabs my hand and holds me there firmly.

"What was his name?" she says again.

The woman is breathing harshly now, almost panting.

"That's enough," Mistress Nadari says. "I didn't want this in the first–"

"One second more," Mistress Coyle says.

"Nicola–" Mistress Nadari warns.

"Todd," says the woman on the cot, the woman I saved, the woman with the infected arm she's going to lose, the woman I now wish was at the bottom of the ocean I've never seen. "The other one called him Todd."

"Get away from me," I say, as Mistress Coyle follows me out of the tent.

"He's alive," she's saying, "but he's one of them."

"Shut up!" I say, stomping across the camp, not caring how loud I'm being.

Mistress Coyle races forward and grabs my arm. "You've lost him, my girl," she says. "If you ever really had him in the first place."

I slap her face so fast and hard she doesn't have time to defend herself. It's like smacking a tree trunk. The solid weight of her staggers back and my arm rings with pain.

"You don't know what you're talking about," I say, my voice blazing.

"How *dare* you," she says, her hand to her face.

"You haven't even *seen* me fight yet," I say, standing my ground. "*I* knocked down a bridge to stop an army. *I* put a knife through the neck of a crazy murderer. *I* saved the lives of others while you just ran around at night blowing them up."

"You ignorant child–"

I step toward her.

She doesn't step back.

But she stops her sentence.

"I hate you," I say slowly. "Everything you do makes the Mayor respond with something *worse*."

"I did *not* start this war–"

"But you *love* it!" I take another step toward her. "You love every-thing about it. The bombs, the fighting, the rescues."

Her face is so angry I can even see it in the moonlight.

But I'm not afraid of her.

And I think she can tell.

"You want to see it as simple good and evil, my girl," she says. "The world doesn't work that way. Never has, never will, and don't forget." She gives me a smile that could curdle milk. "You're fighting the war *with* me."

I lean in close to her face. "He needs to be overthrown, so I'm helping you do it. But when it's done?" I'm so close I can feel her breath. "Are we going to have to overthrow you next?"

She doesn't say anything.

But she doesn't back down either.

I turn on my heels and I walk away from her.

"He's gone, Viola!" Mistress Coyle shouts after me.

But I just keep walking.

"I need to go back to the city."

"Now?" Wilf says, looking up at the sky. "Be dawn soon. T'ain't safe."

"It's *never* safe," I say, "but I have no choice."

He blinks at me. Then he starts gathering ropes and bindings to get the cart ready again.

"No," I say, "you'll have to show me how to do it. I can't ask you to risk your life."

"Yer goin for Todd?"

I nod.

"Then Ah'll take yoo."

"Wilf–"

"Still early," he says, backing the oxes into position. "Ah'll at least get yoo close."

He doesn't say another word as he reharnesses the oxes to his cart. They ask him **Wilf? Wilf?** in surprise at being used so quickly again after thinking their night of work was finished.

I think about what Jane would say. I think about putting her Wilf into danger.

But all I say is, "Thank you."

"I'm coming, too." I turn around. Lee is there, rubbing sleep out of his eyes but dressed and ready.

"What are you doing up?" I ask. "And no, you're not."

"Yes, I am," he says, "and who can sleep with all that shouting?"

"It's too dangerous," I say. "They'll hear your Noise–"

He keeps his mouth shut and says to me, Then they can just hear it.

"Lee–"

"You're going to look for him, aren't you?"

I sigh in frustration, beginning to wonder if I should abandon the idea altogether before I put anyone else in danger.

"You're going to the Office of the Ask," Lee says, lowering his voice.

I nod.

And then I understand.

Siobhan and his mum might be there.

I nod again, and this time he knows I've agreed.

No one tries to stop us, though half the camp must know we're going. Mistress Coyle must have her reasons.

We don't talk much as we go. I just listen to Lee's Noise and its thoughts of his family, of the Mayor, of what he'll do if he ever gets his hands on him.

Thoughts of me.

"You'd better say something," Lee says. "Listening that close is rude."

"So I've heard," I say.

But my mouth is dry and I find I don't have much to say.

The sun rises before we get to the city. Wilf pushes the oxes as fast as they'll go, but even so, it's going to be a dangerous trip back, with the city awake, with Noisy men on our cart. We're taking a terrible risk.

But on Wilf drives.

I've explained what I want to see, and he says he knows a place. He stops the cart deep in some woods and directs us up a bluff.

"Keep yer heads down now," he says. "Don't be seen."

"We won't," I say. "But if we're not back in an hour, don't wait for us."

Wilf just looks at me. We all know how likely him leaving us is.

Lee and I make our way up the bluff, keeping down in the cover of the trees, until we reach the top and see why Wilf chose the place. It's a hill near where the tower fell, one where we've got a clear view of the road coming down toward the Office of the Ask, which we've heard is some kind of prison or torture chamber or something like that.

I don't even want to know.

We lie on our stomachs, side by side, looking out from some bushes.

"Keep your ears open," Lee whispers.

As if we need to. As soon as the sun rises, New Prentisstown ROARs to life. I begin to wonder if Lee even needs to hide his Noise so much. How could it not be possible to drown in it?

"Because drowning is the right word," Lee says when I ask. "If you disappeared into it, you'd suffocate."

"I can't imagine what it's like growing up inside it all," I say.

"No," he says. "No, you can't."

But he doesn't say it in a mean way.

I squint down the road as the sun brightens. "I wish I had some binocs."

Lee reaches into a pocket and pulls out a pair.

I give him a look. "You were just waiting for me to ask so you could look all impressive."

"I don't know what you're talking about," he says, smiling, putting the binocs to his eyes.

"C'mon." I push him with my shoulder. "Give them to me."

He stretches away to keep them out of my grabbing range. I start to giggle, so does he. I grab onto him and try to hold him down while I snatch at the binocs but he's bigger than me and keeps twisting them away.

"I'm not afraid to hurt you," I say.

"I don't doubt that," he laughs, turning the binocs back to the road.

His Noise spikes, loud enough to make me afraid someone'll hear us.

"What do you see?" I say, not giggling anymore.

He hands the binocs to me, pointing. "There," he says. "Coming down the road."

But I'm already seeing them in the binocs.

Two people on horseback. Two people in shiny new uniforms, riding their horses. One of them talking, gesturing with his hands.

Laughing. Smiling.

The other keeping his eyes on his horse, but riding along to work.

Riding along to his job at the Office of the Ask.

In a uniform with a shiny *A* on the shoulder.
Todd.
My Todd.
Riding next to Davy Prentiss.
Riding to work with the man who shot me.

31

NUMBERS AND LETTERS

[TODD]

THE DAYS KEEP PASSING. They keep getting worse.

"*All* of 'em?" Davy asks, his Noise ringing with badly hidden alarm. "Every single one?"

"This is a vote of confidence, David," the Mayor says, standing with us at the door of the stables while our horses are made ready for the day's work. "You and Todd did such an excellent job with permanently identifying the female prisoners, who else would I want to be in charge of expanding the program?"

I don't say nothing, not even acknowledging Davy's looks at me. His Noise is confused with the pink of his pa's praise.

But then there's also his thoughts about banding all the women.

Every single one.

Cuz banding the ones in the Office of the Ask was even worse than we thought.

"They keep leaving," the Mayor says. "In the dead of night, they slip away and cast their lot with the terrorists."

Davy's watching Deadfall get saddled in a small paddock, his Noise clanking with the faces of the women who get banded, the cries of pain they make.

The words they speak to us.

"And if they keep getting out," the Mayor says, "they obviously keep getting in, too."

He means the bombs. One every night for the past two weeks nearly, so many they must be increasing for a reason, they must be leading up to something bigger, and no women have been caught planting 'em except once when a bomb blew up while the woman was still putting it in place. They didn't find much left of her except bits of clothing and flesh.

I close my eyes when I think of it.

Feeling nothing, taking nothing in.

(was it her?)

Feeling *nothing*.

"You want us to number *all* the women," Davy says again quietly, looking away from his pa.

"I've said it before," the Mayor sighs. "*Every* woman is part of the Answer, if only because she is a woman and therefore sympathetic to other women."

The groomsmen bring Angharrad into a nearby paddock. She sticks her head over the rail to bump me with her nose. **Todd,** she says.

"They'll resist," I say, stroking her head. "The men won't like it neither."

"Ah, yes," says the Mayor. "You missed yesterday's rally, didn't you?"

Davy and I look at each other. We were at work all day yesterday and didn't hear nothing bout no rally.

"I spoke to the men of New Prentisstown," the Mayor says. "Man to man. I explained to them the threat the Answer poses us and how this is the next prudent step forward to ensure safety for all." He rubs a hand down Angharrad's neck. I try and hide how prickly my Noise gets at the sight. "I encountered no resistance."

"There weren't no women at this rally," I say, "were there?"

He turns to me. "I wouldn't want to encourage the enemy among us, now would I?"

"But there's effing *thousands* of 'em!" Davy says. "Banding 'em all will take forever."

"There will be other teams working, David," the Mayor says calmly, making sure he's got his son's full attenshun. "But I'm sure the two of you will outwork any of them."

Davy's Noise perks up a bit at this. "You bet we will, Pa," he says.

He looks at me, tho.

And there's worry there.

I stroke Angharrad's nose again. The groomsmen bring out Morpeth, freshly brushed and shiny with oil. **Submit,** he says.

"If you're worried," the Mayor says, taking Morpeth's reins. "Ask yourselves this." He hoists himself up in the saddle in one smooth movement, like he's made of liquid. He looks down at us.

"Why would any innocent woman object to being identified?"

"You won't get away with this," the woman says, her voice almost steady.

Mr. Hammar cocks his rifle behind us and aims it at her head.

"You blind?" Davy says to the woman, voice a little too squeaky. "I'm getting away with it *right now*."

Mr. Hammar laughs.

Davy twists the bolting tool with a hard turn. The band snaps into the woman's skin halfway up her forearm. She calls out, grabbing the band and falling forward, catching herself on the floor with her unbanded arm. She stops there a minute, panting.

Her hair is pulled back into a severe knot, blondy and brown mixed together, like the wire filaments in the back of a vid player. There's a small patch on the back where the hair is gray, all growing together, a river across a dusty land.

I stare at the gray patch, letting my eyes blur a little.

I am the Circle and the Circle is me.

"Get up," Davy says to the woman. "So the healers can treat you." He looks back at the line of women staring at us down the hall to the front of the dormitory, waiting their turn.

"The boy said get up," Mr. Hammar says, waving his rifle.

"We don't need you here," Davy snaps, his voice tight. "We're doing just fine without no babysitter."

"I ain't babysitting," Mr. Hammar smiles. "I'm protecting."

The woman stands, her eyes on me.

My own expresshun is dead, removed, not here if it don't have to be.

I am the Circle and the Circle is me.

"Where's your heart?" she asks. "Where is your heart if you can do these things?" And then she turns to where the healers, who we've already banded, wait to give her treatment.

I watch her go.

I don't know her name.

Her number, tho, is 1484.

"1485!" Davy calls out.

The next woman in line steps forward.

We spend the day riding from one women's dormitory to another, getting thru almost three hundred bands, much faster than we ever did the

Spackle. We start for home when the sun begins to set, as New Prentisstown turns its thoughts to curfew.

We ain't saying much.

"What a day, eh, pigpiss?" Davy says, after a while.

I don't say nothing but he don't want an answer.

"They'll be all right," he says. "They got the healers to take away the pain and stuff."

Clop, clop, along we go.

I hear what he's thinking.

Dusk is falling. I can't see his face.

Maybe that's why he ain't covering it up.

"When they cry, tho," he says.

I keep quiet.

"Ain't you got nothing to say?" Davy's voice gets a little harder. "All silent now, like you don't wanna talk no more, like I ain't worth talking to."

His Noise starts to crackle.

"Not like I got anyone *else* to talk to, pigpiss. Not like I got any *choice* in the situashun. Not like no matter what I effing *do* can I get moved up for it, given the good work, the *fighting* work. All that stupid Spackle babysitting crap. Then we turn right around and do the same thing to the women. And for what? For *what*?"

His voice gets low.

"So they can cry at us," he says. "So they can look at us like we ain't even human."

"We ain't," I say, surprised to find I said it out loud.

"Yeah, that's the new you, ain't it?" he says, sneering. "All Mister No-Feeling-I-Am-The-Circle Tough Guy. You'd put a bullet thru yer own *ma*'s head if Pa told you to."

I don't say nothing but I grind my teeth together.

Davy's quiet for a minute, too. Then he says, "Sorry."

Then he says, "Sorry, Todd," using my name.

Then he says, "What the hell am *I* saying sorry for? Yer the stupid can't-read pigpiss all getting on my pa's good side. Who cares about you?"

I still don't say nothing and *clop, clop*, along we go.

"Forward," Angharrad neighs to Deadfall, who nickers back, "Forward."

Forward, I hear in her Noise and then **Boy colt, Todd.**

"Angharrad," I whisper twixt her ears.

"Todd?" Davy says.

"Yeah?" I say.

I hear him breathe out thru his nose. "Nothing." Then he changes his mind. "How d'you *do* it?"

"Do what?"

I see him shrug in the dusk. "Be so calm bout it all. Be so, I don't know, *unfeeling*. I mean . . ." He drifts off and says, almost too quietly to hear, one more time, "When they cry."

I don't say nothing cuz how can I help him? How can he not know about *The Circle* unless his pa don't want him to?

"I *do* know," he says, "but I tried that crap and it don't work for me and he won't—"

He stops abruptly, like he's said too much.

"Ah, screw it," he says.

We keep riding, letting the ROAR of New Prentisstown enfold us as we enter the main part of town, the horses calling their orders to each other, reminding theirselves of who they are.

"Yer the only friend I got, pigpiss," Davy finally says. "Ain't that the biggest tragedy you ever heard?"

"Tiring day?" Mayor Ledger says to me when I come into our cell. His voice is oddly light and he keeps his eyes on me.

"What do you care?" I sling my bag on the floor and flop down on the bed without taking my uniform off.

"I suppose it must be exhausting torturing women all day."

I blink in surprise. "I don't torture 'em," I growl. "You shut yer mouth about that."

"No, of *course* you don't torture them. What was I thinking? You just strap a corrosive metal band into their skin that can never be removed without them bleeding to death. How could that possibly be construed as *torture*?"

"Hey!" I sit up. "We do it fast and without fuss. There are lots of ways to make it worse and we don't do that. If it's gotta be done, then it's best that it's done by *us*."

He crosses his arms, his voice still light. "That excuse going to help you sleep tonight?"

My Noise roars up. "Oh, yeah?" I snap. "Was that you the Mayor didn't hear shouting at the rally yesterday? Was that you who weren't making that brave stand against him?"

His face goes stormy and I hear a flash of gray resentment in his Noise. "And get shot?" he says. "Or dragged away to be Asked? How would that help anything?"

"And that's what yer doing?" I say. "*Helping*?"

He don't say nothing to that, just turns to look out one of the windows, out over the few lights that come on only in essenshul places, out

over the **ROAR** of a town wondering when the Answer are gonna make
their big move and from where and how bad it'll be and who's gonna
save 'em.

My Noise is raised and red. I close my eyes and take in a deep, deep
breath.

I am the Circle and the Circle is me.

Feeling nothing, taking nothing in.

"They were getting used to him again," Mayor Ledger says out the
window. "They were uniting behind him because what're a few curfews
against being blown up? But this is a tactical mistake."

I open my eyes at "tactical" cuz it seems a weird word to choose.

"The men are terrified now," he's still saying. "Terrified they're going
to be next." He looks down at his own forearm, rubbing a spot where a
band might go. "Politically, he's made a mistake."

I squint at him. "What do you care if he's made a mistake?" I ask.
"Whose side are you on?"

He turns to me as if I've insulted him, which I guess I have. "The
town's," he steams. "Whose side are you on, Todd Hewitt?"

There's a knock on the door.

"Saved by the dinner bell," Mayor Ledger says.

"The dinner bell don't knock," I say, getting to my feet. I unlock the
door with my key *ker-thunk* and open it.

It's Davy.

He don't say nothing at first, just looks nervous, eyes here and there. I
figure there's a problem at the dormitories so I sigh and move back to
my bed to get my few things. I ain't even had time to get my boots off.

"It'll take a minute," I say to him. "Angharrad'll still be eating. She
won't like being saddled up again so soon."

He still ain't said nothing so I turn to look at him. He's still nervous,
not meeting my eye. "*What?*" I say.

He chews on his upper lip and all I can see in his Noise is embarrassment and asking marks and anger at Mayor Ledger being there and
more asking marks and there behind it all, a weird strong feeling, almost
guilty, almost *clear*–

Then he covers it up fast and the anger and embarrassment come
foremost.

"Effing pigpiss," he says to himself. He pulls angrily at a strap on his
shoulder and I see he's carrying a bag. "Effing . . ." he says again but don't
finish the thought. He unsnaps the flap on it and takes something out.

"*Here*," he practically shouts, thrusting it at me.

My ma's book.

He's giving me back my ma's book.

"Just take it!"

I reach out slowly, taking it twixt my fingers and pulling it away from him like it was a fragile thing. The leather of the cover is still soft, the gash still cut thru the front where Aaron stabbed me and it was stopped by the book. I run my hand over it.

I look up at Davy but he won't meet my eye.

"Whatever," he says and turns again, stomping back down the stairs and out into the night.

32

FINAL PREPARATIONS

{VIOLA}

I HIDE BEHIND THE TREE, my heart pounding.

I have a gun in my hand.

I listen hard for the snap of twigs, the sound of any footsteps, any sign that'll tell me where the soldier is. I know he's there because I can hear his Noise but it's so flat and wide I only get a general idea of the direction he's going to come after me.

Because he *is* coming for me. There's no doubt about that.

His Noise grows louder. My back is to the tree and I hear him off to my left.

I'm going to have to leap at just the right second.

I ready my gun.

I see the trees around me in his Noise, along with asking marks wondering which one I'm hiding behind, narrowing it down to two, the one that I'm actually using and one a few feet away to my left.

If he chooses that one, I've got him.

I hear his steps now, quiet against the damp forest floor. I close my eyes and try to concentrate solely on his Noise, on exactly where he's standing, where he's placing his feet.

Which tree he's approaching.

He steps. He hesitates. He steps again.

He makes his choice–

And I make mine–

I jump and I'm ducking and twisting and sweeping my leg at his feet and I'm catching him by surprise and he's falling to the ground, trying to aim his rifle at me, but I'm leaping on him and pinning his rifle arm down with my leg and throwing my weight on his chest and holding the barrel of my gun under his chin.

I've got him.

"Well done," Lee says, smiling up at me.

"Indeed, well done," Mistress Braithwaite says, stepping out of the darkness. "And now comes the moment, Viola. What do you do with the enemy under your mercy?"

I look down into Lee's face, breathing hard, feeling his warmth underneath me.

"What do you do?" Mistress Braithwaite asks again.

I look down at my gun.

"I do what I have to do," I say.

I do what I have to do to save him.

I do what I have to do to save Todd.

"You're *sure* you want to do this?" Mistress Coyle asks for the hundredth time as we leave the breakfast area the next morning, shaking off Jane's last insistences that we have more tea.

"I'm sure," I say.

"You've got one chance before we make our move. *One*."

"He came for me once," I say. "When I was captive, he came for me and made the biggest sacrifice he could make to do it."

She frowns. "People change, Viola."

"He deserves the same chance he gave me."

"Hmm," Mistress Coyle hmms. She's still not convinced.

But I haven't given her any choice.

"And when he joins us," I say, "think of the information he can provide."

"Yes." She looks away, looks out at the camp of the Answer preparing itself. Preparing itself for war. "Yes, so you keep saying."

Even with how well I know Todd, I can also see how anyone else would see him on horseback, would see him in that uniform, would see him riding with Davy, and they would think he's a traitor.

And in the dead of night, when I'm under my blankets, unable to sleep.

I think it, too.

(what's he doing?)

(what's he doing with *Davy*?)

And I try to put it out of my mind as best I can.

Because I'm going to save him.

She's agreed that I can. She's agreed I can risk myself and go to the cathedral the night before the Answer makes its final attack and try one last time to save him.

She agreed because I said if she didn't, I wouldn't help her with anything more, not with the bombs, not with the final attack, not with the ships when they land, now eight weeks away and counting. Nothing, if I couldn't try for Todd.

Even with all that, I think the only reason she agreed is for what he could tell us when he got here.

Mistress Coyle *likes* to know things.

"You're brave to try," Mistress Coyle says. "Foolish, but brave." She looks me up and down once more, her face unknowable.

"What?" I ask.

She shakes her head. "Just how much of myself I see in you, you exasperating girl."

"Think I'm ready to lead my own army?" I say, almost smiling.

She just gives me a last look and starts walking off into the camp, ready to give more orders, make more preparations, put the final touches to the plans for our attack.

Which happens tomorrow.

"Mistress Coyle," I call after her.

She turns.

"Thank you," I say.

She looks surprised, her forehead furrowed. But she nods, accepting it.

"Got it?" Lee calls over the top of the cart.

"Got it," I say, twisting the final knot and locking the clamp into place.

"'At's all of 'em," Wilf says, smacking some dust off his hands. We look at the carts, eleven of them now, packed to bursting with supplies, with weapons, with explosives. Almost the entire stash of the Answer.

Eleven carts doesn't seem like much against an army of a thousand or more, but that's what we have.

"Bin done before," Wilf says, quoting Mistress Coyle, but he's always so dry you never know if he's making fun. "Only a matter a tactics."

And then he smiles the same mysterious smile Mistress Coyle always gives. It's so funny and unexpected, I laugh out loud.

Lee doesn't, though. "Yes, her top secret plan." He pulls a rope on the cart to test that it holds.

"I expect it has to do with him," I say. "*Getting* him, somehow, and then once he's gone–"

"His army will fall apart and the town will rise up against his tyranny and we'll save the day," Lee says, sounding unconvinced. He looks at Wilf. "What do you think?"

"She says it'll be the end." Wilf shrugs. "Ah want it to be done."

Mistress Coyle does keep saying that, that this could end the whole conflict, that the right blow in the right place right *now* could be all we need, that if even just the women of the town join us we could topple him before winter comes, topple him before the ships land, topple him before he finds us.

And then Lee says, "I know something I shouldn't."

Wilf and I both look at him.

"She passed by the kitchen window with Mistress Braithwaite," he says. "They were talking about where the attack will come from tomorrow."

"Lee–" I say.

"Don't say it," Wilf says.

"It's from the hill to the south of town," he presses on, opening his Noise so we can't *not* hear it. "The one with the notch in it, the one with the smaller road that leads right into the town square."

Wilf's eyes bulge. "Yoo shouldn'ta *said*. If Hildy gets caught–"

But Lee's only looking at me. "If you get into trouble," he says. "You come running toward that hill. You come running and that's where you'll find help."

And his Noise says, That's where you'll find me.

"And with burdened hearts, we commit you to the earth."

One by one, we throw a handful of dirt on the empty coffin that doesn't contain anything of the body of Mistress Forth, blown to pieces when a bomb went off too early as she was planting it on a grain house.

The sun is setting when we finish, dusk shining cold across the lake, a lake that had a layer of ice around the edges this morning that didn't melt all day. People start to spread out for the night's work, last-minute packing and orders to be received, all the women

and men who will soon be soldiers, marching with weapons, ready
to strike the final blow.

All they look like now are ordinary people.

I'll leave tonight as soon as it's fully dark.

They'll leave tomorrow at sunset, no matter what happens
to me.

"It's time," Mistress Coyle says, coming to my side.

She doesn't mean it's time to leave.

There's something else that has to happen first.

"Are you ready?" she asks.

"As I'll ever be," I say, walking along with her.

"This is a huge risk we're taking, my girl. *Huge.* If you're caught–"

"I won't be."

"But if you are." She stops us. "If you are, you know where the
camp is, you know when we're attacking, and I'm going to tell you
now that we're attacking from the east road, the one by the Office
of the Ask. We're going to march into town and ram it down his
throat." She takes both my hands and stares hard into my eyes. "Do
you understand what I'm telling you?"

I do understand. I do. She's telling me wrong on purpose, she's
telling me so I can truthfully give the wrong information if I'm
caught, like she did before about the ocean.

It's what I'd do if I were her.

"I understand," I say.

She pulls her cloak farther shut against a freezing breeze that's
come up. We walk in silence for a few steps, heading toward the
healing tent.

"Who did you save?" I ask.

"What?" She looks at me, genuinely confused.

We stop again. Which is fine with me. "All those years ago," I
say. "Corinne said you were kicked off the Council for saving a life.
Who did you save?"

She looks at me thoughtfully and rubs her fingers across her
forehead.

"I may not return," I say. "You may never see me again. It'd be
nice to know something good about you so I don't die thinking
you're just a huge pain in my ass."

She almost grins but it disappears quickly, her eyes looking
troubled again. "Who did I save?" she says to herself. She takes a
deep breath. "I saved an enemy of the state."

"You *what?*"

"The Answer was never exactly authorized, you see." She walks us off in a different direction, toward the shore of the freezing lake. "The men fighting the Spackle War didn't really approve of our methods, effective as they might have been." She looks back at me. "And they were *very* effective. Effective enough to get the heads of the Answer onto the ruling Council when Haven was being put back together."

"That's why you think it'll work now. Why you think it'll work against a bigger force."

She nods and rubs her forehead again. I'm surprised she hasn't built up a callus there. "Haven restarted itself," she continues, "using the captured Spackle to rebuild and so on. But some people weren't happy with the new government. Some people didn't have as much power as they thought they should." She shivers under her cloak. "Some people in the Answer."

She lets me realize what this might mean. "Bombs," I say.

"Quite so. Some people get so caught up in warfare, they start doing it for its own sake."

She turns away, so that maybe I can't see her face or that maybe she can't see mine, see the judgment on it.

"Her name was Mistress Thrace." She's talking to the lake now, to the cold night sky. "Smart, strong, respected, but with a liking for being in charge. Which was exactly the reason no one wanted her on the Council, including the Answer, and why she reacted so strongly to being left off."

She turns back to me. "She had her supporters. And she had her bombing campaign. Not unlike the one we're giving the Mayor now, except of course, that was meant to be peacetime." She glances up at the moons. "She specialized in what we took to calling a Thrace bomb. She'd leave it somewhere soldiers were gathered and it would look like an innocent package. Wouldn't arm itself until it felt the heartbeat in the skin of the hand picking it up. Your own pulse would make it dangerous, and at that point, you knew it was a bomb and that it would only go off when you let it go. So if you dropped it or couldn't disarm it . . ." She shrugs. "Boom."

We watch a cloud pass between the two rising moons. "Meant to be bad luck, that is," Mistress Coyle murmurs.

She loops her arm in mine again and we start walking back toward the healing tent. "And so there wasn't another war exactly," she says. "More of a skirmish. And to the delight of everyone, Mistress Thrace was mortally wounded."

There's a silence where you can only hear our footsteps and the Noise of the men, crisp in the air.

"But not mortally wounded after all," I say.

She shakes her head. "I'm a very good healer." We reach the opening of the healing tent. "I'd known her since we were girls together on Old World. As far as I saw it, I had no choice." She rubs her hands together. "They kicked me off the Council for it. And then they executed her anyway."

I look at her now, trying to understand her, trying to understand all that's good in her and all that's difficult and conflicted and all the things that went into making her the person that she is.

We are the choices we make. And *have* to make. We aren't anything else.

"Are you ready?" she says again, finally this time.

"I'm ready."

We go into the tent.

My bag is there, packed by Mistress Coyle herself, the one I'll carry on the cart with Wilf, the one I'll carry into town. It's full of food, completely innocent food which, if all goes according to plan, will be my entry into town, my entry past the guards, my entry into the cathedral.

If all goes well.

If it doesn't, there's a pistol in a secret pouch at the bottom.

Mistresses Lawson and Braithwaite are also in the tent, healing materials at the ready.

And Lee is there, as I'd asked him to be.

I sit down on the chair facing him.

He takes my hand and squeezes it and I feel a note in the palm of his hand. He looks at me, his Noise filled with what's about to happen.

I open the note, keeping its contents out of view of all three mistresses around me, who no doubt think it's something romantic or stupid like that.

Don't react, it reads. *I've decided I'm coming with you. I'll meet your cart in the woods. You want to find your family, I want to find mine, and neither of us should do it alone.*

I don't react. I refold the note and look back up at him, giving him the smallest of nods.

"Good luck, Viola," Mistress Coyle says, words echoed rapidly by everyone else there, ending with Lee.

I wanted him particularly to do this. I couldn't stand for it to have been Mistress Coyle, and I know Lee will take the best care.

Because there's only one way I'm going to be able to move around New Prentisstown without getting caught. Only one way based on the intelligence we've gathered.

Only one way I can find Todd.

"Are you ready?" Lee asks, and it feels different coming from him, so much so that I don't mind being asked yet again.

"I'm ready," I say.

I hold out my arm and roll up my sleeve.

"Just make it quick." I look into Lee's eyes. "Please."

"I will," he says.

He reaches into the bag at his feet and takes out a metal band marked 1391.

33

FATHERS AND SONS

[TODD]

"DID HE TELL YOU what he wanted?" Davy asks.

"When would I have talked to him when you weren't there?" I say.

"Duh, pigpiss, you live in the same *building*."

We're riding to the Office of the Ask, the sun setting on the end of our day. Two hundred more women labeled. It goes faster with Mr. Hammar watching over it all with a gun. With the other teams around town led by Mr. Morgan and Mr. O'Hare, word is we've got nearly every one of 'em, tho the bands don't seem to be healing as fast on women as they do on sheep or Spackle.

I look up at the dusky sky as we move along the road and I realize something. "Where do *you* live?"

"Oh, *now* he asks." Davy slaps the reins on Deadfall/Acorn, causing him to canter for about two steps and then drop back into a trot. "Five months we're working together almost."

"I'm asking now."

Davy's Noise is buzzing a little. He don't wanna answer, I can tell.

"You don't have to—"

"Above the stables," he says. "Little room. Mattress on a floor. Smells like horseshit."

We keep on riding. "Forward," Angharrad nickers. "Forward," Deadfall nickers back. Todd, Angharrad thinks. "Angharrad," I say.

Davy and I ain't talked about my ma's book since he brought it to me four nights back. Not a word. And any sign of it in either of our Noises gets ignored.

But we're talking more.

I begin to wonder what sort of man I'd be if I'd had the Mayor as a father. I begin to wonder what sort of man I'd be if I'd had the Mayor as a father and wasn't the son he wanted. I wonder if I'd be sleeping in a room over the stables.

"I try," Davy says, quiet. "But who knows what he effing *wants*?"

I don't know so I don't say nothing.

We tie up our horses at the front gates. Ivan tries to catch my eye again as I go inside but I don't let him.

"Todd," he says as we pass, trying harder.

"That's Mr. Hewitt to you, *Private*," Davy spits at him.

I keep on walking. We take the short path from the gates to the front doors of the Office of the Ask building. Soldiers guard those doors, too, but we walk on past 'em into the entryway, across the cold concrete floor, still uncovered, still unheated, and go into the same viewing room as before.

"Ah, boys, welcome," the Mayor says, turning away from the mirror to greet us.

Behind him, in the Arena of the Ask, is Mr. Hammar, wearing a rubber apron. Seated in front of him, a naked man is screaming.

The Mayor presses a button, cutting off the sound mid-cry.

"I understand the identification scheme is complete?" he asks, bright and clear.

"As far as we know," I say.

"Who's that?" Davy asks, pointing at the man.

"Son of the exploded terrorist," the Mayor says. "Didn't run when his mother did, foolish man. Now we're seeing what he knows."

Davy curls his lip. "But if he didn't run off when she did—"

"You both have done a tremendous job for me," the Mayor says, clasping his hands behind his back. "I'm very pleased."

Davy smiles and the pink rush fills his Noise.

"But the threat is finally upon us," the Mayor continues. "One of the original terrorists caught in the prison attack finally told us something useful." He looks back thru the mirror. Mr. Hammar is blocking most of the view but the man's bare feet are curling tightly against whatever Mr. Hammar's doing to him. "Before she unfortunately passed away, she was able to tell us that, based on the patterns of the recent bombings, we can almost certainly expect a major move by the Answer within days, perhaps as soon as tomorrow."

Davy glances over to me. I keep looking at a middle point beyond the Mayor on the blank wall behind.

"They'll be defeated, of course," says the Mayor. "Easily. Their force is so much smaller than ours that I can't see it lasting more than a day at most."

"Let us fight, Pa," Davy says eagerly. "You know we're ready."

The Mayor smiles, smiles at his own son. Davy's Noise goes so pink you can't hardly look at it.

"You're being promoted, David," the Mayor says. "Into an army position. You will be Sergeant Prentiss."

Davy's smile almost explodes off his face in a little boom of pleased Noise. "Hot damn," he says, as if we weren't there.

"You will be at Captain Hammar's side as he rides into battle at the front of the first wave," the Mayor says. "You will get your fight exactly as you want."

Davy's practically glowing. "Aw, man, *thanks*, Pa!"

The Mayor turns to me. "I'm making you Lieutenant Hewitt."

Davy's Noise gives a sharp change. "*Lieutenant?*"

"You will be my personal bodyguard from the moment the fighting starts," the Mayor goes on. "You will remain by my side, protecting me from any threats that may approach while I superintend the battle."

I don't say nothing, just keep my eyes on the blank wall.

I am the Circle and the Circle is me.

"And this is how the Circle turns, Todd," says the Mayor.

"Why does he get to be a lieutenant?" Davy asks, Noise crackling.

"Lieutenant isn't a battle rank," the Mayor says smoothly. "Sergeant is. If you weren't a sergeant, you wouldn't be able to fight."

"Oh," Davy says, looking back and forth to each of us to see if he's being made a fool of. I don't think nothing about that.

"There's no need to thank me, Lieutenant," the Mayor teases.

"Thank you," I say, my eyes still on the wall.

"It keeps you from doing what you don't want," he says. "It keeps you from having to kill."

"Unless someone comes after you," I say.

"Unless someone comes after me, yes. Will that be a problem for you, Todd?"

"No," I say. "No, sir."

"Good," says the Mayor.

I look back thru the mirror. The naked man's head has lolled lifelessly onto his chest, drool dripping from his slack jaw. Mr. Hammar is angrily taking off his gloves and slapping them on a table.

"I am very blessed," the Mayor says warmly. "I have achieved my ambition to put this planet back on track. Within days, maybe even hours, I will crush the terrorists. And when the new settlers come, it will be me who puts out a proud and peaceful hand to welcome them."

He raises his hands, like he can't wait to start putting 'em out. "And who will be right beside me?" He holds his hands out to the two of us. "Both of you."

Davy, buzzing pink all over, reaches out and takes his pa's hand.

"I came into this town with one son," the Mayor says still holding out his hand to me, "but it has blessed me with another."

And his hand is out, waiting for me to take it.

Waiting for his second son to shake his hand.

"Congrats, *Lieutenant* Pigpiss," Davy says, hopping back into Deadfall's saddle.

"Todd?" Ivan says, stepping away from his post as I climb onto Angharrad. "Can I have a word?"

"He outranks you now," Davy says to him. "You'll address him as Lieutenant if you don't want to be digging bogs on the front lines."

Ivan takes in a deep breath, as if to calm himself. "Very well, *Lieutenant*, may I have a word with you?"

I look down on him from Angharrad's back. Ivan's Noise is busting with violence and the gunshot to his leg and conspiracies and resentments and ways to get back at the Mayor, openly thought, as if to impress me.

"You should keep that quiet," I say. "You never know who might hear."

I slap Angharrad's reins and off we go back down the road. Ivan's Noise follows me as I go. I ignore it.

Feeling nothing, taking nothing in.

"He called you *son*," Davy says, looking ahead as the sun disappears behind the falls. "Guess that makes us brothers."

I don't say nothing.

"We should do something to celebrate," Davy says.

"Where?" I say. "*How?*"

"Well, we're officers now, ain't we, brother? It's my understanding officers get *privileges*." He looks over at me sideways, his Noise bright as a flare, filled with things I used to see all the time in old Prentisstown.

Pictures of women with no clothes.

I frown and send him back a picture of a woman with no clothes and a band on her arm.

"So?" Davy says.

"Yer sick."

"No, brother, yer talking to *Sergeant* Prentiss. I may finally be *well*."

He laughs and laughs. He feels so good some of it actually touches my own Noise, brightening it whether I want it brightened or not.

"Oh, come *on*, Lieutenant Pigpiss, you ain't still pining for yer girl, are ya? She left you *months* ago. We need to get you someone new."

"Shut up, Davy."

"Shut up, *Sergeant* Davy." And he laughs again. "Fine, fine, you just stay at home, read yer book–"

He stops himself suddenly. "Oh, damn, sorry, no, I didn't mean that. I forgot."

And the weird thing is, he seems sincere.

There's a moment of quiet where his Noise pulses again with that strong feeling he's hiding–

That something he's trying to bury that makes him feel–

And then he says, "You know . . ." and I can see the offer coming and I don't think I can bear it, I don't think I could live another minute if he says it out loud. "If you ever wanted me to read it for–"

"No, Davy," I say quickly. "No, thanks, no."

"You sure?"

"*Yes*."

"Well, the offer's there." His Noise goes bright again, blooming as he thinks about his new title, about women, about me and him as brothers.

And he whistles happily all the way back to town.

I lay on my bed with my back turned to Mayor Ledger, who's chomping down his dinner as usual. I'm eating, too, but I've also got my ma's book out, just looking at it, lying on the blankets.

"People are wondering when the big attack's gonna happen," Mayor Ledger says.

I don't answer him. I run my hand over the cover of the book like I do every night, feeling the leather, touching the tear where the knife went in with the tips of my fingers.

"People are saying it'll be soon."

"Whatever you say." I open the cover. Ben's folded map is still inside, still where I stashed it. It don't even look like Davy bothered to open the book, not once in the whole time he had it. It smells a bit like stables, now that I know where it's been, but it's still the book, still *her* book.

My ma. My ma's words.

Look what's become of yer son.

Mayor Ledger sighs loudly. "They're going to attack here, you know," he says. "You'll have to let me out if that happens."

"Can't you keep quiet for five seconds?" I turn to the first page, the first entry my ma wrote on the day I was born. A page full of words I once heard read out.

(read out by–)

"No gun, no weapon." Mayor Ledger's standing now, looking out the windows again. "I'm defenseless."

"I'll take care of you," I say, "now *shut the hell up*."

I'm still not turned to him. I'm looking at my ma's first words, the ones written in her hand. I know what they say but I try to sound them out across the page.

Muh-y. My. It's *My*. I take a deep breath. *Dee. Dee-arr. Dee-arr-ess. Dee-arr-ess-tuh*. Which is *Dearest*, which seems mostly right. *My Dearest*. And the last word is *Son*, which I know, having heard it so clearly today.

I think about his outstretched hand.

I think about when I took it.

My Dearest Son.

"I've offered to read that for you," Mayor Ledger says, not able to hide his groan at the sound of my reading Noise.

I turn round to him, looking fierce. "I said, *shut up!*"

He holds his hands up. "Fine, fine, whatever you say." He sits back down and adds a last sarcastic word under his breath. "*Lieutenant*."

I sit up. Then I sit up higher. "What did you say?"

"Nothing." He won't meet my eye.

"I didn't tell you that," I say. "I didn't say a word."

"It was in your Noise."

"No, it wasn't." I'm getting to my feet now. Cuz I'm right. I ain't been thinking bout nothing since I came in for dinner except my ma's book. "*How did you know?*"

He looks up at me but there ain't no words coming outta his mouth and his Noise is scrambling for something to say.

And it's failing.

I take a step toward him.

There's a *ker-thunk* at the door and Mr. Collins lets himself in. "There's someone here for you," he says to me, then he notices my Noise. "What's going on?"

"I ain't expecting no one," I say, still staring at Mayor Ledger.

"It's a girl," Mr. Collins says. "She says Davy sent her."

"Dammit," I say. "I *told* him."

"Whatever," he says. "Says she won't talk to no one but you." He chuckles. "Pretty little piece, too."

I turn at the tone of his voice. "Leave her alone, whoever she is. That ain't right."

"Best not take too long up here then." He's laughing as he shuts the door.

I stare back at Mayor Ledger, my Noise still high. "I ain't thru with you."

"It was in your *Noise*," he says, but I'm already out the door and locking it behind me. *Ker-thunk.*

I stomp my way down the stairs, thinking of ways to get the girl away without Mr. Collins bothering her, without her having to go thru any of that for any reason, and my Noise is boiling with suspishuns and wonderings about Mayor Ledger and things beginning to come clear when I get to the bottom of the steps.

Mr. Collins is waiting, leaning against the wall of the lobby with his legs crossed, all relaxed and smiling. He points with his thumb.

I look over.

And there she is.

34

LAST CHANCE

{VIOLA}

"LEAVE US," Todd says to the man who let me in, not looking away from me when he says it.

"*Told* you she was a piece," the man says, smirking as he disappears into a side office.

Todd stands there staring. "It's you," he says.

But he isn't moving toward me.

"Todd," I say and I take a step forward.

And he takes a step back.

I stop.

"Who's this?" he says, looking at Lee, who's doing his best to act like a real soldier behind me.

"That's Lee," I say. "A friend. He's come with me to–"

"What are you doing here?"

"I've come to get you," I say. "I've come to rescue you."

I see him swallow. I see his throat working. "Viola," he finally says. My name is all over his Noise, too. Viola Viola Viola.

He puts his hands up to the sides of his head, grabbing his hair, which is longer and shaggier than when I saw it last.

He looks taller, too.

"Viola," he says again.

"It's me," I say and I take another step forward. He doesn't step back so I keep coming, crossing the lobby, not running, just getting closer and closer to him.

But when I get to him, he steps back again.

"Todd?" I ask.

"What are you *doing* here?"

"I've come for you." I feel my stomach sink a little. "I said I would."

"You said you wouldn't leave without me," he says and in his Noise I can hear loud irritation at how he sounds. He clears his throat. "You *left* me here."

"They took me," I say. "I had no choice."

His Noise is getting louder now and though I can feel happiness in it–

Oh, Jesus, Todd, there's *rage*, too.

"What have I done?" I say. "We need to go. The Answer are going–"

"So yer part of the Answer now?" he snaps, bitterness suddenly rising. "Part of those *murderers*."

"Are you a soldier now then?" I say back, surprised, heat growing in my voice, too, pointing to the *A* on his sleeve. "Don't talk to me about *murder*."

"The Answer killed the Spackle," he says, his voice low and angry.

And the bodies of the Spackle in his Noise.

Piled high, one upon the other, tossed there like garbage.

The *A* of the Answer written on the wall.

And Todd in the middle of it.

"They might as well have killed me along with them," he says.

He closes his eyes.

I am the Circle and the Circle is me, I hear.

"Viola?" Lee says from behind me. I turn. He's crossed half the lobby.

"Wait outside," I say.

"Viola–"

"*Outside*."

He looks so concerned, so ready to fight for me, my heart skips a little. He broadcast as loud as he could that I was his prisoner on the way here, so loud other soldiers thought he was covering up for a rape he was going to commit and whistled him good luck as we passed. Then we hid by the cathedral, seeing Davy Prentiss riding away from here, thinking things I wouldn't want to see again, thinking about how a *celebration* was due to him and Todd.

And so we pretended to be the celebration.

And it worked.

Kind of upsetting how easily it worked, frankly.

Lee shifts from foot to foot. "You call me if you need me."

"I will," I say, and he waits a second, then steps out the front door, keeping it open to watch us.

Todd's eyes are still closed and he repeats *I am the Circle and the Circle is me* which I have to say sounds an awful lot like something from the Mayor.

"We didn't kill the Spackle," I say.

"*We?*" he says, opening his eyes.

"I don't know who did it, but it wasn't us."

"You sent a bomb to kill them the day *you* blew up the tower." He's almost spitting the words. "Then you came back on the day of the prison break and finished the job."

"Bomb?" I say. "What bomb—?"

But then I remember—

The first explosion that made the soldiers run away from the communications tower.

No.

She wouldn't.

No, not even her. *What kind of people do you think we are?* she said—

But she never did answer the asking.

No, *no*, it's not true and besides—

"Who told you that?" I say. "Davy Prentiss?"

He blinks. "What?"

"What do you mean *what*?" My voice is harder now. "Your new best friend. The man who *shot* me, Todd, and who you ride to work with laughing every morning."

He clenches his hands into fists.

"You been *spying* on me?" he says. "Three months I don't see you, three months I don't hear *nothing* from you and you been *spying*? Is that what yer doing in yer spare time when yer not blowing people up?"

"Yeah!" I yell, my voice getting louder to match his. "Three months of defending you to people who'd be only too happy to call you enemy, Todd. Three months of wondering why the hell you're working so hard for the Mayor and how he knew to go right for the ocean the day after we spoke." He winces, but I keep going, thrusting out my arm and pulling up the sleeve. "Three months wondering why you put *these* on women!"

His face changes in an instant. He actually calls out as if he felt the pain himself. He puts a hand over his mouth to stifle it but his Noise is suddenly washed with blackness. He moves the fingertips of his other hand within reach of the band, hovering over my skin, over the band that'll never be removed unless I lose my arm. The skin is still red, and band 1391 still throbs, despite the healing of three mistresses.

"Oh, no," he says. "Oh, no."

The side door opens and the man who let me in leans out. "Everything all right out here, Lieutenant?"

"Lieutenant?" I say.

"We're fine," Todd chokes a little. "We're fine."

The man waits for a second, then goes back inside.

"*Lieutenant?*" I say again, lowering my voice.

Todd's leaned down, his hands on his knees, staring at the floor. "It wasn't me, was it?" he says, his voice quiet, too. "I didn't–" He gestures again at the band without looking up. "I didn't do it without knowing it was you, did I?"

"No," I say, reading things in his Noise, reading his numbness at them, reading all the horror that sits way down below that he's working so hard to ignore. "The Answer did it."

He looks up fast, filled with asking marks.

"It was the only way I could come and find you safely," I say. "The only way I could get past all the soldiers marching around town was if they thought I'd already been banded."

His face changes again as this sinks in. "Oh, Viola."

I breathe out heavily. "Todd," I say. "Please come with me."

His eyes are wet but I can see him now, I can see him finally, I can see him in his face and in his Noise and in his arms as they drop to his sides in defeat.

"It's too late," he says and his voice is so sad my own eyes start to wet. "I've been dead, Viola. I've been dead."

"You haven't," I say, moving a bit closer to him. "These are impossible times."

He's looking down now, his eyes not focused on anything.

Feeling nothing, his Noise says. Taking nothing in.

I am the Circle and the Circle is me.

"Todd?" I say, and I'm close enough to reach his hand. "Todd, look at me."

He looks up and the loss in his Noise is so great it feels like I'm standing on the edge of an abyss, that I'm about to fall down *into* him, into blackness so empty and lonely there'd never be a way out.

"Todd," I say again, a catch in my voice. "On the ledge, under the waterfall, do you remember what you said to me? Do you remember what you said to save me?"

He's shaking his head slowly. "I've done terrible things, Viola. *Terrible* things–"

"*We all fall*, you said." I'm gripping him hard now. "We all fall but that's not what matters. What matters is picking yourself up again."

But he shakes me off.

"No," he says, turning away. "No, it was easier when you weren't here. It was easier when you couldn't see–"

"Todd, I've come to save you–"

"*No.* I didn't have to think about nothing–"

"It's not too late."

"It *is* too late," he says, shaking his head. "It is!"

And he's moving away.

Away from me.

I'm losing him–

And I get an idea.

A dangerous, dangerous idea.

"The attack's coming tomorrow at sundown," I say.

He blinks again in surprise. "What?"

"That's when it happens." I swallow and step forward, trying to keep my voice steady. "I'm only supposed to know the fake plan, but I found out the real one. The Answer are coming over the hill with the notch in it just to the south of here, just to the south of this *cathedral*, Todd. They're coming right here and I'm sure they're coming right for the Mayor."

He looks nervously at the side door but I'm keeping my voice down. "There are only two hundred of them, Todd, but they're fully armed with guns and bombs and a plan and a hell of a leader who isn't going to stop until she topples him."

"Viola–"

"They're *coming*," I say, moving closer again. "And now you know when and from where and if that information gets to the Mayor–"

"You shouldn't have told me," he says, not meeting my eye. "I hide things but he figures them out. *You shouldn't have told me!*"

I keep moving forward. "Then you have to come with me, don't you? You *have* to or he wins forever and ever and he'll be the one to rule this planet and he'll be the one who greets the new settlers–"

"With his hand outstretched," Todd says, his voice suddenly soft.

"What?"

But he just extends his hand out into the empty air, staring at it. "Greeting it with his son."

"Well, we don't want that either." I look nervously round to the front door. Lee is sticking his head in, trying not to look too out of place, but there are soldiers marching by out front. "We don't have much time."

Todd's hand is still outstretched.

"I've done bad things, too," I say. "I wish everything was different but it isn't. There's only now and here and you *have* to come with me if we have any chance of making this come out any good at all."

He doesn't say anything but his hand is still out and he's looking at it and so I move forward another step and I take it in my own.

"We can save the world," I say, trying to smile. "You and me."

He looks into my eyes, searching, trying to read me, trying to see if I'm actually here, if it's actually true, if the things I say are real, he searches and he searches–

But he doesn't find me.

Oh, Todd–

"Going somewhere?" says a voice from across the room.

A voice from a man holding a gun.

It's a different man from the one who let us in, a man I've never seen before.

Except once, in Todd's Noise.

"How did you get out?" Todd says, surprise rippling through him.

"You wouldn't leave without *this*, would you?" he says. In his non-gun hand, he's got the journal of Todd's mother.

"You *give* that to me!" Todd says.

The man ignores him and waves his gun at Lee. "Come inside now," he says. "Or I will ever so happily shoot our dear friend Todd."

I look back. Lee's got flight all over his Noise but he sees the gun pointed at Todd, sees my face, and comes forward, his Noise saying so loud that he won't leave me here that it almost distracts me from the gun.

"Drop it," the man says, referring to Lee's rifle. Lee sends it clattering to the floor.

"You liar," Todd says to the man. "You coward."

"For the good of the town, Todd," the man says.

"All that moaning," Todd says, his voice and Noise fiery. "All that bitching and moaning about how he's ruining everything and yer just another spy."

"Not at first," the man says, walking toward us. "At first I was just how you saw me, the former Mayor disgraced and left alive in all his inconvenience." The man passes Todd and comes up to me, putting Todd's book under one arm. "Give me your pack."

"What?" I say.

"Give it to me." He swings his arm back and points the gun right at Todd's head. I slide the pack off my shoulders and give it to him. He doesn't even open it the regular way, just feels along the bottom, feeling right for the secret pouch, the secret pouch where if you press right, you can feel my gun.

The man smiles. "There it is," he says. "The Answer don't change, do they?"

"You touch a hair on her head," Todd says, "and I'll kill you."

"So will I," Lee says.

The man keeps smiling. "I think you have a competitor, Todd."

"Who *are* you?" I say, annoyance at all this protection making me brave.

"Con Ledger, Mayor of Haven, at your service, Viola." He gives a little bow. "Since that's who you must be, isn't it?" He walks around Todd. "Oh, the President was very interested in the Noise of your dreams, my boy. *Very* interested in what you thought about while you were sleeping. About how much you miss your Viola, how you would do anything to find her."

I see Todd's face starting to glow red.

"And suddenly he became far more agreeable to me, asking me to pass along certain information to you, see if we could get you to do what he wanted." Mayor Ledger looks ridiculous, all the things he's carrying, a gun in one hand, pack in the other, book under his arm, and still trying to appear threatening. "I must say, it worked like a charm." He winks at me. "Now that I know when and where the Answer are going to attack."

Lee's Noise rises and he takes a furious step forward.

Mayor Ledger cocks the pistol. Lee stops.

"Like it?" asks the Mayor. "The President gave it to me when he gave me my own key."

He smiles again, then sees how we're all looking at him. "Oh, stop it," he says. "If the President defeats the Answer then all this

will be over. All the bombings, all the restrictions, all the curfews."
His smile's a bit weaker now. "You have to learn how to work *within*
the system for change. When *I'm* his deputy, I'll work very hard to
make things better for everyone." He nods at me. "Women, too."

"You'd better shoot me," Todd says, Noise coming off him like
flame. "Cuz there ain't no way yer life is safe if you ever put down
that gun."

Mayor Ledger sighs. "I'm not going to shoot *anyone*, Todd, not
unless–"

The side door suddenly opens and the man who let me in steps
out, surprise lighting up his face and Noise. "What're you–"

Mayor Ledger points the gun at him and pulls the trigger three
times. The man falls back into the doorway and all the way to the
floor until only his feet are sticking out.

We all stand there, shocked, echoes of gunfire still ringing off
the marble floors.

There's a clear picture in Mayor Ledger's Noise, of himself with
a black eye and split lip, of the man on the floor giving him the
beating.

He looks back at us, sees us staring at him. "*What?*"

"Mayor Prentiss ain't gonna like that," Todd says. "He knows
Mr. Collins from old Prentisstown."

"I'm sure the prize of Viola and the Answer's attack will make up
for any other misunderstandings." Mayor Ledger's looking around
now, trying to find a place to free up his hands. He finally just tosses
the book to Todd, as if he doesn't want it anymore. Todd fumbles it
in his hands but catches it.

"Your mother wasn't much of a writer, Todd," Mayor Ledger
says, bending forward and zipping open the pack with his free
hand. "Barely literate."

"You're going to pay for that." Todd looks back at me and I realize I'm the one who said it out loud.

Mayor Ledger digs around in my bag. "Food!" he says, his face
lighting up. He takes out a crested pine from the top and immediately shoves it in his mouth. He digs some more, finding bread and
more fruit, taking bites of almost everything. "How long were you
planning on *staying*?" he asks, his mouth full.

I see Todd starting to edge forward.

"It's not like I can't hear you," Mayor Ledger says, waving the
gun again, digging down to the bottom of the bag. He stops, his
hand deep inside, and looks up. "What's this?" He feels around a

little more and starts to drag something larger out of the pack. At first I assume it's the gun but then he shakes it free of the bag.

He stands up.

And looks curiously at the Thrace bomb in his hand.

There's a second where it can't be true. There's a second where my eyes can't be seeing what they're seeing, not believing that I know what a bomb looks like by now. There's a moment where it's in his hand but it doesn't mean anything, it doesn't mean anything at all.

But then Lee gasps beside me and it all makes sense, it all makes the worst goddam sense I can even think of.

"*No*," I say.

Todd spins around. "What? What is it?"

Time slows down to nothing. Mayor Ledger turns it over in his hand and a beeping starts, a fast beeping, a beeping obviously set to go whenever anyone searched through my bag and picked it up, the pulse in his hand setting it off, a bomb you know is going to kill you if you let go of it.

"This isn't–" says Mayor Ledger, looking up–
    But Lee is already reaching for my arm–
    Trying to grab it so we can bolt for the front door–
    "Run!" he's yelling–
    But I'm jumping forward, not back–
    And I'm pushing Todd sideways–
    Stumbling toward the room where the dead man fell–
    Mayor Ledger isn't trying to shoot us–
    Isn't doing anything–
    He's just standing there, realization dawning–
    And as we're falling through the doorway–
    And rolling over the dead man–
    And curling into each other for protection–
    Mayor Ledger tries to throw the bomb away from himself–

Releasing it from his hand–

And–

BOOM

–it blasts him into a thousand pieces, tearing out the walls behind him and most of the room we're falling into and the heat from the explosion singes our clothes and our hair and rubble comes tumbling down and we force ourselves under a table but something hits Todd hard in the back of the head and a long beam falls across my ankles and I feel both of them break and all I can think as I yell out at the impossible pain is *she betrayed me she betrayed me she betrayed me* and it wasn't a mission to save Todd, it was a mission to *kill* him, and the Mayor, too, if she was lucky–

She betrayed me–

She betrayed me *again*–

And then there's darkness.

Some time later, there are voices, voices in the dust and rubble, voices drifting into my pain-addled head.

One voice.

His voice.

Standing over me.

"Well, well," says the Mayor. "Look who we have here."

PART
VI

THE ASK AND
THE ANSWER

35

VIOLA IS ASKED

[TODD]

"LET HER GO!"

I pound my fists on the glass but no matter how hard I hit it, it ain't breaking.

"*LET HER GO!*"

My voice is cracking from the strain but I'll go and go till it gives out completely.

"*YOU LAY A FINGER ON HER, I'LL KILL YOU!*"

Viola is strapped to the frame in the Arena of the Ask, her arms back and up, the skin around the metal band burning red, her head twixt the little buzzing rods that keep her from hearing Noise.

The tub of water is below her, the table of sharp tools to her side.

Mr. Hammar stands there waiting, arms crossed, and Davy, too, watching nervously from the far door, across the room.

And the Mayor is there, calmly walking round her in a circle.

All I remember is the *BOOM* and Mayor Ledger disappearing in a fury of fire and smoke.

I woke up here, my head aching, my body filthy from dirt and rubble and dried blood.

And I got to my feet.

And there she was

Beyond the glass.
Being Asked.

I press the button again for the speaker in the room. "LET HER GO!"

But no one acts like they can hear me at all.

"I do this with the greatest reluctance, Viola," says the Mayor, still walking in his slow circle. I can hear *him* perfectly clear. "I thought we might be friends, you and I. I thought we had an understanding." He stops in front of her. "But then you blew up my home."

"I didn't know there was a bomb," she says and I can see the pain across her face. There's dried blood all over her, too, cuts and scratches from the explozhun.

But it's her feet that look the worst. Her shoes are off and her ankles are swollen and twisted and black and I just know the Mayor ain't given her nothing for the pain.

I can see it on her face.

See how much she's hurting.

I try to pull up the bench behind me so I can smash it thru the window but it's bolted into the concrete.

"I believe you, Viola," says the Mayor, restarting his walk. Mr. Hammar stands there smirking, watching it all, once in a while looking up to the mirror where he knows I'm standing and smirking some more. "I believe your dismay at your betrayal by Mistress Coyle. Though you can hardly be surprised."

Viola don't say nothing, just hangs her head.

"Don't hurt her," I whisper. "Please, please, please."

"If it helps," says the Mayor. "I'm not entirely sure I would take it personally. Mistress Coyle saw a way to get a bomb right into the heart of my cathedral, destroying it, perhaps destroying me in the process."

He glances up to me at the mirror. I pound my fists on it again. There's no way they can't hear *that* but he ignores me.

Davy looks over, tho, his face as serious as I've seen it.

And even from here I can hear the worry in his Noise.

"You presented her with an opportunity she couldn't pass up," the Mayor continues. "Your extreme loyalty to Todd might actually get you inside where any other bomber might not. She probably didn't wish to kill you, but there it was, a chance to take me down, and weighed up against that, you were finally expendable."

And I'm looking at her face.

It's pulled down sad, pulled down so sad and defeated.

And I feel her silence again, feel the yearning and the loss that I first felt out in the swamp a lifetime ago. I feel it so much my eyes get wet and my stomach tightens and my throat clenches.

"Viola," I say. "Please, Viola."

But she don't even look up.

"And so if that's all you mean to her, Viola . . ." The Mayor's leaning down in front of her now, looking into her face. "Then maybe you finally know who your real enemy is." He pauses. "And who your real friends are."

Viola says something real quiet.

"What was that?" the Mayor asks.

She clears her throat and says it again. "I only came for Todd."

"I know." The Mayor stands again and starts his walk. "I've grown fond of Todd, too. He's become like a second son to me." He looks over at Davy, whose face flushes. "Loyal and hardworking and truly making a contribution to the future of this town."

I start pounding my fists again. "YOU SHUT UP!" I scream. "YOU SHUT UP!"

"If *he's* with us, Viola," the Mayor says, "and your Mistress is against you, then surely your path is clear."

But she's already shaking her head. "I won't tell you," she says. "I won't tell you anything."

"But she betrayed you." The Mayor comes round to her front again. "She tried to kill you."

And at that, Viola lifts her head.

She looks him right in the eye.

And says, "No, she tried to kill *you*."

Oh, good girl.

My Noise swells with pride.

That's my girl.

The Mayor gives a signal to Mr. Hammar.

Who takes hold of the frame and plunges her into the water.

"NO!" I scream and start pounding again. "NO, GODDAMMIT!" I go to the door of the little room and start kicking it as hard as I can. "VIOLA! VIOLA!"

I hear a gasp and run back to the mirror–

She's up outta the water, coughing up liquid and spitting hard.

"We are running short on time," says the Mayor, picking a speck of lint off his coat, "so perhaps we should come right to it."

I'm still pounding on the mirror and shouting while he talks. He turns and looks over to me. He can't see me from his side but his eyes lock right on mine.

"VIOLA!" I scream and pound the glass again.

He's frowning a little—

"*VIOLA!*"

And he strikes me with his Noise.

It's *way* stronger than before.

Like a shout of a million people right in the middle of my brain, so far inside I can't reach it to protect myself and they're screaming YER NOTHING YER NOTHING YER NOTHING and it feels like my blood is boiling and my eyes are popping outta my skull and I can't even stand and I stagger back from the mirror and sit down hard on the bench, the slap ringing and ringing and ringing, like it ain't never gonna stop—

When I can open my eyes again, I see the Mayor stopping Davy from leaving the Arena and then Davy looking back toward the mirror.

And in his Noise he's worried.

Worried about *me*.

"Tell me when the Answer is going to attack," the Mayor says to Viola, his voice colder now, harder. "And from where."

She shakes her head, sending water drops flying. "I won't."

"You will," says the Mayor. "I truly am afraid you will."

"No," she says. "Never."

And she's still shaking her head.

The Mayor glances up to the mirror, finding my eye again tho he can't see me. "Unfortunately," he says, "we don't have time for your refusals."

He nods at Mr. Hammar.

Who plunges her into the water again.

"STOP!" I shout and pound. "STOP IT!"

He holds her there—

And holds her there—

I pound so hard my hands are bruising—

"LET HER UP! LET HER UP! LET HER UP!"

And she's thrashing in the water—

But he's still holding her there—

She's still underwater—

"*VIOLA!*"

Her hands are pulling hard against the binds—

The water is splashing everywhere with her struggling against it—

Oh jesus oh jesus oh jesus oh jesus viola viola viola viola—

I can't–
I can't–
"NO!"
Forgive me–
Please forgive me–

"IT'S TONIGHT!" I shout. "AT SUNSET! OVER THE NOTCH IN
THE HILL SOUTH OF THE CATHEDRAL! TONIGHT!"
And I'm pressing the button as I shout it again and again–
"TONIGHT!"
As she struggles under the water–
But no one looks like they hear me.
He's turned the sound off–
He's turned the *effing sound off*–
I go back to the window and pound–
But no one's moving–
And still she's underwater–
No matter how hard I slam my fists against the gluas–
Why ain't it breaking–
Why ain't it ruddy *breaking*–

The Mayor gives a signal and Mr. Hammar lifts up the frame. Viola swal-
lows air in huge raking gulps, her hair (longer than I remember) stuck
against her face, twisting in her ears, the water falling off her in great
ropes.
"You're in control here, Viola," the Mayor says. "Just tell me when
the Answer are attacking and this will all stop."
"TONIGHT!" I scream, so loud my voice is cracking like dried mud.
"FROM THE SOUTH!"
But she's shaking her head.
And no one can hear me.
"But she betrayed you, Viola." The Mayor's making his voice do that
fake surprised thing. "Why save her? Why–?"
He stops, as if realizing something. "You have people you care about
in the Answer."
She stops shaking her head. She don't look up but she stops shaking
her head.
The Mayor kneels down in front of her. "All the more reason to tell
me. All the more reason to let me know where I can find your mistress."
He reaches forward and pulls a few wet strands of hair away from Viola's

face. "If you help me, I guarantee they won't be harmed. I only want Mistress Coyle. Any other mistresses can remain in prison and everyone else, innocent victims of inflamed rhetoric no doubt, can be released once we've had a chance to talk to them."

He gestures for Mr. Hammar to hand him a towel which he uses to wipe Viola's face. She still don't look at him.

"If you tell me, you'd be saving lives," he says, gently sponging away the loose water. "You have my word on that."

She finally raises her head.

"Your word," she says, looking right past him at Mr. Hammar.

And her face is so angry even *he* looks surprised.

"Ah, yes," the Mayor says, standing. He hands the towel back to Mr. Hammar. "You should look upon Captain Hammar as an example of my mercy, Viola. I spared his life." He's walking again but when he passes behind her he looks over to me. "Just as I shall spare the lives of your friends and loved ones."

"It's tonight," I say, but my voice is a rasp.

How can he not hear me?

"Then again," he's saying, "if you don't know, perhaps your good friend Lee will tell us."

Her head goes right up, eyes wide, breath heavy.

I don't know how he coulda survived the explozhun—

"He doesn't know anything," she says quickly. "He doesn't know when or where."

"Even if I believed that," the Mayor says, "I'm sure we would have to Ask him long and hard before we could possibly be sure."

"Leave him alone!" Viola says, trying to turn her head to follow him.

The Mayor stops just in front of the mirror, his back to Viola, his face to me. "Or perhaps we should just ask Todd."

I pound the glass right at his face. He don't even flinch.

And then she says, "Todd would never tell you. Never."

And the Mayor just looks at me.

And he *smiles*.

My stomach sinks, my heart drops, my head feels so light I feel like I'm going to drop right to the ground.

Oh, Viola—

Viola, please—

Forgive me.

"Captain Hammar," the Mayor says and Viola's plunged into the water again, unable to not scream out in fright as down she goes.

"NO!" I shout, pressing myself against the mirror.

But the Mayor ain't even looking at her.

He's looking right at me, as if he could see me even if I was behind a brick wall.

"STOP IT!" I shout as she's thrashing again–

And more–

And more–

"VIOLA!"

And I'm pounding even tho I think my hands are breaking–

And Mr. Hammar is grinning and holding her there–

"*VIOLA!*"

And her wrists are starting to bleed from where she's pulling–

"I'LL KILL YOU!"

I'm shouting into the Mayor's face–

With all my Noise–

"I'LL *KILL* YOU!"–

And still holding her there–

"VIOLA! *VIOLA!*"–

But it's Davy–

Of all people–

It's Davy who stops it.

"Let her up!" he suddenly shouts, striding forward from his corner. "Jesus, yer gonna kill her!" And he's grabbing the frame and lifting it outta the water and the Mayor gives Mr. Hammar a sign to let him and Davy gets Viola back up and out, her throat roaring from taking in the air and coughing it right back out again with all the water.

No one says nothing for a minute, the Mayor just staring at his son like he was some new kinda fish.

"How can she help us if she's dead?" Davy says, his voice wobbly, his eyes not meeting no one's. "Is all I meant."

The Mayor stays quiet. Davy backs away from the frame and returns to his spot near the door.

Viola coughs and hangs from her bindings and I'm pressed so close against the window it's like I'm trying to crawl *thru* it to get to her.

"Well," the Mayor says, clasping his hands behind his back, looking at Davy. "I think perhaps we've learned what we need to know anyway."

He walks over to a button on the wall and presses it. "Would you please repeat what you said earlier, Todd?"

Viola looks up at the sound of my name.

The Mayor walks back over to the frame, lifting up the little Noise-baffling rods from the sides of her face and she looks all around as she can suddenly hear my Noise.

"Todd?" she says. "Are you there?"

"I'm here!" I yell, my voice now booming thru the Arena so everyone can hear me.

"Please tell us again what you said a few moments ago, Todd." The Mayor's looking at me again. "Something about tonight at sunset?"

Viola looks up to where the Mayor's looking, surprise on her face, surprise and shock. "No," she whispers and it's as loud as any shouting.

"Viola deserves to hear you say it again, Todd," the Mayor says.

He knew. He could hear my Noise the whole time, *course* he could, he could hear my shouting, even if she couldn't.

"Viola?" I say and it sounds like I'm begging.

And she looks into the mirror, searching for where I might be. "Don't tell him!" she says. "Please, Todd, don't–"

"One more time, Todd," the Mayor says, putting his hand on the drowning frame, "or she goes back into the water."

"Todd, no!" Viola shouts.

"You bastard!" I yell. "I'll kill you. I swear it, I'll KILL YOU!"

"You won't," he says. "And we both know it."

"Todd, please, no–"

"Say it, Todd. Where and when?"

And he starts lowering the frame.

Viola's trying to look brave but her body is curling and twisting, trying to keep any part of it outta the water. "No!" she's yelling. "NO!"

Please please please–

"NO!"

Viola–

"Tonight at sunset," I say, my voice amplified over her shouts, over Davy's Noise, over my own Noise, just my voice filling everything. "Over the notch in the valley south of the cathedral."

"*NO!*" Viola screams–

And the look on her face–

The look on her face about *me*–

And my chest tears right in two.

The Mayor pulls back the frame, lifting her away from the water and setting her back down.

"No," she whispers.

And it's only then that she actually starts to cry.

"Thank you, Todd," the Mayor says. He turns to Mr. Hammar. "You know where and when, Captain. Pass on the orders to Captains Morgan, Tate, and O'Hare."

Mr. Hammar stands to attenshun. "Yes, sir," he says, sounding like he just won a prize. "I'll take every single man, sir. They won't know what hit 'em."

"Take my son," the Mayor says, nodding at Davy. "Let him see all the battle he can stomach."

Davy's looking nervous but proud and excited, too, not noticing the odd twist Mr. Hammar's smile has taken.

"Go," the Mayor says, "and leave none alive."

"Yes, *sir,*" Mr. Hammar says as Viola lets out a little sob.

Davy snaps a salute at his father, trying to make his Noise look brave. He sends the mirror a look meant for me, a look of sympathy, his Noise full of fear and excitement and more fear.

Then he's following Mr. Hammar out the door.

And then there's just me, Viola, and the Mayor.

I can only look at her, hanging from the frame, her head down, crying, still tied up and soaking wet and so much sorrow coming from her I can practically feel it on my skin.

"Tend to your friend," the Mayor says to me, just on the other side of the glass again, his face close to mine. "I return to my burned-out home to prepare for the new dawn." He don't even blink, don't even act like nothing's even happened.

He ain't human.

"All too human, Todd," he says. "The guards will escort both of you to the cathedral." He raises his eyebrows. "We have much to discuss about your futures."

36

DEFEAT

{VIOLA}

I HEAR TODD come into the room, hear his Noise come first, but I can't look up.

"Viola?" he says.

I still don't look up.

It's over.

We've lost.

I feel his hands on the binds at my wrists, pulling at them, finally getting one free, but my arm is so stiff from being held back it hurts more when it's released than it did when it was bound.

Mayor Prentiss has won. Mistress Coyle tried to sacrifice me. Lee's a prisoner if that wasn't a lie and he's not already dead. Maddy died for nothing. Corinne died for *nothing*.

And Todd—

He comes around in front of me to take off the second bind and when it's loose and I fall from the frame, he catches me, kneeling us gently down to the floor.

"Viola?" he says, holding me against himself, my head against his chest, the water on me soaking into his dusty uniform, my arms out, not able to grab anything, the metal band throbbing.

And I glance up to see the shiny silver *A* on his shoulder.

"Let me go," I say.

But he still holds me there.

"Let me *go*," I say, louder.

"No," he says.

I try to push him away but my arms are so weak and I'm so tired and everything is over. Everything is over.

And still he holds me.

And I start to cry again and I feel him hold me tighter and I cry harder and when my arms can move a little I put them around him and cry even harder because of how he feels and how he smells and how his Noise sounds and how he's holding me and his worry and his fretting and his care and his softness–

And I didn't know until just now how much I missed him.

But he told the Mayor–

He *told* him–

And I have to try and push him away again, even though I can hardly bear to do it.

"You told him," I say, choking it out.

"I'm sorry," he says, his eyes wide and terrified. "He was drowning you and I couldn't, I just couldn't–"

And I look at him and there I am in his Noise, dropping down into the water with him pounding on the other side of the mirror and worse, I can see what he felt, see the hopeless *rage* of it, see him unable to save me–

And his face is so worried.

"Viola, please," he says, begging me. "*Please*."

"He'll kill them," I say. "Every one of them. Wilf is there, Todd. *Wilf*."

He looks horrified. "Wilf?"

"And Jane," I say. "And so many others, Todd, *all* of them. He'll slaughter them and that'll be the end. That'll be the end of *everything*."

His Noise goes black and barren and he sort of crumples down next to me, splashing in the little puddle that's formed around us. "No," he says. "Aw, no."

I don't want to say it but I hear my voice saying it anyway. "You did exactly what he wanted. He knew exactly how to get it out of you."

He looks at me. "What choice did I have?"

"You should have let him kill me!"

And he's looking at me and I can see his Noise trying to find me, trying to find the real Viola that's deep down in this mess and pain, I can see him looking–

And for a minute I don't want him to find me.

"You should have let him kill me," I say again quietly.

                              *   *   *

But he couldn't, could he?

　　He couldn't and still be himself.

　　He couldn't and still be Todd Hewitt.

　　The boy who can't kill.

　　The *man* who can't.

　　We are the choices we make.

"We have to warn them," I say, feeling ashamed and not looking into his eyes. "If we can." I grab the edge of the tub of water to pull myself up. Pain shoots up my legs from my ankles. I call out and fall forward again.

　　And once more, he catches me.

　　"My feet," I say. We look at them, bare and swollen badly, turning ugly shades of blue and black.

　　"We'll get you to a healer." He puts an arm around me to lift me.

　　"No," I say, stopping him. "We have to warn the Answer. That's the most important thing."

　　"Viola–"

　　"Their lives are more important than my–"

　　"She tried to *kill* you, Viola. She tried to blow you up."

　　I'm breathing hard, trying not to feel the pain from my legs.

　　"You don't owe her nothing," he says.

　　But I feel his arms on me and I'm realizing things don't seem so impossible anymore. I feel Todd touching me and there's anger rising in my gut but it's not at him and I grunt and I pull myself up again, leaning on him to keep me there as I stand. "I *do* owe her," I say. "I owe her the look on her face when she sees me alive."

　　I try to take a small step but it's too much. I cry out again.

　　"I have a horse," he says. "I can put you on her."

　　"He's not just going to let us leave," I say. "He said guards would escort us back to him."

　　"Yeah," he says. "We'll see about *that*."

　　He puts his arm tighter around me and leans down to put his other arm under my knees.

　　And he lifts me in the air.

　　The pull on my ankles makes me cry out again but then he's holding me up, carrying me like he did down the hillside into Haven.

　　Holding me up.

　　He remembers it, too. I can see it in his Noise.

I put my arm around his neck. He tries to smile.

And it's crooked like it always is.

"We just keep on having to save each other," he says. "We ever gonna be even?"

"I hope not," I say.

He frowns again and I see the clouds roiling in his Noise. "I'm sorry," he says quietly.

I grab the cloth of his shirtfront and squeeze it tight. "I'm sorry, too."

"So we forgive each other?" The crooked smile climbs up one more time. "Again?"

And I look right into his eyes, right into him as far as I can see, because I want him to hear me, I want him to hear me with everything I mean and feel and say.

"Always," I say to him. "Every time."

He carries me to a chair and then goes over to the door and starts pounding on it. "Let us out!" he shouts.

"This does mean something, Todd," I say, taking as little breath as possible because my feet are throbbing. "Something we have to remember."

"What's that?" He pounds on the door again and says "Ow" quietly at how it's hurting his hands.

"The Mayor knows I'm your weakness," I say. "All he has to do is threaten me and you'll do what he wants."

"Yeah," Todd says, not looking back. "Yeah, I knew that already."

"He'll keep trying it."

He turns around to face me, fists clenched at his sides. "He won't be laying his eyes on you. Not never again."

"No." I shake my head and wince at the pain. "It can't be that way, Todd. He has to be stopped."

"Well, why's it have to be *us* that stops him?"

"It's got to be somebody." I arch my back a certain way to keep any weight off my feet. "He can't win."

Todd starts kicking at the door. "Then let yer Mistress do it. We'll get to her somehow, warn 'em if we can, and then we're outta here."

"Out of here where?"

"I don't know." He starts looking around for something that

might knock down the door. "We'll go to one of the abandoned settlements. We'll hide out till yer ships get here."

"He'll beat Mistress Coyle and then he'll go right for the ships." I gasp a little as I turn my head to follow him. "There's only a small number of people awake when they land, Todd. He can overpower them and keep everyone else asleep as long as he wants. He doesn't ever have to wake them up if he doesn't want to."

He stops his search. "Is that true?"

I nod. "Once he destroys the Answer, who's left to stop him?"

He clenches and unclenches his fists again. "We have to do it."

"We find the Answer first," I say, trying to pull myself upright. "We warn them–"

"And tell 'em exactly what kinda leader they got."

I sigh. "We're going to have to stop both of them, aren't we?"

"Well, that's easy, ain't it?" Todd says. "We tell the Answer all about yer mistress and then someone new will lead 'em." He looks at me. "Maybe you."

"Maybe *you*." I take a minute to try and catch my breath. It's getting harder. "Either way, we have to get out of here."

And then the door suddenly opens.

A soldier stands there with a rifle.

"I have orders to take you both to the cathedral," he says.

And I think I recognize him.

"Ivan," Todd says.

"Lieutenant," Ivan nods. "I've got my orders."

"You're from Farbranch," I say, but he's staring at Todd, not blinking. I can hear something in his Noise, something–

"*Lieutenant*," he says again in a way that seems like some kind of signal.

I look at Todd. "What's he doing?"

"You have orders," Todd says, concentrating on Ivan. I can hear stuff flying between their Noises, fast and blurry. "*Private* Farrow."

"Yes, sir," Ivan says, standing at attention. "Orders from my superior officer."

Todd looks at me. I can hear him thinking.

"What's going on?" I say.

I see Lee rise in Todd's Noise. He turns back to Ivan. "Is there another prisoner? A boy? Blond shaggy hair?"

"There is, sir," Ivan says.

"And if I ordered you to take me to him, you'd do it?"

"You *are* my superior officer, *Lieutenant*." Ivan's looking harder at Todd now. "I'd have to follow any orders you gave me."

"Todd?" I say, but I'm beginning to understand.

"I've been a-trying to tell you this for some time, Lieutenant," Ivan says, impatience in his voice.

"Are there any higher-ranking officers on the premises than me?" Todd asks.

"No, sir. Just myself and the guards. Everyone else has gone off to fight the war."

"How many guards?"

"Sixteen of us, sir."

Todd licks his lips, thinking. "Would they regard me as their superior officer, too, Private?"

Ivan looks away for the first time, glancing quickly behind him before saying again in a lower voice, "There is some concern with our current leadership, sir. They might be persuaded."

Todd stands up straighter, pulling at the hem of his uniform jacket. I notice again how tall he is, how much taller than the last time I saw him, how his face is lined in a way that's not at all boyish, how his voice is deeper and fuller.

I look at him, and I begin to see a man.

He clears his throat and stands at attention before Ivan. "Then I order you to take me to the prisoner called Lee, Private."

"Even though I have been instructed to take you straight to the President," Ivan says in an official voice, "I feel I cannot disobey your direct order, *sir*."

He steps back out of the door to wait. Todd comes to my chair and kneels down in front of me.

"What are you planning?" I ask, trying to read his Noise, but it's spinning so fast I can hardly keep up with it.

"You said it's us who has to stop him cuz no one else will," he says, the crooked smile inching higher. "Well, maybe there's a way we can."

37

THE LIEUTENANT

[TODO]

I FEEL VIOLA WATCHING ME as I leave and follow Ivan down the hallway. She's wondering whether we can trust him.

I wonder it, too.

Cuz the answer's no, ain't it? Ivan joined the army as a volunteer, saving his own skin in Farbranch, and I remember him slinking up to me all those months ago even before it happened and telling me he was on the side of Prentisstown. He probably couldn't wait to join the army when it marched into town and then he led troops here and was even a Corporal.

Till Mayor Prentiss shot him in the leg.

You go where the power is, he said to me once. *That's how you stay alive.*

So maybe he thinks he's found the new power.

"Exactly what I'm a-thinking, *sir*," Ivan says, stopping outside a door. "He's in here."

"Can he walk?" I say as Ivan unlocks the door—

But Lee's already jumping out with an *AAAAAAAAHHHHHHHHH!!!* and knocking Ivan over and punching him again and again in the face and I have to grab his shoulders and pull him back and he turns to me, fists ready, till he sees who it is.

"Todd!" he says, surprised.

"We need—" I start.

"Where is she?" he shouts, already looking round, and I have to step forward to keep Ivan from smashing the back of his head with a rifle.

"She's hurt," I say. "She needs bandages and splints." I turn to Ivan. "You got those here?"

"We got a first aid kit," Ivan says.

"That'll do. Give it to Lee and he'll take care of Viola. Then tell the men I wanna talk to 'em out front."

Ivan's glaring at Lee, Noise blaring.

"That's an order, *Private*," I say.

"Yes, *sir*," Ivan says, all sour, before he disappears down the hallway.

Lee goggles at me. "*Yes, sir*?"

"Viola'll explain." I push him after Ivan. "You get those bandages on her! She's hurting!"

That gets him moving. I turn about-face and go toward the lobby. Two guards watch me walk past. "What's going on?" one of 'em asks.

"What's going on, *sir*," I snap without turning round. I walk out the front door of the Office of the Ask, down the little path and out the front gate.

Where it's almost peaceful.

And there's Angharrad.

Davy musta brought her.

"Hey, girl," I say, coming up on her slow, rubbing her nose. **Boy colt?** says her Noise. **Todd?**

"It's all right, girl," I whisper. "It's all right."

Hurt, she says, sniffing at the dried blood still on my face. She takes her big wet tongue and gives me the sloppiest lick right across my mouth and cheek.

I laugh a little and rub her nose again. "I'm okay, girl, I'm okay."

Her Noise keeps saying my name, **Todd Todd,** as I move to where my bag is still tied to the saddle. My rifle's still there.

So's my ma's book.

I'll bet Davy brought that, too.

I untie Angharrad's reins from the post and lead her out onto the road a little bit till she's pointing right at the gate with the big silver **A**. "Gotta give a little speech," I say, tightening the saddle. "Better from up top of you."

Boy colt, she says. **Todd**.

"Angharrad," I say.

I put my foot in a stirrup, hop up and swing my leg round till I'm sitting in the saddle, looking up at the sky. It's not darkening yet but the sun's getting down toward the falls. Afternoon is ticking away.

There ain't much time.

"Wish me luck," I say.

"Forward," Angharrad whinnies. "Forward."

The guards look up at me and back to Ivan who's trying to get 'em to stop talking, which would only help if they shut up the clatter of their Noise, too, cuz it's wailing like sheep on fire.

"He's a *lieutenant*," Ivan's saying to 'em.

"He's a *boy*," another guard says, one with ginger hair.

"He's the *President's* boy," Ivan responds.

"Yeah, and you were sposed to take him into town, Private," says another with a big pot belly and Corporal stripes on his sleeve. "Don't tell me yer disobeying a direct order."

"The Lieutenant gave me a different direct order," Ivan says.

"And he overrules the President, does he?" says Ginger Hair.

"Come on!" Ivan shouts. "How many of you got this assignment as punishment for something?"

That quiets 'em.

"Yer an idiot if you think I'm following a boy to face the President," says Corporal Pot Belly.

"Prentiss *knows* stuff," says Ginger Hair. "Stuff he shouldn't."

"He'd have us shot," says another soldier, a tall one this time, with sallow skin.

"By who?" says Ivan. "The army's all off fighting the war while the President sits in his blown-up cathedral a-waiting for me to show up with Todd here."

"What's he doing there?" asks Ginger Hair. "Why ain't he with the army?"

"Ain't his style," I say. They all look up at me again. "The Mayor don't fight. He rules, he leads, but he don't pull no triggers and he don't get his hands dirty." Angharrad feels my nervousness and steps a little to one side. "He gets other people to do it for him."

Plus, I try to hide in my Noise, *he wants to talk to me*.

Which in a way feels worse than war.

"And yer gonna overthrow him, are ya?" asks the Corporal, crossing his arms.

"He's just a man," I say. "A man can be defeated."

"He's more'n a man," Ginger Hair says. "People say he uses his Noise as a weapon."

"And if you get too close to him, he can control your mind," says Sallow Skin.

Ivan scoffs. "That's all just grandmothers' tales. He can't do nothing of the sort—"

"Yes, he can," I say, and once again, all eyes turn on me. "He can hit you with his Noise and it hurts like hell. He can look into yer mind and try to force you to do and say the stuff he wants. Yeah, he can do all that."

They're staring at me now, wondering when I'm gonna get to the part that's helpful.

"But I think he's gotta make eye contact to do it—"

"You *think*?" says Ginger Hair.

"And the Noise hit ain't fatal and he can only do it to one person at a time. He can't beat all of us, not if we all come at once."

But I'm also hiding in my Noise how much stronger it was when he hit me in the Arena just now, how much more potent.

He's been working on it, sharpening his weapons.

"Don't matter," says Sallow Skin. "He'll have his own guards. We'd be walking right into our deaths."

"He'll be expecting you to escort me," I say. "We can walk right past the guards to where he's waiting."

"And why should we follow you, *Lieutenant*?" asks the Corporal, getting sarcastic on my rank. "What's in it for us?"

"Freedom from tyranny!" Ivan says.

The Corporal rolls his eyes. He ain't the only one.

Ivan tries again. "Because as soon as he's gone, *we* take over."

Less eye rolling this time, but Sallow Skin says, "Anyone wanna be ruled by President Ivan Farrow?"

He says it to get a laugh but it don't get any.

"What about President Hewitt?" Ivan says, looking up at me with a weird glint in his eye.

Corporal Pot Belly scoffs and says again, "He's a *boy*."

"I'm not," I say. "Not no more."

"He's the only one a-willing to go after the President," Ivan says. "That speaks for *something*."

The guards look from one to another. I can hear all the askings in their Noise, all the doubts rattling around, all the fears confirming one another, and in their Noise I hear the idea being defeated.

But in their Noise I also hear how it can be saved.

"If you help me," I say, "I'll get you the cure."

They all shut right up.

"You can do that?" Ginger Hair asks.

"Naw," says the Corporal. "He's bluffing."

"It's stockpiled in the cellars of the cathedral," I say. "I saw the Mayor put it there himself."

"Why do you keep calling him *the Mayor?*" Sallow Skin asks.

"You come with me," I say. "You help me take him prisoner and every man here gets all the cure he can carry." They're listening to me now. "It's about ruddy time Haven became Haven again."

"He's taken it from the entire army," Ivan says. "We bring down the President, give 'em the cure, and who do you think they'll start a-listening to?"

"It won't be you, Ivan."

"No," says Ivan, giving me that look again. "But it could be *him.*"

The men look up at me, up on top of Angharrad, with my rifle and my dusty uniform and my idea and my promises and there's a rustle thru their Noise as each man asks himself, is he desperate enough to take the chance?

I think of Viola, sitting in the Arena, sitting there as everything I want to save, everything I'd do anything for.

I think of her and I know exactly how to convince 'em.

"All the women are banded," I say. "Who do you think's gonna be next?"

Lee's pulling the last bandages round Viola's feet when I come back in and her face is looking way less pained.

"Can you stand?" I ask.

"Only a little."

"Don't matter," I say. "Angharrad's outside. She'll take you and Lee to find the Answer."

"What about you?" Viola says, sitting up.

"I'm gonna face him," I say. "I'm gonna take him down."

She *really* sits up at that.

"I'm coming with you," Lee says instantly.

"No, yer not," I say. "Yer telling the Answer to call off their attack *and* yer telling them just how Mistress Coyle works."

Lee's mouth sets firm but I can see his Noise roiling in anger over the bomb. He woulda died, too. "Viola says you can't kill."

I send her a dirty look. She's got the good grace to look away.

"I'm gonna kill him," Lee says. "I'm gonna kill him for what he did to my sister and mother."

"If you don't warn the Answer," I say, "there'll be a lot more dead people to make him pay for."

"He can *have* Mistress Coyle," Lee says but I can already see other people churning in his Noise, Wilf and Jane and other men and other women and Viola and Viola and Viola and Viola.

"What are you going to do, Todd?" she asks. "You can't just face him one-on-one."

"It won't be one-on-one," I say. "I got some of the guards to come with me."

Her eyes open wide. "You *what*?"

I smile. "Got me a little mutiny going."

"How many?" Lee asks, his face still serious.

I hesitate. "Seven," I say. "I couldn't get 'em all to agree."

Viola's face drops. "You're going to fight the Mayor with seven men?"

"It's a chance," I say. "Most of the army's off marching to their final battle. The Mayor's *waiting* for me. It's the least guarded he's ever gonna be."

She watches me for a second, then she puts one hand on Lee's shoulder and one hand on mine and lifts herself to her feet. I can see her catch herself at the pain but Lee's wound the bandages tight and even if they ain't bone-fixers then at least they let her stand for a second or two.

"I'm coming with you," she says.

"No, yer not," I say at the same time as Lee yells, "Not a chance!"

She sets her jaw. "And what makes either of you think you have a say in the matter?"

"You can't walk," I say.

"You have a horse," she says.

"It's yer chance to get *safe*," I say.

"He's expecting *both* of us, Todd. You walk in there without me, your plan is over before you even speak."

I put my hands on my hips. "You said yerself the Mayor will use you against me if he gets the chance."

She grimaces as she tests the weight on her ankle. "Then your plan had better work, hadn't it?"

"Viola–" Lee starts but she stops him with a look.

"Find the Answer, Lee. Warn them. You haven't got much time."

"But–"

"*Go*," she says again, more firmly.

And we both see her rise in his Noise, we both *feel* how much he don't wanna leave her. It's so strong, I have to look away from him.

But it sorta makes me wanna hit him, too.

"I'm not leaving Todd," she says. "Not now that I've found him again. I'm sorry, Lee, but that's the way it is."

Lee takes a step back, unable to keep the hurt outta his Noise. Viola's voice softens. "I'm sorry," she says again.

"Viola–" Lee says.

But she's shaking her head. "The Mayor thinks he knows everything. He thinks he knows what's coming. He's just sitting there *waiting* for me and Todd to show up and try and stop him."

Lee tries to interrupt but she don't let him.

"But what he's forgetting," she says. "What he's forgetting is that me and Todd, we ran halfway across this planet together, by *ourselves*. We beat his craziest preacher. We outran an entire army and survived being shot and beaten and chased and we bloody well *stayed alive* this whole time without being blown up or tortured to death or dying in battle or anything."

She takes her hand off Lee so she's balancing just against me.

"Me and Todd? Together against the Mayor?" She smiles. "He doesn't stand a chance."

38

MARCH TO
THE CATHEDRAL

{VIOLA}

"DID YOU MEAN what you said in there?" Todd says, pulling the strap on the saddle. His voice is low and he's keeping his eyes on the horse work. "Bout him not standing a chance against us?"

I shrug. "It helped, didn't it?"

He smiles to himself. "I gotta go talk to the men." He nods over to Lee, standing away from us, hands in his pockets, watching us chat. "You try and make this easy on him, okay?"

He gives Lee a wave and goes to where our escort of seven soldiers stands huddled by the big stone gate. Lee comes over.

"Are you sure about this?" he says.

"No," I say, "but I'm sure of Todd."

He breathes out through his nose, looking at the ground, trying to keep his Noise flat. "You love him," he says. Not an asking, just a fact.

"I do," I say. Also a fact.

"In *that* way?"

We both look over at Todd. He's gesturing with his arms and telling the men what we're planning and what they should do.

He's looking like a leader.

"Viola?" Lee asks.

I turn back to him. "You need to find the Answer before the army does, Lee, if you can at all."

He frowns. "They may not believe me about Mistress Coyle. A lot of people need her to be right."

"Well," I say, gently taking up the reins of the horse. B**oy colt?** she thinks, watching Todd, too. "Think of it this way. If you can reach them and we can take care of the Mayor, this could all be over today."

Lee squints into the sun. "And if you don't take care of him?"

I try to smile. "Well, then, you're just going to have to come rescue us, aren't you?"

He tries to smile back.

"We're ready," Todd says, coming back over.

"This is it," I say.

Todd holds out his hand to Lee. "Good luck."

Lee takes his hand. "And to you," he says.

But he's looking at me.

After Lee's set off into the woods, running to scale the hills and intercept the Answer before the army does, the rest of us start our march down the road. Todd leads Angharrad, who keeps saying B**oy colt** over and over again in her Noise, nervous at someone new on her back. Todd murmurs things to keep her calm, rubbing her nose and petting her flank as we go.

"How do you feel?" he asks me as we approach the first set of dormitories.

"My feet hurt," I say. "My head, too." I rub my hand on my sleeve where the band is hiding. "And my arm."

"Other than that?" He smiles.

I look at the guards around us, marching in formation, as if they really are escorting me and Todd to the Mayor as ordered: Ivan and another in front, two behind, two to my right and the last to my left.

"Do you believe we can beat him?" I ask Todd.

"Well," he says and laughs, low, "we're going, ain't we?"

We're going.

Up the road and into New Prentisstown.

"Let's pick it up," Todd says, a bit louder.

The men pick up the pace.

"It's deserted," whispers the guard with flaming red hair as we pass through areas with more and more buildings.

Buildings but no people.

"Not deserted," another guard says, one with a big belly poking out in front of him. "In hiding."

"It's spooky without the army," the red-haired one says. "Without soldiers marching up and down the street."

"*We're* marching, Private," Ivan says. "We're soldiers, too."

We pass houses with shutters closed tight, storefronts with locked shutters, roads with no carts or fissionbikes or even people walking. You can hear the ROAR from behind closed doors but it's half the volume.

And it's *scared*.

"They know it's coming," Todd says. "They know this could be the war they've been waiting for."

I look around from atop Angharrad. No homes have any lights on, no faces peep out of windows, no one even curious as to what this band of guards is doing around a horse carrying a girl with bandaged feet.

And then the road bends and there's the cathedral.

"Holy moly," says the red-haired guard, as we come to a stop.

"You lived through *that?*" the pot belly says to Todd. He whistles in appreciation. "Maybe you *are* a bit blessed."

The bell tower still stands, though it's hard to see how, teetering on top of an unsteady ladder of bricks. Two walls of the main building stand, too, including the one with the colored glass circle.

But the rest of it.

The rest of it's just a pile of stone and dust.

Even from behind, you can see that most of the roof has caved in and the largest parts of two walls have been blown out onto the road and the square in front of it. Arches lean dangerously out of balance, doors are twisted off their hinges, and most of the inside lies open to the world, receiving the last of the sun as it heads down to the horizon.

And there's not one soldier guarding it.

"He's unprotected?" says the red-haired one.

"That sounds like something he'd do," Todd says, staring at the cathedral as if he can see the Mayor somewhere through the walls.

"If he's even inside," Ivan says.

"He is," Todd says. "Trust me."

The red-haired soldier starts backing away down the road. "No way," he says. "We're walking to our deaths here, boys. No way."

And with a final frightened look, he takes off running back the way we came.

Todd sighs. "Anyone else?" The men look to each other, their Noises wondering why they came in the first place.

"He'll put the band on you," Ivan says. He nods up at me. I pull up my sleeve and show them. The skin is still red and hot to the touch. Infection, I think. The first aid creams aren't doing what they're supposed to.

"And then he'll enslave you," Ivan continues. "I don't know about you, but that's not why I joined the army."

"Why *did* you join?" asks another guard but it's clear he doesn't want an answer.

"We take him down," Ivan says. "And we're heroes."

"Heroes with the cure," says the pot belly, nodding. "And he who controls the cure–"

"Enough talking," Todd says and I hear the discomfort in his Noise about how this is going. "Are we gonna do this or not?"

The men look to one another.

And Todd raises his voice.

Raises it so it commands.

Raises it so even *I* look at him.

"I said, are we *ready*?"

"Yes, sir," the men say, seeming almost surprised to hear it coming out of their mouths.

"Then let's go," Todd says.

And the men start marching again, *step step step*, crunching through the loose gravel scattered across the road, down a small slope, through the town and toward the cathedral, getting bigger and bigger the closer we get.

We file past some trees and I look to our left, to the hills on the southern horizon.

"Sweet Jesus," Pot Belly says.

Even from here you can see the army marching in the distance, a single black arm twisting up a path too narrow for them, up to the summit of the hill with the notch on top, up to where they'll meet the Answer.

I look at the setting sun.

"Maybe an hour," Todd says, seeing me check. "Probably less."

"Lee won't get to them in time," I say.

"He might. There must be shortcuts."

The snake of the army slithers up the hillside. So many there's no way the Answer will be able to fight them if it comes to open battle.

"We can't fail," I say.

"We won't," Todd says.

And we reach the cathedral.

We march up the side. This is where most of the damage is, the whole north wall having collapsed straight onto the road.

"Remember," Todd murmurs to the men, as we climb over rubble. "Yer taking two prisoners to see the President like you were ordered to do. Nobody needs to be thinking nothing but that."

We pick our way down the road. The pile of stones is so high you can't see into the cathedral. The Mayor could be in there anywhere.

We come around the corner to where the front used to be, now just a gaping hole into the vast lobby and sanctuary, still watched over by the bell tower and by that circle of colored glass. The sun, behind us, shines right into it. Open rooms hang from upper walls, their floors crumbling. Half a dozen redbirds pick through the remains of food and worse in amongst the stones. The rest of the structure leans in on itself, like it's grown suddenly tired and might fall down to rest at any time.

And inside its shell—

"No one," Ivan says.

"That's why there aren't any guards," says Pot Belly. "He's with the army."

"He's not," Todd says, looking around, frowning.

"Todd?" I ask, sensing something—

"He told us *himself* to bring Todd here," Ivan says.

"Then where is he?" asks Pot Belly.

"Oh, I'm here," says the Mayor, stepping out of a shadow that shouldn't have been able to hide him, almost seeming to step straight out of the brick, out of a shimmer where he couldn't be seen.

"What the devil—?" says Pot Belly, stepping back.

"Not the Devil," the Mayor says, taking his first steps down the rubble toward us, his hands open at his sides. The guards all raise their rifles at him. He doesn't even look like he's armed.

But here he comes.

"No, not the Devil," he says, smiling. "Much worse than that."

"Stop where you are," Todd says. "There are men here who would happily shoot you."

"I know it," the Mayor says, stopping on the bottom step of the cathedral entrance, resting one foot on a large stone toppled there. "Private Farrow, for example." He nods at Ivan. "Still seething for being punished for his own incompetence."

"You shut your mouth," Ivan says, looking down the barrel of his rifle.

"Don't look into his eyes," Todd says quickly. "Nobody look into his eyes."

The Mayor slowly puts his hands in the air. "Am I to be your prisoner then?" He takes a look around at the soldiers, at all the guns pointed at him. "Ah, yes, I see," he says. "You have a plan. Returning the cure to the people, capitalizing on their resentment to install yourselves in power. Yes, *very* clever."

"That ain't how it's gonna be," Todd says. "Yer gonna call off the army. Yer gonna let everyone be free again."

The Mayor puts a hand to his chin like he's thinking about it. "The thing is, Todd," he says, "people don't really *want* freedom, no matter how much they might bleat on about it. No, I should think what will happen is that the army will crush the Answer, that the soldiers accompanying you will be put to death for treason, and that you and I and Viola will have that little chat about your future I promised."

There's a loud snap as Ivan cocks his rifle. "You think so, do you?"

"Yer our prisoner and that's the end of it," Todd says, taking out a length of rope from Angharrad's saddle bag. "We'll just have to see how the army reacts to that."

"Very well," the Mayor says, sounding almost cheerful. "But I should send one of your men to the cellar so you can start taking the cure immediately. I can read all your plans perfectly clearly, and you wouldn't want that."

Pot Belly looks back. Todd nods at him and Pot Belly jogs on up the steps past the Mayor. "Just back and down," the Mayor points. "The way's quite clear."

Todd takes the rope and walks toward the Mayor, moving past the guns pointed at him. My hands are sweating into the reins.

It can't be this easy.

It can't–

The Mayor holds out his wrists and Todd hesitates, not wanting to actually get near him. "He tries anything funny," Todd says, without looking back. "Shoot him."

"Gladly," Ivan says.

Todd reaches forward and starts winding the rope around the Mayor's wrists.

We hear footsteps in the cathedral. Pot Belly comes jogging back, out of breath, his Noise a storm.

"You said it was in the cellar, *Lieutenant*."

"It is," Todd says. "I saw it there."

Pot Belly shakes his head. "Empty. Completely empty."

Todd looks back at the Mayor. "Then you moved it. Where is it?"

"Or what?" the Mayor says. "You'll shoot me?"

"I'd actually *prefer* that option," Ivan says.

"*Where did you move it?*" Todd says again, his voice strong, angry.

The Mayor looks at him, then looks around at all the men, and finally looks up to me on horseback.

"It was you I was worried about," he says. "But you can hardly walk, can you?"

"Don't you look at her," Todd spits, stepping closer to him. "You keep yer filthy eyes *off* her."

The Mayor smiles again, his hands still out, loosely bound by rope. "Very well," he says. "I'll tell you."

He looks around at everyone again, still smiling.

"I burned it," says the Mayor. "After the Spackle sadly left us, there was no more need and so I burned every last pill, every last plant that the pills were made from, and then I blew up the processing lab and blamed it on the Answer."

There's a shocked silence. We can hear the ROAR of the army in the distance, marching up that hill, keeping on toward their goal.

"You're a *liar*," Ivan finally says, stepping forward, gun still raised. "And a stupid one, at that."

"We can't hear yer Noise," Todd says. "You can't have burned it all."

"Ah, but Todd, my son," the Mayor says, shaking his head. "I have never taken the cure."

Another silence. I hear suspicions rising in the Noise of the men. I even see a few of them step back, thoughts of the Mayor's power, thoughts of what he can do. Maybe he *can* control his Noise. And if he can do *that*–

"He's lying," I say, remembering Mistress Coyle's words. "He's the President of Lies."

"Well, at least you finally called me *President*," the Mayor says.

Todd gives the Mayor a shove. "Tell us where it is."

The Mayor stumbles back a step, then regains his balance. He looks around at us all again. I can hear everyone's Noise rising, Todd's most of all, red and loud.

"I tell no lies, gentlemen," says the Mayor. "If you only have the right discipline, Noise can be controlled. It can be silenced." He looks around at each of us again, his smile reappearing. "It can be used."

I AM THE CIRCLE AND THE CIRCLE IS ME, I hear.

But I can't tell if it's from his Noise–

Or Todd's.

"I've had just about enough of this!" Ivan shouts.

"You know, Private Farrow," says the Mayor, "so have I."

And that's when he attacks.

39

YER OWN WORST ENEMY

[TODD]

I FEEL THE FIRST STRIKE of Noise fly by me, a *whooshing* of concentrated words and sounds and pictures rushing over my shoulder, straight for the men with rifles. I flinch away and dive for the ground—

Cuz the men start firing their guns—

And I'm right in the way—

"Todd!" I hear Viola shout but the rifles are firing and the men are screaming and I roll on the rubble, jarring my elbow, and whip round to see Corporal Pot Belly on his knees in front of Angharrad, his back turned, both hands on the sides of his head, screaming wordlessly down into the ground, Viola watching him, wondering what the hell is going on. Another guard has fallen on his back, fingers in his eyes, as if he's trying to dig them out, and a third lies unconshus on his stomach. Two others are already running back into the city.

The Noise flies from the Mayor, louder and stronger than anything I've seen before.

Way louder than at the Office of the Ask.

Loud enough to take out five men at once.

Only Ivan still stands, one hand up to his ear and the other trying to aim his rifle at the Mayor but weaving it dangerously around—

BANG

A bullet smacks the ground in front of my eyes, sending dust and dirt up into them–

BANG

Another bounces off stones deep in the cathedral–

"IVAN!" I shout.

BANG

"Stop firing! Yer gonna get us killed!"

BANG

His rifle goes off right by Angharrad's head. She rears up and I see Viola grab the reins, surprised, holding on for dear life–

And then I see the Mayor is walking forward and forward and forward–

His eyes on the men he's attacking–

Coming past me–

And I don't even think–

I leap from the ground to stop him–

And he turns and sends his Noise straight at me–

The world goes all bright, terribly, painfully bright, like everyone can see how much you hurt, everyone watching and laughing and nowhere to hide and YER NOTHING YER NOTHING YER NOTHING all bound up tight like a bullet right thru you, telling you everything that's wrong with you, everything you ever done bad in yer life, telling you yer worthless, yer dirt, YER NOTHING, yer life ain't got no point nor reason nor purpose and you should just tear down the walls of yerself, ripping apart who you are and either die or give it up as a gift, as a gift to the one who can save you, as a gift to the man who can control you, who can take it all away, who can make everything fine fine fine–

But not even Noise can stop a body when it's moving.

I feel all these things and I'm still flying at him and I still hit him and I still knock him over on the steps of the cathedral.

He grunts as the air is crushed out of him and the Noise attack stops for a second. Corporal Pot Belly calls out and falls over and Ivan's gasping for breath and Viola's calling out "Todd!" and then a hand is around my neck and it's pushing my head up and the Mayor is looking right into my eyes–

And this time it hits me full blast.

* * *

"Give me the rifle!" the Mayor is shouting, standing over Ivan, who's crouched on the ground below him, hand over his ear again but the rifle still pointed up at the Mayor. "Give it to me!"

I blink, grit and dust in my eyes, wondering for a second where I am—

YER NOTHING YER NOTHING YER NOTHING YER NOTHING

"Give me the rifle, *Private!*"

The Mayor's screaming at Ivan, hitting him over and over again with Noise blasts and Ivan is sinking to the ground—

But his rifle's still aimed—

"Todd!"

I see horse legs beside my head. Viola's still up on Angharrad. "Todd, wake up!" she's yelling. I look up at her. "Thank God!" she yells and her face is a picture of frustrayshun. "My stupid feet! I can't get off the god-dam horse!"

"I'm okay," I say, tho I don't know if I am, and I lean myself up, my head spinning.

YER NOTHING YER NOTHING YER NOTHING YER NOTHING

"Todd, what's going on?" Viola says as I grab a rein to help me stand. "I hear Noise but—"

"The rifle!" shouts the Mayor, stepping closer to Ivan. "Now!"

"We have to help him," I say—

But I flinch back at the strongest attack yet—

A flare of Noise so white you can almost see the air bending twixt the Mayor and Ivan—

And Ivan grunts sharply and bites his tongue—

Blood spilling from his mouth—

Before he screams like a child and falls back—

Dropping the rifle—

Dropping it right into the Mayor's hands.

He lifts it, cocks it, and aims it at us in one fluid move. Ivan lies twitching on the ground.

"What just happened?" Viola says, too angry it seems to care much about the rifle.

I put my hands in the air, still holding the reins.

"He can use Noise," I say, keeping my eyes on him. "He can use it like a weapon."

"Just so," says the Mayor, smiling again.

"All I heard was shouting," she says, looking at the men lying on the ground, still breathing but out cold. "What do you mean, a weapon?"

"The truth, Viola," the Mayor answers. "The best weapon of all. You tell a man the truth about himself and, well," he nudges Ivan with his boot, "they find they have trouble accepting it." He frowns. "You can't kill him with it, though." He looks back up at us. "Not yet, anyway."

"But . . ." She's not believing this. "How? How can you–?"

"I have two maxims that I believe, dear girl," the Mayor says, coming slowly toward us. "One, if you can control yourself, you can control others. Two, if you can control *information*, you can control others." He grins, his eyes flashing. "It's been a philosophy that's worked out rather well for me."

I think about Mr. Hammar. About Mr. Collins. About the chanting I used to hear coming from the Mayor's house back in my old town.

"You taught the others," I say. "The men from Prentisstown, you taught them how to control their Noise."

"With varying degrees of success," he says, "but yes, none of my officers has ever taken the cure. Why should they? It's a weakness to have to rely on a drug."

He's nearly on us now. "I am the Circle and the Circle is me," I say.

"Yes, you were certainly making an impressive beginning, weren't you, Todd? Controlling yourself while you did the most unspeakable things to those women."

My Noise turns red. "You *shut up* about that," I say. "I was only doing what you told me–"

"*I was only following orders*," the Mayor mocks. "The refuge of scoundrels since the dawn of time." He stops six feet away from us, rifle pointed firmly at my chest. "Help her off the horse, please, Todd."

"What?" I say.

"Her ankles, I believe the problem was. She'll need your help walking."

I still have the reins in my hand. I have a thought I try to bury.

Boy colt? Angharrad asks.

"I assure you, Viola," the Mayor says to her. "If you think about running on that beautiful animal, I will put more than one bullet through Todd." He looks back at me. "However much pain it might cause me."

"You let her go," I say. "I'll do anything you want."

"Now where have I heard that before?" he says. "Help her down."

I hesitate, wondering if I should slap Angharrad's flanks anyway, wondering if I should send Viola riding off into the distance, wondering if I could get her safe–

"No," Viola says and she's already working her leg round the saddle. "Not a chance. I'm not leaving you."

I take her arms and help her down. She has to lean on me to stand but I keep her up.

"Splendid," says the Mayor. "Now let's go inside and have that chat."

"Let us start with what I know."

He's brought us into what used to be the room with the round colored glass window in it but it's now open to the air on two sides and above, the window still there, looking down, but looking down on rubble.

Looking down on a little cleared area with a broken table and two chairs.

Where me and Viola sit.

"I know, for example," the Mayor says, "that you did not kill Aaron, Todd, that you never took your final step toward becoming a man, that it was Viola here who put the blade in all along."

Viola takes my arm and squeezes it tight, letting me know it's okay that he knows.

"I know that Viola told you the Answer were hiding at the ocean when I let you escape to go speak with her."

My Noise rises in anger and embarrassment. Viola squeezes my arm harder.

"I know that you've sent the boy called Lee to warn the Answer." He leans against the broken table. "And of course I also know the exact time and place of their attack."

"Yer a monster," I say.

"No," the Mayor says. "Just a leader. Just a leader who can read every thought you have, about yourself, about Viola, about me, about this town, about the secrets you think you're keeping. I can read *everything*, Todd. You're not listening to what I'm saying." He's still holding the rifle, watching us sit before him. "I knew everything about the Answer's attack this morning before you even opened your mouth."

I sit up in my chair. "You what?"

"I had the army gathering before we even started Asking Viola."

I start to rise. "You tortured her for *nothing*?"

"Sit down," the Mayor says and a little flash from him weakens my knees enough that I sit right back down. "Not for nothing, Todd. You should know me well enough by now to know that I do not do *anything* for nothing."

He sits up from the broken table, showing again that he likes to walk and talk.

"You are completely transparent to me, Todd. From our first proper meeting here in this very room until how you sit before me today. I've known everything. *Always.*"

He looks at Viola. "Unlike your good friend here, who's a little tougher than I imagined."

Viola frowns. If she had Noise I'm sure she'd be slapping him around a bit.

I get a thought–

"Don't try it," the Mayor says. "You're not nearly that advanced yet. Even Captain Hammar has yet to master it. You'd merely end up hurting yourself very badly." He looks at me again. "But you *could* learn, Todd. You could advance far, further than any of those poor imbeciles who followed me from Prentisstown. Poor Mr. Collins barely worth more than a butler and Captain Hammar just another garden-variety sadist, but you, Todd, *you*." His eyes flash. "You could lead armies."

"I don't wanna lead armies," I say.

He smiles. "You may have no choice."

"There's always a choice," Viola says by my side.

"Oh, people like to say that," the Mayor says. "It makes them feel better." He approaches me, looking into my eyes. "But I've been watching you, Todd. The boy who can't kill another man. The boy who'd risk his own life to save his beloved Viola. The boy who felt so guilty at the horrible things he was doing that he tried to shut off all feeling. The boy who still felt every pain, every twitch of hurt he saw on the face of the women he banded."

He leans down closer to my face. "The boy who refused to lose his soul."

I feel him. He's in my Noise now, rummaging around, turning things over, upending the room inside my head. "I've done bad things," I say and I don't even mean to say it.

"But you *suffer* for them, Todd." His voice is softer now, almost tender. "You're your own worst enemy, punishing yourself far more than I could ever hope to. Men have Noise and the way they handle it is to make themselves just a little bit dead, but *you*, even when you *want* to, you can't. More than any man I've ever met, Todd, you *feel*."

"Shut up," I say, trying to look away, not being able to.

"But that makes you *powerful*, Todd Hewitt. In this world of numbness and information overload, the ability to feel, my boy, is a rare gift indeed."

I put my hands to my ears but I can still hear him in my head.

"You're the one I couldn't break, Todd. The one who wouldn't fall. The one who stays innocent no matter the blood on his hands. The one who *still* calls me Mayor in his Noise."

"I'm not innocent!" I shout, my ears still plugged.

"You could rule by my side. You could be my second in command. And when you learn to control your Noise, you may have power to overtake even *mine*."

And then the words thunder thru my whole body.

I AM THE CIRCLE AND THE CIRCLE IS ME.

"Stop it!" I hear Viola shout but it's from miles away.

The Mayor puts a hand on my shoulder. "You could be my son, Todd Hewitt," he says. "My real and true heir. I've always wanted one that wasn't–"

"Pa?" we all hear, cutting thru everything like a bullet thru fog.

The Noise in my head stops, the Mayor steps abruptly back, I feel like I'm able to breathe again.

Davy stands behind us, rifle in one hand. He's led Deadfall up to the steps and is looking over the rubble to the three of us here. "What's going on? Who are the men out there on the ground?"

"What are you doing here?" the Mayor snaps, frowning. "Is the battle already won?"

"No, Pa," Davy says, climbing over the rubble toward us. "It was a trick." He plants his feet next to my chair. "Hey, Todd," he says, nodding in greeting. He glances at Viola but he can't hold her eye.

"*What* was a trick?" the Mayor demands but he's already looking angry.

"The Answer ain't coming over the hill," Davy says. "We marched way back deep into the forest but there ain't no sign, not nowhere."

I hear Viola take a little gasp, a bit of pleased surprise escaping from her even as she tries to hold it back.

The Mayor looks her way, his eyes fierce, his face thinking and thinking.

And he raises his rifle at her.

"Something you'd like to tell us, Viola?"

40

NOTHING CHANGES, EVERYTHING CHANGES

{VIOLA}

TODD'S ALREADY UP and out of his chair, standing between me and the Mayor, his Noise raging so loud and furious the Mayor takes a step back.

"You see the power in you, my boy?" he says. "This is why you watched her being Asked. Your suffering makes you *strong*. I'll teach you how to harness it and together we'll–"

"You hurt her," Todd says, clearly and slowly, "and I'll tear every limb from yer body."

The Mayor smiles. "I believe you." He hoists the rifle. "Nevertheless."

"Todd," I say.

He turns to me. "This is how he wins. Playing us off each other. Just like you said. Well, it stops here–"

"Todd–" I'm trying to stand up but my stupid ankles won't hold me and I stumble. Todd reaches for me–

But it's Davy–

Davy catches me by the arm, stopping the fall and then lowering me back into the chair. He won't meet my eye. Or Todd's. Or his father's. His Noise flushes yellow with embarrassment as he lets me go and steps back.

"Why, thank you, David," the Mayor says, unable to mask his

surprise. "Now," he says, turning back to me, "if you would please be so kind as to inform me of the Answer's *real* plan of attack."

"Don't tell him nothing," Todd says.

"I don't *know* anything," I say. "Lee must have reached–"

"There wasn't sufficient time and you know it," the Mayor says. "It's obvious what's happened, isn't it, Viola? Your Mistress misled you once more. If the bomb went off as it should have, it wouldn't have mattered if you had the wrong information because you and, she hoped, *I* would be dead. But if you were caught, well, then. The best liar is the one who believes her lie is true."

I don't say anything because how could she have misled me if it was only something Lee overheard–

But then I think–

She *wanted* him to overhear it.

She *knew* he wouldn't be able to not tell me.

"Her plan worked perfectly, didn't it, Viola?" The shadow from the setting sun reaches the Mayor's face, covering him in black. "One twist after another, lies building on lies. She played you exactly how she wanted, didn't she?"

I glare at him. "She'll beat you," I say. "She's as ruthless as you are."

He grins. "Oh, *more*, I should say."

"Pa?" Davy asks.

The Mayor blinks, like he forgot his son was there. "Yes, David?"

"Um, the *army*?" Davy's Noise is full of bewilderment and exasperation, trying to make sense of what his father's doing but not finding much relief. "What're we sposed to do *now*? Where're we sposed to go? Captain Hammar's waiting for yer orders."

All around us the low, frightened ROAR of New Prentisstown seeps out of the houses, but still no faces at the windows, and from over the hill with the notch, the blacker, twistier buzz of the army. You can still see them up the hillside, shiny like a trail of black beetles sliding off one another's shells.

And here we sit, alone with the Mayor and his son, in the open ruins of the cathedral, like we're the only people on the planet.

The Mayor looks back at me. "Yes, Viola, tell us. What are we supposed to do now?"

"You're supposed to fall," I say, staring back at him, not blinking. "You're supposed to lose."

He smiles at me. "Where are they coming from, Viola? You're a clever girl. You must have heard *something*, seen some clue as to her real plans."

"She ain't telling you," Todd says.

"I *can't*," I say, "because I don't *know*."

And I'm thinking, I really *don't* know–

Unless the thing she told me about the east road–

"I'm waiting, Viola." The Mayor raises the rifle at Todd's head. "On pain of his life."

"Pa?" Davy says, shock coming out of his Noise. "What're you *doing*?"

"Never you mind, David. Get back on your horse. I'll have a message for you to take to Captain Hammar presently."

"Yer pointing the gun at *Todd*, Pa."

Todd turns around to look at him. So do I. So does the Mayor.

"You ain't gonna shoot him," Davy says. "You can't." Davy's cheeks are red now, so dark you can even see them in the sunset. "You said he's yer second son."

There's an uncomfortable silence as Davy tries to hide his Noise.

"You see what I mean by power, Todd?" the Mayor says. "Look at how you've influenced my son. You've already got yourself a follower."

Davy looks at me, right in the eyes. "Tell him where they are." There's worry all over his Noise, anxiety at how things are playing out. "C'mon, just tell him."

I look back at Todd.

He's looking at Davy's rifle.

"Yes, Viola, tell me, why don't you?" the Mayor says. "Your best speculation. Are they coming from the west?" He looks up toward the falls, the highest point on the horizon, where the sun's disappearing behind the zigzag road carved down the hill, the hill I've only been down once and never gone back up. The Mayor turns. "The north, perhaps, though they'd have to cross the river somehow? Or a hill to the east? Yes, maybe even over the hill where your Mistress blew up the tower and any chance you had of communicating with your people."

I clench my teeth again.

"Still loyal, after all that?"

I don't say anything.

"We could send out troops, Pa," Davy says. "To different parts. They gotta come from *somewhere*."

The Mayor waits for a minute, staring us down. He finally turns to Davy and says, "Go tell Captain Hammar–"

He's interrupted by a distant *BOOM*.

* * *

"That's due east," Davy says, as we all look up even though there's a wall of the cathedral in the way.

It *is* east.

It's exactly the road she told me it was going to be.

She made me think the truth was a lie and a lie was the truth.

If I get out of this, we're going to have words, her and me.

"The Office of the Ask," the Mayor says. "Of course. Where else would they–"

He stops again, cocking his head, listening out. We hear it several seconds after he does. The Noise of someone running at full speed toward the cathedral from the back, up the road we took to get here, around the side of the cathedral and up to the front, coming upon us, gasping.

It's the red-haired guard, the one who fled. He's obviously barely registering who he's seeing as he stumbles into the wreckage of the building. "They're coming!" he shouts. "The Answer is coming!"

There's a burst of Noise from the Mayor and the red-haired soldier falls back, catching himself. "Calm down, Private," the Mayor says, his voice slinky, snakelike. "Tell us clearly."

The guard pants, seemingly unable to catch his breath. "They've taken the Office of the Ask." He looks up at the Mayor, caught by his eyes. "They killed all the guards."

"Of course they did," the Mayor says, still holding the red-haired soldier's gaze. "How many are there?"

"Two hundred." The red-haired soldier isn't blinking now. "But they're releasing the prisoners."

"Weapons?" asks the Mayor.

"Rifles. Tracers. Launchers. Siege guns on the backs of carts." Still the stare.

"How goes the battle?"

"They're fighting fierce."

The Mayor cocks an eyebrow, still staring at him.

"They're fighting fierce, *sir*," the guard says, still not blinking, like he couldn't look away from the Mayor if he tried. There's another BOOM in the distance and everyone except the Mayor and the soldier flinches. "They're coming for war, sir," says the soldier.

The Mayor keeps the stare. "Then you should be trying to stop them, shouldn't you?"

"Sir?"

"You should be taking your rifle and preventing the Answer from destroying your town."

The soldier looks confused but he's still not blinking. "I should . . ."

"You should be on the front line, soldier. This is our hour of need."

"This is our hour of need," the soldier mumbles, like he's not hearing himself.

"Pa?" Davy says but the Mayor ignores him.

"What are you waiting for, soldier?" the Mayor says. "It's time to fight."

"It's time to fight," says the guard.

"Go!" the Mayor suddenly barks and the red-haired guard springs away, back down the road toward the Answer, his rifle up, yelling incoherently, running back to the Answer as fast as he ran away from them.

We watch him go in stunned silence.

The Mayor sees Todd staring at him, mouth agape. "Yes, dear boy, better at *that*, too."

"You as good as killed him," I say. "Whatever you did—"

"What I did was make him see his duty," the Mayor says. "No more, no less. Now, as *fascinating* as this discussion is, we're going to have to settle it later. I'm afraid I'm going to have to have Davy tie you both up."

"*Pa?*" Davy says again, startled.

The Mayor looks at him. "Then you'll ride to Captain Hammar, tell him to bring the army down the road with all speed and fury." The Mayor casts his eyes to the far hillside where the army waits. "It's time we brought this to an end."

"I can't tie him up, Pa, it's *Todd*."

The Mayor doesn't look at him. "I've had just about enough of this, David. When I give you a direct order—"

Boom!

He stops and we all look up.

Because it's different this time, a different kind of sound. We hear a low *whoosh* and a rumble starts to fill the air, getting louder as the seconds pass.

Todd looks at me, confused.

I just shrug. "Nothing I ever heard before."

The roar starts to get louder, filling the darkening sky.

"That don't sound like no bomb," Davy says.

The Mayor looks at me. "Viola, is there—"

He stops and then turns his head.

And we all realize–

It's not coming from the east.

"Over there," Davy points, raising his hand toward the falls, toward where the sky is bright pink with sunset.

The Mayor looks at me again. "That's too loud for a simple tracer." His face tightens. "Have they got missiles?" He takes a step so big he's almost on top of me. "*Have they built missiles?*"

"You *back off!*" Todd yells, trying to get between us again.

"I will *know* what this is, Viola!" the Mayor says. "You will tell me!"

"I don't *know* what it is!" I say.

Todd's shouting and threatening, "You lay a *finger* on her–"

"It's getting louder!" Davy shouts, putting his hands to his ears. We all turn and watch the western horizon, watch as a dot rises, getting lost in the last of the sun before reappearing, growing larger as it comes.

As it comes straight for the city.

"*Viola!*" the Mayor shouts, through clenched teeth, sending some Noise at me but I don't feel whatever it is that men feel.

"I DON'T KNOW!" I yell.

And then Davy, who hasn't stopped watching it, says, "It's a ship."

41

THE MOMENT OF DAVY PRENTISS

[TODD]

IT'S A SHIP.

It's a ruddy *ship*.

"Yer people," I say to Viola.

But she's shaking her head, tho not to say no, just staring at it as it rises over the falls.

"Too small for a settler ship," Davy says.

"And too early," the Mayor says, aiming his rifle at it as if he could shoot it from this distance. "They're not due for another two months at least."

But Viola still ain't looking like she can hear any of this, hope rising on her face so painful it hurts my heart just to see it. "A scout," she whispers, so quiet I'm the only one who hears it. "Another scout. Sent to look for me."

I turn back to the ship.

It clears the crest of the falls, soaring out over the river.

A scout ship, just like the one she crashed in back in the swamp, killing her parents and stranding her here all those months and lifetimes ago. It still looks as big as a house, stubby wings looking too short to keep it in the air, flames coming outta the tail end as it flies flies flies down the river, using it as a road hundreds of feet below.

We watch it come.

"David," the Mayor says, his eyes still on it. "Get my horse."

But Davy's got his face up to the sky, his Noise opening up in wonder and amazement.

And I know exactly how he feels.

Nothing flies on New World except the birds. We got machines that go down the roads, fissionbikes, a few fissioncars, but mainly we just got horses and oxes and carts and our feet.

We don't got *wings*.

The ship comes down the river, nearing the cathedral and flying almost right over us, not stopping, so close you can see lights on the underside and the sky above the exhaust shimmering with the heat. It flies right on past, down the river.

Down east toward the Answer.

"*David!*" the Mayor says sharply.

"Help me up," Viola whispers. "I have to get to them. I have to *go*."

And her eyes are wild and her breath is heavy and she's staring at me so hard it's like a solid thing I can feel.

"Oh, he'll help you up," the Mayor says, pointing the gun. "Because you're coming with me."

"*What?*" Viola says.

"They're *your* people, Viola," the Mayor says. "They're going to be wondering where you are. I can either bring you to them right away. . ." He looks at me. "Or I can sadly inform them that you died in the crash. Which would you prefer?"

"I'm not going with *you*," she says. "You're a liar and a murderer–"

He cuts her off. "David, you'll remain guard over Todd while I take Viola to her ship." He looks back at her. "I think you know firsthand my son's eagerness with a gun if you don't cooperate."

Viola looks furiously at Davy. I look at Davy, too, standing there, rifle in hand, looking back and forth twixt me and his pa.

His Noise roiling.

His Noise saying clearly there ain't no way he's *ever* gonna shoot me.

"Pa?" he says.

"Enough of this, David," the Mayor frowns, trying to catch Davy's eye–

And catching it.

"You will do what I say," he says to his son. "You will tie Todd up with the rope he so helpfully brought and you will stand guard over him and when I return with our newly arrived guests, everything will be peaceful and happy. The new world will begin."

"New world," Davy mumbles, his eyes glazing over, just like the ginger-haired soldier, askings and doubt being pushed outta his Noise.

As he bends to the will of another.

I get an idea.

Forgive me, Davy.

"You gonna let him talk to you like that, Davy?"

He blinks. "What?"

He looks away from his pa.

"You gonna let him point a gun at me and Viola?"

"Todd," the Mayor warns.

"All that Noise you say you hear," I say to the Mayor but I still look at Davy, still hold his eye. "All the way you say you know *everything*, but you don't know yer own son very well, now, do ya?"

"David," the Mayor says.

But *I* got Davy's eye now.

"You gonna let him get his way again?" I say to him. "You gonna let him boss you round with no reward?"

Davy watches me nervously, trying to blink away the mess his pa's put in his head.

"That ship changes everything, Davy," I say. "A whole new batch of people. A whole city's worth to try and make this place something better than the stinking toilet it is."

"*David*," the Mayor says. There's a flash of Noise and Davy flinches.

"Stop it, Pa," he says.

"Who do you want to get to that ship first, Davy?" I say. "Me and Viola to get some help? Or yer pa so he can rule them, too?"

"Be *quiet*!" says the Mayor. "Are you forgetting who has the gun?"

"Davy has one, too," I say.

There's a bit of a pause as we all see Davy remember he's holding a rifle.

There's another flash of Noise from the Mayor and another flinch from Davy. "Jesus, *Pa*, effing quit it already!"

But he looks at his pa to say it.

And his pa catches his eyes again.

"Tie Todd up and get my horse, David," the Mayor says, holding his stare.

"Pa?" Davy says, his voice gone quiet.

"My horse," says the Mayor. "He's out back."

"Get between them." Viola hisses at me. "Break the eye contact!"

I move but the Mayor turns the gun on her without taking his eyes off Davy. "One move, Todd."

I stop.

"Bring me my horse, son," says the Mayor, "and we'll greet the new settlers side by side." He smiles at his son. "You'll be my prince."

"He said that before," I say to Davy. "But not to you."

"He's controlling you," Viola shouts. "He's using his Noise to—"

"Please tell Viola to be quiet," the Mayor says.

"Be quiet, Viola," Davy says, his voice soft, his eyes not blinking.

"*Davy!*" I shout.

"He's just trying to control you, David," the Mayor says, his voice rising. "Like he's done from the start."

"*What?*" I say.

"From the start," Davy mumbles.

"Who do you think's held you back from promotion, son?" the Mayor's saying it and he's saying it right into the middle of Davy's brain. "Who do you think tells me all the things you do wrong?"

"Todd?" Davy says weakly.

"He's *lying*," I say. "Look at me!"

But Davy's overloading. He's just staring frozen at his pa, not moving at all.

The Mayor gives a heavy sigh. "I see I have to do this myself."

He comes forward, gesturing us back with his rifle. He grabs Viola and lifts her to her feet. She cries out from the pain in her ankles. I move automatically to help but he pushes her forward so she's right in front of him, his rifle at her back.

I open my mouth to shout, to threaten, to damn him—

But it's Davy who speaks first.

"It's landing," he says quietly.

We all turn eastward. The ship is taking a slow circle, flying around a hilltop east of town—

Maybe even the one where the tower once stood—

It comes round again and hovers above the treetops—

Before slowly starting to lower itself out of sight—

I turn to Davy, too, see his eyes fogged and confused—

But he ain't looking at his pa no more—

He's looking at the ship—

And then he's turning his head and looking at me—

"Todd?" he says, like he's just waking up—

And his rifle is just there, just hanging from his hand—

And one more time—

Forgive me.

* * *

I lunge forward and snatch it from him. He don't even put up any resistance, just lets it go, lets it go right into my fingers and I'm already raising it and cocking it and pointing it at the Mayor.

Who's already smiling, his gun still in Viola's back.

"So it's a standoff, is it?" he says, grinning from ear to ear.

"Let her go," I say.

"Please take your gun back from Todd, David," the Mayor says, but he has to keep looking at me, watching me with the gun.

"Don't you do no such thing, Davy."

"Stop it!" Davy says, his voice thick, his Noise rising. I sense him putting his hands to the sides of his head. "Can't you both just effing *stop it?*"

But the Mayor's still looking at me and I'm still looking at the Mayor.

The sound of the ship landing screams over the city, over the Noise of the army marching its way back down the hill, over the distant *booms* of the Answer making its way up the road, and over the terrified, hidden ROAR of New Prentisstown all around us, not knowing that their whole future depends on this, right now, right this second, me and the Mayor with our rifles.

"Let her go," I say.

"I don't think so, Todd." I hear a rumble of Noise coming from him.

"My finger's on this trigger," I say. "You try to hit me with yer Noise and yer a dead man."

The Mayor smiles. "Fair enough," he says. "But what you need to ask yourself, my dear friend Todd, is if, when you decide to finally pull that trigger, can you pull it fast enough so that I don't also pull my own? Will killing me kill your beloved Viola, too?" He lowers his chin. "Could you live with that?"

"You'd be dead," I say.

"So would she."

"Do it, Todd," Viola says. "Don't let him win."

"That ain't happening neither," I say.

"Are you going to let him point a gun at your own father, David?" the Mayor asks.

But he's still looking at me.

"Times are changing, Davy," I say, eyes still on the Mayor. "This is where we all decide how it's gonna be. Including you."

"Why's it have to be like this?" Davy asks. "We could all go together. We could all ride up on horseback and—"

"No, David," says the Mayor. "No, that won't do at all."

"Put the gun down," I say. "Put it down and end this."

The Mayor's eyes flash and I know what's coming—

"You stop that," I say, blinking furiously and looking over his shoulder.

"You cannot win this," the Mayor says and I hear his voice twice over, three times, a legion of him inside my head. "You cannot shoot me and guarantee her life, Todd. We all know you'd never risk that."

He takes a step forward, pushing Viola along. She calls out at the pain in her ankles.

But I find myself taking a step back.

"Don't look in his eyes," she says.

"I'm trying," I say, but even the *sound* of his voice is getting inside me.

"This isn't a loss, Todd," the Mayor is saying, so loud in my head it feels like my brain's vibrating. "I wish for your death no more than I wish for my own. Everything I said earlier was true. I want you by my side. I want you as part of the future we're going to create here with whoever steps out of that ship."

"Shut *up*," I say.

But he's still stepping forward.

I'm still stepping back.

Till I'm behind even Davy.

"I want no harm to come to Viola, either," the Mayor says. "All along I promised both of you a future. That promise still stands."

Even without looking right at him, his voice is buzzing in my head, weighing it down, making it seem like it's easier just to—

"Don't listen to him!" Viola shouts. "He's a liar."

"Todd," says the Mayor. "I think of you as my son. I really do."

And Davy turns to me, his Noise rising all hopeful, and he says, "C'mon, Todd, you hear that?"

And his Noise is reaching for me, too, eagerness and worry coming forward like fingers and hands, asking me, *begging* me to put the gun down, put it down and make everything all right, make it so all this stops—

And he says, "We could be brothers—"

And I cast my eyes to Davy's—

And I see myself in them, see myself in his Noise, see the Mayor as my father and Davy as my brother and Viola as our sister—

See the hopeful smile rising to Davy's lips—

And for the third time, I have to ask—

Forgive me.

I point the rifle at Davy.

* * *

"Let her go," I say to the Mayor, not quite able to look Davy in the face.

"Todd?" Davy asks, his forehead furrowing.

"Just do it!" I snap.

"Or you'll what, Todd?" the Mayor teases. "You'll shoot him?"

Davy's Noise is spilling over with more asking marks, with surprise and shock—

With a betrayal that's rising—

"Answer me, Todd," the Mayor says. "Or you'll *what*?"

"Todd?" Davy says again, his voice lower this time.

I look him briefly in the eyes and look away again.

"Or I'll shoot Davy," I say. "I'll shoot yer son."

Davy's Noise is pouring with disappointment, disappointment so thick it falls off him like mud. I don't even read no anger in his Noise, which makes it worse. He ain't even thinking of jumping me or punching me or wrestling the gun away.

The only thing in his Noise is me holding a gun on him.

His only friend holding a gun on him.

"I'm sorry," I whisper.

But he don't look like he hears.

"I gave you yer book," he says. "I gave you back yer book."

"You let Viola go!" I shout, looking away from Davy, anger at myself snapping my voice loud. "Or I swear to God—"

"Go ahead then," the Mayor says. "Shoot him."

Davy looks at the Mayor. "Pa?"

"Never much use as a son anyway," the Mayor says, still pushing Viola forward with the rifle. "Why do you think I sent him to the front line? I was at least hoping he'd die a *hero*'s death."

There's pain on Viola's face still but it ain't all her ankles.

"Never mastered his Noise," the Mayor continues, looking at Davy, whose Noise—

I can't say what his Noise is like.

"Never followed an order he couldn't get out of. Couldn't capture you. Couldn't take care of Viola. Only ever showed improvement because of *your* influence, Todd."

"Pa—" Davy starts.

But his pa ignores him.

"*You* are the son I want, Todd. Always you. *Never* this waste of space."

And Davy's Noise—

Oh, Jesus, Davy's Noise—

"LET HER GO!" I shout so I don't have to hear it. "I'll shoot him, I'll do it!"

"You won't," says the Mayor, smiling again. "Everyone knows you aren't a killer, Todd."

He pushes Viola forward again–

She calls out from the pain of it–

Viola, I think–

Viola–

I grit my teeth and raise the rifle–

I cock it–

And I say what's true–

"I would kill to save her," I say.

The Mayor stops edging forward. He looks twixt me and Davy and back again.

"Pa?" says Davy. His face is twisted and crumpled.

The Mayor looks back at me, reading my Noise.

"You would, wouldn't you?" he says, almost under his breath. "You'd kill him. For her."

Davy looks back at me, his eyes wet but anger rising there, too. "Don't, Todd. Don't do it."

"Let her go," I say again. "*Now.*"

The Mayor's still looking twixt me and Davy, seeing that I'm serious, seeing that I'd really do it.

"Just put the gun down," I growl, not looking at Davy's eyes, not looking at his Noise. "*This is over.*"

The Mayor takes in a long breath and lets it out.

"Very well, Todd," he says. "As you wish."

He steps away from Viola.

My shoulders relax.

And he fires his gun.

42

ENDGAME

{VIOLA}

"TODD!" I shout, the sound of the rifle shot blasting past my ear, erasing everything but him, the whole world reduced to not knowing if he's all right or not, if he's been hit, if–

But it's not him–

He's still holding up his gun–

Unfired–

Standing next to Davy–

Who falls to his knees–

Sending up two small clouds of dust as he hits the rubble–

"Pa?" he asks, his voice pleading, like a little kitten–

And then he coughs, spilling blood down his lips–

"Davy?" Todd says, his Noise rising like he's the one that's been shot–

And I see it–

A hole high in Davy's chest, in the fabric of his uniform, just below the base of his throat–

And Todd runs to him, kneeling down beside him–

"*Davy!*" he shouts–

But Davy's Noise is staring at his father–

Asking marks sent everywhere–

His expression shocked–

His hand reaching up to the wound–

He coughs again–
And gags–
Todd's looking at the Mayor, too–
His Noise railing–
"What did you do?" he shouts–

[TODD]

"WHAT DID YOU DO?!" I shout.
  "I removed him from the equation," the Mayor says calmly.
  "Pa?" Davy asks again, holding out a bloodied hand toward him–
But his pa is only looking at me.
  "You were always the truer son, Todd," the Mayor says. "The one
with the potential, the one with the power, the one I'd be proud to have
serve by my side."
  Pa? Davy's Noise says–
And he's hearing *all* of this–
  "You effing *monster*," I say. "I'll *kill* you–"
  "You'll *join* me," the Mayor says. "You know you will. It's only a mat-
ter of time. David was weak, an embarrassment–"
  "SHUT UP!" I shout.
Todd? I hear–
I look down–
Davy's looking up at me–
His Noise swirling–
Swirling with askings and confuzhun and fear–
And **Todd?**–
Todd?–
I'm sorry–
I'm sorry–
  "Davy, don't–" I start to say–
But his Noise is still swirling–
And I see–
I see–
I see the truth–
Here at the last–
He's showing me the truth–
The thing he's been hiding from me–
About Ben–
All in a messy rush–
Pictures of Ben racing up the road toward Davy–
Pictures of Davy's horse rearing–

Pictures of Davy firing his gun as he falls–
Pictures of the bullet hitting Ben in the chest–
Pictures of Ben staggering out into the bushes–
Davy too scared to go after him–
Davy too scared to tell me the truth after–
After I became his only friend–
I didn't mean it, his Noise is saying–
"Davy–" I say–
I'm sorry, he thinks–
And that's the truth all over–
He *is* sorry–
For everything–
For Prentisstown–
For Viola–
For Ben–
For every failure and every wrong–
For letting his pa down–
And he's looking up at me–
And he's begging me–
He's begging me–
Like I'm the only one who can forgive him–
Like it's only me who's got the power–
Todd?–
Please–
And all I can say is "Davy–"
And the fright and the terror in his Noise is too much–
It's too much–
And then it stops.
Davy slumps, eyes still open, eyes still staring back at me, eyes still
asking (I swear) for me to forgive him.
And he lies there, still.
Davy Prentiss is dead.

{VIOLA}

"You're insane," I say to the Mayor behind me.

"No," he says. "You've been right all along, both of you. Never
love something so much it can be used to control you."

The sun is down now but the sky is still pink, the Noise of the
town still ROARs, there's another *Boom!* in the distance as the Answer approaches, and the ship must have landed by now. Its doors
must be opening. Someone, probably Simone Watkin or Bradley

Tench, people I know, people who know *me*, must be looking out, wondering what sort of place they've landed in.

And Todd kneels over the body of Davy Prentiss.

And then Todd looks up–

His Noise is boiling and burning and I can hear the grief in it and the shame and the *rage*–

And he gets to his feet–

And he raises his rifle–

I see myself in his Noise. I see the Mayor there, too, behind me, rifle pointed, eyes glinting with triumph.

And I know exactly what Todd is going to do.

"Do it," I say, my stomach dropping but it's right right right–

And Todd raises the rifle to his eye–

"*Do it!*"

And the Mayor shoves me hard, sending lightnings of pain up my legs, and I can't help it and I scream out and fall forward, forward toward Todd, forward toward the ground–

And the Mayor does it again–

Uses me to control Todd–

Because Todd can't help it either–

He jumps to catch me–

To catch me when I'm falling–

And the Mayor attacks.

[TODD]

My brain explodes, burning and raging with everything he fires at it and it ain't nothing like a slap at all, it's like fiery metal poked right into the center of who I am, and as I jump forward to catch Viola, it hits me so hard my head snaps back and here it comes again, the Mayor's voice but somehow *my* voice, too, somehow *hers* as well and all of 'em saying YER NOTHING YER NOTHING YER NOTHING YER NOTHING–

Our bodies are still moving together and I feel us tumble into one another, feel the top of her skull crack into my mouth, and YER NOTHING YER NOTHING YER NOTHING she falls into my chest and my fumbling arms and we twist down onto the rubble together, a siren ripping off the roof of my head YER NOTHING YER NOTHING YER NOTHING and I feel the rifle fall and bounce away and I feel the weight of her against me and I hear her as if from the other side of the moons and she's calling my name and YER NOTHING she's saying "Todd" YER NOTHING YER NOTHING she's saying "Todd!" and it's as if I'm watching her from under water and I see her try to rise up on her hands to protect me but the Mayor's above her and swinging his rifle by the barrel and smacking her across the back of her head and she's falling to one side–

And my brain is boiling–

My brain is boiling–

My brain is boiling–

YER NOTHING YER NOTHING YER NOTHING YER NOTHING YER NOTHING–

And I see her eyes as they're closing–

And I feel her against me–

And I think *Viola*–

I think *VIOLA!*

I think ***VIOLA!!!!***

And the Mayor steps away from me like he's been stung.

"Whoo," he says, shaking his head as I blink away the buzz still rocketing from my brain, as my eyes refocus and my thoughts are mine again. "Told you you had some power in you, boy."

And his eyes are wide and bright and eager.

And he hits me again with his Noise.

I fling my hands up to my ears (not holding the gun, not holding the gun) as if that'll stop it but it ain't thru yer ears that you hear Noise and he's in there, inside my head, inside my self, invading it like I don't have any self at all YER NOTHING YER NOTHING YER NOTHING my own Noise swept up and hit against me, like I'm punching myself with my own fists YER NOTHING YER NOTHING YER NOTHING–

Viola, I think but I'm disappearing, I'm falling deeper into it, I'm weaker and my brain is rattling–

Viola–

{VIOLA}

Viola, I hear, as if from the bottom of a canyon. My head is aching and bleeding from the Mayor's blow and my face is in the dust and my eyes are half open but they aren't seeing anything–

Viola, I hear again.

I open my eyes wide.

Todd's scooting back into the rocks, his hands over his ears, eyes squeezed shut–

And the Mayor is standing over him and I can hear the same shouting as before, the same kind of clanging, laser-bright Noise firing right at him and–

Viola, I hear in among all the clatter–

And I open my mouth–

And I shout–

[TODD]

"TODD!" I hear screamed from somewhere out there–
  And it's her–
  It's her–
  It's her–
  And she's alive–
  And her voice is coming for me–
  Viola–
  Viola–
  VIOLA–
  I hear a grunt and the Noise in my head stops again and I open my eyes and the Mayor is staggering back, one hand up to his ear, the same reflex that everyone does–
  That everyone does when they hear an attack of Noise.
  VIOLA, I think again, right at him, but he ducks his head and raises the rifle at me. I think it again–
  VIOLA
  And again–
  VIOLA
  And he steps back and stumbles over Davy's body, falling backward along it and down into the rubble–
  I push myself up–
  And I run to her–

{VIOLA}

He runs to me, his hands open and reaching for me, taking my shoulders and rolling me up to a sitting position and saying, "Are you hurt, are you hurt, are you hurt–"
  And I'm saying, "He's still got the gun–"
  And Todd turns–

[TODD]

And I turn and the Mayor's getting to his feet and he's looking at me and here comes his Noise again and I roll outta the way and I hear it following me as I scramble over rocks, scramble back to where I dropped my rifle and–
  And there's a gunshot–
  And dust flies up in the air in front of my hands–
  Hands that were reaching for the rifle–

And I stop–
And I look up–
And he's staring right back at me–
And I hear her call my name again–
And I know she's understanding–
Understanding that I need to hear her say my name–
And that way I can use hers as a weapon–
"Don't try it, Todd," the Mayor says, looking down the barrel at me–
And I hear his voice in my head–
Not an attack–
The slinky, snaky, twisty verzhun of his voice–
The one that's him taking hold of my choices–
The one that's him turning them into his–
"You won't fight anymore," he says–
He takes a step closer–
"You won't fight anymore and that'll be the end of it–"
I turn away from him–
But I have to turn back–
Have to look into his eyes–
"Listen to me, Todd–"
And his voice is hissing twixt my ears–
And it would be so easy just to–
Just to–
Just to fall back–
Fall back and do what he says–
"No!" I shout–
But my teeth are locked together–
And he's still in there–
Still trying to get me to–
And I will–
I will–
YER NOTHING–
I'm nothing–
"That's right, Todd," the Mayor says, stepping forward, rifle bearing
down on me. "You are nothing."
I'm nothing–
"But," he says–
And his voice is a whisper scratching across the deepest part
of me–
"But," he says–
"I will make you *something*."
And I look right up into his eyes–

Eyes that are an abyss I feel myself falling into–
Up and into the blackness–
And outta the corner of my eye–

{VIOLA}

I throw the stone as hard as I can, praying as it leaves my hand that
my aim's as good as Lee said–
      Praying, Please, God–
      If you're there–
      Please–
      And *wham!*
      It hits the Mayor right in the temple–

[TODD]

There's a terrible *ripping* feeling, like a strip is being torn right outta my
Noise–
      And the abyss is gone–
      It's turned away–
      And the Mayor lurches to the side, holding his temple, blood already
dripping from it–
      "TODD!" Viola shouts–
      And I look at her–
      Look at her arm outstretched where she threw the rock–
      And I see her–
      My Viola.
      And I get to my feet.

{VIOLA}

He gets to his feet.
      He stands up tall–
      And I shout his name again–
      "TODD!"
      Because it does something–
      It does something to him–
      It does something *for* him–
      The Mayor's wrong–
      He's wrong forever and ever–
      It's not that you should never love something so much it can
control you.

It's that you *need* to love something that much so you can *never be controlled*.

It's not a weakness–
It's your best strength–
"TODD!" I shout again–
And he looks at me–
And I hear my name in his Noise–
And I know it–
I know it in my heart–
Right now–
Todd Hewitt–
There's nothing we can't do together–
And we're gonna *win*–

[TODD]

The Mayor is looking up now, half crouched, blood seeping from twixt his fingers held against the side of his head–

He turns to look at me, a scowl on his face–
And here comes his Noise–
And–
VIOLA
I beat it back–
He flinches away–
But he tries again–
VIOLA
"You can't beat us," I say–
"I can," he says, clenching his teeth. "I will."
VIOLA
He flinches again–
He tries to raise the rifle–
I hit him extra hard–
VIOLA
He drops the rifle and staggers back–
I can hear his Noise buzzing at me, trying to twist its way in–
But his head is hurting–
From my own attacks–
From one well-thrown rock–
"What exactly do you think this proves?" he spits. "You've got power, but you don't know what to do with it."
VIOLA
"Looks like I'm doing fine," I say.

And he smiles, teeth still clenched. "Are you?"

And I notice my hands are shaking–

I notice my Noise is flying, sizzling like a bright thing–

I can't feel my feet below me–

"It takes practice," the Mayor says. "Or you'll blow your mind apart." He stands up a little straighter, trying to lock my eyes again. "I could show you."

And right on cue, Viola yells *"TODD!"*

And I hit him with everything I got–

Every bit of her behind me–

Every piece of anger and frustrayshun and nothingness–

Every moment I didn't see her–

Every moment I worried–

Everything–

Every little tiny thing I know about her–

I send it right into the center of him–

VIOLA

And he falls–

Back and back and back–

His eyes rolling up–

His head twisting round–

His legs buckling–

Falling falling falling–

Right to the ground–

And lying there still.

{VIOLA}

"Todd?" I say.

He's shaking all over, almost to the point of not being able to stand, and I can hear an unhealthy-sounding whine cutting through his Noise. He wobbles a little as he takes a step.

"Todd?" I try to get to my feet but my ankles–

"Jeez," he says, crumpling down beside me. "That takes it outta you."

He's breathing heavy, his eyes unfocused.

"Are you all right?" I ask, putting a hand on his arm.

He nods. "I think so."

We look back at the Mayor.

"You did it," I say.

"*We* did it," he says and his Noise is getting a little clearer and he sits up a little straighter.

His hands are still shaking, though.

"Poor bloody Davy," he says.

I grip his arm. "The ship," I say quietly. "Mistress Coyle's going to get there first."

"Not if I can help it," he says. He stands up and he swoons for a second but I hear him call Acorn with his Noise.

ʙᴏʏ ᴄᴏʟᴛ, I hear clearly and Davy's horse tugs free of where he's tied and walks up over the rubble, ʙᴏʏ ᴄᴏʟᴛ, ʙᴏʏ ᴄᴏʟᴛ, ʙᴏʏ ᴄᴏʟᴛ.

ᴛᴏᴅᴅ, I hear from farther out and there's more clopping of hooves as Angharrad follows Acorn in and stands beside him. "Forward," she nickers. "Forward," Acorn nickers.

"Absolutely forward," Todd says to them.

He puts an arm under my shoulders to lift me up. Acorn sees in his Noise and kneels down so it's easier for me to get up top. When I'm in the saddle, Todd slaps his flank gently and up he stands.

Angharrad comes close to Todd and starts to kneel, too, but, "No, girl," he says, petting her nose.

"*What?*" I say, alarmed. "What about you?"

He nods at the Mayor. "I have to take care of him," he says and doesn't meet my eye.

"What do you mean, take care of him?"

He looks past me. I turn. The beetle march of the army has reversed its course and stretches to the bottom of the hill now.

It'll be marching here next.

"Go," he says. "Get to the ship."

"Todd," I say. "You can't kill him."

He looks at me and his Noise is a muddle and he's still struggling to stay upright. "He deserves it."

"He does but–"

But Todd's already nodding. "We are the choices we make."

I nod back. We understand each other. "You'd stop being Todd Hewitt," I say. "And I ain't losing you again."

[ᴛᴏᴅᴅ]

I give a little snort when she says *ain't*.

"I'm gonna have to stay with him, you know," I say. "Yer gonna have to go to the ship as fast as you can and I'm gonna have to wait for the army to come."

She nods, even tho there's sadness there. "And what'll you do then?"

I look over at the Mayor, still sprawled on the rocks, unconshus and moaning slightly.

I feel so *heavy*.

But I say, "I reckon they might not be too unhappy to see him beaten. I reckon they just might be on the lookout for a new leader."

She smiles. "And that'll be you?"

"And if you meet the Answer?" I say, smiling back. "What'll you do then?"

She brushes her hair outta her eyes. "I reckon they may need a new leader, too."

I step forward and I put my hand near hers on Acorn's side. She don't look at my face, just slides her hand till the tips of our fingers are touching.

"Just cuz yer going there and I'm staying here," I say. "It don't mean we're parting."

"No," she says and I know she understands. "No, it certainly doesn't."

"I ain't parting from you again," I say, still looking at our fingers. "Not even in my head."

She pushes her hand forward and laces her fingers in mine and we both look at 'em wrapped together.

"I have to go, Todd," she says.

"I know."

I look deep into Acorn's Noise and I show him where the road is, where the ship landed, and how fast fast fast he's gotta run.

"Forward," he whinnies, loud and clear.

"Forward," I say.

I look back up at Viola.

"I'm ready," she says.

"Me, too," I say.

"We'll win," she says.

"I reckon we just might."

One last look.

One last look where we know each other.

Right down to our souls.

And I slap Acorn hard on the flanks.

And off they go, over the rubble, right down the road, tearing hard toward the people who (I hope I hope I hope) can help us.

I look down at the Mayor, still lying on the ground.

I hear the army marching down the hill, two miles away, if that.

I look for the rope.

I see it but before I pick it up, I take a second to close Davy's eyes.

{ V I O L A }

We fly down the road, and it's all I can do not to fall off and break my neck.

"Watch for soldiers!" I shout in the space between Acorn's flattened-back ears.

I have no idea how far into town the Answer's managed to march, no idea if they'll wait to see who I am before they blow me off the road.

No idea what her reaction will be if she sees me–

When she sees me–

When I tell her and everyone else the things I've got to tell them–

"Faster if you can!" I shout and there's a jolt like an engine firing and Acorn goes even faster.

She'll head for the ship. No doubt about that. She'll have seen it land and gone straight for it. And if she gets there first, she'll tell them how sorry she is that I died so tragically, how I fell so cruelly at the hands of the tyrant the Answer are trying to overthrow, how if the scout ship has any weapons that can be used from the air–

Which it does.

I lean down farther in the saddle, biting hard against the pain in my ankles, trying to make us go even faster.

We get well past the cathedral, down through the rows of shuttered-up shops and bolted-in houses. The sun is completely down, everything turning to silhouette against the darkening of the sky.

And I think about how the Answer will respond when they find out the Mayor's fallen–

And what they'll think when they find out *Todd* did it–

And I think of him–

I think of him–

I think of him–

Todd, Acorn thinks.

And we race down the road–

And I nearly tumble off as a *BOOM* rises in the distance.

Acorn shudders to a halt, twisting round to keep me on his back. We turn and I look–

And I see the fires burning down the road.

I see houses on fire.

And stores.

And grain sheds.

And I see people running this way through the smoke, not soldiers, just people, running past us in the dark.

Passing us so fast they don't even stop to look at us.

They're fleeing from the Answer.

"What is she *doing*?" I say out loud.

Fire, Acorn thinks, nervously clattering his hooves.

"She's burning everything," I say. "She's burning it all."

Why?

Why?

"Acorn–" I start to say.

And a horn blows a deep, long call across the entire valley.

Acorn whinnies sharply, no words in his Noise, just a flash of fear, of terror so sharp I feel my heart leap, echoed by the disbelieving gasps of some of the people running past me, many of them shouting out and stopping, looking behind me, back toward the city and beyond.

I turn, even though the sky's too dark to see much.

There are lights in the distance, lights coming down the zigzag road by the falls–

Not the road the army is on.

"What is it?" I say to no one, to anyone. "What are those lights? What was that *sound*?"

And then a man, stopped next to me, his Noise bright and circling with amazement, with disbelief, with fright as clear as a knife, whispers, "No."

He whispers, "No, it can't be."

"*What?*" I shout. "What's happening?"

And the long, deep horn sounds again across the valley.

And it's a sound like the end of the world.

THE BEGINNING

THE MAYOR WAKES before I even finish tying his hands.

He moans, pure, real Noise ratcheting from him, the first I've ever heard outta his head, now that he's off-guard.

Now that he's been beaten.

"Not beaten," he murmurs. "Temporarily waylaid."

"Shut up," I say, pulling the ropes tight.

I come round the front of him. His eyes are still misty from my attack but he manages a smile.

I smack him cross the face with the butt of the rifle.

"I hear one stitch of Noise coming from you," I warn, pointing the barrel at him.

"I know," says the Mayor, a grin still coming from his bloody mouth. "And you would, wouldn't you?"

I don't say nothing.

And that's my answer.

The Mayor sighs, leaning his head back as if to stretch his neck. He looks up into the colored glass window, still standing, impossibly, in a wall all its own. The moons are rising behind it, lighting up their glass verzhuns just a little.

"Here we are again, Todd," he says. "The room where we first properly met." He looks around himself, at how he's the one tied to the chair now and I'm the one out here. "Things change," he says, "but they stay the same."

"I don't need to hear you talking while we wait."

"Wait for what?" He's growing more alert.

His Noise is disappearing.

"And you'd like to be able to do that, too, wouldn't you?" he says. "You'd like just for once to have no one know what you're thinking."

"I said, shut up."

"Right now, you're thinking about the army."

"Shut *up*."

"You're wondering if they really *will* listen to you. You're wondering if Viola's people can really help you—"

"I'll hit you again with the damn rifle."

"You're wondering if you've really won."

"I have really won," I say. "And you know it."

We hear a *BOOM* in the distance, another one.

"She's destroying everything," the Mayor says, looking toward the sound. "Interesting."

"Who is?" I ask.

"You never met Mistress Coyle, did you?" He stretches one shoulder and then the other against his binds. "Remarkable woman, remarkable opponent. She might have beaten me, you know. She might really have done it." He smiles wide again. "But you've done it first, haven't you?"

"What do you mean *She's destroying everything*?"

"As always," he says, "I mean what I say."

"Why would she do that? Why would she just blow things up?"

"Twofold," he says. "One, she creates chaos so it's harder to fight her as an orderly enemy. And two, she obliterates the safety of those who won't fight, creating the impression that she cannot be beaten, so that everyone's that much easier to rule when she's done." He shrugs. "Everything's a war to people like her."

"People like you," I say.

"You'll be swapping one tyrant for another, Todd. I'm sorry to be the one to tell you."

"I won't be swapping nothing. And I told you to be quiet."

I keep the rifle pointed at him and go to Angharrad, watching us both from a cramped space in the rubble. **Todd,** she thinks. **Thirsty.**

"Is there a trough still out front?" I ask the Mayor. "Or did it get blown up?"

"It did," the Mayor says. "But there's one round the back where my own horse is tied. She can go there."

Morpeth, I think to Angharrad, the name of the Mayor's horse, and a feeling rises in her.

Morpeth, she thinks. **Submit.**

"Attagirl," I say, rubbing her nose. "Damn right he'll submit."

She pushes me playfully once or twice then clops off outta the rubble, making her way round the back.

There's another *BOOM*. I have a little flash of worry for Viola. I wonder how far down the road she's gotten by now. She must be getting near where the Answer is, she must be–

I hear a little stirring of Noise from the Mayor.

I cock the gun.

"I *said*, don't try it."

"Do you know, Todd?" he says, like we were having a nice lunch. "The attacking Noise was easy. You just wind yourself up and slam someone with it as hard as you can. I mean, yes, you have to be focused, tremendously focused, but once you've got it, you can pretty much do it at your will." He spits away a little blood pooling on his lip. "As we saw with you and your *Viola*."

"Don't you say her name."

"But the other thing," he continues. "The *control* over another's Noise, well, I must say, that's a *lot* trickier, a *lot* harder. It's like trying to raise and lower a thousand different levers at once and, sure, on some people, some *simple* people, it's easier than others and it's surprisingly easy on crowds, but I've tried for years to get it to work as a useful tool and it's only recently I've had any level of success at all."

I think for a minute. "Mayor Ledger."

"No, no," he says brightly. "Mayor Ledger was *eager* to help. Never trust a politician, Todd. They have no fixed center, so you can never believe them. *He* came to *me*, you see, with your dreams and things you said. No, no control there, just ordinary weakness."

I sigh. "Would you just be *quiet* already?"

"My point is, Todd," he presses on, "that it's only today that I've been able to even come close to forcing *you* to do what I want you to do." He looks at me, to see if I'm getting it. "Only today."

Another *BOOM* in the distance, another thing destroyed by the Answer for no good reason at all. It's too dark to see the army but they must be marching into town by now, down the road straight to here.

And night is falling.

"I know what yer saying," I say. "I know what I've done."

"It was all you, Todd." He keeps his eyes on me. "The Spackle. The women. All your own action. No control needed."

"I know what I've done," I say again, my voice low, my Noise getting a warning sizzle to it.

"The offer's still open," the Mayor says, his voice low, too. "I'm quite serious. You have power. I could teach you how to use it. You could rule this land by my side."

I AM THE CIRCLE AND THE CIRCLE IS ME, I hear.

"That's the source," he says. "Control your Noise and you control yourself. Control yourself," he lowers his chin, "and you can control the world."

"You killed *Davy*," I say, stepping up to him, gun still pointed. "Yer the one with no fixed center. And now yer *really* gonna shut the hell up."

And then a low and powerful sound rumbles thru the sky, like some giant, deep horn.

A sound God would make when he wanted yer attenshun.

I hear whinnies from the horses out back. I hear a filament of shock race thru the still-hiding Noise from the people of New Prentisstown. I hear the steady marching of the army's feet collapse into a racket of sudden confuzhun.

I hear the Mayor's Noise spike and pull back.

"What the hell was that?" I say, looking up and around.

"No," the Mayor breathes.

And there's *delight* in it.

"What?" I say, poking the rifle at him. "What's going on?"

But he's just smiling and turning his head.

Turning it toward the hill by the falls, by the zigzag road coming down into town.

I look there, too.

Lights are at the top.

Lights are starting to come down the zigzag.

"Oh, Todd," the Mayor says, amazement and, yeah, it's *joy* coming thru his voice. "Oh, Todd, my boy, what *have* you done?"

"What is it?" I say, squinting into the dark, as if that'll help me see it clearer. "What's making that—"

A second horn blast comes, so loud it's like the sound of the sky folding in half.

I can hear the ROAR of the town rising, so many asking marks you could drown in 'em.

"Tell me, Todd," the Mayor says, his voice still bright. "What exactly were you planning on doing when the army arrived?"

"What?" I say, my forehead furrowing, my eyes still trying to see what's coming down the zigzag road, but it's too far and too dark to tell. Just lights, individual points of 'em, moving down the hill.

"Were you going to offer me up for ransom?" he goes on, still sounding cheerful. "Were you going to give me to them for execution?"

"What were those blasts?" I say, grabbing him by the shirtfront. "Is that the settlers landing? Are they invading or something?"

He just looks in my eyes, his own sparkling. "Did you think they'd elect you leader and you'd single-handedly usher in a new era of peace?"

"I'll lead them," I hiss into his face. "You watch me."

I let him go and climb up one of the higher piles of rubble. I see people poking their heads outta their houses now, hear voices calling to one another, see people start running to and fro.

Whatever it is, it's enough to get the people of New Prentisstown out of hiding.

I feel a buzz of Noise at the back of my head.

I whip round, pointing the gun at him again, climbing back down the rubble and saying, "I *told* you, none of that!"

"I was just trying to keep our conversation going, Todd," he says, false innocence everywhere. "I'm very curious to know your plan for leadership now that you'll be head of the army and President of the planet."

I want to punch the smile off his face.

"What's going on?" I shout at him. "*What's coming down that hill?*"

There's a third blast of the horn sound, even louder this time, so loud you can feel it humming thru yer body.

And now people in town are really starting to scream.

"Reach in my front shirt pocket, Todd," the Mayor says. "I think you'll find something that once belonged to you."

I stare at him, searching him for a trick, but all that's there is that stupid grin.

Like he's winning again.

I push the rifle at him and use my free hand to dig in his pocket, my fingers hitting something metal and compact. I pull it out.

Viola's binocs.

"Really remarkable little things," the Mayor says. "I do so look forward to the rest of the settlers landing, seeing what new treats they bring us."

I don't say nothing to him, just climb back up the rubble and hold the binocs to my eyes with my free hand, clumsily trying to get the night vision to work. It's been a long time since I—

I get the right button.

Up pops the valley, in shades of green and white, cutting thru the dark to show me the town.

I raise them up the road, up the river, to the zigzag on the hill, to the points of lights coming down it—

And—

And—

And oh my God.

I hear the Mayor laugh behind me, still tied to his chair. "Oh, yes, Todd. You're not imagining it."

I can't say nothing for a second.

There ain't no words.

How?

How can this be *possible*?

An army of Spackle is marching for the town.

Some of 'em, the ones near the front, are riding on the backs of these huge, wide creachers covered in what looks like armor and there's a single curving horn coming out the end of their noses. Behind 'em are troops, cuz this ain't a friendly march, nosiree, it ain't nothing like that at all, there are troops marching down the zigzag road, troops marching over the lip of the hill at the top of the falls.

Troops that are coming for battle.

And there are thousands of 'em.

"But," I say, gasping, hardly able to get the words out. "But they were all *killed*. They were all killed during the Spackle War!"

"All of them, Todd?" the Mayor asks. "Every single one of them on this whole planet when all we live on is one little strip? Does that make sense to you?"

The lights I've been seeing are torches carried by the Spackle riding on the creachers' backs, burning torches to lead the army, burning torches that light up the spears that the troops carry, the bows and arrows, the clubs.

All of 'em carrying weapons.

"Oh, we beat them," says the Mayor. "Killed them in their thousands, certainly, every one within miles of here. Though they outnumbered us by a considerable margin, we had better weapons, stronger motivation. We drove them out of this land on the understanding that they would never return, never get in our way ever again. We kept some of them as slaves, of course, to rebuild our city after that war. It was only fair."

The town is really ROARing now. The marching of the army has stopped and I can hear people running about and screaming to each other, stuff that don't make no sense, stuff of disbelief, stuff of fear.

I run back down the rubble to him, pushing the gun hard into his ribs. "Why did they come back? Why *now*?"

And still he grins. "I expect they've had time to work on how they might get rid of us once and for all, don't you? All these years? I expect they were only looking for a reason."

"What reason?!" I shout at him. "Why–"

And I stop.

The genocide.

The death of every slave.

Their bodies piled up like so much rubbish.

"Quite right, Todd," he says, nodding like we're talking about the weather. "I suspect that must certainly be it, don't you?"

I look down at him, understanding coming too late like always. "You did it," I say. "Of *course* you did it. You killed every Spackle, every single one, made it look like it was the Answer." I push the rifle into his chest. "You were *hoping* they'd come back."

He shrugs. "I was hoping I'd have the chance to beat them once and for all, yes." He purses his lips. "But it's you I have to thank for speeding the plan along."

"Me?" I say.

"Oh, yes, definitely you, Todd. I set the stage. But you sent them the messenger."

"The messen–?"

No.

No.

I turn and run up the rubble again, binocs back on, looking and looking and looking.

There's too many, they're too far away.

But he's there, ain't he?

Somewhere in that crowd.

1017.

Oh, no.

"I should say, *Oh, no* is right, Todd," the Mayor calls up to me. "I left him alive for you to find, but even with your *special relationship*, he wasn't very fond of you, was he? No matter how much you tried to help him. You're the face of his torturers, the face he took back to his brothers and sisters." I hear a low laugh. "I really wouldn't want to be you right now, Todd Hewitt."

I spin round, looking at the horizon on all sides. I spin round again. There's an army to the south, one to the east, and now one marching down from the west.

"And here we sit," says the Mayor, still sounding calm. "Right in the middle of it all." He scratches his nose on his shoulder. "I wonder what those poor people on the scout ship must be thinking."

No.

No.

I spin round once more, as if I could see them all coming. Coming for me.

My mind is racing.

What do I do?

What do I *do*?

The Mayor starts whistling, as if he had all the time in the world.

And Viola's out there–

Oh, Jesus, she's out there in it–

"The army," I say. "The army's gonna have to fight them."

"In their spare time?" the Mayor says, raising his eyebrows. "When they've got a few free minutes from fighting the Answer?"

"The Answer will have to join us."

"Us?" says the Mayor.

"They'll have to fight alongside the army. They'll *have* to."

"You really think that's how Mistress Coyle is going to play it?" He's smiling but I can see his legs starting to bounce up and down now, energy coursing thru him. "She'll see herself and them as having a common enemy, now won't she? You mark my words. She'll try to negotiate." He catches my eye again. "And where will that leave you, Todd?"

I'm breathing heavy. I don't got no answer.

"And Viola's out there," he reminds me, "all on her own."

She is.

She is out there.

And she can't even *walk*.

Oh, Viola, what have I done?

"And under these circumstances, my dear boy, do you really think the army is going to want you as leader?" He laughs as if it was always the dumbest idea anywhere. "Do you think they'll trust *you* to lead them into battle?"

I spin round again with the binocs. New Prentisstown is in chaos. Buildings burn to the east. People run thru the streets, running away from the Answer, running away from the Mayor's army, and now running away from the Spackle, running all direkshuns with nowhere to go.

The horn blasts again, shaking glass outta some of the windows.

I spy it in the binocs.

A great long trumpet, longer than four Spackle put together, carried on the backs of two of the horned creachers, being blown by the biggest Spackle I've ever seen.

And they've reached the bottom of the hill.

"I think it's time you untied me, Todd," the Mayor says, his voice a low buzz in the air.

I spin around to him, aiming the gun one more time. "You won't control me," I say. "Not no more."

"I'm not trying to," he says. "But I think we both know it's a good idea, don't you?"

I hesitate, breathing heavy.

"I've beaten the Spackle before, you see," he says. "The town knows it. The army knows it. I don't think they'll be quite so eager to discard me and unite behind you now that they know what we're up against."

I still don't say nothing.

"And after all this betrayal from you, Todd," he says, looking right up at me. "I *still* want you by my side. I *still* want you fighting next to me." He pauses. "We can win this together."

"I don't want to win this with you," I say, looking down the barrel. "I *beat* you."

He nods as if in agreement, but then he says one more time. "Things change, but they stay the same."

I hear marching feet getting closer to the church. A troop from the army's finally pulled itself together enough to come into town. I can hear them heading down a side road, toward the square.

There ain't much time.

"I don't even mind that you tied me up, Todd," the Mayor says, "but you have to let me go. I'm the only one who can beat them."

Viola—

Viola, what do I do?

"Yes, Viola, again," he says, his voice slinky and warm. "Viola out there among them, all by herself." He waits till I'm looking him in the eye. "They'll kill her, Todd. They will. And you know I'm the only one who can save her."

The horn blasts again.

There's another *BOOM* to the east.

The feet of the Mayor's soldiers getting closer.

I look at him.

"I beat you," I say. "You remember that. I beat you and I'll do it again."

"I have no doubt you will," he says.

But he's smiling.

VIOLA I think right at him, and he flinches.

"You save her," I say, "and you live. She dies, you die."

He nods. "Agreed."

"You try to control me, I shoot you. You try to attack me, I shoot you. Got it?"

"I've got it," he says.

I wait a second more but there ain't no more seconds.

There ain't no more time to decide nothing.

Only that the world's marching to meet up right here, right now.

And she's out there.

And I ain't never parting from her again, not even when we're not together.

Forgive me, I think.

And I go behind the Mayor and untie the rope.

He stands up slowly, rubbing his wrists.

He looks up at another blast of the horn.

"At last," he says. "No more of this slinking, secret fight, no more running after shadows and all this undercover cloak-and-dagger nonsense." He turns to me, catches my eye, and I see behind his smile the real glint of madness. "Finally, we come to the real thing, the thing that makes men men, the thing we were *born* for, Todd." He rubs his hands together and his eyes flash as he says the word.

"*War.*"

END OF BOOK TWO